This is a work of fiction. All the characters and events portrayed are either products of the author's imagination or, if actual historical persons, are used fictitiously.

INDIA TREASURES: AN EPIC NOVEL OF RAJASTHAN AND NORTHERN INDIA THROUGH THE AGES

Published by TimeBridges Publishers LLC
1001 Cooper Point Road SW, Suite 140-#176
Olympia, WA 98502

On the World Wide Web:
http://www.TimeBridgesPublishers.com

ISBN 0-9707662-0-3

Library of Congress Card Number 00-193605

First U.S. edition

Printed and bound in the United States of America
by Central Plains Book Manufacturing

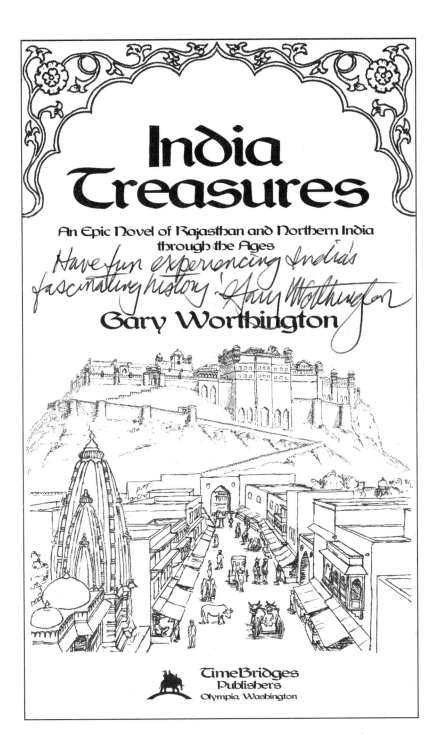

India Treasures

An Epic Novel of Rajasthan and Northern India
through the Ages

Have fun experiencing India's fascinating history!
Gary Worthington

Gary Worthington

TimeBridges
Publishers
Olympia, Washington

Dedication

For Sandra, my own Treasure, my wife, best friend, soulmate, fellow traveler to India and elsewhere, editor and proofreader, my companion on our journey through life.

This book would not have happened without you and your patient, unceasing encouragement and support in so many ways.

Preface

Like so many readers, I enjoy experiencing other times and cultures through large historical novels. Although many fine novels are set in particular time periods in India (the majority during the British Raj or in modern times), I found no fiction that attempted to portray the sweep of Indian history from ancient times to post-Independence. So, having become intrigued with India, I audaciously wrote one myself. I learned as I researched and wrote, taking far more years than planned.

Because so many subcultures collectively make up the large and diverse entity we call "India," I selected a relatively small number of the key historical events, personages, and cultural forces that shaped the most dominant society of the northern two-thirds of the country. I gave considerable prominence to the culturally significant region of Rajasthan and its peoples.

Even with my being so selective, the body of writing became so huge that I divided it into two books. This novel and its sequel, *India Fortunes* (scheduled for publication in 2002), are individually complete in themselves. However, they are interrelated, and each book enhances the understanding of the events and characters in the other. Although I wrote each novel to be enjoyed in its entirety, the individual stories do stand by themselves, so they can be read as time permits.

My Web site at **GaryWorthington.com** has additional background information and comments about India and the stories, as well as answers to frequently asked questions and various links.

In the **Notes** near the end of the book I discuss the extent to which the characters and events in each story are fictional or real.

A **Character List** and a **Glossary**, both with pronunciation guides, are at the back of the book to help readers who are unfamiliar with Indian names and words.

A **Reading Group Discussion Guide** is also at the end.

I'm greatly interested in your comments related to the book. Please contact me by email through the address posted on my Web site at GaryWorthington.com, or else write in care of the publisher at the address on the copyright page. I'll reply to the extent other commitments allow. If you write by regular mail and would like a response, please enclose a self-addressed envelope.

I'd also appreciate copies of any published reviews.

And now, I hope you enjoy experiencing *India Treasures*.

Gary Worthington

Olympia, Washington
March 1983—February 2001

Contents

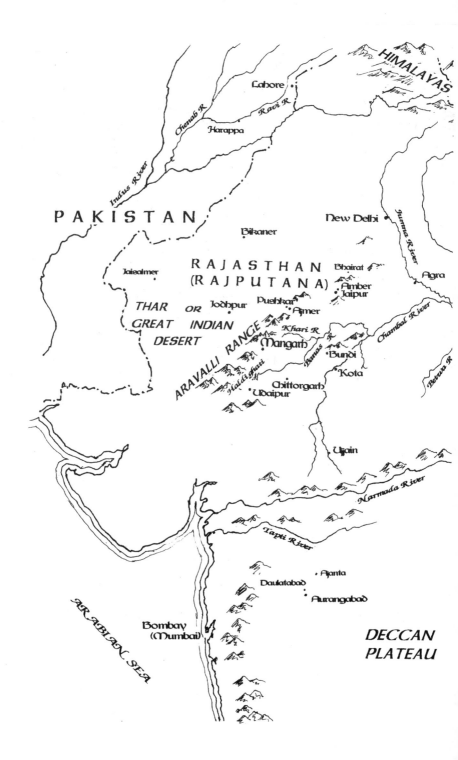

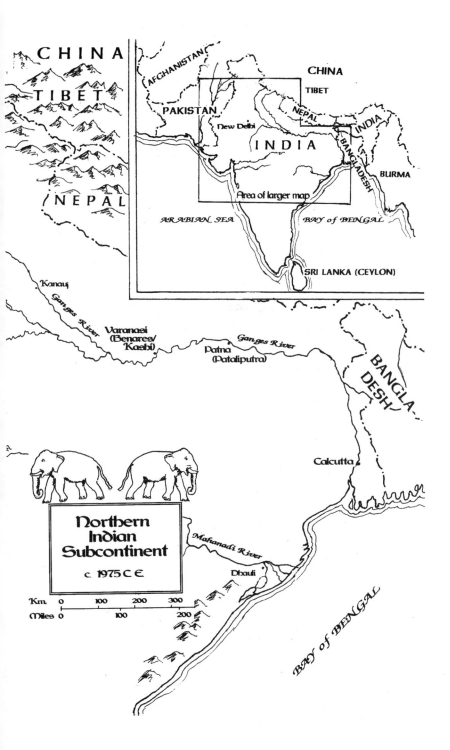

CHINA

TIBET

NEPAL

AFGHANISTAN

PAKISTAN

CHINA

TIBET

NEPAL

New Delhi

INDIA

BANGLADESH

BURMA

Area of larger map

ARABIAN SEA

BAY of BENGAL

SRI LANKA (CEYLON)

Kanauj

Ganges River

Varanasi
(Benares/
Kashi)

Ganges River

Patna
(Pataliputra)

BANGLA
DESH

Calcutta

Northern
Indian
Subcontinent

c. 1975 C.E.

Mahanadi River

Dhauli

BAY of BENGAL

| Km. | 0 | 100 | 200 | 300 |
| Miles | 0 | | 100 | 200 |

Jodhpur

Hanuman Sagar
[Lake]

Cenotaphs

Moti Mahal
[Summer Palace]

Fortress

Mangarh
Old
Town

Mangarh
New
Town

To Amargarh

Mangarh
1975 c. e.

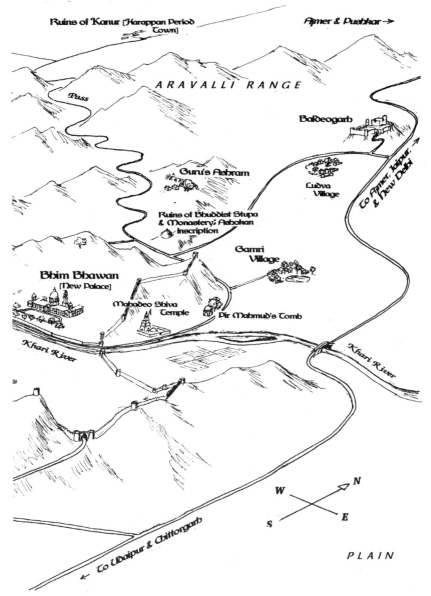

DESERT

Ruins of Kanur [Harappan Period Town]

Ajmer & Pushkar →

ARAVALLI RANGE

Pass

Baldeogarh

Guru's Ashram

Ludva Village

Ruins of Bhuddist Stupa & Monastery; Ashokan Inscription

Gamri Village

Bhim Bhawan [New Palace]

To Ajmer, Jaipur & New Delhi

Mahadeo Shiva Temple

Pir Mahmud's Tomb

Khari River

Khari River

To Udaipur & Chittorgarh →

N
W
E
S

PLAIN

The
Mangarh Treasure
Part One

1

Rajasthan State, 19 June 1975 C.E.

As Vijay Singh drew nearer to Mangarh, the dread of being exposed as an imposter threatened to overwhelm him. He realized how tightly he clenched the seat's sticky vinyl, and he forced himself to let go, to shove his hand onto his lap. Thrusting his face out the window of the raiders' speeding bus, he concentrated on breathing slower and deeper, drawing in the cool, fresh smelling air of dawn.

The dust reddened sun was rising, illuminating a tiny white-washed temple capping an arid foothill of the Aravalli Range, and a crumbling fort crowning the adjacent ridge. Awakening to another scorching day, children dashed from houses with mud walls and thatched roofs. At the edge of a field bordered by thorn fences, an orange tur-baned farmer drew water from a well, his bullock hitched to a rope strung over a big pulley wheel.

Rattling and shaking as if intent on self destruction, the bus was managing to keep up with the jeep. The vehicles hurtled down the potholed highway like a charging cavalry troop, forcing everyone else from the narrow pavement: a line of camels; three bullock carts in a row; a tractor pulling a wagon full of villagers.

At a well sheltered by a *neem* tree, a young man brushed his teeth with a twig, while another, clad only in a white *dhoti*, splashed water over his bare chest and legs from a bucket. Vijay had bathed in a similar manner before leaving his village years ago, except that his caste did not have a well of its own, so water had to be carried from a most inconvenient distance. At least that had changed, now that a new well had been dug with the funds he had sent.

Shortly after 6:30 a.m., the bus labored up a grade in the shadow of a barren hill, and the twin towers of the massive medieval gate of

Mangarh's outer defenses appeared. The jeep and the bus both halted.
Vijay again drew several deep breaths, steeling himself, as he
waited to be handed the envelope containing the detailed orders.

When he had learned their destination earlier in the morning,
he felt as if he were being sent into a war zone where he might be
ambushed at any moment with no place to take cover. The raiding party
had finished breakfast long before dawn, but several officers still sat
drinking *chai* in the dining room of the government rest house near
Ajmer. The warm breeze from the ceiling fan bathed Vijay's face as he
rested his elbows on the table and sipped his *chai*, savoring the sweet-
ness of the sugar and the milk in the thick mixture.

The kitchen door opened and the elderly, barefoot waiter padded in with a teapot. From behind him came the sounds of clattering
dishes and a radio playing a Hindi film song. The old man's face, lined
with cracks like those in the nearby rocky hills, lit with a smile as he
approached the table. Vijay always sensed that serving staff and room
boys intuitively felt a rapport with him, despite his status as a government official. "More tea, sir?" asked the waiter in the local version of
Rajasthani.

Although Vijay was still sluggish from being awakened at 4:30
a.m. after a restless night in a hot room, he returned the smile in an
effort to be pleasant. He replied, also in Rajasthani, "Certainly. It was
good of you to get up so early just to serve us."

The creviced face glowed. "It's my duty, sir."

That was true, of course, but Vijay knew from his own earlier
times when he labored in the fields that a few kind words could lighten
a person's burdens the rest of the day.

After refilling Vijay's glass, the waiter hurried around the table
to Anil Ghosali, who gave an abrupt nod. The old man served Ghosali,
then moved to the next table.

Ghosali peered at Vijay from behind the thick lensed eyeglasses.
He pulled his S-curved pipe from his lips and said, "We're a full day
out from Delhi, and you don't know where our raid will be? Even though
you are second-in-command?"

Vijay struggled to conceal his irritation. As usual for income
tax officers on duty, Ghosali had spoken in English, so Vijay replied in
the same. "Our normal practice, isn't it?"

Ghosali shoved into position some strands of the graying hair
worn straight back and pasted to his scalp. He drew on the pipe and let
out a puff of smoke. "How else to prevent leaks? Nevertheless, I myself
have known for two days where we are going."

Vijay's stomach tightened. An opening for another Assistant
Director of Income Tax was coming up soon. If he got the promotion,
the increased prestige and influence, but especially the added income,
would help him considerably in aiding the lower caste people in his
home village. Ghosali, a Brahmin originally from West Bengal, a few

years older than Vijay's own thirty-four, was the main competition for the position. Recently Vijay felt Ghosali was watching him carefully, as if hoping to catch him in some major error which could discredit him.

Ghosali often alluded to having connections with "big men" in New Delhi. Could he in fact have found out the target of the raid so far in advance? Vijay hesitated, debating whether to ask the question Ghosali obviously expected. But Ghosali apparently had the advantage this time anyway. Vijay forced out the words: "Would you mind telling me where, then?"

Ghosali shrugged, clearly enjoying his edge. "Can't you guess? You're Rajasthani. You're in your home state now."

Vijay rotated his *chai* glass as he considered. Maybe Ghosali really didn't know. One way to find out. The most likely time for a raid was 7:00 or 8:00 a.m. It was now 5:30. What cities lay an appropriate distance away? Possibly Bhilwara. Maybe Beawar. Or beyond....He thrust the thought from his mind.

"I'll tell you," said Ghosali.

Vijay waited.

Ghosali smiled. "Mangarh."

Vijay stiffened.

With a self-satisfied air, Ghosali thrust his pipe back into his mouth, scooted back his chair, casually stood, and left.

Vijay was scarcely aware of him going. True, Mangarh was the right distance. But he fervently hoped Ghosali was wrong.

Ranjit Singh, immaculate as usual in his tightly wrapped turban and gray European-style suit, returned from the room they had shared and sat in the chair Ghosali had vacated. The tall Sikh looked across the dining room to where Dilip Prasad, Deputy Director of Inspection, was apparently rising to leave. With the DDI were the two retired civil servants recruited as unbiased witnesses to the search. Ranjit glanced at Vijay. "It looks like we're about ready to go. Have you found out where we're headed?"

Vijay scowled. "I'm not sure. Ghosali thinks he knows."

Ranjit raised his eyebrows. "How?"

Vijay shrugged, still annoyed that Ghosali could get the information before himself.

Ranjit asked, "Well, can you tell me where?"

Vijay gulped *chai* to moisten the dryness in his mouth. "He says Mangarh."

"Ah, your native place."

Vijay wagged his head yes.

"So you may have a chance to visit your family."

Vijay tensed. "Hopefully."

"And you can inspect the well you paid for."

Vijay tended to forget he'd confided to Ranjit about the well; no one else in the department knew about the donations to his home village. "Right."

"Whom are we raiding?"

"Ghosali didn't say. Maybe he doesn't know *that*."

Ranjit grinned and said with mock seriousness, "And Prasad still hasn't told you? Even though you're in charge under him? How could you lead us if one of those monstrous overloaded trucks hits his jeep and he's killed? You wouldn't know whom to raid."

"I suppose I could telephone Delhi and find out."

"That assumes the phones would be working. You know how unlikely that is." Ranjit laughed. His high pitched giggle normally amused Vijay, but not this morning.

Vijay sighed. "All right. I'll ask him." He drained the last of his tea.

The other officers were shoving back their chairs. Ranjit said, "While you're talking to the DDI, I'll go make sure our kits got loaded on the bus." He stood and strode toward the door.

Vijay's mind was still on the problems posed if they were indeed headed to Mangarh. He put on his navy blue sportcoat, tugged on the bottom to smooth it, and absently fingered his striped necktie to ensure the knot was centered.

He walked outside into the darkness. The air, scented by the profusion of jasmine in the garden, felt refreshingly cool after the stuffy dining room. Vijay stopped in the driveway while the dozen other raiders in the party crunched across the gravel parking area to the bus.

A jackal howled in the sparse jungle not far away. Vijay peered into the distance. The sun had not yet begun to lighten the horizon, and low in the east the tiny constellation of the Karttikas, the Pleiades, twinkled above the black outlines of the rugged hills. Vijay knew many people might think it odd that he would notice the stars at a time such as this. But he had grown up in a village without electricity, and much of his entertainment at night had involved watching and learning to know the sky. The seasonal shifts of the patterns of the stars had become as familiar to him as the changes in the crops in the fields.

The Deputy Director of Inspection, a small man with a pockmarked face and thinning hair, stood smoking a cigarette near the canvas topped jeep, his dark suit blending into the night. Vijay moved close and asked quietly, "Can you tell me now where we're headed, sir?" He held his breath.

Dilip Prasad squinted in the faint light at the slender officer with finely sculpted features and black wavy hair. Vijay Singh had been with the Income Tax Department at least ten years. Although he seemed a little overly tense sometimes, he was loyal and honest, almost to the point of being a little naive in Prasad's opinion. In that sense Vijay was quite unlike Ghosali, whose shrewdness and transparent self-promotion seemed more practical and realistic. But, Prasad thought, one could hardly blame Ghosali for wanting a higher income, burdened as the man was with having to provide dowries for five daughters.

Prasad was mildly amused by the rivalry that had developed between the two men, fueled mainly by Ghosali. It would keep both officers on their toes, pressing hard to show who could achieve the best results in the raid. Prasad knew Ghosali had somehow found out where they were going and was no doubt feeling smug. Maybe it was time to balance the scales a bit. He replied, "We're going to Mangarh, Vijay. To raid the Maharaja."

Vijay's felt light headed; his heart pounded. So it was true. And they would be raiding His Highness! He forced himself to concentrate on what Prasad was saying, "That's one reason you're in charge under me this time. Since you're from the area you must know it well. Have you been to the Maharaja's palace?"

Vijay stood rigid, struggling to think of how best to respond. Although in his earlier years assuming a new identity had seemed the best route to escape the poverty and humiliation of his childhood, it now seemed almost insane to have passed himself off as a Rajput, the high caste of warriors and landlords and princes.

For Vijay came from a family of Untouchable outcastes.

Was there any reason why, if he were indeed a Rajput of the same clan as the Maharaja, he should have visited the palace? Not necessarily. He cleared his throat and said, his voice hoarse, "No, sir, I never went there. My family wasn't high enough...in the nobility."

Prasad shrugged. "No matter. There's a diagram of the building with your instructions. The search should be routine, except for the size of the place. The old fortress is another matter, but Ghosali will lead that part." He lowered his voice. "Confidentially, Vijay, we have a lot of pressure on us this time. You know of Dev Batra?"

Still trying to decide how to deal with going to Mangarh, Vijay had managed with part of his mind to follow what Prasad was saying. "I've heard of him. A cabinet minister?"

"No formal office," Prasad said. "But he's in the Prime Minister's circle. Handles a lot of jobs for the party, and doesn't pay attention to legalities. Anyway, Batra phoned me, insisting we expedite this raid. Says he wants 'results.' As fast as possible."

Vijay now recalled Anil Ghosali claiming to be acquainted with Batra, who was a crony of Indira Gandhi's son Sanjay. He did not know how to respond. Was Prasad telling him this because he expected him to somehow try even harder than usual in the search? Maybe even stretch the law?

"Still," Prasad said, "naturally it goes without saying we'll be strictly legal in everything we do."

Relieved just a little, Vijay replied, "Of course, sir."

An example of those legalities was directly in front of them; the two men recruited as *panch* witnesses, impartial observers of the search, were climbing into the jeep.

Prasad cast down his cigarette, ground it out with his foot, and turned to join them.

Vijay Singh remained unmoving. Although there had always been the remote possibility, he had never considered it likely he would have to go to Mangarh on a case.

He had built his life and his career around a lie. In the huge city of New Delhi, where his chances of meeting anyone previously acquainted with him were minimal, he had succeeded. But exposure was far more likely in the much smaller Mangarh, where so many residents knew him, and he could scarcely bear to think of how disastrous that would be if fellow tax officers were present.

He saw the other raiders were either in the bus or the jeep, and the drivers had started the engines of both vehicles. He forced himself to walk swiftly to the bus, climb aboard, and resume his seat at the front. Across the aisle, Ranjit joked, "You took so long, I thought maybe you'd decided not to come."

Vijay managed a tight grin in response, then realized his friend could probably not see it in the dimness.

The bus jerked into motion and followed the jeep, rattling through the night on the rough roadway. Horns blaring, the vehicles forced a lanternless bullock cart onto the shoulder, then a weaving bicyclist toting a huge can of milk on each side of his rear fender.

Even though the sun had not yet risen and the temperature in the bus should have been comfortable, Vijay took his handkerchief and wiped his perspiring palms, then his face.

Was there a plausible way to avoid going to Mangarh?

A sudden, severe illness? He indeed felt nauseated and weak, his mind slow to function. But to complain or exaggerate his condition would draw too much attention, maybe even arousing Ghosali's suspicions. Anyway, at this late time Prasad would no doubt take him to a doctor in Mangarh rather than attempting to send him back to Delhi.

Ranjit leaned closer. "Did you find out for sure where we're going? Is it Mangarh?"

Vijay hesitated. Prasad hadn't specifically given him permission to tell the others. But there should be no harm now. "Ghosali was right. It's Mangarh. To raid the Maharaja." *Ex*-Maharaja, he thought, now that the recent law had abolished the last of the titles and privileges the princes had retained after India became a democracy.

Ranjit's turban bobbed, barely discernible in the darkness. "That could be interesting—searching forts and palaces, rather than our usual businesses and houses."

Vijay stared ahead.

"And you can visit your family as soon as we're finished," Ranjit added.

The subject had come up again. Vijay sat for a moment, his mind straining furiously. Given their relationship, with Vijay visiting Ranjit and his wife in Delhi so often, even taking their two children to the cinema or the zoo, Ranjit would naturally expect to be invited to the village to meet Vijay's mother. But bringing Ranjit, or anyone else, to his home was unthinkable. He would devise an excuse later. For now, he replied, "I'll visit, assuming there's time, naturally."

The driver leaned on the horn button, dueling with an oncoming truck. The paving was only a single lane wide, and the bus veered to the shoulder. These confrontations happened often, but Vijay flinched from the lorry's blinding headlights and clenched his seat as the bus leaned and bounced. Lord of the highway, like some prince of earlier times, the heavily loaded truck charged past, scarcely a layer of dust away. Not slowing for an instant, the bus, lesser in strength but still a force to be feared, leaped back onto the pavement.

Although the hazard of collision was over until the next encounter, Vijay retained his tight grip on the seat. He wondered just how likely it was that he'd meet someone who had known him previously.

His home village of Gamri was only a few kilometers outside the town; sweepers from his caste went to the small city every morning to clean the streets and dispose of wastes. Women from Gamri gathered firewood and peddled it in Mangarh city, and farmers sold their vegetables and fruit in the market. So if at all possible, he should avoid going out in the town.

Apparently the raid itself would be confined mostly to the Maharaja's palace and his fortress. There, the main danger would be meeting a sweeper or other palace employee who happened to have come from Vijay's village. He could do nothing to avoid that possibility; he would simply have to hope it didn't happen. As an official from Delhi, wearing European-style business clothing, he might look so different from his childhood, and from the way he dressed on his infrequent visits to his people, that he would not be recognized.

He released his grip on the seat and again wiped his forehead with his handkerchief. It would be especially bad if he encountered a previous acquaintance when Anil Ghosali happened to be nearby. Thankfully, he and Ghosali would apparently be searching separate sites.

"Do you know the Maharaja?" Ranjit asked, interrupting Vijay's thoughts.

Vijay was sure he felt Ghosali, seated two rows back, watching him, listening carefully. He struggled to appear calm. "Not really," he said at last. "I didn't normally go in such high circles, you know." A gross understatement, he thought dryly. He hated to have to continue misleading his best friend.

"That's good," Ranjit said. "It could be awkward searching someone you know. I don't suppose that will ever happen to me." He laughed his high giggle. "Nobody I know is rich enough to be worth a raid."

"Same here," Vijay said.

The sun was well above the hills when the driver shifted gears and the bus lumbered like a noisy elephant up the grade along the hillside to the portal of Mangarh's outer wall. Prasad's jeep stopped just before the round gate towers, and the bus halted behind it. Krish-naswamy, the pleasant young income tax inspector who was Prasad's assistant on the raid, stepped from the jeep. The dark skinned native of Tamil Nadu state walked briskly to the bus and handed Vijay the orders.

Vijay tried to appear calm as he broke the seal on the envelope, withdrew the instructions, and silently read:

Half the busload, under Vijay's supervision, was to search the Bhim Bhawan Palace, principal residence of Lakshman Ajay Singh, former ruler of Mangarh. Deputy Director Prasad would oversee the operation as a whole and would serve the search warrant on the Maharaja. As Prasad had said earlier, while the officers under Vijay's direction scrutinized the newer palace, the other raiders under Anil Ghosali would search the old fortress on the hill overlooking the city.

The objective of the raid was to locate undeclared wealth, suspected to be in the form of cash, gold and silver bullion and coins, jewelry, objects of art, antique weapons and clothing.

Stunned, Vijay stopped reading. Everyone in the Mangarh region knew the tales of the fabulous wealth, reputedly hidden in underground vaults in the immense old fortress, protected by the tribe of aboriginal Bhils as their hereditary duty.

He would be searching for the legendary Mangarh Treasure itself.

"Should I continue, sir?" asked the driver, breaking Vijay's train of thought. Still standing at the front of the bus, Vijay glanced ahead and saw that the jeep had disappeared. "Yes—try to keep up with them." He gripped the pole by the door to help keep his balance.

The Mangarh Treasure! Despite his other anxieties, he wished he, rather than Anil Ghosali, were assigned to search the ancient fort. If the trove still existed, it would almost certainly be there, not in the more modern palace.

Vijay wondered if the Bhil guards might resist the raid. That seemed unlikely; the tribal people were more civilized now, and anyway they would realize the futility of opposing government officers.

The light dimmed momentarily as the bus moved into shadow, through the arched gateway of the outer fortifications, the din from the engine reverberating between the two flanking towers.

As the bus emerged from the brief passageway, Vijay resumed reading: The two women in the party would search the ladies' apartments of the newer palace. So far as known, only the ex-Maharajah's daughter, Kaushalya Kumari, and a few maidservants now resided in the women's wing.

The raiders would also scrutinize other, more minor, holdings of the former ruler. Hopefully, the preliminary search would be finished today, but most of the raiders would remain as long as necessary to conduct a more thorough hunt.

A map of the city of Mangarh was attached, with the fortress and the palace each circled in red ink. Also enclosed were rough diagrams of the two complexes, with the entrances and the principal building wings labeled. Vijay wished he'd been given the drawings in advance so he could have studied them longer. The raid was bound to be somewhat less efficient with no opportunity to rehearse. Of course, the fewer who knew of the search, the less chance for someone to warn the Maharaja.

Still, Ghosali had found out.

Vijay shouted to be heard above the engine as he read the instructions to the other income tax officers.

Anil Ghosali was frowning, sitting stiffly erect in his usual high collared, tunic-like *achkan*. "Anil will organize the search of the fortress," Vijay said, striving to control his voice. He recited the names of those assigned to work with Ghosali, then passed him the diagram of the old fort. Pipe dangling from his lips, Ghosali began to study the drawing.

Vijay cleared his throat and resumed: "Everyone else will be with me at the Maharaja's palace." He looked at the two women. "When we arrive, the ladies will watch the main entrance and the front. Ranjit"— he glanced at the Sikh—"will lead the party to the rear and ends, and assign men to watch the doors there. As soon as we've served the warrant, I'll see that you all have specific areas to search. Any questions?"

A couple of men shook their heads "no." The two women watched Vijay but said nothing.

"I love treasure hunts!" said Ranjit. "Can we keep what we find this time?"

Vijay grinned tensely. "Only if you share with all of us." His effort to meet humor with humor sounded feeble to him, but he was too preoccupied to be creative.

No one asked for more details; most of the group had been on other raids, and all knew the basic procedures. The bus jerked as the driver shifted gears at the bottom of the grade, and Vijay stumbled back into his place in the front seat. He reexamined the rough plan of the Bhim Bhawan Palace, a huge structure with several wings and numerous outbuildings.

He again looked out the window as the vehicles entered the fringes of the town. With the population increasing so rapidly all over India, the city had grown dramatically in the last few years. The bus sped past new, nondescript, blocky, concrete and brick houses. Smoke from morning cooking fires hung in the air, a layer of pungent fog. Men bicycling to work and uniformed children walking to school moved aside to make way for the honking motor vehicles.

A couple of women wearing faded, torn clothing were bent over their short handled brooms, sweeping dust and litter to the edge of the street. Vijay jerked his head away from the open window; he recognized the two as from Gamri village and of his own caste. Then he realized there was little danger of them identifying him. Bhangis were too accustomed to keeping their eyes lowered, to not meeting the gaze of their betters.

The raiders entered the gate of the old city, and suddenly they were centuries back in time. Here, everything was exactly as Vijay remembered. The bus slowed in the confined, twisting, streets. In the tiny, open fronted shops lining the lanes, the cobblers and silversmiths and fabric merchants looked up from arranging their wares to watch with curiosity. In the Street of Swordsmiths, the jeep and the bus stopped to wait for a humpbacked white cow that blocked their way as it chewed on some discarded vegetable leavings by the gutter. The jeep's horn tooted. The cow gave a start, stared at the vehicles, then ambled into a side alley. The vehicles resumed their motion.

Vijay thrust his head out the window and looked upward at the sight ahead.

High on the ridge, glowing in the morning sunlight, soared the cupola-crowned palaces and the crenelated battlements of the fort of Mangarh: one of the largest fortress palaces in Rajasthan, and indeed in all of India.

There was where the treasure lay hidden—if it indeed existed. He envied Anil Ghosali the assignment of searching the fort. Vijay's gaze was held captive by the giant structures of honey-colored sandstone that grew from the hill as if placed there to fulfil some storybook illustrator's fantasy. The sight had enthralled him as a young boy, and it still stirred him as a man nearing middle age. To the right of the fortress, the cliff face presented Mangarh's most distinctive natural landmark, a rocky profile resembling an elephant's head and trunk.

When the street wound between the tall, blank walls of crowded *havelis*, the city mansions of the nobility, the fortress disappeared from view, and Vijay felt a vague disappointment. Then it reappeared as the raiders passed the huge rectangular stone-lined tank, now almost dry. Women clad in the bright yellow, green, and red skirt outfits typical of Mangarh bathed and washed clothes on the stone *ghats* leading down

to the water. But the towers and terraces of the old palace still dominated the picturesque scene.

At the lower wall of the fort, the bus stopped, rather than attempting to climb the cobblestoned switchbacks that threaded upward through the consecutive gateways, each flanked by squat, round towers.

Anil Ghosali and the eight men who would search the fortress with him filed out. "Happy hunting!" called Ranjit Singh to the last man off, who waved.

The giant gateway doors, bristling with sharp spikes to discourage ramming by elephants, hung open, ineffective against this modern day assault.

Trying to discern what lay beyond, Vijay peered through the big arched opening, but he could see only an inner wall of huge oblong stones ascending the hill along the edge of the road. As he watched, a troop of monkeys, black faced langurs, bounded off along the top of the wall, perhaps frightened by the invasion.

The bus backed, turned, and rattled away, again following the Deputy Director's jeep. Vijay gave up his effort to plumb the mysteries of the fortress. The vehicles crossed the gentle arch of the ancient bridge over the river. Below, *dhobis* were washing clothes, beating them on rocks alongside natural pools that were almost empty in this season.

Vijay looked back over the tense faces in the bus. The two women sat in the second seat, across the aisle. Mrs. Desai, the heavy, middle aged income tax officer, appeared lost in thought. The large, dark eyes of Miss Das, the attractive young woman who was the newest of the income tax inspectors, seemed unusually solemn; usually she wore a pleasant smile.

Miss Das was also a Buddhist. And everyone knew that in modern India, adopting Buddhism as one's religion almost certainly meant the person was a member of a Scheduled Caste—an Untouchable. Rather, an *ex*-Untouchable, as Untouchability had been outlawed since Independence. Now former Untouchables were often referred to by Mahatma Gandhi's term, "Harijans," Children of God. The laws euphemistically termed them "Scheduled Castes," and activists called them "Dalits," Broken People.

Vijay assumed Miss Das had probably obtained her position in the Indian Revenue Service through one of the slots reserved by law for Scheduled Castes, even though she seemed quite intelligent, possibly even bright enough to have made it on her own against the competition for the opening, as Vijay himself had.

They were nearing the ex-Maharajah's current residence. Going fast to keep up with the jeep, the bus leaned and its tires screeched as it turned into the open gates of the grounds surrounding the palace.

An old man stepped out of the guardhouse at the entrance, then leaped backwards to avoid being struck by the vehicles.

A narrow, paved road wound through an area of giant mango trees where peacocks strutted, their blue plumage iridescent in the morning sun. The road straightened, and the long, buff colored, two storied facade of the Bhim Bhawan Palace appeared. Above the pillared entry, a large dome crowned the central portion of the building. Behind the dome, to one side, soared a clock tower. A smaller dome accented each wing at the ends. As the bus sped by, two *malis*, one an old man and the other a boy, looked up in surprise from watering the flower beds.

Several men, villagers judging from their turbans and *dhotis*, walked toward the palace, perhaps hoping for an audience with the ex-ruler to ask him for help in settling a dispute or in petitioning a government agency. Vijay saw with relief that he did not recognize anyone, so there was no chance they might expose him.

Atop the roof, in front of the central dome, a green flag hung limply from a pole. That must be the ex-ruler's personal banner, thought Vijay, which meant the Maharaja, himself, was currently at the palace. Even though Indira Gandhi had recently engineered abolishing the last of the princes' special legal privileges, many of the former rulers still followed traditions like flying their own flags.

Diagram in hand, Vijay moved to stand by the front door of the bus. He braced himself on the driver's seat and glanced quickly back at the team members to ensure they were ready. All talk had stopped; faces appeared alert.

The driver applied the brakes hard and the bus skidded to a halt. Vijay pushed open the folding door and stepped quickly out. "Everyone to your positions," he called to the five men spilling from the doorway.

"Great riches await us!" cried Ranjit Singh as he leaped to the ground.

Deputy Director Prasad was already climbing the wide steps to the ornate, cusped arches of the main entry. On the broad porch several waiting people, likely more petitioners hoping to see the Maharaja, stared curiously at the new arrivals.

Four tax officers raced to keep an eye on the palace's side and rear entrances. The two women remained by the bus to watch the front of the structure. One of the *panch* witnesses, a tall, skinny, balding man with spectacles, observed from off to the side.

Perspiring, Vijay hurried to join the director.

2

Most days she was in Mangarh, Kaushalya Kumari rose at dawn and climbed the path to the top of the rocky ridge above the palace that was her home. Now, near the end of the hot season, the sun had scorched the sparse, tawny grasses on the hill, and dust covered the scattered, scrubby *babul* trees. But so early in the morning, before the searing heat arrived, the air on the hillside felt cool and fresh.

Kaushalya sat on a flat rock beneath a sheltering mango tree, one of her favorite spots on the hill. She slipped off her sandals, eyeing the inevitable thin film of dust which already coated her gold toe rings and the clear polish on her nails. She spread her legs, smoothed her long, orange skirt over her knees, and placed the large pad of watercolor paper on her lap. The sounds of the awakening city far below her drifted upward: family arguments, barking dogs, crying children, motor scooters and autorickshaws, the continual blasting horn of a bus or lorry. In the mango tree above her the crows cawed, and the flock of small green parrots were returning to their perches in the foliage after wheeling about the sky in great circles.

Several paces away, her elderly maid Gopi squatted and opened up her own sketchpad. In conservative Mangarh it would not be seemly for Kaushalya, as a woman of Rajput royalty, to be alone where she might encounter men not of her immediate family. Likewise, in Mangarh she should not go about without the long, shawl-like veil draped over her head. But she preferred not to wear one whenever she could avoid it. So she glanced around to ensure no one else was near, and she tugged the *odhni* from the top of her head so it fell about her shoulders. She pulled free her single long, thick braid of hair and tossed it so it hung down the center of her back.

Kaushalya took a soft-leaded pencil from her bag and put on her reading glasses, perching them low on her nose. She peered frequently over the top of the glasses as she began to sketch a rough outline of the cupolas and the bastions of her family's ancient fortress, high on the next hillside to the west. The rising sun bathed the uppermost structures of the fort in a warm orange glow. Kaushalya did not have her paints with her this morning, as she planned only to sketch. Maybe tomorrow morning she would begin applying the colors to what she envisioned as a soft, silhouette-like rendering in transparent oranges and pale purples.

"What are you drawing today, Gopi?" she asked her companion.

"The mango tree, with the birds in it."

Kaushalya nodded. Years ago she had convinced Gopi to try drawing and painting, too. Although the woman had no training whatsoever, she showed considerable talent, in a style that might be called primitive, but was refreshingly original in Kaushalya's opinion. Gopi's work expressed an urge to fill every part of the page with shrewdly noticed and often humorous detail.

As Kaushalya drew, the sun touched the profile of the elephant's head rock formation on the cliff guarding the east side of the fort. Gradually the sun bathed the *havelis*, the whitewashed city mansions of the nobles of the Pariyatra Rajput clan, of which her father was the head. While Kaushalya sketched a few lines indicating the defensive walls climbing the hillside to the fortress, the sunlight spread beyond the old walled city to the newer town on the valley floor, and to the three domes and the clock tower of her own childhood home, the Bhim Bhawan Palace residence of her father, the ex-Maharaja of Mangarh state.

As a student working toward her doctorate in art history, Kaushalya preferred the older style of the hillside fortress with its mirrored and frescoed walls and its fluted arches, and the *havelis* with their narrow, twisting staircases and concealed courtyards. But she had grown up in the Bhim Bhawan Palace, and she considered it home, with its fading draperies and cobweb-strewn chandeliers and overstuffed European furniture.

Given her interests in social reform and the arts, the conservative, isolated city of Mangarh might have been the last place she would want to spend her time. In part, the allure of Mangarh was the appeal to her artist's eye—the beauty of the hills and the crumbling ancient forts and palaces, the villages that looked as if they had grown from the land itself. And part of Mangarh's attraction was the sense of time, of history, of people who had lived here and labored and loved and died for centuries upon centuries.

Most importantly, here was her family: her father, whom she dearly loved in spite of his insistence on finding a husband for her; and her older brother Mahendra, and the rest of her clan, and the servants who were virtually part of the family.

She smiled in amusement at the forces that were conspiring to see her married, even though she was not yet ready. Her father simply could not understand her delay, her refusal to even hear of the proposals. But she knew she was more clever than he, and just as obstinate. She would not be married until she, herself, was so inclined. It was not that she objected so much to parents choosing mates for their children. That was the way of India—although all things considered, she preferred to make her own choice in the manner of the West. Still, at least until she had earned her doctorate, she was not the least interested in being anyone's wife.

The sound of the timekeeper's gong drifted over the valley from the main gate of the fort. Seven o'clock in the morning, according to the venerable water clock, which didn't necessarily agree with Indian Standard Time.

She looked again at the fortress. It was truly a shame for such a unique and lovely grouping of historically and architecturally important structures to be slowly deteriorating. She wondered again if part of the complex couldn't be turned into a hotel. The income would provide funds for restoration, while at the same time tourists and others could experience its character and beauty. Of course, it would be easier to do that with a wing of the newer palace instead, since Western style flush toilets and a modernized kitchen were already in place. But her father didn't care for the idea of tourists invading even a part of his home, so she had given up suggesting it.

Although across the fringe of the city, the old fort was close enough that she saw a jeep had stopped by the bottom of the access road. And behind the jeep came a bus, almost certainly too long to negotiate the sharp turns. Indeed, as she watched, the bus halted. Figures, perhaps eight or ten men stepped from it. They hurried on foot up the steep, cobblestoned road toward the fortress.

She frowned. It was odd for anyone to be going to the fort so early in the morning, much less so many persons.

The jeep turned away, and the bus followed. The two vehicles headed roughly in Kaushalya's direction. She lost sight of them after they entered the narrow streets among the *havelis*, and she dismissed them from her mind as she examined her sketch once more. She erased the outline of one of the towers and redrew it so it better matched the identical structures on either side of it. Satisfied, she took off her reading glasses and put them in their case. She folded the cover on her pad and called to her maid: "Gopi, we should head back now. May I see what you've drawn?"

She slipped on her sandals. Both women rose. Gopi smiled and displayed her drawing of the tree, with a single line of dozens of parrots streaming out from it into the sky and forming graceful, symmetrical loops. "The parrots look like they're having fun," Kaushalya said.

Gopi grinned. "That's what I intended."

Kaushalya showed her the drawing of the fortress.

Gopi nodded. "It looks like a scene from hundreds of years ago."

"That's the way I see it." Kaushalya tucked in her braid, pulled the veil over the top of her head, and they started down the rocky path toward the palace below.

Then Kaushalya stopped.

A jeep, no doubt the same one that had paused below the fort, entered the long driveway to the front entrance of the palace and was approaching at high speed. The bus followed the jeep. Kaushalya was certain her father expected no group of visitors other than the normal numbers of petitioners, who usually arrived on foot.

It could be no coincidence that the vehicles were visiting both of her family's main palaces at the same time of the morning. "Gopi, I need to get back quickly," she said. Slowing just enough to ensure the older lady was keeping up with her, Kaushalya hurried down the dusty trail.

3

His Highness is still at his morning *puja*," the retainer at the door said. His deeply wrinkled face must have witnessed at least eighty years, although he stood tall and straight. He wore immaculate white breeches, a long coat of bright green, and a white turban with a lengthy flaming orange tail. His local version of Rajasthani was intelligible to those in the party who knew Hindi, virtually everyone. Vijay had grown up speaking this dialect, although now he also spoke both Hindi and English perfectly.

"I regret we must disturb his prayers," Deputy Director Prasad said in Hindi. "I take responsibility for the interruption."

The retainer stood rigid, apparently uncertain what to do.

A pleasantly modulated feminine voice called from behind them, in English: "What is this all about?"

Vijay turned. A strikingly beautiful young woman, flushed from apparent exertion, climbed the steps. She wore the traditional local Rajput woman's ankle-length skirt with a veil draped over the top of her head. The lustrous black hair peeking from under the scarf contrasted with her light wheatish complexion. She carried a large pad of paper under her arm.

"May I inquire who is asking?" the Deputy Director said courteously.

"This is my home."

"Then you must be Kaushalya Kumari?"

"I am."

"I'm Prasad, Deputy Director of Inspection of the Income Tax Department, New Delhi. I regret to inform you I have a warrant to search your family's residence and other properties, including your own living quarters. I apologize for the inconvenience."

The young woman stared at him, her large brown eyes, glowing with amber highlights in the sun, wide with disbelief. After a moment, she said, "Let me see the warrant."

Prasad nodded, and Krishnaswamy handed her the document. She peered at it a moment, then withdrew some glasses from a case and put them on. She read the warrant quickly and looked up. "It's signed only by your Director. Do you have the Finance Minister's approval?"

Vijay examined her with respect. The girl had to be savvy to know that the Income Tax Department was part of the Finance Ministry. The central government was a complicated bureaucracy. He could not withdraw his eyes from her. He remembered that the Mangarh royal family had a reputation for being tall and light complexioned, and for beautiful women.

"Yes, indeed, Princess," Prasad said, "the Finance Minister is fully aware of our search."

"How about the Prime Minister?"

Her meaning was clear: this was no ordinary family whose privacy was being so rudely invaded. They may no longer rule these lands, but they still had connections at the highest levels. There had better be no mistakes made today.

The Deputy Director shifted his step. He gave a slight smile. "I assume the Finance Minister keeps Mrs. Gandhi informed, Princess," he said casually.

Vijay knew, and obviously Prasad knew, that the princess was now bluffing to some extent. Both her father, a former Member of Parliament, and her brother, a current MP from the opposition Swatantra, Independent, Party, had been strong critics of Indira Gandhi's management of the government and of the Congress (I) Party.

The young woman again looked down at the warrant. Vijay noticed her hands were trembling, in spite of her impression of controlled indignation. At last, she took off the glasses and said, not looking at anyone, "Please wait here. I'll get my father."

An elderly woman, also wearing the Rajput *kanchli-kurti* with a veil and long skirt, was standing with the ancient retainer. The girl spoke to the man in the local dialect: "Shiv, stay here with them. I'll be back with His Highness as soon as I can." She glanced at the staring petitioners who waited on the end of the porch. "You'd better tell these other visitors to come back tomorrow. I doubt anyone will have time for them today."

The old man bowed and quickly raised his hand to his forehead. "As you command, Princess."

Gopi rushed after her, shawl flying. "Princess," she asked when they were some distance away, "why are all these tax people here?"

"They think we have some wealth we haven't declared. I'll talk to you later. They'll be searching my rooms, and you can help me keep an eye on them. Right now I have to get Daddyji."

Kaushalya hurried along the marble-floored hallway and almost collided with her father's khaki-uniformed ADC, Naresh Singh, who abruptly emerged from the palace office. "Pardon me, Princess!" the aide-de-camp said. "I need to see your father right away. The guard at the fort telephoned to say some income tax men have appeared with a search warrant!"

"I know, Naresh. They're here, too. I'll tell him. You wait by the phone. I have a feeling we'll be getting other calls."

Seeming dubious, he looked back over his shoulder at her as he returned to the office. Naresh was thirtyish, unmarried, and pleasant, and his unusually narrow face was handsome in its way. She knew he was strongly attracted to her, but she had made a point of not encouraging him. By long custom he would be ineligible for marriage to her because he was a distant collateral relative, of the same Rajput clan, and she had no interest in him anyway. It also was not appropriate for a woman to have any relationship other than a businesslike one with a man who was not of her immediate family.

Kaushalya slipped off her sandals at the door of the *puja* room. The smooth marble always felt pleasant on the soles of her feet, but her mind was elsewhere this time. The family's priest had already completed his morning ritual and had left. Through the gap between the drapes over the doorway Kaushalya saw her father, clad only in his white *dhoti*, fingering his string of beads as he sat in the glow of the oil lamps. As always, his sacred thread hung diagonally across his torso and over his shoulder. The odor of burning incense drifted into the hallway.

Kaushalya could recall only one other occasion when she had interrupted her father at his prayers. That was years ago when her mother had at last died after an illness of months.

Kaushalya wondered if she should wait. But time could be

critical. What if her father should indeed have something that needed hiding? She pulled aside the curtain and stepped into the room which held the silver image, less than a half-meter high, of a potbellied god with an elephant's head sporting one tusk. The statue was instantly recognizable as Ganesh or Ganapati, the god of good fortune and the remover of obstacles. Known by the Mangarh ruling family as Ekadantji, "Respected One-Tusk," the idol had been their household god for at least five hundred years.

"Daddyji," she whispered.

Her father turned to her, and smiled, not seeming the least upset at the interruption. "What is it, Kaushi?"

Both had been well educated in English medium schools, and they customarily spoke to each other in that language, with occasional words from Rajasthani or Hindi thrown in. Kaushalya said, "Daddyji, people are here from the Income Tax Department. They have a warrant to search our properties."

She held the document out to him.

His face froze. After a moment, he said, "Let's leave Ekadantji, Kaushi." He set aside his rosary and unfolded himself, his face blanching at the effort of rising.

"Daddyji—are you all right?"

His health had not been good the past few years, and she frequently worried about him. He smiled at her, seemingly with effort. "I'm fine, Kaushi. Just feeling a few aches of old age."

"Sixty-five isn't so old, Daddyji." She held back the curtain, and he stepped through, ducking his head to clear the lintel. Kaushalya bent and touched his feet in respect, as customary upon their first meeting each day.

His Highness Sir Lakshman Ajay Singh stood six-foot, two inches tall. He was broad shouldered, but his height lent an impression of slenderness. He now walked with a slight stoop, and his bare chest now seemed almost hollow where his sacred thread crossed it. The twenty-six years since he had given up his kingdom to independent India had taken a great deal from him physically, as well as otherwise. His hair, including his thick mustache, was now almost completely gray. "Would you read the warrant to me, Kaushi—I don't have my glasses."

Kaushalya put on her own eyeglasses and rapidly read. When she finished, he said with a wry smile, "Do you suppose this is the Congress response to my last speech?"

"Quite possibly. I urged you to tone it down, you remember."
He grinned at her. "I thought I was rather mild."

"You call it 'mild' when you compare our Prime Minister to
'the goddess Kali, running amuck, sucking the very lifeblood from her
own poor devotees?'"

His grin vanished. "It may be accurate, but maybe I'm getting
too reckless in my elder statesman years." He was quiet a moment, then
said, as if musing to himself, "So they think they'll find our 'treasure.'"

"Daddyji, *is* there a treasure?" she whispered.

She had studied the family histories more than anyone else
alive. Given the events of earlier centuries, she was fairly sure that at
one time there had been a vast trove of wealth. The guards from the
tribe of Bhils still stood watch at the old fortress. But she was certain if
the treasure still existed, its value must be greatly exaggerated. Otherwise, her father would not have sold most of the horses and all but one
of the elephants, allowed the buildings to deteriorate, and pensioned off
so many of the less-needed servants.

A couple of times she had asked Daddyji about the wealth, but
he'd brushed her questions aside. She assumed he considered the matter not appropriate to share with her, even though he loved her deeply.
As a woman, she would eventually marry and become part of her
husband's family, so her father probably felt she could have potentially
divided loyalties and hence should not know such an important family
secret.

If her father had confided in anyone, it would have been
Kaushalya's two older brothers, whom he no doubt considered his true
heirs—first Karan, the eldest, killed in the 1971 conflict with Pakistan
in the liberation of Bangladesh; and now Mahendra, currently in Bombay
for a political meeting.

He smiled at her. "You're my true treasure."

"Father," she said levelly, "this is serious."

"I know, Kaushi. Let's just say that if there is any treasure, I
doubt they'll find it soon."

Frustrated at his evasion, she said, "They're waiting, Daddyji.
We'd better go." She slipped her feet into her sandals.

"I wonder if I should dress more formally." He gave his old
devilish grin. "No, better to look like an impoverished *sadhu*, a holy
man, than a rich maharaja."

With effort, she returned his smile.

Wearing only his sacred thread and his *dhoti*, he padded down
the long marble hallway to meet the visitors.

4

At the appearance of the Maharaja, Vijay Singh felt warring
emotions. In a genuine sense, Maharaja Lakshman Singh was respon-

sible for the death of Vijay's father. Yet, the people in Vijay's village had considered the Maharaja a god on earth. When Vijay's own Untouchable forebears had been collecting night soil and scavenging the carcasses of dead animals, this man's Rajput ancestors had been commanding armies and making treaties with Mughal Emperors. Vijay had never actually hated His Highness personally for ordering the police crackdown which had resulted in the brutal death of the foremost leader for the rights of Untouchables. But there was no doubt that if the Maharaja had been a more progressive ruler, Vijay would not have grown up never knowing his own father.

"Your Highness," Deputy Director Prasad said, "I regret the imposition. But we have to act on the information we get from our investigators."

"Of course," Lakshman Singh replied. "We each must do our duty as we see it. After all, *dharma* is the foundation upon which our nation is built." He smiled benignly.

Vijay wondered if the old ex-ruler were having a joke at their expense. The half smile seemed almost patronizing, especially combined with the pronouncement on *dharma* which Vijay sensed held an undertone of sarcasm. And he wondered if Lakshman Singh, by wearing only a *dhoti*, hoped to give the raiders an impression of an ascetic no longer interested in material wealth.

"Please come in, Director Prasad," the Maharaja was saying. "I apologize for keeping so many people waiting outside. May I offer you tea? Or perhaps *lassi* or iced coffee since the morning is already hot."

The Deputy Director, who had probably expected strong protests, even demands for lawyers and phone calls to Delhi, appeared uncertain. But composing himself, he said, "Maybe we could take tea later. I think we should first get my men started."

"Ladies, too, I see," said the Maharaja.

"Yes," the Deputy Director said, "they are here to search the women's quarters."

"So thoughtful of you, Mr. Prasad," said Lakshman Singh as he entered the palace.

A man of perhaps thirty with a narrow but handsome face, dressed in a khaki uniform, appeared, looking harassed. "Highness," he said, "your son is on the line from Bombay. Raiders are at your house there with a search warrant!"

Vijay instantly recognized Naresh Singh.

The Maharaja's ADC was the youngest son of the Thakur, the hereditary ruler and owner of considerable land in three small villages including Gamri. Occasionally when Vijay was a schoolboy, Naresh Singh, who was of about the same age, had toured Gamri in the company of his father.

Vijay turned away and pretended to be examining the paintings of former rulers that lined the hall. Would the ADC recognize him? They had never actually talked with each other, but as late as age seventeen or so, Vijay had sometimes been present when the Thakur and his son had held brief meetings with the Bhangis of the village. Vijay had always watched the boy with curiosity, admiring the air of self-possession combined with a good natured smile.

Ironically, as the highest status Rajput boy Vijay had an opportunity to observe in his younger years, it had been Naresh Singh whom Vijay had modeled himself after when he had decided to claim to be of that caste.

Naresh was saying to the Maharaja: "And Shastri has called from your Delhi house, Highness—they're there, too, with a warrant."

Lakshman Singh turned to the Deputy Director. "So many warrants, Mr. Prasad."

Prasad shrugged. "Of course we must be thorough, sir."

"Of course." Lakshman Singh turned to his ADC and said, "Tell everyone to cooperate completely with the searches. I'll talk with them later. And tell any petitioners still on the veranda to come back tomorrow. I doubt I'll have a chance to listen to them today."

"Yes, Highness." Naresh Singh gave a slight bow and hurried off.

Vijay took a deep breath and allowed himself to relax just a little. The ADC had not even glanced at him. Not this time, anyway.

"Your Highness," Director Prasad said, "I have a listing of your assets compiled from your wealth tax and income tax returns. He gestured toward Krishnaswamy, who held two fat briefcases. "I'd like to inventory your strong room and compare its contents with the items listed on your returns. You have the right to search our own persons first, if you wish, to ensure we don't have any incriminating evidence to plant against you. We have our *panch* witnesses along, and you may also have your own observers present at all times."

Vijay noticed that Kaushalya Kumari was watching everything with a wide-eyed expression of near horror. But as one would expect, she left the talking to her father.

Lakshman Singh stopped, turned to face the Deputy Director. "Mr. Prasad," he said, stone-faced, "I won't pretend to like this. But I know you people have the authority to search my properties thoroughly. All I ask is that you follow your procedures to the letter."

Prasad straightened, gave the Maharaja a determined look. "I fully intend to do so. And I appreciate your attitude of cooperation, sir. It can only help you."

Lakshman Singh abruptly turned and padded off. Prasad looked momentarily perplexed, then followed. Vijay went next with Krishnaswamy. Then came Kaushalya Kumari and the two lady income tax officers. The old retainer came last.

They walked a short distance down the huge, marble floored entry hall, then they turned into a branch corridor. The echoes from the stone floor gave a feel of some place no longer inhabited, like an old

Mughal tomb. They went into, and through, a medium sized office which held a couple of desks.

Lakshman Singh stopped by a substantial steel door with three huge padlocks on it. He told his retainer, in Rajasthani, "Shiv, get the keys."

The old man bowed, touched his hand to his forehead, and hurried away.

"Perhaps the princess could take the two ladies to the women's quarters to begin their search there," Prasad suggested.

Lakshman Singh nodded to his daughter. Without a word, she turned and marched off. The two women tax officers, one heavy and one slender, hurried after, their saris fluttering.

The group of men stood in an uncomfortable silence outside the massive door. The old retainer returned quickly. Lakshman Singh nodded at him, and using separate keys for each, the servant undid the three padlocks, removed them, and shoved the bolts on the door aside.

Meanwhile, the ADC reappeared and sat at a desk, where he began using the telephone. Vijay avoided glancing at him, so there would be no chance their eyes might meet.

The old man took hold of the handle and strained at the door's weight as he pulled. Vijay moved to help, and they slowly swung it open. The retainer stepped in, flicked a switch, and then backed out. The light revealed a large, windowless room, its walls lined with thick masonry shelves. On the lower shelves sat boxes, some metal and some wood, and several canvas bags. The upper shelves held ledger books, various old weapons, sculptures, and other assorted antique-looking objects. Dust coated everything.

Lakshman Singh raised his hands, palms together, and bowed his head briefly in respect. He said, "Please remove your shoes. As I'm sure you know, we consider our strong rooms to be sacred ground."

Vijay and the Deputy Director did as asked.

The inside air smelled musty and stale. Director Prasad faced Lakshman Singh and said, "Mr. Vijay Singh, our senior income tax officer"—he gestured toward Vijay— "will supervise the inventorying when I'm not present. We'll confiscate items only when they do not appear to have been listed on your returns."

Lakshman Singh's gaze swung to Vijay, as if he were startled. His mouth opened and he started so speak, then he changed his mind. Regaining his composure, he turned back to the Prasad.

The Deputy Director excused himself to check on the other raiders, and then to go to the old fortress to oversee the search directed by Anil Ghosali. That left Vijay to complete the strong room inventory, with Krishnaswamy's help.

The elderly *panch* witness present watched carefully as Vijay and Krishnaswamy weighed the gold bullion: almost five kilos. Vijay got a mild thrill from handling the gleaming metal, so heavy for its size; it felt a rare privilege for someone who had grown up in poverty to be able to hold these precious bars in his own hands. The gold was worth roughly twelve thousand U.S. dollars or five thousand pounds sterling. But it was listed on the tax returns.

Krishnaswamy wrote the figures on the inventory. Vijay had not worked before with the Tamil; he found the young man to be both competent and affable.

The ex-Maharaja left briefly and returned, having exchanged his *dhoti* for khaki slacks and a blue shirt. He sat impassively in a chair and occasionally smoked a Charminar cigarette as he watched the proceedings. Vijay noted that the brand was a commonly available one, at least in the cities. Although too costly for the laboring classes, who smoked hand rolled *bidis*, he would have expected a relatively wealthy man to choose an even more expensive, imported, cigarette.

A male servant brought tea, which everyone present drank, except for the old retainer, who merely stood watching with a grim expression. Vijay was relieved that Naresh Singh had not reappeared.

Vijay and Krishnaswamy weighed the silver: thirty-five kilos, worth almost two thousand U.S. dollars.

The paper currency amounted to over forty thousand rupees— worth roughly five thousand U.S. dollars. It would be a fortune for an average Indian, but it seemed a modest amount for an ex-Maharaja.

Then they opened the boxes of jewelry. Vijay withdrew a necklace of two strands of pearls. He handled it gently; he had once seen the thread of an ancient necklace break, and the softly gleaming, precious spheres had spewed over the floor.

He examined a set of emerald earrings and bracelets. Then he reverently handled a diamond broach; it was hard not to be awed by the value represented by the hundreds of flashing facets.

One at a time, he held up a dozen rings. Five of them were mounted with diamonds, two with large rubies, one with an emerald. All listed on the tax returns.

Billions of people in the world, including Vijay, would have felt rich beyond all reasonable expectations if they owned such a collection.

But he had assumed there would be even more. Whatever other gold and silver and jewels Lakshman Singh owned must be kept elsewhere.

Even with the door open, the room was hot and stuffy. Sweat ran down Vijay's forehead. He was relieved when a servant appeared with a large, stand-mounted oscillating electric fan and switched it on. The moving air helped considerably.

Vijay turned his attention to the other contents of the strong room. He continued naming items, Krishnaswamy marking the inventory sheet. Often Vijay had to wipe the dust from the objects in order to make out details. "One sword, jewels in handle—appear to be rubies and diamonds. About one meter long."

"Right. One sword, jewels in handle." Krishnaswamy repeated

as he scribbled.

"One sculpture, apparently bronze, approximately six centimeters tall. Looks to be image of Lord Hanuman."

"One bronze sculpture." Krishnaswamy repeated.

They opened a couple of cloth-wrapped portfolios of miniature paintings on heavy paper. Vijay was not particularly knowledgeable about such works, but they appeared to be of a Rajput school, in the style of the Mughal period. His hands were grimy from so many dusty items, so he wiped his fingers as clean as he could and handled the paintings carefully to avoid smudges. He made a point to keep his glass of tea a safe distance away as he compared the paintings with the listings on the returns.

The paintings were reported as being worth a total of over a *lakh*, a hundred thousand, rupees. Probably they would bring much more if they were ever sold in an appropriate art market—old originals were growing ever more scarce as museums acquired them or they disappeared into the homes of wealthy collectors.

The ex-Maharaja made no comment on the inventorying, even when Vijay had difficulty identifying an old clay jug or an ancient garment. Maybe, Vijay thought, he doesn't know himself what they are. The palace must be full of old items, many of them rare and valuable.

In her own apartments in the ladies' wing, Kaushalya had removed her sandals at the door. She sat with her legs drawn up beside her on her swing, a broad, cushioned platform hung on chains from the ceiling. Gopi sat on the bed nearby, watching the proceedings with a hostile expression.

Absently twisting the rings on her toes, Kaushalya seethed as she watched the two women income tax officials go through every item in her jewelry box, every piece of clothing in her closets. She tried to be courteous and pleasant with the searchers, as was her habit with everyone. But it was just too much when the heavy, older woman began pawing through the underwear in the drawers. "Do you truly have to be so thorough, Mrs. Desai?"

"I apologize, Princess," the woman said. "It is our job. Often jewelry and cash are kept in bedroom drawers."

Kaushalya strained to keep her face composed. Through the adjacent broad archway she could watch the attractive younger woman beginning to search the large room that served as a combination studio and study. The blinds of woven slats had not yet been lowered to keep out the heat and glare, so the room was flooded with light from the giant arched windows which opened onto the north balcony.

Mrs. Desai removed—one at a time—all of Kaushalya's numerous art and history books from the shelves and flipped through the pages of Tod's *Annals and Antiquities of Rajasthan*, Ghose's *Ajanta Murals*, Jain's *Ancient Cities and Towns of Rajasthan*, Ghurye's *Rajput Architecture*. Kaushalya was poised to protest if the woman treated the books with anything other than gentleness. But the tax official was careful. She even returned each book to its place on the shelf.

The younger woman was examining the desk, with its typewriter surrounded by stacks of more books. Taped to the wall above the desk was a large color print of the famous Ajanta cave mural, "The Dying Princess." Miss Das gave Kaushalya an apologetic look. "I'm truly sorry. I'll need to look in the desk."

Kaushalya gave a small sigh. "I suppose you must."

The tax officer gestured at the desk. "Are you a student, Princess?"

Kaushalya nodded. "Art history."

"I see." One at a time, Miss Das opened the drawers, carefully looked through the contents. She then removed the drawer, knelt and looked behind. She stood and replaced the drawers.

Kaushalya tensed as the tax officer unwrapped the cloth cover of a small portfolio of miniature paintings that lay on the desk alongside the typewriter. The young woman examined the top one. Then she glanced at Kaushalya with a mild smile. "These are originals?"

"Yes."

"They must be quite valuable."

"They are indeed."

"They belong to you?"

Kaushalya shrugged. "To my family. My father. I'm only studying them."

"Do you know if they are listed on your father's tax returns?"

Kaushalya smiled at the absurdity of the question. "I'm afraid not. I don't fill out his forms, you must realize."

The woman slowly nodded and said politely, "Of course. I'll check the returns later." When she had rewrapped the miniatures, she approached the moveable cabinet that held Kaushalya's painting supplies. She again looked at Kaushalya. "You are an artist, as well as a student?"

"Of sorts. I did the oils on the wall."

Miss Das examined the scenes of the bathers on the stone *ghats* that bordered the tank in Mangarh, rendered in the vibrant colors of a scene illuminated by brilliant sunlight. "I like them very much," she said with her attractive smile. "You've certainly captured the feel of the place."

"Thank you." Normally Kaushalya would have been pleased by such a response; at the moment she was too worried and preoccupied to care.

"And that drawing on the wall of the elephant in different positions? It's quite different in style."

Kaushalya smiled tensely despite the situation, and gestured toward her maid. "Gopiji did those studies of our elephant up at the fort."

Even with their speaking English, Gopi realized the gist of

what was being said and looked pleased despite the solemn expression she'd been wearing.

Meanwhile, Mrs. Desai was removing paintings from the bedroom wall, inspecting their backs, and then minutely examining the wall itself. At times she tapped the wall with a rubber hammer.

Kaushalya could contain herself no longer. "This is all such a waste of your time, Mrs. Desai. If I wanted to hide anything, it wouldn't be *there*."

The woman glanced at her. "I assure you, Princess, I've found items hidden in walls on more than one occasion."

Kaushalya tightened her lips and turned to the view of the hills out the window. Miss Das, finished with the office and studio, came and carefully rehung the artwork as Mrs. Desai moved on.

The platform swayed as Kaushalya shifted her legs to the other side. This was taking forever. Why couldn't they take her word for it that she had nothing hidden here? She called to Gopi to bring tea for everyone. She would show she could be hospitable, despite such incredible provocation.

By noon, Vijay and Krishnaswamy had finished the strong room inventory, and all parties signed and witnessed the list. Ranjit Singh and the others had completed about half the rooms in the ruler's private wing of the palace.

The two women finished searching Kaushalya Kumari's apartments and began on the vacant suites that originally belonged to other royal ladies.

There still remained the public rooms, the apartments of the ex-ruler's sons (one of them now deceased), the guest rooms, the kitchens, the numerous storerooms.

And of course, the outbuildings: servants' quarters, garages, stables, workshops.

Only by covering the other areas in the most superficial manner could the raiders finish by the end of the day.

After lunch, Deputy Director Prasad returned from the old fortress. "God, it's hot up there," he said to Vijay. Sweat glistened on his face, and he had removed his suitcoat.

Vijay refrained from commenting that it wasn't exactly cool down here, either.

Prasad struck a match, lit a cigarette. "That place is a maze!" he said. "Ghosali's got quite a job. The buildings are a hodgepodge, all built at different times. Underground tunnels and rooms in the hillside. It could take weeks to search it thoroughly."

Vijay could have told him that. But he nodded sympathetically. "It's a big job, sir. How long do you expect us to be here?" He tried to sound casual; the longer they were here, of course, the more chance Naresh Singh—or someone else—might notice and recognize him.

Prasad drew on the cigarette, exhaled, looked intently at Vijay. "As long as it takes. But the sooner we get results, the better. I mentioned Dev Batra's phone calls. Apparently the Prime Minister's son didn't like our Maharaja being so vocal against Indiraji. I'm told more pressure will be brought to bear on His Highness if we still haven't found anything within a week."

Vijay tried not to show his disgust. He wondered what could possibly be done that might be more likely to bring results. "So far, His Highness doesn't seem particularly worried about our being here."

"That's true. I'd expect him to be more upset with us."

Vijay thought of the obscenities and threats that had been screamed at him during some other searches. Lakshman Singh was probably the calmest target he'd ever encountered. "It's almost as if he'd been expecting us to show up sometime, sir. Maybe not today, but sometime or other."

Prasad frowned. "Maybe so. I'm not sure exactly what his calmness means, though. That he truly has nothing to hide? Or that he's hidden something so well he's sure we'll never find it?"

"I've no idea. Can you tell me what kind of additional pressure might be brought to bear by Dev Batra?"

"I'm not quite sure. But I'm to keep Batraji informed on our progress. He may come here himself if he thinks we aren't moving fast enough."

"I see."

Prasad glanced around, as if worried about being overheard. "Batra hinted that it could be rewarding for anyone who finds something to embarrass the Maharaja. It hardly seems proper to mention that to our team, though."

"No, they'll do their best anyway."

Prasad looked meaningfully at Vijay. "Still, I don't mind telling you, Vijay, I've thought for some time you'd make an excellent Assistant Director. Finding that treasure could help get you the promotion, if you were directly involved." He gave a short laugh. "Ghosali may need it more, with five dowries to pay for, but you'd do a better job for the department."

Vijay was quiet for a moment. Then he said, "I appreciate that, sir. I'll do whatever I can."

"I know you will."

Was there any implication, Vijay wondered, that the opposite was also true? That if the team didn't find anything, his promotion might be slower? Or that if Ghosali were the one to find it, he might get the Assistant Directorship instead?

Prasad was saying, "Here's a list of the other properties to be searched. I think it would be best to do them quickly, then go back to the more likely ones for an intensive look." He stuck his cigarette back between his lips.

Vijay examined the listing. From his childhood in the area, he knew at least vaguely of most of them. They included a Harappan period archaeological site, a village dating to around 1500 B.C.E. Also listed was a partially excavated Ashokan *stupa*—a masonry covered mound from the 3rd Century B.C.E. reign of the great Emperor Ashoka. Both projects had received funds from one of the ex-Maharaja's trusts.

Vijay tried not to betray his anxiety. The road leading to the two antiquities sites passed within a kilometer of his home village. He looked up from the paper. "These archaeological digs. They seem somewhat of a long shot, sir."

Prasad shrugged, waved his cigarette in the air. "Probably. But where better to hide something, than where digging's been going on? His Highness supported the excavations financially. Maybe he had a purpose besides just an interest in antiquities. Like burying treasure."

Trying hard to sound casual, Vijay replied, "I suppose it's possible, sir."

By the end of the day, the searchers had found no undisclosed assets of any value to matter. Rooms and meals for the tax officers had been arranged in the *dak* bungalow on the edge of the newer part of town. Typical of government-run accommodations for visiting officials, the one story structure had bare concrete floors, and its plastered walls were unadorned except for grimy, pale green paint.

Vijay, Ranjit Singh, and several of the other exhausted raiders changed into thin cotton *kurta* pajamas, floppy and far more comfortable and cooler than Western business clothes. After their evening meal, where there was little conversation due to their weariness, most retired to their rooms.

About 11 p.m. the electricity went out, and the ceiling fans coasted to a stop.

Vijay's bed felt hot to the touch, and he lay there worrying and sweating, wishing he could move up to the roof or out to the lawn. In the village, his family always used to sleep outside on sweltering nights. However, the wood *charpoys* with their stringed webbing were far more portable than the heavy, metal-springed beds in the *dak* bungalow.

Vijay thought about his mother, only a few kilometers away. He must see her. It had been almost six months since his last visit, an unconscionable period of time. But despite the respect many of the villagers would pay him as a university graduate with an office job in the city, he detested having to step so far downward in caste every time he went home. He hated the half-truths, the evasions, necessary to conceal his exact position in the government and the location of his flat in Delhi, so that his relatives could not visit him and accidentally expose him as Scheduled Caste.

The combination of heat and anxiety was unbearable, and he rose and padded barefoot from the room, down the hall, and out onto the long, pillared veranda. Over the rooftops of the city loomed the black silhouette of the fortress. A few points of light glowed here and there on the walls. If there was indeed a treasure, that was where it was hidden, according to legend. He wondered if there was any way to switch places with Ghosali. In the fort, he'd also be unlikely to encounter Naresh Singh again. But he could think of no good way to convince Prasad to send him to the fortress and bring Ghosali to the Bhim Bhawan Palace instead.

A slight breeze on the veranda brought some relief from the temperature, if not from the stress. In Delhi, rather than riding his motor scooter, he often walked to work for exercise and to relieve tension. Should he get his shoes from the room and go for a stroll now? In the darkness, the chances of anyone recognizing him seemed slight. But it was a possibility. And there were the hazards of walking an unfamiliar route in the dark: open gutters, unprotected holes dug for street work, loose paving stones.

He settled for pacing back and forth the length of the veranda. Some distance away a dog barked, and from a house came the sounds of rattling cooking utensils, of a woman shouting at her husband and an angry reply. Similar to the sounds he remembered from Gamri village. He thought of his childhood. He thought of how he had come to leave the place where his family had lived for generations.

His father had been an agitator for rights for the Untouchables—and for his efforts, he had been clubbed to death by a police rifle butt in 1939. Vijay had been born a few months later. At age five, he'd been encouraged to go to school by a grant of tuition and other expenses from an anonymous benefactor. He had often wondered in earlier years about the identity of that generous person, but in recent years he seldom thought about the matter, realizing that as the years went by it was increasingly unlikely he would ever find out.

Vijay still cringed when he thought of the humiliations he had suffered as an Untouchable with the temerity to go to school: sitting in the rear of the class, apart from the children from higher castes; eating and drinking separately; being ignored by the other boys on the playing ground; being skipped over by some teachers for recitations. In spite of it all, Vijay had consistently topped his schoolmates academically. Tenaciously studying his lessons—and reading everything else he could get hold of—had been his avoidance of reality. It had also laid the foundation for his permanent escape from the humiliations of village life.

But an Untouchable was not supposed to surpass those who were his betters. No school term went by without the higher caste children retaliating by playing practical jokes on him, beating him up, or thinking of some other way to embarrass or shame him.

Vijay stopped his pacing. A mosquito whined near his face. In spite of the slight breeze, one had inevitably found him. He swatted to keep it from settling. He listened for the mosquito again, but all was quiet, except for the noises of the town—a distant autorickshaw, a radio somewhere playing loudly. He resumed his walking.

He thought of how he had managed to get a university education in New Delhi. Assured by the headmaster of his high school that the expenses would continue to be paid by the unknown donor, Vijay had applied for admission to college. But he determined he would suffer no further degradations. So he did not request any of the spots reserved for Scheduled Caste students. Rather, he had applied and been accepted solely on the basis of his academic record.

And he audaciously decided to attempt to pass as a Rajput. He therefore adopted the Singh or "Lion" surname, used by virtually all of that high caste.

He was terrified at first of being found out, but the potential benefits seemed worth the risk. At the university, he imitated the demeanor, mannerisms, and dress of higher caste young men—at first of what he remembered of Naresh Singh, and later of some of the students he was around. He would spread his legs and arms more when he sat down, so to take up a larger space and give an impression of confidence. His stipend was large enough that he could eat well, so his face and the rest of his body filled out and could not give him away as coming from a background of poverty. He also bought good clothes, including a navy blue blazer and striped neckties like the ones the boys from wealthier, high caste backgrounds often wore. He studied English hardest of all his subjects, even hiring a private tutor, and he had practiced it until he was as fluent as someone who had grown up attending English medium schools.

So in Delhi he became Vijay Singh the Rajput, not Vijay the Bhangi. The deception worked, and the more time that passed, the less he worried about being exposed.

He excelled in college, and in the civil service examinations afterwards. He achieved a position in the Income Tax Department, and subsequent promotions.

He felt pleased he had done it all on his own merits, without ever taking advantage of any of the Scheduled Caste reservations. He had always been aware, however, of the price: distancing himself from his family, being constantly on guard against a mistake or other incident that might reveal his true origins, avoiding getting too close socially to anyone who might become suspicious.

His long hours at his work still left time to fill on the weekends. He sometimes visited Ranjit's home, or went to the National Museum to look at the sculptures and paintings. Most of the rest of the time, he read books ranging from history to philosophy.

Much to his regret, his living a lie meant he must avoid marriage. Any bride selected in the customary way by his family would be Untouchable, as well as uneducated. If he tried on his own to obtain a wife from a Rajput background, the routine investigation by her relatives would expose his deception. In a society in which family, caste ties, and having sons of one's own were supremely important, the cost had been high—so high he wondered almost daily if it were worth the effort.

But he had committed himself; he had built his life upon the lie. The deception should continue to work, if no one in Mangarh recognized him and inadvertently exposed him in front of a co-worker from the Income Tax Department.

The mosquito again whined, near his ear. Vijay swatted at it. He had grown weary of padding up and down the length of the veranda. He sat in one of the cane chairs. He peered through the darkness at the massive outline of the fortress.

He thought of the search which would continue tomorrow. If they should actually find the famous Mangarh Treasure, it would generate tremendous excitement. The discovery should also bring the raid to an end—and enable him to get safely back to Delhi without being identified. The sooner the better. It was hard enough to lead his life of deception in Delhi; it seemed impossible for any length of time in Mangarh.

Vijay thought of the Maharaja, of how the ex-King had demonstrated such composure under an awkward situation. He wondered how the man would react if the hidden wealth were indeed found.

And the princess. What a beauty! Would he see her again tomorrow? She intrigued him, even aside from her stunning looks. Probably it was because of the way she had reacted to Prasad. Few women of so young an age could have dealt with the Deputy Director so forthrightly, so perceptively. Many men would find that unappealing in a woman. But Vijay always appreciated competence in anyone.

The mosquito returned, determined to feed on him. Vijay decided to go back to his room and try again to sleep. He had an unfortunate tendency—which he hated—to make mistakes when he was exhausted and under stress, and tomorrow would likely be a difficult and challenging day.

5

The search resumed at 8:00 a.m. Vijay felt the tiredness and irritability from his second night in a row with little sleep.

A gathering of petitioners again waited under the porch arches of the Bhim Bhawan Palace. Even though Lakshman Singh no longer had any formal powers, Vijay knew that many people still respected the ex-ruler and relied on him for assistance, whether helping financially, exerting influence on their behalf, mediating disputes, or merely dispensing advice.

Vijay and Deputy Director Prasad met the Maharaja and the princess in the reception room. In contrast to portraits of his ancestors in elaborate jewels and ceremonial dress, the ex-ruler wore a beige open-collared shirt, brown slacks, and *chappals*. Today, Kaushalya

Kumari had discarded the Rajput skirt and veil, wearing instead a blue *shalwar kameez*, the tunic and pants outfit which originated in the Punjab and was now favored by many young urban women. The long, matching scarf of semitransparent fabric was draped around her neck, with an end trailing over each arm. She wore white low heeled sandals. Despite a slight hollowness around her eyes, Vijay thought she looked gorgeous.

"Vijay," Prasad said, "why don't you take the jeep and go inspect those archaeological sites before it gets too hot out?"

Vijay hesitated, thinking. The *stupa* was only a few kilometers from his home village; he had visited it when he was a child. But going there would get him away from the possibility of an encounter with Naresh Singh, at least for a time.

"Archaeological sites?" asked Lakshman Singh.

"Yes, Your Highness," said Prasad. "Apparently there's a prehistoric village and a Mauryan period *stupa*?"

"Oh, those," said the ex-ruler. "Why would you want to look at them? The *stupa*'s nearby, but the Harappan village dig is almost on the northern border of my old state. To get there would take a couple hours each way, maybe longer."

"My instructions include inspecting them," said Prasad. "Just being thorough, Highness." He said to Vijay, "Choose another man to go with you." To the Maharaja, he added, "Naturally, you're entitled to have a representative present, too, sir."

"Too bad I can't send my daughter," Lakshman Singh said. "She knows all about those things."

"Father," protested Kaushalya Kumari. "I've studied the diggings, but I'm hardly an expert on them."

"You know a lot more than I do. But that's irrelevant now."

Vijay felt the young woman eyeing him. Suddenly she tossed her head, pulled her scarf higher on her shoulder, and asked, "Why is it irrelevant, Daddyji? Shouldn't one of us be there, just to ensure everything is done properly?"

The ex-ruler appeared to think for a moment. Then, he said, "Actually, it might be a good idea for you to go along." To Prasad and Vijay, he said, "She can answer questions about the sites, as well as representing me. Of course, there would have to be another lady, too. We can't have my daughter going out to the villages with men unless she's properly escorted. Many people still think it's shocking that she's not in *purdah*."

Deputy Director Prasad mulled over the idea. Then, he said, "I think it would be well for the princess to go along. I can send Miss Das, too, if she is acceptable. Or possibly the princess would like her own maid to go instead?"

"Miss Das will do fine," Kaushalya said, trying not to show her annoyance. That was the worst drawback to being in Mangarh; she certainly didn't bother with a female companion every time she left the house in New Delhi! "We'll need a lunch," she said. "There are no restaurants where we're going. I'll have the cook pack something."

Vijay started to protest, but then he realized the box lunches would not be available from the *dak* bungalow until almost noon. "That's very kind of you," he said.

"Veg or non-veg?" she asked.

Vijay hesitated only momentarily. Rajputs, especially the men, were traditionally meat-eaters, as were Untouchable Bhangis. But he personally adhered to a vegetarian diet for ethical reasons. He decided there was little risk to his deception by sticking to his preferences. And Shanta Das, as a Buddhist, was probably vegetarian. "Veg, please. For Miss Das, also."

Kaushalya Kumari told her maid to go fetch the food and drink from the kitchen. Then she said, "I'll get a few things while we're waiting for the lunch to come." Abruptly she turned, the tail of her *dupatta* flying.

Prasad lagged behind when the ex-Maharaja went toward his office. "Dammit, Singh," he said with a smile, "I would have gone myself, if I'd known there would be a beautiful princess along!" There was a slight pause, and he said, "And Das is rather pretty, too, even if she is Scheduled Caste."

Vijay inwardly cringed.

In half an hour they were in the jeep, an Indian-built Mahindra & Mahindra. Vijay sat by the driver, a small, quiet Muslim about forty years old named Akbar Khan, and the two women shared the back seat. Despite the omnipresent dust in the air and on the roads, when they started out the jeep gleamed and the interior was spotlessly clean; every time the vehicle was stopped for any period of time, Akbar Khan thoroughly dusted it, and if water was available, he would wash the exterior.

As they left the palace grounds, Vijay gazed across the town at the old fortress on its hill. He hated to have to go chasing across the mountains, leaving Ghosali to search the fort. Much as he'd like the treasure located as soon as possible, he didn't want Ghosali to be the one to find it.

No one was speaking in the jeep, partly because unmarried persons of the opposite sex did not traditionally mix freely, except a relative few Westernized elite in the big cities, and partly because Kaushalya Kumari detested the tax people's very presence. It was also noisy in the open-canopied vehicle: the wheels drumming on the rough paved road, the warm air rushing by, Khan continually honking the horn as they met or passed a train of pack camels or a peasant's bullock cart.

The princess had changed into an orange colored outfit, a Rajput long skirt, blouse and veil, no doubt because she would likely be seen by tradition-minded villagers. She also wore sunglasses, definitely a modern touch. Vijay wished he had thought to buy some himself to partially conceal his face. He wondered if dark glasses were even available in Mangarh; as yet, few persons other than the urban elite had access to such luxuries.

The road first wound through the valley, near the bank of the virtually dry river bed. Then Vijay's tension grew as the road veered northerly. Off to the right, only a kilometer away, lay his home village. Across the fields he saw the trees around the tank or village pond, and sunlight bounced off the mud walls and tile roofs. His mother was there in Gamri village, and his uncle and auntie and cousins. He would visit them before leaving Mangarh, but he would need to be careful so none of the other tax raiders saw him and became suspicious.

The road began to climb, and Vijay tried to relax. Up they drove, along a spur of the Aravalli range. Almost every feature of the landscape had some legend attached to it. The sharp hilltop on the right was where Lord Rama and his brother Lakshmana, heroes of the great epic the *Ramayana* had killed a demon. The scrubby forest on one side of the hill was where the two brothers had come to hunt after Rama became King of Ayodhya.

"The *stupa*'s near here," Kaushalya Kumari called loudly. "Do you want to see it now, or on the way back?"

Vijay turned to look at her. The princess had draped part of her scarf over her head, no doubt for modesty in this conservative area, maybe also to protect her hair from the wind and dust. "Let's see it when we come back," Vijay replied, equally loudly. "It will be hotter near the desert, so we'll do that part early."

He turned to face forward again. They passed a tiny village of well kept, tree shaded cottages—the hillside ashram of the well-known sage Guru Dharmananda.

The forest became denser, and the fields in the little valleys were more fertile looking. The air smelled fresher, cooler and less dusty, the scent of pine mingled with the perfume of blossoming shrubs and vines. Farmers drove bullocks around tight circles, pulling the geared shafts that drove Persian wheels with long loops of buckets lifting water from the wells and streams.

The road climbed past a small village of scattered thatched roof huts which Vijay recognized as belonging to Bhil tribals. Then it descended the other side of the mountains, in hairpin curves along arid-looking ravines with water-scoured rocks in their bottoms. Often, between the hills could be seen distant views of the dry, western plain that blended into the Thar, the Great Indian Desert.

The jeep slowed for a section of road repair work. A continual procession of women carried baskets of broken rocks on their heads, tediously moving a section of hillside down to fill in a ravine. Hot, hard, monotonous labor.

In half an hour or so the vehicle reached the lowlands, the sandy fringe of the desert. In the distance lay a couple of farming villages of mud houses, almost the same dusty dun color as the plain. "Turn here," Kaushalya Kumari called as the jeep approached a side road. Vijay told the driver Khan, who didn't understand the English spoken by the others.

The road now was unmetalled, so the jeep trailed a plume of dust. They drove for twenty minutes through a mostly flat, sandy region of scrubby, widely spaced thorn bushes. Occasionally a peacock ran beside the road or a herd of startled antelope raced off. Camels and goats grazed in the distance. The jeep passed a lone bicyclist, and a woman walking with a load of brush balanced on her head.

Abruptly, the princess called, "Over there, to the left."

Vijay saw an area of ground elevated above the surrounding plain, a low, undulating mound a few acres in extent. At its edge stood a long cement-block shed with a corrugated metal roof, and a small house of mud bricks. As the jeep drew near, Vijay saw that the mound had been cut open in a number of places to expose brick walls.

Akbar Khan stopped the jeep by the shed. No fence protected the site, but a dark blue, rusting metal sign with white lettering said in both English and Hindi:

Protected Monument

This monument has been declared to be of national importance under the Ancient Monuments and Archaeological Sites and Remains Act, 1958. Whoever destroys, removes, injures, alters, defaces, imperils or misuses this monument shall be punishable with imprisonment which may extend to three months or with fine which may extend to five thousand rupees or with both.

Archaeological Survey of India

They stepped from the jeep into the blast of the sun, and Vijay stretched his arms and legs. He'd been tense anyway, of course, and even in the heat it felt good to be out of the vehicle after the bumpy ride.

Shanta Das said, "Sir, I've heard you come from this area. Much of what we saw must have been familiar to you."

Vijay glanced sharply at her. She smiled; the remark was obviously innocent. He tried to sound casual as he replied, "I've only been across the hills once." The statement was true. He did not look directly at the princess, but he could tell she was staring at him. She did not comment on the revelation that he came from Mangarh.

From the small house hurried a middle aged watchman, badly in need of a shave and wearing a dirty shirt over a *dhoti*. "You wish a guide, *sahib*?"

He obviously hoped to earn a gratuity. Vijay flashed a copy of the search warrant, which listed the site. The man took the paper and examined it, but from the vacant look on his face it was clear he could not read the English.

Kaushalya Kumari spoke to him in Rajasthani: "This man and that woman are from the government. I am the Maharaja's daughter." The man bowed and pressed his palms together. "I beg your forgiveness, *Rajkumari*. I should have known you." He returned the warrant to Vijay, then backed away.

They looked out over an area of rectangular excavations, at the bottoms of which bricks lay in regular rows, some appearing to be pavings, others walls. Black plastic sheets overlain with sand covered some portions. The whole thing didn't mean much to Vijay.

He saw that Kaushalya Kumari stood poised and calm, her orange *kanchli-kurti* outfit bright in the sunlight, her arms folded, gazing over the site as if it were familiar to her, as indeed it must be. He hesitated to ask for explanations; she must loathe him for the difficulties he and the other income tax officials were causing her and her father. But his preferred manner whenever he dealt with taxpayers on an official basis was to be as courteous and pleasant as possible. He had often been quite successful in his investigations by trying to impress upon the taxpayers that he was just doing his job, that he had no interest in harassment merely for the sake of harassment. He said pleasantly to her, "I'm quite interested in the historical background of this place, Princess. Could you tell me what the Archaeological Survey discovered?"

He could not read her face behind the dark glasses. She remained silent for so long that he wondered if she would answer. But at last, she said tonelessly, "This is the farthest south remnant of the Indus civilization discovered to date in Rajasthan. Of course, some others in Gujarat state and in Pakistan are more southerly."

Shanta Das drew the end of her green sari over her head as shade and asked, "How old is it, Princess?"

"The Harappan town was probably between 1,500 and 2,000 B.C.E. It can't be dated exactly."

Vijay nodded. Every schoolboy knew of the civilization, referred to by the name of the Indus River or of the great ruined city of Harappa, which predated the invasions of the Aryans who had apparently been the precursors of Hinduism. From his own readings, Vijay knew no one could explain with certainty why the society had disappeared in a relatively short period of time. And no one had yet been able to decipher the script those peoples used.

Kaushalya Kumari pointed toward the plain beyond the site. "Over there is a river bed. It's dry except during the monsoons. But thousands of years ago it probably held water all year. That may be why the town was built here. They would have used the river to irrigate their crops. And the civilization seems to have depended on trade by water transport, especially on the Indus River."

"It's fascinating how much a place can change over time,"

said Shanta.

Kaushalya Kumari stood quietly for a few moments. Then she turned to Vijay and spoke, the taunting clear, although her voice was not unpleasant in tone: "Have you decided yet which of the pits holds our buried treasure?"

Vijay had known from a glance that this was a most unlikely hiding place for wealth. It was too remote, too unguarded. Besides, who knew when some amateur archaeologists or looters would come digging?

He smiled self-deprecatingly. "Whatever treasures are here, Princess, they aren't what the Income Tax Department would consider undeclared wealth."

She examined him for a time from behind her dark glasses. He was sure she must be at least slightly surprised at his showing that he could appreciate the larger significance of the site.

At last she said, pointing toward the excavations in front of them, "That long aisle of brickwork is apparently the main street. The higher area over there is thought have been a citadel. Here on the right the diggers have exposed part of the mud brick wall that surrounded the town." Her voice grew quieter as she said, "No one's sure if the wall was for defense, or to keep out the river when it flooded, or merely to keep out wild animals."

"I see," Vijay said. "Has anyone concluded what happened to the town? Why it was abandoned?"

"Not for sure. It could have been destroyed by floods or earthquakes. The archaeologists also found evidence of fires in the top layer of buildings."

Vijay mulled this over. At last, he said, "Well, as long as we're here, I'd like to take a look." He might never again have a chance to visit such a site; most of them were fairly far away, the majority now in Pakistan or near the Pakistani border. He added, "We'll make it fast. It's getting too hot to stay long." He walked into the ruins, between two excavation pits.

Shanta Das followed close behind. In a few minutes she commented, "I think we'd need to have studied the site to really interpret it, sir. Even then, it must require quite an exercise of imagination."

Vijay glanced at her, and nodded. He knew, intellectually, that this was a place where millennia ago thousands of people had spent their lives. These bricks had been laboriously shaped and laid by men long ago, and had witnessed the pains, and the pleasures, of thousands of persons.

But he could feel nothing when he examined the area. The ruins were just old bricks. He wondered how Kaushalya Kumari was affected. He turned to see if she were following.

She had remained near the edge of the site. She stood perfectly still, her arms folded, peering off over the excavations. It was as if she, too, were trying to imagine what the town must have been like 3,500 years before. Or what how it must have felt to have lived then. Or how this civilization could have ended.

Three Peoples

1

Upstanding in the car, the skillful charioteer guides his
strong horses on whithersoe'er he will.
See and admire the strength of those controlling reins,
which from behind declare the will of him who drives.
Horses whose hooves rain dust are neighing loudly,
yoked to the chariots, showing forth their vigor.
With their forefeet descending on the foemen, they, never
flinching, trample and destroy them....

— *Rig Veda*, VI, 75

Kanur, the Indus Civilization, 1503 B.C.E.

The eleven year old girl gazed out over the flat roofs of Kanur. The late autumn sun warmed her bare back, and the still air carried the voices of the other children Sumbari saw playing marbles or dice games on their own rooftops. High above, vultures soared in great circles. At one time Sumbari would have sat and watched them, but she'd had little time for that the past two years, and today her attention was not on the sky.

Despite anxiety over the possible attack, the town of three thousand souls appeared peaceful. White squares of laundry hung from the edges of roofs to dry in the sun. A small striped squirrel flowed along the edge of a neighboring rooftop and onto a *neem* tree branch overhanging the town wall.

A faint odor of burning meat lay in the air. To the west, from inside the elevated temple compound, smoke rose from the fires where goats were being sacrificed to Shiv. Sumbari's father and most of the other adults were at the gathering called by the priests. The adults were worried, especially after hearing that Harappa, the distant capital, had fallen to the invaders in spite of the massive wall around its citadel. Kanur's own mud brick wall had been badly undermined by the floods the past two years, and repairs had not yet been completed on the gaps. Sumbari wasn't sure just how concerned she should be. She knew some foreign tribe posed a threat, but she had difficulty understanding how serious the danger really was. The town had been so quiet, so uneventful all her life.

Sumbari smiled as she pretended to talk to herself, making sure she spoke loudly enough for her five year old brother to hear: "Where can that boy possibly be this time? He finds such good places to hide." Of course, she knew exactly where Pippru was. Even though she played "Find Me" with him at least a couple of times every day, he never tired of hiding in the same few favorite spots. This time he was inside the newer of the two rectangular brick water tanks on the roof. While she was standing in the corner of the main room with her eyes covered she had heard him lift the wooden cover on the tank, which was empty because it hadn't been finished until after this year's rainy season had ended. Pippru would get tired of waiting if Sumbari pretended to be searching the rest of the house, so she had gone directly to the roof.

The rooftop was their favorite place to play whenever Sumbari decided to take time away from the chores which had consumed most of her time after their mother's death two years ago. The roof was also an ideal place from which to watch the stars at night. When Sumbari was small, her mother had taught her to recognize all the constellations and had told her stories about them. Sumbari's favorite stars were the small cluster that her people called the Six Foster-Mothers—even though Sumbari could see *seven* stars herself—because of the way in which the six women of the legend had taken care of the god Shiv when he was a child.

Sumbari was fascinated by the stars moving slowly but continually in great arcs across the sky. Many of them disappeared below the western horizon, only to rise again in the east, a little later on each succeeding night. She had learned to anticipate when most stars and the moon and the sun would rise above certain buildings easterly of her own house, and exactly where those heavenly bodies would set.

Sumbari sometimes told Pippru the stories she'd heard from their mother about the constellations. But usually, after working all day preparing meals and cleaning house and doing laundry and taking care of Pippru, Sumbari was too tired to watch the stars. Still, whenever the Six Foster-Mothers could be seen above the horizon, which was most of the year except for the Hot Season and the Rains, Sumbari would come up on the roof before she went to sleep and say a prayer to them on behalf of her own mother.

Sumbari had been uneasy when she, herself, had been called a "foster-mother" by her older friend Balbutha because of taking responsibility for Pippru. Somehow it didn't seem quite right that someone so young should be a foster-mother, and Sumbari rejected the thought of being one, even though she was in fact performing the duties.

"Where could that boy possibly be?" she asked again. Pippru had lifted the top of the tank and was peering out at her, but she would not spoil his fun by finding him too quickly. She looked at the countryside, beyond the town wall. The cotton and sesamum fields, their harvesting nearly completed, stretched far before meeting the edge of the forest. Crows pecked at the soil and flocks of green parrots wheeled overhead. The plain seemed as quiet as ever.

She knew that for years occasional bands of marauders from over the mountains had raided far to the north of Kanur for cattle and slaves. It was said that this year after the rains had ended, great hordes had poured down from the mountain pass, and many of the invaders had crossed the broad Indus River and were ravaging towns and villages. Last week, the shocking word had come of the sack of Harappa. And now a large band of the invaders was said to be only a day or two away from Kanur.

"I don't see that boy anywhere," Sumbari said for Pippru's benefit as she hurried around the rooftop with exaggerated motions. Then: "I know! He's in the water tank again."

"Nuh-nuh-no, he isn't," came Pippru's stutter, trying to sound gruff, from inside the tank. "He-he-he's down in the workshop!"

"Oh, no, he isn't. He was in the workshop last time. This time he's right here!" Sumbari lifted the lid and tickled his bare side. Pippru giggled and jumped up. He looked at her with bright eyes and a broad grin. His naked front was still covered with tiny stone chips and dust from hiding under the workbench in the front room of the house. Sumbari smiled at him as she brushed him off. Then she gave him a big hug. "That was a good place to hide!" she said.

"Leh-leh-let's play 'Find Me' again!" said Pippru.

Sumbari sighed. If she didn't love him so much she wouldn't put up with him, she decided. "I have another idea. Let's go for a walk. After we get back I'll need to grind the barley for tonight."

"I have to go to the puh-puh-privy."

"Go ahead. But don't miss the hole this time!" Pippru's aim was indifferent; he was as likely to hit the brick seat or floor as he was the opening above the drain. And Sumbari didn't want to have to mop the area yet again today.

Pippru grabbed one of his toys, a hollow clay whistle in the shape of a bird that had been made by their friend Namuci the potter, and he blew into it. The bird cooed loudly, and Pippru ran down the steps to the upper floor and into the tiny latrine room adjoining the outer wall.

Sumbari had already swept the floor of the sleeping area, but while she waited for Pippru she straightened the rope-webbed beds.

She wondered if she should air the blankets on the roof but decided they could wait another day. From behind the latrine curtain came the cooing of the bird, and Sumbari hoped that didn't mean Pippru was being careless in pointing.

When Pippru came out, still blowing his whistle, they continued down the stairs to the ground floor, across the minuscule courtyard and out through their father's workshop, where a row of small square steatite stone blanks lay on his table. Like his own father and grandfather, their father Varchin was a seal carver, the head of the guild now, and Sumbari knew he was considered the best in the area. Everyone admired Papa's renderings of elephants and tigers and rhinoceroses and humped bulls. Naturally, Papa had learned to read and write so he could also carve the lettering on the seals. Even traders from other towns came to buy Papa's seals, which they then used for stamping their signatures on every transaction and for securing every bag of grain or bale of cloth.

Sumbari had heard her father talking, though, about how the past few years the demand for the seals had dropped as trading had declined due to the bad floods, and the raids from the invading tribes, and the river getting shallower so the larger boats could no longer travel on it. Her father had been subdued, often lost in thought, ever since his wife died. And since the recent word of the raiders, he had become distracted and obviously worried.

Sumbari took Pippru's hand and led him out the door and down the tiny ally into the street. A couple of children were playing dice, and a little boy was towing a miniature clay cart on the brick paving, but most of the adults were at the temple ceremonies. Sumbari guided Pippru to the entrance of the elevated, enclosed area where the temple and the priests' houses and the granaries were located. As usual, no one guarded the gateway, but she knew children were not permitted inside at a time such as this. She stopped, holding Pippru's hand, staring at the backs of the crowd gathered before the tall cylindrical stone which everyone worshiped as Shiv. Sumbari, curious about the ceremony, listened for anything of interest. She could hear a priest's voice chanting, but she could not make out what he said.

"Whuh-why are we standing here?" asked Pippru.

"No reason," replied Sumbari, deciding she couldn't learn anything useful. She began walking back toward their own quarter of the town, but by a different route. Just outside the temple area rose the big house of the grain trader Chumuri. Sumbari was surprised to see two bullock carts outside the home. The chubby, scowling merchant was supervising his servants, who loaded furnishings and wooden boxes into the carts. Several children stood watching, and Sumbari and Pippru stopped also. Chumuri paid no attention to the children, which was normal. He considered himself far above most residents of the Kanur in status and only associated with the head priest of the temple, who ruled the town.

"Whuh-what are they doing?" asked Pippru.

One of the older boys, Arsasanas, said in a low voice, "Chumuri is afraid of the attack. He's running away."

"Whuh-what's a 'tack?" asked Pippru.

Arsasanas gave a short laugh. "You'll find out soon enough."

"Never mind," said Sumbari, suddenly filled with anxiety. If Chumuri was leaving, shouldn't everyone else be doing the same?

She led Pippru to the side of the town facing the river. She was glad to see that the laborers working under direction of the masons had remained to repair the wall, rather than attending the temple ceremony. But the flood waters had badly eaten out the earth beneath base of the wall in a number of places, causing sections of brick to fall away from lack of support. The men of the brick masons' guild had been working for months, and even Sumbari could see that it would still be a long time before the wall was completely repaired. The people of Kanur were used to life remaining the same for generation after generation; there was seldom need for haste. Like everything else, repairs moved slowly, too.

"Let's go back home," she said to Pippru.

Pippru was taking a nap when their father returned. Varchin stood inside the doorway, stroking his closely cropped black beard, lost in thought, his dark skin contrasting with the whiteness of the cotton shawl drawn over his shoulder. "What did the priests say, Papa?" asked Sumbari.

He looked absently at her, as if he had not been aware of her presence. He tugged at his shawl, adjusting it. "They uh...said we shouldn't worry. That Shiv will protect us. But just in case, workmen are going to speed up repairing the wall. The priests ordered them and the servants to stand on the wall and defend it if the tribes attack. I and the other artisans will take turns keeping watch. Beginning tonight."

"Do you think the wall will keep the tribes out?"

Her father frowned. "Maybe."

"Harappa's wall didn't stop them."

Her father stared at her. "So it seems."

"Why don't we run away, Papa? Like Chumuri?"

He looked away, started to say something, then closed his mouth. From his annoyed expression Sumbari could tell he didn't approve of Chumuri's action. "We could never come back if we left," he said at last. "The priests would withhold our grain and order everyone not to talk with us."

"Oh," said Sumbari. It made sense that Chumuri could do as he wished; he and his ancestors had always been close partners of the priests. Chumuri held the rights to trade the grain for the temple, which owned all the lands around Kanur.

"Anyway," said her father, sounding as if he were trying to convince himself, "Where would we go? Outside the wall we'd have no protection. And we don't know how long we'd have to be away. It might be days. Meanwhile, the attackers might destroy the town and take everything. That's what the priests said."

Sumbari was twisting the clay bangle on her wrist, first one direction, then the other. Her potter friend Namuci had made the bangle and given it to her a few days ago. She asked, "What will we do if the tribes attack, if they get inside the wall?"

He stared at her, obviously uncertain. Then he said, "You children should hide, I think. Do you know a good spot?"

Sumbari thought. It was difficult to come up with a really good place. At last she said, "The new tank on the roof might be best."

Varchin frowned in thought a moment, then gave a nod. "I can't think of anything better. I hope it doesn't come to that. We must pray that the raiders ignore us and keep on going."

That seemed unlikely to Sumbari. The main road lay only a short distance from Kanur, and the town was clearly visible to anyone traveling. But maybe Shiv would indeed protect the town.

Before bedding down, the family gathered around the little upright cylindrical stone Shiv on the altar on the lower floor of the house. Just as her mother used to do when she was alive, Sumbari lit their oil lamps and incense and made an offering of flowers to Shiv. The family also possessed a small clay image of the Mother Goddess, but this time they did not offer the customary grain to her. This time they were not praying for abundant harvests; they were praying for protection from armed warriors.

A day passed with no sign of invaders. As they did so often, Sumbari and Pippru went to the potters' lane to visit Namuci and his wife, who had no children of their own. Namuci sat in his courtyard by his stone wheel, on which he was forming wet clay into a big jug. His black eyes had a sleepy look most of the time, but they lit with pleasure at the sight of Sumbari and Pippru.

"I have a new toy for you," Namuci said. "Balbutha, would you get it?" His wife gave the children a welcoming smile, and she set aside the basket of grain she was sorting through. The clacking of her many bracelets against each other as she stepped into the house reminded Sumbari of the sound of her mother's jewelry.

Balbutha came back out with a small clay object and a length of string. "Oh!" said Pippru. "A muh-muh-monkey!"

"You know how it works?" asked Namuci.

"Sh-show me!" said Pippru.

The potter, smiling with pride at his creation, stepped away from his wheel, leaving it to gradually coast to a halt. He rinsed his hands in a bowl of water and dried them with a rag.

A long string ran through a hole in the tiny clay monkey, and Namuci handed one end of the string and the monkey to Pippru. "Here," he said. "You hold your end as high as you can. I'll hold the other." The potter knelt on the brick paving, so the string was stretched at a shallow downward angle. "Hold the string tight," he said, "and let the monkey go." Pippru did so. Namuci gave light jerks on the string, relaxing and tightening it. Each time he loosened the string, the monkey would slide down a little, only to halt again when the string was tightened.

Pippru was laughing with joy. "It cuh-cuh-climbs down the string!" he shouted.

"It took Namuci three tries to make a monkey that could do it right," said Balbutha to Sumbari. "But come, let's get some of the honey cakes I've just made."

Another day passed with no evidence of raiders. Sumbari was beginning to feel that maybe there was really nothing to be so concerned about. When she and Pippru again visited the potter and his wife, Namuci asked with a concerned look, "Have you children made plans in case of the attack?"

"We'll hide in the new tank on our roof," replied Sumbari.

Namuci stared at her for a time, pressed his lips together and gave a nod. Sumbari had the impression he wasn't entirely pleased with her answer but didn't know of anything better to suggest.

When she left, she wore another clay bangle he'd made her. There were craftsman who specialized in creating only bangles and earrings and such, but to Sumbari's mind Namuci's bangles were every bit as good. As she and Pippru walked home, she deliberately swung her arm high and low in rhythm with her legs so as to enjoy the sound the two bangles made when they clacked together.

Back at their own house, their father returned after a visit to the market. His eyes were dazed, his forehead even more lined with worry than before. He told Sumbari, "A trader in bronze came through today. He said that the tribe attacked Kaller. You know that's only a half day's walk from here. So they could come any moment. The priests have told all the watchmen to be alert."

His eyes at last focused on Sumbari: "You children be ready to hide!"

"We will, Papa," said Sumbari.

By nightfall the invaders had not appeared. Sumbari went to bed as usual after going up on the roof and praying to the Six Foster-Mothers. But now that the threat was imminent, she woke frequently as she twisted and tossed on her rope-webbed cot. She dreamed Kanur was being attacked. Though the night was cool, she awoke perspiring, certain the assault had begun. It was some time before she realized that the town was quiet, and that her father was still sleeping in the far corner.

She decided to avoid more nightmares by staying awake. She took her blanket and climbed the stairs to the roof. She wrapped the blanket around her and sat near the new water tank as she watched the sky lighten in the east. She thought about the times she had sat on this roof with her mother, listening to the stories about the stars. Tears came to her eyes.

"Why did you leave me, Mama?" she whispered. "Are you somewhere up there in the stars now? I need you. Why did you die?"

Sumbari rubbed at her tears. She suddenly realized she was getting angry at her mother for leaving, and she felt ashamed. She knew her mother hadn't wanted to get sick or die. So why get angry? But she couldn't stop herself. She was sad and loving and angry all at the same time. It was confusing.

Then she heard the first shouts of warning from the men on the walls. She jumped up, dropped her blanket. "Papa!" she called as she dashed down the stairs. She saw he had heard, and he was already up, throwing his cloak around his shoulders.

"Should we go up on the roof now?" asked Sumbari.

Her father hesitated. Then he came, put his arms around her, and held her so tight it almost felt like he was crushing her. "Do as you wish," he murmured. "Just make sure you get up there in a hurry if you need to."

"I will, Papa." Sumbari blinked back more tears. What if he got hurt? Even killed. Papa let her go. He stepped over to Pippru, stroked the sleeping boy's shoulders for a moment. Then, after a final look at Sumbari, he hurried down the stairs.

Sumbari panicked at a sudden thought: what if she never saw Papa again? But she was in charge of the house, and she had her duty. She decided the roof was where she wanted to be, just in case. Anyway, she could see better from up there. She shook Pippru awake, pulled him from his bed. He stumbled from drowsiness as she shoved him ahead of her up the steep stairway. In the dim light she saw his eyes were wide with anxiety as he looked back; he seemed to climb each riser slowly and reluctantly. She pushed him onto the roof. "Get into the tank," she ordered.

"Do we have to get in now? Can't we wait?" Pippru's small voice asked.

Sumbari thought a moment. There should be plenty of time to climb into the tank if the attackers should get inside the town's walls. "All right. But keep out of sight!"

They squatted behind the low brick wall surrounding the edge of the roof. Already in the distance were sounds of yelling and clashing of weapons, and screams. The children found it difficult to see what was occurring on the outskirts of town, even though daylight had come.

"That suh-suh-sounded like Papa!" Pippru wailed after a distant male voice yelled in agony.

"Be quiet!" Sumbari ordered. "It didn't sound like him at all." She wished she felt more sure.

In only a few minutes the sounds of fighting seemed closer. Sumbari was puzzled—could the invaders be inside the wall so soon? Suddenly, she heard horses' hooves clattering on the street. No one in

Kanur had a horse! "Get down! Quick—into the tank!" she commanded. She boosted Pippru over the side, then climbed in herself and pulled the cover of wooden planks over the top. She fervently hoped no one had seen them climb in; she had not intended to wait until the attackers were so close.

What's happened to Papa? she worried as she squatted, shifting positions to try to get comfortable in the confined space. And to Namuci and Balbutha and their other friends? She wore only a thin white cotton cloth wrapped around her hips, and the brick side of the water tank felt rough to the bare flesh of her back. The interior of the tank smelled dank, like the clay from which the bricks were made. She heard distant crashing sounds, as if doors were being broken open, and a woman screamed. The sounds seemed close, even though they were muffled by the wooden cover.

And then she felt the floor of the tank vibrate as the door of their own house crashed in.

"Keep quiet and don't move!" she whispered to Pippru. She tried not to let her voice show her terror.

Occasional sounds of items being smashed came from below, and she heard male voices. After a short time there were heavy footsteps on the stairs. The door to the roof creaked open.

Sumbari held her breath and hoped fervently that Pippru would stay quiet. He was not noted for obeying her orders. She heard the top of the other tank lifted, then—after a pause—dropped.

Close by her own tank, a man's voice spoke loudly in a strange tongue, and a reply came from not far away. She heard footsteps on the roof, but they did not seem headed toward the hiding place. Maybe it worked, she thought—they saw the water in the other tank and won't bother to look in this one.

Then she remembered the blanket she had dropped previously when she'd been on the roof.

Right by this tank.

What if they saw it? She took another deep breath and held it, hoping. She prayed to Shiv. She prayed to the Six Foster-Mothers, even though they were no longer visible in the sky. She prayed to her own mother.

After ages of torment, she again heard footsteps come close. She willed herself to be small and invisible, and bent her face toward the floor of the tank. Suddenly the lid was lifted, and daylight flooded the tank's interior. She sat still, willing herself not to be seen.

The lid remained raised. A loud, deep voice broke the stillness, directly above her ear, in the unfamiliar tongue.

She realized it was hopeless to pretend she had not been found. She fearfully raised her head. A man stood over her, his huge form silhouetted against the sky.

Through eyes squinting to adjust to the brightness, she saw he was like no one she had ever before encountered. She had heard of the paleness of the invaders, but it was quite another matter to see one herself. His skin was so light she could scarcely believe it was real. His long hair and beard were the color of ripened wheat. The blue-gray of his eyes matched the sky behind his head. Maybe a little younger than her father, he smelled of sweat and of damp wool.

In a deep, booming voice he spoke a command. Then he backed away slightly, motioning upward with the sword she now saw in his hand. Fresh blood covered the weapon's blade—and the hand gripping the hilt. Her eyes wide with fright, she shrank away, pressing her back into the wall of the tank.

His forehead wrinkled in irritation, the man again barked the command, again gestured with the reddened sword. Sumbari hesitated, almost certain the weapon was about to be used on her and Pippru. But she had no choice. Numbly she braced her hands on the floor of the tank and shoved herself erect. The man pointed his sword at Pippru and spoke another command, clearly ordering the boy out of the tank.

Pippru whimpered and shrank into his corner. The man spoke loudly and abruptly, and again gestured with his weapon. Hoping they would be spared if they did as ordered, Sumbari took hold of Pippru's arm and drew him up.

Another man shouted from the doorway. Their captor turned and replied, anger in his tone. Sumbari saw that the other man was about the same age as the first, but he was shorter and had slightly darker hair. He strode over and roughly grabbed Sumbari's arm. She cried out at the pain.

The first man's deep voice shouted a sharp protest, his face contorted in rage. The other man snarled equally loudly, and Sumbari saw that he, too, appeared angry. The two argued forcefully for some seconds. Suddenly, the first man grabbed Sumbari's other arm, his blood-coated fingers deep in her flesh. The men stood in stiff confrontation, scowling eye to eye.

Slowly, the second man released her. He spoke a burst of furious words. Then he turned, stalked to the doorway, and disappeared down the stairs.

The first man gave an order to Sumbari and tugged her toward the stairs. He waved his sword at Pippru in a gesture beckoning him to follow. Sumbari stiffened; she must protect her brother. "Let us stay!" she demanded, her voice high pitched with fear.

He spoke a short angry phrase and pulled harder. "No!" she screamed, straining to hold back. The man tightened his grip and dragged her to the doorway, shoved her through. Behind them Pippru began wailing. Afraid of tumbling down the steep stairs if the man continued to push, Sumbari stopped struggling. She weakly called to Pippru, "Come on—do what he wants." She added: "For now."

As she descended the steps, she gasped at seeing the wrecked interior of the house. The sleeping cots had been overturned, the bedding tossed aside. The red clay water jugs lay shattered and the liquid flooded the floor. Stunned, she continued past the sleeping level, down to the lower floor. The man still gripped her arm tightly.

She stopped to gape in astonishment at the devastation of the living area: the clay figure of the Mother Goddess lay in many pieces; Shiv's phallus rested where it had been thrown, in the corner opposite its altar. How could the gods have allowed such a thing! Why hadn't they struck the offenders dead?

She glanced through the door of her father's carving shop. The tools that her father treated with such care had been dumped to the floor, the workbench overturned.

The man pushed her out the door into the alley. She glanced back and saw that Pippru followed. They turned right at the street. The strong smell of smoke hung in the air, and she saw dark gray billows rising from several places in town.

A wheeled conveyance with two brown horses attached sat in the street. She was astonished at how flimsy the cart looked. The only wheels she had seen before were of thick, solid wood. But the two wheels on this cart seemed to be mostly air: only thin, round wooden rods fanning out from the center supported the narrow, hoop shaped rim. The man waved at them to climb into the cart.

"No! We won't leave!" Sumbari said loudly.

He scowled. He spoke brusquely, and grabbed her wrist. Part of his big, red-stained hand covered her clay bangles, pressing them painfully into her flesh.

She sat on the ground, trying to look fierce, though she was terrified.

The man seemed momentarily puzzled, then his face hardened. He pulled on her arm. Sumbari cried out from the pain as a bangle snapped, its pieces falling to clatter on the paving bricks. Mild surprise in his eyes, the man let go, but he yelled at her, gesturing firmly for her to get up.

She sat obstinately, trying hard not to cry. The man wiped his bloody sword on a scrap of cloth from the floor of the cart, shoved the weapon into its scabbard, and then took Sumbari by each of her shoulders and jerked her roughly to her feet. He shouted a command at her and pointed. She tried to look defiantly at him, but her eyes were wet with tears.

He pushed her, forcing her to scramble up onto the cart's wooden floor. Pippru slowly climbed in also. A bow and a mostly empty quiver of arrows lay on the bottom. The man seized some thongs of hide from the chariot's corner and quickly bound Sumbari's wrists together. Curiously, he seemed to take care to avoid the abrasion from the broken bangle. He then tied her ankles. He did the same to Pippru.

He easily lifted the two children aside on the floor, then climbed in himself. After leaning the bow and quiver upright against the leather front of the conveyance, he took the reins in one hand and seized a whip in his other. He cracked the whip over the two horses, who surged into motion.

Sumbari had opened her mouth to protest again, but the sudden movement of the cart threw her off balance, and with her limbs bound she had to struggle to stay upright. She saw determination in the face of her captor and realized there was no point in trying to change his mind. She looked back through her tears in disbelief as the man drove them down the street of homes, houses with their doors battered in, the dim interiors gaping vacantly. A group of pale skinned men were hauling small items out of the home of Chumuri the merchant. She heard a woman screaming from within a dwelling. Sumbari wondered if Namuci and Balbutha were safe, but their house was beyond the view from the route of the cart.

Twice, men looting homes called out to the man who was driving them. Each time he laughed, and boomed out a reply. They drove past the temple, and through the gateway Sumbari was stunned to see that the big stone column of Shiv had been toppled from its flat foundation. She whimpered in dismay. How could Shiv have allowed such a thing?

As they neared the town wall, she saw more results of the fighting. Bodies littered the street. Almost none were the light skinned attackers. Shocked almost beyond the ability to comprehend what she saw, and fearful of recognizing her father, she avoided looking closely at the remains.

Suddenly, her father's voice cried out ahead: "Wait! Don't take them!" Sumbari turned with relief. Her father limped toward them, half-hopping, dragging a leg drenched in blood.

"Papa!" she screamed.

Their father leaped, managed to grab the side of the vehicle as it rolled past. "Let them go!" he shouted. His face was contorted with pain as he hung to the side with both hands, letting the cart drag him.

Their captor looked down and frowned in annoyance. He swung the whip, its leather strands slashing across Varchin's forearms. Varchin grimaced, but he did not let go. Strips of red appeared on the dark skin of his arms. Again the man lashed the whip. Still Varchin clung to the side, lines of blood oozing from his hands and arms.

The man now dropped the whip into the vehicle, and withdrew his sword.

"No!" screamed Sumbari. "Nooooo!"

The man raised the sword, brought it down. It smacked with great force on the top edge of the vehicle's side.

But it did not strike Varchin's hands; he had let go at the last instant. Sumbari realized the man had not struck with the sharpened edge of the sword, which would have cut deeply into the vehicle; rather he had hit with the broad part of the blade. Still, it would have hurt terribly had Papa not let go.

The man flicked the reins and the horses increased speed. Sumbari quickly turned back toward her father, sprawled in the street.

He raised himself with both hands to look after his children, and he cried out: "Be careful! Try to come back!"

They sped through the open gateway. Sumbari panicked at being snatched from the town that had always been her home. "I want my papa!" she shrieked. She began sobbing in earnest, tears flowing down her cheeks.

The man looked puzzled, and spoke a few loud words in response.

"My papa," Sumbari bawled, her words muffled from her sobs. "I want my papa!"

The man shook his head, his lips tight. A group of the attackers stood a short distance away, near several townspeople huddled on the ground. Five or six more of the odd two wheeled vehicles stood nearby, attached to horses.

Sumbari's loud crying attracted the attention of some of the other townspeople in the forlorn looking group guarded by the strangers. She wiped the tears from her eyes enough to recognize some of the captives; they were mainly children, but also some women, distraught and battered, and two discouraged looking men, squatting with their heads in their hands. One of the men had a blood-soaked bandage on his upper arm. Namuci and Balbutha were not among them.

Her captor shouted to a guard, who called in reply. Sumbari expected that she and Pippru would be made to join the group of prisoners, but instead her captor drove past. He cracked his whip again, and the cart quickly gathered speed. Although the vehicle seemed light and flimsy compared to the oxcarts she had occasionally ridden in, it moved much faster, so fast she felt an increased terror. But her tearful gaze remained fixed on the small group of captives by the main gate as they dwindled into the distance.

She again opened her mouth to protest, but she once more realized it was useless. She started to squirm her way out of the cart even though it would have meant a painful drop to the ground, but she then realized she could not leave Pippru alone. She wiped her eyes once again and examined her captor's face more closely, knowing that her future and that of Pippru depended upon him. She was unable to read those strange blue eyes, now intent on the road ahead. But he held his head high, and his lips seemed to smile faintly, as if he were pleased with himself. His long nose arched out from his face like the beak of some bird, quite in contrast to the flat, broad noses of the inhabitants of her community. The pale brown skin of his arms seemed so light compared to her own dark hue.

And everyone she had ever known had black hair. The lightness of this man's would have been unbelievable were she not seeing it with her own eyes. Rather than cotton, he wore a wool shawl around his shoulders and another wool cloth around his hips. A leather belt held his scabbard and sword. His feet were shod in heavy-looking leather sandals.

She glanced at Pippru, who was trying to stay upright on the other side of the bouncing vehicle. His face showed utter terror. The tears again streamed from her own eyes, and her body shook with heavy sobs as the rooftops of Kanur disappeared far behind, and with it her father and everyone else she had known.

2

We have drunk the Soma and become immortal!
We have attained the light, we have found the Gods!
What can the malice of mortal man
or his spite, O Immortal, do to us now?

— *Rig Veda* VIII, 48, 3

Bhira reached the encampment with his captives. He examined the girl as he drove in. He agreed with his friends that in general the natives were ugly, with such dark skin and stubby, broad noses. This girl was almost pretty in a way, though, with her fine features and large eyes. The little boy had a certain delicate, bright eyed cuteness. Unfortunately they'd probably outgrow it eventually and be as unattractive as the other adults of their people.

The girl, he thought, couldn't know how lucky she was. That scoundrel Trita had been ready to rape her until Bhira made it clear the girl and the boy were his captives alone. He wished Trita had forced a fight over them. Bhira would have killed him, clearly showing who was the tribe's greatest warrior. And Bhira would have rid himself of his main rival.

The encampment spread over a broad field on high ground above the river. The herds of cattle, sheep, and goats grazed around the outskirts, watched over by children. As Bhira and the two captives arrived, women and children ran out to meet them, anxious for news of the assault. Bhira drove to his own tent, where he reined the horses to a halt. "Lord Indra made it easy!" he told his greeters. "We conquered them in minutes. Their wall had big holes in it, and those godless people didn't even know how to fight! Our bronze swords cut right through their flimsy copper weapons."

His wife Visala held out a bowl of cool water for him. Her smile, often twisted at the corners in scornful amusement at the foolishness of her husband and others, this time seemed to show she was glad to see him. He quickly drained the bowl and wiped his mouth with the back of his hand. He grinned at her. "I brought a couple of slaves to help with your work. They're a little young, but they should be easier to handle than older ones."

Visala raised an eyebrow as she looked skeptically at the two children. She brushed a wisp of light brown hair away from her gray eyes to examine them more clearly. Like most of the other warriors, on previous raids Bhira had foregone taking slaves in favor of building up his herd of cows, or bringing back other domestic animals or food-stuffs, or looting valuable housewares or weapons. But recently it had become fashionable for warriors to seize human prizes.

Now Visala's skepticism seemed to soften. "What darling children!" she said. Her usual sardonic air returned, and she said, "I might be able to use one, but I don't know what I'd do with two of them."

Bhira shrugged. "We can always trade one of them for cows."

"They look terrified, Bhira! What did you do to them?"

Annoyed, he deposited the two children on the grassy ground. "I didn't do anything! They should be grateful. I saved the girl from Trita."

"Hmm. Well, as long as we have them, I'll put them to work." Bhira untied the thongs on their ankles, and Visala beckoned to the children to follow her. They stood for a moment. The girl, her wrists still tied together, wiped her moist eyes with the edge of a hand and glared. Visala, frowning, beckoned more curtly.

The girl at last came to her, and the boy followed the girl.

While Bhira unyoked his horses he glanced appreciatively at the cows grazing beyond his tent. Although he was a warrior rather than a herder, he prided himself on his growing number of animals. They were beautiful in themselves, but mainly they were the measure of his wealth. He and Visala bartered the surplus milk for whatever they might need in the way of supplies. And if he lived to an age at which he could no longer join the raiding parties, the cows would provide for his sustenance.

Bhira watched as Visala unbound the girl's wrists and showed her how to churn butter. The girl at first refused to work. Bhira stepped over and gave her a light cuff on the side of the head. The girl whirled about and glared at him. But he saw fear in her eyes, too. Then the girl abruptly turned and began working the handle of the paddle with vigor, as if taking out her anger on it.

As the morning progressed other warriors returned with their booty and slaves from the newly sacked town. All day the air was filled with merriment. The attackers had almost no dead and few injuries, and the town had been ripe for looting.

They didn't try to make the little boy work right away. He sat on the ground, wiping the tears in his eyes, watching his sister.

That night the tribe held its customary post-raid celebration around the campfire. Bhira lay back, contented after gorging himself on the roasted goat meat and baked chicken, washed down by huge quantities of *sura*. He felt confident he was still holding his *sura* well when the gambling began.

Trita, his enemy since childhood, sat near him, appearing to have forgotten the earlier dispute over the slaves. But when the brown nuts used for dice were brought out, Trita said, "I'd still like that girl you took today. I'll wager a cow against her."

Bhira squinted, trying to read Trita's round face in the firelight. That Trita was a clever bastard. He was shorter and less strong than Bhira, but he made up for it by being more cunning. "Only one cow? Ridiculous!" Bhira replied.

"Well...two, then. But no more!"

Bhira thought. He didn't yet know how good a worker the girl would be. In any event, he'd never consider less than three cows. He knew Trita was goading him. "I'd rather be rid of her little brother," he said.

Trita spat. "I prefer girls in my bed."

"Can't your wife find some work for him?"

Trita examined Bhira's face. Bhira realized his rival was trying to decide if the question had been a veiled insult about Trita's own capacity in bed. Eventually Trita said firmly, "No. It's the girl I want."

Bhira shook his head. "I'm not ready to wager her yet. She's too young, anyway."

Trita laughed. "They're never too young. I may capture one myself in the next town. Then you'll be stuck with this one. And she's too young yet to give you a son."

Bhira's hand shot to his sword. "You're going too far!" he growled. Trita knew that Bhira's wife still being childless after five years of marriage was a sore point; the suggestion Bhira might turn to a mere *dasi*, a black, to produce children, was a serious insult.

Trita laughed uneasily. "You know I was joking!"

Bhira rose. "Find someone else to joke with!"

He moved to join a group of men on the far side of the fire who were singing ribald songs, accompanied by drums and a flute. There, the others loudly welcomed him.

The next day, as the tribe prepared to decamp and move on, Santanu, one of the wealthiest herders, approached Bhira. Santanu held well over two hundred cows; people seldom bothered to count cattle exactly when one reached so many. "I saw the boy you took yesterday," Santanu said. "Would you take two cows for him?"

Bhira pondered before replying, "No, my wife can use him. I wouldn't part with him for less than four."

Santanu shook his head. "Far too much for someone so young and inexperienced. I'd like another cowherd, but I'd be taking too much of a chance on someone so small." He paused, as if considering. "I could go three cows," he said, "but that's my final offer."

"Sold!" Bhira felt pleased. With three new cows, his own herd would number twenty-three. Unless he was mistaken, that put him two cows ahead of Trita. Not a significant margin, but better than being behind by one cow as he had been the past weeks.

Bhira led Santanu to where Visala was supervising the two slaves in packing up the gear. In spite of the language difficulties, the girl seemed to be at least some help. "I just sold the boy to Santanu," he told Visala.

His wife's face registered dismay, quickly turning to annoyance. "It's not good to separate him yet from his sister! He's too young."

Bhira's mouth hung open in surprise. "I thought you said you couldn't use both."

Her gray eyes shifted away. "Well, I changed my mind."

"You haven't grown attached to them already? They're only *dasas*, after all."

She turned her back on him and stood looking at the two children. They had stopped working and were talking with each other in their odd-sounding tongue. "Anyway, the boy won't be far away," Bhira told her. "The two can visit each other."

Visala did not reply.

"I want some *sura* to celebrate," he said. "I have more cows than Trita now."

"Get it yourself this time. Can't you see I'm busy?" She strode over and spoke to the children, beckoned for them to help her take down the tent.

He stared at her back. God, she was hard to please!

He had not expected such a commotion when they tried to take the boy away. The girl held tightly onto her brother; it took all three adults to separate them. Then the boy started crying. The girl kept screaming and had to be restrained as Santanu dragged her brother off. She then seemed to quiet down, so they cautiously released her, but she instantly shot off in the direction in which her brother had disappeared. Swearing, Bhira ran after her, and he caught up just as she approached Santanu's encampment.

Santanu had seen the chase and turned to wait. "Might as well let her see where her brother will be, so she knows he's all right," he said to Bhira.

Bhira nodded, softening his anger.

"Why not leave her with me for a while—I'll send her back later with one of my older girls," Santanu said.

Glad to be rid of the nuisance of dealing with the matter, Bhira agreed.

Sumbari, realizing she had no choice, reluctantly accepted for the moment that her brother would have to live with the cowherder's family. At least it appeared she would be able to see Pippru every day.

The big difficulty was that escaping was now more complicated. She would run off at the first chance, and naturally she would take Pippru along.

She worried about how badly their father was injured. She should be there to take care of him. Pippru needed her, too, though. She wondered if Namuci and Balbutha were all right.

Even though she was exhausted and drained, she found it impossible to sleep that night. Her captors bound her hands and feet when she went to bed. Not so tight as to cut into her flesh, but tight enough that she was unable to loosen the knots or work the ropes off, though she tried for hours.

Both the camp and the people were upsettingly different from what she was used to. Here the cooking odors were more of roasted meat than of spiced grains. The ground was hard to sleep on, not at all like her webbed cot back home. It was also strange to be sleeping in a tent, with the fabric rustling in the light breeze and her captors sleeping near her. The sounds in the camp were also unlike the noises of the town. The voices were unintelligible and harsh-sounding. The horses staked outside whinnied and shuffled, and the cattle mooed and shifted positions.

Eventually Sumbari tried chewing on the leather strands binding her wrists. The remaining bangle pressed into her cheek, reminding her of Namuci and Balbutha. She again worried about them. She chewed until her teeth ached, and chewed more, but she made little progress against the tough leather.

In the morning the man came to untie her. He frowned at the sight of the damp, marred thongs. He pointed to them, his eyes blazing. Then he cuffed her on the side of the head. Sumbari saw it coming but couldn't duck fast enough. It hurt, and it enraged her.

During the daytime, when she was unbound, the woman watched her closely and did not allow Sumbari near the edge of the encampment. As the tribe began traveling easterly, taking Sumbari farther away from Kanur, she realized she must flee as soon as possible. The greater the distance to go back, the more difficult and dangerous the escape would be.

Her father had told her to return; but also to be careful. It seemed like it would be difficult to follow both his directions. At the first opportunity, she asked the few other captives from Kanur if Namuci and Balbutha had survived, but none seemed to know. In any event, she desperately wanted to return to Kanur, where she could be with her own people, not these strangers she couldn't even talk to, who had so ruthlessly destroyed her town and her home, injured her father, abducted her and her brother.

Yet, both time and distance passed with no good chance to escape. At night her captors now took care to tie her into a position where she couldn't reach her bindings with her teeth. The woman put her to work herding their cows as the tribe traveled. Sumbari tried to devise ways to be close to Pippru, but his own herd was far to the rear, and the woman called Visala made it clear to Sumbari with gestures that she was not to leave the cows put in her care.

Moving slowly because of the cattle and chariots, the tribe wound northeasterly on a main trade road. The plains eventually gave way to low ridges covered by scrubby, thorny trees. Then the hills grew taller, and the trees and other vegetation more lush. Mango trees towered among tamarinds and wild figs. In this rugged terrain the road narrowed and became steep and stony. Often the travelers had to ford small streams that tumbled through the bottoms of the many ravines. Occasionally the two wheeled vehicles had to be pushed up inclines or over rocks, and often it was difficult coaxing the cows and bullocks along such a difficult route.

Sumbari constantly watched for a way to escape, even though she feared being alone in the deep forests. Back home she had heard stories of the fierce tribes living here, of the tigers and lions and panthers and elephants that roamed these jungles. Whenever she started to lag behind as they walked, Visala would call to her and gesture for her to hurry, the meaning obvious even though the words were foreign. When Visala was occupied with some task, she tied Sumbari's hands or feet or else asked other nearby women to keep an eye on her. In the evening, even when Sumbari visited Pippru, an older girl always escorted her both ways and watched the two children when they were together.

Despite the dangers of the jungle, Sumbari considered sneaking away in the middle of the night, but Pippru told her that he was made to sleep in the center of a tent, tied to a pole, with family members grouped around him. He sorrowfully said he wet himself every night. He never used to do that, and Sumbari was sure it was because he was so upset at being taken away from home and Papa.

To ensure she could find their way back when they did manage to escape, Sumbari took care to memorize the forks in the road, as well as major landmarks on the route such as prominent mountain peaks or unusual rock formations. From the fact that they were traveling toward the spot where the sun rose in the mornings, she knew they were headed generally east, in spite of the many twists and turnings of the track as it wound through the mountains.

She additionally reassured herself as to the positions of the familiar stars in the sky at particular times. Every night she prayed to the Six Foster-Mothers for help in returning home. The constellation rose above the horizon after sunset, followed by the nearby Deer's Head. Sumbari remembered that around midnight this time of year, the Six Foster-Mothers were always due south relative to a point directly overhead, so this fact, too, was a good indicator of the direction the tribe was traveling.

Sumbari also kept count on her fingers of the number of days of travel so she would know how long it would take to get back to Kanur. She had counted ten days when they at last reached the plains on the other side of the range of low mountains. There the men attacked a town, and they brought in more cows and loot and slaves. Seven days later, the tribe raided yet another village. But now the farmland tapered out, and they entered the fringe of a vast forest.

Bhira rose from his bed, full of anticipation. He burst from the tent opening and looked about. Surya the sun god was just above the horizon, and the sky was clear. Perfect weather for the festivities. For it was also the day of the full moon, the day of the *soma* sacrifice.

As soon as the morning meals were finished, the sounds of pounding drifted across the encampment. Bhira strode about, watching the preparations. Under the supervision of priests, Visala and Sumbari and the other women and girls used the sacred stones to crush the stalks of the precious *soma* plants which the priests had gathered in the mountains weeks before. The resulting juice was carefully saved in large bowls.

By midmorning, the pounding stopped. The women began the first of the three pressings of the day, forcing the juice through a filter of sheep's wool, then mixing it with water, and finally adding milk for sweetening.

Meanwhile, the priests had started a huge bonfire. Bhira impatiently joined the other men at his traditional position in the circle around the fire, awaiting the start of the sacrifice. The spreading branches of a mango tree sheltered the area where he was seated, next to Kasu, an older warrior, who in turn sat several places away from the *raja*, the chief. Trita's place was on the other side of Bhira. Each man held his bowl, anticipating his share of the *soma* pressing.

Kasu sat with a slight slump. His hair had gone gray, and his vigor had noticeably declined in the past year or so. He said to Bhira, his voice sounding tired, "Have you wondered if we should keep traveling, now that we're in such a rich land?"

Bhira stared at him as Kasu continued, "This is the type of place we hoped to find one day. Plenty of pasture land. The hunting's the best I've seen."

Bhira could understand how a man who had grown old might find it easier to stay in one place. Out of sympathy for Kasu, he gave a nod and said agreeably, "I've never seen better myself." Indeed, both he and Visala liked this well forested, lush area. The grass was well-watered by the streams, good for cows, the plains flat enough both for pasture and for driving chariots.

And game was plentiful in the hills and woods. Bhira had shot several deer, but more thrilling by far, he and several other men on horseback had chased wild boar. Now *there* was hunting! He loved the danger of racing over the uneven ground after prey that could suddenly turn on the hunters and disembowel a horse or a man.

But was Kasu truly serious? "You're not really suggesting we stay here?" asked Bhira.

Kasu shrugged. "Is that such a bad idea? We don't know what's beyond this forest. How could it be better than this land, right here? What if we find it's not nearly so good? I doubt we'd turn around and come back. That isn't our nature. We'd keep moving forever, or we'd settle for second or third best."

It was clear that such a rigorous existence had lost most of its appeal for the aging Kasu. But remaining in one spot was almost unfathomable to Bhira. All his life the tribe had traveled, attacking towns, always moving on. He looked down into his empty bowl, then up at the flames leaping from the crackling dried wood. He remembered how far his people had already come. When he was a small child, his tribe and others separated from the rest of the Aryan peoples on the plains of central Persia. His own group traveled eastward, moving slowly because of the need to let the cattle and sheep graze along the way. The tribe won many battles with their swift chariots, even conquering several walled cities in the lands of plateaus and mountains.

In contrast, taking most of the towns in this land had been children's play. Only the city the natives called Harappa, now far away on the other side of the small mountains, had been strong enough to give serious resistance, and that, too, had crumbled fast. It had been too long since these *dasas* had fought battles; they had gone soft.

Trita had been listening to the interchange. Now he said, loud enough for Kasu to hear, "I couldn't even consider staying here. We'll find lots more towns somewhere ahead. That means more cows. And more slaves. I intend to find a girl like that one Bhira took."

Bhira agreed, of course, that remaining here was out of the question. Hardly anyone besides a few old or sick people would support the idea. But he found it difficult to say so. Not when it meant concurring aloud with Trita. And he hated the thought of Trita getting more cows and a slave girl of his own. So he said to Kasu, "Maybe you're right. Maybe it's not such a good idea to take a chance on what's ahead. Not when we have all we could want right here."

Trita snorted. "Maybe *you* have all *you* want. But I'd guess most of us would love to have more." He asked Bhira pointedly: "You want to give up raiding?"

"Of course not. If we stay here, there are villages only a day or two away we can attack. But what if we go on, and there are no more boars to hunt?"

Trita smiled, obviously pleased he had goaded Bhira into supporting such an odd opinion as to favor ending the trek. "Other tribes are close behind us," he pointed out. "When they get here, there won't be enough land for us all. Someone will have to move on anyway."

"The latecomers could be the ones to move on," Bhira said, reluctant to give in now that he had stated a position. "We're here first."

Trita looked slyly at him and said to those within hearing, "Maybe Bhira is worried that he's getting too old to travel and raid villages. But I don't think he's too old at all."

Bhira glared at him. He knew Trita had insulted him, but when the insult was worded as a compliment, how should he reply?

Kasu, apparently seeing what was happening, said placatingly, "Of course our brother Bhira is not too old."

The chief priest, the *purohita*, faced the assembly and raised his hands to indicate the ceremony was about to begin. The onlookers fell quiet. Annoyed though Bhira was with Trita, his irritation fell away as he returned his attention to the pleasures to come.

The *purohita* began chanting a mantra and feeding the *ghee*, the clarified butter, to Agni the fire god. The fat-fed flames crackled and shot high into the sky, showing Agni's pleasure. Agni would bear the sacrificial offerings to the other gods.

The *purohita* offered the first draught of *soma* to the great warrior god Indra, lord of thunder and lightning, who had helped the Aryans conquer so many cities and forts along the route of the march. *Soma* was Indra's favorite offering, and the Aryans must ask his blessings for continuing the trek that had become their way of life.

As the *purohita* cast the fluid into the flames, he sang *mantras* in a rhythmic voice that rose and fell:

> *Indra, the fire is kindled, the soma pressed,*
> *Let your best horses draw you here.*
> *Indra, with concentrated heart I call on you.*
> *Come, be with us for our prosperity.*
>
> *Indra, come here: Your arrival is always*
> *Heralded by our desire to drink soma.*
> *Listen, hear the prayers we now offer;*
> *Let this sacrifice increase your power....*

Now that the *soma* had been consecrated, the priests divided the remainder among the men of the tribe: first the *raja*, then the senior members of the council, then to Kasu and Bhira, and finally to the lesser ranking warriors.

At last, Bhira raised his bowl to his lips and eagerly sipped his own portion of the draught of immortality. A feeling of lightness, of well being, swiftly spread throughout him. A wonderful numbness crept to the extremities of his limbs.

His thoughts sped quickly, seeming separate from his body. He was aware that he periodically sipped from his bowl, but the action seemed distant, as if it were someone else taking the drink.

He began to expand, growing until he was of enormous size. He slowly reached up his hand until it pierced the blue bowl of the sky. He had become a god himself; he was one with them; they would bless his future. Any moment now, he would see them in their heavens.

As a god, there was nothing he could not do. He could destroy cities single-handedly, just as could Indra. He could wave his sword and shout, and the heavens would thunder. His arrows could pierce the farthest target. He could drive his horses to victory in any race.

His *soma* bowl, now empty, dropped unnoticed from his hands. His racing thoughts briefly touched on Trita, but his rival was no longer important. The problems Trita had posed had become irrelevant when the universe was such a place of ecstasy.

Gradually, the effects of the first *soma* pressing began to wear off, and Bhira became aware in brief snatches that he was seated with the men of his tribe about the circle. By that time the next pressing was ready, and after pouring the gods' share into the fire, the priests refilled the men's bowls. Bhira again drank, and again he became a god.

In early evening the men drank the third and final pressing. And so it went, until the bright immensity of the full moon rose to preside over the close of the sacrifice.

The tribe continued easterly through the forests. It spread out into a long, winding line along the narrow tracks, often only wide enough for a single chariot or oxcart. At intervals, the Aryans came to open areas of farmland where they seized more cattle and replenished the fodder for their herds.

Daily, the nights grew colder, although the days remained pleasantly warm. Sumbari had grown accustomed to being around the cows she tended. They were slow, stupid animals, but Sumbari understood why her captors prized them. Leather from the cows' hides had a multitude of uses—from binding the hands of slaves, to making reins and whips and sandals. The milk was a favorite drink at every meal as well as a frequent ingredient in cooking. From the milk the Aryans obtained butter and curds. The butter was not only eaten on bread and various dishes; when clarified by heating, it kept without spoiling, and it was tossed on the fire as an offering to the gods.

Visala had taught Sumbari to help with the milking. One teat was held in the left hand and another in the right hand. The teats had to be squeezed in just the right way, and at first Sumbari's fingers ached from the unaccustomed use. It had taken a few days to become proficient. Then she had the knack: squeezing the left teat, then the right, in a steady rhythm so milk flowed almost constantly into the wooden bucket.

One day while Sumbari was milking the cows, she was startled when the very earth beneath her began to shake.

She screamed.

The milk danced in her bucket. The cow she was milking bellowed in protest and tried to pull away. Sumbari, squatting by its udder, lost her balance and fell to the ground.

Still the earth rumbled, violently jarring her.

Baffled, panicky, she looked about. The tents were actually swaying on their poles! Several collapsed as their pegs pulled free from the churning soil. Horses whinnied and tried to pull loose from their tethers.

Still the earth convulsed. The cows were bawling, shuffling about.

Then, gradually the tremors subsided.

Sumbari saw that the tribal people seemed confused and unnerved. Many were trying to catch animals that had gotten loose, others were frantically throwing water onto tents that had fallen into campfires. Shaken though she was, she realized this could be her best chance. She dashed to the area where Pippru was watching his own cows along with a number of older boys. She knew he'd be upset by the trembling earth and all the commotion, and indeed, he sat on the grass crying. She grabbed his arm and pulled him up. "Come! We're leaving!" she said urgently.

He resisted, unable to forget his terrifying experience, so she began to drag him. At last he realized what she wanted him to do, and he began to run along with her, but he was slower with his smaller steps.

A couple of the older boys saw what the children were doing and began to chase, yelling.

"Run as fast as you can!" Sumbari shouted to Pippru.

He did. But it wasn't nearly fast enough. Quicker than she would have believed possible, the older boys caught up, grabbed hold of them.

"Let us go!" Sumbari screamed. She tried frantically to pull away.

The boys held her tightly. One even slapped her. Furious and frustrated, she glowered at him. Of course, it did no good. They dragged her back to Bhira, and Pippru back to Santanu.

Visala watched while Bhira slapped Sumbari hard on one side of the face, then the other. "Enough!" the woman said after the fourth slap. Bhira started to strike Sumbari again, but he caught himself and stopped. They bound her wrists and ankles together, and then tied her to a tent pole for the rest of the day. Her head ached terribly from Bhira's cuffing.

They kept her bound all night. In the morning, they released her. "Don't do it again," Bhira growled, glaring at her. Sumbari stared at the ground. After a while she gave a curt nod.

The Aryans asked each other why the earthquake had occurred. Was it a sign of some kind from the gods that they were angry? Even the priests seemed unsure. The tribe resumed its eastward trek.

Sumbari still yearned to return home. Every day she thought about her father, about Namuci and Balbutha, about the others. What was happening to them? Had her father's wounds healed? Were they repairing the town? Who was cooking for her father now that Sumbari was gone? She was sure he was worrying about her and Pippru. But what could he possibly do?

She had no more realistic opportunities to escape, though she still watched continually for a chance. Her captors didn't treat her badly, for the most part. The only times they struck her now were when she obstinately refused to work. That wasn't very often any more, just whenever she decided it was time to show them she still didn't like what they'd done to her and her brother and their home. Even though they casually kept an eye on her, she would have at least made an effort to run off except for the problem of getting Pippru away, too.

Both she and Pippru were quickly learning their captors' language, and she discovered they called themselves "Aryans." Although she understood the words used in daily life, she had trouble understanding these people's thoughts. There were a few minor similarities with her own people, such as the fact that these Aryans worshiped their gods by building fires and by throwing substances into the fires as sacrifices.

But the differences seemed greater. The firepit was the focus of each family's camp, both for worship and for roasting meat for meals. They had words relating to all aspects of their herds. There were even separate words for "cows barren after giving birth to a calf" and "a cow with a strange calf." She sensed the Aryans had never lived in a town and thought the idea of doing so was stupid. Though they herded sheep and goats, they put little value on anything other than their cows. And Sumbari greatly resented the fact that they seemed to despise her own people and anyone with dark skin.

As Kanur receded farther and farther into both distance and time, despite the fact that she was no longer watched so closely, it was becoming highly difficult for her to go back, even if she could spirit Pippru away, too. If they did succeed in escaping, the men in the chariots would almost certainly search for them. She and Pippru would have to somehow cross the wide rivers unassisted. They would need enough food to sustain them on the long trek. Traveling alone, they would be vulnerable to wild animals and roving bandits and the primitive tribals in the hills. If they traveled during the day time, they could easily be spotted by searchers or bandits. But if they traveled at night, the air would be cold, and they would have a difficult time seeing their way. The menace from wild beasts would be even greater.

So Sumbari gradually, with almost unbearable frustration, came to accept that it might be a long time before she again saw Kanur. Her life there seemed more remote as each day passed. It surprised and troubled her that she was unable to escape. She felt she was failing Pippru and her father, as well as herself. Pippru still wet himself every night when he slept, and she knew he often cried while he watched his cows.

*

Sumbari did not know that Trita was still trying to acquire her from Bhira. Bhira remained unwilling to put her up as stakes in dicing, so Trita tried an outright purchase, offering as many as four cows. But Bhira no longer felt such an urgency to increase the size of his herd now that he had more cows than Trita.

Trita changed his approach. "I'm better than you now at chariot driving," he bluntly told Bhira one night as the men drank *sura* by the fire. "I challenge you to a race. If you win, you get five of my cows. I win, I get your *dasi*."

Bhira was getting tired of Trita pestering him about the girl. True, he could understand it a little better now—the child was older than he had thought at first; her breasts were definitely forming. She had a fiery liveliness that was attractive if you overlooked her dark skin and short nose. Visala was clearly fond of her, probably because of having no child of her own.

Bhira had been reluctant to take a chance on the dice, even for the possibility of more cows. But chariot racing....That was another matter. He was good at it, definitely better than Trita. His own horses were faster than Trita's, and he took better care of them.

Five cows couldn't be given up easily. Feeling expansive under the influence of the *sura*, he said loudly, "We race tomorrow!"

Trita was momentarily surprised; he had grown so use to Bhira's refusals that he had not really expected him to accept. He laughed heartily. "We'll race at sunrise, before the day's too hot!"

Bhira said, "That clear area south of camp should be a good place."

Trita laughed again. "It's taken me a long time to get her from you. She'd better be worth it!"

Bhira snapped, "I'll be glad to reduce your herd by five cows!" He rose and left the circle.

"You didn't!" Visala shouted when Bhira told her of the wager.
"Don't get upset. I'll win!"
"But what if you don't?"
Bhira said with irritation, "You're supposed to encourage me! I tell you, I'll win! I always do!"
Visala buried her face for a moment. Then she raised it, sighed, and prepared for bed.

Sumbari, already lying on her pad in the rear of the tent, had overheard. She knew enough of the Aryan language to understand, and the betrayal hurt deeply. She had seen how Trita looked at her, how he treated his wife. It would be far better to remain with Bhira and Visala.

She had often been furious at herself for not trying again to escape and go back to Kanur. Now, she vowed, the time had arrived. Just as soon as she could prepare Pippru, and get some food and water ready.

3

It grieves the gambler when he sees another
with wife and happy home untouched by trouble.
He yokes the brown steeds in the early morning,
And when the fire goes out he sinks degraded.

— *Rig Veda*, X, 34, 11

Despite all he had drunk, Bhira's sleep was restless. You'll win, he kept telling himself. And you can use those five cows.

The aftertaste from the *sura* still fouled his mouth as Usas, the goddess of dawn, began to lighten the sky. Bhira rose and went to look over his chariot. There was a remote chance that Trita might have tried to tamper with the vehicle, so Bhira pulled hard on the wheels, testing them. It wouldn't do to have one come off during the race. He examined the rest of the car carefully, tugging on the sides, on the yoke. Everything seemed in order. He felt foolish having suspected Trita— just because he didn't like the man, it didn't mean his rival would try to cheat.

He strode over to where Vata and Apah were staked and untied them; Vata meant "Wind" and Apah meant "the Waters." He led them over to the chariot. "Come on, come on, don't be so sluggish," he told them. Both of the dark brown horses seemed slow to respond, as if they resented being asked to work so early in the morning.

He drove around the edge of the encampment. People were beginning to be up and about, feeding their fires. When he reached the ground where the race would be held, he drove the horses down and back, loosening them up. They still seemed slow to him, but he ascribed it to his own impatience.

Surya, the sun god, had risen above the horizon in his own flaming chariot, beginning his drive across the sky. Naturally word of the race had spread, and people were starting to gather. Bhira heard a thundering of hooves as Trita approached at high speed, drove in a tight circle around Bhira—covering him with dust—and then reined to a quick halt. Trita stood in his vehicle, grinning at Bhira. Furious, Bhira clenched his fists but pretended indifference for the onlookers' benefit.

It was necessary to agree on a course. Trying not to let Trita hear the anger in his voice, Bhira pointed, and said, "We can go around that tree, and that big round rock. Then back to here."

Trita nodded. "That's fine." He called to the older warrior Kasu, who was standing near. "Kasu! Kindly put down a mark for our finish line. You can start us."

Kasu removed his cloak, folded it, set it on the ground to indicate the line.

Bhira called to Trita: "How many times around?"

Trita laughed easily. "Once should be enough."

"A trial run first?"

Trita negligently waved his arm. "No need. I limbered up my horses on the way over."

Bhira began to feel uneasy. Why did Trita seem so lazily confident? The cunning bastard must be putting on a front to unnerve him! Well, it wouldn't work.

They stepped briefly from their chariots to toss the dice. Bhira won the inside position. His luck had already begun! With that advantage, there was no doubt whatsoever of his winning. They lined their chariots up side by side. Bhira glanced at the onlookers and saw Visala there with the others, her face grim. The slave girl was not with her.

He called loudly to Kasu, "Start us!" Kasu raised his sword high. It glinted as Surya's flame touched it.

"Run hard! Like you always do!" Bhira whispered to his horses.

The sword dropped. Bhira instantly snapped his whip. The horses sped off, but for some reason, they seemed slower than usual. Incredibly, Trita was leading by a full chariot length!

Bhira's horses still seemed sluggish. Trita was slowly increasing his lead. Bhira cracked the whip. "Faster! Faster!" he screamed at the Vata and Apah.

As they rounded the scrubby tree, he pulled almost even with Trita, who was at a disadvantage being on the outside.

They sped toward the rock. It was a long, straight run, and Bhira was sure he could pass Trita now. But somehow, Trita again pulled farther ahead, steadily increasing his lead.

How could it be? Bhira was bewildered to see Trita cut in front of him as they approached the turn. Skidding around the rock, Bhira blinked his eyes to clear them of Trita's dust. He was stunned at being behind, but he hadn't yet lost the race.

He desperately urged the horses faster. They were better horses, better cared for. They should be able to catch Trita yet.

Still, Trita increased the gap. Trita's dust was billowing back over Bhira, irritating his eyes, making it hard to breath.

He cracked his whip furiously. He urgently asked himself, What's wrong? Why can't I gain on him?

They were nearing the finish line. Bhira realized that he could not win.

Trita crossed the line over two chariot lengths ahead.

Dazed, Bhira reined in his horses. That bastard! He was furious, but there was nothing to be done now. He was aware of all the people watching, chattering loudly to each other in their excitement.

He forced his lips into a tight smile. "A good race!" he shouted to Trita. He thought he had managed to sound sporting. He carefully did not look toward where Visala had been standing.

"Where's my prize?" Trita demanded, a broad, satisfied grin on his face.

Bhira unclenched his teeth and took a deep breath. "At my camp. I'll send her to you."

Visala had immediately left when she saw that Trita would win. Before coming to the race she had asked her neighbor to keep an eye on Sumbari in case the girl should try to run away. Now she returned to her tent and saw Sumbari seated on the ground in front, staring at the smoking embers of the campfire.

Sumbari looked up, her eyes haunted. She could tell from Visala's face what the outcome of the race had been. Sumbari buried her face in her hands.

Visala put an arm around Sumbari and did her best to comfort the crying girl. After several minutes, Visala said, "We have to go." Sumbari made no response. Gently, but firmly, Visala pulled the girl to her feet and guided her in the direction of Trita's tent.

"How could you have done it?" Visala later demanded of Bhira. She tried to keep her voice low so it would not carry to the other tents.

"I don't know." He shook his head sadly. "I don't know. Visala, I should have won!"

She turned away, and did not speak to him the remainder of the morning. The hours passed slowly. Bhira found himself continually looking in the direction of Trita's tent. I shouldn't have lost, he kept saying to himself. My horses are better. Why weren't they faster?

He told himself he would never have agreed to the wager if he hadn't drunk so much *sura* last night. But the urge for more of the drink came over him again: *sura* had gotten him into this, *sura* would at least help him forget.

He entered his tent. Ignoring Visala, he seized a jug. Not bothering with a cup, he drank straight from the container. It seemed like only seconds before he had emptied it. He grabbed another.

Just as his mind began to feel sluggish from the drink, a thought came. His horses, too, had been sluggish this morning. As if they'd drunk some *sura* themselves. Not enough to make them stagger, but enough to slow them down.

That was the answer!

He surged to his feet. Furious, he sped from the tent and ran through the gathering darkness toward Trita's camp. As he approached, he heard Sumbari's screams.

"Trita!" he yelled. He drew his sword as he ran. "Trita! You fed my horses *sura*, you bastard!"

He burst into the tent, where in the gloom the astounded Trita lay naked over a small, dark, bare form. Suddenly realizing his danger, Trita leaped for his own sword, but he was far too late. Bhira's practiced swing, with all his strength behind it, sent Trita's head flying in a spray of blood.

Bhira stood for a moment, breathing hard. He saw the nude, frightened form of the girl lying there, her eyes wide in horror. He reached out his left hand. "Come," he said gruffly. He handed the girl's garment to her and waited while she fumblingly put it on. "Did he have time to rape you?" Bhira asked.

He wasn't sure if the girl understood the word, but she shook her head no.

Outside the tent, Trita's wife was screaming. Bloody sword still in his right hand, Bhira took Sumbari's arm with his left and led her out, past Trita's stunned family, past the onlookers who were swiftly arriving, to his own camp.

Visala waited outside, her eyes anxious. Her voice was hoarse: "What happened? Did you kill him?"

"Yes." His own voice seemed to come from a distance.

"You know what that means! The *raja* will soon be here."

"I suppose. Yes." He struggled to clear his mind from the effects of the drink.

"You know the penalty—they'll take all our cows! They'll take everything, and it still won't be enough!"

Bhira nodded, his head pounding. The penalty for killing a man was a hundred cows, far more than he had, so they would take his horses, his chariot, his slave, everything. Without cows, especially, a family was destitute. It might as well be a sentence of death.

Sumbari had heard the last of the exchange, and she slipped away in the darkness with her blankets. Somehow, she *must* get Pippru away. If she waited, tomorrow she would be given to some other man, and she wanted no repeat of what Trita had tried to do to her.

Keeping in the shadows, away from the campfires, she crept to Santanu's tent. In the light of the flames she saw Pippru leaving with a water jug, apparently on an errand. Relief flooded over her—maybe it would not be so hard to get him away after all. She caught up with him. "It's time to leave," she whispered. "We're going back home."

"Huh-huh-home!" Pippru exclaimed, more loudly than Sumbari preferred. "I'll suh-see Papa again!"

She clamped a hand over his mouth. She hesitated, then whispered, "I hope so. We'll try. Now be quiet!"

Avoiding the light of the fires, they swiftly left the encampment. No one seemed to notice; most people appeared to have gathered around Trita's tent.

The moon shone enough for them to see the road. Stumbling occasionally on a rut, they hurried along toward the west, toward Kanur, the direction from which they had come with the tribe. As they entered the dense forest, it became much darker. The road was only barely visible, much of it in shadows. A jackal howled, and another replied.

Sumbari shivered, and she became aware of the coldness of the night. It was a long way back. She had counted forty-three days of travel to date. But they must keep going. She could not allow herself to be given to another Trita.

4

O Varuna, what was my chief transgression
That would destroy a singer of your praise?
....
It was not my own will, but malice, Varuna,
Gambling, drinking, anger, that betrayed me....

— *Rig Veda*, VII, 86, 4,6

Visala spoke rapidly, her normally calm voice shrill: "We should leave now, before anyone comes! They probably won't follow us if we leave everything behind. They know Varuna will be angry at you."

Bhira slowly nodded, numb. Varuna was the god of *rita*, the laws holding the universe together and governing men's relationships with the order of the world. Bhira's killing of his own tribesman had upset the balance of this natural order. Since he was unable to pay the full penalty of a hundred cows and thereby put the fabric of the universe back in balance, who knew what consequences Varuna would bring upon him? Although Bhira himself had frequently sacrificed to Varuna, it was doubtful the sacrifices would make up for killing Trita.

But to leave the tribe! To leave everyone he'd known since birth! Although his own parents no longer lived, he still had uncles and cousins. And whom else could he live with, in this land of *dasas*?

Death might be better than what now faced him—and Visala. He had disgraced her, as well as himself, and if he were no longer with her, maybe another man would do better for her.

Although he had no fear of death, his pride would not let him deliberately kill himself, much less let him die from starvation or any other cause he could control. Nevertheless, he looked at Visala and felt shame. He had already badly humiliated her. If she left the tribe with him, he would be tearing her, too, away from her kin and the life she had known. He could never ask so much of her. "You'd better not come," he mumbled, his gaze at the ground.

She sighed and looked away. She held back the anger at the devastation he had brought her, and said bluntly, "I go where you go."

Mixed with his guilt, he felt relief. Still, he summoned the strength to say hoarsely, "You don't have to."

She looked sharply at him and said in a mixture of ire and resignation, "I will anyway. We'd better hurry."

Finally, he said, "Yes."

Visala began grabbing items of food. "Be fast," she said again. "Get blankets, clothes, whatever else we can carry." Suddenly she stopped. "Where's the girl?"

Bhira looked around in surprise. He stepped to the door of the tent and glanced outside. "I don't see her. She must have run off."

After a moment, Visala shrugged. "That may be better for her. Anyway, we don't have time to look."

"Should I harness the chariot?" Bhira asked, though he already knew.

"No! They'd come after us for certain. But if we're walking, they'll know we haven't taken much with us."

They strode rapidly all night toward the west, the direction from which they had come with their tribe. Hearing the many wild sounds in the darkness, Bhira wondered what the Lady of the Forest, the goddess, thought of their flight through her domains.

The moon shone brightly enough for them to see the narrow, rutted road, though much of it was lost in black shadows. When they heard the roar of a lion nearby, Bhira's hand tightened on his sword and they hurried as fast as they could.

Bhira cursed himself for not bringing a spear. But he had thought it would be too much to carry, so he brought only his bow and arrows, sword, and knife. They were questionable protection against a lion. Even so great an archer as himself would have difficulty shooting a moving lion at night.

He breathed more easily after several minutes. They apparently had left the lion behind, as they heard no more from it. Suddenly Visala stopped. "What's that?" She pointed to a small patch of white gleaming in the moonlight a short distance off the road.

Bhira cautiously stepped into the brush to investigate. He stood, peering for a moment. Then he beckoned to her, and whispered loudly, "Come here!"

Sumbari and her little brother were asleep in each other's arms, blankets wrapped tightly around themselves.

Sumbari stirred. She opened her eyes and saw the two dark shapes above her. She shrank in panic. Then, gradually in the dim light she recognized Bhira and Visala. Tears came to her eyes. It just wasn't fair! Why couldn't she have been able to get away this time? Only Pippru's exhaustion had led her to rest for a while. Why did those people keep after her? Hadn't they done enough to her already?

They were talking in low voices to each other. Sumbari looked at them and saw that each carried a bundle of possessions. Why? Had they planned to spend a long time chasing her and Pippru?

Then she realized they, too, might be fugitives after Bhira killed Trita.

They stopped talking and looked at Sumbari. "Come with us," Visala said firmly. "You need protection. It's too dangerous to travel alone."

Sumbari started to refuse. Then she thought again. She had heard the lion's roar and was indeed worried. She gave a nod.

"We need to hurry," Visala said.

Given his and Visala's own situation, Bhira was not pleased to be responsible again for the two *dasas*. But arguing with Visala would delay them all even longer, and he knew she wouldn't change her mind.

So they continued along the dark track. Some time later, as they were growing weary from the long flight with no sleep, a dark shape startled them as it swished and flapped through the air across the road, barely missing their faces. With relief, Bhira recognized it as an owl.

At last Usas, the lovely goddess of dawn, came in her radiant garments, but still they continued, taking turns now carrying Pippru. When Sumbari could stumble no farther, and even Bhira was tired, they left the road and slept behind the concealment of a brushy hillock.

In late afternoon, after they resumed their trek, the four passed a shallow valley where they saw a large encampment. The horses, and the parked chariots, marked the group as another tribe of Aryan migrants. Bhira crept to a rise and, hidden by brush and rocks, examined the camp for a long time.

He knew there was no point in trying to join the group. They would ask many questions. Even if the tribe were at first fooled into taking in an exiled killer, eventually they would discover the truth, and they would again drive Bhira away.

For a time he carefully examined how the people had fenced and tied their horses. The soreness of his feet and his legs from the past day's walking had reaffirmed that no warrior should ever be forced to walk more than a few steps. A true fighting man rode wherever he went. If not in a chariot, then on a horse.

Bhira cautiously returned to the side of the road, where Visala and the children waited, and the party continued on, apparently without being seen. That night, however, Bhira rose from his bed and left the camp. He returned just before dawn, leading a brown mare. He immediately roused Visala and the two children. They blinked the sleep from their eyes and looked in astonishment at his acquisition.

"A warrior needs a horse," he said bluntly.

Visala exploded. "God, Bhira! Haven't you brought us enough trouble? You got us cast out of our own tribe, and now you have another tribe mad at us, too! How can you be such an idiot?"

Bhira backed away from her; she had never been a docile woman, but she seldom challenged him so forcefully. "Haven't you done enough?" she persisted. "Take it back! Maybe they haven't missed it yet!"

"Take it back?"

"You fool! We don't need this other tribe after you, too!"

He realized she had not taken their exile as calmly as he had thought. And he understood her anger at him. But to return the horse? "I can't take it back now," he said. "It's light out. They'd catch me for certain."

"Tell them you found it running loose! Tell them anything! Just don't give them a reason to come after us!"

Bhira took a deep breath. "I'm sorry," he said. "It's too late now. We need to get moving as fast as we can."

Visala glared at him. Then, she sighed deeply. "We'd better go."

Bhira at first led the party in a shallow stream to hide the horse's tracks, but then he tried to cover as much distance as possible, heading southwesterly on a wide, deeply rutted trail that bore numerous wheel tracks and hoofprints. Much of the time he carried Visala or one of the children with him on the animal, giving each a chance to rest from the fast pace on foot. Good fortune had apparently returned to him, for there was no evidence of pursuit. The next day, Bhira slowed the pace. But still they kept moving toward the southwest, as neither Bhira nor Visala saw any point in retracing the same route they had traveled before.

"Is th-th-this the way home?" Pippru asked Sumbari.

"Not exactly," she said.

"Then wh-wh-why are we going this way?"

"Be quiet! We have to go this way first. But then we'll go home."

"I wa-wa-ant to go home *now*!"

"So do I. But we can't quite yet. We'll go back soon."

"When?"

Sumbari decided to ignore him. Fortunately, they had spoken in their own tongue, so Bhira and Visala could have no idea what was being said.

Pippru continued to pester Sumbari about going home. She resolved to take the first good opportunity to turn northward. But she was worried about her ability to find her way back to Kanur. Even though she was fairly sure about the general directions they had traveled, she had no idea what obstacles might now lie directly between her and Kanur, in addition to the range of small mountains the tribe had crossed on its way east.

Bhira soon shot a deer with his bow, and the meat kept them in food for a time. Once they encountered a large group of a hundred or more *dasas*, people like those who had lived in Kanur and its neighboring towns. Bhira steered his party away from them. Sumbari wondered if she and Pippru should try to join the larger group, since the people were so similar to her own. But she was reluctant to leave the known for the unknown, and she doubted Bhira and Visala would let her and Pippru go anyway. Most importantly in her mind, the group was headed northeasterly, away from the general direction of Kanur.

After a couple weeks' travel, the small mountain range again rose before them. When they drew close, the track skirted the edges of the hills through heavy, lush forest. Occasionally Bhira's party saw bands of a few hunters, dark skinned and nearly naked, carrying crude bows and arrows.

They traveled though the foothills for most of a day. Suddenly Pippru pointed and exclaimed, "There's an eh-eh-elephant's head!"

A dramatic ridge rose at one end of a valley through which a small river meandered. The easterly end of the ridge was a bare rock face with a profile like an elephant's forehead and trunk. The remainder of the hill resembled a crude sculpture of the animal's body. "Yes, it does look like an elephant!" replied Sumbari. "Part of the cliff even looks like its ear, and another part like an eye!"

But Bhira was not looking at the animal shaped rock. He was examining the community of forest dwellers on the valley's hillside. Initially, he had not even recognized it as a village. First he saw one hut of woven branches, on a rise overlooking the trail. A dark form watched quietly from within its low doorway. Then, he spotted another dwelling, back in the trees. A short distance away was another. He saw a naked boy run between these two huts, no doubt carrying word of the travelers on the trail.

Soon, a group of men appeared, bearing bows with arrows strung but not yet aimed. The men were short and wiry, dressed only in loin cloths. Their noses were longer than those of the *dasas* Bhira had seen before, and their skins were not so dark. A man with graying, bushy hair who appeared to be the leader stepped forward and spoke.

Bhira could make nothing of the language. To Sumbari, however, the dialect was similar enough to that spoken in Kanur that she could understand. "He says we have to pay if we want to pass through here," she told Bhira.

Bhira glanced at her quickly, surprised that a *dasi* child could know anything he didn't. He looked back at the men. From the appearance of them and their crude stone-tipped weapons, he could charge through them with ease. Why, he could probably defeat them all, by himself alone. But he'd rather not chance injuring Visala. "Tell them we have nothing to pay them with," he told Sumbari.

She did so. The leader replied, pointing as he did so at Bhira, and at the horse. Sumbari told Bhira, "He says then we can't pass. But he says they'd accept clothing, or any of your weapons. Or your animal. I think maybe he doesn't know what a horse is."

Bhira thought a moment, before replying, "Tell them we need everything we have. But maybe I can shoot some game for them."

The chief replied with an amused smile that they were good

hunters themselves, so they didn't need anyone to hunt for them. But Bhira's bow appeared to be a fine one. They'd like to see him shoot it. Maybe, in the meantime, they could think of a suitable toll to impose.

"Ask them what they'd like me to shoot at," Bhira said.

The men consulted. One of them hurried to a mango tree with low hanging foliage, twenty paces or so away. He pointed out one of the elongated leaves, the outermost leaf of one of the bottom branches, and tore off its tip to mark it. Then he stepped back.

One of the others raised his bow, took aim, and released the arrow. It ripped the leaf from the tree. Bhira looked at the men with new respect.

The chief gestured at him, and at the tree. The man near the tree was pointing out another leaf as Bhira's target. He again tore off the tip. Bhira glanced at the faces of the men. They were exchanging smiles with each other, clearly doubting the stranger could hit such a small target. "That was nothing," Bhira growled. He called to Pippru. "Boy! See the cup by that door? Get it."

Sumbari, already on edge over the encounter with the Bhils, felt apprehensive as she wondered what Bhira had in mind. Pippru got the cup, which was quite small, woven of bamboo.

The Bhils began talking loudly. Sumbari spoke to Bhira: "They think you want to steal the cup."

"Just tell them to watch me," ordered Bhira.

Sumbari told them.

Pippru was walking toward Bhira. "Stop there," Bhira directed. "Hold out the cup so I can see it. That's good. Now don't move if you value your hide!"

He nudged his horse into motion. It trotted about fifty paces away. The men began muttering to each other that he was running away, maybe even trying to escape the toll. Then Bhira stopped the horse. "Bhira!" Visala screamed. "Don't do it! What if you miss?"

Sumbari abruptly realized what Bhira was going to do. "No!" she shrieked.

Bhira ignored them. He strung an arrow in his bow.

Pippru was standing with a terrified look on his face, the lip of the cup held by the very tips of his thumb and forefinger, as far away as he could reach. "No!" screamed Sumbari again. Tears were streaming from Pippru's eyes. Sumbari began running toward him.

Bhira whirled his horse about and sped toward the forest dwellers. Startled, and certain the foreigner had decided to attack them, some leaped away, fearful of being run down. Two or three raised their bows to defend themselves. But Bhira galloped past the disarrayed group and let fly his arrow.

It tore the cup from Pippru's hand, sent the object spinning through the air.

Bhira slowed his horse, turned about, and trotted back. He halted in his original position.

The forest dwellers' eyes were wide with amazement. They turned to look in awe at Bhira, then at Pippru, who was lowering his arm. He was crying. Sumbari reached him, hurled her arms around him, and held him tight.

The tribals considered themselves excellent archers and even called themselves the "Bhils,' meaning "Bowmen." But to hit such a target while riding a fast-moving animal!

"Bhira, how *could* you!" said Visala, her eyes blazing. "What if you had missed? You might have killed him!"

"Quiet! You know I almost never miss."

A Bhil boy came running back with the retrieved arrow, and the men examined it, exclaiming over the keenness of the bronze tip. The Bhils' gestured toward their own arrows, some of whose points were made from horn, and some of chipped stone.

Bhira let them examine his bow and test its pull. Their own were made of bamboo, and they were clearly not as powerful as his, which was made from a tree he doubted grew here. The men chattered for a time among themselves, and then returned the bow. They led Bhira and his party along a winding path to the chief's hut. As they passed a large banyan tree, Sumbari let out a small cry. She ran and knelt at the tree's base. There, among the thick, arched roots was a tall, rounded stone, dyed a vivid red, with small portions of grain on leaves placed in front of it. So these people, too, worshiped Shiv!

The Bhils remarked to each other that if this girl who understood their tongue also respected their god, maybe these people were not so strange as they appeared. But how did the strangers happen to have such different colored skin? The girl and the boy were so much darker than the man and the woman.

That night, Gajlyo, the chief, hosted the four refugees for a meal featuring fresh venison. Then he invited them to spend the night. The hut was small and crowded inside, but the chief assigned the guests a place to sleep on the ground by the dwelling.

The next day, Bhira accompanied a party of Bhils into the forest. He proved his skill once again—and the power of his bow—by shooting a deer so far away that the tribals would not have made the effort.

The next day, too, he went hunting with them. And the next. He was especially thrilled to join with them in bringing down some of the dangerous, tasty wild boar.

Soon he and his fellow refugees had been guests for a week. Visala felt relieved at the respite from trudging along dusty, rutted roads, and began to wonder if they had not gone far enough.

On a warm afternoon, she drew Bhira aside, gesturing for him to sit on a large, comfortable flat stone. Overhead spread the shady foliage of a giant *pipal* tree, lush with large, rounded leaves sporting long narrow tips. When he was seated, Visala said, "I think we should stay here. We've been lucky so far. If we keep traveling, we could be attacked by bandits or a lion or a tiger any time. We need a larger group to help protect us. And you know none of our own people would have us!"

The idea of joining a tribe of mere *dasas*, even ones with a somewhat lighter skin and thinner noses, appalled Bhira. But he had grudgingly grown to respect their wiry strength and their hunting skills. He wiped the his brow with a hand. "I don't know," he said. "They worship those stone pricks, just like the *dasas* we've conquered. And they don't know anything of our fire sacrifices! It's one thing to visit them a while. But to stay the rest of our lives?"

Visala said, "Then find me some Aryans who'll accept us."

Bhira fell silent. He thought for a time, staring at the elephant shaped ridge at the end of the valley. Very reluctantly, he agreed there was little point in continuing to travel. No Aryan tribes would have them, and the only other groups they were likely to encounter would be *dasas*.

These Bhils weren't bad men. They seemed to have their own sense of honor. They certainly respected him as an archer and horse-man, even though his knowledge of stalking animals in the forest didn't begin to approach their own. He half smiled at how they persisted at mispronouncing his name: they called him "Bhairava."

He said, "I wish they kept cows, Visala."

She sighed. "We could probably manage a few for ourselves."

Resigned to their apparent fate, he quietly spoke one last re-gret, shaking his head: "We'll never again take part in a *soma* sacrifice. Never. Even if we could find a priest, I'm sure *soma* doesn't grow around here. It needs higher mountains."

She made no reply, and he knew she was no doubt thinking it was his own fault they would never again be one with the gods, feeling the power, walking with them in their heavens. That's what he would be thinking, if he were Visala.

Bhira sat on the rock for a time, lost in memories of a way of life now gone for him. Then, suddenly, he leaped to his feet and said loudly, "By the gods, Visala! I can show these people how to *really* hunt and fight! I bet they'll make me their chief in a few years! Any-way," he said more calmly but with a gleam in his eyes, "I can chase all the boar I want!"

Sumbari was more anxious than ever to return to Kanur. The differences between these forest dwellers and her own people were less than those with the Aryans, but the Bhils were still hunters, not town folk. She detested the idea of living in the hilly jungles. Pippru still wet himself at night when he slept. She was sure it was because he was so unhappy. And Bhira's risking Pippru's life just to prove how great an archer he was showed how little he really cared about them. She would never, ever, forget how Pippru looked, holding out that little cup while Bhira shot at him while riding horseback.

She still feared the dangers of the wild. She feared losing her way. She worried about not knowing what obstacles she might encounter. It would take weeks to get back to Kanur, and she doubted her ability to protect Pippru, much less her own self, on such a long journey.

But when she learned Bhira and Visala had decided to stay with the Bhils, Sumbari realized it was time to again take Pippru and attempt to return home. If they were killed on the way or were recaptured, at least they would have tried.

She dreaded the thought of retracing the route they had traveled for so many weeks. She knew that with Pippru's short little steps they could not travel much faster, if any, than before. And she couldn't possibly carry enough food to last so long a time.

But she had been thinking. Maybe Kanur was closer than it seemed. She had watched the position of the sun and the stars carefully the entire time they had been traveling, so she knew the directions they had headed.

She took a stick and began to scratch a diagram in the dirt. Using the width of a convenient stone for the measure of a day's travel, she drew the route they had traveled easterly from Kanur and then southwesterly from the point at which they had fled from the tribe. She knew these high, sharp hills were part of the same range that she had seen every day from the rooftop of her house in Kanur.

So far as she could tell, if she could just manage to get across the mountains, Kanur should then be no more than a day or two of traveling to the north. Maybe five days' travel from here, maybe a week. But surely no more than that.

One of the Bhil boys had pointed out a trail which headed northerly to a pass across the mountains. She would be in entirely unfamiliar territory, and the idea of finding her own way through the jungle-clad hills terrified her. But the thought of almost two month's travel retracing her route was even worse.

She drew and redrew her diagram. Each time it came out very much the same. She hoped she was right—Pippru's life probably depended on it. And her own, of course.

Now that she had decided to leave, she saw no reason for delay. She gathered some dried meat, some grain, some radishes, bread saved from the evening meal, and their blankets. No one watched them any more, so that night they found it easy to sneak away. Sumbari felt a slight regret at not having a chance to say farewell to Visala; the woman had not been unkind except when Sumbari had tried to escape.

Sumbari had no regrets whatever about leaving Bhira. He was the one who'd torn her from her father and her friends and her home, and slapped her, and shot at Pippru, and made this whole fearful journey necessary.

More than once that night after they left the Bhil village, as they heard the cries of jackals or the swishings of wings or crashings in the brush, Sumbari wondered if she were being foolish.

There was little moonlight, which made it difficult to see the trail. Pippru cried when he stumbled and hurt his knee, and only the hope of seeing his father again lured him to continue. They walked north less than two hours before lying down to sleep on a high rock overlooking the trail. They awoke just before sunrise, and continued on.

Sumbari wondered if Bhira would try to follow them on his horse. If so, she hoped they could hear him in time to hide off the trail. But there seemed to be no pursuit.

On the second day, the trail joined a larger, more heavily traveled one. She assumed it must be a trade route crossing the range. The way was still difficult: up along the side of rock-strewn hills, through canyons with big boulders on either side, across rushing cascades of water—fortunately not very deep so long after the rains.

Then downhill again. And uphill. And down, down, down.

Jackals howled at night, owls screeched, occasionally a tiger or a lion roared. Somehow Sumbari and Pippru escaped becoming prey.

Three days later, they at last reached the plains on the other side. Now the traveling was easier, and Sumbari again used the sun and the stars to guide her.

Starving, their feet sore, almost exhausted, they approached Kanur.

The road into the town appeared little used now. The fields were untended, taken over by weeds. The town itself looked so different that Sumbari at first wondered if she had mistaken the location. The wall had crumbled in several more places. She could not see the temple on its elevated mound. Buildings stood here and there in various states of ruin; others had disappeared.

And no people were visible.

She and Pippru stopped while she tried to make sense of what she saw. Could the Aryans have done all this? Why would they have gone to so much effort?

Taking Pippru's hand, she resumed walking and entered the devastated town. She was stunned. Where had everyone gone? Had the Aryans killed them all after she and Pippru had been taken captive? What had happened to her father?

Tearfully, she led Pippru around and over piles of crumbled mud bricks from ruined buildings toward their own house. The neighborhood was so changed she had to keep checking, comparing the location relative to the temple hill and the outer wall, to make sure she was in the right spot.

At last they stood before what she was certain was their own house. Part of the upper floor had crumbled away, and the rooftop she

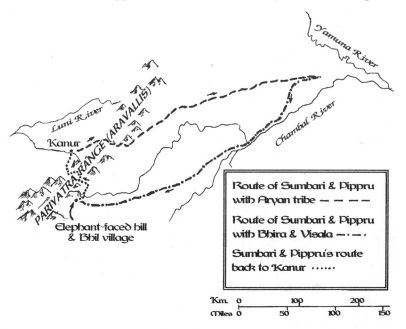

had loved was now unusable. Still, the house was in better condition than many of the other buildings.

The doorway was there, same as ever, an open dark rectangle. Sumbari hesitantly approached, afraid of what she might find within.

She let go of Pippru's hand and entered. As her eyes adjusted to the dimness she saw that the interior looked better than she would have expected. It was orderly, even clean. She went further into the room, Pippru a step behind her.

The house gave an odd feeling, as if it were occupied but yet empty. On the floor of the kitchen area stood a clay jar that normally held grain. She lifted the lid and saw that the contents were partly consumed. She was sure the kitchen was being used. Did that mean her father was still alive?

"Look!" said Pippru. "It's still here!" He held up his bird whistle to show her, then put it to his lips and blew. The cooing echoed loudly about the brick walled room.

"Be quiet!" said Sumbari in a loud whisper, terrified that the sound would alert some dangerous person of their presence.

Abruptly a figure loomed in the doorway, startling her. A voice said loudly, "Sumbari! Pippru! Is it you?"

"Papa!" She ran and threw herself at him, put her arms around him and held him fiercely tight. Then she began to cry. She cried and cried.

He was stroking her back and saying over and over, "It's all right, Sumbari. It's all right." Pippru had his arms around his father, too. Papa was saying, "I knew you'd come back. I knew."

"I'm so glad you're still here, Papa!," she said between sobs. "Are you still hurt?"

"I'm all right, Sumbari."

Eventually, she stopped crying long enough to ask, her voice hoarse and weak: "What happened to everyone else, Papa?"

"We had an earthquake, you know. It was bad. It ruined almost everything those Aryans hadn't already destroyed. Many people died. The river even lost almost all of its water."

She tried to absorb the revelations. How could the river go so dry?

Her father was saying, "A traveler told us the earthquake caused a big landslide a long way upstream that made the river change course. Everyone said the gods didn't want us to stay here anymore. The floods, the attack, the earthquake—they were all signs the gods wanted us to leave. So most of the people who were still alive left. They decided to travel far to the south, so the Aryans would never attack them again."

"But you didn't go, Papa!"

"The others told me not to stay here by myself. I knew, though, if I left with them I'd never find you and Pippru again. I knew you'd come back if you could. I was injured when the Aryans took you, so I couldn't follow. When I got so I could walk again, Namuci and I went to try to find you. But we didn't know which tribe had taken you, or where they'd gone. The first group we found, the men chased us away. We were sure they'd kill us if we kept on. So I finally decided to come back here and wait." Tears filled his eyes. "I'm so glad you've come. I worried and worried all day long, every day, wondering what had happened to you, and if I'd ever see you again."

She wiped at her own tears. "Where are Namuci and Balbutha?"

"They went with the others. I know they were worried about you, but they felt they couldn't stay. Oh, they left this for you." He pulled a small clay cow from beneath his workbench and showed it to them. "Namuci made it."

The head was formed from a separate piece of clay and attached to the body by a wooden pivot. Varchin tugged on a string and the head bobbed up and down, up and down. He handed it to Pippru.

Sumbari started crying again, and so did Pippru, even as he tugged on the string and made the clay cow's head move.

At last, Sumbari asked, "What will we do now, Papa? Will we

live here all by ourselves?"

"No." He shook his head. "It would be hard to live here, to get more food. There's no work for me. No one wants to buy seals any more, so I stopped carving. I think we need to follow our people. It's only been about a month since they left. They'll have to travel slowly since there are so many old people and children. We should be able to find them."

Sumbari absorbed this. She was disappointed not to be able to live in Kanur, just as before. She felt a great sadness, a terrible loss, that Kanur was no more, that it would never be again.

And she was tired of traveling.

But maybe it wouldn't be so bad, now that she had Papa to help her, so she wouldn't have to decide everything all on her own.

***

Centuries later, Bhil tribes of the Aravalli hills would worship a horseback archer named "Bhairava" or "Bheru," considered by many to be a form of the great god Shiva.

The cows which the Aryans prized so highly would eventually be held sacred, and the very thought of eating beef would be abhorred.

The mantras sung in Sanskrit by the Aryans at their fire sacrifices would be collected into books called the Vedas, the earliest and most sacred scriptures of the Hindus.

Over the years other northerners like the people of Kanur would migrate from their homelands because of natural disasters, the decline of the northern civilizations, and, perhaps in some cases, the invasions of the light skinned, Sanskrit speaking Aryans. Those who settled in the southern region of the subcontinent would be collectively known as Dravidians, a dark skinned people speaking their own group of languages.

The Aryans and the Dravidians would greatly influence each other's societies, including absorbing each other's gods and forms of worship. And the hundreds of forest dwelling indigenous tribes like the Bhils would adopt, at least in part, many aspects of the resulting culture.

The
Mangarh Treasure
Two

6

Kaushalya had visited this place on two occasions when the digging was going on. Each time, it seemed as if the site held some meaning for her, whether about the impermanence of life itself, or the temporary nature of all things made by humans, or of living the present moment to the fullest. In any event she usually felt a sort of timelessness here.

But today, she was too wrought up over the income tax raid. For a second, she had almost been able to imagine what the town must have looked like in its prime. Perhaps at least in part because of her art training, her visual imagination was well developed. Today, though, she was unable to let loose of the present sufficiently to feel more than a fleeting impression of the past.

She watched the two tax people and wondered how long they would stay out in such scorching heat. An interesting pair. The law gave revenue raiders considerable power to deal with suspected violators, so she would have expected them to be arrogant and arbitrary like so many government officials. Much as she wanted to dislike the handsome Mr. Singh because he was trying to find something to incriminate her father, she had to admit he treated her courteously.

Even though his manner was poised and proficient, she noted that he often seemed tense, his smile forced. Sometimes his eyes appeared haunted by some worry, although the look abruptly disappeared whenever he focused on his duties.

From the brief exchange between him and Miss Das, it seemed he was originally from the Mangarh region. Since his name was Singh, she wondered if he was a Rajput. Of course, he could also be a clean-shaven Sikh—in spite of the requirements of the faith, some of the younger Sikhs occasionally gave up their beards and turbans. And occasionally persons from lower castes adopted the "Singh," the "Lion" surname, as part of an effort to raise their status.

The other officer, the pretty Miss Das, also seemed capable, and pleasant to the extent her role allowed. She sometimes appeared reticent or unsure, but maybe that was because she was young and new to her job.

The two began walking toward her. Kaushalya grew wary; the fact that her companions for the day presented themselves as amiable did not in any way diminish the fact that they were her adversaries.

Miss Das held up a slightly curved, slender, cylindrical grayish fragment, about the diameter of a small finger. "This was lying on the ground. Do you have any idea what it is, Princess?"

Kaushalya took the piece. "There are shards all over. Too many for the archaeologists to collect them all." She rubbed her finger along its curve, dislodged some dusty soil. "I'm no expert, but it's probably part of a bangle, a bracelet. A lot of them have been found here." She handed it back to Miss Das, who took it carefully, as if it were of great value. It wasn't; it was too fragmentary, and too many had been discovered.

"We'd better get out of the sun," Vijay Singh said. "Do you suppose we can find some shade for lunch?"

"There's a small old temple just off the road, back at the base of the hills," Kaushalya said. "It's surrounded by trees, so it should be as cool as anywhere else we're likely to find."

They spread out the food on two blankets in the shade of a giant *pipal* tree, its pointed, heart-shaped leaves dull with the dust. Kaushalya thought it ironic that she should be picnicking with tax raiders, but it would have been both awkward and unthinkably rude to go off by herself.

On a hillside possibly a half kilometer off, a tree cutting operation was under way. The raucous noise of a chain saw snarled intermittently. The sound, and what it represented, grated on Kaushalya's already overwrought nerves.

Twenty or so paces away stood the tiny temple, its masonry platform holding the red-smeared idol of Bheru, sheltered by a flat stone roof supported by four pillars. Kaushalya removed her sandals, took a couple of mangos, and walked to the shrine. The sunbaked soil burned the tender soles of her feet, so she hurried to the shade of the little stone roof. She deposited her offering of mangoes before Bheru, then put her palms together and bowed her head, paying her respects.

She did it more as a matter of custom than out of belief that she would benefit; she had been brought up to feel the royal family had a duty to honor the deities worshiped by the local people. This time, she prayed silently that the Bheru would use his influence to preserve the adjacent forest from the loggers—as well as to protect her family from the income tax raiders. She returned to the shelter of the *pipal* tree and sat on the blanket with Shanta Das.

Vijay at last removed his sportcoat and loosened his tie; it was just too hot, and there seemed little point in adding to his discomfort merely for the sake of formality. Although the food had been prepared by a maharaja's cook, it was not exceptional or unusual: tomato and cucumber sandwiches, vegetable *samosas*, bananas, and mangos.

Vijay found it intriguing that the princess was calmly eating with two Untouchables—although, of course, she did not know their caste backgrounds and it wouldn't be proper to ask. Sometimes surnames provided a clue, but in Shanta's case "Das" could be derived from a number of sources. The very fact that no one present showed concern illustrated how different such matters were now among urbanized people. In most rural villages, however, the old rules regarding intercaste relations retained strength.

They ate in silence for the most part. He was quite aware of the princess seated so close that he could see the fine dark hairs on her arm contrasting with that light, flawless skin.

He finished a tomato and cucumber and coriander sandwich, then bit off the end of a mango to suck out the flesh and juice.

There came the crashing and splintering of a tree on the far hillside. "It sounds like the Forestry Department is busy," Vijay said. He took a cloth napkin and wiped the sticky juice from his fingers.

"They're extremely misguided," said Kaushalya Kumari icily.

"Why is that?" asked Shanta in a tone of sincere interest.

Kaushalya set down a half finished sandwich. She removed the length of scarf covering her head and pushed back her heavy braid. She took off her sunglasses and gestured with them. "These mountains have been forested for thousands of years. The contractors are cutting down most of the trees in a decade or two. Do you realize what that means?"

She did not wait for a reply, but rushed on: "The Bhil tribal people are forced to become farmers or to hire out as laborers, instead of hunting game or harvesting wood products and fruit. They don't even get most of the money from the trees now. The rich contractors do. And corrupt Forest Department men. The climate will change, too— we'll see more droughts without the forests to retain moisture and help precipitate rain. The hills will erode without trees to hold the soil."

"That sounds bad," said Shanta Das with a frown.

"That's not half of it! These hills are all that hold back the sand. The desert's already growing, moving into the gaps in the hills. You'll be getting more sandstorms in Delhi without the trees to keep the winds on this side of the mountains. My father would never have allowed the cutting—that area used to be a strict preserve."

Vijay was staring at her, intrigued by the sudden vitality in her face, by the spark in her eyes. The princess obviously felt strongly, almost fanatical, about the matter. But of course she was on edge over the tax raid, so maybe she came across as more fervent than she would have at a less stressful time. Vijay ventured, "I've read that deforestation may well rank with too many people as our main environmental problems. So much of the flooding and destruction during the monsoons comes from not having enough forests to absorb the excess rainwater."

She stared at him, as if surprised that he would be knowledgeable about such things, or possibly unsure whether he was sincere or merely trying to win her good opinion. At last she said in a tone ending the conversation, "That's true."

When they had finished eating and were packing the food containers, Shanta Das glanced toward the shrine and asked, "Which god is that? I glimpsed the image as we drove in. It looked like a rider on a horse, with a woman standing by him."

"He's worshiped mainly by the Bhil tribals," replied Kaushalya Kumari. "They call him 'Bheru,' or 'Bhairava.' He's often shown with his consort. Some people consider him a form of Shiva. They say Bhairava rode and hunted and conquered in the forests long ago, even before the Rajputs conquered the Bhils. There are shrines to him all over these hills. The Bhils make little clay images of him to put in the shrines." She smiled slightly. "The Bhils usually offer liquor to him, but I didn't have any today." Before stepping out of the shade, she put her sunglasses back on and again drew the scarf over her head. "He's usually depicted as an archer on horseback, but don't ask me why."

They returned across the Aravallis. Although the jeep's canvas top shielded them against the direct sun, the ride was still hot. And dusty.

Vijay could not help but wonder if, back at Mangarh city, the treasure had already been found in the old fortress—maybe by Ghosali. He pushed the thought of the haughty Brahmin from his mind.

A string of camels appeared ahead, laden with huge sacks on each side. Their drivers urged them onto the shoulder to make way for the honking motor vehicle. Soon afterwards the jeep passed a line of heavily loaded bullock carts.

"I wonder if they're going all the way across the mountains," said Shanta Das.

"This is an ancient trade route," replied Kaushalya, trying to respond as briefly as possible without obvious rudeness.

"Where did it go?" asked Shanta.

Kaushalya again felt annoyed that a tax official, even an agreeable one, expected her to answer questions as if she were a tourist guide. But it would be discourteous not to reply. And it was probably best to continue to cooperate with the "enemy," hopefully reinforcing the impression she had nothing to hide. She said, "This is a fairly easy pass through the mountains, so caravans used it on their way to the seaports on the coast. Traders spent the night near the fort at Mangarh for protection from robbers."

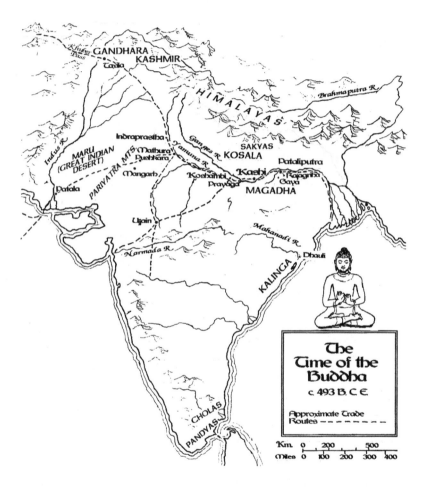

The
Time of the
Buddha
c. 493 B.C.E.

Approximate Trade
Routes - - - - - -

A Merchant
of Kashi

1

Kashi, later known as Varanasi and Benares. Near the end of the rainy season, 493 B.C.E.

The afternoon monsoon rains pattered outside the ornately carved, pillared, teakwood pavilion where the barber was trimming Samudradatta's beard. With the merchant's prominent jowls and his short, well fattened physique, to some persons he resembled an image of Lord Ganesha, the potbellied, elephant-headed god, who was worshiped in a few locales but had not yet become widely popular. The wealthy trader sat on his customary cushions on the mezzanine floor overlooking his main gate. Nearby, his clerks worked with the aid of mustard oil lamps. His servant Jajali, a tall, skinny, sun browned man of forty years, squatted patiently within reach. From the open door of Samudradatta's ground floor storerooms rose the scent of cinnamon, overpowering the odors of other spices and of bales of muslin. The merchant was smugly pleased with this huge supply of goods, which he had obtained on last spring's caravan to the southern kingdoms.

Samudradatta heard footsteps on the veranda fronting the avenue and looked down. The elder of his two sons, twenty-two year old Arthadatta, removed his sharp toed shoes inside the gateway. The young man stamped his bare feet to shake the water from his legs, then he climbed the wooden stairway and entered the office pavilion. His white shawl and turban soaked from the rain, Arthadatta bent his slender body and touched his father's feet.

Arthadatta straightened and stood quietly. His eyes, normally sleepy looking, now shifted about uncertainly. "Well?" demanded Samudradatta in his raspy voice. His son's slow-moving manner annoyed him today, as it so often did. The merchant observed that Arthadatta was again wearing clothes of coarsely woven cotton, unadorned by embroidery or patterned borders, and his earrings were of cheap baked clay. Recently, Arthadatta had been dressing in this less expensive, simple clothing, rather than the finest Kashi-woven cottons which he had previously worn. He also no longer wore the shoes decorated with peacock feathers that were former favorites. Samudradatta supposed there was nothing improper in less costly attire. It could give the impression of being serious and unconcerned with frivolity, so long as Arthadatta didn't carry it to an extreme so people thought he couldn't afford better.

Arthadatta's eyes widened with anxiety. "Have you heard, Father, that Paravata's caravan disappeared in the Great Desert? It never arrived in Pushkara. Paravata hasn't been seen for months. All the drivers were lost, too, of course. Everyone. Just vanished into the desert!"

"All lost?" Samudradatta felt an uneasiness in his gut. The disappearance of such an experienced trader emphasized the perils of the caravan journeys which Samudradatta himself undertook every year. He shook his head and sighed. "Those desert crossings are the most dangerous of all. So much depends on the pilot keeping watch on the stars. If he falls asleep and misses the next water source, it can mean death for everyone in the caravan."

Arthadatta's lips, usually hanging in a slack, lazy smile, trembled as he said, "Pe—people are saying that the demons must have led Paravata astray."

A tingling chill ran through Samudradatta. The demons took delight in confusing the pilots at night and sending the caravans off track. Then they fed on the bodies after everyone died, and looted the cargo. They were often on the minds of merchants and cart drivers whenever a caravan was in a deep forest or in the midst of wastelands. Samudradatta himself had never actually seen a demon, but he had heard them on more than one occasion when the winds were shrieking about his encampments. "No doubt we'll never know for sure what happened," he said, trying not to think further about that particular menace. "It's seldom anyone ever finds a trace of a caravan lost in the desert."

The barber finished with the scissors and began rubbing Samudradatta's beard with the usual sandalwood-scented perfume. The trader seldom bothered to have the small fringe of hair beneath his bald pate cut; there was so little of it, and anyway it was covered by his turban most of the time.

Arthadatta changed the subject, but his eyes did not lose their aura of anxiety. "I've arranged for hiring eight more carts, Father."

Samudradatta shoved aside his thoughts about the lost caravan and focused on his son. He scowled. "Only eight! I specifically told you we need twelve. Why have you come to me with only eight?"

"There were no more to be had today, Father. I visited all the usual places. We still have a few weeks before the caravans leave, so I thought there was no hurry—"

"—No hurry! What if other traders contract with all the cart owners in the meantime, so there are no more carts left?"

"That hasn't been a problem before, Father, so—"

"—Son, if I send you to get twelve carts, then you get twelve carts. Why are you always trying to get out of work? Did you spend the entire time today on getting the carts?"

"Uh, not exactly, Father."

"What do you mean, 'not exactly?' Have you been off listening to one of those teachers in the Forest of Bliss again?"

Arthadatta's eyes flicked away to gaze at a corner of the room. "No, I was in the Deer Park, Father. But only for a short time."

Samudradatta gave a heavy sigh. That particular forest, to the north of the city, was another place where spiritual leaders congregated. "How could it be only for a short time? It must take you most of the day just to get there and back, especially with the road so muddy these days."

Arthadatta looked down at the floor.

The barber bowed low and quietly left.

"I just don't understand," Samudradatta said, shaking his head. "When I send you to do something, you come back without doing it. Don't you appreciate what I've done for you, making this business for you and your brother, so you don't have to start out poor as I did? All my own father ever did was beat me, you know. I swore I'd never be like him. That's why I've tried to teach you boys what I know."

Arthadatta, who had heard the speech so many times before, said, "I realize that, Father. But one thing you've taught us is to listen to all kinds of teachers when you've invited them to give talks at our house. I don't see a difference between that and going to hear them in the Deer Park or the Forest of Bliss."

"The difference," said Samudradatta, his eyes igniting, "is that I invite them to my house after my day's work is done!"

And it was a lot of work organizing the two upcoming caravans: one to Rajagriha in the east, which he was entrusting to Arthadatta, and the other to Indraprastha in the northwest, which Samudradatta himself would lead.

As usual, Samudradatta had obtained commitments from other traders to join their own trains of bullock carts with his caravans, dividing the costs of hiring guards and guides. To avoid carrying large quantities of copper coins or of gold, he had arranged for letters of credit with leading merchants in the cities along the routes. And now, to be able to transport more goods, he had sent Arthadatta to negotiate agreements to hire additional bullock carts and drivers.

Samudradatta took pride in being expert at the long, involved process of organizing caravans, but he doubted his sons would ever be as competent at it as he—they just didn't exert themselves with the same concentration to details. Maybe that came from growing up comfortably, rather than starting out poor as Samudradatta himself had. Still, some day he would turn over the business to the boys, and hopefully they could summon up enough sense between the two of them to continue accumulating wealth.

Arthadatta fingered the vine carvings on a teak pillar. "Father," he said in an unusually solemn voice, "I need to talk with you."

"That's what we're doing, son, in case you hadn't noticed."

Arthadatta looked away, avoiding his father's eyes. Samudradatta knew the boy feared him a little. Both sons did. That wasn't necessarily bad; a little anxiety kept a person alert, so long as it wasn't carried so far as Samudradatta's own father had. As a boy Samudradatta had run away from home, rather than face the daily lashings and browbeatings. He had fled all the way east from Indraprastha to Kashi, just to make sure he would be safe.

But although Samudradatta had been a hard disciplinarian with his own boys, they must know he loved them—otherwise, why would he keep telling them that the business would some day be theirs? "Go on, son," he urged.

Arthadatta glanced at his father's servant Jajali, at the two clerks who were seated on the floor at their small writing tables, and at the pair of office boys who sat waiting to run errands. In a hushed voice he said, "Maybe we should be alone, Father."

"Whatever for? These men are always here. They're like family, you know that."

Arthadatta, eyes downcast, hesitated a few more moments. Then he said, "Fa-Fa-" Flushing with embarrassment at his nervous tripping over words, he tried again: "Father, it's hard to tell you this. In the Deer Park I've been going to talks by the teacher whose followers call him the Buddha, the Enlightened One."

"And?"

Arthadatta's eyes suddenly glowed with life. "Father, he's amazing! He's the most—the most saintly person I've ever seen. As soon as he began to speak, I knew that he had the truths I've always wanted."

Samudradatta said dryly, "I've heard you say that about a few other teachers in the past."

Arthadatta grinned sheepishly. His glanced at his father's face, then away again. "But they were nothing compared with the Buddha. As soon as I heard him, I knew that he had what I needed, even though I hadn't realized it before."

Samudradatta shrugged. "Well, if not him, you'd be following someone else. Just so long as it doesn't interfere with your work."

Arthadatta said, "You—you know I've tried to work hard at the business, Father."

Samudradatta frowned and said, "Sometimes."

Arthadatta wiped his wet forehead and continued, "I know the bu-business is a wonderful opportunity for me, as you've always said. But I've never been as interested in it as you are, Father. It always seemed to me there should be more to life than earning money, or having a big house with lots of servants."

Samudradatta scowled as he replied, "That's because you've never had to do without them. But why shouldn't you follow this Buddha? The Buddhist traders we know are all fine men. The master shouldn't do you any harm."

Arthadatta hesitated a moment, absently fingering the carvings on the pillar, then plunged boldly. "Father, I've decided that being a merchant isn't for me. I want to be a monk."

Samudradatta stared at him. "You *what?*"

Arthadatta again wiped his forehead with the back of his hand and repeated quickly, "I want to join the Buddhist Order, Father."

Disbelieving, Samudradatta still stared at Arthadatta. Then, watching Arthadatta's face, he asked, "You're joking, son. Aren't you?"

"Nuh—no, Father."

Samudradatta sat scowling at the young man. He'd had no hint of such an interest, had he? True, Arthadatta had often disappeared for large portions of the day. Samudradatta had thought nothing of it, other than frequently being annoyed that the boy wasn't working. There was indeed this recent matter of wearing cheap clothes. And Arthadatta had always been the gentler of the two sons. He would rather watch a squirrel play in a *neem* tree or parrots circling the sky than come inside and count bolts of muslin. He preferred talking about his guru's lessons on the *Vedas*, instead of concentrating on adding up the figures in a ledger.

But to leave the business! "No!" said Samudradatta.

Arthadatta stood rigidly, his eyes straight ahead.

"I won't hear of it," said Samudradatta. "I've planned on you and your brother taking over the trading." Samudradatta rose to his feet. His servant Jajali was watching him and Arthadatta with wide-eyed fascination, but the clerks were pretending to be intent on their work, rather than the conversation. The office boys had discovered an engrossing spot on the opposite wall.

Samudradatta padded over to where he could look down into a storeroom at the bales of goods. He whirled about and all but shouted, "You can become a Buddhist layman only! I know many businessmen who are Buddhists, but they aren't monks!"

Arthadatta shrunk backward. He said in a weak voice, "The Buddha says it's so difficult to achieve enlightenment that most laymen can't do it. There are too many distractions. Only by being a monk can a person concentrate fully on the path."

"When you get to be my age," said Samudradatta, "if you still want to be a monk, you can feel free!" He sat down again, and said more calmly, "Meanwhile you must do your duty. Work in the business, get married, have sons of your own."

Arthadatta blinked at a tear, then wiped it away.

"If there's anyone who's entitled to go off and be a wandering seeker, it's me," said Samudradatta. "But I know my duty to my family. I would never even consider running off until I knew my sons were ready to take over the business."

Arthadatta made no response. Below in the street, cart wheels drummed on the cobblestones and a driver called to his bullocks

"Besides," said Samudradatta sternly, "what about your betrothal? Your mother would never stand for breaking it. Don't even mention it to her!" Ambalika had evolved into a vicious woman, and Samudradatta shuddered when he thought of how his wife would scream if Arthadatta did not go through with the marriage she had arranged.

A visitor appeared at the top of the stairs and entered the pavilion. "Am I interrupting anything?" the trader Chamikara asked. He seated himself on a floor cushion without waiting for a reply.

Samudradatta tried to hide his annoyance at the timing of the visit as he replied automatically, "Of course you're not interrupting. You know this is your place as much as it is mine. After all, you're family." Like Samudradatta, Chamikara was a trader of the Vaishya class of merchants and farmers, the third highest social group, below the Brahmin priests and scholars and the Kshatriya princes and warriors. Chamikara considered himself a near-equal of Samudradatta in business, an evaluation Samudradatta did not share, even though he had agreed to Chamikara and his bullock carts joining the Rajagriha caravan with Arthadatta this year.

Chamikara also considered himself Samudradatta's good friend, and he dropped by the business often for visits. Chamikara was similar in height and bulk to Samudradatta. Although when they were together it was obvious that they resembled each other only superficially, when they were apart people who did not know them well sometimes mistook one for the other, a fact which irritated Samudradatta.

Jajali handed the visitor a copper cup of rice beer, while one of the office boys placed a bronze tray of sugared sweets nearby on the floor. Chamikara drank deeply of the beer, then said, eyes bright with excitement, "Did you hear? Paravata of Rajagriha was lost with his whole caravan in the Great Desert!"

Samudradatta was slow to reply. "Yes, we heard."

"It's thought the demons tricked him off course so they could feast on flesh and steal the trade goods!"

"We know," said Samudradatta. Arthadatta stood awkwardly in front of the two men.

"You look as if something's wrong," Chamikara said to Samudradatta with an exaggerated look of concern. "Has Paravata's disappearance upset you so much, then? You didn't have any goods in his caravan, did you?"

"No," said Samudradatta, trying to think of some way to avoid telling the man what was happening. Not only would Chamikara enjoy learning of Samudradatta's difficulties, he would spread the word among all the other merchants of Kashi.

Chamikara finished the cup of beer. Jajali poured another as

Chamikara's eyes shifted from Samudradatta to Arthadatta and back to Samudradatta again. "You're quite sure nothing's wrong?"

Samudradatta gave a shrug as if to dismiss the matter. "My son came up with a foolish notion. That's all."

"Nothing important, I hope," said Chamikara. "You know how concerned I am about you. How can I be happy myself, if my best friend is unhappy?"

Samudradatta sighed. There seemed to be no way out. He said, "My son tells me he wants to be a Buddhist monk."

Chamikara peered at Samudradatta, then at Arthadatta. "Is it really so?" he asked Arthadatta.

"Yes, Uncle."

His beer forgotten, Chamikara sat immobile, a glint of delighted fascination growing his eyes. Then he looked at Samudradatta and said, "Well. Imagine that!"

Samudradatta said, trying to keep his voice under control, "I told him to forget that nonsense. It's one thing for him to renounce the world after he's fulfilled his obligations to his family. It's quite another to become a monk at so young an age."

Chamikara glanced at Arthadatta, then back at Samudradatta. "Well. It must have been quite a surprise."

"It was."

"He's explained his reasons to you, I assume?"

"No," said Samudradatta. "Why should he? I told him to forget the idea."

Chamikara looked as if he could hardly believe his good fortune in being present at a time when Samudradatta confronted such an awkward situation. He recomposed his face into a grave expression and said to Arthadatta, "You must know that this hurts your father deeply."

Arthadatta glanced quickly at him, then said, "I know, Uncle. I regret that very much."

"Hmm. Well, since your father has refused his blessing, I suppose that's that."

"So it is," said Samudradatta with finality. "I need my son to lead the Rajagriha caravan. He must give his full attention to getting ready for it."

"Yes," said Chamikara. "Yes, organizing a caravan does indeed require one's full attention. I have my own son working on the same matters right now."

Samudradatta's younger son Durvasas entered the room. Durvasas glanced at his brother, then at his father and Chamikara. He quickly bent and touched his father's feet, then straightened. "Is something wrong, Father?" In many ways, nineteen-year-old Durvasas had always been the more promising of the two boys—intelligent, industrious, serious. With a thin, pinched looking face, he was also the stronger willed, stubborn in his quiet way.

Samudradatta said, "Your brother tells me he wants to be a Buddhist monk."

Durvasas stood immobile, emotions flickering across his eyes. Then he looked at Samudradatta and gave a nod.

"You knew about this?"

"Yes, Father."

"But you didn't tell me? Well, I suppose that's to be expected."

Durvasas said, "I felt it was between only you and my brother, Father."

Samudradatta said loudly, trying to control his anger, "I told him to forget about it!"

Durvasas' eyes flicked toward his brother, then quickly away.

Arthadatta had been standing silently, his eyes downcast, a hurt expression on his face. "May I leave, Father?" he asked quietly.

"Yes, go. Find the rest of the carts."

The young man left without looking at anyone.

When Arthadatta had gone, Chamikara hurriedly drained the beer cup, handed it to Jajali, and put an arm on Samudradatta's shoulder. He said, "I know how hard this must be for you, my friend. But he's a good boy. You have two good sons. That's one more than I have. Be grateful for that."

Samudradatta replied stiffly, "I am."

Chamikara said, "You've always invited so many gurus to your house for dinner. Maybe your son got the wrong ideas from listening to them."

"I didn't invite them to give ideas to my sons!" said Samudradatta. "I invited them because I find their teachings entertaining." He added more quietly, "And to gain merit, of course. After all, charitable deeds do build up good karma."

Chamikara asked, in an apparent effort to lighten the mood, "Ah–so you want to be reborn even higher in caste in your next life! Maybe as a Brahmin?"

Samudradatta shrugged. "Who doesn't?"

Chamikara sat a moment, then gave a nod. He rose to his feet. "I'll leave now. But you know you can call on me any time if I can be of help." He hurried down the steps.

Samudradatta sighed deeply. Most likely, Chamikara was going to tell the entire city what happened. He asked Durvasas, "How could your brother even think of doing such a thing?"

Durvasas quickly looked away. "It uh...it's something he wanted very badly, Father."

"Well, you talk to him. Try to see that he behaves more sensibly. After all, some day this business will be yours, too, and it will be much easier with someone else to share the load."

"I'll try, Father."

To Samudradatta it seemed Durvasas spoke without much conviction. With a big outpouring of breath, Samudradatta stood. "Get my palanquin," he ordered Jajali. Although it was cooler out than he preferred, the rain had stopped, and bathing in the Ganges at the bottom of the bluff below the city wall would provide just the soothing, refreshing escape that he needed. He had bathed at sunrise this morning, of course, as he did every day of his life. But he needed to do it again.

The river was high due to the monsoons. Wearing only his white cotton *dhoti*, with a gasp of relief Samudradatta waded into the refreshing chill of the sacred waters. Jajali and the palanquin bearers waited on the shore. Samudradatta saw only a couple other local people in the water; virtually everyone bathed at sunrise each morning, and the pious also at sunset. Several parties of pilgrims, most likely from nearby kingdoms, were in the Ganges. But few people traveled long distances in the rainy season, when the roads turned to mud and the rivers flooded, so the numbers were far fewer than at other times of the year.

A thin haze of smoke drifted over from downstream, where funeral pyres smoldered at the burning ghats. It was everyone's wish to die in Kashi and to be cremated on the banks of the most holy of rivers in this sacred city. Or, at the least, to have their ashes carried to Kashi and cast into the Ganges here.

Farther downstream yet, oars flashed in the sun and sails flapped as the ferries crossed and recrossed the river, bearing the traffic of the Northern Highway, the trade route which crossed the entire subcontinent.

Without conscious decision, Samudradatta began following the same ritual he did every morning soon after rising from his bed, cleansing himself in the river and worshiping the rising sun. He did not have a *neem* twig such as he normally used to scrape his tongue and scrub his teeth, but he gulped water and swished it about, thoroughly rinsing his mouth and throat.

Then he splashed water over himself while reciting his traditional mantra: "May I possess the lovely splendor of Lord Shiva that he may inspire my mind." His palms pressed together, he respectfully bowed toward the bright area in the clouds that marked the location of the sun.

As he left the water, he thought with a smile of Chamikara. His merchant friend had an altogether different way of relaxing. He would have relieved his anxieties not by bathing in the Ganges, but rather by the ministrations of his favorite courtesan while he drained cup after cup of rice beer. That was not Samudradatta's way, despite his growing distaste for his wife.

While Jajali dried what little remained of Samudradatta's hair and refitted his turban, the merchant debated whether or not to return to his business affairs. In the end he decided to make a round of visits to other traders. One never knew what details one could pick up which might be useful. His presence might also minimize whatever gossip about him Chamikara was spreading.

It was late that night when Samudradatta returned to his luxurious teakwood home. He took great pride in its pillared facade, its barrel-vaulted tile roofs, and its pleasant garden adjoining the rear of the warehouse and office. Since Kashi occupied a high plateau, from the top floor pavilion of his house Samudradatta could look down over the wooden city wall at the broad flat expanse of the Ganges, an especially lovely sight at sunset. But because of the presence of his wife Ambalika, Samudradatta avoided his own household whenever he could, treating the living quarters as if they were across the city from his storerooms instead of merely down a stairway and through a courtyard. He had wondered how long it would take Ambalika to hear of Arthadatta's request.

As he both expected and feared, Ambalika awaited him when he at last entered the house. She wore massive gold jewelry which gleamed in the lamplight, and beneath her shawl her huge breasts hung over roll after roll of fat. With her hefty legs and broad feet, she stood as immovable as an elephant in his path. He tried to hurry in past her, but she blocked him and screamed, "How could you have let him say such a thing? Why didn't you order him not to?"

"You're, uh, referring to our son?"

She planted her hands on her bulging hips. "Of course I am! Who else did you think I meant?" Samudradatta said nothing, but he waited, knowing she would not let him off easily. Ambalika had become the main shadow in his life. As she had gained in social status over the years due to the steadily increasing wealth from her husband's business, she had grown ever fatter and increasingly argumentative and conceited. It seemed to him that Ambalika always blamed him for anything that went contrary to her wishes. Samudradatta now spent as little time in her company as possible while still fulfilling his obligations as head of the family. She shouted, "If you'd kept him busier at trading, and answered all his questions yourself, he'd never have wandered off to listen to that 'Buddha!'"

"How could I have expected anything like this to happen?"

"You've invited all those teachers with their odd ideas to our home. Did you think it would have no effect on our son?"

Samudradatta said, "I did refuse him permission to leave."

"How can I ever face Chundala?" Ambalika wailed. "She may even call off her daughter's marriage to him!"

Samudradatta spread his hands in a gesture of futility. "I doubt it. Anyway, that's hardly my fault."

"You could have stopped it all!" said Ambalika. "Our son has always been like that—sitting around daydreaming, watching birds. You should have known what he was thinking."

"I thought I did! But I didn't know he felt so strongly."

Ambalika glared at him. Then she sniffed and padded off.

His dinner was waiting. Fortunately, the cook had fixed some of his favorite dishes, including barley with curds, and venison with rice and fish. Eating it helped him feel better.

2

Chamikara continued his daily visits, no doubt eager for new information to spread about Samudradatta, but giving the appearance of being sympathetic. "There are so many teachers in Kashi these days," he said, shaking his head. "All of them trying to win converts to some new doctrine. Anyone's son could have fallen for one." He quickly finished his cup of beer and held it while Jajali poured another.

In spite of his frequent annoyance with Chamikara, Samudradatta found himself both appreciative of the apparent sympathy and eager for someone to talk to about the subject. He nodded. "That's true. Many of those I've invited to my house to speak have had quite interesting ideas."

"The next thing we hear, you'll be giving up your wealth and family to be a disciple yourself!"

"Not likely. I know my duty, much better apparently than I've been able to teach it to my son. That's what makes me so angry. What are these boys thinking of when they go off to follow some teacher before they've fulfilled their obligations to their families?"

It was not uncommon for older men of status and wealth, even kings sometimes, to renounce their worldly belongings and families and go off to seek the meaning of life. But that was only after they had married, fathered sons, seen their daughters safely married, and made provisions for the financial security of their own wives and other dependents. Samudradatta had never seriously weighed doing such a thing himself, although in the back of his mind was a vague thought that some year, far in the future, he might consider it. At the very least, such a life might have some appeal in that it would free him from the necessity of daily contact with Ambalika.

Chamikara took a sweetmeat from the tray between them and said, "I remember you once feasted the leader of the Jains, the one they call Mahavira, Great Hero. Maybe you should be glad your son didn't want to be a Jain. They seem even stricter than the Buddhists."

"I suppose. They do go to extremes." Mahavira and his monks went about totally naked, striving like many ascetics to be completely indifferent to the material world, including heat and cold, and to give up unneeded possessions like clothes. To keep from building up bad karma, the Jains tried to avoid killing any living thing. Many of the monks swept the path ahead of themselves with brooms so as not to step on insects and wore cloth face masks to keep from accidentally inhaling bugs. "But," said Samudradatta, "it's bad enough that Arthadatta wants to be a Buddhist monk. Imagine—never to get married or have a son of his own!"

"Maybe you should have stayed in Indraprastha after all," said Chamikara. He sipped at the beer, more slowly now. "I've heard that the young people there don't have so many new ideas to seduce them. The Brahmins' influence is still much stronger there, and nobody ever challenges their teachings about the *Vedas*."

"At least we aren't in Mathura," said Samudradatta. "That city's even worse than here. The other day a trader told me that more and more people in Mathura are worshiping Krishna. They say Lord Krishna actually loves them and will answer all their prayers, and that he doesn't need sacrifices."

Chamikara stared at him. "No sacrifices at all? You're joking."

"No! I swear that's what he said."

"But how could anyone believe such things?"

"Oh, I agree, of course. It seems nowhere is safe. I'd watch your own son, my friend. Tell him to stay away from all those new ideas." Samudradatta was thinking about his own younger son Durvasas. He didn't need to be concerned about losing him, too, to some guru, did he?

At least he did not have to worry now about Arthadatta spending too much time in the Deer Park; not for many months. With the end of the rainy season, the Buddha left his hermitage. As he did every year, the teacher resumed his wanderings until the next monsoon time, visiting other cities to spread his message.

Several days before Samudradatta's first caravan of the year left, he called upon his Brahmin priest Sudeva to conduct a sacrifice for the success of his ventures and to establish an auspicious time for the departures. Although costly, the rituals were always satisfying to Samudradatta: the purification of himself and his wife through bathing and prayers; the preparation of the grounds by the priest and helpers by digging the pit and building the fire; the death of the goat by strangulation so as not to spill any blood; the offerings of flesh and ghee to the gods by way of the fire....

Samudradatta always felt that the continued success of his ventures must be due to some large extent to the fact that he took so much care to first obtain the blessings and support of the gods.

On a day and time the priests determined to be favorable for the undertaking, Arthadatta and Chamikara left Kashi with their caravan, ferrying the carts across the Ganges, and then traveling east on the Northern Road toward Rajagriha.

Then Samudradatta departed with his own long line of carts, carrying the cinnamon and other spices that he had acquired from the south to Indraprastha, far to the northwest on the Yamuna River. This well-established portion of the Northern Road through the prosperous Ganges plain was not so difficult as the routes that went through wild jungles or unmarked deserts. Samudradatta had less fear of attack by bandits in these wealthy kingdoms, less chance of coming under the influence of malevolent demons. There were ferries to move the carts across the larger rivers. Still, in many sections the roads were ill-maintained, and there was the annoyance of frequent tolls and customs duties to pay.

3

Samudradatta was ready after five months of travel to return to the comforts of home, even with Ambalika's unpleasantness and the city sweltering in the midst of the hot season. Caravans were uncomfortable at best, with the unavoidable dust and the long, harsh rides on the carts. He had driven good bargains at Indraprastha, acquiring dates and almonds and wines and woolens to transport east on the return trip. Arthadatta and Chamikara had arrived back a month earlier, as the distance from Kashi to Rajagriha was so much less than the distance to Indraprastha.

During the long days on the road he had thought a lot about Arthadatta's wanting to follow the Buddha. The idea still pained Samudradatta immensely. But he did wonder whether Arthadatta could even carry on the business satisfactorily now. To be successful at trading required one's full commitment. Could it be better to let the boy follow his obsession, in the hope he would eventually decide he'd made a mistake and return to the business?

After bathing and seeing to the unloading of his own carts, Samudradatta listened to his son's report on the Rajagriha journey and was relieved to learn that a good profit had been made. A boy was fanning them, but the heat was still oppressive. "What mishaps did you endure?" asked Samudradatta, not really caring; the main concern was the wealth that now lay in his storerooms.

"Oh, the usual, Father," said Arthadatta, sounding like an experienced trader now. "Several carts lost wheels and spilled their loads. A few drivers injured other drivers when their arguments turned into fights. One driver got drunk and fell off a ferry, but he was rescued from the river. The roads got muddy after some rains—it mired the carts and slowed us for a week or so."

"All that's to be expected. You've done well, son! And you said Chamikara's satisfied, too?"

"Very much so, Father. His part of the caravan probably didn't do quite as well as ours, since he didn't get nearly so much ivory. But he seems pleased."

"Yes—the ivory. I want to look it over more carefully."

The ivory from Rajagriha waited in the storeroom, guarded by a strong-looking young Kshatriya warrior with a spear and a sword. The servant boy fanned them as Samudradatta sat on a bench, with

Arthadatta standing near, both looking at the stacks of pale, gently curved wealth. "So valuable," Samudradatta murmured. "And so beautiful when they're carved."

Arthadatta's face lost its usual lazy smile, and his eyes took on a look of concern. "Yes, but have you thought, Father, that the elephants are usually killed so we can get the tusks?"

Samudradatta stared at his son in surprise. He had never considered the matter. He frowned. "Yes," he said slowly, "It's unfortunate for the elephants. But if we don't trade in ivory, someone else will."

"That way of thinking could excuse almost anything, Father."

Samudradatta scowled. "The ivory trade has always been an honorable one. Think of all the beautiful things that will be carved from these tusks."

There was silence for some time. Then Arthadatta said, "Father, if you feel rested enough, there's something I need to discuss."

Reluctantly, Samudradatta turned away from the ivory, the sight of so much of which had given him a secure feeling. "Go ahead."

Arthadatta wiped the sweat from his forehead with a cloth. "Father, the Buddha is back in the Deer Park after his wanderings. He plans to spend the next rainy season there again. Won't you come hear him?"

Samudradatta froze. "So you're still interested in being a monk," he said coldly.

Arthadatta's eye twitched. "Why don't you just come hear him, Father. That's all I ask."

Samudradatta shook his head no. "I have too much to do. After all, I've been away for months. It's also hot out, and it would take well over an hour each way, just going and coming."

Arthadatta sat, motionless. Samudradatta thought. He was indeed curious about this teacher about whom he'd heard so much for so long. He gave his son a look that was still skeptical. "All right. I warn you, though, that I may not stay long. When does he preach?"

Arthadatta's face lit with joy. "Usually late afternoon, after his midday rest. When the sun's not quite so hot."

"We might as well go today, then. Order the palanquins ready."

Arthadatta's smile broadened and his eyes shone bright with delight, but he remained motionless, as if not really believing his father was ready to go hear the Buddha at this very moment.

The familiar figure of Chamikara appeared, perspiring from the heat. Samudradatta rose, forced a smile, and the two embraced heartily. "Welcome back!" said Chamikara. "I heard you'd just arrived."

Samudradatta stepped back and gave a nod. "You had a successful trip, I understand."

"Oh, quite. Quite successful." Chamikara seated himself, took a drink of his customary rice beer. He glanced at Arthadatta and said, "As did your son. I assure you he did you credit. Anyone would have thought he'd been leading caravans for years."

Samudradatta hesitated. Then: "Yes, I'm quite pleased with him."

"And how was your own journey?" asked Chamikara.

"Worthwhile," said Samudradatta, preoccupied with the problem of Arthadatta and the Buddha.

Chamikara appeared perplexed at the terseness of Samudradatta's replies.

Arthadatta said happily, "Uncle, Father has agreed to go with me today to hear the Buddha."

Chamikara stared at Samudradatta. "How interesting. Well, I suppose there's no harm in listening. Maybe I should go hear him myself sometime, just to satisfy my curiosity. Unfortunately I have another commitment today, however."

Samudradatta did not reply.

Chamikara rose, let Jajali take his cup. "I must leave you, I think. I'll drop by tomorrow to hear your reaction to the Buddha."

Samudradatta said nothing. Chamikara left.

The palanquin bearers moved at a slow trot through the narrow streets of Kashi, their bare feet slapping on the pavement stones. Jajali ran alongside, sweating heavily, but his long, skinny legs had little difficulty keeping pace. Samudradatta himself lay back in his cushions, with the canopy shading him from the sun, and he tried not to think about Arthadatta, whose palanquin followed his own.

They passed the teakwood mansions of other rich traders, then the much smaller houses of the less wealthy. Barefoot *sadhus* wearing skimpy loincloths and carrying only staffs and begging bowls leisurely roamed the streets. A whiff of incense drifted from the base of a giant banyan tree, where local residents were offering grain before a large, oblong rock in which dwelled the spirit who reigned over that particular neighborhood. At the adjacent pond, other worshipers were bathing to purify themselves before their own offerings to the deity.

The palanquins passed through the bazaar, where the stalls were less busy now than earlier in the morning when all the vegetables and fresh flowers were purchased. Then Samudradatta's party exited though the main, western gate in the timber wall, slowing in the press of heavy traffic from the Northern Road, bullock carts, horse-drawn carriages, soldiers, pilgrims.

Samudradatta unconsciously averted his eyes as he traveled past the filthy hovels beyond the city walls where the Untouchables lived, so low in status that they were not even considered as belonging to a caste. It was said by some that the dark skinned outcastes were descendants of primitive tribals who inhabited the lands long before the coming of the more civilized peoples.

For a short distance the palanquins followed the Northern Road with the stream of other travelers, then they turned off to the right onto the less busy track to the Deer Park. The road cut through part of the

Forest of Bliss, and on the left lay a series of ponds draining into the Varana River. It felt noticeably cooler here in the shade of the huge, ancient banyan and mango and teak trees.

The forest was home to a great many teachers imparting "Upanishads" to their disciples: question and answer sessions with the followers seated at the feet of their master. Many of the teachings were too complex for Samudradatta's taste, with their philosophical doctrines about the nature of a man's *Atman* or soul and its oneness with *Brahman*, the fabric of the universe; or the idea that good and evil did not exist as separate components in actuality, but were inseparable and an integral part of the one underlying reality. However, some of the masters were good entertainers, and Samudradatta often enjoyed listening to teachings which were amusingly presented or gave rise to intriguing speculations.

A party of naked ascetics was coming toward the city, and at their head Samudradatta recognized Mahavira, leader of the Jains, a dinner guest two years ago. The great teacher's followers strolled along behind him. Mahavira was in his mid-forties, his body thin but healthy appearing and well-built. Like the Buddha, he came from a princely Kshatriya background rather than from a Brahmin priestly heritage. This guru who had attracted so much attention and so many followers the past few years walked at a moderate speed, his expression calm and self-possessed.

Mahavira lived on the earth but had no real interest in it, and he gave no sign of remembering his former dinner host. Samudradatta did not mind. For him, the Jain leader's talk had been interesting, but too intellectual, too impractical, with its emphasis on striving to avoid taking actions of any kind, its stress on noninvolvement with the material world. Jainism held no further appeal for a man such as Samudradatta.

This time of year the water in the small Varana River flowed shallow, so the bearers could splash across at the ford. Most of the way to the Deer Park the road went through cultivated areas intermixed with more forest land.

Samudradatta watched his palanquin bearers for a time. Dark skinned Shudras, the lowest class of the caste system, the men were breathing heavily on such a long jaunt in the heat. The odor of their sweat filled the air, and perspiration ran in tiny rivers down their backs and chests. Samudradatta regretted it wasn't practical to use palanquins on caravans. The conveyances were so comfortable compared to the bullock carts, which crept along at slower than a walk and jolted and tossed their occupants at every unevenness in the road. But it would be extremely expensive to use palanquins on long journeys—a large number of bearers would have to be brought along to spell each other off frequently.

The Deer Park, so called because the King had given it as a forest preserve for those particular animals, was also called

"Rishipatana" for the many *rishis* or sages who inhabited it. Once again the air immediately felt cooler when the road entered the trees. Arthadatta directed the palanquin bearers to an area of bamboo huts. When the bearers had deposited Samudradatta's conveyance on the ground, he boosted himself from his cushions. Jajali immediately held an umbrella to shade him, even though the sun was filtered by a huge mango tree overhead. Samudradatta looked with a smile of irony at Arthadatta, already out of his own palanquin. "You wouldn't be traveling that way any more if you joined the Buddha's Order," he told his son. "You'd be walking the whole distance in the heat."

"I'm capable of walking, Father," Arthadatta said lightly.

Samudradatta gazed at his son, habitually so slow and easygoing. The idea of Arthadatta traveling large distances every day by foot was difficult to comprehend.

Arthadatta grinned. "Walking is better than riding a bullock cart, Father. I won't get my rear end battered about on a hard seat. And usually there's not so much dust kicked up."

Samudradatta thought, and shrugged. "Maybe."

A surprising number of persons were converging on the Buddha's teaching center. Some of them were richly dressed, some poorly. Arthadatta led his father past a few tree-sheltered huts to a clearing, where several hundred people had already gathered, squatting on the earth. Jajali placed a mat from the palanquins on the ground, and Samudradatta and Arthadatta seated themselves. Jajali squatted, holding the umbrella to shade his master and the young man. "Have you heard the story of the Buddha's life, Father?" Arthadatta asked.

"I know he's said to be a Kshatriya prince who gave up his inheritance to be an ascetic. Like Mahavira of the Jains." Samudradatta's tone indicated he had no desire to know more.

Nevertheless, Arthadatta informed him with enthusiasm, "The Buddha's name is Siddhartha Gautama, but they call him Sakyamuni, the Sage of the Sakyas, because he's from the Sakya tribe. Even though his father was a wealthy raja, Gautama decided he didn't want to live in luxury, that he wanted to find the meaning of life. So he left home and became a wanderer. For six years he tried living as an ascetic, almost starving himself to death."

Samudradatta suppressed the urge to voice a wish that the master had succeeded, so Arthadatta couldn't have come under his influence.

Arthadatta was rushing onward: "But the Buddha decided he could gain nothing by that, except weakening his body so much he almost died. When he regained his strength, he sat under a *pipal* tree near Gaya, in Magadha, determined not to move until he found what he sought. After forty-nine days, he achieved Enlightenment, and then he became a teacher. He preached his first sermon right here in the Deer Park."

"I've heard of him for years," Samudradatta admitted reluctantly. "He must be getting somewhat old by now."

"He's said to be about seventy. He seems much younger."

They realized all conversation had stopped. The heads of the crowd turned to the right as the Sage of the Sakyas appeared at the edge of the clearing. Eyes lowered, making no acknowledgment of the crowd, the man who was acclaimed as the Buddha, the Enlightened One, slowly, smoothly, walked to a low raised platform and seated himself on a mat. For what seemed a long time, he merely sat, his face pleasantly composed, eyes closed, apparently in meditation. The man was muscular and quite handsome, his skin light with a golden hue. Samudradatta knew from his own travels that the Sakyas, the Buddha's tribe, came from different stock than the lowlands people; their coloring was more like that of the people to the far north, beyond the vast range of high, snow covered mountains.

Eventually, the Buddha opened his eyes, raised his head, and casually examined the crowd. His voice, when he began, carried easily over the assembly. He sounded calm, confident, friendly: "Always seek to do what is good. Do not allow yourself to think of doing evil things, or your mind will fall into evil ways.

"Do not consider a good deed to be of little worth, because it seems small. Just as falling drops of water will eventually fill a water jar, so the wise man becomes full of good, even though he gathers it little by little.

"Likewise, do not consider a bad deed to be excusable because it is small. Bad deeds, like good deeds, accumulate, and the accumulation of wrongdoings is most painful."

Although the Buddha said little that seemed new, Samudradatta found himself listening intently. Something about the teacher's voice was compelling. "Let us avoid the dangers of evil," the Buddha said, "just as a man who loves his life avoids drinking poison. Strive to live in joy, in peace among those who struggle. Live in joy, although you may have nothing.

"Remember that victory brings hate, because the defeated man is unhappy. But a man who surrenders both victory and defeat is happy.

"Health is the greatest possession. Contentment is the greatest treasure. Confidence is the greatest friend.

"Cravings give rise to sorrow and fear. If a man is free from cravings, he is free from both sorrow and fear." The Buddha's eyes swept slowly over the crowd.

He concluded, "Again, always remember the importance of doing good." He nodded, smiled at the crowd, and then unhurriedly rose and left the platform.

"What do you think of him, Father?" Arthadatta asked anxiously.

After a moment of judicious silence, Samudradatta replied, still watching the Buddha's yellow robe until it disappeared into the trees, "He's an excellent speaker. I certainly can't fault what he said." He turned to his son. "I was disappointed he didn't say more, though. How does one attain enlightenment, such as he claims for himself? He never said. He just said to do good deeds."

Arthadatta replied, "When he's talking to newcomers, he often does speak only about living a good life. I think he saves the more difficult teachings for those he knows are serious. I learned about his Four Noble Truths and the Eightfold Path from some of his followers."

Samudradatta furrowed his forehead, thinking. "I'd like to hear more. Just out of curiosity. I know he accepts invitations to meals, so I'll invite him to our home."

"You'd do that?"

Samudradatta shrugged. 'I've done it with other teachers, haven't I? It doesn't mean I approve of all he says. I've heard he opposes sacrifices, and says the *Vedas* aren't important. But if you want to be a disciple, I need to hear more. Do you know where he went?"

"Probably to his hut, Father. He instructs his monks there most of the evening."

They found a senior monk, who led them a short distance along a mango and *pipal* tree-shaded path to another small clearing. There, some thirty or forty saffron robed monks were seated before the Buddha, who appeared to be in a discussion with several men in the front row. Their guide whispered to Samudradatta, "I'll present you to the master, and you can give your invitation. If the Buddha accepts, he'll do so by remaining silent."

They waited several minutes until the Buddha acknowledged the presence of their guide, who stepped close and whispered. The disciple then beckoned the two forward and said, "Blessed One, this is Samudradatta, a merchant of Kashi, and his son, Arthadatta, who would like to take his vows."

Samudradatta bent to touch the Buddha's feet. "Master," he said, "I respectfully ask the honor of yourself and your monks dining at my house tomorrow." The Buddha's lips curled slightly into a smile. He looked at Samudradatta, but said nothing.

Pleased at the Buddha's acceptance of the invitation, Samudradatta nodded, turned and left, with the delighted Arthadatta close behind.

Early the next morning, Samudradatta sent Arthadatta to the Deer Park to inform the Buddha that all was ready. A venerable monk told Arthadatta that only twenty disciples would accompany the Blessed One today. Arthadatta hurried back to the city and informed his mother.

Ambalika gave a clap of her hands and ordered the servants, "Twenty-one tables in the garden. Be quick!" It was her duty to oversee the arrangements. Any deficiencies would reflect unfavorably upon her management, and this she would not tolerate.

An hour before noon, the Buddha and his entourage appeared, perspiring and dusty from the lengthy walk. All had brought their begging bowls. As outcastes, however honorable, their use of Samudradatta's dishes would have rendered the dishes impure, to be destroyed afterwards. Samudradatta welcomed the guests and seated each of them before a separate tiny table in the courtyard. He and Ambalika and their two sons poured water over the visitors' hands to rinse off the dust. The family and their servants then spooned the food into the bowls: rice with a sauce, and a mixture of vegetables. The Buddha and his followers themselves did not believe in killing animals for food, so Samudradatta was careful not to serve anything that might cause the monks distress.

Samudradatta noticed with a mixture of amusement and annoyance that one of the young monk's eyes were riveted on the swaying of a servant girl's full, high-nippled breasts as she bent before him to spoon the food into his bowl. After she moved on to serve others, the young monk still stared at her. An older monk seated beside him nudged the younger *bhikkhu*. The boy, realizing he'd been caught thinking about something forbidden, reddened and quickly turned his attention to his food.

When the guests had finished dining, servants brought water to wash their hands and bowls. Samudradatta and his family then seated themselves before the Buddha, who smiled benevolently and calmly began his talk: "Suffering and hardship are inherent in all of life. No one, no matter how rich or powerful, can avoid all illness, or the pains of old age, or the loss of loved ones. That is the first of the Four Noble Truths." The Buddha paused, giving time for reflection on his words.

Samudradatta thought of his own experiences. He'd had many good times, but he agreed that at least some unhappiness was unavoidable. He'd felt forced to flee from home as a child. The possibility of one of his own sons leaving to become a monk was definitely painful, as was being married to a difficult wife. The Buddha continued, "The cause of the unhappiness is selfish desire, a person's own wants and cravings. That is the Second Noble Truth. The Third Noble Truth is that one can rid oneself of these desires, and thus be rid of the causes of the unhappiness. The Fourth Noble Truth is that of the Eightfold Path, the course of action a person can take to eliminate his selfish wants."

"The Eightfold Path involves leading a good life, and a well-disciplined one. It is a middle way between asceticism and self-indulgence. The eight steps on the Path are Right Knowledge, Right Resolve, Right Speech, Right Conduct, Right Livelihood, Right Effort, Right Mindfulness, and Right Meditation. All of these steps are intended to help in disciplining the mind, and to eliminating the boundaries of the selfish ego, so that one rids oneself of the causes of unhappiness. They all must be practiced regularly, over a person's lifetime.

"One reason I counsel a person to do good deeds is that helping other people makes him identify himself more with others, thereby decreasing the importance in his mind of his own self and its desires." He waited a few moments, then concluded, smiling, "A more detailed explanation of each of the steps on the Eightfold Path takes considerable time, and regretfully it must be left for another day."

The Buddha stopped, and Samudradatta had the impression he was finished. The discourses at a home were usually quite short, intended primarily as a way of thanking the host. The monks always wanted to be back to their living quarters by noon. But Samudradatta said, "Master, is it permitted to ask a question?" The Buddha inclined his head slightly to one side and waited.

Samudradatta said, "Master, it sounds to me as if most of your teachings primarily involve living a good life. Can't this be done by a layman, as well as a monk?"

With no change of expression, the Buddha replied, "Living a good life is part of the Path. But the goal is to become completely selfless—to break down the boundaries separating the individual self from other people. To be free from selfish desires, one must give up wanting anything at all for himself. That is very difficult. Because it is so difficult, it is important to avoid as many distractions as possible by living a simple life, and to live with other men who are trying to live the same way, so they can encourage each other. It is much more difficult for laymen to give up all desires and gain enlightenment."

He paused, before continuing, "By this, I do not mean to minimize the importance of everyone, including laymen, living a life of good deeds." He looked directly at Samudradatta, and smiled gently. Samudradatta felt the full force of the Buddha's personality boring into him as the teacher said, "You are reluctant to have your son join the Order, because you feel he will be lost to you. You are attached to your children, as if they are your possessions. Remember that man's possessions always bring worry to him. Without possessions, he has no worry."

He stopped, and once again Samudradatta thought the Buddha was finished. But the Buddha then looked at Ambalika. "Ambalika, what kind of wife are you?" he asked, still smiling.

Ambalika gasped. Utter silence filled the garden. Ambalika appeared astonished by the question, and uncharacteristically she made no response. The Buddha did not insist on a reply, but rather continued, calmly, softly, "There are many kinds of wives. There are those wicked in mind, ill-disposed, without pity, intent on harassing their families. There are those who squander a husband's profits from his work. There are those who are lazy, gluttonous, and domineering.

"On the other hand, there are those who are kind, compassionate, and protective of their husbands and families. There are those who are respectful toward their husbands. There are those who rejoice in their husband's presence and companionship. And there are those who endure all things, including hardships, calmly, without anger, and free from hatred.

"Ambalika, what kind of wife are you?"

The Buddha sat, smiling at her for a moment. Then, he rose, turned, and led his monks off in the direction of the monastery.

Samudradatta sat frozen in his place, dumfounded by the Buddha's singling out of Ambalika. He waited resignedly for the burst of outrage he knew would come. After some time passed, with no sound from her, he timidly glanced at her. He was astonished to see tears in her eyes. She looked at his face, and she burst into sobs, burying her face in her hands. He sighed. It was many years since he had seen her cry. He knew it would not last long, that her anger and resentment would soon be loosed to punish the household for her humiliation.

Arthadatta and Durvasas tactfully left. The servants remained out of sight. After several minutes of sobbing, she looked up at him, her eyes red and wet. "I want to be a good wife. I did all along..." her voice broke. In a moment she continued, "I didn't like it that all my friends' husbands came from good families, and I had to marry you just because you had money, even though I never even knew who your father or mother were. The Buddha made me realize I was wrong...." She again buried her head in her hands, and shook with her crying.

Samudradatta awkwardly watched her, uncertain how to respond.

What a remarkable being that Buddha is, he thought. He now understood why Arthadatta wanted to be a follower. Samudradatta had not become reconciled to the fact. But he could understand.

"Father," said Arthadatta the next day, "I still want to leave to join the Buddha's Order."

Samudradatta examined him for a time, then looked away.

"May I have your blessing, Father?" asked Arthadatta.

Samudradatta realized that he, himself, was still under the Buddha's spell. What was it about this teacher? Part of it was the Buddha's saintliness; he so obviously embodied love and compassion. It was clear that he had risen completely above any wants for himself, that he had totally dedicated himself to nourishing the well being of others. How could Samudradatta refuse his son the possibility of following such a path?

But what about the trading business? Could Durvasas alone ever manage it? Samudradatta knew other traders such as Chamikara who had only one son. A few merchants had only daughters, or even no children at all. Was it being too selfish to insist on *both* of his own sons taking over the business? Clearly, the Buddha would say yes. Samudradatta knew in his heart that the Buddha was right. Reluctantly, he said to Arthadatta, "Just don't be hasty."

Arthadatta stared wide-eyed at his Father. "I—I have your permission?"

Samudradatta desperately wanted to say, "No!" But he struggled with himself. At last he managed to say in a low voice, "As you wish."

Arthadatta's body sagged in relief.

Samudradatta said, "I don't like it. But if you lack the will to completely immerse yourself in trading, you won't do well at it. So I see no advantage in continuing to refuse you. Just think about it again, carefully. It would a hard life. You've always lived in comfort. Even traveling on caravans isn't as uncomfortable as how you'd be living."

"I won't change my mind, Father. I'll miss you and the rest of our family. But I'm grateful you're giving me your blessing."

Samudradatta sat stiffly, still not quite believing it could happen.

There was silence in the room. Arthadatta rose and frowned. "Now I suppose I'd better tell Mother. May I leave, Father?"

Samudradatta numbly gave a nod.

4

Ambalika cried quietly for some time. Samudradatta still could not quite believe that she did not openly blame him for Arthadatta leaving, or even scream at him. The improvement in Ambalika's attitude compensated somewhat for Samudradatta's sadness. Although she never again mentioned the Buddha or his comments, she was obviously trying to improve how she treated her husband.

Samudradatta wondered why his wife had reacted so strongly to the Buddha's words. Because no one else had ever confronted her so directly about herself? Had she somehow wanted all along for someone to peer within her and see what really lay beneath her facade of unpleasantness? If so, how had the Buddha discerned that?

And how had the Buddha so clearly ascertained Samudradatta's feelings about Arthadatta joining the Order? Maybe, Samudradatta thought, I was more transparent than I realized when I asked about the possibility of being a layman rather than a monk.

The Buddha had greatly impressed Samudradatta, although not enough to become a follower himself. Samudradatta felt a casual interest in the Buddha's ideas, but that was all. Even with his elder son gone, he still hoped for the continued prosperity of his business and for the future of his family. He had not grown wealthy by being pessimistic. He still had his wealth, his friends, and a fine son in his younger, Durvasas. Many men had much less.

He endured the hot season. He was glad for Ambalika's more pleasant disposition; otherwise, the oven-like weather might have been unbearable. The monsoon came on schedule and was, as usual, a welcome relief.

In preparation for the caravan season, Samudradatta called upon Sudeva, his Brahmin priest. Jajali led a fine milk cow as a gift to the priest. Sudeva was a big man, tall and lumbering, who carried a large part of his weight in his bare belly which bulged out over his *dhoti* like a bag of grain about to fall from an overburdened cart. His sacred thread, which would normally have hung diagonally across his chest, was supported almost horizontally at the lower end by this protuberant stomach. The Brahmin always wore a smile, but it was without humor, as if his facial muscles had merely stiffened into that particular configuration.

Sudeva's eyes glittered at the sight of the valuable cow. He accepted the animal as nothing more than what was due to him. After all, as the giver of the gift, Samudradatta would gain in merit at least as much as the Brahmin would benefit from the gain in wealth. When the two men were seated, Sudeva said, "Prior to discussing ceremonies, I would like to bring up another matter." His eyes took on a stern look which contradicted any impression the fixed smile might have given. "Everyone knows you hosted the so-called Buddha at your home. And you allowed your son to join his Order. This is a matter of deep concern to me."

Samudradatta raised his eyebrows in surprise. "Of course I had the master for a meal. But only so I could learn more about his views, since my son was so interested."

"Has it occurred to you that it gave this Buddha considerable legitimacy to be invited to the home of one of Kashi's wealthiest traders, and to give your elder son to him?"

"I, uh, hadn't considered the matter in that light. I often have teachers to my house, you know. And I was quite upset at my son leaving to follow him."

The priest's eyes softened just slightly. "Ah, I'm glad to know that. I detest that man and the other teachers who ridicule the *Vedas* and the sacrifices."

Samudradatta frowned. "I see. To a large extent, of course, I share your views."

Sudeva's smile broadened, appearing more genuine. "You must know I consider you a friend, as well as a generous client. I was worried that you might be thinking of following this 'Buddha' yourself, and that you might think you had no more need for my services."

Samudradatta's eyes widened in consternation. "Why, such a thought is inconceivable! I could no more conduct my business without your first satisfying the gods and all the spirits than...than I could transport my goods without carts!"

The priest's face relaxed. "Well, then, I see no further need to talk about the matter."

Sudeva and his assistants handled the ceremonies with great pomp and precision. Their endless Sanskrit chants grew tedious and trying to the patience of the family members required to be present at the sacred fire, but Samudradatta kept assuring himself it was worth any amount of boredom to ensure the gods would smile upon the upcoming ventures.

Samudradatta felt sure he didn't have to worry about Durvasas leaving the business. Like Arthadatta, Durvasas was intrigued by new ideas and philosophies, but rather than sitting around thinking about them, he would expound them with enthusiasm. Surely if Durvasas had any doubts about being a merchant, he would have told his father long ago.

Recently, Durvasas had seemed to realize that he was now the sole eventual heir to both the business and the household. He made no objection when Ambalika began searching for a suitable wife for him. He accompanied Samudradatta to the storerooms every morning, and he willingly did whatever Samudradatta directed. He often disappeared for much of the evening, but Samudradatta did not mind Durvasas taking time for diversions. After all, the boy would be facing ever-increasing responsibilities over the coming years.

5

Two years later. Maru, the Great Indian Desert, northeast of Patala, in the spring of 490 B.C.E.

The sun at last descended to touch the horizon, a most welcome time after the glare and sizzling heat of the desert day. It was the sixth such day since the caravan had left the port of Patala, at the mouth of the Indus River. The drivers were yoking their bullocks to their carts and getting into line behind the land-pilot. As prime organizer of the caravan, Samudradatta traveled immediately behind the pilot's cart. His other eighty-three carts followed him, laden with dates from Egypt, with almonds and jugs of wine from Persian lands, and even with some well-concealed gold from Africa. Durvasas accompanied the caravan to learn the route, and Samudradatta had assigned him to keep watch from the rearmost of their carts.

After Samudradatta's part of the caravan came Chamikara, who had joined on this particular journey with his own fifty-odd carts, and then the other traders with their own conveyances. Ten horseback Kshatriya warriors hired as guards rode to their positions near the front and the rear.

The driver of the last of Samudradatta's carts lifted the lid from the big clay water jar it carried. Samudradatta looked in, assured himself the container had not lost any of its contents. He always checked the water personally, every day, on each of his carts. Some of the caravan leaders assigned specific carts solely to carrying water, but Samudradatta always divided the supply up among all his vehicles. That way even if a cart overturned or lost a wheel, the amount of water lost from broken jars would be small relative to the quantity carried by the entire caravan. Samudradatta returned to the front of the line, with

Jajali following close behind as always.

Vairochaka, the land-pilot Samudradatta had engaged, approached. "Shall we set out, sir?"

Samudradatta carefully examined the man. "Yes, let's be on our way," he replied at last. But something about the pilot still bothered him, besides a carelessness in the man's dress. Vairochaka's eyes were always bloodshot, and his thin face held an appearance of slackness, as if he habitually imbibed too much intoxicating liquor. However, the first choice for a pilot had fallen seriously ill, and no others could be found at the port. Samudradatta's contacts at Patala assured him about the man's experience as a pilot, and they said he never became drunk while on duty.

Still, Samudradatta had reservations about hiring Vairochaka. The lives of the hundreds of men in the caravan would depend upon that one person for the three weeks it took to cross Maru, the great desert. Samudradatta kept thinking of the trader Paravata, whose caravan disappeared in this same desert, on the same route, only two years previously.

The choice had been between hiring Vairochaka or waiting until some other pilot returned from a journey, whenever that might be. Chamikara and the other traders strongly wanted to get underway. So Samudradatta agreed to hiring the man.

Samudradatta had become especially uneasy because of two ill omens. Just as the caravan had gotten underway, he spotted two Untouchables crossing the roadway in front of them. That was followed almost immediately by the bullocks on one of his carts bolting, and it took the driver several minutes to bring them under control and then calm them. Two inauspicious happenings at the very outset. Not good at all.

Samudradatta kept a close watch on Vairochaka, but so far, after six day's travel, the pilot seemed satisfactory. During the daylight Vairochaka kept to himself, eating alone and sleeping away from the others. All night, he lay on his back on his pad in his cart, watching the stars as he guided the caravan across the wastes. His navigation seemed faultless; each dawn found the caravan at precisely the water hole or camping spot toward which they had aimed.

Now Vairochaka climbed into the lead cart and ordered the driver to begin today's journey. The cart squeaked into motion.

Samudradatta got into his own cart. Jajali clambered in also, and the driver started the bullocks. All along the line, neck bells tinkled as the animals began padding across the sands.

The air was still hot from the scorching day. Samudradatta beckoned to Jajali, who handed him a wet cloth to wipe his face. He wished he could drench his entire body with water. But it had been two days since the last well, and he estimated only two day's water remained in the giant jars. Better save as much as possible for drinking and for watering the bullocks, or in case something went wrong.

Some caravans had begun using those strange creatures, camels, for transporting goods across deserts. Odd though they appeared, with their long thin necks, their tall legs, their lips curled in looks of disdain, they seemed uniquely suited to desert travel. Compared to bullocks the camels needed little water, and their wide, soft footpads seemed almost intentionally designed for sandy tracks. Samudradatta had hoped to hire some camels just to try them for himself, but there were none available in Patala at the moment.

The cart creaked and rumbled, and sand crunched under the wheels. Samudradatta was glad that, being at the front of the caravan, he was subjected to comparatively little dust. They passed the skeletons of several large animals, bullocks from the looks of them. Apparently a prior caravan had run short of water and perished.

Could it be the remains of Paravata's band? Possibly. There was probably no way to know. Bleached bones such as these, partially buried by the sand, were a common sight in the desert. Samudradatta wondered if the ghosts of the men from this particular caravan remained nearby, haunting this area still.

The glow from the sun faded, and the sky became totally black. This was the time when the men of the caravans worried about demons, those evil spirits which inhabited the deserts, coming out at night to lead caravans astray. The disappearance of at least one caravan every year was blamed on the demons, like the loss of the unfortunate Paravata.

There was no moon, so the landscape was lit only by the dim, vague luminosity of the starglow. Ahead shone the lantern on the pilot's cart, and behind came a long string of hundreds of other lanterns, one on each of the other carts. That was all to be seen.

Except for the stars. In the desert the stars shone as thousands of bright but distant beacons, a wondrous, dazzling display, as well as the only "landmarks" to guide the caravan.

Samudradatta was familiar with the configurations they formed from traveling so many nights in the past in the desert, and from camping under the stars during the autumn and winter, when the actual traveling was done by day. He now looked up for quite some time, noting the locations of old friends: the constellations of the Deer's Head and the tight cluster of the Six Nymphs; the long milky band of the Celestial River; the reddish star Rohini. He'd learned long ago that with his keen eyesight he could see stars that were too dim for others to discern. There was even a star which his vision could resolve into two stars, where other men saw only the one.

Eventually his neck began to ache from looking up, so he focused on the lantern ahead. He had more than enough time to think on these all-night treks, and he usually found it difficult to sleep with the cart continually jolting and lurching. He now thought back over the past couple years.

He had continued training Durvasas to succeed him in operating the trading enterprise. Durvasas was competent enough, though he somehow seemed to lack enthusiasm for the work. A year had passed, and then another. Arthadatta did not visit his former home, and his family heard nothing from him. Even though this was not unusual for wandering monks or ascetics, it nevertheless disappointed Samudradatta.

While Ambalika was more pleasant as a companion, the house and warehouse both seemed bleak with no family members present except Durvasas. Samudradatta still retained a hope that Arthadatta would tire of his strenuous life as a mendicant and would return home, just as a trader returned home with his caravans.

Samudradatta had previously tested this new trade route to the western coast that passed through the range of low mountains in the area called Pariyatra, and he found it profitable. He frequently saw wandering holy men as he traveled: the naked Jains, Buddhists in their saffron robes, ascetics in loincloths or less. Always, he hoped that one of the Buddhists would turn out to be his son, but always he was disappointed.

All over the land he saw wandering older men, too, who had left their homes. Having faithfully fulfilled their duties as the heads of households for many years, they at last relieved themselves of the distracting burdens of family and work responsibilities. They gave up their castes to become, in effect, respected outcastes, searching for something more lasting, more significant, than could be found in material pursuits.

More and more, as he thought about the fact he was growing older himself, Samudradatta wondered about these wanderers. Occasionally he invited one or more of them to share his meals, or to ride with him in his cart, and he questioned them. They seemed to have no serious worries, having given up their possessions and their homes and families. Some were clearly lazy and irresponsible, ignoring their obligations to their families and living off the charity of others. But most were sincere, totally involved in their personal quests: searching out a meaning for their own lives; learning more about the nature of the universe; attaining spiritual powers or enlightenment; becoming one with god; doing good works; sharing their knowledge with others.

The cart lurched over some object, bringing Samudradatta back to the present. How long had he been lost in thought? He looked up at the sky. The stars moved slowly in their paths, but it seemed to him they had traveled considerably across the sky since he had last looked. Had he dozed off, fallen asleep? He didn't think so.

Well, it was difficult to judge time out here. In the desert it was almost timeless, almost outside of time, especially at night. He imagined it would be the same way out on the ocean, where there were no landmarks by which to measure one's progress.

The carts continued rolling across the desert darkness, hour after hour. Despite having slept earlier during the day, Samudradatta dozed for a time, then awoke. He again looked at the sky.

Something was wrong. It was as if the stars had moved backwards in their paths. But that could not be—not if the caravan was on course. Could he be mistaken?

No. Samudradatta called ahead, his voice abrupt above the sounds of the creaking carts and the bullocks' bells, "Pilot! Is anything wrong?"

No reply. Samudradatta jumped to the sand from the slowly moving cart and hurried ahead to the pilot's vehicle. In the lamplight he saw Vairochaka's driver upright on the seat. The pilot himself, lying on the floor, was in the shadows cast by the side of the cart. "Vairochaka!" Samudradatta shouted again.

The driver of the cart turned to look at Samudradatta. No response came from the pilot. The driver looked down at the pilot, and called to him, "Sir! Is everything all right?"

No reply.

"Sir!"

Still no response.

Samudradatta boosted himself into the still-moving cart. The pilot lay quiet, his eyes closed. Samudradatta took hold of the man's shoulder. "Pilot! Vairochaka!"

The pilot stirred. "Wha—" His eyes opened. He started at the sight of Samudradatta. He sat up, rubbed his eyes.

"You were asleep!" shouted Samudradatta, trying to control his panic.

"No...no...just resting."

"Look at the stars!"

The pilot looked. He turned his head to gaze again.

"We're off course!" said Samudradatta.

The pilot took a moment to answer. "Maybe a little. Driver— stop! Stop the caravan."

The cart halted, and Samudradatta's cart behind it, and one-by-one the hundreds of others.

"What does this mean?" asked Samudradatta, his mouth gone dry. He was afraid he knew only too well.

"We...uh....we need to wait until daylight," said the pilot. " I'll see if I can spot a landmark."

"You fool!" shouted Samudradatta. "You may have killed us all!"

The pilot sat stolidly for several moments. Then he spoke in a mumble: "Wait until daylight."

Samudradatta started to say something. But he choked it back. Nothing he could think to say was equal to the provocation.

"The demons must have cast a spell on me," said the pilot, holding his face in his hands. "I saw them last night, laughing as they led me astray. Otherwise this could never have happened!"

Outraged, Samudradatta shouted, "I never saw them, and I was awake the whole time right behind you! You fell asleep. They may have visited you only in your dreams."

"No, I tell you, they were here."

"Then why did I not see them? Or hear them?"

Chamikara and Durvasas appeared, each carrying a lamp. "Why have we stopped?" asked Chamikara.

"This idiot fell asleep. We're off course."

"No!" said Chamikara. "How far off course?"

"It was the demons," insisted the pilot. "I tell you, they came not long ago!"

"He doesn't know how far off," said Samudradatta. "It depends partly on how long he was asleep. And we don't know that."

In the lamplight Chamikara's eyes had gone wide with fear. Durvasas, too, looked worried. "We have to wait until morning," said Samudradatta.

The Kshatriya guards rode up and were told; then one by one the other merchants appeared. They reacted with varying degrees of shock, anger, fear.

Then everyone waited for dawn. No one talked. Samudradatta thought of the ill omens at the beginning of the journey: the Untouchables crossing the road, the bullocks bolting. He fervently hoped that the portents predicted only minor troubles, not disaster for the entire caravan. He knew that the other traders, like himself, were gazing into the darkness, listening for the slightest sounds, wondering if the demons were watching and waiting.

The eastern horizon began to grow light. The pilot was standing in his cart to get up as high as possible, peering into the distance. He said nothing. The sky grew lighter until it clearly revealed the landscape. Still the pilot looked.

Samudradatta stood in his own cart. So far as he could tell, no one feature stood out. Low rolling dunes, dotted with scrubby bushes, as far as he could see. "Well?" called Samudradatta, too impatient to wait longer.

The pilot shook his head. "I don't recognize anything. We'll have to keep going until I do."

"How do you know which direction to go?" asked another of the traders.

The pilot pointed. "We need to go that way. Easterly."

Samudradatta said angrily, "The direction isn't a problem. Even I know the direction to Pushkara. The problem is finding the next well.

And the one after that. We need water." He had checked the levels in the jars, and he now estimated no more than a day and a half's supply.

The caravan set out. With no significant landmarks to sight upon, it was difficult to keep going in a straight line for much more than a half hour or so. But at least the sun provided a relative measure. The sun that grew more searing by the minute. It was for good reason that caravans traveled only at night in the desert during the hotter part of the year.

They kept moving while the brilliant, blazing tormentor rose higher into the sky. The heat was getting unbearable, even beneath the big umbrella that shielded Samudradatta and his driver from the direct sunlight. The water supply was too limited to use it for cooling. And it was impractical to keep the sun off the bullocks.

Still the pilot saw nothing familiar.

"We'd better stop," Samudradatta called to him. "The heat will kill the animals."

Vairochaka gave a nod, and his driver halted. Drenched in sweat, the men moved the carts into circles, unyoked the bullocks, and as usual during the daytime, both man and animals used the vehicles and canopies hung from them for shade. Chamikara and Durvasas and the other merchants joined Samudradatta, and they talked with the pilot at his cart.

Vairochaka put on a show of confidence. "There's no serious problem," he said, wiping the perspiration from his brow with a rag. "We'll keep going. I will eventually find a landmark, or we'll run across a well."

Samudradatta didn't believe him for a second. "It's too hot to travel by day. And how will you see to find a landmark at night?"

"We, uh...we must travel at dusk and at dawn. When the sun isn't so high."

One of the merchants, a heavy man from Kalinga on the eastern coast, said in a strong accent, "It takes long after dusk before the sand cools down."

The pilot did not reply.

"We must do something!" said the Kalingan merchant, the sweat on his forehead running down his face.

"What do you suggest?" asked Samudradatta dryly.

The trader was silent. Then, eyes large, a note of panic in his voice: "I don't know!"

Durvasas seemed somewhat less affected by the heat than most. "Father," he asked, "can't we follow our tracks backward until we find where we veered off course? Our path should still be quite apparent."

Samudradatta shook his head. "There'd be no way to tell for sure where we went wrong, since we don't always follow a straight line. And we may have drifted off course gradually."

"Then could we return all the way back to yesterday's campground, and start over from there?"

"Maybe," mused Samudradatta. The air was so hot it was almost painful to talk. "But that means at least two more days without water. One day to return to the campground. And another to get to the water hole we were headed for originally. The bullocks will begin dying of thirst before then."

"But if we continue blindly," said Durvasas, "couldn't we wander much longer than that, without ever finding water? If the demons indeed led us astray, they might do it again."

Samudradatta said reluctantly, "That's possible." He shuddered at the thought of how the demons might feast on the bodies of himself and the other men, not even conducting a cremation ritual. Without a *sraddha* ceremony, his ghost and that of the others in the caravan might haunt these wastes at night forever. But he would do everything possible to avoid giving them the chance. Jajali held the umbrella to ward off the sun. Samudradatta shaded his eyes and looked into the distance. "If only we could see farther."

Vairochaka used his hand to shield his eyes from the glare, and he took quite some time, scanning the horizon. At last he shook his head no. "I don't see anything helpful."

Samudradatta knew his own eyesight was keen, possibly better than the pilot's. He pointed. "What's that there, on the horizon? It looks like it might be a cone shaped hill."

Vairochaka looked, again shading his eyes. Eventually, he said, "I can't see anything but a darker spot. But if it's indeed a cone shaped hill, then I know where it may be. It's a landmark on the way to a well about a quarter day's travel from it."

Samudradatta thought for a time. He squinted at the spot. It still appeared to him as a possible pointed hill. "Could you get us to the well from there?"

The pilot gave a nod. "If we go to the hill first, and if it's the right one."

There should be no difficulty getting to the hill. Samudradatta was confident that even he could navigate the caravan to it using the stars. "Are there other hills that might be confused with that one?"

The pilot thought. "There are not many real hills in this section of the desert. And most of them are long ridges. Not cone shaped."

"If we saw a ridge from the end instead of the side, it might appear cone shaped."

Vairochaka gave a nod. "It might." He pondered a time. Then he said, "Most ridges here run from southwest to northeast. This hill is east of us. So if it were a ridge, we'd likely be seeing a longer side."

Samudradatta thought about this. He told the other traders the situation.

"I still think we should backtrack and start over, Father," said Durvasas.

"We're too short on water for that," said the Kalingan trader in his strong accent. "I say we take a chance on that hill." He appeared as if he were ready to collapse from the heat.

Chamikara, who also looked miserable, had been continually wiping his face with a cloth. He said, "It may be certain death if it's the wrong hill. What if the demons are trying to confuse us again? Then they'll eat our corpses and steal all our goods."

Horror shone in the eyes of the Kalingan. "Why don't we divide into two groups?" he asked, a note of panic in his voice. "One can backtrack, and one try the hill."

"The heat has clouded your mind, my friend," said Chamikara with effort. "We only have one pilot—such as he is."

Samudradatta beckoned to the two Kshatriya guards who stood nearby. "Do you think you can ride to that hill, and see whether it's cone-shaped or a long ridge?"

The men mounted their horses. One shaded his eyes, and peered off in the direction Samudradatta indicated. He said, "I think I see it. We'll have to be careful to ride in a straight line toward it, so we don't get lost."

The other Kshatriya said, "After we get there, can follow our own tracks to find our way back here."

Samudradatta said, "Take some extra water, in case you're longer than you expect."

He noticed several men shielding their eyes as they peered into the west. He turned to look himself.

The sky was turning brown.

"Gods, no!" said Chamikara.

A sand storm.

"Get under cover!" Samudradatta shouted. He damned the storm; now the guards wouldn't be able to ride to the hill for a closer look until the winds died down.

The other merchants hurried to their vehicles. Samudradatta started to quickly check his own carts and drivers and animals. The storm hit before he could finish. He drew the tail of his turban over his face, but sand driven by the hot wind stung his exposed skin, worked into his eyes.

The wind tore at the encampment, and it carried a sound like the voices of the demons, furious at the possibility of their plans for the caravan being thwarted.

Samudradatta dove under his own cart, into the shelter formed by the drapes his driver and cook and Jajali hung from the sides and weighted at the bottom.

Hour upon hour the storm continued. The wind whirled and whistled and hurled sand through even the smallest gaps in the curtains. Particles gritted between Samudradatta's teeth. He rubbed at his eyes and kept blinking, trying to alleviate the irritation.

And he fretted at the delay. It meant more water consumed, and even longer before replenishing their containers. The sandstorm persisted through the night, allowing no possibility of the scouts heading for the possible landmark. Into the next morning the storm continued, as if the demons were determined to harass the caravan until there was no possibility of survival.

Then the shrieking gradually diminished. At last all was quiet. Filthy with the abrasive sand, drenched with perspiration, near-exhausted from the heat and worry, Samudradatta burrowed out from under his cart. Without the sand in the air as a shield, the sun again bore down.

The two Kshatriya warriors rode off to examine what Samudradatta thought might be the hill that would serve as a landmark.

But once more the caravan itself would have to wait until sunset before setting out, even assuming the guards' report was favorable. More time lost, more water gone. Almost certainly it would not last until the next well. And in this heat, that might well mean deaths.

Samudradatta went off to squat and relieve himself. When he had finished, he scrubbed himself with sand, rather than use more precious water.

Durvasas, strain lines in his perspiring face, looked as if he had lost weight the past couple of days. He joined Samudradatta in the shade of the cart while they waited for the sun to go down. Seated on the sand and with his back against one of the wheels, he asked, "We're almost out of water, aren't we, Father?"

"Yes."

Durvasas sat for a time in silence. "Those demons who led the pilot astray," he said after a while. "They're always a danger."

"I don't know if it was the demons or only the pilot's carelessness this time," Samudradatta replied.

"Still, caravans are dangerous."

"They can be. Desert crossings are the worst, of course."

"Caravans are always uncomfortable and tiring, even when they're not dangerous."

Samudradatta gave a shrug. "I suppose. Usually. But they can also be extremely profitable." God, it was hot. Why was Durvasas persisting in this line of talk?

"Father," Durvasas said hesitantly, "I know how much you count on me to help with the business."

"I certainly do." Samudradatta wiped his forehead with the already soggy and grimy cloth. "I still find it hard to believe I've lost one of my sons. I don't know what I'd do without you now. But it will be rewarding for you as the sole heir."

Durvasas looked pained. His eyes shifted away. "Father," he said, "that makes it all the more difficult for me...."

Samudradatta stared at him. "What do you mean?"

Durvasas hesitated. Then: "Father, you know that back home I visited some of the gurus in the Forest of Bliss."

"Yes, what of it?"

"If we survive the desert, I want to try living with them."

"What do you mean?"

"I want to go live in the Forest of Bliss."

Samudradatta clenched his teeth. If this desert wasn't the death of him, these teachers would be. Durvasas was talking almost like Arthadatta had. After several moments, he looked at Durvasas and said, carefully, "I don't mind your spending time in the Forest of Bliss. You can keep up with the business by coming in every day. When you've learned what you want in the forest, you can devote yourself fully to trading again."

Durvasas looked pained. He fell silent for a time. Then he said, "Father, you don't understand. I want to live there all the time."

"All the time?!"

"Yes, Father."

"But you still have a lot to learn about trading! You can't just leave!"

Durvasas sagged against the cart wheel. He looked as if he were about ready to faint from the heat.

Samudradatta continued, "How can you succeed me in the business if you haven't involved yourself fully?"

Durvasas said in a voice so low Samudradatta wasn't sure if he heard correctly: "I don't think I want to succeed you, Father."

"What? Did I hear you right?"

"I don't want to take over the trading, Father."

Samudradatta peered at him in horror. "But—there's no one else!"

"I know, Father. I'm sorry."

"You *have* to stay! I need you!"

Durvasas looked stricken.

"Don't you think one monk in the family is enough?" demanded Samudradatta.

"Not when I want to be one, too. I realize how hard it must be for you, Father. But I know it's what I have to do."

Samudradatta sat dazed, breathing heavily. Not *two* sons as monks! Arthadatta, he could understand. Arthadatta's temperament was monk-like anyway. But Durvasas was so outgoing.

Samudradatta sat in misery. From time to time he glanced at his son. His *only* son now. He wiped his forehead again. "Tell me," he said, straining to not sound too gruff. "What's the appeal of these men?"

Durvasas replied, "There are many teachers in the Forest of Bliss, but I haven't found the right one for me yet. So I want to look further. I want to travel, to meet as many teachers as I can. The first thing I want to do is to try being an ascetic."

"An ascetic? You want to be an *ascetic*?" After the recent tortures of the desert, Samudradatta found the idea incomprehensible.

Durvasas nodded. His eyes suddenly aglow, he said, "I want to practice *tapas*, to see what magic powers I can gain, Father."

"Magic powers?"

"I've been thinking about it for a long time. Then, those demons that led us astray made me realize how powerful I could be if I was able to bend them to my will."

To bend demons to one's will. For centuries, rigorously strict disciplining of the body had been considered a way to control the powers of the gods; in some ways, it was an alternative to conducting sacrifices. *Tapas* involved the accumulation of one's energies to focus them in desired channels. All sorts of powers could be attained by a man willing to subject himself to severe enough deprivations, whether enduring hunger, or cold, or intense heat, or a bed of thorns.

Samudradatta drew in a breath of hot air. "I can understand why you might want the powers. But look what you'd give up! Wealth brings its own power, if it's power you want."

"That's not the type of power I mean, Father. You remember what the Buddha said when he was at our house, about how a man's possessions bring him worry? I don't want possessions to worry about. I want to control the weather, to be able to fly, to walk on water, to foretell the future..." In spite of the strain of the heat, in his narrow face Durvasas's eyes were bright, much brighter than when he talked of business matters.

Samudradatta stared at him. Then he said, "The Buddha did impress you."

Durvasas gave a nod.

Samudradatta shouted, "He was an ascetic for six years! His will was so strong that he went without food until he almost starved himself to death. But he gave *tapas* up as being fruitless." He shifted position after the exertion, wiped his face again.

Durvasas replied, "Father, he was looking for something different. I'm not interested in his path to enlightenment. He seems to teach that men should give up wanting anything for themselves. For me, self-denial is merely a way to gain all the powers that will come. It's not an end in itself."

Samudradatta gestured at the burning desert. "It's one matter to *endure* this type of hardship. It's another to seek it out. You've never willingly suffered before. Make sure it's what you want. Before you talk this nonsense of leaving home for good!"

Durvasas said firmly, "If it's not what I want, I'll try something else, Father."

"Listen to me! I need you in the business. Why are you trying so hard to avoid it?"

"Father, I can never be satisfied as a trader. These caravans are tiresome, traveling day after day just to haul goods somewhere. And look at where it's gotten us right now. Waiting to see if we survive another day."

Samudradatta sat, still staring at his son. "We'll talk again," he said gruffly, after a long time.

Durvasas eventually left to go seek shade with someone else. Later, Chamikara came by, moving slowly in the heat, drenched with sweat like everyone else.

Samudradatta told him what Durvasas had said. "How did it all come to this?" Samudradatta asked, still in shock. "What went wrong?"

"Who's to say?" said Chamikara, seeming genuinely distressed at Samudradatta's difficulties. "The gods must have their plan for you."

"If I have no sons to inherit my wealth and all the trading contacts I've worked so hard to build, then my work no longer has any point."

Chamikara slowly nodded. "It must seem that way."

"Maybe the gods no longer favor me. In spite of all my sacrifices to them, my rituals!"

"We'll find out," said Chamikara, looking away into the glare. "If we survive this, it will be difficult to say the gods don't favor you."

The two Kshatriya guards returned and reported that the hill was indeed cone-shaped. Although there was not complete certainty the hill was the one Vairochaka assumed, it seemed likely, as he knew of no others in the region with that shape. So Samudradatta decided to take a chance on heading toward it, and the other merchants agreed.

At last the sun set, and the caravan got underway. On through the night, toward a hill they could not see in the darkness. Samudradatta watched the stars, ensuring that they remained in their expected directions, alert in case any demons might come up with some ingenious way to trick him. Periodically, he walked ahead and checked on the pilot. Vairochaka showed no resentment; he knew he had betrayed his trust. Whenever Samudradatta looked, the pilot was awake.

Sometime after midnight, Samudradatta and his driver and Jajali shared the last drops of their water. Farther back in the caravan, first one bullock, then another fell, their bones soon to become bleached additions to the desert landscape. Their drivers could not delay for fear of being left behind, so they either continued with their remaining bullocks or abandoned their carts.

The eastern sky began to grow light. Ahead and slightly to the right rose a pyramid-shaped dark outline. Dawn revealed it as a hill, conical in shape.

Samudradatta waited, watching Vairochaka. The pilot gave a smile, although strained, for the first time. "This is the hill. I'm sure of it."

Samudradatta allowed himself to relax just slightly. No doubt more bullocks would be lost, unable to last even the few hours to the well, but the men and most of the animals should survive.

6

Near Mangarh

Ten days later, with the change in route from being lost in the desert, the caravan reached the Pariyatra range well south of the original destination of Pushkara. Instead, the traders crossed the hills by way of the low pass north of the small town of Mangarh. The near-disaster had clarified Samudradatta's thoughts. Durvasas was right in one respect: organizing and leading caravans was a hard, dangerous life. And the rewards no longer seemed worth the effort and the hazards.

Samudradatta had determined that this was his final caravan through the desert. But now he even wondered if he should continue to organize other caravans, with less risky routes, such as the ones from Kashi to Rajagriha or Indraprastha?

There seemed little point any more in keeping on with trading, especially with Durvasas wanting to leave. Samudradatta already had more wealth than he could ever spend. If Durvasas went away, neither son would be considered members of his family. Samudradatta would be in the unenviable position of being a sonless man. When he died, there would be no son to officiate at his funeral or at the later *sraddha* ceremonies in honor of himself and the other ancestors of the family. Although it was permissible for him to find a boy to adopt as a replacement, that idea held little appeal for him. Even if he found a suitable young man, he would have to start at the very beginning in training the boy. It would take years and years.

One possibility was for Samudradatta to give up family life altogether, to renounce his caste and its duties, to become a seeker himself. Earlier, he had not seriously envisioned himself doing so, even though he had been mildly interested in the various conflicting teachings of the gurus. But he had never expected to be without sons. Now, the more he recalled of his talks with other men who had become wanderers, the more the idea of doing the same grew within his own mind.

He was thinking about the implications of such an act when he saw a pair of Buddhist monks on the dusty road, not far from the elephant head cliff of Mangarh. The shorter of the two monks looked familiar. Samudradatta stared hard to be certain—the shaved heads changed a man's appearance. The monk, returning his gaze, smiled in recognition. "Father!"

It was Arthadatta. Samudradatta sat on his cart and looked awkwardly at his son for a moment. Then he smilingly dismounted. Arthadatta bent to touch his father's feet, but Samudradatta reached out to restrain him. The two embraced hard, for a long time. Then they separated. "You look good," he told the young monk. "Different, but good."

"You look as if you've had a hard journey, Father. You've lost weight, I think."

"So I have," Samudradatta replied. He was pleased that Arthadatta still addressed him as "Father," even though their family relationship supposedly no longer existed. "Our desert crossing was difficult. We were lost for a time."

"Then you're fortunate to be here! You must tell me about it. But first, how is Mother?"

"Fine, the last I saw her."

Durvasas joined them and embraced his brother.

Samudradatta said, "Well. How do you like being a monk?"

Arthadatta smiled. "As much as possible, I'm trying to eliminate my likes and dislikes. But I find it agreeable. I'm doing important work, learning from the Buddha and bringing his message to others. I think it's the most worthwhile thing I could do." He spoke simply, matter-of-factly. After a pause he gestured to his companion. "This is the Venerable Kumbha. He joined the Order shortly before I did, and we've been together ever since we first met."

The other monk and Samudradatta respectfully acknowledged each other. Then, Samudradatta asked Arthadatta, "Why are you on this particular road?"

"Maybe you haven't yet heard—the Buddha has been teaching near here."

"This far west? I didn't realize his wanderings would take him such a distance."

"Maybe you'd like to pause for the night and hear him speak."

Samudradatta thought for only a moment before replying, "Why not? We planned to stay at the camping field near Mangarh anyway."

The Buddha would speak under a large *pipal* tree in a clearing on a hill overlooking a forested valley near Mangarh. Darkness was falling, and the night would be cool. But for now the air was still pleasantly warm, and after the dryness of the desert it smelled fresh from the green trees and shrubs. The meeting was much the same as when Samudradatta had gone with his son to hear the Buddha in the Deer Park near Kashi. A large crowd, people of all ages, gathered and sat on the hillside.

Eventually the Buddha appeared, saffron-robed like his disciples, his stride unhurried but deliberate as he walked to his dais and seated himself. To Samudradatta, the teacher's physical appearance was the same as two years ago, his handsome face glowing with the same aura of bliss and peace.

Today, the Buddha's topic was the ephemeral nature of material goods. To some extent he repeated what Samudradatta had heard him say in Kashi: "Man's possessions bring him worry," said the Buddha. "Without possessions, he has no worries."

He elaborated on the theme, and Samudradatta listened intently to every word, every nuance. In the same way that men held gold or ivory or other physical items as possessions, said the Buddha, men often considered other persons as their possessions. Likewise, places, or even ideas, could be possessions. Attachment to any of these things led to wanting to preserve them, and consequently to fearing their loss. But one way to reduce these attachments and concerns was for a person to regularly do good works to help others, so he would gradually think more and more of other persons and less and less of himself and his own possessions.

When the Buddha concluded, he said, "Just as a man who has long been far away is welcomed with joy on his safe return by his relatives, well-wishers, and friends, in the same way the good works of a man in his life welcome him in another life, with the joy of a friend meeting a friend on his return."

Samudradatta could not help but feel the words were meant for him. As on the previous occasions in Kashi, the Master's speech was compelling, sincere, persuasive.

Afterwards, Samudradatta approached Arthadatta. He still had difficulty comprehending that this same young man, bald headed and wearing a saffron robe, had once been his son. Samudradatta asked, "Can you arrange for me to talk again with the Blessed One?"

Arthadatta looked pleased. "I'm quite sure he'll be willing, Father."

"I remember you well, from Kashi," said the Buddha, gazing warmly into Samudradatta's eyes. "You were concerned about losing your son. Now he is in fact lost to you."

Samudradatta, seated before the Master, nodded. "That's so, Blessed One. And I also seem to be losing my other son."

The Buddha's face radiated understanding and compassion. "But in relinquishing them, you need no longer be attached to them. You've given up a source of worry."

Samudradatta said, "I didn't see it that way at first. Now, maybe I am beginning to. But I also have another concern."

"You have many worldly goods," said the Buddha, smiling benevolently. "And you want to know what to do with them."

"That's correct, Master."

The Buddha looked into the distance. "I, too, had a son," the teacher said. "He came to me to claim his inheritance. I told him my gift was not worldly possessions. If it were material objects, he would have to strive to protect them, and in the end they would be stripped from him—if not by other men, then by death. But the inheritance I could give him was a gift that could not be measured, a gift which would increase with use."

Samudradatta bowed his head. "I think I understand, Master."

The Buddha bathed Samudradatta in a sympathetic smile as he said, "By allowing your sons to go their own ways, to find their own paths, you have given them a valuable inheritance. Now you have an opportunity to do many good deeds with your remaining wealth, if you so choose."

"I do choose that, Master. Can you give me guidance?"

The Buddha smiled more broadly, a loving, warm, knowing smile. "You do not need guidance from me. Ample opportunities will present themselves."

Others were waiting to talk with the Master. Samudradatta nodded, and he rose. He realized he had made a decision. It had been slow in coming, but it now felt right to him.

He'd had considerable time to think on his long journeys. He was weary of being a caravan merchant. The desert crossing that had almost ended in disaster had been the final factor. No more responsibilities for organizing and leading caravans.

All his wealth....What good did it now do him? What was the point in continuing to generate more? He had paid the Brahmins for many sacrifices, and he had prospered. But the results were like mud walls left exposed to the rains: they appeared substantial and lasting, but the appearance was only an illusion; one good storm could wash them away.

He would return to Kashi with the caravan. He would try to help Ambalika understand his decision. Durvasas could leave for the Forest of Bliss. Chamikara would be glad to take over Samudradatta's trade routes and contacts.

Samudradatta would then again seek out the Buddha, to learn more about the master's teachings. If Samudradatta continued to like what he heard, he might even join the Order himself and wander with the other monks, spreading the Buddha's message. Otherwise he would look for a guru until he found the right one.

In the meantime, he would use his wealth to do good works.

The years passed. The Buddha himself died, but his teachings spread throughout the north of the subcontinent.

Samudradatta never again organized a caravan. But he built inns for wayfarers, and he sponsored the planting of shade trees along roads and the digging of wells for travelers. As the last of his philanthropic works, before he renounced his wealth to become a Buddhist monk himself, he financed a monastery on the hill near Mangarh where he had met with the Buddha.

Samudradatta lived the remainder of his life a contented man. And for many centuries the monastery he built would be a retreat for the monks while they rested from their wanderings during the rainy seasons.

The
Mangarh Treasure
Three

7

In another twenty minutes the jeep arrived at the site of the ancient Buddhist monuments, on a low hill above the eastern plain.

Vijay deliberately did not look at his old home village below on the valley floor, less than two kilometers away. He fervently hoped nobody he knew would come to see who the visitors were. But most inhabitants of the village would probably be resting in the shade during the height of the afternoon heat.

Khan parked the jeep by a monolithic rock face with the Ashokan inscription. A tall fence of heavy wire mesh protected the monument.

The sun hit them brutally when they stepped from the shelter of the jeep, but Vijay intended to keep the visit short. He had seen the site before, years ago, on several occasions as a village lad, when he and his friends ventured up here.

Still, he now understood much more about the stone's significance, so he paused to examine it. Literally everyone in India knew of the rock inscriptions of the great Emperor Ashoka of the Third Century B.C.E. The writings were scattered throughout what had been Ashoka's vast empire, from Afghanistan to almost the southern tip of the Indian subcontinent. Ashoka had converted to Buddhism, so the nearby ruins of the Buddhist monastery and *stupa* explained the placement of this particular edict.

"What does it say?" asked Shanta Das, peering through the wire mesh. The writing was in an ancient script, unreadable to anyone but a scholar of the period. She and Vijay both turned to Kaushalya.

Unable to remember the exact translation, and again annoyed at the necessity of being polite to government agents who were harassing her and her family, Kaushalya at first did not reply. But her duty to remain courteous reasserted itself and she briefly summarized what she knew of the inscription's background.

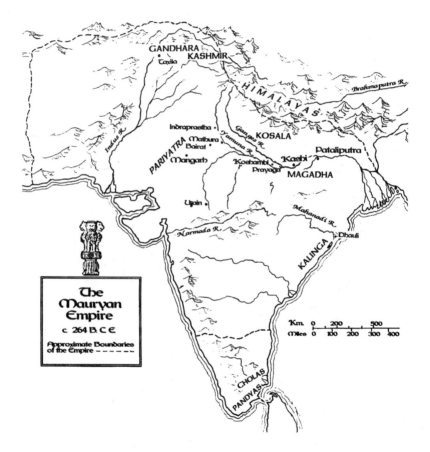

GANDHARA
KASHMIR
Taxila •

H I M A L A Y A S

Brahmaputra R.

Indus R.

Indraprastha •
Mathura
Bairat •
Maingarh •

Ganges R.

Yamuna R.

KOSALA

PARIYATRA

Koshambi •
Prayaga •
Kashi •

Pataliputra

MAGADHA

Ujjain •

Narmada R.

Mahanadi R.

Dhauli

KALINGA

The
Mauryan
Empire
c. 264 B.C.E.

Approximate Boundaries
of the Empire - - - - -

Km. 0   200   500
Miles 0 100 200 300 400

CHOLAS
PANDYAS

Elephant Driver

1

Amarpur village, Pariyatra (later known as the Aravalli Range), in the winter of the eighth year of the reign of Emperor Ashoka Maurya, 264 B.C.E.

Jimuta shivered in the cool morning air despite his shawl and turban. He scuffed a bare foot in the dust by the tracks of his uncle and two older cousins, who walked ahead along the edge of the wheat field. Although the air smelled fresh from last night's dew, and mist lingered in some lower areas, the small amount of moisture did not change the dry, powdery feel of the soil.

Each of the four still carried the small earthen pot which had held the water used to wash themselves with their left hands after their bowel movements in the fields. At least there was still water at the very bottom of the well for this daily necessity, even if there was not enough for the crops.

Like the others, fifteen year old Jimuta had not yet had anything to eat this day. The last of the mangos and other fruits from the summer's harvest had been consumed over a week ago. Jimuta would eat nothing until their tiny evening meal, and in his stomach he felt the dull pangs that had become so familiar the past two years.

A flock of crows settled onto the edge of the field and began to peck at the soil. Jimuta ran at them, screaming to chase them away, so they would not steal any of the grain that might otherwise feed the family. The crows flapped off into the nearby *neem* tree, and Jimuta returned to his uncle and cousins.

His uncle, a short, sinewy man with skin burned dark from so many years working in the sun, gave a nod of approval. But the two older boys, Suchaka and Chekitana, whispered to each other, watching Jimuta from the corners of their eyes, and snickering. Ever since he had come to live with his uncle and aunt's family after his widowed mother died, Jimuta's cousins ridiculed him for whatever he did, and they played tricks on him like putting a dead cobra in his bedroll and hiding his water pot. Jimuta understood their not wanting to share the family's meager food supply with him. The two older boys apparently also resented Jimuta's working harder in the fields than they did themselves. Even though having to feed and clothe another person was an added burden, at least Jimuta's uncle and aunt had been kind.

Jimuta's uncle spotted some tiny weeds. He bent, and tugged them from the dust so they would not steal further moisture from the crops. "May we go back to the house, Father?" asked Suchaka, the elder son, who was seventeen years old, and taller and stronger than his brother.

Jimuta's uncle shook his head no. "We'll stay and weed."

"Again?" asked Chekitana, age sixteen. He wrinkled his broad forehead as if in pain and put his hand on his stomach. "I don't feel well." He lay down on the ground on his back, in the shade of the *neem* tree by the edge of the field and closed his eyes. No one commented that this was his favorite excuse for not working.

Suchaka said, " I don't see why we should bother weeding, Father. We won't get much of a crop anyway." He squatted beside his younger brother. Only Jimuta stooped and began pulling at the weeds that were just barely appearing above the layer of dust.

Out of the last five years, in only one—three years ago—had the rains come in adequate amounts. The wheat and gram reserves from that time were consumed long ago. And locusts had come last spring to devastate the fields. This season, the family had drawn water from the well and painstakingly watered the crop of winter wheat and millet, but then the well went mostly dry. Even the Khari River was only a trickle in the center of its channel.

Jimuta's uncle was weeding a nearby row. "I don't see how much longer we can keep Mango Blossom," he muttered about the family's cow, apparently to no one in particular. "There's so little fodder now. Her milk's gone as dry as our well."

They were working at the edge of the field near a small shrine, a rough clay image of an archer on horseback, the god Bhairava. Jimuta thought about how Uncle and the other farmers of the village had petitioned Bhairava and the other gods for rain. For whatever reason, the deities had failed to respond.

Jimuta glanced up to the top of the nearby hill, at the long, low wooden buildings of the Buddhist monastery. As long as he could remember, the early morning visits of the orange-robed monks, heads shaved, eyes averted to avoid seeing women, begging bowls extended before them, had been a regular part of each day's routine. When the villagers went hungry, the begging bowls also received little. But the monks' prayers, also, failed to bring rain.

Something hit his back and shattered. Startled, Jimuta began to straighten and to turn to see what had struck him. Then he realized one of his cousins, probably Suchaka, had thrown a dirt clod at him. He resumed the weeding.

Another clump of dirt struck, knocking his turban askew. This time his uncle noticed. "You boys stop that! You should be ashamed! Your cousin does ten times as much work as both of you put together. Get over here and help with the weeding."

Neither young man moved.

Uncle said in irritation, "Do you want The Mugger's men to thrash us all when we don't have a big enough harvest to pay our ruler's share?"

They all well remembered The Mugger's last visit. "The Mugger" was what the farmers called the brutal warrior who sometimes accompanied the tax collector sent by their local lord, Kumara Aja, the prince who ruled their village and the neighboring ones. "Mugger" was the term for a crocodile, and the warrior's nickname came from fact that, unlike the prey of animals such as tigers who killed quickly, a crocodile's victims sometimes took a long time to die.

The Mugger's most recent visit was all too typical. When the farmers insisted they could not pay as much as The Mugger demanded, he and his men forced their way into houses, taking whatever they found of value, supposedly to pay the assessments. But the men also discovered a thirteen year old girl named Ambika hiding in the storage shed of her family's home. Her screams were heard all over the village while The Mugger and his men took their pleasure from her. Afterwards, she refused to be seen outside her house, and her parents soon took her to live with distant relatives.

Jimuta had been fond of Ambika, who'd had lively, intelligent eyes and a charming lilt to her speech. Whenever he thought of her fate, he grew angry, although normally he was quite even tempered no matter what the provocation.

Usually, Jimuta's uncle did not bother to try to force his sons to overcome their indolent ways, except on rare occasions when they aroused his ire, such as now. Jimuta thought his uncle's approach was not a wise one, as it had resulted in the boys turning into lazy, thoughtless bullies. Still, it was not his own place to criticize his elders. He determined to think about something else.

He thought about how, after Prince Aja had refused to hear their requests for lower taxes, Uncle and the other farmers had gone to petition the Raja of Mangarh for cart loads of grain. However, the Raja's own lands had the same difficulties as those of his subjects, and his one-fourth share of the crops from the lands in his domains was not enough to maintain his own huge household with its servants and warriors.

In desperation, the village elders eventually sent a delegation to the Mauryan Emperor Ashoka's governor in the district capital at Bairat. However, they were given a mere single cartload of seed grain, because the rains had failed not only in the Pariyatra region, but over much of the rest of the vast empire which encompassed most of the subcontinent.

Jimuta's thoughts were interrupted by the approach of Kuvera, one of the village boys, who came at a half run. Jimuta could remember, years ago, when Kuvera was plump. But he was as thin now as the rest of the villagers.

The boy respectfully greeted Jimuta's uncle and then announced, "There's going to be a battle by the river! The Raja from Ramgarh is attacking our own Raja. I'm going there now."

Jimuta's cousins scrambled up with new-found energy and were already leaving. Suddenly he himself had also found purpose in the day. Watching a battle was the most exciting entertainment one could hope for. "Uncle! May I go watch?"

Uncle gave a quick nod. "They're warring over who gets to use the most water from the river. Just be sure to keep away from the fighters!" There was no danger to the onlookers, provided they took care to keep well out of the paths of the warriors and the weapons. Weeding the field had receded in importance for Uncle, also. "I'll go see that the rest of the village knows," he said.

The boys hurried along the road toward the river, past areas of sandy soil with dry looking, thorny *babul* trees and purple-blossomed, cactus-like *akkra* plants. "I hope we get there in time," shouted Suchaka. "I'd hate to miss any of the fighting!"

A peacock ran from their path as they climbed the rocky hill toward the Buddhist monastery. Now that Jimuta was higher up, he could see the two armies approaching each other on the plain, each surrounded by a huge cloud of dust. The normal quiet of the valley was replaced by the sounds of drumbeats and rattling weapons and armor. "We're in time!" Suchaka said. "They haven't started fighting yet."

More and more villagers climbed the hill for a good view. Most of the inhabitants of the monastery were traveling in this season, but the few saffron-robed monks who remained appeared from their buildings and stood to watch.

The boys reached the top of a rock outcropping near the highest point of the hill, where they had a view in three directions. Through the dust they saw that their own Raja Balarama had perhaps a dozen elephants in his front line, and behind them were ranked at least fifty chariots. Then came a couple hundred or so horse cavalry, and maybe a thousand foot soldiers. In the middle of the array, protected by the cavalry, rode the Raja, in a four-horse chariot with a white umbrella and white pennants. The opposing Raja had his own army arranged similarly. He appeared to have more elephants, but otherwise the armies were of about the same size.

The invading Raja of Ramgarh blew a long note on his conch shell, answered by a blast from the Raja of Mangarh. The armies charged. Dust billowed high into the air. Men shouted as they ran toward the enemy and brandished their weapons. Elephants' great feet hammered the earth. Horses' hooves pounded. Jimuta sensed the vibrations even so high on the hill.

First to meet were the elephants in the front ranks, colliding with thuds and shrieks and clashing of metal. Then the chariots and horsemen and foot soldiers joined the fray. Jimuta gaped in fascination mixed with unease as, on both sides, men fell into the dust, some screaming from pain. He flinched as a chariot overturned, its wooden frame snapping with a loud crack. Its driver and warriors pitched onto the ground, their arms flailing in a futile effort to protect themselves. Suchaka and Chekitana whooped with delight at the sight.

"Look," Jimuta shouted, pointing off to the left. "That one elephant's running away, coming this direction!"

"He's not coming here," Suchaka said with derision. "He's headed toward the next hill."

The others turned their attentions back to the main battle. Jimuta, however, continued watching the runaway elephant. He wasn't sure, but it looked like the animal didn't have a driver, or even any warriors in the box on its back. Soon the great beast disappeared into the trees on the hillside. Jimuta watched a few moments longer, but there was much more happening on the battlefield itself, so he, too, resumed watching the fighting.

"I think our Raja's winning," Suchaka said.

"Yes—he's shoving back Ramgarh's men," said Chekitana, with the confident air of an expert on warfare.

The battle continued. More men lay scattered on the ground; a chariot lost a wheel and was dragged by the horses a considerable distance through the dust; even an elephant fell, shrieking in pain. Then the Ramgarh Raja blew several blasts on his conch, wheeled his chariot about, and swiftly drove toward his own territories. His warriors disengaged and followed.

"I think it's over already," Suchaka muttered in disgust.

Chekitana said, "They hardly killed anybody."

"I've heard that sometimes battles can last all day," Jimuta said. "The rajas must not have wanted to lose too many men or animals." The others ignored him. He decided to count bodies on the ground, and came up with about twenty men, plus four horses and an elephant. Possibly twice as many more warriors were limping or being carried away.

A few Mangarh cavalry and chariots chased their enemy a short distance before giving up and returning. The boys watched the Mangarh forces assembling to count their losses and aid their wounded. Crews began salvaging arrows, spears, and other weapons and debris.

Jimuta looked toward the hill where the runaway elephant had vanished, half expecting it to reappear. But he saw no sign of it.

He glanced at the sky. High above, vultures had gathered and were circling about, waiting for the chance to feed on whatever remained from the carnage of the battle.

2

The arrow in Rudra's shoulder burned, and whenever he moved he felt sharp pain from the spear in his side. He raised his trunk and trumpeted a protest. Today when his keepers had thrown the colorful blanket over him, and strapped the big wooden box on his back, and began painting decorations on his head, he had assumed he would be in a parade. That was fine with him. He enjoyed all the attention when he walked in a parade. The people would shout encouragement to him. Sometimes he would bellow or raise his trunk and blow a raucous burst of air from it just to hear the laughs and shouts from the people watching.

This morning, though, his driver and his keepers hadn't seemed as happy as they were before parades. They hadn't hung the bells around his legs, and they had been quiet most of the time. When they spoke, their voices sounded harsher. The people who cheered when the procession had left the fort had sounded different, too. Loud like they were excited, but not having as much fun as at a festival or parade.

When groups of men riding horses and carrying the metal-pointed sticks joined the procession outside the town, Rudra realized he was going to a place where men would fight other men. When he had done that before, he had usually gotten hurt. That was how his ear had gotten the big rip in its edge.

Rudra hated being where men were fighting other men. Even the mere sounds of men shouting at each other in anger, of their metal weapons clashing together, disturbed him. The smell of blood and the screaming when men and other elephants got hurt especially upset him.

He was quite willing to carry as many men on his back as could fit in the box, but he hated it when other men threw the long, metal-pointed sticks at him. The ones that stuck in him always hurt terribly. So did the smaller sticks with the points on the end, the ones that were hurled from far away by bent wooden branches and flew at him so fast he could scarcely see them, much less move to avoid them.

He didn't mind so much when the other elephants ran at him, trying to show who was boss. All he had to do was charge at them, and they usually gave up before he even hit them. Whenever elephants got together there was usually a boss, and almost always it was Rudra, since he was the biggest and had the longest tusks. And elephants almost always quit fighting before one of them got badly injured.

But it was different when *men* tried to show each other who was the boss. Then a lot of the men always got hurt, even killed. And often elephants got badly hurt or killed, too. Their drivers would make them run at other elephants when it was obvious the other elephants were bigger and stronger. Rudra had never understood that. Why didn't the weaker men just give up and submit to the stronger men as soon as they realized who would win?

At first today the fighting hadn't been too bad. The men who were trying to hurt him were a long way off, and so were the elephants who faced him. But then his driver had made him run directly into the line of the other elephants and men.

In the beginning, Rudra had followed his rider's commands, but when he got close to the other elephants, he and the one his driver aimed him at had each turned a little and run past each other instead of hitting head on. He hadn't been injured then, but the loud clashing of metal, the screams of the men, the shrieks of the other elephants began to unnerve him.

Suddenly, he was surrounded by men who were trying to hurt him. Mingled with the smells of men's sweat and fear, of elephants, of horses, was the scent of warm blood. A man with one of the flat, shiny, sharp edged weapons swung it at his trunk, and Rudra quickly moved his head aside to avoid being cut. Another man with one of the long, sharp sticks tried to poke Rudra in the eye. Rudra bellowed in outrage and swung his head, and the man fell backward to get away from Rudra's giant tusks.

So far Rudra had avoided stepping on anyone, but all the sharp, harsh noises, the worrisome odors, the people trying to hurt him confused him—and he suddenly felt his rear foot squash a man. Rudra could not see beneath his huge body; normally he relied on his trunk to sense what was below so he would not step on anything he shouldn't. He immediately stopped and raised the foot.

He then realized the usual weight of his driver was no longer behind his head. Where had his friend gone?

He smelled a familiar odor from below, along with the scent of fresh blood and of warm guts. He moved sideways and looked backward at the ground.

He was horrified to see he had stepped on his own driver! His friend lay there, one of the small metal pointed sticks in his body, head and shoulders smashed flat by Rudra's foot!

Rudra shrieked in bewilderment. He liked his driver. For a long time, the man had fed him, had inspected him every day for injuries, had helped rub him down every day in his bath.

Rudra again shrieked. Men were still trying to hurt him, and one jabbed a sharp stick into his side. When a man again tried to cut off his trunk, Rudra decided to leave. He briefly wondered if any other men were still in the box on his back, but he decided that didn't matter. If they were there, they weren't giving him any signals.

He began to run. He knocked some humans over as he ran, but by then he no longer cared. He just wanted to get away.

Soon there were no more men or elephants or horses near him. The ground was no longer level; he was lumbering up a hill covered with broadly spaced trees which smelled good. He kept going, over the hill, and down the other side, and along a trail in a valley with the scents of many smaller animals.

Some time after his keen ears could no longer hear the sounds of the fighting, he slowed. One of the sharp sticks still burned in his shoulder, and another hurt in his side. He tried to reach them with his trunk to pull them out, but he couldn't turn his head enough. He shook himself, trying to get rid of them, but they were stuck too deep. He gave up for the moment.

He raised his trunk and waved it this way and that. The aroma of the leaves, dry though they were from the heat, tantalized him. He wrapped his trunk around a nearby branch and pulled along its length, stripping the foliage, which he then thrust into his mouth. He tore off a smaller branch in its entirety, quickly chewed it and swallowed.

Then he lifted his trunk again and sniffed the air. Mixed in with the scents of vegetation, of deer, of squirrels, of jackals, of a tiger, he smelled water!

He began to run, following the odor. Soon his eyes confirmed what the smell had told him. He had found a pond. It was mostly mud, mostly dry, but there was a pool of liquid in the center.

He was hot from the running and from the sun. The water smelled good. Gingerly, he tested the shore before putting weight on the foot, one step at a time to make sure he would not sink too far. The mud was dried out, hardened from the sun, so he continued.

At last he stood in the water. He cautiously splashed into the middle. He'd have preferred to lie down, especially since the pond was so shallow, but he knew he shouldn't, not with the box on his back. And he didn't want to risk pushing the sharp sticks in even further.

He stuck his trunk under the water, drew in as much as he could hold, and sprayed it all over himself. Then he began to drink.

When he'd had enough, he stopped, and he rested, and he thought. He was extremely upset at killing his driver, even though he hadn't intended it.

"That elephant's back at the Raja's stables by now," Suchaka said dismissively to Jimuta. "I'm going to go see if I can find an arrow or spear or something left from the battle."

"Me, too," said Chekitana.

"I'm sure he didn't have a rider," Jimuta repeated. "So he must not have gone far."

"Listen to the elephant expert!" Suchaka said. "For all you know, they trained him to go back to the stables if he ever lost his driver."

"Maybe." Somehow, Jimuta felt sure the elephant must be in the hills somewhere close, waiting. "I'm still going to go look for it."

"What will you do if you find it?" Suchaka asked with a sneer. "You can't feed it, and anyway only the Raja can have one!"

Jimuta knew Suchaka made sense. But he felt compelled to go look. He headed down the hill, away from the Buddhist monastery.

"I know," Chekitana called after him. "You think the Raja will reward you if you bring it back!"

Jimuta paused in mid-stride. He hadn't thought it out completely, but now that words were put to it, he recognized truth in the accusation. But yet, there was something more. Ignoring his cousins, he continued on.

"Let him go," he heard Suchaka say. "There'll be more for us to eat at supper if he's not back yet."

Jimuta was soon out of hearing. He suddenly realized he was feeling tired, even weak. In the excitement of the battle he had forgotten his hunger, but it now returned full strength. He began to regret his refusal to return.

Still, he continued. Up hill, and down, through the forest. The ground seemed totally devoid of any moisture, and his footsteps crunched through the layer of dry leaves and twigs. He sweated from the exertion, and from the heat of the afternoon sun, only partly filtered by the scattered trees.

He began to feel foolish, wondering if he should give up. But the thought of Suchaka and Chekitana's ridicule when he returned—exhausted, hungry, and with nothing gained—kept him plodding up the next hill.

He topped the rise. There, below him, in the center of a mostly dry pond, was the missing elephant. The animal stood there, still wearing the boxlike howdah on its back, as well as its armor: a piece of heavy leather covering its forehead and upper trunk, and a thick, quilted blanket. The elephant was swaying gently back and forth, flapping its gigantic ears and swishing its tail. The blanket looked wet, as if the elephant had done a lot of splashing.

Jimuta approached slowly, trying not to startle the animal into running off. It turned its head toward him and waved the tip of its trunk as if sniffing the air.

He saw that the shaft of an arrow protruded from the great animal's shoulder, near the edge of the thick blanket. And the haft of a spear dangled from the buttock on the other side.

Jimuta came up quietly, and he saw that the elephant was watching him from its nearer eye. It stopped flapping its ears. Jimuta continued across the dry, cracked mud to the water. He hoisted his waist cloth, tied it higher on his legs and waded in, feeling his way carefully in the bottom.

As he neared the animal, he realized how truly big it was. The elephant towered above him like some moveable gray mountain. Despite its wounds, he sensed the immense power in its huge bulk.

Yet, he felt caution more than he felt fear. He stopped an arm's length from the elephant's head, and watched. The elephant let out a low, rumbling sound. "Don't worry, I won't hurt you any more," Jimuta said. Although he could not keep the excitement from his voice, he hoped the elephant found the tone soothing.

The trunk darted toward Jimuta, startling him. He forced himself to stand still, surprised, as the elephant thoroughly sniffed Jimuta's entire body with the tip of its trunk, bathing his skin with blasts of moist, warm air.

Then, suddenly the trunk wrapped around his arm and pulled. The skin felt rough, and Jimuta felt the strength in the muscles. "What are you doing!" he protested. The elephant released his arm, but instead reached down and grabbed Jimuta's lower leg. "Stop!" Jimuta ordered.

The elephant kept fondling him, so Jimuta pulled out of reach. He realized it was probably the animal's way of finding out who he was, and Jimuta was thrilled but disconcerted at the same time. "Let's see if we can get that arrow out of you," he said as he tried to duck the waving trunk.

He splashed through the water to the elephant's shoulder. He could just barely reach the arrow. He seized it, and pulled, hard. At first it resisted, but then it popped out as the head exited the wound. The elephant raised its trunk and let out a high pitched blast, clearly protesting the pain.

Jimuta waded to the other side, going around the elephant's rear to avoid its trunk. He examined the spear for a moment. It was so much larger than the arrow. Would the pain of pulling it out upset the animal, maybe even anger the elephant enough that it might attack him?

It didn't seem right to leave the spear in. It had to be painful, and if the elephant moved, the weight of the shaft could cause the point of the spear to shift around inside, maybe making the wound worse.

Jimuta took a deep breath, gripped the shaft tightly with both hands. He jerked, hard and fast. The spear came out, scarlet blood glistening on the metal tip and a short distance along the shaft. The elephant shuddered momentarily, but it made no sound. It stood, eyeing Jimuta.

He let out his breath. The elephant apparently understood he was trying to help, even if he caused some pain at the same time.

What to do next? The wounds bled, obviously needing treatment. He knew he couldn't take the elephant home. Aside from the fact it belonged to the Raja, feeding it for even a day would probably consume their cow's entire remaining stock of fodder. The only sensible course was to take the elephant to the Raja's fortress at Mangarh.

Jimuta had looked up at the wooden stockade of the fort many times from the town below, on market days and celebrations such as the festival of Indra's Standard. The castle was perched on the crest of the hill with the elephant-shaped cliff, on the far side of the river from Mangarh town. He had never before had cause to ford the river or climb the steep, narrow switchback road to the top. Not until now.

He looked over the elephant carefully. It was a long way to the fortress, and Jimuta was tired and weak from hunger. It would be much better if he could ride in the box on the animal's back, or on the elephant's neck like the driver normally did.

But how could he get up there? He'd never seen anyone mount an elephant before. Maybe he could grab hold of the big strap around the elephant's belly and climb up that way. But the strap was tight around the animal's body, and it would be hard to keep a good grip on it as he moved up.

Another thought came. How would he tell the elephant which way to go? He didn't have any idea what sort of commands the driver gave.

The day wasn't getting younger, and he knew he had to get to the fort before the gates closed for the night. He would have to walk.

Only how did he get the elephant to follow? He didn't see a rope to lead it. And what if it didn't want to come? He could hardly shove it along in front of himself!

"Follow me!" he at last called to the elephant. His voice sounded weak and hesitant. He tried again more firmly, "Come, fellow—follow me!"

The elephant eyed him, flapped its ears once, and remained in its spot in the pond. Jimuta thought some more. He began to walk away. He half turned, beckoned with his hand, and called again, "Come. Follow me!"

The elephant stood watching. Jimuta continued walking. Suddenly, the animal raised its trunk and trumpeted. Startled, and a little worried, Jimuta stopped. He eyed the elephant. The elephant watched him, but made no effort to move.

Time was passing. Jimuta didn't want to be here when night fell. With the drought, this pond probably held the only water in the area, so tigers and wild boars would come to drink. There might even be muggers, crocodiles, around. At the thought, Jimuta glanced uneasily about. To his relief, he didn't see any. Maybe they'd keep away if they knew the elephant was here.

Did he dare try to drive the elephant just as he drove his cow? He wasn't sure. He didn't have to worry about docile Mango Blossom trampling or goring him if he struck her on her rear end. Still, he could think of no better idea. He found a suitable stick at the edge of the pond, splashed over to the rear of the elephant, and swatted its rump, not hard, but not lightly. "Move!" he demanded.

Nothing happened. He hesitated to hit the animal any harder, for fear of angering it.

Another idea came. He splashed up to stand alongside the elephant's left front shoulder. He reached out the stick and poked firmly at the top of the massive leg. "Go!" he commanded decisively.

The elephant lifted its head, trumpeted, and began to walk ahead. Surprised and pleased, Jimuta watched it splash its huge bulk forward out of the pond. It was even headed in roughly the right direction.

Jimuta hurried to catch up. He walked fast at first, keeping at the elephant's side near its front leg. He still could not quite believe the largest creature he had ever seen was actually doing as he directed.

Then, because of the lateness of the day, Jimuta broke into a slow half-walk, half-run. He prodded the animal again. "Faster!" he commanded.

The elephant did as he asked.

Rudra hadn't known what to think about the young human who appeared. But the boy removed the pointed sticks that were causing so much pain, something Rudra could not have done by himself. Rudra was grateful and quickly decided the boy was a possible friend, and someone who could be useful.

The sun was getting low, so it seemed time to go back to the stables. He'd rather not spend the night out in the forest. He liked his accustomed routine every day, and that included sleeping in his own pen under a roof. He also missed the comforting presence of the other elephants nearby, even though he had never developed a close friendship with any of them.

The young human was swatting at him and shouting. The boy obviously didn't know how to talk to him. Maybe the boy could learn if he stayed with Rudra long enough.

The young human shouted and poked Rudra at almost the exact spot his driver touched to tell him to move forward. Apparently, the boy was trying to get him to leave the pond, which was exactly what Rudra wanted to do now anyway.

Rudra began to slowly splash his way out of the water. Then the boy was walking alongside him, at the same spot his driver would be, and the two were moving through the forest. Rudra headed in the direction of the stables. The boy seemed to want to come along, too, which was fine.

The wounds hurt, but they weren't so bad as to interfere with his moving. Soon, the boy prodded him once more, and shouted again. The boy seemed to be in a hurry, and to want him to move faster. That was fine with Rudra. The sooner he got back to the stables, the happier he'd be.

And he decided it was an amusing game, doing what the boy who had helped him seemed to want him to do.

3

In honor of the Raja's victory that day, the town of Mangarh was festooned with banners, and flowers covered the streets. At sunset, the weary Jimuta proudly drove the great animal down the narrow lanes winding between the wooden houses of merchants and craftsmen. Most of the stalls in the marketplace had been taken down for the night, and the shutters were closed in the shop fronts. But the streets were busy with gossiping villagers. A gathering of townspeople listened to a small group of musicians. Vendors of roasted nuts and grains were circulating through the crowd, and the aromas made Jimuta's stomach yearn for food. Despite his hunger, he enjoyed the surprised looks of the inhabitants who quickly moved aside to let the giant elephant pass.

He and the animal crossed the bed of the river, now almost entirely dry, and began the ascent to the fortress. From the walls high above came the sounds of drums, horns and loud talk. The Raja's warriors must be celebrating their triumph, Jimuta realized. He heard a lookout shouting above, and a crowd of men assembled at the gate to watch him urging the elephant up the switchbacks of the narrow road.

When he reached the entry he saw that most of the men carried drinking cups. "It's Rudra, all right!" one of the men shouted. "That big coward!"

The men laughed raucously. "Looks like all he needed was a farm boy to show him the way home!" said another man.

More laughter. Jimuta cringed in sympathy for the elephant that was the target of the ridicule.

So his name was Rudra.

Suddenly the men gave way to each side as a short, broad man followed by several others pushed through to where Jimuta stood with the elephant. The tallness of the man's turban, its jewels flashing in final rays of the setting sun, indicated his extremely high status. Jimuta recognized the round faced, mustached, thick lipped man as his Raja and threw himself to the ground to touch the ruler's feet.

"What is all this?" the Raja of Mangarh asked loudly but in good humor. "I thought we had men searching for this guy!"

"Most of the elephant keepers are still out looking, Highness," said one of the men.

"I half hoped they'd never find him. The big baby!" said the Raja.

The men laughed uproariously.

The Raja's thick lips were smiling as he looked down to where Jimuta still sprawled at his feet. "Get up, boy. You're the one who found him?"

Jimuta scrambled to his feet. "Yes, Your Highness," he managed, fearful now that he faced his ruler. In a weak voice, Jimuta explained, "He was in a pond in the hills. I pulled an arrow and a spear out of him."

The Raja's eyes observed him briefly, then appeared to lose interest. "You did, did you? Good! There'll be a reward for you." The Raja called to his officers, "Someone take care of them." He took a long drink from his cup, turned and strode toward the great wooden hall and the sounds of music: drumming and a flute and stringed vina. Most of the men followed him.

Jimuta stared after the ruler, bewildered over what to do next. The elephant still stood beside him. A reward, the Raja had said! What could that mean? Better not expect too much; then there was less likelihood of being disappointed.

A boy not much older than Jimuta appeared, carrying a short pole with a metal hook on one end. The boy was tall and thin, with friendly eyes in a pockmarked face. He smiled amiably at Jimuta and said, "Come." With the blunt end of the pole he firmly prodded the elephant at the back of a foreleg, almost the same spot where Jimuta had poked. The boy led the elephant, with Jimuta following, to the stables, where unusually thick, round wooden posts supported a long thatched roof. "You brought Rudra back by yourself—alone?" the boy asked as he led the animal along the row of stalls, most of which were occupied by other elephants.

"Yes," said Jimuta, trying not to sound as proud as he felt. "There was no one else." The stables smelled of elephant urine and dung, not unpleasant to Jimuta, who was used to farm yards.

The boy looked Jimuta over, obviously impressed. "Most people would be afraid. He killed his driver Kumbha today, you know."

Jimuta's eyes widened. "He did?"

The boy's face turned somber. "Someone said they saw Rudra step on him."

Jimuta went numb. He looked up at the huge gray beast lumbering beside them. He wiped his brow with a hand, suddenly realizing how foolish he must have been to take such a risk.

"I'm sure it was an accident," continued the boy. "Rudra wouldn't have done it intentionally. He liked Kumbha."

Jimuta felt slightly better.

A small, sober looking, old man walked toward them with an unusual gait, his legs wider apart than normal. "Come, Nakula," said the elderly man to the boy. Jimuta watched with interest as they chained the rear leg of the elephant to one of the posts in a stall. The links of the chain were the thickest he had ever seen, and it was clear why the wooden posts were so massive. The elephant could no doubt pull an ordinary sized post right out of the ground.

The man and the boy examined Rudra's wounds. "I'll take care of them," said the man.

The boy Nakula smiled at Jimuta. "You want to stay here tonight?"

Jimuta thought. He'd rather not try to get back to his own village in the dark. "I think I'd better," he said.

"We're celebrating the victory," said Nakula. "There's plenty of food. Come. I'll show you." Jimuta's head suddenly felt light from not eating in so long, and he worried he might faint as he followed Nakula to the big wooden hall, where the music was originating. When he approached the open doorway and the odors of spices and roasted meat assaulted his nose, so desperate was his hunger that he became nauseous.

Inside, oil lamps had been lit and hung around the walls. Not since the drought began had Jimuta seen so much food, even at weddings. Placed in central locations about the many noisy men seated on the floor were various dishes. "Lamb, venison, peacock," said Nakula, indicating the types of meat from which to choose. Jimuta saw three different kinds of bread, and too many varieties of sweets to count.

The two found a spot to sit on the wooden planked floor at the rear of the hall, between a couple of groups of reveling soldiers, some of whom bore wounds dressed with cloth bandages. Jimuta eagerly grabbed a millet cake and dipped his fingers into a platter of goat meat in a spicy sauce. While he ate, he and Nakula watched the drunken men harass the dancing girls who were trying to perform while the small orchestra played.

As he was gorging himself, and beginning to feel ill from eating such rich food, and so much more than he was used to, Jimuta tried to think of a way to save some of it for his family. Maybe he could at least bring a few of the small cakes and a little bread in his waist cloth.

The raucous festivities were quite a spectacle for a farm boy from a tiny village. But it had been a long, exhausting day. Eventually he fell asleep.

In the morning, Jimuta was one of the first to awaken. Nakula had disappeared from the hall, but numerous men sprawled about, apparently sleeping off the effects of their drinking.

Jimuta wondered what to do. He should probably return to his village, but the Raja had promised him the reward. He wandered outside.

High up in under the eaves of the wooden towers, pigeons cooed. A huge flock of crows flapped across the courtyard and settled to peck for food. For want of a better idea, Jimuta went to the elephant stables. In the daylight, he saw his charge from the day before, in the middle of the line of twelve wooden stalls, each of which was occupied. He was surprised to see that Rudra was the largest of the elephants.

No one was around, so Jimuta went over to him. Warily—remembering that the elephant had killed his driver only yesterday—Jimuta patted the elephant's rough side. Rudra turned his head, reached back his trunk, and darted the end of it here and there, all over Jimuta, spraying warm, moist air. Jimuta stood stiff, marveling at the unique tickling sensations on his skin. Then, as yesterday, the elephant grabbed hold of Jimuta's arm, firmly. "Stop!" Jimuta demanded.

"He's just getting to know you better," came Nakula's voice. "They always explore a new person with their trunks."

Jimuta forced himself to try to relax. The elephant let go his arm, grabbed his leg, and pulled hard, but almost certainly not as hard as he was capable of. Jimuta braced himself, straining to remain in place. "How are his wounds?" he asked.

"We've treated them, so they should heal quickly," said Nakula, his amiable smile illuminating the pockmark scarred face.

"What do you use?"

"Mainly just water, for rinsing, and in a compress. If the wounds are kept clean and free from flies there should be no problems."

The elephant let go, and Jimuta moved quickly out of reach. "I see." He thought for a time. Then, he asked, "How do you get to be an elephant keeper?"

Nakula shrugged. "Most of us are born to it. My father was one, and his father before him." The answer was what Jimuta had expected. Most occupations were passed from father to son, generation after generation. There was no reason elephant keepers should be different. Still, he felt a vague disappointment that there was no possibility he might be able to continue to work with Rudra.

Nakula was saying, "We elephant handlers come from a village back in the hills. We all worship Ganesha."

It made sense that they would pray to the elephant-headed god. "I see."

Jimuta helped Nakula clean the stalls. It wasn't much different from cleaning up after cows, except the chunks of dung were a lot bigger. He again regretted that there was no possibility of him staying. He thought briefly of whether he might ask the Raja to give him a job in the elephant stables, but he knew there was no point. Any new positions would go to family members of those who already did that type of work.

He kept wondering if someone would come to give him his reward, or if he needed to go ask for it. Jimuta knew exactly what he would request, though, assuming he was given a choice. "How can I get to see the Raja?" he at last asked Nakula.

"You want to see the Raja himself?" the boy raised his eyebrow in astonishment.

"He told me I could have a reward for bringing Rudra back."

"Oh. I suppose you need to ask one of his officials. I'm not sure which one. But I know His Highness is busy. A delegation from the Raja of Girnar came to see him."

Jimuta realized the ruler might well have forgotten the matter, especially with the distraction of important visitors. There was probably no point in trying to see the Raja while he was so preoccupied. So Jimuta resigned himself to waiting as long as it took. He hoped Uncle and Auntie wouldn't be too upset. At least the family would have one less to feed today.

He went with Nakula and the old man, Uttara, and the other elephant keepers and drivers when they took the elephants down the hill to bathe them in the almost-dry river below the fort. Jimuta noticed that many of the drivers walked with a gait similar to Uttara's, their legs wider apart than normal. He suddenly realized that it must be because they spent so much time straddling elephants' broad necks.

The fact there was so little water made the job of bathing the animals more difficult. Nakula gave a command and shoved Rudra firmly. Rudra immediately lowered himself into the river and rolled onto his side, displacing a huge surge of water. "See," said Nakula.

"It's easier to wash him this way." He took a flat stone and demonstrated how to scrub the elephant's hide.

"You like this, don't you, Rudra?" Jimuta asked the great animal as he vigorously rubbed the elephant's back with the rock. Rudra rumbled with pleasure. Jimuta was thrilled to be working with the huge beast and didn't mind getting his feet and legs muddy and the rest of himself wet. Occasionally Rudra would suck up a trunkfull of water and spray over his own back, not caring if he soaked Jimuta at the same time.

The sound of music came from high on the hill, and a small procession of horsemen trotted down, banners flying. "It's the representative sent by the Raja of Girnar," said Nakula. "He must be heading back. Seems like he's in more of a hurry than most. Usually officials sent from other rajas want to have a big procession and ride in a palanquin or on an elephant." Jimuta watched with the other drivers as the horsemen splashed across the river and then disappeared into the narrow streets of the town.

When the elephants returned to the castle, word came that the Raja was coming to the stables to inspect the animals. Quickly, the animals were secured in their stalls, and the drivers ensured the floors were clean and equipment was properly stowed. Jimuta remained near Rudra, whose stall was next to the elephant belonging to the older driver, Uttara.

There was a long wait, but at last the Raja arrived, his flywhisk and umbrella bearers immediately behind him, and the Chief Minister at his side. An entourage of a dozen or so warriors trailed them. Jimuta observed that the minister was a Brahmin, as the rotund man had no turban, and his shiny round head was shaved except for a tuft of hair hanging from the upper rear. Both exalted men wore sour expressions, as if engaged in an annoying task.

The officer in charge of the elephant stables joined the Raja and his minister, who began at the end of the row of stalls, spending only a brief time glancing at each animal. When they arrived at Rudra, they halted, looked closely at him, and began conversing. The Raja's cold gaze swept past Jimuta, but the ruler showed no hint of recognition.

Jimuta assumed the Raja and the Chief Minister must be speaking Sanskrit, the language normally used among the nobility and educated persons. He recognized many of the words, but their speech was different enough from the local dialect that he could not follow what they were saying. He did recognize the name "Ashoka Raja" several times, and he assumed they must be referring to the famous Mauryan Emperor Ashoka. Eventually, the Chief Minister switched to the local dialect and demanded of the officer in charge of elephants: "Have you assigned a new driver to Rudra?"

"Not yet, your honor," said the man, hanging his head in apparent apology. "We had no extras available. We may have to bring in one from elsewhere."

The Raja and the Chief Minister exchanged frowns. The minister ordered: "Find one. We may need to send this elephant away."

The official appeared to hesitate, then asked, "You're sending Rudra away, your honor?"

The Chief Minister glanced at the Raja, who nodded in confirmation. The minister said, "His Highness is thinking of sending Rudra as a gift to King Ashoka. He...uh...assumes the great King may be upset about our fighting with the Raja of Ramgarh, and the gift of such an elephant may help placate him."

The official gazed at Rudra for a moment, then said, "As you say, your honor. I'd hate to lose our noblest animal. But I suppose he's not much use in war any more, anyway."

The ruler and his party moved on, perfunctorily looking at the other elephants, then left the stables. Jimuta was disappointed that the Raja hadn't mentioned the reward again. That meant he must pursue the matter himself.

Uttara agreed to help Jimuta locate the proper person to ask about the reward. Eventually, they found a scribe who informed them that the Chief Minister was the likely one to handle the matter. Remembering the official's cold demeanor, Jimuta wished there were someone else he could ask instead. But there seemed no other choice.

After the evening meal, Jimuta sat with Nakula and Uttara and the other elephant handlers, who had gathered round a campfire against the chill of the night. The drivers argued about whose elephants had done best in the battle, and they discussed the conditions of the wounds of both the animals and the drivers. They especially talked about Rudra's accidentally killing his driver Kumbha, and about the elephant's running away and returning.

"Rudra probably would have come back anyway," said one mahout. "They usually do. Why, I know of a cow elephant, Sunderbala was her name. She was gone for five years and still came back. She went right back into her old routine. Acted as if she'd never been gone. That's another example of how they never forget anything."

"Except when they *want* to," said Uttara, and the drivers all laughed knowingly.

The next morning, Jimuta entered a large room where the Chief Minister was granting audiences to various waiting men. A young aide, clearly another Brahmin from the shaved head with a tuft of hair on the back, ignored Jimuta for a while, then finally deigned to ask what he'd come for. After Jimuta told him, the assistant brusquely ordered him to wait.

Jimuta watched the minister, who sat on a luxuriously embroidered cushion, his sacred Brahmin's thread exposed where it wasn't covered by his shawl of finely woven wool. The aide called the petitioners forward one at a time. Each visitor would bend and touch the great man's feet, then state the request. A scribe squatted near the minister and recorded the proceedings.

Jimuta had always been intrigued by the idea of writing. The only one in his village who knew how to write was the man who kept the records of the land for Prince Aja's tax collectors to examine. If a villager needed a letter written to someone far away, for a fee the man would do the writing and would dispatch the letter.

As he watched the scribe, Jimuta saw yet another use for writing: keeping a record of decisions made by important men, so it would not be necessary later to find someone who had been present and remembered the details. He wished there were some way he, too, could learn such a useful skill. But that was obviously impossible. It would clearly take a long time to learn such things. Anyway, who would ever teach him?

After at least twenty persons had been received, the assistant looked to Jimuta. "Boy!"

Jimuta hurried forward and made his obeisance. He was nervous in the presence of such an exalted man, who surveyed Jimuta without warmth. But with no hesitation, Jimuta said, "Your honor, His Highness the Raja promised me a reward for returning the elephant Rudra. Please, may I have some food for my family as the reward?"

Jimuta felt the minister scrutinizing him. "Take all the grain you can carry," said the official eventually. He waved a hand in dismissal.

Jimuta decided he had little to lose by boldly saying, "I could carry more if I had the use of a cart, your honor. May I borrow one for a day?"

The Chief Minister raised an eyebrow in surprise. His face reddened as his annoyance grew. Then Jimuta saw the man's eyes soften slightly, and interest sparked in them. A smile curled at the corner of the minister's lips, as he tilted his head to one side, obviously thinking. At last, the man said: "You did return a valuable animal. His Highness has decided to send that very elephant to King Ashoka as a gift. So I'm sure His Highness would want to be generous in this case. Very well—I'll order a cart sent to the storehouses. You may take as much grain as you can carry in it."

An entire cartload! Jimuta could scarcely belief he'd been so successful. It would help feed his whole village! Did he dare make the additional request? He hesitated, but he doubted he would never have another opportunity. "Honorable sir," he said, "I was wondering, too, if you might need another elephant driver."

The minister stared at him and scowled. Then the official laughed harshly. "An elephant driver? All our mahouts are born to their work. They learned it from their fathers, who learned it from their own fathers. How could you ever suppose you could do such a thing?"

Jimuta swallowed his fear and persisted: "Your honor, I was

able to bring Rudra back here by myself. I'm sure I could learn quickly."

The Chief Minister shook his head, his lips twisting in amusement. "The idea's absurd. Go back to your fields."

Although Jimuta had expected to be refused, he could not help but feel disappointed. He bowed and backed away. "Yes, your honor." He turned and hurried past the scribe and the aide, and out the door.

At least he had the cartload of grain. A whole cartload! For once, his uncle and auntie and cousins would be glad to see him. He walked swiftly across the courtyard toward the storehouses. He'd better see to getting the grain before that Chief Minister changed his mind.

"Boy!" came a shout from behind.

He stopped, and turned, and saw the Chief Minister's aide. "Don't you know you must wait for the scribe to write out the order? You don't expect the keeper of the grain to take your word for an entire cartload?"

Flustered, Jimuta hurried back. He waited as the Chief Minister dealt with two more petitioners. Then the scribe beckoned to him, extending a piece of palm leaf on which he'd been writing.

The room was at last empty of persons seeking audiences. Jimuta was aware of the Chief Minister staring at him, but he did not dare to return the look. Jimuta took the order the scribe had written, and turned to leave.

"Boy!"

Jimuta whirled about. The Chief Minister himself had called. "Boy! Come here. So you want to drive an elephant."

Jimuta approached and quickly touched the minister's foot, then straightened. "Uh, yes, honorable sir."

"It takes men who are born to the work many years to learn."

Jimuta looked down at the teak planked floor. "Yes, your honor."

"What do you say to that?"

"I...don't know, your honor. I would do my best and work hard at it. I learn most things quickly."

The minister gave a curt nod, and appeared to be thinking. At last he asked, "Could we trust you to be completely loyal to His Highness the Raja, even if you were far away from the him?"

Jimuta struggled to keep his composure. Why would the minister be asking such a question? He realized the official was staring intently at him. "Of—of course, your honor. He's my Raja."

"Good. And could you follow your Raja's orders without question, no matter what those orders were?"

"I...of course, your honor." Jimuta realized there could be some orders that might be difficult to obey, but he couldn't think of what those might be, at least not right now.

"Good. It would be very troublesome for you if you did not obey."

Jimuta sensed potential danger in the minister's blunt words, but he lacked the experience to judge exactly what the hazards might be.

The minister continued, "I think we could use another elephant driver after all. But you must leave your village."

Jimuta had known he'd have to move to the fortress if he were to become an elephant handler. While he would regret leaving Uncle's family, it did mean their food would stretch farther. And Jimuta could send his wages to them. Whether in cash or in grain the remittance would be more helpful than whatever work Jimuta could do on the land itself, where his two cousins would remain to help with the labor.

"I'm can do that, your honor," he replied.

"You also need to leave Mangarh."

"Your honor?"

"You'd go to Pataliputra. With the elephant you brought back to us. Probably permanently. His Highness' brother, Kumara Aja, will lead the escort."

He wondered if he had heard right. "Pataliputra, your honor?"

"Yes, yes. I told you His Highness is giving the elephant to King Ashoka. A driver must go with it. There are problems in sending one of our regular mahouts; problems we wouldn't have if we sent you."

Jimuta still had difficulty grasping what was being said. No one had ever left his village before for more than a few days. And not for such a long journey. Not for *any* reason. "I, uh, am not sure I should leave my family, your honor."

"Nonsense. You said yourself they're short of food. If you left, they would have one less person to feed."

Jimuta couldn't think of how to respond. How could he possibly refuse the Raja's own Chief Minister?

He thought of the hard life on the farm, of the continual hunger the past two years, no matter how hard one worked. The fact that he was indeed a burden to his uncle and aunt.

The wages as an elephant driver in the great King's army would probably be even higher than whatever Raja Balarama would pay.

He thought of Pataliputra. Everyone had heard of that city, said to be the largest and richest in all the world. The very name had the same ring as the heaven of the gods. Its palaces, overlooking the sacred Ganges River itself, were said to have walls of silver glittering with gems.

He could probably find a way to return to the farm some day, if he truly wanted. But never again would he have such an opportunity to leave his prescribed place in this life.

And he would be with Rudra. "I'll do it, your honor. If my uncle will agree."

The Chief Minister snorted. "He *must* agree. I'll send someone to tell him." He casually waved Jimuta off. "You may go."

Jimuta made his obeisance. He was stunned by the fact that the minister had changed his mind, and by the implications of the great change he was on the verge of. As he left the room, he was so unsteady on his feet that he had to concentrate so as not to stumble.

Jimuta could not see that the Chief Minister, with eyes narrowed, was watching him leave and evaluating him with care.

The minister saw a thin looking peasant boy, with the sun darkened skin and the rough feet and hands from hard work in the fields. However, the minister was thinking that he was far more impressed than he would have expected with this particular farm boy's self-possession and persistence and apparent intelligence. It almost seemed, the minister thought, as if the boy had been a higher caste in a previous lifetime.

But did that mean there was a possibility the boy might begin to think independently once he was far away from the oversight of his Mangarh lords?

The plans that had been worked out with the envoy from the Raja of Girnar and with the other allies were so critical. Indeed, it might not be exaggerating to say that the future of the empire ruled by King Ashoka was at stake, as well as Raja Balarama's control of Mangarh. What if the boy decided not to obey the Raja's orders at critical moment?

Or, worse yet, what if he betrayed them all?

It would be best not to tell the boy any more than he needed to know. And the minister decided he would ensure Kumara Aja knew what to do if it ever appeared the boy couldn't be trusted. The Raja's brother had a ruthless streak, as did most of the Kumara's officials, and they would not hesitate to kill someone who had become a threat.

4

Jimuta kept wondering why the minister had reconsidered so quickly. In the courtyard the next day, he and the driver of the two wheeled cart waited half the morning for the escort sent by Kumara Aja to guard the food and deal with Jimuta's family.

An entire cart load of grain! Jimuta could hardly wait to see the surprised and delighted reactions from his uncle and aunt and cousins, and the rest of the villagers.

At last they heard hoofbeats, and six mounted warriors thundered into the yard. Their leader was a broadly built man with a hunched over posture and long, thick, dangling arms.

Jimuta instantly felt light headed and nauseous. His breath caught, and his heart pounded hard.

The Mugger! Previously, Jimuta had seen the feared warrior only from a distance, and that was by far the safest way to view him. The Mugger had a blunt, bent-down nose that didn't look anything at all like the long snout of a crocodile, the animal after which the villagers had given the man his nickname. But the officer's soulless eyes pierced Jimuta with suspicion and menace. Jimuta thought again of what The Mugger and his men did to the girl Ambika after they found her hiding in her house. How could he be so ill-starred as to have to go all the way to the village and back with the brutal warrior?

The Mugger glared down at him and muttered loudly to his men in a deep rumbling voice, "What will our lord think of next? Being nursemaids to a stupid farm boy!"

One of the soldiers was staring at the fully loaded cart of grain. He edged his horse closer to The Mugger and murmured something that Jimuta could not hear. The Mugger turned toward the cart and eyed it for a moment. A smile tugged at the corners of his lips. He gave a quick nod.

"Be off, then!" he ordered the cart driver. Without a further glance, The Mugger wheeled his horse about.

The driver and Jimuta climbed onto the seat of the cart, and the driver sent the two bullocks into motion. The Mugger rode ahead with one of his men, while the other warriors flanked each side of the cart. The vehicle lumbered down the hillside, splashed across the ford, and rumbled through the town and out the gate in the wooden palisade.

Why, Jimuta wondered, had The Mugger been given this particular task? The warrior's own chief was Kumara Aja, who ruled Jimuta's village, not the greater ruler, the Raja of Mangarh. And guarding the cartload could have been assigned to any of the Raja's soldiers.

About halfway to the village, at the track that turned off to lead to Kumara Aja's fort, The Mugger halted them all. "Driver!" he shouted. "Take the cart and follow these men." He gestured to three of his warriors, who turned off onto the track.

"But, sir!" said Jimuta. "My village is straight ahead."

The Mugger glared at him. "I know that, you idiot! Grab a bag of grain, and come with me."

Jimuta gaped. The Mugger was stealing almost all of the cart load of food! "But sir, the honorable Chief Minister said—"

"—I know what he said, you fool! You expect me to take you to your village and get nothing for it? Get moving, or I won't let you take even the one sack!"

"Your honor, my family and everyone in my village are hungry."

The Mugger laughed, and so did his men. "Then they should work harder and grow more food! That's what farmers do!"

Stunned and outraged, Jimuta tried to think of what to do. Complain to the Chief Minister when he returned to the Raja's fort and Mangarh?

The Mugger rode close and stared down at him coldly. "Don't think of telling anyone about the rest of the grain. The Chief Minister himself will get half of it as his share, you know! Otherwise he'd never have told you to take so much. Even if someone believed you, they wouldn't do anything. And very soon you'd die in an accident—after I and my men had some fun with you."

Jimuta swallowed.

The officer smiled nastily and asked, "Do you know what all those louts in the villages call me?"

Jimuta turned numb throughout his whole body. Should he say? Or should he pretend not to know?

The man laughed, harshly, and for the first time amusement shone in his eyes. "They call me 'The Mugger!' *'The Crocodile!'* Have you ever seen what a crocodile does when it gets hold of its prey?" He waited a moment, as if expecting a reply, then he laughed and laughed as he wheeled his horse about.

Jimuta, covered with dust and carrying the bag of grain, stumbled tiredly behind the three horsemen as the party approached the village.

Normally, curious children would run out to see any unusual visitors. But this time, the hamlet was deathly quiet. Nothing moved. Obviously someone had recognized The Mugger and spread a warning.

The Mugger and his men halted. "Farm boy!" came the deep voice. "Where's your house?"

Jimuta hesitated, hating to bring his uncle's family to the attention of the notorious officer. But there appeared no choice. He let the bag of grain drop to the ground. "There, your honor," he pointed out the two-room, thatch roofed wooden hut. His voice was dry and hoarse, and not solely because of the dust and heat.

The Mugger and his men rode in the direction indicated. Jimuta hoisted the bag again and trudged after them. "This one?" asked The Mugger.

Jimuta tried to clear his throat. Reluctantly: "Yes, sir,".

"You'd better get them out here. They're probably pissing in their clothes for fear of what I'll do to them. Tell them I want nothing from them except you." He glanced at Jimuta momentarily. "Although I can't understand why anyone would want *you* for an elephant driver."

Jimuta dragged the bag to the hut and pulled at the door of rough-hewn boards. As he'd expected, it was barred from the inside. "Uncle! Auntie!" he called. "It's me."

He heard murmuring inside. There was a short wait, then he saw an eye appear at a crack between the boards. He heard the bar being withdrawn, and the door creaked open slightly. "You—you're with The Mugger?" whispered his uncle.

"Yes, Uncle. I'm sorry. May I come in?"

After a moment, the door opened farther, and Jimuta quickly tugged the heavy bag into the dim, earth floored interior. Wide-eyed with fear, his aunt and cousins were standing against the far wall. His uncle slammed the door and thrust the bar into its notches.

"I'm sorry," Jimuta repeated. "I didn't know *he'd* be bringing me here. I brought some grain. There would have been a lot more, but The Mugger took the rest for himself and the Chief Minister."

Sweat glistened on his uncle's forehead. "Why did he come here? Where have you been?"

Jimuta moistened his lips. "The Mugger came to tell you the Raja wants me to be an elephant driver and to go to Pataliputra."

Everyone gawked at him.

"He, uh, wants you to come outside," said Jimuta. "He says he won't hurt you."

His uncle started to ask another question, then thought better of it. "I—I'd better go out. The rest of you stay."

He again unbarred the door. It creaked as he tugged it open. Followed by Jimuta, he slowly went out to the bright daylight where the soldiers waited.

Still on his horse, and looking as if he had swallowed something bitter, The Mugger fixed those frigid eyes on Jimuta's uncle and said, "His Highness the Raja commands that your nephew join his elephant corps and be trained as a driver. The boy will then take an elephant to Pataliputra with His Highness, Kumara Aja, as a gift to His Majesty, Emperor Ashoka Maurya. Your nephew will probably stay there some years. I assume you don't object?"

Jimuta's uncle blinked at the sweat that had dripped into his eyes. After a time, the man's mouth moved, but no words came.

"Good," rumbled The Mugger. "The matter's settled." He said to Jimuta, "Be at Mangarh fort by midmorning tomorrow." He and his men turned their horses and sped off.

Eventually, Uncle wiped his forehead and took a deep breath. He turned to stare at Jimuta. "I think...you'd better tell us about this."

Seeing that The Mugger and his men had left, the other villagers quickly began to appear, and soon Jimuta and his family were surrounded by a curious crowd. Jimuta explained how he had returned the elephant, and how his request to be a driver had been turned down at first, and then, for some mysterious reason, granted. He was aware of his cousins Suchaka and Chekitana, as well as Kuvera and the other boys, watching him in disbelief—and maybe with some envy.

When he told about how The Mugger had stolen the grain that could otherwise have helped feed the entire village, people muttered about the theft. But of course there was nothing to be done.

One of the village council members, a middle aged man named Pushan, whom everyone respected for his wisdom and good judgment, voiced the question so many of those present had: "Why would our Raja want someone with no training in handling elephants to take such a valuable animal all the way to Pataliputra?"

"I don't know, sir," Jimuta admitted. "I think they didn't have any extra drivers."

"Still," continued Pushan, "why would the Raja send an elephant as a gift to Emperor Ashoka, if the elephant might run away in battle? That seems likely to anger the great King, rather than please him."

Jimuta lowered his eyes. "I don't know why, sir."

Pushan frowned. "It makes no sense. I would be watchful and careful if I were you, my boy. You're somehow being used to further a scheme of these great men. I hope you don't end up being badly hurt by the time they're finished with you.

Jimuta trudged back to Mangarh town the next day, leaving behind perplexed relatives and bewildered fellow villagers. On the long way to the fortress, he thought about Pushan's words of caution. But the actions of the lordly ones were beyond the comprehension of a simple farm lad, no matter how agile his mind. He did not have the knowledge or experience, he realized, to discern their motives or plans. The best he could do would be to keep his ears and his eyes alert, so he would not miss any hints that did present themselves.

At the Raja's stables, an elephant driver around thirty years in age named Kunala had been directed to train Jimuta in elephant handling and care—in only a month. He glared at Jimuta for a time. Then, he said angrily, "I won't train you. It can't be done. Especially not in a month! Our knowledge was learned over many lifetimes by our fathers, and by their fathers before them."

The old man Uttara came near. "I agree it's the most foolish thing I've ever heard of," he said. "Still, His Highness ordered it. How can you refuse?"

"The order's impossible!" said Kunala. "Let the Raja do with me as he will. If he throws me in his jail, he'll be short two drivers, not just one." He glanced about, and lowered his voice. "Why would His Highness send *Rudra* as a gift to the Emperor, anyway? He may be big, but he's almost worthless in battles, since he usually runs away."

"His Highness must have had a good reason," said Uttara.

"And why would His Highness send the elephant with a driver who's had no experience?"

"Would *you* want to spend the rest of your years in Pataliputra, away from all your kin?" asked Uttara.

"Of course not," replied Kunala. "I probably couldn't even understand the way everyone talks there. But I still don't see..."

The boy Nakula came over. "Jimuta did bring Rudra back by himself. He seems to have a way with Rudra."

"It's still ridiculous!" said Kunala.

"You could at least try," said Nakula.

Kunala snorted. "Never." He turned and walked off.

"Uncle," Nakula said to Uttara, "you and I can teach Jimuta as much as we can, in the time we have."

Uttara shook his head in annoyance. "You should know it can't be done. Oh, I've known of one or two drivers who weren't born to the work. But it took years and years for them to learn. Even then, they probably weren't as good as we are."

Nakula said, "So how is Jimuta to learn? What will happen when the Raja learns we refused?"

The old man shook his head sadly. He shrugged.

Nakula stood, watching him. Jimuta observed them both, and wondered what to do.

Uttara said, annoyance still in his voice, "There's something about this I don't like. His Highness is no fool. He knows our work is not something to be taught in a short time. So why is he asking us to do it? And why is it so urgent to send Rudra to the Emperor *now*?"

Nakula and Jimuta exchanged glances, and remained silent.

Uttara mused, half to himself, "It's odd, but I think His Highness must not *care* if Rudra's driver has any experience or not. And I think our lord would be quite angry if no one tried to train Jimuta as he asked. Our Raja must have his reasons, strange though they appear to us."

Nakula said, "What reasons could he have?"

Uttara gave him a stern look. "Better we not ask. There are things we aren't intended to know. The ways of the lordly ones can be impossible to understand."

"But shouldn't Jimuta know the reasons, if he's so involved?"

Uttara frowned. "He'll be told what His Highness' officials think he should know. It's better," he said to Jimuta, "that you simply do as you're told."

Jimuta nodded. That was what he'd usually tried to do, anyway.

After a time, Uttara again shrugged. "I suppose we might as well do as much as we can in the time we have." He looked hard at Jimuta. "But if you get hurt, or the elephant does, it's not due to us!"

"I understand, sir," said Jimuta, relieved that the matter had been resolved.

Uttara said, "I'll meet you at the stables after meal time."

"Yes, sir. I'm grateful, sir."

Uttara shook his head and muttered, "For your sake, I hope you are a very fast learner."

They approached Rudra's stall.

Uttara said, "You've seen that elephant drivers worship Ganesha as their main god. The first thing we do before we mount the elephant each day is to pay our respects to Lord Ganesha." He reverently touched his fingers to Rudra's side, then to his own forehead. He glanced at Jimuta and waited.

Jimuta duplicated the short ritual, honoring the elephant god whose spirit the mahouts believed was embodied in each of the great animals.

"Now," said Uttara, "The main rule in elephant handling is that you can make the animal do anything *it* wants to do. You understand what I mean?"

"I think so, sir," said Jimuta. "The elephant's so much bigger and stronger than me, I can't actually force him to do anything. If I tried to hurt him to get him to do what I want, he might get mad and attack me."

Uttara's expression softened. "That's part of it. But it doesn't mean you can't make him do something he'd prefer not to do. You should have such a good friendship with him that he trusts you and believes that what you want him to do will usually be in his best interests. Or, it helps if what you want him to do is part of his daily routine, so it's a habit he won't question, such as taking him to the river to bathe, or inspecting his feet to make sure they stay healthy."

"I see, sir. But once in a while, wouldn't I need to make him do something he didn't want to do? Like...fighting in a battle."

"Sometimes you have to fool him. You have to make him *think* you might be able to force him to do something, even though you in fact couldn't. You understand?"

Jimuta scratched his head through his turban. "How can I fool him into thinking I could force him? I'm so much smaller!"

"With this, when you need it." Uttara handed him a goad, one of the short wooden poles with a sharp pointed iron hook on an end. "This *ankus* is your tusk. Now you are a big male elephant, too." Nakula laughed. Even Uttara gave a grim smile. Jimuta was trying to decide if they were playing a joke on him. Uttara explained, "When you give him an order, give it to him as if you were another male elephant. Your goad is your proof to him that you can enforce what you command."

"But I can't! Even with this." Jimuta examined the *ankus*.

"Of course you can't. But the elephant must never know it. Sometimes drivers who forget this are killed by their elephants."

After a moment, Jimuta said hesitantly, "I think I'm beginning to see."

"It works for us," Nakula said.

"Most of the time," said Uttara, "if you go about it the right way."

"*Most* of the time?" Jimuta asked, his doubts growing.

"An elephant has his own mind. Sometimes he gets excited or afraid and runs away—like Rudra did in the battle. Or he could be uneasy about doing what you command, such as if you want him to cross a river and he thinks the bottom could be too soft. He might ignore you. Then you can only do your best to try to outwit him, to trick him into obeying."

"Another matter," continued Uttara with a sober look. "To my mind, the best of the drivers never actually use the *ankus*, at least not to actually cause the elephant pain. The ones who are unkind to their animals often end up with angry elephants who are slow to obey."

Jimuta slowly nodded. "I think I see."

"The best driver," said Uttara, "is such a good friend with his elephant that the animal is naturally eager to please him."

Jimuta gazed at Rudra. "I hope he and I can be such close friends."

"Also," said Nakula, "don't try to order an elephant who's in musth."

"In 'musth'? What's that?"

Uttara said, "See the small hole on each side between his eyes and his mouth? Once a year or so, they begin to drain. Then you won't be able to handle him. That's when many drivers are killed. Then he must be firmly chained, and no one must come close to him. But come—I'll teach you the basic commands."

Uttara demonstrated on Rudra. Jimuta learned the voice commands for moving the elephant forward (*"agit!"*) and backward (*"peechay!"*), for making it stop (*"dhuth!"*). "Always give the orders loudly—and firmly," said Nakula. "That way, you know he hears you. And that you mean it."

There were commands for telling the elephant to kneel, to raise its foot, to turn left and right. There were also pressure points for using the goad while walking or standing by the animal, such as on the front of the elephant's feet.

Jimuta began to practice with Rudra. Occasionally the elephant would hesitate, but when Jimuta repeated the command louder and with more determination, Rudra obeyed.

"That's enough for now," said Uttara at last. "Rudra may be getting tired of us telling him what to do today. And even though time is short, you can only remember so much at once."

The next morning, after they bathed the elephants, Nakula showed Jimuta how to mount Rudra. "The riders in the howdah usually use a ladder," he said. "But you can choose one of these other ways, so you don't need to keep a ladder with you."

First, the boy had the elephant bend a foreleg at the knee and raise it. Nakula used the leg as a step, grabbed Rudra's ear, and boosted himself behind the neck.

He then dismounted and had Rudra lower his head so the tusks were near the ground. Nakula stepped on the nearer of the two tusks, the elephant raised his head, and Nakula scrambled around to back of the neck.

Nakula dismounted again, gave a command, and Rudra wrapped his trunk around the boy's waist, lifted him high, and deposited him on the elephant's neck.

"One more way," said Nakula. He went to the elephant's rear, grabbed the tail, and using it as a rope, walked hand over hand up a back leg until the boy could grab the edge of the blanket and scramble on top.

Then Nakula showed him how to straddle the huge neck, how to place his feet in the exact position so that he could use them to signal

Rudra. Pressing hard with both big toes told Rudra to "go." Pressing with the left big toe told Rudra to "turn right." Poking Rudra with both heels told him to "stop." And so it went.

Although a couple of men would be going on the journey to cut sufficient fodder to satisfy the animal's immense appetite, the two elephant keepers gave Jimuta a continual stream of advice on what to feed Rudra and how often, as well as how long to let him rest, what to do if he should become ill, how to chain him under various conditions, and other assorted knowledge. Despite a retentive memory, Jimuta felt his mind strained to its capacity by trying to absorb so much in so little time.

In the evenings, before the elephants were fed, several of the mahouts always gathered in a corner of the barn yard before a small stone image of Ganesha, the god with the head of an elephant and the body of a man, who was also the son of the great Lord Shiva. Jimuta would watch while some of the older drivers placed tiny offerings of food and flowers in front of the image and chanted prayers.

When the elephant drivers sat around the fire every evening, Jimuta listened to the conversations with great interest, but little was said of immediate use to him. None of the drivers seemed inclined to offer him helpful advice; indeed, they ignored him. When they did look at him, he was sure it was with a mixture of amusement and annoyance. Clearly they considered it absurd for someone so young and inexperienced to take a tusker on such a long journey by himself.

He had the impression they felt insulted that anyone would presume to acquire in a month the expertise that had taken them their entire lives to accumulate.

Jimuta wasn't so sure they were wrong.

After remarking upon Rudra's gigantic size, Jimuta learned that elephants had castes just as did people. An elephant's caste was determined by his physical features. Uttara informed Jimuta that Rudra, with his great girth and length, his tawny eyes and tusks, his dignified demeanor, was of the *bhadra* or "noble" caste, suitable for use by royalty. That fact made Jimuta even more impressed by the huge animal.

With every waking moment packed with details to learn and exercises to practice, the time passed as fast as a tiger streaking after a deer. By the week of the departure from Mangarh, Uttara and Nakula were both surprised at how much Jimuta learned in such a short time. "I think you must have been an elephant driver in your last life," Uttara told him solemnly. "Otherwise, you couldn't know so much so quickly."

Jimuta flushed with pleasure at the unexpected compliment. He glanced down at his feet, and rubbed the top of one with the sole of the other. His toes had gotten over being raw from contact with Rudra's neck, and were forming calluses on spots that had previously been sore.

Uttara looked about to make sure no one else was near. Then the old man said in a quiet voice, "You must be careful on your journey.

There have been unusual happenings. His Highness the Raja has been visited by more messengers than normal from some of the other rajas. I've heard rumors they're plotting something. Our Raja hates Emperor Ashoka, you know. Our Raja would like to expand the area he rules, but Ashoka won't allow any of the rajas under him to fight each other to gain more territory. I think His Highness would not be sending the Emperor an elephant as a gift unless there was some reason for it we don't understand."

Jimuta frowned. There was so much about the goings on of the lordly ones that he didn't have the knowledge to understand. "But why would I need to be careful, sir? How could I be hurt myself?"

Uttara again glanced about. "I don't know. But I'd hate to see you harmed. So just be watchful."

Jimuta looked toward the Raja's quarters, thinking. "I'll try, sir."

Afterwards, he worried. How could he truly be careful if he didn't know the nature of the threat? What, exactly, did he need to be on guard against?

The day before they were to leave, Kumara Aja, who would command the traveling party, appeared at the elephant stables. The prince was a short, heavy warrior with thick, unsmiling lips like his brother the Raja, and a scar across a smallpox ravaged cheek. The Mugger and several warriors were with him.

Although the prince was the ruler of Jimuta's village and several others, never had Jimuta been so near to him. Jimuta immediately threw himself on the ground and touched the great man's foot.

"Get up," ordered the prince in an irascible voice. Jimuta did so, and uneasily stood next to Rudra. The prince speared Jimuta with a dark look. "You've never ridden an elephant before?" he demanded.

"N—not before a month ago, Your Highness."

Kumara Aja shook his head in disgust and said to The Mugger, "This looks like a fool's mission. But I suppose we have no choice. Be sure you have that elephant ready tomorrow at dawn." He stalked off, followed by his retainers.

The Mugger tossed Jimuta a look of disgust as he left. Jimuta hoped it would be the last time he saw that feared and hated warrior.

But why, he wondered, was Kumara Aja undertaking the journey if he was uncertain about its even being desirable?

There seemed no way to know, at least not yet.

5

At dawn the next morning, the traveling party began assembling in the big courtyard of the fortress. Filled with excitement, Jimuta waited with Rudra and with Uttara and Nakula. The servants who would accompany the travelers either patiently awaited the departure by squatting on their heels, with their bundles of possessions, or else rushed around loading items onto bullock carts or pack asses.

Jimuta still felt far from expert as an elephant driver. Having sole responsibility for the care of a big male elephant that was to be presented to the great King was an intimidating role for someone so young and inexperienced.

And never having been beyond Mangarh, he felt both thrilled and apprehensive at leaving on such a great adventure. He had promised his uncle and aunt to return some day, but he had no idea when or how that might happen, because he had no idea what would occur in Pataliputra, or on the long journey to that far off legendary city.

Jimuta felt at the little bag tucked into his waist cloth. It held the few small coins that were left from his first wages as a mahout. He'd given most of the money to his uncle to help the family. It was not very much, but it was the first he'd ever earned.

Eventually, horsemen thundered into the yard. The Mugger was leading them. Jimuta felt a sinking feeling in his stomach. Surely the feared officer would not be going on the journey?

The Mugger dismounted and began stomping about shouting orders at whomever was nearest to him at the moment. Eventually he noticed Jimuta. "Farm boy!" came the loud, deep voice.

Jimuta hurried to the warrior.

The cold eyes fixed on him. "Is that elephant ready?"

"Yes, sir."

"He better be. I'll be unhappy if he causes us any problems. And you don't want me unhappy."

"Yes, sir." It indeed sounded as if The Mugger would be on the journey. Jimuta's already tight stomach contracted into even more of a knot.

At that moment, Kumara Aja, followed by yet more retainers, rode into the courtyard. The Mugger hurried to bow and touch the prince's foot. They exchanged words while the prince looked over the party.

Then the Raja of Mangarh appeared, accompanied by a huge entourage trying to crowd into the courtyard. The ruler conversed briefly in Sanskrit with his brother.

Finally, The Mugger spread the word to prepare to leave. Warriors shouted at each other as they climbed onto their horses, which were nervously shifting about in their places in the confined space.

At last, *ankus* in hand, Jimuta mounted Rudra to begin the journey. He had decided the way he liked best to get atop the elephant was to have Rudra lower his tusks so Jimuta could step onto one. The elephant then raised his head, and Jimuta scrambled around to straddle the neck.

Nakula and Uttara and the other drivers stood by as he bid farewell to them. Some of them smiled knowingly at each other; clearly they still felt he was embarking on a journey that could only be a fiasco.

Kumara Aja set out on his horse, followed by The Mugger and twenty cavalry men armed with bows and swords. Then came Jimuta on Rudra. Jimuta had a rising fear that Rudra would refuse to obey him, that the journey would be over before it even started. But Rudra immediately responded to Jimuta's foot command to "go." On Rudra's back, behind Jimuta, were strapped the elephant's blankets, chains, buckets, and other gear. A caparison and a howdah and a ladder were carried separately in a wagon.

The elephant's ankle bells jangled in time to his steps. The two fodder cutters, wiry brothers in their mid-forties in age, walked in back of Rudra, carrying their sickles, knives, and personal belongings. Then came the two dozen or so bearers and cooks. Ten creaking bullock carts carried cooking equipment, tents, bedding, and other supplies.

By chance, a merchant's caravan headed east was camped at Mangarh, and the prince, who had been no further than Bairat (less than a fifth of the distance to Pataliputra) had decided to accompany the experienced travelers. At the camping area outside the town, Aja's party joined the caravan, which was made up of perhaps a hundred two-wheeled carts, narrow so as to negotiate the tracks which were often little more than heavily traveled paths. Soon the entire column got under way with a squeaking of the large wooden wheels and shouts of drivers to their bullock teams.

As the procession passed over the rise between the low wooded hills, Jimuta took a last look at the fort on its elephant-faced ridge and at the town below, golden in the early morning sun. Would he ever see this place—and his family—again?

The road descended, and his home valley was lost to view. Although excited by the prospect of the journey, he felt quite alone, even with Rudra as a companion. The prince and his men paid no attention to Jimuta once they were on their way. The dust kicked up by the warriors' horses was unpleasant, but somehow it didn't seem so bad high up astride Rudra's neck.

Jimuta realized he had the best vantage point of anyone in the caravan. From his height he could see farther, and somehow the landscape was different, looking over walls and down on bushes and fields and houses and people, rather than seeing them more or less at their own level.

And in spite of his apprehensions about the journey and about being in charge of Rudra, riding astride such a huge beast gave him a feeling that was unusual and strange: a feeling of being much more powerful, almost invulnerable. It was as if nothing could harm him up here, as if the animal's strength and size had somehow become his own.

When the caravan reached the plains, the road angled northeasterly, paralleling the Pariyatra hills, the long, broken range of small mountains that stretched from horizon to horizon in both directions. Rudra plodded along in the dust, apparently undisturbed at the thought of leaving the place that had been his home. On either side lay fields of sick-looking winter wheat. Occasionally groups of men could be seen working to deepen a well, or carefully hand-watering a row of plants, or resting in the shade of a mango grove. High overhead, hawklike kites glided in wide circles around the blue immensity.

The caravan halted for the midday meal by the bed of a stream. The channel was mostly dry, but small pools held sufficient water for Rudra and the bullocks and horses to drink. Rudra happily began pulling up tufts of grass from the edge of the stream bed with his trunk, knocking the dirt from the roots, and thrusting the stalks into his mouth.

Jimuta assumed he would eat with the fodder cutters and the other servants. But to his great surprise, Shantanu, the middle aged trader in charge of the caravan, strolled by and invited him to share a meal. Shantanu was a big man with a broad, pleasant face and a heavy gait when he walked. Jimuta instantly liked him. But why would a wealthy merchant, the leader of the entire caravan, show any interest whatsoever in a young elephant driver?

Thrilled, but also uneasy over such an unusual invitation, Jimuta followed Shantanu to where a cook had laid out a lunch of cooked lentils and bread on a cloth on the ground. After checking to assure himself that he could keep watch on Rudra, Jimuta sat down where the trader indicated. "Please eat all you'd like," Shantanu said. "I'm Buddhist, so I don't take meat, but my cook is quite accomplished."

Following the trader's lead, Jimuta broke off a piece of bread and used it to scoop up some lentils. They had been cooked with an unfamiliar spice, and he found them delicious. He could not help but remember that his own family was probably without food for any meals other than supper, as they would sparingly ration the grain he'd brought.

Shantanu apparently loved to talk. Jimuta noticed that Shantanu's highly arched eyebrows and open facial expression gave the impression he had asked a question even when he hadn't. "I'm from Kashi," he told Jimuta with no prompting. "My family have been traders there for hundreds of years. In fact, one of my ancestors gave the funds for the Buddhist monastery at Mangarh. Every few years I travel all the way from one coast to another, but this route through Mangarh is my specialty. I bring rice, spices, lac, sandalwood, to the west. Sometimes gemstones, too. To the east I carry wool from Kashmir, saffron from the hills, salt from the Salt Range. Sometimes dates and almonds. Even gold."

When the trader paused in talking, Jimuta, still not at ease, searched for something to say to such an important man. He finally asked, "How long do you expect our journey to take, sir?"

"Normally, it's a little over four weeks to Kashi, and then another three or four days to Pataliputra. If we get a lot of rain it can slow us down, but that's unlikely this time of year."

Jimuta asked a question that had been bothering him. "Sir, how likely are we to run into bandits?"

Shantanu laughed good naturedly. "You've probably heard a lot of stories about them. Robbers are mainly a problem in the wilderness areas, especially where there are rugged hills or ravines for them to hide in. But the entire route we'll be traveling is ruled by the Mauryan King. Ashoka has all the highways patrolled. He doesn't tolerate bandits." He smiled broadly at Jimuta. "We traders love him. Of course, his taxes aren't light, but they're no worse than anyone else's. At least we get something for our money with him."

When they both had finished eating and had washed their hands, Shantanu asked, "Would you like to see some samples of the wool I'm carrying?" Not waiting for an answer, he signaled his servant, a chubby, smiling, fast-moving man. "Agastya, get the wool samples." The man went to Shantanu's cart and came back with a large bundle. Shantanu withdrew a piece of cloth and said, "Feel this! It's fine goat's wool."

Jimuta fingered the fabric. "It's so smooth and thin, sir."

"Exactly! Now feel this. See how much heavier? It's sheep's wool. And this yak's wool is the heaviest of all."

Shantanu sent the samples back to the cart. He looked intently at Jimuta, and his tone changed. "So you're driving that elephant as a gift for King Ashoka."

"Yes, sir."

"Hmm. Any idea why your Raja is sending the gift?"

"No, sir."

Shantanu eyed him for a time. "I see. Well, no matter. I was just curious." The trader stood. At that signal, the drivers and servants in his caravan also rose. He went to take his place on the seat beside the driver of the lead bullock cart, while Jimuta remounted Rudra.

Again, the elephant resumed his place in line and lumbered along as if he knew exactly what he was supposed to do. Jimuta's confidence grew—at least there shouldn't be any problems with the routine marching. "I never would have expected the leader our caravan himself to invite me to share his meal," he murmured to Rudra. "We've barely left Mangarh, and already something so different has happened!"

Rudra raised his trunk and let out a raucous blast of air, which Jimuta took as Rudra's way of showing he understood the excited tone, if not the exact words. Jimuta continued to wonder about Shantanu's unusual invitation, but he think of no reason for it that made sense.

Peacocks scurried into the brush or the fields to get away from the route of the procession. A flock of small green parrots took off from a grove of trees, wheeled about overhead, and then returned to their resting places. At a well, camels and cows had gathered to drink from the adjacent trough.

The caravan passed numerous clumps of tall, plumy *kucha* grass, good for thatching roofs, and scattered *khejari* trees. At the base of a huge banyan tree was a tiny shrine to Lord Shiva, the stone *lingam* dabbed with red powder by worshipers. In the distance, a village of thatch-roofed houses slept in the pleasant warmth of the afternoon winter sun.

The caravan pitched camp at the "cow dust time," so called because it was when cowherds brought their animals in from pasture, hooves stirring up dust that caught the golden orange rays of the setting sun. Shantanu had selected the camping spot because of the grove of sheltering mango trees, and because of a deep hole in the nearby river which would provide water for drinking and bathing and for watering the animals.

The drivers arranged the carts to form several circles and unhitched and tethered the bullocks. The carts then rested with the rear ends on the ground and the yoke shafts high in the air. Within the circles the drivers and servants built their cooking fires.

Jimuta rode Rudra a short distance downstream and began bathing him. "How did you like our first day of travel?" He asked his big friend. Rudra eyed him and rumbled pleasantly. Jimuta took that to mean the elephant was reasonably content. "It's exciting!' Jimuta told him. "Especially meeting Shantanu. But I'm tired." He finished the bathing more quickly than usual, then tethered Rudra to a large mango tree, beneath the thick, leafy canopy. The two fodder cutters approached and dropped their bundles of grass and branches. Rudra began eating.

Jimuta was astonished when Shantanu again invited him to share a meal. As night fell they squatted before a small camp fire, blankets wrapped around their shoulders, their faces illuminated by the flickering glow against the surrounding darkness. Jimuta could hear the elephant happily breaking up branches and munching them. Occasionally a bat swooped overhead, barely glimpsed in its swift passage through the dark.

Jimuta still could not understand why an obviously wealthy trader would have any interest in him. He knew from hearing comments about the Buddhists in the monastery near his village that followers of the Buddha had no caste distinctions. But still, for an older, worldly man of the merchant class to even notice an ignorant farm boy was beyond his comprehension. "I have two daughters, but no son," Shantanu mentioned, his eyes turning momentarily sad in the firelight. So Jimuta wondered if this fact, coupled with the merchant's love of talk, explained his attentions.

When Shantanu found out that Jimuta was going to remain in Pataliputra, he informed him, "The language spoken there is rather different from your own. You should learn the Magadhi dialect so you can talk to people once you get there."

"How could I learn it, sir?" Jimuta was vaguely aware of other ways of speaking, such as that of the Bhils back in the hills, but everyone he knew spoke exactly the same tongue.

Shantanu waved his hand in dismissal of the matter. "You learn fast and have a good memory. I'll teach you some. It will pass the time."

"I'd like that, sir. But won't it take a long while to learn?"

"Oh, you won't be able to speak like a native Magadhan, not by the end of our journey. But there are enough similarities to your own dialect that you should be able to carry on conversations."

"I'll do my best, sir. But—why would you do this for me? Won't it take a lot of your time?"

The trader laughed. "Time is something we have plenty of on this journey. I've traveled this route so often, I know every rock and tree along the way. It will be good to do something different."

"I'm grateful, sir."

"The King and his highest officers speak Sanskrit among themselves, just like your own Raja and Kumara Aja when they're talking with other nobles. But you shouldn't need to know any of that since you won't be in such high circles."

"I'm sure I won't!"

Shantanu laughed. "Actually, any men who have the ability can rise quite high in Ashoka's government, regardless of their caste or how poor their family was. So it's quite different from the way your own Raja rules. Still, you're probably unlikely to need Sanskrit."

Jimuta tried to grasp the idea that a man could acquire a high position without having been born as a Brahmin or a Kshatriya or into a wealthy family. It seemed so improbable, he wondered if Shantanu might be exaggerating. Ever since he himself had been born there had never been any question but that, if he did not starve to death or die from illness as a child, he would always be a low caste farm worker. It was only a moment of good fortune granted from the gods, an extremely rare event, that had enabled him to leave his home and drive an elephant. The trader was saying, "There's one word you should know right now. Have you learned *'Apehi'* yet?

"No, sir."

"You may need it in one of the cities on the way. If you have to make Rudra move fast, and there's danger to people who might be run over by him, you should yell, *'Apehi! Apehi!'*—'Get out! Get out!' It's the same thing a chariot driver would shout. Then you won't be punished if someone is injured because they didn't move out of the way."

"That's easy to remember."

Jimuta looked about the camp. All around, men squatted by their fires, trading stories. Bullocks contentedly chewed their grass.

Overhead, through the haze of smoke from the campfires, and beyond the canopies of the trees, a multitude of stars adorned the black sky. Jimuta easily picked out his favorite constellations: the Deer's Head, and the Six Foster-Mothers. Across the heavens flowed the milky ribbon of the celestial river Ganges.

When he lay down near Rudra under the mango tree to sleep and wrapped his blanket around himself, he was exhausted. From a life in the farming village in which virtually nothing changed from day to day, he had plunged into a life in which it seemed everything changed moment by moment.

He was aware of Rudra's huge dark bulk nearby, somehow a comforting and protective presence. Jimuta fell asleep to the pleasing sounds of the elephant chewing on branches.

The next morning, the air was crisp but clear. Shantanu invited Jimuta to share breakfast. "This is the season to travel!" the trader said, looking about the cloudless sky with obvious pleasure. "I love being on the road in the winter. It sometimes rains enough to settle the dust, but seldom enough to make the roads impassable. The nights are a little colder than I'd like, but the mild days make up for it."

When Jimuta had finished honoring Lord Ganesha and was preparing to mount Rudra, The Mugger's manservant, a sour faced, scraggly bearded, unusually tall man named Darsaka appeared. "His honor wants you. At once!"

Jimuta's stomach contracted into a knot and his mouth went dry. He cleared his throat. "Yes, sir."

He followed the servant to where The Mugger stood, inspecting the blade of his sword. The officer did not bother to look at him. "Farm boy! You've been talking to the trader."

Puzzled—and worried over what he might have done that he shouldn't—Jimuta swallowed, and replied, "Uh, yes, sir."

"Why could he want to talk with a stupid boy?"

"I don't know, sir."

"What could you possibly say that he'd care about?"

"I—I don't know, sir. But I have a lot of questions, and he doesn't seem to mind answering them."

"Hmm. Very odd. You can't know anything useful. I just don't understand why he'd pay any attention to you." The Mugger sheathed his sword, and speared Jimuta with the usual cold look. "If he talks to you again, find out about his business. Report to me what you learn." He gestured toward Darsaka. "You can tell my man, and he'll pass it on to me."

"Uh, yes, your honor. But..."

"What?" snarled The Mugger.

Jimuta wanted to ask why the warrior was so interested in the trader, but he quickly realized it wasn't his place to question such an exalted person. Instead, he said, "Shantanu talks quite a lot, sir. How will I know what's important to you?"

The Mugger scowled. "Don't tell the trader this—or anyone else, if you value your skin. His Highness the prince and I want to know what the merchant's business was in Mangarh. He didn't trade any goods there, but he still visited some men in the fort and in the town. I want to know why. And report to me about anyone else he speaks to on this journey. Anyone besides his own drivers and servants. And that's all you need to know!"

Jimuta again swallowed. "Yes, your honor."

"Now, get that elephant ready to move."

"Yes, your honor."

Once again, Jimuta grasped his *ankus*, mounted Rudra, and soon the caravan set out. This early in the morning, mist still hung in the depressions. The constant rhythm of Rudra's ankle bells provided a pleasant, lulling sound. Jimuta had heard that many drivers slept while riding astride the necks of their elephants. But his own mind was too active. Why did Kumara Aja and The Mugger want him to find out those details of Shantanu's business?

Jimuta liked the trader, and the idea of reporting on him bothered him greatly. But how could he disobey the prince's and The Mugger's commands?

Maybe, he thought, he could just give a general report, not including any details that might hurt Shantanu. But he knew so little. Could he report something that might betray Shantanu without even knowing it?

Abruptly the elephant stopped.

Startled, Jimuta signaled with his feet for Rudra to continue.

Instead, Rudra backed up. Jimuta glanced behind, and to his consternation he saw that the entire line of carts was coming to a halt, their progress blocked by the elephant. He frantically signaled Rudra. The elephant had his head down, and paid him no attention. Jimuta grabbed the goad. "Rudra!" he called loudly. "Rudra! You must keep moving!"

Just then, Rudra raised his head, and his trunk curled backward so the tip was directly before Jimuta's face. Gripped by the flexible finger on the tip of the trunk was a small cloth bag. Puzzled, Jimuta took reached up and took it.

Rudra's ankle bells jangled as he resumed his march.

The bag looked familiar, and it felt like it contained coins. With a sudden pang of anxiety, Jimuta felt at his waist. His purse was missing. It had apparently fallen to the ground. Rudra had realized the fact and stopped to retrieve it.

Grateful and relieved, Jimuta rode for a time in amazed silence. "I'm sorry, Rudra," he said at last. "I should have known you wouldn't stop without a good reason. It would have been terrible if I'd lost all our money!" At the next halt, he obtained a clump of raw sugar from Shantanu's cook and fed it to Rudra, with many pats and strokes, as a small reward.

Jimuta was especially interested in the travelers his caravan met on the road. He would scrutinize their faces, their clothes, their mannerisms, trying to guess their personalities and their purpose in journeying—all from what little information he could glean during the short time they were close enough he could examine them.

There was a band of four Buddhist monks heading for who knew where; undoubtedly they had spent the previous rainy season in a monastery some months' walk in the direction from which they were walking. One of them looked joyous, one looked glum, the other two somewhere in between.

A lone ascetic, naked except for a brief loincloth, approached with a long, loping stride, a cloth bundle slung over his back. From under a matted mass of hair, and above an unkempt beard, poked a pointed nose with a mole on one side. His eyes closely examined the caravan as he passed, especially Shantanu's cart, which was the most finely crafted one. Jimuta guessed the man hadn't been a *sannyasin* for long, as he hadn't yet acquired the emaciated appearance of most of those ascetics who walked all day and ate only what they could beg from the villagers.

They met another caravan, laden with cotton and silk fabrics and with teak and ebony logs. Both rows of carts had to slow to ease past each other on the narrow track, so it was quite some time before Jimuta saw the last of the other vehicles.

At the midday halt, The Mugger strode over to where Jimuta was tethering Rudra. "Can that elephant go any faster?" he demanded. "His Highness is getting annoyed." He glowered fiercely.

"Only—only for a short time, your honor. And he'd have to rest afterwards."

"Are you sure? You've never traveled with one before!"

"Th—this is what the driver Uttara told me, your honor."

The Mugger shook his head. "This caravan's so damned slow, we'll all be old men by the time we reach Pataliputra." Without waiting for a response, he stomped off to rejoin his men.

The terrain changed little that day, or the next. The track was mostly level, cutting through the forests or farmlands, occasionally climbing over a foothill that was an extension of the mountain range to the left. They passed small villages of wooden huts, and more fields of wheat and millet, always sparse due to the lack of rain.

At dawn of the fourth day out, Shantanu's cook was preparing the morning meal when a Buddhist monk came by with his begging bowl. Jimuta was watching Rudra devour the ration of fodder. He looked over at the monk, scrutinizing the man as was his habit. The monk had the usual shaven head, and a pointed nose with a mole on it. As the cook was depositing pieces of bread in the bowl, the monk was looking at Shantanu's cart.

That's odd, Jimuta thought. Most monks would stand with their eyes downcast while receiving donations of food. He looked more closely at the man.

He'd seen him before.

The monk strode silently off—any expression of gratitude for the food would have been inappropriate because it was the monk who was doing the favor by giving Shantanu a chance to earn merit through the gift.

Jimuta joined Shantanu at the fire and said, "I don't understand, sir. Two days ago that monk was a *sannyasin* with long hair and a beard. Now his head is all shaved. How can someone become a monk so fast?"

Shantanu stared at Jimuta. "What? You're sure? Those shaved heads make men look so different."

Jimuta gave a nod. "I look at faces carefully, so I don't forget them. And people walk differently—this one takes sort of long, smooth steps. Both times I saw him, he seemed interested in your cart. And before, he was going the opposite direction from us, so he must have turned around and caught up with us again."

Shantanu slowly turned about and watched the monk's retreating back. For some time the trader sat in thought, looking more solemn than Jimuta had ever before seen him. Then Shantanu resumed his usual amiable expression and turned back to his meal. "Well," he said to Jimuta, "if you see him again, would you mind letting me know?"

Still puzzled, Jimuta said, "Of course, sir."

So now he was reporting something to Shantanu, as well as to the prince. Whatever was all this about?

That day and the next Jimuta did not see the *sannyasin* who had so quickly become a monk.

The prince and The Mugger did not again try to increase the pace of travel. But in early morning and late afternoon, the prince and most of his men would ride off into the woods in search of game. They would rejoin the caravan some time later, almost always with a deer or boar or bird that became part of their meals. Jimuta would longingly sniff the aroma of the cooking meat that drifted from their fires, but it had become accepted that he would eat with Shantanu, so always his fare was vegetarian.

He did not really mind, as he was learning so much from the friendly merchant: not only the Magadhi dialect, but facts about the cities they would visit, the customs of the peoples Shantanu had encountered in his travels, the ins and outs of making profits in trading, the politics of the Mauryan empire. Shantanu's knowledge seemed endless.

At last, an appropriate moment came. Casually, Jimuta asked, "And do you find trade goods in Mangarh, too, sir?"

"Not normally," said Shantanu without hesitation. "It's merely a convenient stop on the route. I usually visit an acquaintance or two as I'm passing through, but I haven't found anything worth trading yet."

Later that night, Jimuta reluctantly reported the conversation to The Mugger's servant, Darsaka. The dour man merely frowned and gave a nod. "I'll tell the master. You may go. Tell me if you learn anything more."

Jimuta felt uneasy, and he hoped he would never again hear anything that seemed worth reporting.

Late in the seventh night, the last night before they would reach their first major halt, the district capital of Bairat, Jimuta was awakened by the sound of Rudra, who was swaying and making more noise than usual. The elephant seemed agitated for some reason, and Jimuta rose and went to stroke him and murmur reassurance.

While he tried to comfort Rudra, Jimuta looked about. The camp as a whole was utterly silent. The stars shone brightly overhead, and there was a sliver of a moon. A bat swept swiftly across the sky. Jimuta glanced toward the spot where, perhaps sixty paces away, Shantanu slept in the tent made by fastening hangings to his cart.

The dark figure of a man was approaching Shantanu's tent. The figure quietly lifted a flap of the tent, and raised a hand. Moonlight gleamed briefly on smooth metal: a knife.

Jimuta instantly began to run, but he quickly realized he might get there too late. "No!" he screamed.

The figure froze and looked toward Jimuta. The man's face was in shadow, and even as Jimuta drew close he could not see details.

The man drew back his hand. Jimuta again saw a flicker of moonlight on metal as the knife was hurled at him.

Jimuta threw himself to the side and sensed the weapon fly by. Off balance, he stumbled. Recovering, he saw that the assailant was running out of the encampment.

Shantanu now had burst from his tent. "Sir!" said Jimuta, realizing the trader might not recognize him in the darkness. "That man was going into your tent with a knife!"

Without a word, Shantanu gave chase, and Jimuta saw the flash of a knife in the merchant's own hand. Jimuta ran after. Other men were rising from sleep, and a dog began to bark.

At the edge of the camp, Shantanu stopped. He stood, appearing to listen. Jimuta stopped a few paces behind.

The assailant had disappeared into the forest.

Several men, some of them Shantanu's drivers, gathered round. The trader told them, his voice calm, "Apparently it was a robber. I doubt he'll bother us again."

One of the drivers asked, "Who was on watch?"

Another replied, "I was. I was awake the whole time, and I didn't see a thing. Or hear anything, until the shouting."

"It's a large area to guard," said another. "It wouldn't be hard for someone to sneak in."

Shantanu's manservant Agastya said to the trader, "I'll keep awake the rest of the night by your tent, just to be sure, sir."

"A good idea," said Shantanu. "But I don't think he'll come back this night." He said quietly to Jimuta, "I'd like to talk with you."

They returned to the tent, and when no one else was within

hearing, Shantanu said in a quiet voice, "I owe you much. He might well have killed me. I won't forget that."

"I'm glad to have helped sir. It was Rudra who woke me up."

"Was it! He has my gratitude, also, then. Tell me: did you get a good look at the man's face?"

"No, it was too dark, sir. I have no idea who it might have been."

Shantanu was silent for a time. Then: "Well, as I said, he was probably just a robber. In any event, it worked out well, thanks to you and Rudra. We'd best get some sleep now."

"Sir—I think it was more than robbery. It looked to me like he was trying to kill you!"

After a few moments of silence, Shantanu said, "That's possible. Anyway, he failed. I plan to be more careful in the future, I assure you."

In the morning, before the caravan set out, the Mugger's servant Darsaka appeared and demanded, "Come at once. His Highness and my master wish to speak to you."

Jimuta hurried to where the prince and The Mugger were preparing to mount their horses. Jimuta bowed low and touched Kumara Aja's foot. The prince thrust out his jaw and ordered Jimuta, "Tell me exactly what happened last night, boy!"

Jimuta did. Unable to keep from stuttering, he was brief.

Kumara Aja glared at him. Then the prince nodded to The Mugger.

The Mugger said stonily, "So you saved that trader from being robbed. It *was* a simple robbery. The trader might have been hurt if he'd woken up and resisted. But you have no reason to think someone tried to kill him. Remember that!"

Baffled by the man's insistence, Jimuta responded, "Yes, your honor."

"Good. And also remember your loyalty is to *His Highness the prince*. Stay clear of matters that don't concern you. It could be dangerous to you."

"Begging your pardon, sir. I'm not sure what you mean."

The Mugger glowered at him, then said in an annoyed tone, "I mean that you don't know anything about anything! It could be dangerous if you involve yourself in matters that don't concern you. Like last night. That...robber...can't be pleased at your interference, and he may decide to kill *you* if he thinks you're a danger to his plans."

Jimuta's eyes widened.

The Mugger continued, "You weren't sent to Pataliputra as a boon to yourself. His Highness and I will give you orders, and you will follow them. And His Highness is commanding you not to interfere with anything you don't understand."

"I, uh, think I see, sir." Did that mean the prince and The Mugger didn't want him acting to save Shantanu's life? But that was clearly unreasonable! "Shall I stay away from Shantanu then, honored sirs?" "No!" said The Mugger. "Continue to watch him. But remember, if you're killed, His Highness will be delayed because I'll need to find another elephant driver! And that will make both of us *very* angry."

Jimuta stopped breathing for a moment. His mouth had gone dry, and his voice was hoarse as he replied, "I see, sir, I think. Yes, sir. I'll try to be more careful."

"One more thing," said The Mugger. "His Highness will want to ride the elephant into Bairat. And into all the other cities we visit also. Have the animal ready."

"Yes, sir."

The caravan arrived on the outskirts of Bairat. Jimuta and the two grass cutters decked Rudra in the caparison and fancy blanket and howdah and ankle bells, and then Kumara Aja rode the noble animal in through the city gates, with his horseback Kshatriya retainers and his servants as his retinue. As they marched along, two of the servants beat drums in time with Rudra's footsteps. Bystanders stopped to watch, chattering among themselves about what a grand man the prince must be to be making such an impressive entrance to the city.

Only on festival days in Mangarh had Jimuta seen so many people at one time as in the crowds coming and going at the bazaar. He was impressed at the size of the Mauryan governor's palace, a collection of brick buildings with barrel-vaulted roofs in a large walled compound on the hillside.

Shantanu arranged accommodations at an inn near the outskirts, a large rectangle of low wooden buildings enclosing a big courtyard. After assuring himself that his trade goods were secured in the sheds, Shantanu excused himself to spend an afternoon at the Buddhist monasteries on the hills outside the town. Jimuta led Rudra out to bathe in one of the two small, almost dry rivers flowing nearby. Then, with the fodder cutters, he purchased food for the elephant at the rest house stables.

He tethered Rudra and left the elephant munching contentedly. Then he wandered around in the bazaar, examining the goods for sale: iron knives and plow tips, silver jewelry, carvings of wood and ivory, lengths of cotton and wool cloth, clay toys, confections. There even appeared to be plenty of grain and meat, but Jimuta listened to the haggling between a number of sellers and their disgruntled buyers. He soon realized that the prices were extremely high, and the sellers were blaming the crop shortages.

In late afternoon, he was watching the guards at the city gate as they assessed duties on a peasant's cart coming into the town with a load of firewood. He happened to glance at a side street just in time to see Shantanu with two soldiers who, one holding each arm, were firmly escorting a loincloth-clad ascetic into the gate of the governor's palace. Jimuta stared in fascination. The prisoner was the long-nosed Buddhist monk. But now he had shed his saffron robe and reacquired the beard and the thick matting of hair!

The party went straight into the palace compound. Jimuta was both fascinated and intrigued. Was the ascetic the one who had tried to rob or kill Shantanu? He could think of no other reason for the merchant to be involved in taking the man into custody.

And how could the man regrow his hair and beard so fast?

The hair must not be real! Jimuta knew that sometimes actors in plays wore false hair to help them look more like their roles, but he'd never heard of anyone else doing so. He could hardly wait for Shantanu's explanation.

Then he had an unpleasant thought. Was this the type of incident he should report to The Mugger and Kumara Aja? He definitely did not want to inform the prince about Shantanu's activities. But Aja was his ruler, and Jimuta was probably obligated to pass on the information.

He decided he'd wait, though, until he heard what Shantanu said about the matter. Surely that should be part of the report to the prince.

Back at the encampment, after Shantanu's return, Jimuta hung close to him, eager for the trader to tell him what had occurred. To his immense disappointment, Shantanu did not make the slightest mention of the incident. Instead, the trader talked of the history of the Buddhist monastery he had visited, of the reasons why Bairat was a caravan stopping place, of why the city had been chosen for a provincial capital. Several times Jimuta was on the verge of asking Shantanu about the ascetic-monk. He could think of no reason why Shantanu would not be anxious to tell about a robbery attempt, if indeed one had occurred.

But at last Jimuta decided, with great reluctance, that it was better not to inquire. Apparently Shantanu had a good reason for not discussing the affair.

What about reporting the matter to The Mugger and Kumara Aja? Probably, loyalty required him to do so. But didn't he owe some sort of loyalty to Shantanu, also? And Jimuta hadn't actually learned *anything* from Shantanu himself; Jimuta had just happened to be in a location where he saw something involving the trader. No one else need know Jimuta had seen anything, and maybe the matter had no relevance to Kumara Aja's interests at all. Since Shantanu had made no mention of it, it might have no importance whatsoever.

The reasoning wasn't entirely satisfactory, but Jimuta decided that, this time anyway, he would say nothing to The Mugger.

Jimuta continued to ponder the attempt to kill Shantanu, and the occurrence involving the ascetic who was also a monk. He could think of no reasonable explanation, and to his frustration Shantanu never brought up the matter.

Another five day's travel took them to Mathura, on the banks of the Yamuna River. This was a center of worship for the great god Krishna, who was said to have been born nearby and spent his childhood in the area. Again, Kumara Aja rode Rudra into the city, making a grand procession of entering the gates. Mathura was even larger than Bairat, and its temples and mansions and markets fascinated Jimuta. Again, Shantanu assured him it was nothing compared to Pataliputra.

Here they crossed the Yamuna, the first river that was too large to wade, even though the level was unusually low. Ferrymen took the carts and bullocks and horses and men across on large rafts and on boats.

But Kumara Aja decided to have Rudra swim across, rather than trying to accommodate his huge bulk on a raft. Jimuta, even though he could swim, was uneasy when it came to riding the elephant across the river. He worried that Rudra would submerge completely, in which case Jimuta might be forced to abandon his charge until they reached shallow water.

Rudra set out each new day reluctantly. He had to walk much farther every day than he was used to. All along the way there were new smells, new noises.

He preferred to avoid new things. He'd rather just stay in one place. He liked the comfort of knowing all the smells and sounds, of tasting the same familiar grass and leaves every day (although a treat now and then was nice, too).

He missed the companionship of the other elephants, even though he had never become close friends with any of them.

If he'd known how much he would dislike such a long journey, he might have balked at going. But he hadn't understood just how far he would be traveling. He was used to cooperating with the humans, particularly with his driver, so it didn't even occur to him to refuse to set out on the road. First one day passed, then another. By the time he realized he would be traveling so many days, he was already so far from his old home there didn't seem to be any point in trying to turn around and head back.

Rudra did like his new driver. The young human had been nice to him ever since the first when he'd removed the sharp sticks from Rudra's flesh.

At first it had been hard sometimes for Rudra to understand what the new driver wanted him to do, but the boy had gotten much better now at giving directions.

He still thought a lot about how he had killed his former driver. Even though it had been an accident, the matter had been very upsetting. Rudra was usually careful about where he put his feet. Even though he couldn't see underneath himself, he usually knew what was below. If he had any doubts, he skimmed the ground with the tip of his trunk so it could tell him what was there, just like when he had picked up that tiny bag and given it to his new driver. He had trouble accepting that he could have accidentally stepped on something so large as a man. Especially his own driver.

It must have been because there were just too many things going on at one time. That was one of the things he didn't like about wars. They confused him and upset him. He didn't like to hurt anyone, and lots of men and elephants got hurt in battles. Rudra liked it much better when things were quiet and he easily could be aware of everything that was going on. Then he could also think his own thoughts without being distracted.

Even though he would have preferred to stay in one place, in a way, he was now getting used to the traveling. At least all the new smells along the way did provide some distraction.

Rudra liked to eat. It often wasn't easy to do that while traveling—his driver got impatient if he stopped or tried to leave the road to nibble on some bushes. Sometimes Rudra could raise his trunk and grab some leaves off a tree branch overhead, but usually they were out of reach on the sides of the road.

So Rudra got the idea of saving a bundle of some of the dried grasses from his morning meal. He would curl his trunk around the bunch and carry it for quite some time, occasionally thrusting it into his mouth to nibble, until at last he had consumed it. He would then have to wait until the next stopping place before he could eat any more.

The travelers frequently came to streams which they had to cross. Rudra didn't mind wading across the little rivers. He took his time, feeling each step, making certain the bottom was solid enough to hold his weight.

Then they came to a big river, one that was too deep to walk across. He got to swim when he reached the deepest part, in the middle. He enjoyed it because he got all wet. Sometimes when he was in deep water he would swim completely under the surface, with only the end of his trunk sticking out for air. But this time he was careful not to go all the way under, as he was sure his driver wouldn't like it. He swam so the water never reached his driver's head, and soon he felt the firm bottom underfoot.

Whenever he wasn't crossing rivers, he had to walk and walk and walk. This got tiresome.

By the end of each day his feet would be starting to get sore. But the men seemed to know just when he was getting to the point of thinking about refusing to go further. They would stop for the night, and Rudra's driver would bathe him and let him play in the water for a time. Then his driver would feed him as much as he wanted to eat. Rudra always felt much better afterwards.

By morning his feet had always recovered. And although he would rather not start out on those long all-day walks, he always did so. He didn't understand why he needed to travel so much, but he assumed the men must have their reasons. So long as they did not try to make him walk to the point of hurting or exhausting himself, he would do as they wished.

Especially so long as he always got bathed and fed at the end of the day.

The caravan was traveling easterly and somewhat southerly on the Royal Highway, over the broad, flat plain between the Yamuna and the Ganges Rivers. On both sides lay farmlands, tinged green with winter wheat or dotted yellow with mustard. "The crops aren't as lush as usual because of the drought," Shantanu told Jimuta at one of their halts. "Even with the rivers nearby, I can see there hasn't been enough water."

"They still look better than in my own village," Jimuta replied.

Shantanu said, "The King's revenues are down, since they come from a share of the crops. You can tell the highway's not in as good repair as usual."

To Jimuta, the highway was so far superior to any he had before seen that he had difficulty seeing any defects. The broad road was elevated above the surrounding land to provide good drainage, and the imperial government had set milestones showing the distances to the next major towns. Every few miles there were wells for the use of the travelers, and rest houses. The government had planted shade trees virtually the entire length of the route.

The caravan rested a day in the prosperous commercial center of Koshambi. Then, two weeks after Mathura, the travelers reached Prayaga, at the confluence of the Yamuna and the Ganges, a major pilgrimage spot because of the joining of the two sacred rivers. Here Rudra luxuriated in the vast quantity of water flowing by.

Shantanu was now clearly anxious to reach Kashi, only a few days away, where he would spend several weeks with his family before organizing another caravan. As they drew closer to that city, they passed groups of pilgrims walking on foot to bathe in the Ganges at the sacred spot and worship in the temples.

Kashi was the largest and richest looking city of all those they had yet seen. Shantanu told Jimuta that not only had the city accumulated wealth from the countless thousands of pilgrims over the centuries, it had also been the home of the greatest concentration of traders in all the land. Donations from the rich merchant families had built temples and tanks, parks and pavilions, monasteries for monks, ashrams for gurus, and bathing *ghats*, wide stone steps, along the Ganges riverfront.

When they arrived at the inn where the prince's party would stay, just within the walls of the city, Shantanu approached to bid farewell. "You can speak Magadhi well enough now to get along fine," he assured Jimuta. "I'm amazed at how fast you've learned!"

Jimuta shook his head. "I still feel there's a lot I don't know, sir. And you speak slowly with me. Won't the people in Pataliputra talk faster?"

"Be assured, you'll learn more after you get there."

Jimuta was sad at having to part from the merchant, who had become such a mentor to him, almost a true guru. As he struggled to find words to express what he felt toward the man, Shantanu handed him a small pile of clothing items of obviously high quality, tied in a bundle. "If you're to see the King, you need to be able to dress well," Shantanu explained with a smile. "And it's a small expression of my gratitude for your saving my life. As I told you, I'll never forget."

Jimuta took it, speechless.

Shantanu next handed Jimuta a small, carved wooden box. "You'll be seeing King Ashoka personally, you know, when Rudra's delivered to him. It's always appropriate to give the King a present. As a favor to me, would you mind presenting this to the King as your own gift? By the way, the proper way to greet him is to say loudly, 'Victory to the King!'"

"I'll remember that, sir."

"Be sure to hand the box to the King personally—don't let some official relieve you of it." Jimuta wondered about the reason for this last part of he request. But he felt awkward asking Shantanu to explain, and after all the merchant's kindnesses, Jimuta certainly couldn't refuse even if he didn't understand the reasoning. He nodded.

"I *know* we'll meet again!" Shantanu said firmly. He turned and left before Jimuta could respond. Jimuta indeed hoped they would encounter each other in the future, but it seemed so unlikely. How could Shantanu sound so confident about the likelihood?

Jimuta untied the clothing bundle. On top, in individual cotton wrappings, were a silver belt, silver earrings, and a silver bracelet. While not anywhere near the value of the jeweled items Kumara Aja wore, they appeared at least as fine as the best he had seen any of the villagers wear at the Mangarh festivals.

The jewelry lay on a folded turban, of obviously fine quality white cotton. He lifted the top items aside. Beneath lay a wool shawl, and two white waist cloths of fine cotton. He would be a handsome figure, indeed, when he dressed up for celebrations now.

He examined the small teakwood box he was to give the King. It was the size to hold a necklace or a couple of bracelets. Its lid and sides were carved in a pattern of forest creepers.

Curious as to what it contained, he opened the box. It was empty; the inside was lined with a finely woven red cloth. Puzzled, he squinted closely at it. The box itself was probably of a value appropriate for a junior mahout to present as a gift. But why would Shantanu bother with it? And why be so insistent on Jimuta giving it to the King personally?

He scrutinized its every detail, but he could see nothing unusual. It was just a small carved wooden box.

*

Kumara Aja stayed in Kashi only three days, long enough for him and The Mugger and their men to visit courtesans, bathe in the Ganges, and view the bazaars. Jimuta saw as much of the city as he could in such a short time. He wandered through the markets, strolled past the mansions of the wealthy, visited temples, inspected parks.

He took Rudra to the river twice a day. Here, too, the water level was unusually low. But each time he walked down the gray clay bank and entered the waters, he felt a thrill that he should have this experience that everyone in his home village talked about as a goal to reach someday before their deaths, but which few would actually accomplish. Usually, death claimed them before they had saved enough money or could manage to take enough time away from their labors.

The party left Kashi and continued along the Ganges on the Royal Highway. Traffic was heavy on this main arterial of the central part of the empire. Frequently they met merchants' caravans and companies of soldiers.

Four days after leaving Kashi, the great wooden palisade of Pataliputra at last appeared. Their journey from Mangarh had taken five weeks.

6

The size of Pataliputra awed Jimuta: nine miles in length, the wall with its regularly spaced watchtowers seemed to stretch across the entire horizon. Traffic on the highway grew ever thicker as they drew close, with Kumara Aja again riding on Rudra, and his retinue forming a procession.

The King's officials had been informed of their approach, and in honor of the prince and the Raja he represented, a minister from the King's council came outside the city to welcome them, with musicians playing and an escort of cavalry.

Aja's party waited while a palanquin deposited the minister. Jimuta sat stiffly erect, trying to be a driver worthy of an important prince. The ladder was quickly brought from its wagon and Aja climbed down from the elephant. Jimuta watched the prince and the minister embrace and exchange a few words in Sanskrit. Then Aja remounted Rudra, and the minister climbed back into his palanquin. At The Mugger's command, Jimuta nudged Rudra, and the procession crossed a bridge over the moat, one of many such bridges, and entered the main gate.

Guards and customs officials stood aside and observed. Jimuta had the impression that if it weren't for the official escort, the guards would be questioning the party's intentions.

The procession continued down a broad avenue, through the busy marketplace. The colors of the clothing seemed brighter than what people wore back in Mangarh. Everywhere were people, soldiers, cows, horses, elephants. Snake charmers and jugglers and bear tamers were entertaining crowds. Jimuta noticed the *rakshinah*, the police, patrolling in pairs, carrying sturdy bamboo staffs. Leaving the market area and continuing toward the King's palace complex, the party passed through a neighborhood of the barrel-vaulted mansions of the wealthy, where the numbers of people and animals in the streets thinned somewhat. At the corners of many intersections stood piled rows of large pottery jars. Jimuta remembered Shantanu, in one of his many long, detail-filled talks, mentioning that Pataliputra had hundreds of stacks of these containers filled with water for extinguishing fires. The party passed numerous small shrines to various gods, as well as a couple of larger wooden temples.

The King's palace appeared to be virtually a town in itself, surrounded by its own wall, overlooking the bank of the Ganges. Officials directed Kumara Aja and his men to guest quarters, and Jimuta and Rudra to the elephant stables.

Another guard patrolled the entrance to the stables, and he sent a boy to locate the official in charge, who assigned Rudra to the section reserved for transient elephants.

Jimuta was amazed at the size of the establishment, which held literally hundreds of elephants in wooden stalls, divided by the massive posts to which the animals were tethered. Most of the long, high buildings were thatch roofed, but one row, which appeared to house only especially large elephants, had a tiled, barrel-vaulted roof.

"There are so many elephants!" Jimuta commented to the attendant who came to lead them to Rudra's stall.

The man shrugged. "Other stables at the edge of the city hold thousands more. The largest army in the world, it's said."

Thousands? Jimuta found such numbers almost impossible to grasp.

"Don't see many drivers as young as you. Where are you from?" asked the attendant.

Jimuta told him. The man shook his head. "Never heard of Mangarh."

Jimuta gestured toward the tile-roofed section. "Why are those stables so much finer than the others, sir?"

"Those elephants are the King's favorites. The best of everything for them."

Jimuta wondered if Rudra could ever become a favorite of the King. It seemed unlikely, given that there were thousands of other elephants.

"You've been informed of the curfew?" asked the attendant.

"No, sir."

The man shook his head. "Someone should have told you. The city has a curfew at night. The conch will sound six *nalikas* after sunset and again six *nalikas* before dawn. Except in emergencies, you must not be about on the streets during that time unless you have a pass."

"I don't think I'd be out that late anyway, sir."

The man laughed. "Probably not, at your age."

Rudra had never been with so many other elephants at one time. He hadn't realized there could be so many. But it was a comfortable feeling to be among them, especially when he saw that he was the biggest elephant of all.

His driver took him through the winding streets to bathe in the river, and there were even more elephants, lots of them, bathing also. It was almost as if there were more elephants than people in this city, although there were many humans, too.

Rudra liked spending the night again in a building where there were the sounds and smells of lots and lots of other elephants.

In the morning, his driver came rushing in, faster than ever before. He and some other men quickly began dressing and decorating Rudra. Rudra briefly worried that maybe he was going to another field where men would fight other men. But while his driver and the others seemed in a hurry, they did not have the same smells of covered-up worry, or the same loud manner in their voices that men usually did before such an event.

His driver and another man began painting Rudra's forehead and ears while two others hung the bells around Rudra's ankles. Then the men flung the big embroidered, brightly colored pieces of cloth on Rudra's head and back.

A parade! Rudra thought. This was how he was always dressed when he was going to be in a parade. So he would have some fun today!

Rudra's driver quickly led him from the stables. What was happening? If he was going to be in parade, the men always put a big box of some kind on his back for other men to ride in. Why wasn't there any box this time?

To show honor to the delegation from the Raja of Mangarh, the audience with the King at which the elephant was to be presented was set for the next day after arriving.

Jimuta carefully bathed and dressed in the fine outfit given him by Shantanu. When he led Rudra from the stables he held the wooden box that was the gift for the King in one hand, and his goad in the other.

Jimuta waited with Rudra—and with The Mugger and the rest of the prince's retinue—outside the double doors plated with hammered gold. Inside the magnificently carved wooden audience hall, the prince was presenting himself to King Ashoka and offering the gift from the Raja of Mangarh. Jimuta had hoped to be allowed inside to see if the walls of the hall were truly plated with silver and studded with gems. And he'd heard that the King's personal bodyguards were women, who were thought to be more loyal than men. Jimuta hoped to see them for

himself.
 But he was not needed at the ceremony. Although the doors stood ajar, two soldiers blocked the opening, and he was not close enough to see what was occurring within. He wondered if he would have an opportunity to present the King with the box.
 The blast of a conch shell at the door of the hall startled him. He looked toward the sound in time to see the two guards step swiftly aside. A handsome, slender man of around thirty years in age, wearing a richly embroidered shawl and waist cloth and a tall, jewel-draped turban, appeared at the door of the audience hall. Two pretty girls followed closely, one holding a gold fringed white umbrella over him, and another waving a flywhisk. Then came Kumara Aja, several armed women guards, and various finely dressed men. Jimuta knew the first man could only be the great King Ashoka himself.
 "Victory to the King!" Jimuta said, his voice hoarse, and he threw himself to the dusty ground.
 "Up, up!" said the King pleasantly.
 Jimuta unsteadily rose to his feet as Ashoka approached.
 The King walked around Rudra, examining him. All the while, Jimuta was enthralled at being so close to the greatest ruler in the world. King Ashoka's expression was calm and dignified, yet somehow cordial at the same time. Eventually, the King came to stand in front of Rudra's head. He reached out a hand. Instantly, an aide gave the ruler a sweetmeat, which he handed to Rudra.
 Rudra swiftly grabbed the sweetmeat with the tip of his trunk and thrust it into his mouth. Then he again extended his trunk. "Sorry, fellow, no more this time," said King Ashoka with a laugh. Jimuta was able to understand, as the King was speaking in the dialect of the common people of Magadha, rather than the Sanskrit normally used by the royal court. "Obviously the elephant is of the noble caste," the King said to one of his companions. "See the high tusks and the thick neck? An outstanding animal!"
 The King turned to Jimuta and said slowly, "What is his name?"
 "Rudra, Your Majesty," replied Jimuta, trying to control his trembling.
 "You've learned to speak like a native Magadhan. Good!"
 Jimuta could not help smiling in pleasure. To think that the great King had spoken to him, even complimented him! He suddenly remembered the gift and, bowing, held it toward the King. "A—a small token of esteem for you, Your Majesty."
 King Ashoka took it, glanced at it quickly, and nodded. His face kindly, he looked at Jimuta a moment. Then the King turned back to Kumara Aja. "Please tell Raja Balarama I'm most pleased with his gift. Rudra is a magnificent elephant. Truly noble! And the driver seems an astute young fellow."
 Ashoka waited while an interpreter relayed his words to the prince. Then, the King swept back into the audience hall. An official

remained behind long enough to tell Jimuta, "You may return the elephant to the stables."

As Jimuta passed The Mugger, the warrior muttered, "You young fool! Don't you know you never hand anything to the King himself? You always give it to one of his officials!"

Jimuta stepped backward, mortified. He'd committed a serious breach of etiquette! He felt so stupid, so ignorant!

But hadn't Shantanu told him specifically to hand the box to the King and no one else? Why would Shantanu want to embarrass him that way? And the King hadn't seemed upset, or even surprised....

It was most puzzling.

Jimuta assumed in the future he would see the King only from afar, and he turned his attention to learning the routines in the elephant barns.

Kumara Aja and The Mugger and their men remained, sampling the courtesans and other delights of the capital. So far as Jimuta knew, he and they were the only persons in Pataliputra who had ever been to Mangarh. There would still be new experiences in this great city, he was sure, but they could hardly compare with the adventures of Shantanu's caravan and of meeting King Ashoka in person.

Rudra was assigned to a group of elephants, under the supervision of an officer named Rajasena who was the *Padika*, the commander of the ten elephants as well as the accompanying ten chariots, fifty horsemen, and two hundred foot soldiers. Rajasena was a short, husky Kshatriya warrior who examined Jimuta in disbelief upon their first meeting. "You're only a boy. How can you drive a war elephant at so young an age?"

"Rudra's driver before me was killed, and I suppose there was no one else to send, sir."

The commander frowned. "Hmm...I'm skeptical about you having enough experience. But, normally I never change drivers for an elephant. It takes too long to build the bond between elephant and mahout. And you brought Rudra all the way from...where?"

"Mangarh, sir."

"Where might that be?"

"Five weeks to the west, in the Pariyatra mountains, sir."

"A long journey. Well, as I said, I'd never change drivers without a very good reason. Still, a lot of officers will think I'm crazy to have so young a mahout handling one of my animals. Especially when you'll likely go into war. You'll have to show they're wrong."

"Yes, sir. I'll do my best." Jimuta realized he should probably tell the officer Rudra didn't like battles and tended to run away from them. He hated to say such a thing about the elephant, but it was probably something the commander should know. Jimuta opened his mouth, but the officer was already striding off.

Later, Jimuta would occasionally think of saying something

about the matter, but the moment never seemed quite right. And as time passed, he became more and more embarrassed at the thought of bringing the issue up after having waited so long.

The majority of elephant drivers came from forest tribes who specialized in capturing and handling the animals. But with a need for thousands of handlers, there were still many mahouts who, like Jimuta, had obtained positions on other than hereditary grounds. Jimuta soon gained friends who were helpful in rounding out his training.

His favorite was a shy, slight, gray-haired man named Vidura who walked with the mahout's gait. Vidura's large male elephant Gajendra was in the stall next to Rudra. Like Jimuta, Vidura's ancestors had not been mahouts, so he had acquired his knowledge after being hired to help in the elephant stables. But after so many years of experience, he knew a tremendous amount about the animals and could answer virtually all of Jimuta's questions. He lacked a son of his own, and he seemed pleased to informally adopt Jimuta.

"You're so young!" observed Vidura in his thin, reedy voice, as he eyed Jimuta at their first meeting. "I think you must be the youngest of all the elephant drivers."

Jimuta glanced around the stables and saw many boys, some clearly even younger than him, working at various tasks.

Vidura guessed what he was thinking and said, "All those others are just helpers. They clean the stables and help bathe and feed the animals. A few of the assistant drivers are your age, but none of the drivers themselves."

Jimuta explained how he had come to be in his position.

"Ah, I see," said Vidura. "Well, since you're already Rudra's driver and can handle him so well, the officers will probably let you keep the job. But you should consider yourself graced by the gods. All those other boys will have to work for years before they have full charge of their animals."

Vidura had a small green pet parrot named Lakshmi, and he perched it on Gajendra's trunk, about midway down.

"Won't Gajendra move his trunk and frighten Lakshmi?" asked Jimuta.

"Oh, no," replied Vidura. "In fact, that's one way I can keep Gajendra from moving if I want to inspect his skin or his feet for sores. So long as Lakshmi is sitting there, Gajendra won't move at all. He's very careful not to do anything that might scare the parrot."

Jimuta digested this. Then he said, "Rudra seems careful about little things, too. I dropped my purse once on the road. He knew it had fallen, and he stopped and picked it up for me."

Vidura nodded and smiled. "That's quite common. Many elephants will do the same. I once dropped a piece of fruit from my lunch while I was riding. Gajendra gave it back to me. He didn't even try to eat it."

*

Vidura lived nearby with his wife in a row of huts which housed elephant drivers and their families. Like a number of other mahouts without families, Jimuta slept in the stable near his elephant and cooked his meals over a fire outdoors.

The morning after he had met Vidura, he and the older driver were discussing their animals. Two younger boys had come up and stood listening. "Ah," said Vidura. "Here are the helpers I recommended for Rudra. They're the sons of my wife's brother's daughter. She has been widowed for some years, so they work to help feed her and their younger sisters. The older boy is called Devrata and his little brother is Mangala."

Both boys were thin and wore only dirty, ragged waist cloths. Devrata, who carried a leather bucket, was perhaps a year younger than Jimuta. Mangala, maybe two or three years younger yet, held a short handled broom. "What should we do first?" asked Devrata, his pleasant smile revealing a mouth of crooked teeth.

Jimuta's surprise lasted only a moment. He had grown accustomed, of course, to the help of the fodder cutters on the journey, although he had never actually had to try to order them to work. But now he was quick to take advantage of the situation: "As you can see," he said, "the floor needs cleaning. And Rudra needs more grass. After that, you can help me bathe him."

There would be time later for getting to know more about his helpers. First there must be no doubt as to who was in charge.

Jimuta was amazed to learn that the King himself often came around to inspect the elephants. Indeed, the first time Ashoka visited Rudra's stable was only a few days after their arrival.

The King was accompanied by a giant officer who was apparently a personal aide, by the women bodyguards, and by the two beautiful young women who held the royal umbrella and fly whisk. Followed by his entourage, the King strode down the rows of assembled elephants, stopping at first one, then another. To Jimuta's surprise, he greeted both the elephant Gajendra and the driver Vidura by name.

When he got to Rudra and Jimuta, he again halted.

"This big fellow is my generous gift from Raja Balarama," the King observed in the common Magadhi dialect, apparently to no one in particular. He looked at Jimuta, and said, "The elephant is called Rudra. And your own name is Jimuta?"

The astonished young driver said evenly, "Yes, Your Majesty." *How had the King known his name?*

King Ashoka walked all around Rudra, looking him over. "He's a magnificent elephant. I see he's had some wounds, but they've healed well." He stopped and fixed a pleasant but firm gaze on Jimuta. "If I were Raja Balarama, I wouldn't have parted with such a fine bull.

How is the elephant in battle?"

Jimuta hesitated an instant. He knew he should be truthful, yet he should not embarrass Raja Balarama by seeming to disparage the ruler's gift to the great King. "I've never been with him in battle myself, Your Majesty," he said. "I've only been Rudra's driver for about two months."

King Ashoka gazed at him for so long a time Jimuta began to feel uncomfortable. Had the King sensed the evasiveness in the reply?

"You're young to be a driver," the King said at last, still eyeing him.

"I, uh, was very fortunate, Your Majesty."

"Indeed you were. But you must have talent for it, or you wouldn't still be in the job. Rudra would have given you too much difficulty."

Jimuta smiled at what appeared to be praise from the King.

The King's expression remained calm, but his gaze was sharply focused on Jimuta. "You may have to drive him into a battle, you know. Do you think you can handle that?"

"I...think so, Your Majesty. I'll do my best."

At last, Ashoka nodded, and moved on.

Jimuta could scarcely believe the experience had happened. To have the great King speak to him yet again! After the inspection was over, Jimuta commented on the fact to Vidura.

Vidura's smile crinkled the skin below his eyes. "There are thousands of drivers and keepers, but he can recognize most of them."

The amazed Jimuta digested this. Surely the King didn't scrutinize every one of the elephant drivers so thoroughly!

He went over the encounter with King Ashoka again and again in his mind. At the presentation of the gifts outside the audience hall, Jimuta had given Rudra's name in response to the King's questioning. But he had not been asked his own name. How, and why, would the ruler have found out? And why had the King examined him for so long?

Jimuta could think of no good reasons whatever.

7

The days grew hotter as winter gave way to spring, with the festival of Holi. The celebration in Pataliputra was similar in many ways to that in Mangarh, particularly the wild, playful battles in which participants threw colored water and powders on other persons in the streets. But the folk dances in Pataliputra were quite different from those performed by the Bhils, and the Pataliputra festival drew far, far more people—so many it was often difficult for Jimuta to force his way through the densely packed crowds.

The curfew was suspended for the duration of the festivities, and Jimuta stayed out much later than usual the first two nights. As he and a couple of young assistant mahouts ran through the less busy streets on the outskirts of the main bazaar, tossing their pink powders on other revelers, Jimuta thought of his cousins, of his uncle and aunt. They were almost certainly at festivities at Mangarh village this very evening. More than at any other time in the two months since he had arrived in Pataliputra, Jimuta missed his home valley.

The week of Holi passed quickly, and then there was only the routine of caring for Rudra. Jimuta's two assistants were eager workers. Devrata did most of the talking with Jimuta, while little Mangala merely smiled quietly in the background. Like most of the drivers, Jimuta shared in the work of bathing Rudra, but he left the stable cleaning and the feeding to the two helpers.

Rudra had found a friend, a big bull elephant in the stall next to him. The name the men had given him was Gajendra. Gajendra was healthy and strong with cream colored spots on his forehead and ears.

Rudra was particular about his friends and did not make them readily. With other bulls, especially, there was always the need to establish who was boss, and even then they tended to want to stay clear of each other.

But Gajendra was smaller in size, and he readily accepted Rudra's dominance. The two had similar calm, relaxed temperaments. They rumbled for long periods of time, exchanging small pieces of information, stroking each other with their trunks for companionship and comfort.

They often talked late at night, when the keepers and most of the other elephants were sleeping. There wasn't a great deal to talk about, so mostly they just shared their feelings.

Both of them were content to be in the stables, where every need was taken care of. They liked the daily outings for exercise, the daily bathing in the river.

Rudra learned that, like himself, his friend had been captured by men at a very young age, far away in the jungles, and that the men had trained him. He been in the stables here for a long time. It was mostly a good life.

Like Rudra, Gajendra didn't care for the training for war, where the men tried to get the elephants accustomed to loud noises and confusion. And Gajendra didn't like helping men hurt each other. Not only was it noisy and upsetting, but men got killed. Often elephants got hurt or killed at the same time.

Gajendra was glad it had been a been very long time since he'd had to be in a battle.

Rudra told Gajendra of how he had accidentally killed his own driver in a battle.

Gajendra was shocked, but he assured Rudra he could see how

that could have happened. Rudra felt better, now that he knew someone understood.

One morning, The Mugger's glum manservant Darsaka appeared and said to Jimuta, "His honor told me to ensure that you are doing your job as expected."

The surprised Jimuta said, "I, uh, believe so, sir. I'm taking care of Rudra, and driving him wherever he goes."

The tall man scrutinized Jimuta as if trying to determine if he were being truthful. Then he said, "Good. See that you continue. His Highness and the master command that you are not to neglect your duties or do anything that might cause you to be replaced by another driver. And you are to await further orders, and carry them out as directed when you receive them. Any questions?"

"No, sir. Only..."

"What?"

"I—I'm working for the King's elephant corps now. How is it that I'm supposed to follow Kumara Aja's orders, too?"

"Your loyalty is to Their Highnesses, the Raja of Mangarh and Kumara Aja. Never forget that!" Darsaka looked sternly at Jimuta. "It could be dangerous for you—and for your family—if you fail to follow the prince's orders. My master said to tell you that if you do anything disloyal, he'll visit your family in the village and punish them. He said you have an idea what that means."

Jimuta wet his mouth. "I'll do my duty, of course, sir."

"You'd better." The man stared hard at Jimuta. "His Highness and my master are leaving tomorrow for Mangarh. However, don't assume you can ignore their orders. They'll be back here, and they will expect your complete obedience to whatever they tell you to do."

"Yes, sir."

"I'm also instructed to tell you that you'll be watched while we're gone."

"Sir?"

'Someone will be keeping an eye on you and reporting to us. Never forget that."

"Uh, yes, sir."

The manservant left, and Jimuta peered after him. What orders might the prince or The Mugger possibly give? And what if their orders conflicted with the orders given by his superiors in the elephant corps?

And why the warning, a threat really, about the dangers to him and his family if he failed to obey the prince?

And why was he being watched? By whom?

Anyway, he felt a definite relief at their leaving Pataliputra. Hopefully they wouldn't be back for an extremely long time.

Another week passed.

At first, Jimuta couldn't get out of his mind that someone was supposed to be watching him. He would casually glance behind as he walked about the stables, or he would look about when his was eating his meals, hoping to catch someone staring at him.

So far as he could tell, no one paid him the slightest undue attention. Gradually, he tired of trying to spot the watcher. He began to wonder if Darsaka had even been telling the truth. After all, why would anyone want to go to the trouble of watching someone so unimportant as he clearly was?

Then, completely unexpected by Jimuta, Rudra was selected as one of the elephants in the King's own entourage on a visit to a hunting preserve outside the city.

Gajendra hadn't been chosen for the outing, so Vidura helped Jimuta decorate Rudra with the painted designs. With the help of Devrata and Mangala, they draped the caparisons on the elephant and hung the ankle bells. "I wonder why Rudra was picked," mused Vidura. "Normally the elephants in this barn aren't used by the King himself."

Jimuta was wondering that too, but he merely shrugged. "Maybe it's because Rudra is fresh in the King's mind." The reason probably didn't matter; he was just glad his elephant had been selected.

When Rudra was ready, Jimuta led him to the stables where the elephants assigned for the King's personal use were housed. There he watched as attendants hoisted a gilded howdah onto Rudra's back. The howdah, with its rounded roof, golden fringe, and soft bolsters, was similar to the one Jimuta had seen the Raja of Mangarh ride in, but this one was larger.

Jimuta climbed to his usual position astride Rudra's neck, and an official led them into a position fourth from the front of a line of two dozen or so other elephants. Attendants placed a ladder against Rudra's side. The line waited some time before conch shells sounded, and the King's musicians appeared around the corner of the stables. Everyone standing on the ground bent to touch the earth as King Ashoka approached following the musicians. The King strode to the lead elephant, which he mounted by climbing the golden ladder to the howdah.

The big officer who always accompanied the King on inspections of the elephant corps strode over to Rudra's ladder and climbed up and seated himself in the howdah. Jimuta had learned before that the man was Siddharthaka, the King's own charioteer and favorite companion. "A good day for a hunt, driver," commented Siddharthaka in a deep voice.

Surprised at being spoken to by a man of such exalted rank, Jimuta turned and responded merely, "Yes, your honor." He glanced briefly at the officer's face—somewhat ugly, he thought, but friendly-appearing, in spite of the man's status as a Kshatriya, the class of warriors and princes.

The procession began when the King's musicians marched across the open square, playing loudly to alert people of Ashoka's coming. The musicians were followed by attendants swinging censers of sandalwood incense to perfume the air for the King. Women body-guards on horses formed a screen along each side of the King's elephant.

Outside the palace grounds, as the party neared the main bazaar, crowds of people formed to cheer the King. Siddharthaka ignored them, and instead questioned Jimuta.

"Where are you from, driver?"

"A village near Mangarh, your honor. In the Pariyatra hills."

"How did you get to be a driver? And to come so far from your family?"

Jimuta was puzzled as to why a confidant of the King could be interested in a mere novice elephant driver. But he outlined the events that had brought him to Pataliputra. Whenever he glanced back at Siddharthaka, he saw that the officer's eyes showed interest. When Jimuta had finished, Siddharthaka laughed. "Quite a story. And your Magadhi is almost good enough to pass for a native's!"

Outside the city, the procession passed the shabby bamboo huts of the Untouchables, who were not permitted to live within the walls, and then turned onto a side road which cut through fields of mustard being harvested. Siddharthaka entertained Jimuta with his own stories about how he and the King had fought the King's own brother for the throne, only a few years previously. Jimuta's grasp of Magadhi was such that occasionally he didn't know a word Siddharthaka used, but almost always he understood the meaning from the context.

Even in his home village, Jimuta had heard stories about the war that had gone on for years before King Ashoka had killed his own brother in combat, thereby consolidating his hold on the vast empire. Jimuta could hardly believe that he, a village lad from so far away, was hearing the story from one who had been at the King's side the entire time. Gradually, the feeling grew within Jimuta that Siddharthaka must be an unusual man, one who paid little attention to status, who would be as comfortable in the company of the workers in a stable or the soldiers in army camp as with the King and his ministers.

Eventually the procession arrived at the large forested area that was the King's hunting preserve. They followed a wide path winding among the trees. The day had grown hotter, so the shade was welcome. "Won't be long before we're eating fresh mangos," said Siddharthaka, gesturing toward a big tree heavily laden with small green fruits. "I can taste them already!"

"Me, too, sir," said Jimuta with a smile. He'd heard the mangos in this area were different from those grown in the Pariyatra region, and he was eager to try them.

The procession halted by a large, elevated wooden platform. Attendants brought ladders, and Ashoka and his guests and Siddharthaka dismounted. Jimuta watched the party climb the stairs to the hunting platform, where attendants handed them bows and arrows. The drivers then moved the elephants some distance away along the path, barely in sight of the platform, so as not to distract the game animals.

Jimuta heard the thumping of many drums far off in the woods as the beaters drove the deer toward the hunters. The sounds gradually became louder, and several times he heard a cheer and laughter from the hunting platform, presumably as one of the shooters hit or missed a target. But he was unable to see what was occurring and so had to wait patiently, as was often the case for drivers.

When the hunt was finished, and elephants were summoned for the party to mount up, Jimuta had yet another surprise. Siddharthaka approached and told him, "The King's switching elephants. He'll ride with me on yours this time."

Jimuta was incredulous.

"A routine precaution," Siddharthaka told him with a wry smile as servants brought the King's golden ladder over and placed it against Rudra's side. "In case someone's poisoned the cushions of his own howdah." By now, Jimuta had heard enough about intrigues in the palace that the information did not surprise him as much as it would have originally.

King Ashoka climbed the ladder to the howdah, followed by Siddharthaka and the flywhisk and umbrella girls.

While they were traveling back to the capital, Jimuta could hear the King talking casually with Siddharthaka. Rudra was now the first elephant in line, directly behind the servants swinging the censers, and the aroma of sandalwood was strong. The midday sun was hot, and Jimuta was aware of the yak tail flywhisk swishing back and forth as the servant girl tried to keep the ruler cool.

Then, the King spoke to Jimuta: "My friend is impressed with you, Jimuta," he said. "And so am I."

The comment threw Jimuta into pleased confusion. He half turned toward the King, whose eyes seemed amused. At last Jimuta managed, "I'm honored, Your Majesty!" He'd heard it was not proper to turn one's back on the King, so he remained facing Ashoka as best he could while still straddling Rudra's neck.

After a short pause, Ashoka said casually, "You may know I have agents all over the empire, to keep an eye on people for me."

He seemed to be waiting for a response, so at last Jimuta said, "Governors, and such, Your Majesty?"

"Officials, yes. But also, agents you might call spies. People who work for me in secret. I can't be everywhere myself, so I need others to be my eyes and ears."

He again was quiet, and Jimuta said, "I understand, Your Majesty."

Ashoka fixed his gaze on Jimuta's eyes and said quietly, "I'd like you to be one of my agents, Jimuta, if you're willing. It must be kept secret. No one else must ever know your role. But if you do well, you'll be paid well. And you'll eventually receive higher positions."

Jimuta's mouth fell open. He wondered momentarily if he had

heard correctly. An agent for the King himself! Finally, he managed to say, "I—I'm honored, Your Majesty!"

"Then you're willing?"

"I—of course, Your Majesty! Only—" Jimuta broke off, realizing he should not question the King.

"Only, what?" Ashoka grinned at Jimuta's confusion.

"Your Majesty, I'm only an elephant driver. And I've just turned sixteen. What could I do that would be useful to you?"

The King smiled reassuringly. "I don't expect you to provide any information that will shake my empire. But you can listen to what people are talking about. One difficulty I have is that my ministers and generals often tell me only what they think I want to hear. What I need most, Jimuta, is accurate information on what people in all castes are thinking and saying. They're unlikely to guard what they say around a mahout, especially a young one. You can overhear conversations I'd never hear myself. And you're clever enough not to be obvious about it."

Jimuta digested this, then asked hesitantly, "Your Majesty, how did you decide to ask me? How do you know enough about me?"

The King's lips curled in amusement. "Since you're now an agent, I suppose I can tell you. But you must keep it absolutely in confidence! You traveled all the way to Kashi with one of my key spies. He talked with you every day. When he reported to me, he said you'd even saved his life. He said you were unusually fast at learning Magadhi, and he recommended you as a likely prospect. Siddharthaka agreed after his chat with you today."

Jimuta was speechless. So Shantanu was a spy for the King!

King Ashoka said, "Shantanu also informed me that it was your keen observations that led to the capture of an enemy spy from Kalinga."

Jimuta was dumfounded. So that explained why Shantanu had captured the ascetic and escorted him to the governor's palace at Bairat!

The King added, "The report he wrote under the lining of the box you presented me was quite informative. Of course, you didn't know we had agreed one way of sending me a report might be by a box of that type."

Events had moved so fast that Jimuta felt overwhelmed. At last, he managed, "What would you like me to do first, Your Majesty?"

The King laughed. "I'm glad you're eager. For now, just listen. Be my ears in the elephant stables. Every month I want a report. Frank information on what people think of me and my policies, or conditions in my empire. Once a month—or any other time you hear anything you think I should know—go to the house of the courtesan, Satyavati. She'll see that either Siddharthaka or myself gets the information."

A courtesan! Jimuta had always assumed he would see these beautiful, well-educated—and extremely expensive—women only from a distance. Now he would actually be meeting one in person! After some hesitation, he said with forced boldness, "How do I find this courtesan, Your Majesty?"

Siddharthaka replied for the King: "You *are* new in Pataliputra, aren't you? Just ask anyone on the streets. They'll direct you."

"I see, your honor."

In his excitement, it did not even occur to Jimuta that the loyalty demanded of him by Kumara Aja might ever conflict with his new duties for the King. When he did think of it the next morning, it was too late to inquire about the matter, and he eventually decided that, in the unlikely event a problem did occur, he would concern himself about it then.

Also, too late, he wondered if should have told the King or Siddharthaka about the fact that someone might be watching him. He decided he would simply have to be careful, and ensure he wasn't being followed whenever he did something obviously out of the ordinary, such as reporting to the courtesan's house.

8

Vidura was surprised to hear that the King had actually ridden on Rudra. He held some bits of grain in his hand for the parrot Lakshmi to peck at and said, "That's most unusual. But maybe he just wanted a change. And Rudra being so large and of noble caste, he's certainly an appropriate mount for the King."

"Siddharthaka said His Majesty often changes elephants in case the cushions of his howdah had gotten poisoned."

"Well, that's true, so I've heard. But he usually has just a couple of favorite elephants and he changes back and forth between them. Maybe he's looking for another favorite."

Jimuta wished he could tell Vidura another reason—that the King had probably ridden Rudra mainly in order to have a private conversation with Jimuta himself! But he knew he could never reveal that fact. He wasn't even sure Vidura would believe him. He sometimes wasn't sure he believed it himself.

Being a spy was already proving to have its disadvantages. Unlike his job as a mahout, there was no one whom he could talk with about his work as a spy. No one at all to ask for advice.

Jimuta had always learned by observing and by listening. Now he was being paid for it. He'd known that the drought affecting his home village was widespread. Partly because of it, all was far from well in the empire, and much of the talk concerned the crisis. The successive crop failures had brought many rural people to the edge of starvation. Poor crops also meant poor revenues. That meant the King's government had less money to spend on roads, irrigation works, opening up new farmlands—and on its huge army.

One day, Jimuta noticed that Rudra was growing less attentive to commands, less quick to obey. When Devrata and Mangala piled up the grass and branches for Rudra, the elephant started briskly tossing the fodder across the stall, rather than eating.

Jimuta wondered if the giant animal might have contracted some sort of illness, although he could see nothing obviously wrong. He glanced about to seek Vidura's advice, but the driver was not in the stable at the moment. Jimuta resolved to keep a closer watch on the elephant, just in case.

Anyway, it was time for Jimuta's first monthly report, and he was unsure what to say. Surely the King already knew about the problems in the empire! Indeed, Jimuta had heard that the ruler had sponsored great sacrificial ceremonies to influence the gods to bring rains.

Jimuta had also learned, simply by overhearing a conversation, that the courtesan the King had mentioned, Satyavati, held the official position of chief courtesan of Pataliputra. Ashoka himself was her principal patron, although many other important men frequented her house and the girls who lived there. Her mansion was not far from the royal palace, in a wealthy residential area.

Jimuta realized he should not be seen acting unusual in any way when he walked to her house, so he wore his normal cleanly laundered but worn-looking clothes. He was visiting in the heat of late afternoon, when he assumed she would be likely to be at home, but probably also finished with any midday nap. Glancing about frequently to ensure he wasn't being followed, Jimuta approached the service entrance on a side street, just as a servant boy would. A short, broad man, somewhere in his thirties in age, armed with sword and dagger, guarded the gate. "I need to talk with the courtesan Satyavati," Jimuta told him.

The guard examined at him. "Is that so? Your name?" The guard was missing most of his front teeth, so the words, though understandable, came out somewhat slurred.

"Jimuta of Mangarh, sir."

"Your work?"

"Elephant driver, sir."

The guard motioned him through. "You're expected. Go to the main house."

"Yes, sir." Jimuta found himself in a courtyard, with stables along one side, and storehouses on the other. He headed for the door into the house, a tall structure with the typical round-vaulted roofs.

Here another armed guard stood in attendance. "I must see Satyavati herself," he told the man. The guard summoned a boy who must have been ten years of age or so, and sent the messenger inside.

Shortly, Jimuta heard the tinkling of anklets, and an elegantly dressed, extremely lovely girl, perhaps about the same age as Jimuta, came to the door. "Follow me, please," she said in a pleasant voice.

Jimuta stood with his mouth agape, entranced. A few of the girls in his village were comely, but never, ever, had he seen one so beautiful as this.

Perfume lingered to mark the path behind her. He hurried to catch up. He could not take his eyes off the smooth, slender bare back, the rounded buttocks that beckoned through the filmy cotton cloth hanging from her jeweled *mekhala* or waist girdle.

They walked down a teakwood floored hallway and into a large courtyard garden. Here, a woman of perhaps thirty, whose beauty rivaled that of the younger girl, was seated on cushions in a pavilion. At one edge of the raised stone floor, two women musicians, one with a stringed *vina* and another with a flute, played softly. The scent of blossoming jasmine filled the air, overwhelming the more subtle perfume of the girl who had guided Jimuta.

Jimuta desperately wished he had worn the clothing Shantanu had given him; the garb of a poor mahout seemed out of place here. Never before had he seen a setting of such luxury, or women so lovely. The older woman smiled graciously. "Please sit. I'm Satyavati. His Majesty said you'd be visiting soon. What do you have to report?"

Jimuta told her of the talks he'd overheard complaining of high food prices and poor weather. She listened attentively, and he immediately saw that her eyes, though outlined in the customary black kohl makeup, were themselves a striking blue; a rare color in a land of brown eyed peoples.

"That's really all I have," he said, feeling ashamed that he couldn't report more. He was getting much better at understanding Magadhi, but there had still been occasions when people talked so fast he couldn't follow them. He hoped he hadn't missed anything important.

He noticed that the girl who had led him in was writing with a stylus on palm leaf sections. So she knew how to write! And the girl must be taking down what he was saying! It was an odd feeling. Especially since the writing was probably going to go to the King.

"Excellent," Satyavati said, again smiling, with kindness in her incredible blue eyes. "That's exactly what the King wants from you. Soon you'll develop a talent for overhearing things, and you'll learn even more. But for now, that's very good." She paused, and seemingly as an afterthought added, "You're a mahout. What do you hear around the elephant stables in particular?"

Jimuta thought a moment. "Nothing especially important. Everything seems normal, I suppose. I've heard a rumor that the elephants may be fighting in a war. Probably in Kalinga. People say that so long as Kalinga is ruled by King Vadhukha, King Ashoka will be in danger. They say King Vadhukha encourages King Ashoka's vassals to unite in overthrowing his rule, and he also sends agents to try to assassinate the King and his ministers. But no one knows anything definite."

Satyavati appeared deep in thought. "So there are already rumors about a war," she mused. The blue eyes again seemed to bathe him in their warmth. "That's valuable to know. Keep listening for more about Kalinga. When you report again, let me know what you hear. And if I'm not available, you may tell Renuka anything you have for me." She waved toward the young woman with the stylus. "In fact, you'll usually be reporting to her, though I wanted to meet you today since this is your first time here." She examined Jimuta a moment, and then said, "Do you have any questions before you go?"

Jimuta asked, "Do all the King's spies report here to you?"

She laughed. "Not at all. Only a few. You must know that the prime minister, the commander-in-chief of the army, many others have their own spies. But you're special. You're one of a very few who report directly to the King."

"I still don't understand why the King chose me," Jimuta said, shaking his head.

She looked solemnly at him. "His Majesty was told you're both astute and trustworthy. It's true you're youthful, but the King is still a fairly young man himself. He plans far ahead, and he seeks out good men who'll serve him for many years. I'd guess you may not always remain a mahout."

Jimuta was trying to digest the implications of this as Renuka showed him out. Her scent lingered with him long after he had returned to the elephant stables. And he could not get the vision of her graceful, superbly shaped body out of his mind.

9

He was thinking of Renuka when he approached Rudra the next morning to lead the elephant out to bathe. He patted Rudra on the side as usual, and bent to undo the leg chain. Devrata and Mangala stood waiting to help.

The normally docile Rudra let out a blast from his trunk that startled Jimuta. The elephant rumbled and stamped his feet and strained at the chain. He shrieked and trumpeted.

"What's wrong, Rudra?" Jimuta asked, trying to speak calmly.

A mountain of fury, the elephant screeched and pulled at his chain.

Then Jimuta saw the fluid draining from the tiny pit below Rudra's eye. *Musth!*

Rudra tore with all his might at his chain. He wanted to break free, to run away as fast and hard as he could. He wanted to stomp on things, especially anything that got in his way. He wanted to spear something with his tusks, anyone or anything. He wanted to grab trees with his trunk and tear them from the ground. He wanted to bash in doors, to knock down buildings, to trample them into the earth.

He knew his driver was near and was saying something to him, but he didn't care. He just wanted to burst free and run and break things.

He thrust against the ground with all four feet and strained in hatred at the chain.

He was aware that he was now surrounded by frantic, yelling men, but they weren't important.

In the next stall, Gajendra had moved as far away as possible and was watching him wide-eyed, but Rudra wanted nothing to do with him right now.

He just wanted to break free, to run wild, to destroy.

Jimuta screamed for help, even as he was racing to get another leg chain. An elephant in musth should be confined by all four legs. Rudra was held by only one.

Jimuta seized a heavy chain from the pile of extras and ran, the end of the chain whipping up dust where it dragged behind. Devrata and Mangala grabbed other chains. Back at Rudra's stall, Jimuta thrust the shackle pin through the end of his chain, attaching it to the heavy timbered post near Rudra's right rear leg.

Rudra heaved his huge bulk at Jimuta, who quickly dove aside to avoid being crushed against the post. Now to get the other end around Rudra's leg! Normally it was an easy one-man job, but it was virtually impossible with the elephant stomping and constantly lunging from one side of the stall to another. He was reluctant to put Devrata or Mangala in danger by telling them to help.

With relief, he saw that at last aid had arrived, Vidura and three or four other drivers, a couple with their own fetters. Vidura was telling him, "Get the chain around as far as you can! I'll grab the end!"

Jimuta waited until Rudra had finished moving the leg in one direction. Then, he ducked partly under the animal's rear and extended the chain as far as he could. He felt it grabbed and pulled from the other side, and began to scramble backward to safety.

Just then, Rudra shoved the leg backward, hard and fast. Jimuta was aware for only an instant of the thick gray tower flashing toward him.

Then it slammed him, and all went black.

Jimuta painfully returned to consciousness. He heard voices around and above. He opened his eyes, and saw Vidura and another man bending over him. Vidura looked worried. The other man was gently feeling Jimuta's arms and prodding his chest, and Jimuta realized he must be a *vaidya*, a physician.

"How do you feel?" the man asked.

Jimuta squirmed in the dust. His limbs seemed to function. But his head felt as if it had been smashed flat, and he told the man so.

The *vaidya* chuckled. "If the elephant had actually stamped on you, you wouldn't be talking now. His leg was slowed by the chain, so it didn't hit you full force." He looked Jimuta over, had him again move his arms and legs. At last the physician said, "You should rest for a day or two. You have some bad bruises, especially where the chain hit your hip. But I think you'll recover with no problems."

Rajasena, the commander of ten, had been watching. He shook his head. "How could you not know your elephant was in musth?"

"I'd never seen Rudra that way before, sir."

Rajasena sighed. "Well, I knew there were dangers in having someone so inexperienced in charge of an elephant. Still, you'll know better in the future."

"Yes, sir. I certainly will."

Vidura was standing near. "Sir," he said, "I'm glad to help Jimuta with whatever he hasn't learned about elephants. I can see I should have been paying some attention to Rudra as well as Gajendra."

Rajasena gave a nod. "Excellent." To Jimuta, he said, "You have a good teacher. I'm sure there won't be any more problems."

Rudra was in musth for a week. By the time he came out of it, Jimuta's bruises were fading.

Jimuta realized that, through his own inexperience, he had failed to see that Rudra's earlier restlessness was a sign of musth coming on. Rudra could easily have killed him or the two assistants or even others. Once again, the gods had been generous.

Jimuta warily renewed his friendship with the animal. He knew Rudra had not meant to hurt him, that the elephant had been totally under the influence of the musth.

But the driver now had a new respect for his big companion. And he began consulting Vidura even more about caring for Rudra.

Jimuta wanted to wear the fine clothing and jewelry given him by Shantanu to the next meeting at Satyavati's house. However, he knew that some of the other drivers, possibly including Vidura, would see him leave the stables, and he had been unable to think of a good explanation for dressing in his best on a day when there were no festivals.

He disliked keeping so many of his activities secret from Vidura, but he knew he had no choice. Although he was quite sure Vidura could be trusted with confidences, Jimuta had been specifically directed not to reveal his status as a spy to anyone.

And there was good reason for the rule, he had come to realize. Everyone knew there were hundreds, perhaps thousands of spies in Pataliputra. Many of them worked on the side of the King, but many of them worked for Ashoka's enemies—foreign Kings such as Vadhukha of Kalinga, as well as persons at Pataliputra who would rather see someone else on the throne. Since there was no way to be certain who was a spy and who wasn't, the only safe course was to be as discreet as possible.

When Jimuta appeared at the garden courtyard, Renuka was seated on a wide, low swing under the shade of a banyan tree. In the heat she was bare above the long waist cloth and the jeweled *mekhala* encircling her hips. With her toe she gently pushed the swing back and forth.

She saw Jimuta and smiled. His heart beat faster at the thought that he might join her on the swing for their meeting, so close together that their bare arms might sometimes touch!

She stopped the swing. Jimuta tried to ignore his disappointment as she rose, anklets tinkling, and gracefully walked the few paces to the pavilion and ascended the two wooden steps to the cushion-strewn floor.

There, Jimuta joined her, and they seated themselves facing each other. The pillows were so soft that Jimuta felt as if he were sinking through them to the thick carpet beneath. When Renuka gracefully folded her legs beneath her, he noticed how attractive her feet were. Her toenails were shiny and clean and neatly trimmed, and her soles were dyed with thin red lac. What a contrast to the soil-encrusted, roughened soles of the feet of the girls in his home village! She took up her writing materials, looked at him with a smile, and said, "You may begin."

He gave her a self-deprecating grin and said, "I wasn't able to spend quite so much time this month gathering information because of my injuries. But I'll tell you what little I did overhear."

He paused, watching her. He had carefully planned that introduction, and it achieved the result he'd hoped. She looked up at him, her eyes wide with concern. "Your injuries? I hope they weren't serious."

Jimuta shrugged, with just the right amount of casualness, he was sure. "It wasn't much. My elephant went wild with musth and kicked me unconscious. But fortunately he didn't break anything. I'm mostly recovered now."

She smiled and nodded. "I'm glad." She looked back down at her palm leaf.

Warmed by her response, but unsure whether it was due to anything more than ordinary good manners, he began his report.

He had spent much of his time trying to improve his knowledge of elephants by questioning the more experienced drivers and listening to their stories. At the same time, he remained alert for information that might be useful to the King. Now he watched Renuka's slender fingers—so smooth and well-kept—as she manipulated the stylus to write down his words: "People are still complaining about the poor crops. Some mahouts have heard that people in their home villages even say the King's out of favor with the gods—that the gods are sending poor weather to show they're displeased with him."

The scent of the jasmine blossoms flooded the garden. Jimuta's eyes kept returning to Renuka's breasts, following the graceful curves of the pale undersides up to the dark, prominent circles with points in the center. He imagined cupping one of those ripe half-melons in the palm of each hand. Would they feel firm? Soft? Or in between?

"I've heard more talk of war," he continued. "Some people assume we'll fight Kalinga eventually, but probably not for a while." His eyes caressed the contours of her face. He wished he could somehow kiss those lac-reddened lips, so moist from the gentle strokes of her tongue as she concentrated on her writing.

When Jimuta had finished, Renuka raised her head. Her dark, bright eyes seemed friendly as her smile spread to them. "Is that all?" she asked.

He wished he had more to tell her, both to prolong the visit and to impress her with his competence. But he had to answer, "That's all. For this time." He smiled with what he hoped was a combination of sophistication and shared secrets. "Uh, I was wondering," he said, "have you been writing in Sanskrit, or in Prakrit?"

Her own smile broadened. "In Sanskrit. But of course the script is the same." She lay aside her writing materials and rose with a tinkling of anklets and a swaying of lovely breasts. She gave no hint of receiving any messages other than that which he had dictated as she said, "Until next month, then. I hope you continue to heal well. Please be careful of your elephant—he sounds dangerous!"

Jimuta straightened himself. "Oh, really he's not. He's normally quite calm. But once a year he goes into musth."

"I see. Well, until next month then."

On the street, when he was out of sight of the guard at the gate, he tore off his turban and threw it to the ground with all his strength. A couple of people walking by smiled in amusement. He ignored them.

What had he really expected? For Renuka to suddenly offer her time to him free, when rich merchants or nobles no doubt paid hundreds of *panas* for a night?

Eventually he retrieved his turban and shook the dust from it.

Jimuta could not forget her.

He realized he was in an unusual situation. Back in his own village, there would be almost no opportunity to be alone with any girl other than a small child. At some time in the next few years, his family would have begun looking for a wife for him from a family of his own caste from some nearby village.

But in Pataliputra, so far from his relatives, they could make no arrangements for his marriage. And no respectable family would let a daughter roam where he would be likely to encounter her. What did that leave for him besides prostitutes, of whom he could afford only the lowest class? Unless he were to return to his village, he seemed destined to remain unmarried and celibate—and frustrated by his longing for a girl who was completely unattainable.

He also felt disheartened that he had not gathered better information as a spy. He wanted to seek out something that would help the King. And he wanted to be able to tell Renuka something important.

He would be more likely to learn valuable information if he did not limit his listening to the elephant stables. So he began to frequent places where he could overhear conversations without feeling he was conspicuous: the main markets in the city, the riverfront where passengers waited for the ferries and boats unloaded their cargos, the temple courtyards where both pilgrims and residents congregated.

One day, Vidura casually remarked upon Jimuta's frequent disappearances from the stables. "Where do you find to go so often?" he asked. "The other elephant boys say they haven't seen you."

Jimuta had prepared a reply in case of such a question. "I've never been in such a huge city. There are so many interesting places to visit. I want to see them all!"

"Ah, I see," Vidura said. He spoke to the parrot. "You hear that, Lakshmi? He wants to see everything in Pataliputra. That would take years! No wonder he's gone so much."

The parrot tipped its head and eyed her master. Vidura looked back to Jimuta and gave a light laugh. "Maybe you'll get tired of running around the city after a while. I know I did."

"Maybe. I doubt it. Everything is so different from my village. Back home, I never saw anything like those big jugs of water on the street corners for firefighting. It's clever the way the potters make the tops and bottoms so the jars can all stack one atop the other as high as a man can reach, but yet the piles don't fall over."

Vidura examined Jimuta thoughtfully. "I suppose that's true. It *is* clever. Yet, I never thought about it before. You're really quite shrewd yourself, to notice such things. But then," he added with a smile, "I already knew that, since you learn so quickly about elephants."

10

With his prowling the areas where people congregated, the volume of Jimuta's information increased, if not the quality. He felt he should be doing more. But what?

One morning after bathing Rudra, Jimuta left the stables and wandered past the two storied, arched roof building housing the offices of the commanders of the four branches of the army—the elephant corps, the chariots, the horse cavalry, and the foot soldiers. A guard armed with sword and spear stood at each side of the entrance. As Jimuta passed, a palanquin approached, escorted by a squad of soldiers. The party halted by the guarded doorway, and a scowling man of perhaps fifty, dressed in fine sandals, a sparkling white waist cloth with jeweled belt and scabbard, and a tall turban stepped out. The guards raised their spears in a salute as he strode into the building.

Clearly the man was a high ranking official. Jimuta could easily imagine him meeting with one of the army generals, or maybe even with the *hastyadhyaksha*, the superintendent of elephants. Perhaps his business was legitimate, but it was also possible he was planning a scheme the King should know about—such as defrauding the government by taking a bribe from one of the contractors supplying fodder for the elephants, or diverting army supplies to his own use. Jimuta would never know; there was no way for him to overhear what went on in the building.

He sat on the hard ground in the shade of a *pipal* tree opposite the entrance. He was so deep in thought he almost failed to notice the young man, apparently a scribe, who walked in carrying a small stack of palm leaf sections with an ink pot balanced on top.

Jimuta had come to realize that here in Pataliputra, unlike in his home valley where the rigid hereditary traditions prevented most persons from changing occupations or status, in King Ashoka's government, someone with sufficient skills and ability could advance to quite high levels in the King's government. Satyavati had hinted that Jimuta might expect higher positions if he did well.

Jimuta loved Rudra and enjoyed caring for him. However, it had become increasingly obvious that an elephant driver was not well placed for overhearing information of real value. A good spy should be able to meet people in trade or government, or even to travel, as did Shantanu.

Jimuta had been learning everything he could about elephants: the methods of capturing them in the jungle; how they were trained for work and for war; how to recognize and treat their illnesses; their diets under varying conditions; their mating habits. But when elephant handling was his only skill other than farming, how could he ever hope to expand his range of contacts?

Then there was Renuka.

Although as a courtesan she was not of high caste, any visits with her other than at the time of his monthly reports seemed impossible. Even if Jimuta were not sending most of his money to his family, he doubted his salary as a mahout would buy more than a few moments per month of her time.

And she seemed so refined, so elegant, so educated. She could even write. And she knew Sanskrit.

He remembered the young man who had entered the building. A scribe. Jimuta himself had always been fascinated by the idea of writing, and here, he suddenly realized, was a skill which might be the very means for his own advancement! All important men used scribes to do their writing. If he could obtain work as a scribe in the government, and if he could learn Sanskrit, those skills would not only put him in a position to overhear conversations at a higher level, they could also bring him to the attention of men who might promote him if they were favorably impressed.

But how would that fit in with his work with Rudra? He wasn't sure. The two occupations were so different from each other. He only knew that at last he saw a way to learn how to write, and a highly desirable use for the skill.

He waited outside the palace offices at the end of the day, when the workers and officials were leaving. Soon he spotted and approached a junior scribe, who agreed to sell him an old stylus, some ink, and some defective palm leaf sheets. And the young man agreed to teach him to write, and to understand Sanskrit, in exchange for two *panas* a month.

Jimuta felt reluctant to use up the costly writing materials for mere learning exercises, so he practiced the characters in his mind and by writing in the dirt.

Vidura and Devrata and Mangala often watched him as they played dice games to pass the time. In the beginning, Vidura asked with a smile of amusement, "Why do you want to learn how to write? Elephants can't read, so what good can it do an elephant driver to write?"

Jimuta replied, "I want to be able to write to my family without paying a scribe's fee."

Vidura nodded knowingly. "You can save a lot that way if you write often. Maybe you can even earn extra money by writing letters for other men. A lot of the drivers would use your services."

"Exactly," said Jimuta agreeably. That thought had occurred to him, but he had something more in mind.

He offered to teach Devrata and Mangala what he was learning about writing, but they refused. Devrata, the elder brother, said solemnly though his prominent crooked teeth: "It wouldn't be fitting for mere elephant helpers. It's not our *dharma*." Mangala, the quiet one, merely smiled.

"You could get a scribe's job when you're older," said Jimuta. Devrata shook his head. "Oh, no. That wouldn't be right. Our caste works as laborers. Our uncle Vidura is the only one who's tried anything else. Maybe we can be elephant drivers like him someday."

Not everyone, Jimuta realized, was as eager as he to obtain a higher position in life. But maybe their stomachs had never been so empty for so long as his own had been, back in his old village.

Month after month he continued his meetings with Renuka. He had come to realize she had many skills. Once when he had arrived, she had been playing the *vina*, her slender fingers racing over the strings quite expertly in his opinion. Another time, she had been reading a palm leaf manuscript of the *Arthashastra*, a textbook of government written by Kautilya, a former chief minister. Yet another time, she was checking account records for Satyavati's business. Yet another time, she was decorating a wooden door frame with a painted design of intertwined vines.

He was quite aware that he had become obsessed with her, but he doubted he could help himself, even if he had wanted to. He felt frustrated that he had no one with whom he could talk about her. He could tell no one that he was an agent for the King, and he could think of no other explanation for having even met such an expensive courtesan.

Since he could envision no way she could become a larger part of his life given his current status, he often fantasized about running off with her. Maybe when the drought was over they could return home to Mangarh, where they could be married and farm part of his uncle's land. He would smile to himself as he imagined the looks on the faces of his family when he appeared, a grown man now, with an incredibly beautiful city woman at his side.

Or maybe he could become a mahout in the service of the Raja of Mangarh, and he and Renuka would live in a room in the fortress itself.

But he knew these were merely pleasurable daydreams. A lovely courtesan, raised in luxury, was not going to abandon the soft cushions of her secluded garden pavilion in the capital of the empire to become the wife of a poor farmer—or of a poor mahout—in a tiny, remote kingdom.

On a morning in the heat of the summer, Jimuta was bathing Rudra in the Ganges. Devrata and Mangala both were ill with a fever that was striking many people in the city, and Jimuta had sent them home. The elephant lay on his side in the shallow water near the shore, on the downstream end of the group of other elephants and drivers. A short distance away, Vidura was bathing Gajendra. High above the bank, a short distance further down the river, the tiles on the arched roofs of the King's palace shimmered in the sun.

Jimuta always talked to Rudra while bathing him, usually murmuring about nothing of importance. "I just don't know what to do about her," Jimuta now said in a quiet voice, as he leisurely scrubbed Rudra's neck with a stone. "Even if I went back home alone, I could never be happy with a village girl after seeing Renuka. And any prostitutes I could afford in the city don't interest me. The ones I've seen are nothing compared to her.

"But how can I ever afford her? Other men, rich men, must often be buying her time. Maybe one of them is with her now." This idea so frustrated him that he had usually avoided thinking of it. Renuka always appeared so pure, so untouched. Yet, she had probably lain with numerous wealthy lovers.

He furiously threw the stone into the water and said, "Why does she have to be a courtesan? Why couldn't she have been raised on a farm? Why couldn't she be free to marry *me*?" Rudra had been lying quietly. Now his eye looked at Jimuta, and his trunk suddenly blasted a stream of water out into the river.

Jimuta started, and realized the foolishness of this one-way conversation. He had been speaking in a low voice, but still—what if one of the other drivers had overheard? He guiltily looked around, and he felt relief that Vidura was looking away, out of hearing range, and that no one else was near. He quickly retrieved the stone and gave Rudra a vigorous scrubbing.

Late one afternoon, the buzzing flies and intense heat in the stables were making it difficult for Jimuta to concentrate on practicing his writing and his Sanskrit. He was puzzled, but also somewhat relieved at the distraction, when a messenger appeared and told him, "You're wanted at the gate."

He arrived there to find a guard from Satyavati's house, the one with the missing teeth and distorted speech, whose name he had earlier learned was Bhasuraka. The guard was perspiring heavily in the heat. "My mistress instructed me to tell you," Bhasuraka said, "that you're to report to the King's section of the palace immediately. Show this to the guards. But don't show it to anyone else outside the palace." He handed Jimuta a small piece of palm leaf, with writing on it. "Any questions?"

Jimuta hesitated. Then: "You don't know why I'm supposed to go there?"

Bhasuraka took a cloth from his waist and wiped his forehead. He smiled in mild amusement, fully exposing the big gap in his front teeth. "No one felt I needed to know. I don't question my orders, and you shouldn't, either."

Jimuta nodded. The guard left.

Jimuta hurried the short distance through the baking sun to the entrance to the royal compound. On the way, he glanced at the palm leaf. He could make out that it was an order to admit him, but it didn't say to where. There were several words he didn't know. Maybe, he thought, the part he couldn't understand was in some sort of code so if anyone other than the guards saw it, they wouldn't know what it was.

The soldiers at the first portal examined the pass and admitted him to the compound. A soldier escorted him past the big, wood pillared public audience hall to a set of guards at another gate. One of the men escorted him to an outer room of the building containing the smaller private audience hall, where a pair of dwarf guards admitted him.

It was dim and somewhat cooler inside. A scribe was seated on a mat, writing on palm leaf sections. And near him sat a familiar figure.

Jimuta's mouth fell open.

"I told you we'd meet again," said Shantanu with a grin.

Jimuta hurried forward and bent to touch his mentor's foot. As he straightened, the merchant who was also an agent for the King rose and embraced him.

Jimuta was speechless, but Shantanu said, "Come, we can talk later. Right now, the King is waiting for us."

He led Jimuta into the audience hall, where King Ashoka sat on cushions with Siddharthaka, and with an older man, clearly a Brahmin from the shaved head with a tuft of hair on the back. All held goblets, and plates of fruit were on mats. Behind the King stood a girl attendant slowly waving a flywhisk, and two girls were waving long handled fans against the oven-like heat. Four of Ashoka's women guards stood along the wall behind him, two on each side.

Jimuta somehow remembered to say, "Victory to the King!" He quickly did his obeisances. Here, at last, he saw what he had heard legends of, even back in Mangarh: walls plated with silver and gold, inlaid with gems that sparked as they caught the shafts of filtered sunlight. But he had no time to examine the room's details.

Indeed, after the surprise of encountering Shantanu, and then being taken immediately to the King, he had to take firm hold of his racing mind to concentrate as the King spoke. "Jimuta, would you care for some refreshment? This mango juice is still cool from the cellars. And have some fruit and dates if you wish."

Yet another serving girl appeared, and she handed Jimuta a brass goblet of the juice. The King was saying, "I've been having discussions with Siddharthaka and Shantanu, and with my teacher of many years, the honorable Vishvamitra"—he gestured toward the Brahmin—"as well as others. I'm concerned about how to prevent the local rulers of villages from overexploiting the farmers and other common people. Frankly, we don't know many persons who've come from villages. Shantanu suggested we call on you since you are from a village ruled by the brother of the Raja of Mangarh."

Jimuta tried to grasp that the most important men in the empire had apparently summoned him *because he was from a village*. The idea was almost inconceivable. It had been obvious to him from an early age that men of high position, and virtually *anyone* from a town or city, almost always viewed farmers and other villagers with disdain.

The King was continuing, "I'm considering appointing a new type of official. These men would go about and ensure that all the people are being treated fairly by those who rule them. They would be official representatives of myself, with full authority to correct any wrongs they find. Siddharthaka and my teacher think the idea will never work, that as soon as my officials left a village everything would revert back to the old ways of doing things, and any villagers who'd complained to the officials would likely be punished."

Jimuta reluctantly found he was agreeing with the latter view as the King went on: "I don't see any good way to send these officials to kingdoms ruled by independent Rajas who've sworn allegiance to me, such as the Raja of Mangarh. Those rulers would be outraged if I tried to interfere in the internal workings of their kingdoms. But Shantanu and I think it might at least be worth trying some day here in Magadha and in the other regions I rule directly. Since you lived in a village, I wonder what you think of the idea. Would those officials be able to help the farmers?"

Jimuta could still scarcely believe such a great King would

care about common farmers, much less be interested in a young elephant driver's opinions. But he must do his best to answer.

He immediately thought of The Mugger, and of Kumara Aja. "I, uh, think, Your Majesty, that your officials might possibly be able to help some people if you gave the officials enough power, and if they got to know the villages well and kept coming back to see that their orders were being followed. But there are some villages where the rulers would punish anyone who complained about them. Your officials would have to stay around a long time to make sure that didn't happen." Jimuta's mouth was dry, and he suddenly remembered the goblet of mango juice. He took a quick sip. It was both delicious and surprisingly cool,

King Ashoka nodded thoughtfully. "What you say supports Siddharthaka and my teacher on that aspect. I admit I see the point. My representatives would have to remain in a particular area permanently, and the rulers would have to know that I would punish them if they didn't comply with my officials' orders."

"It still wouldn't work," said Siddharthaka. "Your officials would have too much power, and they'd become corrupt themselves. Soon they'd be as bad as the local rulers they were supposed to be watching."

"Not necessarily," said the King calmly. "If the officials were selected properly, and if they were well trained and well paid, and if they knew that they themselves would be punished severely for misusing their powers, I think the plan would work."

"However," said the Brahmin, "you would have to make the system permanent. If the officials ever left, some of the rulers would take revenge on any of the people who'd made complaints."

"That's probably true," mused the King. He looked to Jimuta. "Does your own experience support that?"

Jimuta was again thinking of The Mugger, and of Kumara Aja. "Unfortunately, yes, Your Majesty. But it still seems worth trying. Many people suffer because of tax collectors and others who take too much from them."

"Are you aware of any particular incidents back in your own village that might help us understand that?" asked Siddharthaka.

Jimuta hesitated. Then: "Yes, sir, only, perhaps I shouldn't be saying...." He didn't want to be disloyal by disparaging Kumara Aja before the King.

"You may speak freely," said King Ashoka. 'I assure you I won't be interfering in such matters in Mangarh."

"Well, Your Majesty, our lord's tax collectors didn't lower their demands when crops failed, even though it was impossible for the farmers to pay the lord's share and still feed their own families—" He stopped, reluctant to speak even more critically of the ruler of his village.

"Yes, go on," said the King.

Jimuta shuddered inwardly at the memories. "When the farmers couldn't pay, our lord's men went into the houses and took whatever they wanted, to make up for not getting enough grain, and—" He again hesitated.

"Continue," ordered King Ashoka.

Jimuta's mouth was again dry, and his voice was hoarse, as he remembered Ambika. "Sometimes people were hurt. There was one time when the lord's men found a girl hiding in her house. They, uh, took unfair advantage of her." He took another quick sip of the juice.

"They raped her?" asked Siddharthaka bluntly.

"Yes, sir."

Siddhartha gave a nod, his eyes hard. "It seems there are always those who make unjust use of their power."

The King said, "Exactly why we should try my plan. Even if it helps only a few, it's worth the effort. And if it works reasonably well, it might help many of my people."

The Brahmin Vishvamitra said, "A noble sentiment, Beloved of the Gods. Still, I seriously question whether it won't harm more than it would help.

There was silence, and Jimuta took a deep breath, then spoke again: "Your Majesty, if I may suggest...."

"Of course."

"I'm sure you aren't going to act only on what I alone have said. But before you decide exactly how to go about your plans, I think it would be well for you or your agents to try to talk to as many farmers and other villagers as you have time for. Some of the older people, especially, are wise and experienced. They can make good suggestions."

The King nodded. "We'll seriously consider that. I realize that living in palaces, we don't get much sense of exactly what the problems are in the villages. Your comments are useful, Jimuta. If you have nothing else to say, you may go. And Shantanu also. No doubt you have much to talk about."

Jimuta hurriedly finished the juice in the goblet. He and Shantanu made their obeisances and left the relative coolness of the hall.

"We should probably remain here," said Shantanu, "so no one else sees you with me. We shouldn't be disturbed if we sit in the garden for a time." They seated themselves by the edge of a small reflecting pond, in the shade of a cluster of date palm trees. He glanced at Jimuta and smiled. "It's been quite some time since we've seen each other. You're taller now. Have you found Pataliputra to your liking?"

"Oh, yes, sir. And I'm glad you recommended me to the King as one of his agents."

"It was my duty. I'd have been failing His Majesty if I hadn't taken the opportunity. He needs capable persons working for him. And how is Rudra?"

"Rudra is well, sir. And I've learned a lot more about caring for him." Jimuta related the incident of the musth. "I've also." he added, "been learning to write, sir."

Shantanu raised an eyebrow. "That can be quite useful for an agent. I'm pleased. I'm sure His Majesty will be, also."

The time passed quickly in conversation, with Shantanu asking numerous questions about Jimuta's activities. Eventually, Jimuta realized he must be getting back to the stables to bathe Rudra. Shantanu would be leaving the next day with one of his caravans, so once more he and Jimuta took leave of each other.

Afterwards, bathing Rudra in the river, Jimuta happily went over and over the conversations with Shantanu and with the King. He kept returning, in amazement, to the thought that King Ashoka truly cared about the people of the empire.

How different that seemed from the rulers of his own village back in Mangarh. And he could still scarcely believe that the greatest King in the world had summoned him to ask his opinion on how to help farmers. He could never, ever, imagine the Raja of Mangarh or Kumara Aja doing such a thing.

The month of his eighteenth birthday, as had become customary, Jimuta met with Renuka alone for his monthly report. The monsoon had come, bringing lower temperatures that were most welcome, and out the windows he could see rain pouring from the roof. While Jimuta dictated, he gazed with admiration and longing at Renuka's lowered head, at the richness of her shining dark hair with delicate white jasmine flowers woven into it.

At the end, as usual, she looked up and smiled at him. "Anything else?"

After more than a year of their meetings, Jimuta had still said nothing to her of his desires. He assumed any use of her time not related to his reports would be far too costly. She would typically ask him when he arrived, "How is Rudra?" He would save up some brief little anecdote to tell her about the elephant. But then she would turn to the business of transcribing his report, and he would watch the tip of her tongue wetting her delectable lips while she wrote.

When he was away from her, he nourished the hope that perhaps she had fallen in love with him, too, and so maybe she would decide to give her time to him free. But he also feared, especially when he was in her elegant presence, that she might see him as a mere country lout—that underneath her pleasant demeanor she might compare him with her wealthy, sophisticated clients, and view him with scorn.

Now, Jimuta wondered if perhaps he might have been mistaken about how costly she was. After all, he really didn't know how much she charged. Maybe the amounts he had been able to save over the past year were sufficient to purchase at least a small portion of her time.

He hesitated, but he decided he had little to lose. He summoned all his boldness and said quickly, "How much are you?"

She appeared puzzled. "How much...?"

"How much do you charge for a night? Or for only a *nalika*."

She examined him closely, then lowered her eyes. A smile flickered across her lips. "If I understand you, Satyavati hasn't yet made me available to clients alone."

Jimuta blanched. How could he have made such a blunder! Had he insulted her? "I didn't know! I thought—" At the same time he felt overwhelming relief. She hadn't yet been touched by another man!

She looked up at him and smiled reassuringly. "I understand. You see, Satyavati's saving me. She's raised me from when I was small. My own parents were poor and couldn't take care of me. I'll eventually go to a wealthy man, either as a wife or a permanent companion."

Jimuta digested this while he tried to sort out the swirl of feelings within himself. "And he'll pay for you?" he asked at last.

Renuka laughed as if to dismiss the matter. "I'm afraid so. A lot, so Satyavati says."

Boldly, Jimuta asked, "How do you feel about it?"

She examined him, a slight frown on her forehead. "It's my *dharma*, of course. My duty. It's no different from parents arranging the marriage of a daughter to an older man she's never met. It's just that instead of Satyavati giving the man a dowry, the opposite will happen—he will give money to her."

Jimuta could think of no response to that. So he asked, "How long—when will it happen?"

A cloud seemed to flit momentarily across her eyes, then she was gently smiling again. "I think probably soon. Most girls are married by my age, you know. It's already past the time when Satyavati expected me to leave her house, but I think maybe she's grown a little reluctant for me to go. We're quite fond of each other."

Jimuta sat for several moments. "I see," he said. None of the other questions he longed to ask seemed likely to result in the type of replies he wanted to hear. He rose with as much dignity as he could summon. "Until next time, then."

When he turned away, she was staring at him with a half smile— and a look in her dark eyes that he could not interpret.

11

Now that Jimuta knew she was still a virgin, obtaining her for himself became even more urgent. She could be bought by a rich man at any moment! He fantasized even more about convincing her to run away with him, even of abducting her. But always, he would return to reality, realizing he had no way whatsoever to support her in the luxurious style of Satyavati's mansion. And if he ran away with her, he would not even have his income as a mahout or as the King's spy.

There was also his own *dharma*. He was obligated to care for Rudra, who had been entrusted to him so long ago and so far away by the Raja of Mangarh. And King Ashoka had bestowed a great honor upon Jimuta by choosing him as an agent. How could Jimuta betray that trust, break that bond, by running away?

Every day, in his prayers to Ganesha, he would ask the god for a satisfactory solution. Every day, he would ponder the problem, searching for a way around the fact that he had no realistic choice but to remain and fulfill his duties, no matter how high the personal cost.

Rudra observed that sometimes, when his driver returned to the stables, the young human would be in an especially cheerful mood, and Rudra would smell a faint, lingering, trace of sandalwood and flowers. Those times the driver would be also giving off the odor Rudra had learned to identify with human males who were eager to mate.

Rudra decided his driver had found a possible female partner, and that it was her perfume that clung to the young man after he visited her. However, Rudra also assumed that the young woman was resisting his driver's efforts, because her odors would been much stronger if his driver had actually been in lengthy contact with her body.

Since his driver was so obviously happy and excited when he returned from these visits, Rudra hoped his driver would soon succeed in the mating.

After more than a year of study, Jimuta felt proficient at writing in the script used throughout the main part of the Mauryan empire, and he knew enough Sanskrit to follow conversations in that language and record them. He should therefore be able to obtain a position as a scribe, either in Pataliputra or elsewhere. However, he still would likely earn a relatively low salary.

And Jimuta did not want to leave Rudra. Especially when there was no one else whom he felt was worthy of caring for his big friend.

The next two visits with Renuka were difficult. He felt certain he saw a change in the way she looked at him. Her gaze now seemed to linger on him, her smile seemed more intimate. But neither of them mentioned their previous conversation about her status.

He still could see no way out of his dilemma. And any day, he knew, Satyavati might sell Renuka to some wealthy patron.

When the monsoons ended, orders came for the drivers to prepare the elephants for war. There was no official mention of name of the enemy, but everyone knew the army would march far to the southeast to invade Kalinga, the most powerful of the Kingdoms which still remained independent of King Ashoka's empire. There had long been rumors of King Vadhukha of Kalinga plotting with other rulers to try to remove Ashoka from his throne, and most people of Magadha thought Ashoka had no choice but to try to rid himself of such a constant major threat.

Rudra was given a set of leather armor made especially to size for him. One piece covered his forehead and the upper part of his trunk. Other pieces, tied together, hung along his sides beneath the howdah to protect the main part of his body.

Several times the drivers took their elephants out to a forested area for training. Mostly the exercises were intended to get the animals used to noise and confusion, such as in battle. So in the beginning, men would run at the elephants beating pieces of metal together and shouting. Gradually both the level of noise and the numbers of men were increased until they approximated what might occur in the war.

Then, troops of cavalry making as much noise as possible rode at the elephants. Finally, lines of elephants charged toward each other. Unlike in battle, the drivers tried to avoid actual collisions, but the exercises got the elephants accustomed to confronting other elephants.

Jimuta could tell Rudra didn't like any of this. The elephant was slow to respond, and it was clear he wasn't putting his full effort into charging toward the other elephants. But he never actually refused to cooperate.

Vidura, always somewhat quiet, became even more silent. "War's not good," he abruptly told Jimuta as he was checking the elephants' traveling gear. "I've been in two battles now. A lot of elephants get killed. Men too, of course. But somehow it bothers me more about the elephants dying. They don't have any choice."

"Are you worried about Gajendra?" Jimuta asked.

"Yes." Vidura glanced at him with a look of concern. "Gajendra could get hurt bad. Maybe killed. So could I. But I'm responsible for him. If anything bad happened to him I'd feel like I failed to take care of him."

"There's nothing you can do about it," said Jimuta. "He belongs to the King's army. So if he's told to fight, he has to."

"I know," said Vidura, shaking his head and turning away. "But I still feel responsible for him. He doesn't know any better—he does what he's told. He trusts me not to tell him to do anything bad."

"It's his duty to fight for the King," said Jimuta. "Isn't it?"

Vidura sighed. "Of course. I shouldn't be talking this way."

But Jimuta realized he had the same concerns about Rudra. He knew for a fact Rudra didn't like battles, that the elephant might even run away. And Rudra could get injured or killed. So could Jimuta himself, for that matter.

Realistically, he could see nothing he could do to keep either himself or Rudra out of the war, even if it weren't their *dharma* to fight. He greatly admired and liked King Ashoka, who had sought him out and placed so much trust in him. He couldn't imagine Ashoka fighting a war without good reason. If King Ashoka needed his and Rudra's help to defeat the King of Kalinga, it was the least they could do to help to the best of their abilities.

So there seemed little point in dwelling on such doubts. Jimuta rechecked Rudra's armor and traveling gear and supervised its packing by Devrata and Mangala.

On his next visit to Satyavati's house before leaving, both the courtesan and her protege were present in the garden, where the foliage was a lush green from the recent rains. Jimuta's report concerned mostly talk he'd heard about the war. He finished by telling Satyavati, "You probably know this is my last report for some time. I'm leaving for Kalinga in a week." He carefully did not look at Renuka to observe her reaction. What if he saw none?

"I wish you well," Satyavati said, seeming sincere. "Renuka speaks highly of you. We'll miss your reports."

So Renuka had spoken "highly" of him! Jimuta's pulse quickened. What exactly did that mean? Did he dare to seriously entertain any hope of a closer relationship, assuming he returned after the war? He expected to come back and resume his previous positions as mahout and spy, but he knew there was a possibility he might not: he could be wounded or killed, or perhaps his company of elephants might be ordered to remain in Kalinga.

He wondered whether, if he asked the question on his mind, it might impair any future role as an agent who reported to Satyavati. He decided to take the chance, although for once he wished Renuka were not present.

Trying to act as if it were a matter of impersonal curiosity—though he strongly doubted Satyavati would be fooled—he asked, "How much do you intend to ask for Renuka? When you find a man for her."

Satyavati raised her eyebrows, and the blue eyes appraised him. At last, she said, "It's a matter for negotiation, of course. I've trained Renuka myself, since she was seven. No man has yet had her. As you can see, she's quite exquisite, and well educated. I love her like a younger sister, and I would miss her. I would want at least fifty thousand *panas*, maybe more. It would depend on the man."

Jimuta had known it would be a lot, but he was aghast. As a junior mahout he earned ten *panas* a month. Being a spy for the King added five *panas* a month more. He had been sending most of it to his family.

He rose. "I see." He tried to keep his face expressionless and to leave with dignity. Both Satyavati and Renuka wished him well in the war as he departed. His glance swept past Renuka, and he was certain he saw tears in her eyes.

Back at the stables, someone was waiting for him: The Mugger's tall manservant, Darsaka.

Anxiety swept through Jimuta. Even though The Mugger had expected to return, after so long a time Jimuta had come to almost assume that he would never again hear from the despised officer.

Darsaka asked bluntly, "Where were you?"

"Just out walking around the city."

Darsaka scowled. "No one knew where you had gone. I've been waiting a long while. The prince and my master are back in Pataliputra. They order you to come."

Jimuta nodded, and Darsaka led him out to the streets, and to a mansion not far from Satyavati's. A guard admitted them through a courtyard gate, and yet another admitted them to the house.

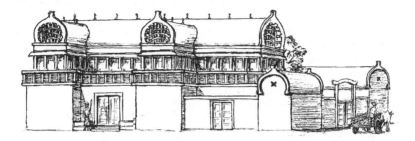

They entered a room that was open up to the high vaulted ceiling, where daylight filtered in though latticed openings in the gable ends. Kumara Aja, looking as ill humored as ever, sat on embroidered cushions. Near him sat The Mugger. An attendant fanned the prince, and two of Aja's armed warriors stood nearby.

Jimuta hurried to touch the prince's feet. Aja waved him up, and looked to The Mugger. "You may question him."

The Mugger glowered at Jimuta and that deep, menacing voice said: "We received reports that you are often gone from the stables. No one knows where. What do you do at these times?"

So someone had indeed been spying on him! Jimuta tried to appear innocent. "Various things, sir. Sometimes I visit friends. Sometimes I go to the markets. Sometimes I just wander around looking at the city. It's so different from my village."

The Mugger snorted. "It certainly is." He stared hard at Jimuta. "We're also told that you are learning to write. Why would you want to learn such a thing?"

"So I can earn extra money, sir, by writing letters for people. Then I can send more back to my family to help them buy food." Jimuta was thinking furiously. Who could have been sending these reports about him?

The prince and The Mugger exchanged looks. The Mugger laughed. "Ambitious, are you? Well, you'll earn far more some day by continuing to work for His Highness and the Raja of Mangarh than if you just write letters for workers around the elephant stables."

Uncertain how to respond, Jimuta said, "I see, sir."

"This war that's coming up," The Mugger said. "We will have work for you. And you must follow our orders exactly, whether you understand them or not."

Jimuta's breath caught. He nodded. "Yes, sir."

"If King Ashoka loses the war, your own Raja will become a great king, ruling a much larger area. And Kumara Aja will become an even greater prince than he is now. You understand?"

Jimuta swallowed. "I think so, sir."

"Good. Remember, you are being watched. Don't do anything foolish. I will kill you if we think you've betrayed us." The Mugger paused, glaring at Jimuta. Then: "You may go. But make sure we can find you after this. His Highness doesn't like waiting. Neither do I."

"Yes, sir."

All the way back to the stables, and the rest of the evening, Jimuta wondered: What should he do? Should he inform Satyavati about the meeting? But he really didn't know any details about whatever the prince and The Mugger were planning.

And what if he were being followed? He thought long, and in his anxiety he had difficulty getting to sleep. He heard the conch sound the beginning of the night curfew; normally he was sleeping well before that time.

He had at last fallen asleep when he was awakened by someone shaking him. He looked up at the tall form of Darsaka.

Still groggy, he worried. What would they ask of him so soon?

Darsaka was whispering, "The prince and my master order you to come."

Jimuta rubbed his eyes and quickly rose and put on his turban. "Hurry!" said Darsaka. "His Highness doesn't take kindly to waiting."

Fully awake now, but still sluggish, Jimuta followed him out of the stables. "What about the curfew?" he whispered to Darsaka.

"The master got a pass for us, of course," said the man. "Did you think me foolish enough to risk arrest?"

"Do you know why His Highness wants me?"

"To translate, naturally! What other reason could there be? You can't expect His Highness to understand the ridiculous way these people speak here! I can't understand a word they say, myself."

"I see." Actually, now that he'd grown accustomed to Magadhi, Jimuta didn't think it was truly much different from the dialect spoken back in Mangarh.

They rushed through the darkened and nearly deserted streets, to the mansion where he had visited the prince and The Mugger before. More warriors stood guard than previously: three at the outer gate, and two more at the doorway to the house. Darsaka mumbled something to each set, and they were readily allowed to pass each point.

They entered the high ceilinged room Jimuta had visited before. In the glow of oil lamps, Kumara Aja and The Mugger sat on cushions with three other men. The prince beckoned Jimuta forward. "These men speak only Magadhi. You will tell me what they are saying," ordered Aja. "And you will say nothing to anyone else of what you hear tonight. Nothing!"

Jimuta knew the prince must have at least one other interpreter in his entourage for use by his servants in dealing with the necessities of daily interactions in the city, and he wondered why the prince wasn't using that person. But he said merely, "Yes, Your Highness, I understand." He remained standing, of course, in the presence of such a grand man.

"Tell these...envoys," Kumara Aja indicated the three, "that His Highness the Raja of Mangarh and all his allies are prepared to act as soon as word is received of success here."

Jimuta relayed the information.

The leader of the three men said in Magadhi, "Prince, to ensure we prevail, we have a number of plans under way at the same time. Only one of them need succeed. Assassination is the preferred route, as it will make the others unnecessary. But as you can imagine, it is also difficult to accomplish."

As Jimuta interpreted, he wondered, assassination of *whom*?

The man was continuing, "When the war comes, there will be a number of opportunities. One plan involves killing the King in battle. But causing him to lose the war is the preferred route. And our plans for the elephant corps are still the most important factor. As you know, we are depending heavily on you in that matter."

Jimuta translated, and thought: They must be talking about killing King Ashoka! And the elephant corps is a key.

The conversation continued. Not many details were stated about the plans, but "drugs" and "confusion in the battle" were mentioned several times in regard to the elephants.

While one part of his mind did the translating, another wondered: How could the well-guarded elephants be poisoned? And how could the animals be deliberately confused?

At one point, Aja gestured toward Jimuta and said, "This boy here is the driver of the Mangarh elephant, and he's also my own contact in the elephant stables."

Suddenly, Jimuta wondered if the plotters were counting on *him* to somehow drug some of the elephants' food with a substance that could cause them to be confused. Or to help one of their agents gain access to the stables to do it?

Either way, the actions could indeed influence the entire course of the battle. If enough of Ashoka's elephants charged the wrong direction, trampling men on their own side, it could be devastating.

The three Magadhi men were scrutinizing Jimuta. Then their leader said, as if Jimuta were not present, "He seems quite young. And can you trust him completely?"

The prince replied, with Jimuta feeling awkward translating about himself, "He's clever enough to know how to follow orders. He understands he'll be killed if he doesn't."

"But you're sure he won't tell anyone what he learns of us?"

Kumara Aja said firmly, "He's from Mangarh, so he's loyal to me and to my brother the Raja. He has no reason to betray us." The prince waved toward The Mugger. "Also, my officer is quite talented at ensuring loyalty." The leader of the plotters peered at Jimuta for a time, then nodded acceptance.

There was more conversation, none of which revealed useful details. Jimuta was aware of The Mugger piercing him with a menacing glare the entire time.

At the end, Kumara Aja told Jimuta bluntly, "Remember— not a word of this to anyone! If I so much as think you *might* have leaked any information, I'll send my officer—" he gestured toward The Mugger "—and you'll die." The prince's eyes were cold.

Jimuta swallowed hard. He wondered: Was there also suspicion, or doubt about him? "I understand, Your Highness," he replied, his voice hoarse.

The prince waved him off, and Jimuta respectfully bowed and backed away.

On the way through the dark, quiet streets, he anguished over what he should do. His *dharma* required that he be loyal to his own Raja, who ruled the land of his birth, and he owed the same loyalty to Kumara Aja.

Yet, he'd become part of King Ashoka's elephant corps, and the King had personally recruited him as an agent. His *dharma* also required that he be true to his oath to King Ashoka.

He definitely felt more kindly toward the King than toward the prince, who could likely order The Mugger to slit Jimuta's throat without a qualm.

And the entire outcome of the war, even Ashoka's throne, might depend on this information about the elephant corps being the key to the Kalinga agents' plots, about Prince Aja's involvement, about the Raja of Mangarh being secretly allied with Kalinga, and about the location of the plotter's mansion!

Should he tell Renuka about the meeting tonight, so she would pass the information to Satyavati, and thus to the King? But what if Kumara Aja should find out?

Should Jimuta wait, and try to decide later? There wasn't much time before the army left.

Unable to sleep that night, he struggled to decide. Betray the King? Or betray Kumara Aja and the Raja?

Neither course was acceptable.

By the time the conch shell sounded the end of the night curfew, he had made a decision, though he wasn't completely pleased with it.

The Raja of Mangarh and Kumara Aja did have the right to assume he was their servant. After all, he was born in the prince's lands and had agreed to be a driver for one of the Raja's elephants. Most men never left the village of their birth and remained subject to the rulers of their area their entire lives. The first one to claim a person's loyalty was the one to whom loyalty was owed, unless permission was given to release the claim. And even though Rudra and his driver were given to King Ashoka, Kumara Aja and The Mugger had made it clear that Jimuta was still to serve the Mangarh rulers.

In the excitement of agreeing to become an agent of the King, Jimuta had been naive in overlooking the prospect of a conflict in duties. He had assumed the prince would make no more serious demands on him. Had he realized the problem, he would either have told the King, or else come up with a way to inform Kumara Aja that he no longer considered himself in the Mangarh rulers' employ.

But the Mangarh rulers no longer provided him with his pay. Rather, they apparently assumed that past loyalty and a vague promise about the future—and intimidation by The Mugger—were sufficient to keep him in their service. Jimuta knew they regarded him as a mere tool and they might well kill him anyway so he could not reveal what he knew, especially if the plot should fail.

He had subsequently given an oath to the King, and now he took regular pay, both from Satyavati as the King's agent, and from the army as an elephant driver. Rudra was in his charge, and Rudra belonged to the King. Those factors alone could be enough to justify the change in allegiance.

However, there was more. He greatly admired King Ashoka, who seemed genuinely concerned with the well-being of his people. The King had great presence, but this quality was different from the arrogance of Kumara Aja and his brother, and from the viciousness of their agent The Mugger. And all Jimuta's friends were now in Pataliputra. In a way, Vidura and others had become his family. He could no longer imagine living in Mangarh; at most, he would return some day to visit his uncle and aunt.

A main difficulty was that he felt he did owe it to Kumara Aja to inform the prince of the change in loyalties. However, that could well result in Jimuta's death, as well as in the plotters disappearing to come up with other plans equally dangerous to the King.

So he decided on a reluctant compromise. He would tell the King's agents of the plot and request protection in the palace. He would like to send word to Aja of his resignation from the prince's service, but that would be far too dangerous.

It wasn't entirely satisfactory, but he could think of nothing better.

His information about the plotters seemed so important that he briefly thought of trying to directly contact the King's confidant Siddharthaka, or even Ashoka himself. But without a new pass, it would be difficult to get past the many layers of guards, who would be unlikely to believe that a mere boy could know anything significant.

So as dawn began to lighten the sky, he hurried to Satyavati's house. He was concerned about the person who was apparently watching him, so he occasionally glanced back to make sure he saw no one he recognized. The streets were already growing busy with servants and women on their way to buy the day's food from the markets, with Buddhist monks and their begging bowls, and with all types of persons on their way to bathe in the Ganges or to pay respect to their gods at the neighborhood temples. Even a few elephants were being driven to bathe in the river by early-rising drivers.

As he turned the last corner before Satyavati's mansion, he glanced back, and he saw a tall man far behind, partly hidden by a small group of soldiers who were headed in the direction of the city gate. He thought he recognized Darsaka, but he could not see enough of the face below the turban to be sure. Then a bullock cart ground its way between them, blocking the view. When the cart had passed, he could no longer see the man. He stood for a moment, then hurried on.

At Satyavati's house, he saw Renuka just leaving the gate with two other young women. Jimuta remembered Renuka mentioning she liked to start each day by going to a nearby Shiva temple.

At his approach her face brightened. Before she could speak, he said quickly, "I have something I must tell you."

"Yes?" Her smile changed to concern when she saw how agitated and tired he looked.

He glanced about. "Inside the gate would be better."

"Of course." The other young women continued on. Jimuta and Renuka went into the courtyard, and the gate guard moved a discrete distance away. "Is Satyavati available?" Jimuta asked. "She should hear this, too."

"Why, no—she spent the night at one of the King's gardens outside the city."

So Jimuta told Renuka alone what he knew. She listened in growing astonishment, frowning. When he had finished, she said, "And you must be a key part of their plans, since you are the prince's own contact in the elephant corps!"

Jimuta grimaced. "Yes, I suppose I am."

"We must get word to the King at once."

"How will you do that?"

"I'll go there personally. I know passwords that will get me past the guards."

"Shall I come?"

Renuka's frown deepened. "I think maybe you'd better not. If you're seen there, it would make the plotters suspicious of you."

Jimuta pondered. Was there any danger for Renuka in what she was doing? It seemed slight, provided she was careful. "Can you take someone else along?" he asked, just to be cautious.

"I doubt there's a need. But Bhasuraka's free this morning. I know he'll come."

Jimuta's anxiety lessened considerably. The guard, who usually carried a sword and dagger, would be far more protection than he himself could be. Reluctantly, he decided she was right about going without him. He said, "Be careful who you tell. Try to get an audience with the King himself, or with Siddharthaka."

She smiled thinly. "I will."

He looked into her eyes for a moment. She glanced downward, still with a strained smile. He backed out through the gate. Then, he sighed, turned, and slowly walked toward the stables.

Some distance away, a nagging thought grew. What if he had indeed seen Darsaka earlier, and the servant was so skillful at following him that he'd seen Jimuta arrive at Satyavati's and reported the matter? The plotters' mansion was close by.

He decided to follow Renuka and Bhasuraka at a distance until he was certain she'd been safely admitted to the King's section of the palace.

He returned to Satyavati's street—just in time to see The Mugger and another man forcing Renuka into a carriage. The Mugger was cupping his hand over her mouth and helping the other man lift her in. Two more men were dragging the limp form of her own guard Bhasuraka into the gate of a small public garden. It was all being done so quickly that he doubted any of the few passersby noticed.

Jimuta remembered what The Mugger had done to the defenseless girl Ambika back in his home village, and he impulsively started to run to Renuka's aid.

Then he realized he could do little by himself. Not against The Mugger and three other warriors. He reluctantly halted.

The two men who had dragged Bhasuraka into the garden dashed back to the carriage and leaped inside.

Jimuta knew he had to summon help, fast. But how would he find where Renuka was being taken? Her captors could hide her almost anywhere in the huge city.

The carriage drove away, and he realized he'd better try to follow. He ran after, trying to keep it in sight. As he passed garden gateway through which Bhasuraka had been dragged, he saw a trail of blood on the paving stones. He hesitated momentarily. Should he try to aid the guard?

A group of three women were approaching, headed in the direction of the market. He continued running and shouted to them as he passed: "A man's lying in the garden. He may be hurt! See if he needs help!"

He overtook and ran past a couple of armed soldiers. He was managing to keep the carriage in sight. It turned a corner and continued in the direction of the plotters mansion.

He rounded the corner just in time to see it turn into the courtyard of that house. Two guards closed the gate, and one remained standing outside.

Jimuta stopped, his heart pounding, his breathing hard from the running.

He saw the guard at the gate glance up the street one direction, then look toward Jimuta. Jimuta turned and edged back around the corner out of sight, hoping he hadn't been recognized. What to do?

Renuka was in grave danger. The Mugger might well torture her for information, as well as raping her. If the plotters thought her knowledge was dangerous enough, they might even kill her immediately.

But surely he couldn't rescue her by himself, even if he could get inside the guarded house. He must get aid!

The two soldiers he had passed earlier were approaching. Desperate, he hurried to them. "Sirs! A girl has been just been taken by force. She's held at a house around the corner! Can you help me free her—quickly, before she's hurt?"

The two men stopped, glanced at each other. Both looked at the nearest houses, obviously extremely expensive, then at Jimuta. They smiled, and one said, "This is a wealthy neighborhood. You expect us to break into some rich merchant's mansion with no proof? What kind of fools do you take us for?"

"But, sirs, I saw her taken myself! They could be killing her this very moment! They've already stabbed her guard."

One of the men turned sober. "You do seem worried. But my friend's right. We can't just break into someone's house. You'd better run and tell the *rakshinah*. They'll know what to do."

"That might be too late!"

The man shook his head. "Sorry. You'd better just hurry as fast as you can." He and the other soldier moved on.

Jimuta hesitated. No one else was likely to believe him either, at least not enough to help right away. And the only ones who knew he was an agent of the King were Satyavati, who was out of the city, and Siddharthaka, and Ashoka himself.

Jimuta broke into a run, through the increasingly crowded streets to the entrance to the King's compound in the palace, where he hurried up to the guards at the gate. Out of breath, he managed to gasp, "I must see the King at once! It's urgent. I know he'll want to see me."

The guards exchanged amused glances. "I'm sure His Majesty would be delighted to see you," said one. "However, you may know that he has many matters to occupy him. Maybe you should come to the next public audience and wait your turn there."

"But this is important! A life is in danger! Maybe the King's life, too!"

The guard's smile broadened. "The King's life is always in danger. That's why this other guard and myself are here. And all the other guards inside. To protect His Majesty."

Jimuta thought furiously. Should he tell them he was an agent? He'd been ordered to keep the matter secret. Anyway, they would be unlikely to believe him. "Then may I see His Majesty's general, Siddharthaka?"

The guard shook his head. "Not a chance. He's usually with the King. And if you can't see the King, obviously you can't see someone with him."

Jimuta looked about in frustration. Whom else could he see? How would he convince someone in authority of the urgency of the matter, even assuming he could get an audience? And since he had apparently been followed to the courtesan's house, he himself was in danger.

Suddenly he knew what he had to do. There was a way to quickly multiply his own strength by many times.

He dashed to the stables, and he released Rudra.

Jimuta was so agitated he almost forgot to invoke Lord Ganesha's aid, but he remembered in time, hastily touching Rudra's side and then his own forehead before virtually leaping atop the elephant. At his command, Rudra hurried away from the barns, and out the gate of the compound. The two guards at the entrance appeared surprised at such haste, but they recognized Jimuta as being the driver who had care of such a big elephant at such a young age, and they merely shrugged at each other.

Jimuta kept shouting the warning, *"Apehi! Apehi!"* Surprised people leaped from Rudra's path as the elephant thundered down the streets.

Jimuta talked loudly to Rudra, explaining what must be done. He knew his friend couldn't understand the words, but Jimuta was sure he conveyed the seriousness, and that Rudra would do as instructed.

The street ahead was blocked by a crowd. Jimuta realized the people had gathered at the spot where Renuka had been forced into the carriage. Although the onlookers eased aside to let Rudra by, the elephant had to slow and slip through to avoid colliding with anyone.

Jimuta called to a young man standing near: "What is happening?"

"A man was killed here!" came the reply. "They found the body inside that gate."

Bhasuraka!

Jimuta felt a pang of anguish at the thought that the not unfriendly man with the missing teeth and slurred speech was no more. Could he have done more to help the guard, who had died serving Renuka, quite possibly as a result of Jimuta's own carelessness in leading the plotters to her?

He didn't see how; not when he himself was probably Renuka's sole remaining source of aid. He'd asked the approaching women to help Bhasuraka. Hopefully they'd done whatever they could.

He wrenched his thoughts back to Renuka.

He *must* ensure *she* would not die, too. Free of the crowd now, Jimuta again urged Rudra into a run. Soon, they rounded a corner of the street, and Jimuta could see the mansion where Renuka had been taken, with the guard standing by the courtyard gate.

Rudra didn't understand why his driver was in such a hurry, but there was urgency in the young human's voice. Rudra smelled a trace of the perfumes that always lingered on his driver whenever the young man returned to the stables in a happy mood and bearing the odor of human males eager to mate, presumably after visiting the young woman. This time, however, his driver's sweat smelled of worry and fear.

Rudra dashed through the streets in the direction his driver ordered. People hurriedly moved from his path, which was good, since it would be awkward to avoid hitting them when he was moving so rapidly.

They had to slow for a large group of humans. Rudra smelled the people's excitement.

He also smelled blood; probably that had something to do with the reason for the people's agitation. While Rudra was moving slowly, his driver exchanged talk with a man standing near.

Then they were out of the crowd, and his driver told him to run again.

His driver guided him to a large building of the type humans lived in. Among the many odors in the air, including the scent of several men, Rudra smelled the strong aroma of the young woman's perfume. She had passed by recently, and the scent also was drifting strongly from inside the structure, so he decided she must be inside. There was a man apparently keeping watch by a gate in a high wall attached to the building. Rudra was surprised when his driver guided him to face the gate and gave the command for pushing it in.

Were these men rivals for the female's attentions? If so, Rudra was glad to help his driver defeat them. Still, he sensed there was much more involved. His driver was far too fearful and agitated for a mere fight over who would get a woman.

Rudra hesitated for a moment, but the command came again, definite and clear. There were two wooden sections to the gate, and Rudra rushed at the point where they met in the center. He struck them with the blunted ends of his tusks, and the doors easily splintered and fell away.

His driver was urging him through the gateway, so Rudra continued on in, to a small open area, where a wheeled vehicle was parked to one side, with two oxen attached to it. The oxen saw Rudra, and one of them bellowed.

His driver told him to turn, so Rudra did, and he faced another, smaller, doorway in the side of the building. A human inside the structure looked out the window and screamed when he saw Rudra.

The man from the gate rushed in, and he held his weapon as if he were going to try to injure Rudra or his driver. His driver's order was an unusual combination of the commands for "fast' and "push left with your trunk," but the intent was obvious. Rudra quickly tossed the man away.

At his driver's order to push the door in, Rudra complied. But the opening was too small for him to continue through. The driver guided him to face an edge of the doorway and told him to "push ahead." Rudra did so, and the door frame splintered and fell away.

At his driver's direction, Rudra did the same thing to the top of the door frame. Then to the other side. Now his driver told him "move ahead." The opening was just big enough for him to enter it if he hunkered down. So he squeezed inside the building. Fortunately, the ceiling inside was quite high, so Rudra could stand at his full height again.

Four men were in the room, two facing him with weapons held ready.

And there, at last, he saw his driver's intended mate. A man was restraining her, and her odor of fear was even stronger than the familiar scent of her perfume. Rudra now knew for certain why his driver had brought him here.

The guard at the gate saw the elephant hurtling toward him, and his mouth dropped open. Rudra was moving so quickly that they reached the watchman before he realized the elephant wasn't going to continue down the street.

Hardly slowing Rudra, Jimuta had him quickly turn and charge the gate. It fell inward with a crash.

The watchman shouted, but by then they were in the courtyard, where Jimuta saw the carriage sitting empty. Jimuta turned Rudra toward the door of the house.

The watchman ran in, shouting, his sword drawn. His heart pounding, Jimuta called to Rudra, who fortunately understood the complicated command. The elephant turned his head and flipped his trunk, sending the guard smashing into the courtyard wall.

Jimuta hoped the main room of the mansion was as high as he remembered. He had to be careful now; he didn't want to bring the whole house crashing down on Renuka.

He saw Darsaka's face in a ground floor window, and the servant shouted a warning just as Rudra nudged the door inward, snapping hinges and shattering wood.

Unless it were enlarged, the opening was far too small for the elephant. Jimuta had him push on the left side of the door frame. The wood splintered and crumbled. Then Rudra did the same to the right side. Then the top of the frame.

The elephant lowered his head and bent his knees. Jimuta pressed himself down into Rudra's neck while the elephant squeezed through the enlarged opening and into the high-ceilinged room. There, as Jimuta had anticipated, Rudra was able to stand upright.

Jimuta tried to stifle his panic at what he faced. The Mugger and another soldier confronted them with swords poised. Another soldier was in a corner—holding Renuka. Nearby was Darsaka, his face contorted with shock.

The Mugger's eyes opened wide at recognizing Jimuta astride the elephant. Recovering his composure, he thundered: "How dare you, boy!" He darted forward and swung his sword at Jimuta's leg.

Jimuta instinctively blocked the blow with his *ankus*, but his arm went numb from the impact. He shouted to Rudra. The elephant's trunk seized The Mugger and threw him into the adjacent wall, hard. The sword flew from the warrior's grasp, and he slid to the floor.

The swordsman by him turned and ran, escaping out the door in the side wall.

The man holding Renuka began dragging her toward the same doorway. She screamed and kicked and bit at him.

Rudra moved quickly toward them. Consumed with the urgent need to free Renuka, Jimuta readied his *ankus* as if it were a spear, intending to jab the man.

The Mugger, rising from the floor, shouted, "Don't let her go!" He darted around Rudra's rear and seized Renuka from the other side.

Rudra let out a bellow. The terrified soldier released his hold on the girl, leaving her to The Mugger, and ran out through the doorway.

The Mugger drew his dagger, and he held the blade to Renuka's neck. "Keep back or I kill her!" Darsaka, also now holding a dagger, grabbed her arm on the side vacated by the soldier who had fled.

Petrified by the new crisis, Jimuta halted Rudra and hesitated. The Mugger might well be able to cut Renuka's throat before the elephant could grab him or before the *ankus* could be used. For certain, both men could not be dealt with before one or the other of them could seriously wound her.

The Mugger and his manservant began dragging Renuka out the side door. "Don't you move that elephant or I'll kill her, you young traitor!" shouted The Mugger. They were now through the doorway, which was far too small for Rudra to follow without demolishing the entire wall around it. And that, Jimuta realized, might bring the roof down on their own heads. From outside, the Mugger boomed: "I'll be back to kill you, you traitor!"

It was awkward turning the elephant completely about in the confined space, and before the maneuver was completed, through a window Jimuta saw The Mugger and Darsaka dragging Renuka across the courtyard. The noise of Rudra demolishing the gate and the doorway had attracted attention, and people were entering the yard to see what was occurring.

"Stop them!" Jimuta yelled to the onlookers.

"Stay away from us, or we'll kill her!" Jimuta heard The Mugger roar. The captors, tugging Renuka along, hurried out the gate.

Jimuta tried to suppress his panic. He *must* not let them escape. Despite the danger they might kill Renuka when they saw him pursuing, he knew The Mugger would kill her anyway—after extracting any information they wanted.

At last Rudra emerged though the previously enlarged door opening. *"Apehi! Apehi!"* Jimuta shouted. The stunned onlookers leaped aside as Rudra charged out the gate.

The two men, knives held ready, were rapidly dragging Renuka down the street, ignoring the shocked looks of passersby.

"Apehi! Apehi!" screamed Jimuta, and people scrambled from their path. Darsaka glanced back, saw the elephant closing in, and screamed to The Mugger.

Jimuta was terrified they would kill her right then.

They didn't, and he realized: they knew using Renuka as a hostage was probably their best chance for escape. If the *rakshinah* didn't arrive in time to arrest them, then the guards at the city gates would try to seize them. The Mugger would no doubt threaten to kill her if they weren't provided horses and safe passage away.

But where could they possibly go that would be out of the reach of Ashoka's soldiers?

Kalinga! That was a likely place, since the Raja of Mangarh was allied with Kalinga's ruler in the plot to kill or defeat Ashoka. They'd take Renuka along, of course.

And they'd kill her eventually, when they felt they had reached safety and had no more need of her. Maybe after torturing her or raping her, knowing The Mugger.

The two men and their victim were approaching a street corner where a huge supply of the big water jugs stored for fighting fires were stacked high in rows. Rudra was now right behind the three. Scarcely able to suppress his dread, Jimuta hoped the elephant would understand as he directed Rudra to grab The Mugger and jerk the man away from the girl.

He was terrified that The Mugger might have time to use his dagger on Renuka, but he could think of no better option. And he realized he would also have deal with Darsaka quickly, before the servant decided to use his own knife.

Rudra's trunk seized The Mugger's upper arm and chest, hindering the man's use of the dagger. Then Rudra pulled hard.

The elephant jerked the officer backward and to the side, but The Mugger gripped Renuka so firmly he pulled her along with him, breaking Darsaka's hold.

The servant whirled toward the elephant and swiped with his dagger at Rudra's trunk. The blade glanced off a tusk, and Darsaka stumbled. Jimuta jabbed his *ankus* at the man but missed.

Rudra surged forward, dragging The Mugger and also Renuka. At the same time the elephant struck Darsaka with the side of a giant foreleg, throwing the servant against the stack of large pottery water jars. The man's head struck a container and he fell to the paving stones.

The Mugger was struggling to break his arm free so he could use his dagger. Giving up, he at last released Renuka so he could grab his weapon with the hand that had imprisoned her.

Renuka ran.

"I'll kill you for this, boy!" snarled The Mugger, straining against the grip of the trunk.

Jimuta clubbed him with the *ankus*, but The Mugger's turban cushioned the blow. "*No one* does this to *me*!" roared The Mugger. Seeing the man was about to stab Rudra's trunk in an effort to free himself, Jimuta reluctantly shouted to the elephant to release him.

Rudra let go. The Mugger darted behind the highly stacked rows of water containers, between them and the tall, blank wall of the adjacent house. "I'll be back with all my men, and I'll kill you!" thundered The Mugger. The space was far too narrow for Rudra to follow, and Jimuta realized the man might escape around the corner. Alone, and freed of the need to drag Renuka, The Mugger might even succeed in hiding himself in the crowds and escaping!

"First I'll put out your eyes, boy! Then you'll die slow, one part of you at a time!" came the enraged shout from behind the water jugs.

Jimuta flinched at the thought. He yearned to see if Renuka were all right. But so long as The Mugger was loose their lives were in peril. If not now, then later.

Desperately, he directed Rudra to shove the nearer end of the stack of big jars toward the wall. Rudra did so, managing to avoid having them fall, and sealing the end of the passage. Jimuta had feared the jars might tumble from the stack and roll, but they remained nested together as designed.

Fearful The Mugger would realize what was happening and dart out the far end, Jimuta hurriedly urged the elephant there. They reached the end just as The Mugger edged from the opening. The man saw the elephant and darted outward, but Rudra's trunk shot over and knocked him onto his back. The Mugger rolled to his hands and knees and scrambled behind the pile of jars again.

Rudra shoved the end stack of containers against the wall, closing the gap.

The Mugger was trapped.

Jimuta watched the pile of vessels for several moments, anxiously wondering what to do next. He glanced toward Renuka, and he saw she was watching wide-eyed, apparently uninjured, except for absently rubbing an arm where she had been grasped so hard.

A water jar smashed on the paving stones. Jimuta whirled toward the stacks of containers and saw a gap in the upper row. Then an adjacent upper jar tumbled to the ground and broke, releasing a surge of water, as The Mugger dislodged it from behind. Jimuta could now see the top of the man's turban. A container in the next row down of the gap fell outward and smashed, revealing The Mugger's furious face.

If The Mugger dislodged only another jar or two, he would be able to scramble free. Jimuta again urged Rudra forward, this time tumbling several of the remaining upper containers onto the man. "That's for Ambika, as well as for Renuka!" Jimuta muttered. A couple jars broke, but the rest remained intact. Rudra shoved several more jugs onto the right side of the pile, then, as directed, moved and pushed more onto the left side.

There was no more sign of movement from the man buried beneath the mass of heavy containers.

A shout came from some distance: "Stop in the name of the City Authority!" It was the *rakshinah*, at last.

Ignoring the police for the moment now that The Mugger appeared captured, Jimuta slid from Rudra. His legs were so weak he almost stumbled, and he felt faint, but he managed to get to Renuka.

She was fingering her neck where the knife had been held to it. Her face pale, her hair and clothing disheveled, Jimuta thought she looked lovely. She gave him a strained smile, and her eyes were lit in admiration. He asked hoarsely, "You're all right?"

She dropped her hand from her neck, and her smile widened. "Yes, I'm fine. What a spectacular rescue!"

Jimuta struggled against his light-headedness.

"Where is everyone else, though?" she asked.

"Who?" he answered in a daze.

"The men in the house thought the army had come to attack them!"

He was trembling. "No. Only me."

Renuka's jaw dropped. "You did this alone?"

With great effort Jimuta raised a hand toward Rudra, who was standing patiently. "He helped. A lot."

With a look of wonder, Renuka stared at the elephant a moment. She turned back to Jimuta. "I owe you *both*. More than I can say." Her smile left. "Bhasuraka was with me, but they attacked us so fast he couldn't defend us. Do you know what happened to him?"

To keep from fainting, Jimuta squatted, bent over, and lowered his head. "He...I'm sorry. He was killed."

She let out a muffled shriek. He glanced up and saw her eyes filling with tears. She put her face in her hands.

One of the *rakshinah* interrupted to shout angrily, "Why are you causing this disturbance?"

Jimuta's mind was too numb to think of an answer.

The area was filling with curious onlookers.

The *rakshinah* stood over him. "Tell me what is happening! Now!"

Jimuta felt his senses slowly returning. Still squatting, too unsteady to be sure he could stand without falling, he looked up at the policeman. He managed to say weakly, "Sir, we've captured a couple of murderers. They're also traitors to the King."

*

With Renuka's accusations, in between sobs, it took little time to persuade the *rakshinah* to arrest The Mugger and Darsaka for abducting her and killing her guard. But convincing the head officer that the two men were dangerous Kalinga spies, without revealing Jimuta's and Renuka's own roles as imperial agents, was considerably more difficult.

At last the policeman agreed to at least postpone deciding on that matter until he could consult with officials of the King. After ensuring that Jimuta and Renuka could be easily found to obtain further evidence, they were allowed to leave.

Although steadier on his feet, Jimuta still felt as if he'd barely survived a week of utter terror. A part of his mind was thinking clearly again, and he said to Renuka, "It's time Rudra and you met."

She stood briefly, wiping at her eyes, while Rudra's trunk sniffed all over, bathing her in warm, moist air, then grasped her around her waist. "Enough!" said Jimuta. "We need to go." He nudged the trunk, and the elephant released her.

Jimuta helped Renuka onto Rudra, then climbed astride the elephant's neck. He was very aware of Renuka's closeness behind him as the crowd parted to let the huge animal through. "Can you get us in to see the King?" he asked in a low voice.

Renuka murmured near his ear, "Yes, I know the passwords." Her breath on his neck sent shivers over his skin. "And I have my coin," she added. He wasn't sure what she meant by the latter, but he assumed he'd find out.

They rode to the palace, and across the outer courtyard. Jimuta left Rudra tethered to a post by the gate to the King's section. To the soldiers on guard—the same ones who had refused to admit Jimuta earlier—Renuka asked, "Have you seen a stray peacock come this way?"

The men stood aside and waved them past, surprised looks on their faces at seeing Jimuta again, this time with a lovely young woman with tear-reddened eyes who knew the password phrase. "Sorry," said one of the soldiers. "We were just obeying orders earlier."

Jimuta gave a nod.

The next set of guards responded to the same phrase, and then they faced two more soldiers. Renuka gave the phrase again, and this time she handed one of the men a small copper coin. The guard examined it carefully, then nodded, handed it back to Renuka, and waved them through.

Relatively quickly, after passing the scrutiny of four layers of officials, they were in the private audience hall relating their tale to the King himself and to Siddharthaka.

Ashoka immediately began issuing orders in Sanskrit to search for the other plotters and to increase the guards at the many elephant stables. Jimuta and Renuka's eyes met in a shared look of relief while the King was giving the directives.

"Jimuta, I'm most grateful," said the King at last, switching to Magadhi. "You've certainly justified my confidence in you. I was aware of various of my vassal rulers—including the Mangarh Raja—agreeing to an alliance against me, but my agents hadn't yet been able to discover the details. It was clever of the plotters to decide to use the elephant corps. Short of killing me personally, widespread confusion among my elephants would probably be the best way for my enemies to make the odds more favorable to themselves when I battle against Kalinga."

Pleased at the King's gratitude, Jimuta said, "Your Majesty, there are still the other plans mentioned at the meeting where I was the interpreter. I'm sorry I didn't learn any details."

Ashoka looked to Siddharthaka, who was frowning. The King's confidant said, "We simply must use every precaution against assassination. And you have to stay well protected during battles in Kalinga. You tend to expose yourself too much. The enemy must know that."

The King shrugged. "Thousands of my soldiers will be exposing themselves to the enemy. If I expect them to fight for me, the least I can do is share their risks."

"But if one of *them* is killed," said Siddharthaka firmly and loudly, "it makes a difference to him and a few others. If *you* are killed, we'll not only lost our King, we'll probably lose the war!"

Ashoka looked away, a grin twisting at the corners of his mouth. "I'll try to remember that."

"I'll help remind you!"

Jimuta had the impression the King and Siddharthaka had engaged in a similar conversation numerous times, and that the King liked the thought of joining his men in their perils. There was silence now, and Jimuta said, "Your Majesty, may I mention another concern of my own?"

"Of course. Always speak freely with me."

"Your Majesty, Kumara Aja and His Highness of Mangarh have been relying on me to be loyal to them. I see that when I became your agent, I should have informed them that I no longer considered myself in their service. But they threatened to hurt my family, as well as me, so I was afraid to refuse them. I'm glad I obtained information from them that was helpful to you, but I'm still worried about them hurting my family. And even though they threatened me, I can't help but feel I, uh, misled them somewhat."

The King examined Jimuta with interest, then exchanged looks with Siddharthaka. Ashoka said, "I'm favorably impressed that you feel your duty to your prior rulers strongly. It makes me even more confident that I can trust you myself in the future. I'm quite sure Kumara Aja now realizes you're no longer working for him. If he has a chance before we capture him, he'll probably convey that information to the Raja of Mangarh. So I'll inform the Raja immediately that I hold him personally responsible if anything happens to you or your family, whether by accident or not. Needless to say, I'm also most upset with the Raja for plotting against me, and I intend to think of a good penalty for him."

"Your Majesty, I still don't feel well about the way I handled everything."

"Good. I might be worried if you could change loyalties easily without informing those who were counting on you, even if you were working for them because of a threat. If you ever decide to leave my own service, I hope you'll tell me."

"Oh, I don't plan to leave, Your Majesty!"

The King smiled. "Good. Now," he turned to Siddharthaka, "Satyavati's house needs some extra guards for a while. And is this young man safe if he leaves the palace?"

Again, Jimuta and Renuka exchanged looks, while Siddhartha replied, "He should be safe enough in the stables, especially with the increased guards there."

"Your Majesty," said Jimuta with a glum expression, "I'm wondering if I'm still of any use to you as an agent. Everyone will hear how I went to rescue Renuka, and they may figure out the reason I knew her."

"Maybe," said Renuka to Jimuta, "you can just tell everyone you saw me being abducted and there wasn't time to summon the *rakshinah*. So you took matters up yourself."

"That *is* what happened," Jimuta said. "Still, I suppose a lot of people will probably be talking about me for a while. Things may never be quite the same."

"I'd hate to lose Satyavati as someone for my spies to report to," mused the King. "I think Jimuta should stay away from her house now, so no one will see him going there. Unless, of course, something extremely important comes up again."

Jimuta tried not to show his consternation. Not to see Renuka again, for who knew how long!

"I think," said Siddharthaka with a smile, "maybe Jimuta has additional reasons for going to Satyavati's house."

Ashoka raised an eyebrow.

"It would be a shame," said Siddharthaka, "to penalize him for rendering us such important services."

"Quite true," said the King, with a tight grin. "Any suggestions?"

Everyone was silent. Jimuta was embarrassed, and Renuka's face had reddened.

Siddharthaka said, "I think Jimuta's proven he deserves access to the palace. He can report here in the future as an alternative to Satyavati's."

"Agreed," said the King.

"You must know the current passwords at all times," said Siddharthaka to Jimuta. "As you may have heard from Renuka, the phrase this month is: 'Have you seen a stray peacock come this way?'" He reached into his waistcloth and handed Jimuta a small copper coin. "And if you have occasion to come directly to the King's section of the palace again, this will get you through the first layers of guards and officials."

Jimuta looked at the coin, apparently identical to Renuka's. At first glance, it appeared like any other small piece being commonly used for money, except that it had a little round hole near one edge. As did many such coins, this one bore a simple, stylized peacock, the symbol of the Mauryan dynasty, as well as an Ashoka tree inside a railing, the symbol of the King personally. There was also a horse and an elephant on the side with the tree.

Siddharthaka said, "The hole in it should help prevent you from spending it accidentally. To anyone who casually sees it, it looks like thousands of other coins. But the other coins don't have *both* a horse and an elephant along with the tree. They have other animals, often including an elephant, but *never* a horse and an elephant together. The King's senior guards know this and will ensure that anyone presenting it will be passed through to a higher level immediately."

"Hopefully," said Ashoka, "Jimuta won't be barred from Satyavati's house for long. We're leaving for Kalinga soon, anyway. After we're back from there, I think maybe he should resume reporting to uh...Satyavati."

12

On the day the astrologers declared to be auspicious, the great army set out for Kalinga. Jimuta rode Rudra with the rest of the elephant corps behind the King and his generals, who led the long, wide column. And behind Rudra came Gajendra, with Vidura astride his neck. Devrata and Mangala and the other helpers trudged alongside.

The constant dust was an irritation, and he was glad he was near the front of the vast horde, so he avoided at least part of the dirt plume. Even high up on Rudra, Jimuta could not see far back through such thick dust, but he knew that behind the thousands of elephants with their jingling leg bells came the chariot corps, followed by the horse cavalry. Then came the foot soldiers. Far to the rear were the support personnel: supply wagons, merchants, physicians, entertainers, prostitutes.

Most of the other elephant drivers seemed in good spirits, glad to be leaving the routine of the stables at Pataliputra. Aside from his regrets at leaving Renuka, Jimuta shared much of their excitement. He barely remembered the only battle he had ever witnessed, long ago near Mangarh. He was thrilled to be embarking on such a great adventure as part of a huge and powerful army, participating in a grand mission on behalf of the greatest King ever to rule. The feelings supplanted any memories of the wounded and dead men and animals he had seen in that one brief war.

However, as he rode, he frequently was sobered by thinking of his encounters with The Mugger, especially of how careless he, himself, had been to lead the enemy to Renuka. And of how she could easily have met a similar fate to that of her guard Bhasuraka. The Mugger might well have emerged the victor and continued to plot against the King. Jimuta often gave Rudra extra attention and treats, deeply grateful to his big friend for making it possible to overcome such a serious menace.

Jimuta's thoughts of the coming war itself were vague; he did not know the extent to which he and Rudra would be involved in the actual fighting. He was more than a little worried that if they did find themselves in an intense battle, Rudra might again run away, and humiliate both of them.

He wondered again and again if he ought to inform the commander in charge of his company of elephants about Rudra's reputation in Mangarh. But Jimuta felt embarrassed he had delayed so long. Maybe it would be better to continue to wait. From the fact that Rudra was often among the two dozen elephants selected for the retinue whenever the King traveled outside the palace grounds, it appeared he had become one of the King's favorite animals. So maybe he would not even be risked in battle.

The Kalinga King Vadhukha had decided to meet the invading Mauryan army at Dhauli. The battlefield would be the broad, fertile plain through which the Mahanadi, the Great River, slowly meandered before reaching the coast. Vadhukha had established himself and his army on a great elongated outcropping of rock which rose from the flatlands like an island from the sea.

The soil here was reddish, and the vast armies stirred up a haze of red-tinged dust that hung in the air and coated the palm trees and banana groves. There was constant noise from so many men and animals and so much equipment gathered in one place: hammering of tent pegs, clanging of blacksmiths working on armor, the cries of vendors selling supplies, the trumpeting of elephants, the whinnying of horses, the creaking of cart wheels.

The night before the first battle, because of his noble size and bearing, Rudra had the honor of being one of the few elephants chosen to take part in the great ceremonies. Jimuta and his helpers fitted Rudra with armor and ankle bells and caparison and painted the elephant's face and ears. Then, Jimuta rode Rudra to the site of the sacred fire where the ritual would take place.

There, in the presence of the King and the top commanders, with the entire army assembled, the *purohita*, or chief priest, anointed the foreheads of Rudra and the other elephants with ghee while chanting mantras. The oily spots of clarified butter glistened in the light of the flames from the firepit.

The priest then chanted mantras and blessings invoking victory for the King, his commanders, their weapons, and their chariots. Jimuta was relieved to learn that Rudra had not been selected for the initial fighting. For one day, at least, there would be no chance for Rudra to run away.

The fighting that day was fierce. Jimuta watched from the height of Rudra's back as Ashoka's army, with many of its elephants in the front line, splashed through the shallow river under heavy enemy archery fire and established a hold on the far shore. In the distance Jimuta saw the glinting sparks of sunlight that were thousands of flying arrow tips, the bright flashes from the swinging sword blades and the shields held high for protection, the moving lines of dark mountains that were elephants charging in formation, the dancing brightly colored standards of the chariot knights as they circled and wove in and out of the fray.

When the fighting ended at sundown, as customary, and the surviving warriors returned to their camps, they left behind on the battleground on the far side of the river the bodies of thousands of men and animals. The *chandalas*, the Untouchables who traditionally cremated dead bodies, would have much work that night.

Before the darkness fell completely, Jimuta saw on that distant field what appeared to be literally scores of huge mounds—the elephants who had died in battle. The low caste scavengers who cut up the carcasses and the crews who salvaged the howdahs and other trappings would be laboring until dawn.

The second day of the war, Rudra again was not selected for fighting, nor was his friend Gajendra. Jimuta found it difficult to see what was occurring from such a long distance away, and rumors of the course of the fighting tended to be unreliable, often contradictory.

Although Jimuta had reservations about getting involved in the battle, given the dangers—and especially given Rudra's questionable reliability—he was here to help King Ashoka defeat Kalinga. He disliked having to wait passively when so many thousands of others were actively engaged in the fighting. He had not come such a great distance to merely sit under the hot sun and listen to the stories of others. He also wanted to have at least a small taste of the battle so he would know what it was like to take part in war. He wanted to return to Pataliputra—and Renuka–to tell his own first hand stories of heroism.

Ashoka had offered a huge reward for anyone capturing King Vadhukha or any of the top enemy commanders. Jimuta was too far back to see when many of Ashoka's elephants and cavalry attempted, but failed, to break through the Kalinga lines to attack the enemy king. The result was a fiercely fought melee in which thousands of men, hundreds of horses, and dozens of elephants died on both sides.

Everyone assumed Ashoka's much larger forces would quickly overcome the Kalingans. But King Vadhukha was proving to be stubborn. He had chosen his site well for defense, and he was making the invasion costly for the Mauryan invaders. Clearly it would be virtually impossible to get close to Vadhukha on the top of his strongly defended hill.

Rudra and Gajendra were held in reserve again on the third day, when fierce fighting on the plain further reduced the numbers of Ashoka's troops as well as the numbers of his enemy's. Even the unwounded soldiers returning from the fray appeared tired, dirty, discouraged that the battle had continued so long.

The smoke from the vast numbers of funeral pyres and the moans and cries of the multitude of wounded sometimes made Jimuta wonder if he shouldn't hope to continue to remain away from the fighting. But he did have the feeling that if he went into battle he would not be one of those injured or killed. He knew that the cause he had come to fight for was just, and that he and Rudra were instruments in the larger plans of the gods and the King. Although the risks were real, and some of the men and animals around him might unfortuanately fall, he felt confident he and Rudra would contribute in at least a small way to King Ashoka's ultimate victory, and that they would emerge from the fighting unharmed.

Ashoka himself frequently drove his four-horse war chariot to mingle with and encourage his men, but much of the time he sat in the howdah of his personal elephant, Ganesha, in order to observe the battlefield from a higher position.

Jimuta was pleased when, in the afternoon of the fourth day, Rudra's howdah was selected as Ashoka's observation post. It was a welcome break from the monotony of waiting, without the hazards of actually participating in the midst of the fighting itself.

When the King approached, he gave Rudra a sweetmeat and patted his trunk hard. "You're one of the biggest men in my army," he told the elephant. "So I'll have a good view from your back."

Jimuta, already seated on Rudra's neck, was surprised at how tired the King looked. Ashoka and his aide Siddharthaka mounted the gilded ladder to the howdah, followed by servants with the royal flywhisk and umbrella.

It was the first time Jimuta had been close enough to the King for private conversation after the incident with the spies. When they were on their way, Ashoka said to Jimuta, "I wanted to tell you again how grateful I am that you discovered that plot against me. If anyone managed to sow confusion in the elephant corps here, it would be disastrous."

"I'm glad to have helped, Your Majesty."

"I thought you'd like to know—although we weren't able to get much useful information from the agent you called The Mugger, he died after several days of questioning."

Jimuta looked away. "I see, Your Majesty." It was usual practice, of course, to torture a captured enemy spy, both to try to get information from him and to discourage other such agents.

"Also," said the King, "Kumara Aja will trouble you no longer. He was captured and executed for his own part in the plot. Hopefully that sent a strong message to his brother the Raja."

His mouth dry, Jimuta could think to reply only, "Yes, Your Majesty."

"And those were fine reports you sent me all along, Jimuta. I'd like you to continue them when we return to Pataliputra." The King gave a strained smile. "I think perhaps you wouldn't mind seeing Renuka again."

Jimuta reddened. "Not at all, Your Majesty."

The King sobered. "In the meantime, if you learn anything here in Kalinga you think I should know, send word to me through Siddharthaka."

"Of course, Your Majesty," Jimuta said.

Ashoka clearly had other, more major, matters on his mind. He turned to Siddharthaka. Though the two talked in low voices, and in Sanskrit—which they did not realize Jimuta knew—he was able to overhear much of their conversation.

"I just don't understand how Vadhukha can hold out after such heavy losses!" the King said wearily. It was hot in the howdah, even with the aide waving the flywhisk, and Ashoka's face glistened with sweat.

"It's so obvious he can't win," Siddharthaka replied. "Not when he's outnumbered this badly. He's sacrificing his men needlessly."

"And that means I can win only if a lot more of my own men die." Jimuta was surprised at how pained Ashoka sounded.

"You have no choice. You can't leave now."

"I know." The King's voice sounded resigned. "I only wish I could think of a way to end it quickly."

13

The seemingly endless battle continued. Although the immediate events of the war kept Jimuta's attention more than occupied, he occasionally thought briefly about The Mugger, and about Kumara Aja, and how their lives had ended. It was difficult to truly believe that the two would no longer oppress villagers back in Mangarh, nor would they ever again trouble Jimuta personally.

On the fifth day, Rudra and Gajendra were at last ordered to join the other elephants of their company in a charge at the Kalingan forces. Both elephants were in the Mauryan army's left flank, which was protected by a long bend of the river, the Mahanadi.

Jimuta's mouth was dry, and his stomach was queasy. He scarcely breathed as he approached the elephant's head. "Rudra," he said, his voice unsteady and weak. He swallowed and tried again, his voice lower and more firm, while he slowly rubbed the coarse skin of his friend's trunk and looked into the big, wise-appearing eye. "The King is depending on us. I want you to do just as I tell you. It's important we do well, so we can help the His Majesty win this war."

Rudra shifted on his feet, returning Jimuta's gaze. Jimuta was sure the elephant understood. He patted the trunk hard. "We—we'll just do our best for each other."

By the time they were ready for battle, behind Jimuta in Rudra's howdah sat a Kshatriya knight with bow and arrow and an armload of spears, and two other archers of lower caste.

Despite his tension, Jimuta felt the full glory of war as the elephants moved into their positions in line, with a band playing loud music. It was late morning, and the sun beat down, but Jimuta ignored the heat even though he had wrapped an extra layer of cloth in his turban and donned a heavy quilted coat, similar to that of the foot soldiers, for greater protection from spears and arrows.

The company commander's conch shell sounded, cutting like a sword through the music of the band. Jimuta gave Rudra the signal to charge. On either side of him, the other huge armored mountains surged into motion.

Rudra listened carefully as his driver talked with him. He could smell the young human's fear, and he heard the agitation in the unsteadiness of his driver's voice. Rudra sensed he was being reassured about the dangers they would soon face, and that he was being told to obey all the commands, even if he didn't want to

When his driver signaled him to run, Rudra obeyed. But he didn't like this battle any better than the earlier ones he'd been in. He felt his driver's foot pressure behind his ears, urging him toward where he could see fighting going on. He didn't like it, but he went.

He could see Gajendra, some distance away, moving in the same direction. Up ahead, he saw a line of other elephants facing him. His driver was urging him faster, straight at them.

Rudra ran right up to the other elephants, but then he saw men in the boxes on their backs throwing metal pointed sticks at him. Most of them were bouncing off his armor, but he felt one strike his leg and stick there with a sharp pain.

And the noise! Only in his other battles, long ago, had he experienced such a clamor: the clashing of metal against metal, the screams of other elephants and of men who were hurt, wooden howdahs splintering as they struck the ground.

Rudra decided he *must* get away. He turned aside, and he began to run, desperate to flee as far from the fighting as possible. His driver was screaming at him, but Rudra paid no attention.

Suddenly, he heard Gajendra calling him, screaming for help. Rudra's driver was still shouting at him, but that didn't matter. Gajendra needed him, and that was more important.

Rudra called loudly in reply as he ran toward his friend, bursting through a mass of fighting soldiers who were in the way. When he got to Gajendra, he was shocked to see his friend lying on the ground, shrieking in agony. Rudra moved near, stood with his foreleg against Gajendra's, stroked his friend's face with his trunk.

Rudra smelled blood, a lot of it. Then he saw that Gajendra no longer had a trunk. Blood gushed from the gaping raw hole right at the bottom edge of Gajendra's head armor. A long sharp stick jutted from Gajendra's head by his eye, and another from his side in between his armor plates.

Rudra raised his own trunk and trumpeted in outrage.

Gajendra's shrieks became moans. Rudra kept stroking Gajendra's face. Gajendra groaned and whimpered.

Again Rudra raised his trunk and blasted a protest. Tears formed in his eye. He saw Gajendra's driver, his own driver's friend, kneeling by Gajendra's head, sobbing.

He heard his own driver shout something to Gajendra's driver. Gajendra's driver did not look up, but shook his head from side to side.

Rudra's driver was shouting at Rudra to turn and leave. But it was Rudra's duty to guard his friend. He had no intention of leaving.

His driver was prodding at him with the goad. Still Rudra stood firm. Gajendra would not be hurt any further. Not so long as Rudra was there to prevent it.

"What's wrong with that idiot elephant?" screamed the knight from the howdah.

"I don't know, sir!" Jimuta called back. "I think he doesn't want to leave his friend." Although he could understand Rudra's feelings, he was furious that the elephant didn't obey.

Jimuta had quickly realized he did not like being in the fighting himself. Except for the quilted coat and thick turban, a mahout was almost defenseless against arrows and javelins or even against a mounted swordsman. Blood seeped from a shallow cut in his exposed leg; in the noise and confusion and violence of the battle he had not even known when he had gotten the minor wound. But Jimuta would do his duty, in spite of the risks.

That was more than he could say for the elephant. Once again, Rudra was avoiding battle. This time, he had Jimuta with him, and three warriors.

Jimuta desperately tried to think of what to do. He opened his mouth to call to Vidura for advice. But then he reconsidered. Vidura was lost in grief over Gajendra.

The fighting had moved away from them, so there seemed no immediate danger. Jimuta looked about, trying to see what course the battle was taking. He saw the King's chariot, with its white umbrella and its small cavalry guard heading in his direction.

He silently groaned. What a time to have the King see them, when Rudra was refusing to obey. And Jimuta had thought they both had impressed the King so favorably!

He noticed Ashoka's cavalry bodyguard seemed agitated; the mounted warriors were practically bumping into each other in their haste to race to the far side of the King's chariot.

Jimuta looked in that direction—and gasped.

It appeared as if half the Kalinga army was thundering down upon them.

The enemy cavalry were after the King.

The Kalingans must have seen Ashoka was away from the bulk of his army and had decided to try to kill or capture him. Jimuta remembered the conversation back in the palace at Pataliputra when Siddharthaka had tried, without apparent success, to convince the King not to expose himself to such unnecessary risk in battles.

That was the one way Kalinga could win. The enemy could never hope to defeat the Mauryan army itself, but they could render it headless. With no King, Ashoka's generals would almost certainly withdraw to their own territory. The Kalingan commanders must have known of Ashoka's tendency to go off on his own, and they may even have been watching for such an opportunity.

And the river blocked Ashoka's escape.

"To the King!" the warriors in the Rudra's howdah were yelling. "Go to the King!"

"Go!" Jimuta screamed at the elephant, signaling hard with his toes. Still Rudra stood, stroking Gajendra.

Jimuta jabbed Rudra with the point of the goad. Jimuta screamed, "The King! We have to save the King!"

The elephant eventually raised his head.

Rudra was overwhelmed with grief over Gajendra. He could tell his friend was dying. So he ignored the shouts of his driver and the other men. This time what Rudra himself wanted was more important. The men could try all they wanted to push him into doing their will, but he knew they couldn't make him do anything unless he chose to. And right now he needed to be with Gajendra to comfort his friend's last moments of life. Gajendra was trembling, letting out horrible muffled shrieks of pain.

Dimly, Rudra realized his own driver was getting far more frantic than usual. But Rudra was concentrating on Gajendra, sympathizing with his pain, telling him he cared. Then Gajendra's trembling ceased. He was still.

Rudra realized his friend was no more, and he raised his head, lifted his trunk and shrieked his outrage.

Rudra's driver was jabbing him with the goad, screaming and

screaming at him. Rudra was full of both grief and anger, but he decided since he could comfort his friend no more, he would at least look to see what was happening that his driver felt was so important.

When Rudra looked up, he saw the big wheeled vehicle with the white umbrella and flags, and he knew the only one who rode in a vehicle like that was his man-friend, the boss of all the other men, who always spoke to him and often brought him treats.

Rudra hadn't wanted any part of the fighting before, where many men he didn't even know were trying to prove who was boss. But now, he could see lots of other men were challenging his friend's right to be boss. And his friend might even get killed, with so many other men challenging him all at one time.

Gajendra's spirit was standing beside his discarded body. You should go help, said Gajendra. I no longer need you.

Are you sure? asked Rudra.

Quite sure. I have moved on, but you still have your duty here.

I don't want to leave you, said Rudra.

I will be with you always. Even when you are not aware of me, I will be there.

Rudra understood. I'll go, he said. He again raised his trunk, and he trumpeted his own challenge as he began to run. His felt his driver's signal for more speed, and he ran even faster.

He quickly approached his friend's vehicle, which was wheeling around in a turn. But what should he do?

There were too many men and horses to stop them all. He felt his driver directing him, so his driver must know what to do.

Rudra obeyed.

Vastly relieved that at last Rudra had responded and begun running toward the King, Jimuta's mind raced trying to discern how to best help Ashoka. Jimuta was close enough now to see Siddharthaka between the two other drivers at the reins of the King's four horses.

The Kalinga cavalry were almost upon them.

The King's chariot had swung about and he was trying to escape, but the bend of the river prevented him from going directly away. The Kalingans were about to intercept him.

"Charge them!" the warrior behind him was screaming.

Arrows zipped past Jimuta. Rudra slowed, and Jimuta could tell the elephant was uncertain what to do.

Despite the warrior's command, Jimuta saw little point in turning to meet the horde head on. He and Rudra could eliminate a few of the enemy, but the others would pour past to overwhelm the King.

Thinking quickly, Jimuta signaled Rudra to continue the same direction. The elephant could run unbelievably fast for short spurts. Within moments they had overtaken the King's chariot and moved alongside, inserting Rudra as a moving shield in front of the Kalingans.

"Go, Rudra!" Jimuta screamed. The elephant ran exactly where he was supposed to, beside the King's chariot. The enemy could reach the King only by wounding Rudra enough to cause him to slow, or else by awkwardly managing to go around him.

Showers of Kalingan arrows flew at them. Jimuta felt one rip through his turban. A warrior in the howdah behind him screamed in pain.

An arrow lodged in Rudra's neck, next to Jimuta's bare leg. Rudra shrieked, but he kept moving. Kalingan cavalrymen now half surrounded Ashoka's chariot, and Rudra charged through them, knocking horses aside as if they were flies to be swatted.

Spears struck the howdah, clattering as they bounced off. Behind him, another of the soldiers screamed. Jimuta did not have time to turn to look. A short distance away, he saw Mauryan cavalry and elephants racing to save their King. But it would take far too long for them to arrive.

Again came a shower of arrows and spears. Jimuta glanced toward the King, who was wielding a spear against a big enemy horseman with a sword. Ashoka's arm was bleeding. Siddharthaka had fallen against the side of the chariot, blood soaking his chest.

Arrows bounced off Rudra's thick leather armor. Jimuta felt something slice his forearm through the heavy sleeve of his coat. A burning sensation cut across his thigh.

Again, Rudra knocked horses and men aside. Once more the elephant shrieked in protest, but Jimuta couldn't see the cause. It appeared to him that most of the enemy were intent on targeting Ashoka so they could claim their reward, and they therefore were simply trying to avoid Rudra, not to waste valuable moments attempting to kill the giant beast.

A spear struck Jimuta's right hand with stunning pain and bounced away. The hand hurt terribly, but he had no time to attend to it.

The rescuing Mauryan forces arrived at last, with shouts and volleys of arrows. Horses collided with horses, elephants smashed through the frustrated enemy troops. Wave after wave of Ashoka's forces flooded around their ruler.

If the King was not too badly wounded he should be safe, Jimuta decided. He signaled Rudra to slow and turn, veering away as the fighting moved off. He was dimly aware of the King's chariot only a short distance away, protected now by his own troops.

At last Jimuta looked at his blood-drenched hand.

His two smaller fingers were gone.

The hand throbbed horribly, and blood dripped from the raw edge where the fingers had been severed.

He glanced at his thigh. Blood flowed from a long, deep gash. He thought of pulling up his wet, reddened sleeve to look at his arm, but he didn't have the strength.

He was feeling light headed. It must be from losing so much blood....

He needed to look at Rudra, to see how badly the animal was wounded. He must dismount to do that. He signaled Rudra, and he was aware of himself falling before his mind went blank.

Jimuta heard voices near his head. Too weak to move, he ached and hurt all over. Someone was wrapping cloth around his hand. With great effort, he raised his eyelids. A *vaidya* and an assistant were kneeling beside him. "Good!" said the physician. "You're conscious. Can you understand what I'm saying?" Jimuta tried to talk, but succeeded only in letting out a croak. "Don't talk, then, if it's hard for you," said the *vaidya*. Jimuta felt them cleaning his leg wound. "This cut's deep," said the *vaidya* to his assistant. "Bring the ants. The King's ordered the best care for him." Jimuta vaguely realized they were going to use ants to tie the wound together.

One insect at a time, the physician applied an ant's head to the cut, and the ant bit the wound with its mandibles. The assistant instantly severed the ant's body with a small pair of scissors, so the mandibles were left binding the edges of the cut tightly together.

Abruptly, a blast of warm moist air swept across Jimuta's face. Rudra! The elephant was examining him with his trunk. "Rudra..." Jimuta managed weakly, his voice hoarse.

"What did you say?" asked the *vaidya*.

"Elephant..." Jimuta croaked. He tried to sit up to see how badly Rudra was hurt.

"Don't move! Your elephant has some wounds, but he should recover. I've seen much worse today."

Jimuta relaxed some.

"You and the elephant were lucky," said the *vaidya*. "The soldiers in your howdah are all dead."

Jimuta fainted again.

14

When he regained consciousness, he still lay on the ground. The physician had left; no doubt he had much more work to do today. Something big moved not far from Jimuta's ear. He turned his head and saw Rudra's massive leg. He looked up; the elephant stood protectively by him. In the distance he heard the battle continuing.

Devrata and Mangala abruptly appeared, sweating and out of breath from running. They carried stretcher poles and blankets which they placed on the ground. "We were sent to help you," said Devrata. "Do you feel like we can move you?"

Jimuta tried to sit up, but the pain made it difficult. He lay back again. "I think so," he said weakly. "Check Rudra's wounds first."

He could hear the two boys talking in low voices as they examined Rudra. Devrata said at last, "We counted six cuts—one on his trunk, two on his neck, a couple on his rear, one on a leg. Somebody must have already pulled out any arrows. He should be all right until we can get him treated."

They made the poles and blankets into a stretcher, lifted Jimuta onto it. Then they began carrying him toward the encampment, with Rudra following.

Abruptly Rudra stopped.

He refused to respond to Devrata's prompting.

"I think he wants to go to Gajendra," murmured Jimuta. "Over there to the right. Take us there."

Devrata and Mangala began carrying him toward where the big body lay. This time, Rudra followed.

Vidura was still sitting with the dead elephant; he agreed to take responsibility for Rudra while Devrata and Mangala carried Jimuta to the camp and then came back to clean and treat Rudra's wounds.

Rudra stood guard over his friend Gajendra the remainder of the day. In the distance, the fighting continued. As darkness fell, the salvage crews arrived to retrieve Gajendra's howdah, his caparison, his bells, his armor. Then came the crew to saw out Gajendra's tusks for their ivory, and to cut up Gajendra's body for meat to feed the army, and to burn whatever remained.

Rudra knew what the men were going to do. He'd seen it happen with another elephant.

He came back to the camp reluctantly with Devrata and Mangala, but he came.

Beneath the thick cotton bandages, Jimuta hand and leg throbbed, and his arm hurt. He slept little during the night. But the next morning he felt good enough to sit up, and even—from his seat—to supervise treating Rudra's wounds.

King Ashoka had Jimuta carried to his tent, where the injuries of both the King and his friend Siddharthaka were being tended.

"How are your wounds, Jimuta?" asked the King from his seat on the edge of a bed.

Jimuta felt pleased that the great ruler should inquire. He didn't really feel very good. And he would miss those fingers. But he said, "Not so bad, Your Majesty. Others are much worse."

Ashoka's eyes lowered. He was quiet for a time. Then, without looking up, he asked, "How is Rudra?"

"His wounds aren't bad ones. He should recover, too, Your Majesty."

The King nodded. "I'm glad." He again looked at Jimuta. "I doubt I'd be here, if it hadn't been for you and Rudra. Each time I thought the Kalinga cavalry was overwhelming me, Rudra knocked them aside."

Jimuta inclined his head. "I'm glad to have helped, Your Majesty."

The King slumped, seemingly exhausted, as well as in pain. "You'll have a reward," he said, "as soon as the battle is over." He flinched as a physician tightened a bandage on his arm. Then, he eyed Jimuta curiously. "I don't know how you and Rudra happened to be so far away from the other elephants. But it was lucky for me. And for Siddharthaka. Fortunately, he'll recover, too." Jimuta nodded. He did not trust himself to make a proper reply if he spoke.

Ashoka weakly raised a hand, and Jimuta was carried out.

He was glad, of course, that he and Rudra had been so crucial in saving the King's life. But his feelings were tempered by the death of Gajendra—and of so many others.

And by the loss of two of his own fingers. He kept wishing he could go back, do something different, so Gajendra wouldn't have gotten killed, and so the spear would have missed his hand. But some events could not be undone.

Rudra was subdued, his eyes dull, his movements sluggish, now that his part in rescuing the King was over, and now that Gajendra's body was no more. He seemed not even to notice Jimuta's efforts to comfort him.

Jimuta also felt helpless to console Vidura, who sat in the elephant encampment, head down, tears in his eyes, absently stroking his parrot Lakshmi. Jimuta sat for long periods by Vidura's side, with Rudra tethered nearby.

Now that he had experienced the true reality of war, Jimuta could think only of its horror. The pain of the dead and injured men, of the dead and injured elephants. Of Gajendra in particular.

It was the *dharma*, the life's work, of Kshatriyas such as the King and Siddharthaka and the other warriors to fight battles. Jimuta realized that if Rudra were ordered to fight again, he himself would have little choice but to go. But he truly hoped he would never have to be involved in more fighting of any kind.

For the rest of his life, probably every day, his two missing fingers would remind him of the terrible experience.

The war ended the next day, the sixth, when Mauryan cavalry captured the Kalinga King as he attempted to escape.

Each day that followed, Jimuta continued to gain strength, and his wounds hurt just a little bit less. Three days after the end of the war, the King summoned Jimuta to an audience.

Jimuta could walk now with the aid of a crutch. The large open-sided cloth pavilion was crowded with officers and soldiers who would receive awards from the King. Jimuta had expected Ashoka to look jubilant after the victory. But though the King smiled as each recipient was escorted forward, the pleasant demeanor appeared strained, and Ashoka seemed weary. It was almost as if he were the defeated King, rather than the victor.

An aide approached Jimuta and whispered, "You're next." Turning to face the throne, the aide announced loudly, "The elephant driver Jimuta of Mangarh, Your Majesty."

Jimuta hobbled forward and made his obeisance.

"Jimuta," Ashoka said with the strained smile, "You've helped me more than I would ever have believed. I now owe the fact that Siddharthaka and I are seated here today to you. And to Rudra, of course. You may know that at the beginning of the battle I offered a hundred thousand *panas* as a reward to any of my warriors who captured or killed the King of Kalinga. It seems only appropriate that my own life should be worth at least as much as that of my former enemy. I'm therefore directing my treasurer to pay you a reward of twenty-five thousand *panas*. The remainder will be divided among the others who played important parts in my rescue." He gazed fondly at Jimuta. "That's a lot of gold to carry. You'll want to wait until your return to Pataliputra to claim it."

Jimuta gaped at the King. Had he heard right? *Twenty-five thousand panas?*

The King continued, "That's too much wealth for an elephant driver. I'll ask my ministers to find another position for you, one more in keeping with your new riches. Do you think you can give up Rudra?"

A new position! And twenty-five thousand *panas*!

Not in his wildest imaginings had Jimuta expected the reward to be so much.

The King had asked if he could give up Rudra. Jimuta had thought vaguely of that matter from time to time. "Only if I can still see him every day, Your Majesty. And if I can make sure the new driver is a good one for him."

Ashoka nodded. "I think that can be worked out."

"Your Majesty," Jimuta said, "I'm overwhelmed by your generosity. So I hope you will not be offended if I make another request. I've learned to write, and I now know Sanskrit, and I would like my new position to be one in which I can make use of those skills. As soon as my hand heals, of course."

Ashoka examined him with obvious interest. "So you've learned Sanskrit! And to write. My ministers will find an appropriate position for you."

Relieved, Jimuta again made his obeisance, and he backed away from the throne, careful not to lose his balance and fall.

His mind churning, he followed the aide to a spot at the fringes of the onlookers.

Twenty-five thousand *panas*!

Surely, it must be enough to live comfortably for the remainder of his life, if he were careful not to develop a taste for too many expensive luxuries.

Could it possibly enough to buy Renuka's contract? Unfortunately, that seemed doubtful. Fifty thousand was the amount Satyavati had mentioned, and that was a minimum. She might well insist on much more.

And Renuka was accustomed to a luxurious style of living. Even if he paid Satyavati everything he had, how would he still have enough *panas* to provide anything like the comforts Renuka would expect?

15

At Jimuta's suggestion, Vidura agreed to share responsibility for Rudra on the long journey back to Pataliputra. Jimuta felt an odd guilt whenever he was with Vidura or the other drivers who had lost their elephants or received even more severe wounds than his own. It somehow seemed unfair that Jimuta should come out of the war as a wealthy young man, and he and Rudra with relatively minor wounds, while some of the drivers had lost so much.

True, the King had been generous in compensating them, too, for their injuries. But the elephants belonged to the state, not to the individual drivers, so there was no way of making up for that particular type of loss—the sacrifice of a friend, a companion, the main focus of one's life.

At a night halt on the journey, Jimuta said to Vidura, "You know I probably won't be an elephant driver much longer after we get back to Pataliputra."

Vidura gave a slight nod; his demeanor had been solemn and subdued ever since losing Gajendra. "I'll miss you," he said in a quiet voice.

"I'll come by often to visit. But I've thinking about Rudra, too. I was given responsibility for him back in Mangarh. I can't leave him unless I'm sure he'll be well cared for. I wouldn't trust him to just anyone. He likes you. And most of what I've learned about taking care of him, I've learned from you. Would you be willing to take him over from me?"

Vidura gave a strained smile. He nodded. "I'm honored. He's a fine elephant."

They sat in silence for a time. Then, Vidura said, looking at the ground, hesitation in his voice: "Before we settle the matter, there's something I need to tell you."

Jimuta waited.

Vidura's gaze remained on the ground. "I took money to report on your activities to a man from Mangarh."

Jimuta's mouth dropped open. Speechless, he stared at his friend and mentor.

"I should have told you immediately," Vidura said. "I didn't want to report on you in the first place, and I told the man that. It was that tall manservant Darsaka, but he said he had trouble understanding the way I spoke, so he'd always bring another man with him to interpret what I said. At first I thought Darsaka's masters just wanted to ensure that you were taking good care of Rudra. But Darsaka wanted to know *everything* you did, whether or not Rudra was involved. And when I told him I didn't want to do it, Darsaka threatened me. He told me I already knew too much, and that an 'accident' might happen to me and my family if I didn't do as he asked."

Jimuta felt a surge of anger: anger at the Mangarh prince and his agents who had intimidated Vidura into spying on him; anger at Vidura for complying so easily and not informing him. Then he realized that he'd been put in a somewhat similar predicament himself, when he was expected to serve two masters and he had not informed either of his obligations to the other.

Vidura continued, "I should have told you. But I couldn't see that anything I said to Darsaka about you could hurt you in any way. And I was afraid of his threats, especially for my family. I also felt I needed the money to pay for my niece's wedding. So I didn't see any actual harm in it."

Jimuta sighed. "I suppose there was no real injury done."

Vidura now looked at Jimuta. "It was still wrong of me. If you want to reconsider about me being Rudra's driver, I'll understand."

Jimuta smiled tightly at the irony. "I gave Darsaka's masters some information, too, when I didn't want to. So I think I understand how you came to do it. And I still wouldn't trust anyone else but you with Rudra."

Jimuta visited Satyavati's house the day after returning to Pataliputra. The wound on his leg was an ugly, scabby stripe. A bandage still covered his right hand for protection, and the hand often ached. But he walked without the crutch, with only a slight limp.

The weather was turning hot, and the familiar jasmine odor powerfully scented her garden. He had requested an appointment with the head courtesan personally, and she met him and the armed guards who accompanied him in the small outdoor pavilion. He was struck again by her unusual beauty, and by those distinctive blue eyes.

"Everyone has heard how you and your elephant helped save His Majesty's life," Satyavati said. "We're all most grateful." In an aside to a servant girl, she ordered, "Bring wine and some of those new melons."

Jimuta smiled in acknowledgment. The refreshments indicated she was aware of his intention to discuss a matter of business.

He and his companions deposited the boxes of gold on the carpeted floor of the pavilion. The guards withdrew to wait by the gate.

Satyavati indicated for him to be seated on the cushions facing her. She pointedly ignored the nearby wealth. Her eyes turned serious as she said, "I've never had the opportunity to tell you how grateful I am that you rescued Renuka. I wish I had been here to see it. It's still talked about by everyone I meet!"

She had been speaking in Magadhi. Jimuta looked down, but he replied in Sanskrit. "It was the only thing I could think of to do."

Her eyebrow rose in surprise, but she didn't acknowledge his ability, except to switch to Sanskrit herself: "Still, it must have been quite a spectacle. Renuka is teased about it constantly. And I think you'll hear about it the rest of your life."

Jimuta smiled in embarrassment. "I hope not."

The courtesan said, "I was quite concerned when I heard of your wounds. How are you feeling now?"

His stomach was knotted like the girth rope on an elephant. "I'm healing quite well, thank you. And your own health?"

"Oh, I'm quite well. But will your leg recover completely?"

"Except for a scar, I'm told."

"And your hand?"

He smiled grimly. "I can't restore the fingers I've lost. But I'll be able to use the hand, even to write with it. A small loss, compared to His Majesty's life."

The serving girl reappeared and handed them each a gold-inlaid cup of wine. Another servant set down trays of sliced melon, both orange and green.

They sipped at the wine. "And is Renuka well?" he asked at last, trying to keep his voice even.

A slight smile curled at Satyavati's lips. "Quite well. I'll tell her you inquired about her. I assume you would like to see her sometime?"

Rivulets of sweat were running in his armpits. He realized he should take some of the melon for the sake of courtesy. But his stomach felt like it did just before entering the battle at Kalinga. "I'm wondering if...if you'd consider an offer for her contract."

Satyavati smiled. "I'm always open to discuss such a matter."

He gestured toward the boxes of gold. "I would like to offer twenty-five thousand *panas*."

"That's your entire reward," Satyavati said.

"Yes."

After a moment she sighed. "I told you, I think, that although the price is a matter for negotiation, fifty thousand is the minimum."

He took a gulp of wine, but his voice was still a croak as he said, "This is all I have. I hoped it might be enough." He had thought that perhaps the sight of so much money, so close, so easy to take, would be enough to convince her.

Satyavati's face turned impassive. She said after a time, "I've assumed she'll go to a wealthy husband. If I sold her to you, you'd then be poor. You must want her badly to give up such a fortune."

"I do. I've loved her since I first saw her."

"How would you support her, if you give up all your wealth?" He drank more wine. "You should also know that the King's given me a higher position. I'm now assistant scribe to His Majesty himself. I earn two hundred *panas* a month."

Satyavati examined at him for a time, and then she nodded. "Two hundred is a lot for someone your age. But," she smiled to take away the sting, "it would be a day's expenses for the type of man I've expected Renuka to marry."

"It's enough to live well on, even if not in great luxury." He drank more wine, and discovered the glass was empty. The servant girl poured more.

Satyavati, who had not touched her own cup after the first sip, said pleasantly but bluntly, "Renuka has been accustomed to great luxury ever since she came to live with me. I feel obligated to look after her best interests. How could I justify letting her go for far less money than I know she could get?"

Jimuta thought for a time. He had been unable to eat over worry about this meeting, and with the empty stomach his head was starting to feel light from the wine. Even though he had no more funds, maybe there was a way to increase his offer. "I'll pay you half of everything I earn until I've reached the total of fifty thousand *panas*. Hopefully, His Majesty will eventually feel that I'm worthy of an even higher position. Then I could pay larger amounts, and I'd reach the fifty thousand sooner."

She smiled gently. "Obviously, that doesn't solve the problem of your properly supporting Renuka. In fact, if you'd already obligated half of your pay, it would add to the difficulty."

Jimuta wiped with the back of his bandaged hand at the sweat on his forehead. He started to sip more wine, then thought better of it. He needed his head clear.

Everything was going wrong.

All his love, all his high regard, for Renuka was being reduced to a matter of not enough *panas*.

Did his overpowering feelings count for nothing? Did *Renuka's* feelings count for nothing? He asked, "May I make a suggestion? Why not ask her if she'd be willing to accept less luxury, in exchange for a husband she knows would value her above all else in the world?"

Satyavati raised an eyebrow, and contemplated him. "I don't mean to ignore her wishes. However, she may be unduly influenced by her emotions of the moment. Especially given your famous rescue of her by elephant. I doubt it would be useful to ask her opinion at this time. She and I have talked about you a number of times before, so I think I know what she would say."

Jimuta tensed even more. What, indeed *would* Renuka say? He'd felt almost certain she'd give up a luxurious life for him. But could he have badly misjudged her feelings for him?

And did he even have the right to make such a request of her?

To make her face such a choice? He thought furiously, desperate to devise another way to increase his offer even more, or to find a way to obtain a larger income. He could think of nothing else likely to sway the courtesan. To have so much wealth fall into his hands unexpectedly, and yet to have it not be enough!

Satyavati, too, was silent, staring out into the distance. Eventually, she said, "You probably don't know that I started out poor, like you did, and like Renuka did. I was on my own when I was only a child, and I was completely alone when I arrived in Pataliputra. I came into my work because it seemed my best chance to survive. In many ways, the gods have been good to me since then."

She stopped talking, glanced at Jimuta, who was puzzled as to why she was revealing this information.

Her blue eyes softened as she resumed: "I'd always planned that Renuka would have the best patron I could find for her. Not only a rich man, but one who would treat her well. Renuka has often talked with me about you. I've been fond of you, but it was obvious that you could never provide her with more than a life of hard work. I frankly advised her to forget you." Satyavati smiled at him. "She says she can't do that."

Jimuta's breath caught.

"Renuka also says she'd prefer her husband to know what it's like to be poor—as she was when she was a small child. She doubts a man who'd been wealthy all his life could ever truly understand her."

Jimuta stared at the courtesan in astonishment. He had become increasingly certain his cause was lost.

Satyavati continued, "Renuka is special to me. I don't want to disappoint her. I quite realize that she might not even be alive today if you hadn't saved her. And I think you'll treat her kindly." The happiness in her decision was evident in her voice as she went on: "I'm already wealthy enough myself. Anyway, I wouldn't even have the possibility of receiving payment for her if those Kalinga agents had killed her. So the money will be Renuka's dowry. If you manage it well, you and she can afford many luxuries. And I *am* impressed that you've learned Sanskrit. I think eventually the King will trust you with even higher positions. It will be a good match."

Rudra now occupied the fanciest of all the stables. The boss of all the men visited him almost every day, bringing him a treat. And often it was Rudra whom the boss rode in parades.

Rudra knew from all the attention and special treats he received that he had done well in the battle.

But he had hated the fighting. He would never forget Gajendra's screams for help, or the mutilated body as his friend lay dying.

Gajendra's spirit often visited Rudra at night, when Rudra was drowsy, not quite asleep, but not quite awake. And the two would talk.

Afterwards, Rudra would feel comforted.

But he felt deeply saddened whenever he thought about never seeing Gajendra again in the flesh. Good friends were difficult to find. Not long after Rudra was placed in his new home stable, the young man he had grown so fond of stopped riding him and grooming and bathing him.

Gajendra's former driver took over instead, and he treated Rudra very well. Rudra liked him.

Rudra didn't understand why he had a different driver. But at least his old driver and friend returned to see him almost every day, dressed in nicer clothes, and smelling strongly now of the young woman Rudra had helped rescue. On every visit he brought Rudra a treat, just like the boss of all the men did, and often both his old driver and his newer one would go out riding on Rudra.

Sometimes his former driver would bring his mate. She carried his scent mixed with the smells of her own body, as well as the odors of the familiar perfume and of the flowers in her hair. Rudra liked her. She always spoke to him in a pleasing voice, and she brought sweets for him.

After the next season of rains ended, the two came for a different kind of visit. Rudra could tell from the tone of their voices, and the way the former driver hugged him so hard, that the man and the woman were going to go away for a time.

Many, many days passed when they did not come again to visit.

The weather turned cooler for a long time, and then it gradually turned warmer again.

At last his former driver returned with his mate, who carried a tiny child. Rudra trumpeted with delight at seeing his old friends. And at the big load of food which the helpers carried in for Rudra. The grasses and branches were dry, because they had come a such a long distance. They carried the distinctive odors of the soil and the air that he remembered fondly from his old home, at the big wooden buildings on the top of the hill so far away.

The years passed. Rudra never again had to be in a battle, which was just fine with him. Nor did any of the other elephants.

Rudra thought that was probably because the boss of all the men—who continued to visit Rudra and bring treats, and often to ride him—had finally realized there was no need any more to prove he was stronger than the other bosses.

The time of poor harvests was over; the rains came regularly each year. The empire entered a new period of prosperity.

By the time Jimuta was thirty he held the position of *hasty-adhyaksha*, superintendent of elephants, only a level below that of a Minister in the King's cabinet. It had helped that he worked for the

King himself, and thus was well known to Ashoka personally. But it also helped that never before had there been such opportunities for men with no family connections to obtain government promotions solely on the basis of merit.

When Jimuta returned to Mangarh for another visit, he was accompanied by his beautiful wife and four children in a giant curtained carriage with an entourage of servants. He came as a representative of the King and stayed as an honored guest in the Raja's castle.

One purpose of the visit was to oversee arrangements for an edict of the King to be inscribed on a nearby rock face.

Another was to present the local Buddhist monastery a grant from Ashoka. The King was a recent convert to Buddhism, and the funds were to be used to build a *stupa*, a large dome shaped, masonry-covered earth mound over a sacred relic of the Buddha.

Years before, the aged Raja of Mangarh had narrowly escaped being deposed from his throne for his part in the plot against King Ashoka. His own brother had been captured and put to death for trying to bring about the King's demise. So the Raja took great care to ensure the Emperor's representative was treated as royalty.

The Raja, of course, had discovered that the distinguished visitor came from Mangarh originally, and that the village which the official visited was the man's place of birth. But the Raja simply could not comprehend why such an esteemed personage as the *hastyadhyaksha* would spend so much time in the humble Mangarh elephant stables, or why the supervisor of all the elephants in the imperial army would engage in such long conversations with a mere elephant driver named Nakula.

***

Emperor Ashoka felt great remorse over the tremendous loss of life in the Kalinga War. After more than a year of searching for solace for his troubled soul, he become a follower of the teachings of the Buddha, who had lived some two hundred years before. Ashoka sent missionaries to other Asian Kingdoms, spreading the Buddha's message far beyond its original homeland. Had it not been for Ashoka's patronage, Buddhism might well have disappeared from the earth.

The King also embarked upon one of the grandest experiments in the history of humankind. He decided to never again wage war, although he did continue to maintain a large army so no enemy ever dared attack him. The greater part of his long reign was a period of peace and prosperity such as the Indian subcontinent probably had never enjoyed before, and would never enjoy again for so long a period.

Ashoka developed his own concept of Dharma or Dhamma, a rule of conduct based on compassion and respect for all other beings.

As perhaps the most powerful ruler ever on the subcontinent, he had a unique opportunity to try to improve both the moral and material lives of his people. He established a special corps of government agents to visit all parts of his empire and promote his program of Dharma.

As a devout Buddhist, Ashoka endowed many monasteries throughout his territories. He became known both for his stupas, large hemispherical structures of masonry and earth, and for his edicts carved on rock faces and pillars throughout his empire.

A depiction of the capital from the top of his pillar at Sarnath, with four lions and the wheel of Dharma, eventually became the official seal of the modern nation of India, and his chakra disc adorns the center of the Indian flag.

The ending of an edict inscribed in stone at a number of locations in his territories said:

This inscription on Dharma has been engraved so that my sons and great grandsons should not think of gaining new conquests. For them, the true conquest should be by Dharma, for that is what is of value both in this world and the next.

Unfortunately, his sons and grandsons were not so able as he; the Mauryan empire soon disintegrated after his death.

Its memory, however, has been kept alive for over two millennia in the legends of a glorious golden age—which India could once again experience if its rulers were to have the unselfishness, the wisdom, and the will.

Ashokan Lion
Capital

The
Mangarh Treasure
Four

"I can't give you a literal translation from memory," Kaushalya Kumari said as she gazed at the rock face, "but this is a version of the famous inscription in which Emperor Ashoka tells of his remorse for causing the loss of a hundred thousand lives when he conquered the kingdom of Kalinga. And how he regrets deporting a hundred fifty thousand more people."

She moved her scarf to better shield her face from the fierce sun. "He speaks of giving up war, and of his own concept of *Dharma* which he wants everyone to follow. He says that anyone who does wrong should be forgiven. He wants all beings to be gentle. He ends by saying that he has engraved the inscription so that his sons and grandsons should not think of gaining new conquests. Instead, their conquests should be by *Dharma* since that is what is of value both in this world and the next."

Vijay enjoyed listening to the princess' charmingly modulated voice, watching the changes in expression flit across her exquisitely sculpted face. Despite the discomfort of the intense heat on the hillside, he hoped she would say more, but she did not. It was understandable, of course, given the animosity she must feel toward Vijay and Shanta.

Shanta Das slowly shook her head as she gazed at the rock. "What an amazing king. It's too bad modern rulers don't follow his example."

Kaushalya Kumari gave her a sharp look, as if wondering if the tax inspector was criticizing Lakshman Singh's former rule in Mangarh. But she quickly composed her face, apparently realizing Shanta Das probably knew no details whatever of the Maharaja's reign before independence.

Vijay was growing exceedingly anxious here, so close to his home village, where someone who had known him might come by at any moment, drawn by curiosity about the strangers in the jeep. "We'd better look at the monastery and the *stupa*," he said, "before the sun fries us." They left the rock face and its inscription.

To the untrained eye, the hilltop ruins of the monastery resembled a smaller version of the ruins of the Harappan town: undulating mounds of earth, exposed remnants of low brick walls forming small rectangular enclosures.

"Does anyone know what the bricks were?" asked Shanta. From the tone of her voice, Vijay had the impression she was becoming intrigued by the archaeological sites.

"All the little square rooms were probably cells where the monks lived," replied Kaushalya Kumari.

"Interesting," commented Vijay. But not a likely hiding place for wealth, for much the same reasons the Harappan town was not a good place. Too remote, and too little security.

He walked on to the *stupa*. The big domelike, masonry-encased mound appeared to be crumbling back into the dust. It had been constructed of large bricks covering a hemispherical hillock of earth about ten paces in diameter. Many of the bricks were gone, and those remaining sagged irregularly into the soil of the mound. A deep, now-eroding trench sliced into one side, exposing a partial cross section.

"Did the archaeologists dig into the *stupa*?" asked Shanta Das.

"I saw them working at it when I was a small child," said Kaushalya Kumari.

"Was anything interesting found?" asked Shanta.

The princess shrugged. "Not that I recall. The *stupa* is supposed to have been built by Ashoka after he became a Buddhist. I'm sure you know legends say he ordered eighty thousand of them made, all over India. They were intended as focus for worshipers. Most of them probably held some sort of relic of the Buddha, like a hair or a tooth. But nothing was found in this one. Maybe it was looted by some invader."

"Possibly Muslims," said Vijay, "since their invasions are blamed so much for Buddhism's disappearance."

"Maybe," said Kaushalya Kumari. "There's no way to know."

Vijay slowly shook his head as he gazed at the mound. "It's curious how Buddhism died out in the land where it was born."

Shanta Das said, seeming a little tentative, "We can't say it's died out altogether in India. I'm Buddhist."

Vijay noted that saying she was Buddhist was a clear indication she was Scheduled Caste. Most modern Indian Buddhists were low caste converts from Hinduism who hoped to better their place in society by embracing a religion that didn't recognize classes. He said, "But if Ashoka's missionaries hadn't spread Buddhism to other countries, it would probably be a dead religion now like that of the Egyptians." He felt Kaushalya Kumari's eyes on him, and as he continued, he realized to his consternation that he was trying to favorably impress her with his historical knowledge: "The decline was probably caused by other factors, too, besides the Muslim invasions." He quickly concluded, "Such as Hindus accepting the Buddha as an incarnation of Vishnu. That must have made it harder for Buddhists to maintain a separate religion."

Kaushalya Kumari responded, "Buddhism was still strong in the 7th Century when the Chinese pilgrim Hiuen Tsang visited here. And when the Ajanta cave murals were painted. The last of them were probably 6th Century, in the time of the Gupta Emperors. I'm doing my doctoral thesis on one of the murals called 'The Dying Princess.'"

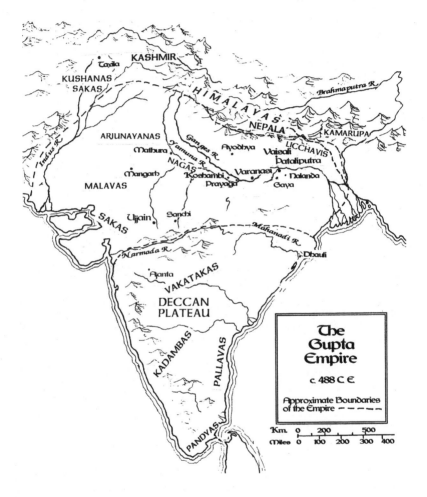

The Gupta Empire

c. 488 C.E.

Approximate Boundaries of the Empire – – – –

Km. 0   200   500
Miles 0 100 200 300 400

The Art of Love

1

Dhavala extended the mirror to Guhasena, who eyed himself critically in the polished brass. "A little more collyrium on my eyelids," Guhasena told his valet.

The short, thin man with a dignified bearing and a delicately featured face held the cosmetic tray so it was convenient to his master. "Unfortunately, sir, that won't hide the redness below them."

"That's what we need, Dhavala," Guhasena said cheerfully, dipping the small, pointed brush into the mixture. "Something to take the red out of our eyes the morning after. If you can discover an eyeball whitener, you'll be a wealthy man. Everyone in Ujjain will seek you out!"

Dhavala sniffed. "Not everyone is dissolute enough to stay out until all hours drinking."

"I'm firmly convinced you were never young, Dhavala."

Dhavala formed a mock scowl. Forty-one years was not exactly ancient, even though he'd experienced significant ordeals. When he was not much older than Guhasena's twenty-one years, through a poor investment he had lost what little money he'd inherited from his father, forcing him to become a domestic servant. And only a year after that, he had lost his wife when an epidemic had swept the city. He replied, "Not so long ago, I, too, was young like yourself. But I aged quickly when I entered your service, sir."

Guhasena laughed. "Well said!" He once more examined himself in the mirror for reassurance that he looked his best. Indeed, his long dark hair fell to his shoulders with just the right amount of curl. His white turban was tied just right. The gold earrings and necklace matched perfectly. He added a touch more of red lac to his lips, then returned the cosmetic tray and mirror to Dhavala. "But life will be easier for you when I'm married. You'll be amazed at the sudden change in me."

Dhavala looked at him with interest. "I thought her father still hasn't agreed."

"He hasn't. But he will. His family has been friends with mine for too many years. Besides, he could never refuse Shashiprabha something she really wanted. And she really wants me!" Guhasena lowered his head, allowing a garland of marigolds to be draped around his neck, to hang midway down his bare chest.

"That says little for the young lady's intelligence," Dhavala observed, "especially when she's known you for so long. Tell me...if you married would you suddenly develop an interest in your father's trading ventures? As a painter, you might find it difficult to support the daughter of one of Ujjain's wealthiest men. She's used to having as many attendants as a princess."

Guhasena rose from his stool. He strode over to his latest effort at portraiture. He picked up the wooden board, turned it slightly to catch the light from the window, then gently set it down again. "It's a good likeness of her," he said. "But I still can't quite capture the spark in her eyes when she's watching me."

Dhavala shook his head, though Guhasena was not looking at him. "You should give up painting for sculpture. I have to admit you're not bad, but painting's only a craft, not an art. If you're determined to be an artist, then be a real one. Take up the hammer and chisel."

For the first time that morning, Dhavala caught Guhasena's interest. "Why should sculptors have all the prestige, just because stone lasts longer than wood or plaster? It's the expression that makes the art, Dhavala, not the medium."

Dhavala snorted. "Everyone in Ujjain who can afford a paint box fancies himself an artist. A painting can be turned out in hours. But the really serious, the dedicated—those who are willing to spend months on a piece—take up sculpting."

Guhasena sighed. "I intend to change that attitude, Dhavala." The sound of the nearby temple watchman's hymn drifted in the open window, suddenly making him aware of the time. "Oh! It's the end of the watch. I'm late!" He ran for the doorway. Dhavala, shaking his head, followed.

The household's groom was waiting in the courtyard with their horses. They quickly mounted and rode out the gateway. Guhasena dug his bare toes into his horse's sides and shouted, urging it into a gallop. Servants and sweepers scampered aside as the two sped down the street lined with large, whitewashed, vaulted-roofed mansions, and over the short bridge spanning the tiny stream which emptied into the larger Sipra River.

Turning left now onto the wide Royal Avenue, they passed the high stone wall surrounding the huge palace of Budha Gupta, Emperor of most of northern India. Ujjain had long been a principal city; in ancient times it had been the capital of the major kingdom of Avanti. For a hundred years, ever since the conquest of Ujjain by the great Chandra Gupta II, the Gupta emperors had used Ujjain as a capital, sometimes ruling from it, sometimes from their original capital of Pataliputra. The Guptas had brought prosperity, peace, security, and a flowering of the arts to those they ruled, and Ujjain was a showpiece of their reign.

A short distance beyond the palace, Guhasena and Dhavala turned onto a side street. They had reached their destination, the large forested park known as the Pushpakaranda Garden. They wound their way on a trail through the woods to a small dense grove of mango trees and creepers by the bank of a stream. Guhasena hurriedly dismounted and entered the thicket, leaving Dhavala to watch the horses.

Guhasena found Shashiprabha waiting, seated on a wooden bench with Menaka, her favorite maidservant. Seeing him, Shashiprabha's face lit. She jumped to her feet and raced into his arms. Guhasena was dimly aware of Menaka discreetly leaving. His mouth sought Shashiprabha's, red painted with lac like his own. "I'm sorry I'm late, dearest," he whispered between kisses. As usual, she wore only a striped waist cloth, and her bare breasts pressed into his chest. He inhaled the perfume in her oiled dark hair.

After a time, they sat side by side on the bench, his arm around her, holding her warm smooth flesh to his own. He looked down at the top of her breasts, rubbed with sandalwood paste and saffron, his artist's eye appreciating the way the painted design of delicate vines on her light skin accentuated the outward curves.

She looked up at him coyly and said with a smile, "I heard you were at a party last night at Sagaradatta's house. And the courtesan Madanika was there with some of her girls."

Guhasena stiffened and looked at her in surprise. Then he relaxed. "Oh! Your brother must have told you. I'd forgotten he was there for a while."

Guhasena tried to recall anything he had done that would be embarrassing for Shashiprabha to know. "I really don't remember much," he admitted at last. "I must have drunk more than I realized at the time."

"Oh, don't worry," she said, laughing, her dark eyes lively. "My brother would never tell me any details. And I wouldn't want to know them, anyway."

He felt a warm rush of pleasure at his good fortune in finding such a good natured future wife. So many women were bad tempered; harridans at an early age. But he had known Shashiprabha since she was a small child, and there was no meanness whatsoever in her.

She extended a leg encircled by a gold anklet and appeared to examine the lac painted on the sole of her bare foot. Then, she placed her foot on top of his own and began slowly stroking with her toes as she snuggled closer to him. He felt the familiar stirring at his groin.

So far, they had never actually made love, though he found the possibility most tempting. He had studied Vatsayana's treatise on the subject, the *Kama Sutra*, in great detail. He had carefully memorized the chapters on courtship and wooing a girl, but he had been pleased to find that much of it was not needed with Shashiprabha, who had been quietly in love with him for years.

With courtesans he had tried his knowledge of some of the other chapters of the *Kama Sutra*, so he was familiar with practices such as the "twining position," the "congress of a cow," the "churning manner," and the "ramming manner." Even Vatsayana, though, wrote that it was preferable for a girl to be a virgin when she entered marriage, and with Shashiprabha, Guhasena had so far limited himself to the chapters on embracing and kissing.

Her foot stopped stroking, and Shashiprabha said, "I've been talking with my father. I think he'll agree now to our marrying!"

He looked down at her in pleased surprise. "That's wonderful, dearest!" He held her more tightly. "At last! What made him decide?"

She grinned. "I did. I told him again how you'd been the only man I'd ever loved, ever since I first saw you when I was five years old and you were nine. I told him I knew right from that moment we were destined for each other in this lifetime. I told him if he really cared about my happiness, he couldn't even so much as consider marrying me to someone else!"

"Hadn't you told him that before?"

"This time, I told him I'd run away and we'd have a *Gandharva* marriage if he wouldn't agree."

Guhasena laughed. "So that's what really decided him."

"I think so. My mother would never forgive him if I got married secretly. She naturally wants the biggest wedding Ujjain's ever seen."

That evening, Guhasena's father summoned him for a talk in the garden of their home. They sat on a stone bench in the small pavilion, where servants had set up the coconut oil lamps. Vasudatta smiled good naturedly and said, "My friend Dharmagupta says his daughter insists you're the only one she'd ever consider marrying."

Guhasena returned the smile. "That's what she tells me, too, Father."

"Your mother and I both think she's an excellent choice. We couldn't have found better if we'd tried. And even aside from being so wealthy, Dharmagupta's the best trading partner I've ever had."

"I'm glad you agree, Father."

Vasudatta's face became more solemn. "If you're to be a householder, you need some means of support. Do you truly think you can earn enough from your painting to keep Shashiprabha and all her servants?"

"I don't know," Guhasena admitted. "But I think I can do well with my art. I intend to try."

Vasudatta looked out into the night. After a time, he said, "You probably inherited some of your talent from me. I have some skill in the arts myself, you know—or at least I used to. Business hasn't left me much time to indulge in it, except as a patron." He looked back at his son. "Have you found a wealthy sponsor, or do you intend to rely solely on individual commissions?"

"I don't have a patron, Father," Guhasena replied. "I haven't even tried to find one—I assume no one would sponsor me, since they know I come from a wealthy family."

Vasudatta smiled wryly. "So they'd assume your support will come from me, eh?"

Guhasena shrugged. He watched the small clouds of insects swarming around the lamp flames.

Vasudatta said, "You've never brought up the subject. But I've thought about it. I'm convinced you have talent. And you work hard at it. Oh, I know you indulge in your amusements such as drinking parties and courtesans. But you don't let them run your life." Vasudatta again stared into the night, seeming lost in thought. Then he returned his gaze to his son. "To do well as a trader, I had to give up all ideas of life as an artist. But there's no reason you should have to. So I'll be your patron, for as long as you need me."

It took a moment for Guhasena to recognize the import of the words. Then he quickly moved to embrace his father. "Your confidence in me means a lot. And I *was* worried about where I'd get enough money, Father, especially since Shashiprabha is used to so much wealth."

Vasudatta hesitated, then said, "I wonder about your emphasis on painting, though, son. It has a much lower reputation than sculpture. Everyone dabbles in painting. Competition's so keen that the commissions tend to pay little, unless you're doing large murals. Have you seriously considered being a sculptor?"

"Not really, Father. I like painting much better. I know I'd probably gain more prestige as a sculptor. But stone feels so cold and hard. Paintings are warmer, more alive. I can be more spontaneous."

Vasudatta sat in silence a moment. Then he shrugged. "I respect your decision, of course." He rose. "Well. Your mother and I had better set up a meeting with Shashiprabha's parents to work out your wedding details!"

2

The astrologers determined that the couple would be a good match, and that an auspicious date would be three months hence. Planning and preparation for the wedding began.

Whenever he wasn't meeting Shashiprabha in the park, Guhasena applied himself diligently to his painting. Determined to be a success, he convinced his father to sit for a portrait, and then he painted his friend Buddhila. When the chubby, cheerful Buddhila arrived for the final sitting, he said, "My father's adding a new room to our house. He's looking for a good muralist to do scenes from the *Ramayana*. I suggested you, and he's interested!"

Even had he wanted to try, Guhasena could not have suppressed the grin that flooded his face. His pulse raced. "I've never done a complete mural," he admitted. "But I helped another artist do one. I know I can manage."

"Then bring some samples of your work. I'll convince him to hire you."

"It's more than I ever dreamed of!" he exclaimed to Dhavala when he returned from Buddhila's house. "The room will be the new entertainment hall. That means every guest who comes to the house will see my work."

"A great opportunity for you, sir."

"Yes! I'm supposed to have it finished for Buddhila's sister's wedding, only a little over two months from now. *Shakuntala* will be performed in the hall to entertain the guests."

Dhavala raised an eyebrow and said, "That's not much time for such a large project."

"True, but I can manage. I paint fast when I'm forced to. And I'm only doing the walls, not the ceiling,. At least it will be finished before my own wedding."

"No drinking parties for a while, sir?"

"No drinking parties for a while."

Ideas for the scenes churned wildly in Guhasena's mind. He immediately began overseeing the preparation of the walls in the large hall. First, workmen whitewashed the surfaces. Then, carrying pails as they worked from ladders, they used brushes to apply a mixture of sand and plaster for a proper ground.

As the walls dried, Guhasena sat for hours in the center of the room planning his composition—how it would fill the spaces with movement, how it would curve naturally around the windows and doors. He would present some key episodes of the *Ramayana* in sequence, from left to right around the room, beginning with the scene in King Dasharatha's palace when the King agonizingly fulfilled his promise to grant a boon to his junior Queen, Kaikeyi: the exiling of Prince Rama for fourteen years.

When Guhasena was certain the ground was dry, he took up his brush and began boldly outlining the palace scene in red ochre. Only when the entire segment was drawn to his satisfaction did he begin to fill in the outline, contouring the figures with red, overlaid with the various local colors, resulting in fully modeled, rounded figures that appeared to leap forth from the walls into reality.

He was pleased with the result of his first scene. Even Dhavala admitted, "I could understand the story from their gestures alone, sir. The King is so obviously unhappy, the Queen so clearly self-satisfied. Your ability to convey feeling is unexcelled, sir!"

His patron, too, was delighted. But Guhasena felt especially gratified when his own father stopped by for a look. Obviously impressed, Vasudatta said, "Guhasena, I want you to know I'd be proud to be your patron even if you weren't my son. As it is, I feel doubly honored."

Guhasena continued to see Shashiprabha briefly almost every morning, and he kept her informed on his progress. "You must come by soon to see it," he kept telling her.

And finally, she did. He had just completed painting Sita's abduction by the demon Ravana. Shashiprabha stood surveying the scenes with a broad smile on her face. At last, she looked into his eyes. "It's marvelous, Guhasena. I knew you were good, but I never realized just how superb you are!"

"You mean as a painter, I assume?"

Her eyes twinkled at his teasing. "In every way."

He turned to look at his work. "What do you think of my Sita?" he asked her.

Shashiprabha frowned in thought as she looked at the fresco. "I noticed her right away. You've shown her essence so clearly! In the scene when she leaves for the exile with Rama and Lakshmana, she's so obviously...well, pure and good, as well as beautiful. And when Ravana abducts her, she looks absolutely terrified."

Guhasena forced a straight face. Casually, he asked, "Does she resemble anyone you know?"

Shashiprabha examined the figures. "I think so," she replied hesitantly, "but I can't quite..." Suddenly her hand flew to her mouth. "*Guhasena!*" she gasped. "You *shouldn't* have!"

He laughed, enjoying her consternation immensely. "I had no choice. Whenever I envisioned her, I saw you."

"But—what will everyone think?" she whispered.

"That she's the loveliest Sita they've ever seen."

One morning, he entered the grove in the park for his daily meeting with Shashiprabha to find her seat empty. He sat down to wait, puzzled. It was unlike her to be late.

Suddenly, her maid, Menaka, came hurrying in. "Sir!" she said breathlessly. "My mistress awoke ill this morning. She asked me to come tell you she's sorry, but she can't see you today."

Guhasena frowned, hiding his disappointment. "It's not serious?"

Menaka hesitated. "I hope not, sir. She's running a fever, so I summoned the *vaidyas* right away."

Guhasena started to say he would come see her immediately, but then he realized it was not appropriate to visit a young woman, even his betrothed, in her bedchamber. "Keep me informed, Menaka! And tell her I'll be thinking of her every minute and praying for her recovery!"

When Menaka had gone, he sat for some time on the bench. Finally, he rose and left to work on his mural. He heard nothing more about Shashiprabha until that evening, when Menaka sent word that her mistress's condition was unchanged, and not to plan on a meeting in the park the next morning.

He was surprised at how depressed he felt at not being able to meet with her two days in a row. He stayed out late that night drinking for the first time since he had begun the mural. The next morning, he rose desultorily, did his ablutions, and went to continue his work. In midmorning, Menaka suddenly appeared, looking solemn. "Sir," she said, "my mistress has been asking for you, and her parents agreed to your coming."

When they arrived at Dharmagupta's elegant mansion, Menaka led him quickly to Shashiprabha's rooms. There, his beloved lay on her bed, surrounded by her servants. Her mother and brother were also there, and two physicians.

He quickly rushed to her side. He saw how flushed her face was. She opened her eyes to see him, and he was astounded at the change. How dull, how lifeless, those eyes now seemed!

"Dearest!" he said.

She tried to force a smile, but soon closed her eyes. She reached out her hand, and he took it. "How do you feel?" he asked.

She was a moment answering. "Hot..." she murmured. "I can't think...."

He told her of his progress on the mural, and he thought she heard, but apparently responding was too much effort. After a time she appeared to drift off to sleep.

He became aware that the two *vaidyas* had begun chanting *mantras*. He vaguely recognized that the words were from the *Artharva Veda*. Suddenly, he felt conspicuous, squatting there beside her. He realized she would no doubt be asleep for some time. He slowly rose.

Her brother escorted him to the door. "Tell her I'll come any time, the instant she calls," Guhasena said. "I'll be by again this evening."

He tried to continue his work on the mural, but he was unable to concentrate. Eventually, he gave up and left, walking the streets of the neighborhood, not seeing anything about him. Dhavala was off on his own pursuits, assuming Guhasena would be absorbed in the mural, so he was alone.

Twice he walked past the small stone Shiva temple that served his area. He had seldom visited it, not being particularly interested in performing *pujas*, and knowing that his father and mother regularly took care of the rituals on behalf of the family. But now, he paused by the temple, thinking. After a moment, he stepped into the porch and peered into the gloom of the chamber, where the priest squatted before the *lingam*, the symbol of Shiva. He entered the room, felt in his purse for some coins, handed them to the attendant. Then, he knelt before the *lingam* and prayed for Shashiprabha.

3

He returned to Shashiprabha's room that evening. Three *vaidyas* were present now, different ones. Dharmagupta, Shashiprabha's father stood by, and several aunts, uncles, cousins. It seemed to Guhasena her condition was no better. She was unaware of his presence for a while, and then her only acknowledgment of him was to open her eyes briefly and try unsuccessfully to force a smile.

He looked up to meet the worried eyes of her father. Dharmagupta beckoned to Guhasena, who reluctantly rose and followed him out of the room.

"She's not well at all," Dharmagupta said. "The physicians say this particular fever is a bad one. Many people die from it."

"No!" Guhasena said. "I *know* she'll recover."

Dharmagupta looked weary. "I hope so, Guhasena. I hope so."

Guhasena returned to sit by her bed. As the hours crept by, the family members came and went. Guhasena sat in a daze. Once, as Menaka held Shashiprabha's head, his vision cleared for a moment. It was as though he were an outside observer, almost as if he were a god, seeing this scene from the perspective of an impartial observer. The tableau was a moment frozen in time: all these people gathered to watch a girl who was terribly ill.

Very late, well after darkness had fallen, her father came to him. "You'd better go rest at home. I'll send word if she wants you, or if there's any change."

After a night when he had difficulty sleeping, he visited her sickroom again. She was in the grip of the fever, sweating, constantly changing position, trying to gain some relief. Guhasena felt a growing fury at the demons who were doing this to his beloved. Why didn't they take their vengeance on someone else? Why on Shashiprabha, who couldn't possibly have done anything to anger them?

He left, and he again visited the Shiva temple.

That evening, she was worse. He left for his own home reluctantly, feeling he should be with her, but knowing it made little sense to stay up all night. He heard the temple watchman sing out the end of one watch, and three hours later the next. He had not realized he had fallen asleep, until he felt Dhavala shaking him. "A servant is here from Dharmagupta's house, sir," he said.

Guhasena quickly rose to his feet and went to the front hall. The messenger was a man of about thirty years, and he looked distraught, his eyes were moist. "How is she?" Guhasena asked urgently.

"The young mistress is gone, sir."

The next day, he stood with the other mourners on the banks of the Sipra and watched his beloved's body consumed by the flames of her funeral pyre until he could stand to watch no longer.

He did not return to his *Ramayana* fresco that day, nor did he return the following day, or the next. He sat in his rooms, eating little, seeing little. Sometimes, memories of Shashiprabha would come to him. Her smile when she met his eyes, the lightness of her step when she walked. He remembered the first time he had seen her, when she was a strikingly beautiful child of only five years old. He remembered seeing her happily playing ball outdoors once, when she was ten or eleven; and gracefully dancing and playing her *vina* when she was thirteen and almost a woman.

He had often had the feeling over the years that they had known each other in previous lives, and he had somehow known that they were meant for each other in this lifetime. But fate had played a cruel trick. What terrible thing had he done, what had she done in previous lives, that karma would dictate such a horrible revenge?

He thought of her ashes, now flowing down the Sipra, then into the Chambal, then down the Yamuna and the Ganges, and ultimately into the sea. The idea of such separation was too painful, and he forced the thought from his mind.

Dhavala quietly served him. But one morning, he said, "Sir, hadn't you better complete your mural?"

Guhasena did not reply for some time. Eventually, he said, "I no longer have inspiration, Dhavala."

"I understand, sir. But you did accept the commission."

"You obviously do *not* understand, Dhavala! I no longer feel like painting. That means my work would be no good."

After a time, Dhavala said, "I understand more than you think. I know how I felt when my own wife died."

Guhasena looked at him with remorse. "I didn't mean to imply you'd never felt sad," he said quietly. "But if I'm not inspired, my art will show it. That's not fair to the man who commissioned me."

"Neither is not finishing the work. The wedding is only a month away. How would it look if someone else had to complete the mural? Can you imagine it executed in two different styles?"

Guhasena had not let himself consider that possibility. But now he faced it. "No."

"Besides, you may feel a little better if you're doing something constructive.

*

Guhasena forced himself to complete the mural. At first, it was difficult. He would suddenly realize that he had been standing, wet brush in hand, for some time, staring at the outline on the wall. He would begin filling in the contours in color, only to find himself again lost in a daze. But he did complete the mural, barely long enough before the deadline for the paint to dry, and he was surprised at how good it was.

He had been invited to the wedding of Buddhila's sister, and of course to the featured entertainment: the presentation of *Shakuntala*, the most famous drama of the great playwright and poet Kalidasa. As traditional for a play whose main theme was love, the performance was held in the evening. Guhasena entered the hall in the state of numbness he had felt ever since Shashiprabha's death. He was only dimly aware that a white curtain, the color for a play in the erotic *rasa*, or mood, had been stretched across the dais at the far end.

He heard a voice say, "Your murals are exquisite, Guhasena. The figures are so real, the flickering of the lamplight actually makes them seem to move!"

Guhasena turned to see one of his father's wealthy business friends. He folded his hands and bowed. "I'm glad you like them," he said blandly, unable to think of the man's name. He was aware of acknowledging the many other compliments paid him by guests who were seeing his mural for the first time. But he felt no sense of accomplishment, no glow of warmth from all the praise. It was as if someone else had painted the hall.

He seated himself on a low couch next to Buddhila, whose wide, round face was grinning. "I was worried for a while," Buddhila said, "that you wouldn't finish the walls in time. But I should have known you'd keep your word."

Guhasena smiled wanly. "How could I have not finished, after you were so kind as to get me the commission?"

Buddhila looked about. "The room still smells of fresh paint, but at least it's dry enough not to smear if someone touches it. And such a grand new room does show the groom's family how much importance we place on the wedding."

Guhasena could not help but think of how he should have been anticipating his own wedding in another three weeks, and the sense of loss was overwhelming.

A hush came over the room as the stage manager appeared and recited the invocation to Shiva, patron god of the dance and theater. After the stage manager's prologue and a song by an actress, the play, based on an incident from the *Mahabharata*, began.

The noble and heroic King Dushyanta appeared on the stage, dressed for the hunt, riding in his chariot. Though no actual chariot was used, the actor playing the part of the King was so skilled that his gestures and motions clearly conveyed that he was chasing an animal through the woods.

Near a hermitage in the forest, the King met the lovely young woman Shakuntala, the daughter of a sage and a celestial nymph, and they fell in love. As traditional, the King and the other upper class men spoke in Sanskrit, while the women and lower class characters spoke in the local tongue.

Lost in his indifference, Guhasena had paid little attention to the opening of the drama. But now, in spite of himself, he was being drawn into the play's *rasa*, its mood, the dominant emotion of love. He found himself reliving his own falling deeply in love with Shashiprabha, almost as if she were still alive, as if he felt her near.

The play almost absorbed Guhasena into its substitute world, but not quite, due to his nearly continual awareness of the parallels in his own life. Frequently, the actors emphasized a passage by singing rather than speaking, and their stylized gestures often turned into actual dance. King Dushyanta and Shakuntala were united in an informal *Gandharva* wedding. Although Guhasena was reminded of his own wedding that was not to be, the feeling of loss was somewhat lessened by his being engrossed in the love of the two characters on the stage.

The King returned to his palace, leaving his ring with Shakuntala, who would follow later. But Shakuntala was so absorbed in her love for the King that she failed to pay proper attention to an irascible sage, Durvasas, who visited the hermitage. He had acquired many powers by his ascetic disciplines. Angered by Shakuntala ignoring him, Durvasas invoked a spell so the King would forget ever having met her. The spell could be broken only when the King saw the ring he had left with her.

In the next acts, when Shakuntala finally left the hermitage for Dushyanta's palace, carrying the son born of her union with the King, she accidentally lost the ring while crossing a river. King Dushyanta, failing to recognize her because of Durvasas' spell, brusquely sent her and the infant away. The *rasa* of love was superseded in Guhasena by the mood of sadness, and he felt again his deep sorrow of losing Shashiprabha.

King Dushyanta's memory returned when some fishermen found the ring and brought it to him. But he was too late; Shakuntala and the boy had disappeared, having been taken to the celestial regions where Shakuntala's mother lived.

As the King became despondent at his loss, the feelings in Guhasena grew almost unbearable. His attention returned to the room, where he was surrounded by the audience raptly absorbed in the happenings on the stage. He shifted in his seat, searching for a way to the doorway without requiring anyone to move or otherwise drawing attention to himself. But leaving now would be a conspicuous distraction.

So he remained seated, wishing he were elsewhere, as on the stage the King agreed to a request from the god Indra for help in fighting some demons, and a flying chariot carried His Majesty to the celestial regions. There, by chance King Dushyanta encountered his son. A drama always strove for overall harmony, for a sense of equilibrium. Thus, Dushyanta was reunited with Shakuntala and their son, completing the circle begun at their first meeting.

Unable to share their happiness, Guhasena thought of how the loss of Shakuntala and Dushyanta to each other earlier in the play was doubtless a karmic retribution for acts done in a previous life. Likewise, his own loss of Shashiprabha must have been payment for some dire deed he had done in a prior existence.

Knowing that he must have deserved such a penalty did almost nothing to lessen its pain. And unlike in the drama, there would be no reunion between himself and Shashiprabha—at least not in this lifetime. He left the play feeling only a deeper sense of unhappiness and loss.

4

After seeing the *Ramayana* mural, one of the wealthy wedding guests approached him to paint a similar hall with scenes from the *Mahabharata*. Guhasena refused the commission. But he felt guilty doing so. He could not live forever on his fee from the *Ramayana* fresco. And when those funds were gone, he did not see how he could justify taking money from his father if he were making no effort to earn anything by his painting.

Finally, he decided he must leave Ujjain and its memories of Shashiprabha. He had no destination in mind. He simply knew he could not continue living in Ujjain, especially in his father's house, if he were not working.

Dhavala insisted on accompanying him. "Don't be absurd," Guhasena told his valet. "You don't want to live that type of life! I have no idea where I'll spend my nights, or even when or where I'll take my next meal."

"Sir," Dhavala said with a smile, "I've served you almost all your life. I don't want to have to learn someone else's idiosyncrasies." His face became more serious as he said, "And I, too, want to travel while I'm still young enough to survive it."

They journeyed first to Sanchi, then to Koshambi, then along the Ganges to Varanasi, and then to Pataliputra, the other capital of the Gupta emperors. Guhasena lived simply, careful to make his money last as long as possible. During the rainy seasons, he and Dhavala stayed in various religious communities, or in the ashram of some holy man, learning a great deal about varying philosophies. But no message seemed meant for him personally.

"Sir," Dhavala said to him one afternoon while they were sitting in a park in the great city of Pataliputra, "it seems to me that running away from one's pain seldom works."

Guhasena nodded. "True." In many ways, Pataliputra reminded Guhasena of Ujjain: the broad boulevards, the many parks, the huge mansions in the finer residential districts, the great palace complex of the Guptas, originally built in the time of Emperor Ashoka Maurya. It had been two years since the two had last seen Ujjain. Guhasena added, "You once told me time can heal the pain. I'm letting time do its work."

Dhavala sighed. After a while, he said, "Forgive me if I speak too harshly, sir. You're not only in love with a young woman who has passed on. You're in love with a vision, a dream of what your life with her might have been. You feel cheated that you couldn't live your dream, and that's understandable. But there are other women who can share your life."

"So why didn't you marry again, Dhavala?"

Dhavala shrugged. "I have my memories. That seemed enough."

After a time, Guhasena said, "I loved her, Dhavala. I doubt I'd have much chance to find another girl I love. My parents would almost certainly arrange my marriage. That's not the same."

Eventually, Dhavala said, "It doesn't have to be so different. I loved my wife, you know. My parents arranged our marriage. The love just came later, after we were together a while."

Guhasena remained unconvinced.

They left Pataliputra, heading south. Season followed season.

Four years after leaving Ujjain, they had traveled across the Narmada River to the hilly regions of the Deccan plateau, beyond the borders of the empire of the Guptas, in the region ruled by Harisena of the Vakatakas. Though their route had taken them only a few days travel to the east of Ujjain, Guhasena had deliberately not returned to his home, even for a visit, knowing he was not ready.

It was a fine winter afternoon, sunny and quite hot as he and Dhavala ascended a rocky, dusty road through a low range of mountains. Other travelers had told them of the Buddhist monastery at Ajanta, and they decided to visit the settlement, and perhaps to stay a while.

They turned off the main caravan route and followed a trail which wandered along the Waghora River. They climbed through a narrow ravine, where the stream tumbled down a waterfall in a series of steps. Soon they saw saffron robed *bhikkhus* going about their business. Above the river the dark openings of the caves contrasted with the brightness of the cliff front; the Ajanta monastery was carved out of the rocky hillside along the concave side of a bend in the river. Guhasena and Dhavala had occasionally seen other cave settlements on their journeys, so Ajanta did not appear particularly unusual.

They were weary from the heat and covered with dust. As they approached the settlement, a monk directed them to a cave near the center of the row. They passed between two large stone elephants and climbed the rock stairs to the entrance. A young *bhikkhu* stepped from the doorway. "Welcome to Ajanta," he said, speaking in a dialect quite similar to that of the Ujjain region. "I am called Jeta." Jeta was both overweight and tall, making him an impressive size.

Guhasena introduced himself and Dhavala, and said, "As you can tell, we aren't Buddhists. But we're searching for knowledge, and we'd like to spend some time with your *bhikkhus* if you'll have us."

"Of course. We often have visitors who aren't followers of the Buddha. We have an empty cell where you can stay. Come, and I'll get some water for you to wash. We don't take food after noon, but I'll get you some juice to drink."

When Guhasena and Dhavala had refreshed themselves, Jeta took them on a tour of the complex. "We'll start with the oldest caves," he said, as they descended some steps toward the river. He led them through a doorway. It was considerably cooler inside, and while their eyes adjusted to the gloom, Jeta said, "This cave is the lowest one to the river. We use it as a residence now. It's thought to be the first one built, perhaps six centuries ago."

Dimly, Guhasena could see a rectangular room with a series of doorways opening off, all carved from the solid rock. The visitors paused only briefly before Jeta again led them out, where they squinted in the sunlight. "The next two," Jeta said, "are almost as old. As you can see, they're *chaityas*, halls of worship."

They approached the first of the *chaityas*. Above the doorway was a large, arched window, its sculpted frame tapering at the top into a narrow point, representing a stylized *pipal* leaf. A wooden lattice covered the opening. Entering the cave, Guhasena saw a long, narrow room, with a small hemispherical stone *stupa* at the far end. A line of pillars paraded down each side and around the *stupa*, but Guhasena's eyes were immediately drawn to the frescoes on the walls, which depicted various scenes from the life of the Buddha. He nodded approvingly; the artists had been quite competent.

The next cave, higher in the side of the cliff, was a much larger *chaitya*, also with a larger *stupa* at the far end, carved out of the same rock as the room itself. Here, too, paintings covered the walls. Guhasena remarked, "Dress in those days was quite different from now."

"Yes," Jeta replied. "I've been told the murals date from the time of the Satakarnis, a few hundred years ago. Are you especially interested in painting?"

Guhasena was silent for a moment. Then he replied, "At one time I was a painter myself."

Jeta eyed him speculatively, but soon turned to continue the tour. "The next three caves are *viharas*, residences," he said as they moved on.

Of varying sizes, the caves all had large central rooms with cells for the monks opening off the outer walls. "How many monks live at Ajanta?" Dhavala asked.

"We have about a hundred and fifty at the moment," Jeta replied. "I'm sure you know that in the Buddha's time, most *bhikkhus* stayed in monasteries only during the rainy season. The rest of the time they journeyed about teaching, and they begged their food. But now most monks live year round in monasteries funded by laypersons who want to acquire merit by their donations. Kings have given many monasteries the rights to the revenues of local villages. So we no longer beg our food—we either buy it or raise it ourselves."

They came to the cave Guhasena and Dhavala had first approached, where Jeta had greeted them. "This is our latest *vihara*," he said. "It was finished only last year, when it was dedicated by King Harisena's minister, Varahadeva. As you can see," he gestured toward the river, "there's a good view of the waterfalls from the veranda." Inside the cave, stone pillars delineated aisles around the outside of the large square assembly and living hall. Rows of cells for the monks opened off the painted outer walls of the aisles. Through a doorway in the center of the rear wall Jeta showed them a smaller room, a shrine with a large statue of a seated Buddha.

Guhasena examined the hall's murals more closely. On the back wall was a large scene of rajas riding elephants, attended by musicians and soldiers. Another scene depicted the seated Buddha teaching a large group of princes. To Guhasena, it seemed that the figures, unusually large in size, were competently executed—the modeling was good, the shading well done. But the depictions of persons were not as graceful, as poised as they might be.

He moved to the right wall, where he saw various scenes from the life of the Buddha. Jeta and Dhavala followed as he crossed the hall to the left wall. It was mostly blank, the bare rock exposed. His study was interrupted by a new voice at his ear: "You seem quite interested in our frescoes." He turned to see an elderly monk.

"This is the Venerable Devasharman," Jeta said. "Our supervisor of new works. He's in charge of overseeing the excavation of the caves, as well as decorating them." Guhasena and Dhavala bent to touch the monk's feet as Jeta informed Devasharman, "Guhasena has been a painter himself."

"Indeed!" Devasharman examined Guhasena with obvious interest.

"Honorable sir," Guhasena asked, gesturing toward the left wall, "why hasn't this surface been painted yet?"

"We haven't yet received a donation to pay for it. The artists we hired to do the other two walls have returned to their home cities."

"I see."

They took their leave of the older monk, and Jeta led them to an adjacent cave, which was still under construction. "Here you can see how our rooms are built," he said. "First the face of the cliff is smoothed and the outline of the facade is drawn on it. Then the workmen start tunneling into the hill at the height of the ceiling. They gradually hollow their way downward from the top of the room, so they don't need any scaffolding. All the ceiling ribs, the pillars, the rough shape of the statues are carved at the same time out of the same rock, working from the top down."

"A tremendous job," Guhasena remarked in awe. "Obviously one that takes many years."

"Indeed it does."

But Guhasena's mind was only partially on the labor involved in hollowing out a community from solid rock. He kept seeing in his mind the blank wall in the room next door.

Several days went by, and he and Dhavala slipped easily into the routine of the monastery. They shared a small room carved from the rock, one of the cells off the left side of the newest cave. After rising early in the mornings, they bathed in the river with the *bhikkhus*, then they attended the morning lectures or readings from the Buddhist scriptures.

Occasionally, Guhasena would discuss the lessons with Dhavala. Both found the teachings interesting, but not enough for Guhasena to give up being a lukewarm follower of Shiva, or Dhavala of Vishnu.

The two often worked in the kitchens helping to prepare the one meal of the day. Taken shortly before noon, it consisted of rices, curries and vegetables, cakes and fruits. Then, after a brief nap, came more lessons for most of the *bhikkhus*, and Guhasena and Dhavala worked in the gardens or swept the halls or paths. In the evening, they attended the worship service in a *chaitya*, when the images of the Buddha were washed and flowers and incense were offered to the likenesses and to the *stupa*. They often went for evening walks with those monks who did not use the time for meditations. They retired for the night early, not long after sunset.

Whenever he came and went from his cell, Guhasena looked at the unpainted wall of the *vihara*. The emptiness seemed to beg to be filled, and he felt an increasing urge to act on that need personally.

One morning, he happened to walk to the river to bathe at the same time as the elderly monk Devasharman. He casually asked, "Honorable sir, do you have any subject in mind for the blank wall in the newest cave?"

"Yes," Devasharman replied, looking at him curiously. "Our committee has agreed it should illustrate the scene when the princess Sundari dies from grief because her husband, Prince Nanda, has left her to become a follower of the Buddha."

"I see."

A dying princess....Guhasena could easily envision that scene. He himself had seen a "princess" dying. And it had robbed him of all desire to paint.

Or had it?

He and Devasharman removed their robes and lay them on the rocks by the river bank. As he did his ablutions, Guhasena suddenly asked, "Would you allow me to do that mural, sir? I'd be glad to do it in exchange for my keep here."

Devasharman appeared unsurprised. "Quite possibly. Naturally, I'd need to see some of your work."

"I don't have any with me. But if you can make some paints available, I'll give you a demonstration."

Guhasena and Dhavala watched as workmen hired from a nearby village plastered the rough but porous rock surface. An odor of wetness from the powdered rock, clay, cow dung, and chopped rice husks permeated the air in the cave.

Dhavala said, "I'm glad you obtained the commission, sir. But I would expect the subject matter to be painful."

Guhasena was silent for some time before replying, "Maybe that's why I need to do it, Dhavala. I've been trying to forget. If I face the source of my pain directly, maybe I can finally exorcize it."

Dhavala appeared dubious.

When the first coat was done, the workers added a second. While it was still wet, under Guhasena's close supervision they smoothed and polished the surface with trowels. Finally they applied a wash of white lime.

It took longer for a wall to dry in the confined space of the cave than if it were in a room in a normal structure. So the air was warmed with a fire, carefully watched so the smoke would not coat either the murals already completed or the freshly plastered wall. Several monks took turns waving large fans to keep the air moving and draw out the moisture even more quickly.

When the wall was at last dry, Guhasena began. Except for the blue pigment made from lapis lazuli, his paints were obtained locally: red ochre and yellow ocher; lampblack; white from kaolin, lime and gypsum; green from glauconite.

The scene was vivid in his mind. He had personally observed it all, in detail. He first did the red ochre outline of the composition on the wall. In the central focal point of the composition he drew a bed, and on it lay a reclining young woman, leaning on her left arm, with a woman attendant supporting the upper part of her body. He drew another woman attendant fanning the sick girl. He drew two older men on the left, looking sadly at the scene. Nearby were various other family members and servants.

When he was satisfied with the composition, Guhasena began filling in the figures. As he rendered the anxiety in the faces of the two women attendants, he felt his own grief well up once more. Occasionally, he had to stop briefly, walk out to the cave entrance, and let the bright light of the outdoors bathe him. Then he would return to the mural, and as his eyes adjusted to working by the dim lamplight, he would resume painting on the faces. His reactions were similar when he painted the older men, one of whom was based on Shashiprabha's father.

Dhavala frequently watched the progress, but he said nothing.

As Guhasena had expected, he found it easier to paint the more distant household members, who looked appropriately saddened, but who weren't quite so devastated by the impending death.

He left the ill young woman for last. Until he actually began detailing her, he didn't know if he would paint her as Shashiprabha. He made no effort to precisely control the brush; rather, he let the paint flow as if it possessed its own will.

As the face took form, he saw that it was not strictly Shashiprabha. There were elements of her in the overall structure of the face, but it was not her. It was a composite of the faces of several girls, a blending of the personhood of many young women.

The Dying Princess

When he made himself think of witnessing Shashiprabha dying, the memory pained him yet. He could have forced himself to depict his recollection in precise detail on the wall. But that was not how he wanted to record the scene.

*

Upon the mural's completion, Dhavala quietly, slowly, appraised the whole. Finally, he said, "It's good. *Very* good."

Guhasena nodded. After a time, he asked, "How do you like my dying princess?"

Dhavala hesitated. He looked at the scene and eventually said, "You did an excellent job of conveying her imminent end. The head drooping, the eyes half closed, almost clouding over." He took a deep breath and continued, "But she doesn't look like Shashiprabha."

Guhasena smiled. It was the first time Dhavala had seen him smile at her name since her death. "No. I once painted Shashiprabha as Sita. *That's* how I want to remember her."

Dhavala peered at him and said, "And I don't see you in the scene."

"I'm not, Dhavala."

Eventually, Guhasena said, "I think I'm ready to go back to Ujjain, and take up my life of painting again. Would you care to come with me?"

The
Mangarh Treasure
Five

9

The Aravalli Hills near Mangarh, 1975 C.E.

A doctoral thesis on an Ajanta mural, no less! Vijay was even more impressed with the princess.

He had begun glancing frequently in the direction of Gamri village, fearful of someone coming to see who was looking at the ruins. "We'd better get back to the palace," he said.

While they walked to the jeep, Shanta Das said to Kaushalya Kumari, "So that's why you have so many books in your studio about Ajanta. Your thesis."

The princess' face hardened at the reminder of the search of her rooms. "Yes."

Vijay wiped the sweat from his forehead with his handkerchief. He glanced toward his old village, down on the plain. It was almost impossible to stop anywhere in India without someone soon coming by, and indeed a couple of men in turbans and *dhotis* were walking toward them across the fields, three or four minutes away.

As he and his party drove past the two men, he carefully looked in the other direction so they would not see his face, just in case. When the jeep had left the vicinity of the village, he allowed himself to relax a little. The outing had been interesting in its own way. It might even have been enjoyable, with the lovely princess and Shanta Das for companions, if he had not been so on edge and the day had not been so hot. But the excursion had completely failed in its purpose of finding concealed wealth.

When they arrived at the Bhim Bhawan Palace, Ranjit Singh, who had apparently been watching for them, approached from somewhere outside the building. Even Ranjit had removed his suit jacket in the heat, although he kept his necktie tightly knotted. "Are you laden with treasure, *yaar?*" he asked Vijay.

"No. We're just hot and dusty." Vijay glanced uneasily toward Kaushalya Kumari. She was climbing the steps to the palace and was unlikely to overhear, so he asked, "Have you found anything yet?"

Ranjit wore a grin as if he were holding something back, but he said, "Not much of interest. I trust you yourself had an otherwise pleasant outing?"

"Tolerable. I learned a few things about the Harappan culture and about Emperor Ashoka and Buddhist monuments. The princess has been a cooperative and knowledgeable guide."

"Good!" Ranjit paused for dramatic effect. He then said, "I have news. I have had the honor of being team leader in charge of our search operations this afternoon. But now that you are back, that exalted position is yours."

"What? Where's Prasad?"

"His father died, so he had to return quickly to Delhi. He said that you, as the senior income tax officer present, are to take full responsibility for the remainder of the search in Mangarh. He'll be in touch with you by telephone. He left you this note." Ranjit handed an envelope to Vijay, and smiled wryly. "I think the DDI regretted that you had his jeep. But the Maharaja was kind enough to lend him a car and driver."

Vijay shook his head, and gave an ironic smile. "We seem to grow more indebted to our hosts the longer we're here." He tore open the envelope.

My Dear Vijay,

By now you know that a higher duty has called me away. Do whatever you feel appropriate to locate concealed assets. As mentioned before, some very big men in Delhi would like fast results. Remember the one week deadline.

I'll try reaching you at the palace by telephone tomorrow afternoon. Phone our Delhi office if you need me. I'll call the office daily. Good luck.

D. Prasad

Vijay crumpled the note and stuck it in his pocket for later disposal. With the references to the "very big men," it was not the kind of correspondence one put in an office file. "So I'm in charge now. I haven't even been up to the fortress yet."

"Nor have I. Ghosali, of course, has been overseeing the search at the fort in Prasad's absence."

Vijay withdrew his handkerchief and wiped the perspiration from his forehead. When he refolded the cloth he saw it was filthy from the dust mixed with his sweat. He absently returned the handkerchief to his pocket. He now felt the full weight of the pressure on him to find something to justify the search. "I'd better take a drive up there," he said, gazing at the huge fortress sprawling on the opposite hillside. "Anything I should see here first?" He waved a hand at the palace. "Nothing that can't wait. His Highness went to take an afternoon nap. I haven't seen him since."

Kaushalya Kumari had reappeared. "I should go to the fort also. May I ride with you?"

Vijay saw that her forehead, too, glistened from the heat. "Of course, Princess." He straightened as he said it. On the trip to the archaeological sites, he had felt himself merely a civil servant with some limited police authority. But now, he, the former Untouchable, was the representative of the central government in dealing directly with a royal family. And in spite of bearing the responsibility for the outcome of the search, he felt more secure. No longer was anyone present who could order him to go where he might encounter someone who could expose him. He could stay away from the newer palace as much as possible, and thereby more easily avoid Naresh Singh. "Miss Das will come, too," Vijay said, remembering that the ex-ruler's daughter should not be seen traveling alone with men.

"I had hoped to freshen up a little," Kaushalya Kumari said wistfully, "but that can wait."

Vijay knew he should leave at once for the fort; he was now responsible for a search that was underway in a place he had seen only from a distance. But he said, "I'd be glad to wait a few minutes, Princess."

She glanced at him, obviously surprised that he would be so considerate. Then she composed her expression. "I won't be long."

Shanta Das said, "I would like to wash off the dust also. Is there a place I could use?"

Kaushalya Kumari gave a nod and said as she turned away, "Of course. Gopi will show you a guest bathroom."

A quarter hour later, the princess returned to the jeep. She had changed into a clean pink *shalwar kameez*, and her face glowed as if it had been scrubbed. Vijay had washed the dust from his own face and hands, and Shanta, also, looked refreshed for the moment.

The jeep, too, was again gleaming; Akbar Khan had worked his small miracle with his dusting cloth. They drove through town to the old fortress. The streets were virtually deserted while people took shelter from the late afternoon sun.

Then Vijay saw a man walking who looked vaguely familiar. He stared, trying to discern if he had known the person previously. The man turned toward the jeep, as if feeling the scrutiny. Vijay quickly faced the opposite direction. Suddenly he remembered: he had last seen the fellow almost twenty years ago—only the man had been a boy in his mid-teens. They had attended secondary school together, in the same class, and the boy had been an eager participant in tormenting Vijay. Arjun was his name; Arjun Oswal.

Vijay felt a surge of anger as he remembered Oswal's cruel laughter. He and some other boys had hidden Vijay's mathematics book and refused to return it. Their only reason, of course, was that Vijay was a Harijan. Oswal had thought the joke was quite amusing. And Vijay vividly recalled his own fury and humiliation, which he had covered by pretending indifference. Fortunately they had eventually returned the book; it was worth the equivalent of a month's food.

He was relieved when the jeep reached the fort, where it seemed much less likely he would again encounter someone from his past. They passed under the massive arch in the lower wall, an opening built high enough to permit the passage of an elephant with a howdah on its back. Khan shifted down, and after tight turns to the left and then right, the vehicle lumbered up a bumpy, cobblestoned road cut into the side of the hill.

A sharp left turn, and the roadway hugged the base of the foundation wall of one of the palace wings which soared high above. Vijay leaned out in order to look upward at the structure. Pierced only by an occasional window or gallery, the facade was mostly blank. At the very top a balcony rail overhung the wall, and below the railing, hugging the wall, were several large, dark bee hives, a common accretion on old buildings.

The jeep turned sharply right, then left, to enter the gate of the main part of the fortress itself. As on the lower gate, Vijay noticed

Main Gate, Mangarh Fort

another set of numerous long iron spikes protruding from the massive wooden doors, to prevent elephants from ramming if the fort were under attack. Above the gate were two stone elephants facing each other, and cupolas flanking a balcony. The gate opened into a huge courtyard, where a green-coated, white-turbaned guard with an old looking rifle watched them as they came to a stop.

In the shade by the far wall stood an unusually large, long tusked elephant eating from a pile of dry grass. A chain held the animal by a rear leg. Vijay stepped from the jeep into the harsh sun and walked toward the elephant, halting just out of its reach. He had always liked elephants, but the sight of them was increasingly rare. He stood for a moment, watching it. An odor of straw and of dung hung in the air, not unpleasant to someone from a farming village. Shanta came to stand with him. "What a magnificent animal!" she said.

Kaushalya Kumari walked to the elephant and began talking to it in a low voice, patting and stroking its trunk.

"What is his name?" Vijay asked, assuming it was male from its size, and from the length of the tusks.

"Airavata," she replied, her attention still on the elephant, whose eye was clearly watching Vijay. The name was that of the legendary elephant ridden by the god Indra.

"May I come closer?"

She shrugged. "If you like. He won't harm you."

Vijay stepped up beside her. Immediately the end of the trunk shot out and prodded his arm, startling him. He recovered and stood still. A rush of moist, warm air surged over him as the end of the trunk darted here and there, exploring, lingering embarrassingly at Vijay's crotch. Vijay rubbed the side of the trunk and was struck by how rough the skin was, how stiff and bristly the hairs. The elephant abruptly grasped Vijay's arm and pulled.

"He's just getting to know you," said Kaushalya Kumari. "But you don't need to let him drag you around."

Vijay managed to pull free and backed out of reach. He turned as Anil Ghosali strolled near, the ever-present pipe in his lips. From the frown, Vijay got the impression Ghosali was annoyed at the interference with his work in the fort. Ghosali gave a slight nod and stood, waiting for Vijay to speak.

"Any luck?" Vijay asked, moving farther away from the princess and the elephant.

Ghosali removed the pipe from his mouth. He forced a strand of hair back into conformance with the rest of those pasted to his scalp. "We have as yet found nothing of note," he reported in the stiff manner which irritated Vijay whenever it didn't amuse him. "We have found lots of old weapons and such that aren't listed on the wealth tax returns, but they probably are not of high value, either."

Vijay nodded and glanced to see if Kaushalya Kumari had come near enough to overhear. She was still stroking the elephant's trunk and talking to him. Vijay led Ghosali into the shade of the line of low buildings surrounding the courtyard. "We'll keep at it," he said quietly. "No one's had much luck at the newer palace or anywhere else, either." He was watching the princess. She had let the covering fall from her head and she no longer wore the sunglasses. She was a fetching sight in her pink *shalwar kameez* as she petted the big elephant.

Ghosali took a puff on his pipe. He said, "I have certain sources in the Finance Ministry who tell me they are very interested that we find something."

Vijay's stomach tensed; Ghosali was making sure Vijay knew he was better connected with higher-ups, even though Vijay might be in nominal charge of the search. "That's my understanding, too," he said. He looked pointedly at Ghosali. "We'll do our best. But no stretching the regulations. I want everything completely legal."

Ghosali raised his eyebrows and shrugged. "Of course. I have no doubt I will find the treasure anyway. If it exists, of course."

Vijay clenched his teeth. Before could think of an appropriate response, Ghosali asked, "Why are the ladies here?"

Vijay turned toward the princess and the elephant. She had stepped away, and the animal was seizing pieces of hay in its trunk and then tossing the dried grass over its back. Vijay replied without looking at Ghosali, "Kaushalya Kumari is His Highness' daughter. I think she wants to make sure we aren't planting anything incriminating. And I thought Miss Das should be along as a witness so the princess can't try to embarrass us by accusing the men of any immoral advances down in the dark dungeons."

He glanced at Ghosali, who was staring at him as if trying to decide if Vijay were serious or joking. Vijay had sensed that Ghosali, as a Brahmin from an orthodox family, still felt uncomfortable when he was in close proximity to an ex-Untouchable such as Miss Das. "I see," Ghosali said at last. He looked at the princess again. "She is quite beautiful."

Vijay thought of responding to the comment, but instead he said, "I'd like a quick look at what you've searched so far."

"That would take considerable time." said Ghosali. "We're most busy."

"I'd still like to see for myself."

Ghosali frowned. Then he again shrugged and took the pipe from his mouth. "As you wish." Abruptly, the sound of a gong shattered the stillness and reverberated across the court. Vijay glanced toward the source and saw a turbaned old man in a small balcony to one side of the main gate. Ghosali asked, "Can you believe it? They still use a water clock here! A brass bowl with a hole in the bottom, floating in a basin of water. Every half hour the bowl fills enough so it sinks, and that man strikes the gong. What a waste!"

Kaushalya Kumari and Shanta Das had moved close enough to overhear. The princess said, her eyes cold, "He has done that work all his life. And his father and grandfather before him. The people are used to hearing the sound. Mangarh would not be the same without it."

Ghosali shrugged. "It's so useless in modern times. Like the elephant. But who am I to question?"

Vijay quickly gestured toward the animal and said to the princess, "I've always liked elephants. You keep him as a pet?"

Kaushalya Kumari, obviously still irritated at Ghosali, said stiffly, "We used to have a dozen. Airavata is the last. My father couldn't part with him. I usually bring him a treat, but I forgot this time. I can tell by the way he's looking at me he's annoyed."

"Pachyderms must be quite expensive to keep in these times," said Ghosali.

The princess eyed him a moment, apparently wondering why he didn't call the animal an "elephant" as most people would. Then, she said, in a calmly controlled voice, "Ganesh is our household deity—we call him Ekadantji. He appears on the Maharaja's personal flag. So the elephant is a symbol of our family."

Ghosali raised an eyebrow. "You can not have much use for such an animal any more."

Kaushalya Kumari said in obvious irritation, "Must everything have a practical use in order to be valued?"

Ghosali frowned as if pondering a new concept.

Vijay hurriedly asked the princess, "Would you care to join us on a tour of the fort? Maybe you'd be kind enough to answer any questions we have." She gave a curt nod, and he began walking across the sunbaked courtyard. The women followed, their heels clacking on stones smoothed by countless other footfalls over the centuries.

Ghosali stood for a moment, clearly still puzzled. Then he quickly strode to catch up with the others. Suddenly assuming the role of resident expert on the fortress, he took his pipe and pointed with it to the arched openings in the buildings lining the edge of the court. "These are garages, and old stables for the elephants and horses. We looked through there quickly, but it did not seem a likely hiding place."

Pigeons fluttered from their path as the group crossed the courtyard. One of the guards approached and saluted Kaushalya Kumari. A small man perhaps in his fifties with a pleasant, round face, he wore a bulky white turban and a tense expression. He carried a large ring of keys. The princess said in Rajasthani, "Show them whatever they want, Captain Surmal."

The guard bowed and said, "As you wish, *Rajkumari*."

Ghosali led the party through an arched gateway. On either side of it, set into the masonry, were panels of stone,

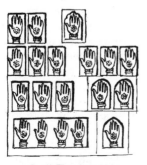

Sati Handprints

each carved with rows of hand prints, dabbed with red dye. Ghosali did not comment on them, but Vijay knew why they were there.

The princess certainly knew, too. Many years ago each hand print had been placed by a woman leaving the security of the women's quarters in the *zenana*—on her way to becoming a *sati*, burned alive on her husband's funeral pyre.

The group entered a smaller, though still sizeable, courtyard. On the wall each side of the gateway was painted a large elephant in profile. More pigeons flapped away. At one side stood a big, squarish roof supported by tall, graceful, carved white marble pillars and arches. "The old public audience hall," said Ghosali.

The three men and two women continued past the row of pil-lars. Overhead, stone elephants ornamented the corbels supporting the roof overhang. Black faced langur monkeys scampered along the top of the wall parapet, unconcerned about the sheer drop on one side.

"What are those for?" asked Vijay. He gestured toward a set of two rectangular vertical stone uprights, a meter or so apart from each other, with a round iron rod joining them near their tops. They hugged the outer surface of the wall and extended perhaps a meter above its top edge. "I don't have the faintest idea," said Ghosali, as if the items were beneath his notice.

The princess answered dryly, "A pulley wheel was fixed on the rod between the two stone pillars, with a rope over the wheel. It was used to raise water buckets from the base of the wall below."

"Ridiculous," said Ghosali. "There had to be a simpler way."

Kaushalya Kumari's eyes narrowed at him. She said, "That was the only way to get water up here until an aqueduct was built from the reservoirs on top of the ridge. And in the old days there were plenty of servants to hoist the buckets." She turned her back to Ghosali.

They walked through yet another gateway, with a stone elephant on each side, into a smaller paved courtyard. On the left was a wide, low, balcony-like platform with a ceiling supported by more arched marble pillars. "The private audience hall," said Ghosali. They passed by it quickly, although it was a beautiful place, its columns inlaid with semiprecious stones in reds, blues, blacks, and with displays of weapons on the rear walls in mandala-like arrangements of old rifles and spears and daggers.

They climbed a flight of steep, close steps, and stooped to pass through a small doorway. "The narrow stairs and low lintels were intended to make the palace easier to defend if an enemy gained access," said Ghosali.

Vijay already knew that, but he said nothing. Ghosali continued his lecture, "As an enemy bent over to come through the door, it would have been quite easy for the defenders to cut off his head."

Surmal, the guard, hunted on his ring for the key to open the next door. "I'm told this is called the Sheesh Mahal," said Ghosali.

Sheesh Mahal, thought Vijay, the Hall of Mirrors. The Bhil found the key, removed the padlock, and they walked in. The long room glittered with a multitude of tiny reflections. Its walls and arched ceiling were intricately decorated with thousands upon thousands of small pieces of mirrors and colored glass embedded in ornately sculpted and painted plaster designs.

"It's beautiful," whispered Shanta Das.

"Lovely," agreed Vijay.

"A number of palaces in Rajasthan have rooms like these," informed Ghosali in a tone of dismissal. "But then, you'd know that, being Rajput."

"Of course," replied Vijay. He glanced at Kaushalya Kumari. She was staring at him with a bemused expression, as if not quite knowing what to make of him being Rajput, too. Still, there were Rajputs and there were Rajputs. He would never be so foolish as to try to pass as actual nobility, much less as royalty. If you were part of those circles, you either knew, or knew *of*, most other members, at least in your own area of the country.

He stood, looking about the hall, reluctant to leave such a place of beauty. Every surface sparkled as if it were inlaid with gems. Or with multicolored stars. Miss Das, too, was clearly still enthralled. Kaushalya Kumari, although she must have seen it many times, was lingering also, gazing at the walls and ceiling. But Ghosali strolled back out, apparently unmoved by the splendor. Vijay slowly followed, continuing to glance at the room until he was through the door.

"The ruler's apartments," said Ghosali as they entered a huge, rectangular three-storied structure. "It seemed a good place to hide something, so we searched thoroughly. Even the underground levels." They walked quickly into the first floor, a series of small, bare rooms lighted in colored patterns from tiny stained glass windows.

At a branching of corridors, Ghosali slowed and halted. "These wings are quite confusing," he said, sounding uncertain. "I pride myself on my sense of direction, but I confess I still get lost. Momentarily, of course."

"This way," said the princess dryly. They passed through more rooms, down more twisting corridors and stairways. The elephant motif appeared often: elephants depicted in pieces of semiprecious stones in the mirrored mosaics, elephants in the painted murals in wall recesses.

Vijay had a sense of continual enchantment and surprise, and of dislocation. Like Ghosali, he sometimes realized he had no idea of where he was in the building. Halls intersected at odd angles. Forests of columns obscured what lay on the far side of dimly lit spaces. Successions of rooms served as hallways. Stairways appeared to lead to dead ends. Broad hallways ended at tiny rooms; narrow corridors ended at large open pavilions. From doorways, numerous L-shaped rooms gave no hint of what lay around their corners. Stone lattices over the windows diffused and scattered the light, making it difficult to discern details. "What a maze! But it's wonderful," said Vijay.

"I sometimes think," said Kaushalya Kumari, "that it was deliberately intended to confuse enemies who might gain access. But mainly, I think the architects just had a sense of playfulness. And of course, over the centuries new rooms were attached to the old ones with no particular sense of order."

She led them up a narrow stairway, and along a balcony that overlooked a garden courtyard. They passed through another low doorway, and came out on a small, secluded garden terrace shaded by an overhanging *pipal* tree. A couple of striped squirrels were chasing each other around the trunk. In the center of the oblong grass terrace lay a rectangular marble pool, now dry, the bottom littered with leaves. A row of round metal water spouts for tiny fountains lined a stone channel leading into the pool. A low marble railing bordered one side of the terrace, and over the barrier lay Mangarh city, spread out far below like a toy town.

Vijay moved to the rail and looked down. The edge of the terrace overhung its supporting wall by a good half meter, and below was a sheer drop of five or six stories to the cobblestoned roadway that ascended to the main gate. The myriad noises of the city drifted upward to him, blending into a drone. At eye level, a few hundred meters away, a hawk spiraled lazily on a hot air current. Vijay didn't normally think of himself as fearing heights, but he quickly moved backward a meter or so. The carved marble rail was a little too low for him to feel comfortable leaning over it.

"It's a beautiful spot," said Shanta Das. "It must have been even more lovely when the pool was full of water and the fountains were spraying."

They crossed the terrace past a small pillared marble pavilion. Beyond lay another short stretch of grassy terrace, with two small trees of a type Vijay didn't recognize. Affixed to the outer wall was another set of the stone uprights for the water pulleys. "Undoubtedly to bring up the water for the pool and the fountains," said Ghosali, stating the obvious as if it were a clever deduction. No one responded.

"Where does that go?" asked Vijay, pointing to a narrow stairway that cut downward into the ground at the inner edge of the terrace.

Ghosali puffed on his pipe, hesitated, then removed the pipe and replied, "Frankly, I don't remember. There are so many of these ridiculous little stairways and passages."

"It goes to some storerooms below," said Kaushalya Kumari in a tone of annoyance.

"What's in them?" asked Vijay.

"I now remember," said Ghosali. "They are mostly empty. What's there appeared to be a lot of old junk. It would not be profitable to explore the place."

Vijay said, "I'd like to see the rooms anyway."

Ghosali scowled, looking as if he wanted to object at such an infringement on his valuable time. Then he sighed, pulled an electric torch from his pocket, and led the way down the narrow stone steps. The guard followed. Vijay gestured Kaushalya Kumari to precede himself, but she shook her head no, and waited to be last. The door at the bottom scraped as the guard pulled it open.

A dim hallway revealed itself, with light coming from a few small, high windows. The doors to three rooms hung open, and the air smelled of dust and decay and bat droppings. Ghosali flashed the torch into the first room. Scraps of cloth littered the floor, along with odds and ends of other debris.

A pile of random-length boards. A machine with a "squirrel-cage" blower attached to a rotary crank by a belt; Vijay recognized it as an old air cooler of the type operated by hand labor. A couple of large pulley wheels stacked in a corner. A picture frame with nothing in it leaned against a wall. A large, sturdy wicker basket.

Obviously, no treasure here, Vijay observed to himself. Not even any chests to pry open in the hope of finding something valuable. He scanned the walls and ceiling but saw no openings in the roughly finished stone. "Let's move on," he said.

He quickly searched the other two rooms. One was totally empty, except for some accumulated dirt and rubble on the floor. The other contained a pair of *charpoys*, the simple cots used for sleeping and sitting, made from rope webbing strung across the wooden frames. Also in the room were an assortment of large pottery jugs. "All empty," said Ghosali, indicating the jugs. "Naturally we checked."

Some coils of rope. A cabinet with tall doors, hanging open, obviously empty. More assorted scraps of debris littering the floor. "Anything else on this level?" asked Vijay.

"Nothing," said Ghosali.

"I don't think so," said Kaushalya Kumari, sounding bored.

"Then let's go back up," said Vijay. They climbed the stairway to the sunlit glare of the terrace. After crossing the open space the guard unlocked another doorway. "The ladies' apartments," said Ghosali. "The *zenana*, as it was commonly called. We intend still more searching here. Again, it's most confusing inside." They walked through series of rooms, up and down narrow stairways. The rooms were empty of furniture, but many of the walls were painted with murals: scenes of palace life, scenes from the life of the god Krishna, scenes of hunting. Another small courtyard, and another terrace overlooking the city. They were all sweating profusely from the exertion in the heat, and Vijay wished he had thought to bring something to drink. They turned a corner and entered a narrow hallway with intricately carved, pierced sandstone screens along one wall. "The ladies were in *purdah*," volunteered Kaushalya Kumari in a dry tone. "These openings let them watch what was occurring in the audience hall without anyone being able to see them."

Vijay nodded, peering through the lattices and trying to imagine what it must have been like to be virtually imprisoned in the harem. At the end of the hallway, they ascended a narrow stairway and left the ladies' wing at a level closer to the top of the ridge. "We haven't had time to search any more up here," said Ghosali, "except for the old treasury itself and some tunnels."

"I can understand why. What a confusing tangle!" replied Vijay. On it went, seemingly endless rooms after rooms, with narrow passages or stairways connecting them.

They turned right and entered a warren of smallish rooms, built of much rougher stonework than the previous sections. "What is this area?" asked Vijay.

"The kitchens, I believe," said Ghosali.

"And servants' quarters," said Kaushalya Kumari.

Vijay gave a nod of thanks. Even though she was perspiring in the heat, her beauty drew his gaze, and she looked graceful in the pink outfit with its flowing scarf

They swiftly moved through the section, making no attempt to see it all. They crossed a small court scattered with litter. Vijay glimpsed a mongoose flowing across a section of the court and disappearing behind some rubble. "The armory, I'm told," said Ghosali, gesturing with his pipe. A row of doorways lined the courtyard, each door opening into a separate storeroom. In some of the rooms lay stacks of spears and rusty ancient rifles, in some sat small, dust covered cannons. Vijay recognized swivel guns of the type meant to be mounted on the backs of camels. Some of the rooms were bare.

The courtyard abutted a squarish castle-like structure with rounded towers at each corner and twin higher towers in the center. "The old treasury is in there," said Ghosali. Vijay looked about. They had reached the highest level of the fortress, on the very top of the ridge.

"The style of this building is quite different," said Vijay. "Much simpler."

"This is the oldest part of the fort," said Kaushalya Kumari, her voice more pleasant and expressive now, as if she had decided to dismiss Ghosali's distasteful observations from her mind. "It's been rebuilt more than once, but it goes back at least a thousand years, maybe much longer. An archaeologist found remains of wooden buildings and walls from even earlier times."

Vijay gave a nod. "I see."

They passed through an arch in the wall, crossed another small court. Yet another squirrel played at the base of a big *pipal* tree. Atop the wall several more monkeys bounded off. "Jail cells and storerooms here," Ghosali said.

"We'll see that later," said Vijay. "I'd like to look at the treasury now." He was anxious to be done with the survey and to find a cool drink, but he felt he could not leave without seeing the place where so much wealth had once been hoarded. They continued through an arched passage to another, similar courtyard. Surmal unlocked a doorway opening off it. They passed through two rooms, the first of which appeared to be a guard station, and the second an office, which still contained a table and a desk.

Ahead stood three massive metal doors, all hanging open. From each door dangled a set of big padlocks, none of them secured. "The vaults," said Ghosali.

Vijay examined the first, a deep, medium sized room with masonry shelves lining the walls. It was completely empty. He went to the second. It, too was barren. As was the third vault. He turned to Kaushalya Kumari. "How long since this treasury was used, Princess?"

She shrugged. "It's been empty as long as I can remember."

Vijay thought it odd that absolutely nothing was stored in the rooms. It seemed a waste of spaces which could be so securely locked.

"I think a tunnel might have taken off from here," said Ghosali, leading them through a heavy metal door at the end of the hall. An uneven pile of stone rubble filled a sizeable square opening in the floor. Part had been dug away to reveal rock steps leading downward. "I intend to excavate this," Ghosali said.

Vijay again turned to Kaushalya Kumari. "Do you know what it was, Princess?"

She stood with her arms folded, quiet and collected, seemingly unperturbed by the heat, as if above the mundane concerns of the others in the party. She replied, "It used to be the entrance to an underground passage. But it's been filled in ever since I can remember." After a moment's hesitation, she added, "There was supposed to be a network of tunnels through the ridge, for escape in the old days if the fort was attacked. I haven't seen any passages that could still be used."

Vijay said to Ghosali, "It may be quite a job digging it out. But I agree we should try." He glanced at the princess, and continued, embarrassed to say in her hearing: "This could be a logical place to leave some treasure, since the tunnels were already here."

"I'll set about hiring some laborers," said Ghosali. He drew on his pipe, seeming satisfied that Vijay did not question his suggestion to excavate the passage.

It was mind-boggling, Vijay thought as they returned to the big lower courtyard where the jeep waited. With such a multitude of places to search, they would have to be lucky or clever, or both, to find the Mangarh Treasure quickly.

The dining room of the *dak* bungalow was hot, even with the ceiling fans whirring at top speed. The main topic of conversation—virtually the only topic among the men—was where the treasure might be hidden. It seemed to Vijay that everyone except himself had a pet theory. And maybe excepting the two women, who were quietly eating together at a separate table. He listened as he drank one bottle of Limca after another; the pale, citrus flavored soft drinks were pleasantly cool from the refrigerator.

Ranjit Singh thought the wealth had to be hidden near one of the water supplies. "They almost always hide it in a well, or near one." He poured a measure of rum into the bottom of a glass, then added part of a bottle of Campa Cola. He resumed, "Even the villagers have always thrown valuables down a well if they had to flee in a hurry. Wells are a favorite spot for rich people, too. The water conceals whatever's underneath, whether it's the loot itself or a hidden doorway to an underground vault. And it slows down anyone trying to search there—discourages them if they're in a hurry."

"Your point is nonetheless true for being obvious," said Anil Ghosali. "But you have not yet seen the fortress. In this case the reservoirs are up on top of the ridge. They're too far away to be convenient. I don't think there is even a well in the main palace complex—it's all built on solid rock. The water had to be hoisted on pulleys or carried in, or piped in."

"They still must have had storage tanks in the palace area," insisted Ranjit. "I'd look there."

Ghosali was quiet for a few moments, stuffing wads of rice and *rotis* into his mouth. "Perhaps," he said finally. "But if it were my wealth, I would want it close by, where I could watch it. I would search the areas near the Maharaja's living quarters, both in the old palace and in the newer one. Of course, the tunnels are quite likely possibilities, especially the one by the old treasury."

"I'd look in the women's wings," said Krishnaswamy, his dark skin glistening in the heat. He sipped from an orange soft drink.

Ghosali stared at the young Tamil. "Whatever for?" he asked. He drank from a bottle of water, his personal supply which he had brought with him from Delhi.

"Because it was the best guarded area in the whole palace," said Krishnaswamy, appearing not to have noticed Ghosali's condescending tone. "No man other than a close relative would have dared to enter it. And many rulers trusted their favorite women with their most important secrets."

"Interesting theory," mused Ranjit. He swirled his rum and cola.

Mrs. Desai spoke up for the first time. "And one I like, personally. I'm sure the women held more influence than the men would have cared to admit."

A couple of the men laughed.

"Just as the women do now?" asked Ranjit.

"You were the one to say it," said Mrs. Desai, with an uncharacteristic smile.

More laughter. She gave the appearance of glumness most of the time, but the men generally liked her, and as the only woman tax officer in the Delhi office other than Shanta, she sometimes was the subject of good natured teasing.

Ranjit looked over at Vijay. "Our leader hasn't said much yet. Vijay, you should have some idea how Rajputs think, being one yourself."

Vijay had been tracing a design with his fingertip on the plastic laminate table top while he sipped occasionally from his Limca. He smiled, trying to cover his tension, and he forced himself to sound light. "Everyone knows Rajputs are men of action, not great thinkers."

"In your case, you're both," said Ranjit with a laugh. "So what are you thinking of doing?"

Vijay had wondered that himself as he listened. The others could hold their opinions, but the ultimate responsibility for finding the treasure was his. The more he thought, the more possibilities had come to mind. Everything from false ceilings in the domes of the cupolas to false floors in the stables. And depending on how much rubble had been dumped into the tunnel entrance, it could take days, maybe even weeks, to dig the passage out.

He took a breath, and said carefully, "With our limited time we obviously need to set some priorities for the most thorough searches. You all have good ideas. So I think we'll concentrate in both palaces on the water storage areas, the Maharaja's apartments, and the rooms where the queens and the favorite concubines would have lived. And also the area around the old treasury, especially the tunnel."

"That is still a large area to search," said Ghosali, his eyes narrowed.

"True," said Vijay, trying not to sound annoyed at Ghosali's clearly implied criticism. "But not nearly so large as if we tried to search everywhere."

That night, he lay awake in the hot room he shared with Ranjit in the *dak* bungalow. At least the ceiling fan was working. He again thought about the hidden wealth. With so many structures to search, this was by far the most extensive operation of his career. Success was by no means assured.

He had been fortunate so far in not having to converse with the ADC, Naresh Singh, and in not encountering anyone else from Mangarh who knew him. He fervently hoped his luck would hold.

He thought about Kaushalya Kumari, so attractive and knowledgeable. His admiration of her hadn't interfered with his work, of course. But he hoped he wouldn't be forced by his duties to take some action that could seriously harm her or her family.

10

Early the next morning, Vijay decided on a quick visit to the summer palace, just to assure himself that it wasn't a likely hiding place for treasure. He again took Shanta with him, and Kaushalya Kumari as guide and observer. The princess wore a pale pastel blue *shalwar kameez* and medium-high-heeled sandals. Vijay thought she looked stunning, although she did appear tired.

The entire way, Vijay surreptitiously watched the faces of the people on the road, so he could be sure to turn away to avoid possible identification by anyone who had previously known him. He saw no one he recognized.

On the final leg of the short drive, the roadway bordered the calm waters of the artificial lake, the Hanuman Sagar. Then the jeep drove up the approach lane through orange and mango and palm trees. "What a lovely building!" Shanta exclaimed as the structure appeared before them.

To Vijay's eye, the Moti Mahal, the Pearl Palace, was exquisite and appropriately named. A row of finely sculpted white marble archways formed each side, giving the impression of a huge garden pavilion. The pale domes gleamed, their glass finials sparkling in the morning sun. Red bougainvillaea wrapped itself over one corner, contrasting with the whiteness of the walls. Beyond the building, the lake reflected the blue of the sky.

After stepping from the jeep Shanta stood gazing at the sight. "This is where I'd want to live," she stated firmly. Indeed, Vijay reflected, it seemed the type of place that people would spin fantasies about.

Shanta turned to Kaushalya. "Did you ever think of moving here yourself?"

Kaushalya gave a tight smile. "Often. I did spend some time here during the summer holidays. My family came here for picnics."

The caretaker appeared, an old man in a white turban, a long white shirt, and a *dhoti*. He respectfully welcomed Kaushalya and then hurried to unlock the door.

"Is that why it was built?" asked Shanta. "For holidays and picnics?"

"Probably," Kaushalya replied. To avoid seeming too rude or uncooperative, she felt she should say more. "From time to time various women of the palace lived here. The last was one of my grandfather's wives. An American lady."

Inside, the structure was virtually empty. The usual odors of unused buildings hung in the air: of mildew; of bat or bird droppings; and faintly, of urine. The bare marble floors were dull from lack of cleaning and polishing.

The visitors' footsteps, particularly Kaushalya's heels, echoed as the party walked through a succession of interconnected rooms, all of them high ceilinged, all with giant arched windows and doors opening to the verandas and balconies. Vijay and Shanta were scanning the walls, the ceilings, the floors, for signs of anything that might give a hint of a hiding place. But the very design of the building, with its openness and relative simplicity, and the lack of guards except for the caretaker, argued against hiding anything much larger than a jewel casket.

Vijay decided he might send a couple of men later for a more careful examination of places such as the interiors of the domes and of the surrounding gardens. But for now, he was satisfied that the Moti Mahal was an unlikely hiding place for something so major as the Mangarh Treasure.

Vijay returned Kaushalya Kumari and Shanta Das to the newer palace, then he had Akbar Khan drive him to the old fortress. The elephant Airavata stood in the same spot in the big courtyard. He was eating hay, which his mahout, an old, turbaned man with a lush, white mustache, and a young helper were carrying in big bundles from the adjacent storeroom. Airavata clearly saw Vijay, and the elephant kept an eye on him while stuffing the fodder into its mouth. When the mahout and his assistant were out of sight in the storeroom, Vijay walked closer and said, "*Namaste*, Airavata. How are you today?"

Vijay glanced about, feeling slightly foolish, not at talking to the elephant, but at the idea that someone else might overhear him. The only persons visible were Khan at the jeep and a Bhil guard on the wall. Vijay watched Airavata a minute or so longer, then wandered past the audience hall toward the entrance of the Madho Mahal. He wanted time to think, to try to put himself in the place of someone who wanted to hide a fortune. Abruptly, the pleasant faced Bhil guard captain, Surmal, appeared and began walking with him.

"Can I be of help, sir?" asked Surmal.

"No, I'm just looking around again." Vijay continued walking, and thinking. The captain almost certainly knew if the treasure existed, and if so, exactly where. The guards could hardly protect the wealth without knowing its location. Vijay glanced pointedly at the Bhil, and smiled. "Unless, of course, you want to tell me where the treasure is, and save us all a lot of trouble."

Surmal's amiable expression did not change. "I'm sorry, sir. I'm unable to do so."

Unable and unwilling, thought Vijay, even if the man did know. "There's really no need for you to come along," he said.

"It's my duty, sir. You may need a guide inside the buildings, as they can be confusing to outsiders. His Highness directed me to ensure there was someone to help you at all times."

To *watch* me, you mean, thought Vijay. He shrugged. "Very well." He began looking about, trying to ignore the guard. Once in a while Vijay would stop, jot something in his notebook when a potentially useful idea occurred to him, and then he would continue. He occasionally glanced at Surmal, trying to read the man's facial expression. Would the Bhil get a worried look in his eyes if Vijay appeared to get close to the hiding place? But always the guard captain gave an impression of calm composure.

After an hour, Vijay had superficially covered only perhaps an eighth of the main fortress complex, when Krishnaswamy approached. "Telephone call for you from Ranjit Singh, sir," the Tamil said. "The phone's in the guard office by the main gate."

Vijay followed him. Halfway across the courtyard, the Bhil left them. Vijay entered the office and picked up the receiver from the table. "Ranjit? Vijay here."

Ranjit's voice cut through the static: "Vijay, we may be onto something. I overheard the Maharaja talking to his son in Bombay on the phone. His Highness mentioned he hoped we didn't find the secret tunnel under the new palace. So I thought we ought to ring you up."

Vijay frowned as he considered. At last, he said, "Good, Ranjit. I'll be over shortly to have a talk with His Highness."

He mulled over the development as Akbar Khan drove him to the Bhim Bhawan palace. Despite the risk of encountering Naresh Singh, this could possibly be his big chance. He hoped he wouldn't get into a major confrontation with the Maharaja. What if Lakshman Singh denied knowledge of a tunnel?

Ranjit met him at the palace entrance. In the main hallway, Kaushalya Kumari appeared, still in the blue *shalwar kameez*. Vijay pressed his hands together in greeting, and she returned the formality. "May I see His Highness please, Princess?"

"Of course. He's in his study. I'll take you there." Her voice was cool though not impolite; her face was expressionless.

"Airavata sends his greetings," Vijay said, and immediately felt embarrassed, even though he had seen the princess herself speaking to the elephant the previous day.

Kaushalya Kumari shot him a startled look.

"I talked with the elephant for a minute this morning," Vijay explained hurriedly.

"I see." Her eyes registered brief puzzlement before she composed them.

Vijay was disturbed at himself for trying to joke with her. There was probably nothing wrong with a light jest which couldn't possibly cause offense. Still, he didn't normally try to ingratiate himself with someone who was a target of an investigation.

Kaushalya Kumari led them to a large room with a multitude

of stuffed animal heads hanging on every wall and numerous tiger skin rugs on the floor. Framed photographs of Lakshman Singh with various famous political leaders and royalty crowded the tops of several small tables. There her father, seated in an overstuffed armchair, was sipping a clear beverage from a glass. Shiv stood stiffly by the door. Lakshman Singh did not rise. "Good morning, Mr. Singh," he said. "I understand you're in charge of the search now."

Vijay hoped he was covering up the fact he felt so ill at ease encountering a king. Especially a king who was largely, if unintentionally, responsible for his father's death. "I'm team leader for the income tax officers in Mangarh, Your Highness," he replied. "Naturally, I answer to my superiors in New Delhi."

"Of course. May I offer you anything to drink? *Chai*? *Lassi*?"

"Thank you, Your Highness, not at this time."

Lakshman Singh smiled slightly. "I understand you're from near Mangarh, Mr. Singh."

Panic gripped his gut. "Yes, Highness." He knew the next question would be: *Which village*? The ex-ruler would naturally know all of them, no matter how small, that had been located in his former state. And then he would ask about Vijay's family to see if he knew any of them.

But the Maharaja surprised him by merely asking, "Have you discovered anything of interest yet in your search?"

Vijay answered cautiously, concerned that if he committed himself to a definite position, his words might be used against him at a later date. Dev Batra might well wish to take a minor discrepancy and blow it up into something major. "Several items that weren't listed on your returns, sir," he replied. "Probably nothing of great importance."

Lakshman Singh nodded. "That's about what I expected."

"So far, Your Highness," Vijay said, "we've limited our search to the more obvious places. However, it's commonly known that most palaces have at least a few well-disguised hiding spots. There's been a rumor that you have some hidden chambers or passages in this building."

He paused, and watched Lakshman Singh's face. He saw no change in expression. Vijay continued, "Your Highness, we can usually discover those types of places by taking detailed measurements of the inside and the outside of the structure. But that's time-consuming. I'm sure you'd like to be rid of us as soon as possible. Also," again he paused, "sometimes in the process of locating hidden chambers, we of necessity do considerable damage to the building. If we are reasonably sure we know where a hidden passage is, but we can't find the entrance, we may be forced to break through walls in a number of spots until we find access."

He waited. Lakshman Singh was staring at him as if in disbelief. Vijay didn't look at Kaushalya Kumari; he was afraid of what he might see. He went on, "So to save a great deal of effort and expense and frustration on both sides, Your Highness, I'm going to ask you outright. Do you have any hidden rooms or passages in this palace?"

Lakshman Singh took out his pack of Charminars, shook one free, and slowly lit it. He stared out the window. At last, he turned back to Vijay and said, "Yes, I was hoping you wouldn't find it. And that you wouldn't ask. But I do have a secret tunnel, and some small chambers that open off from it." He smiled mildly, and said more quietly, "I probably should also tell you that the passage was built to hide some of my family's most ah...confidential items."

Vijay allowed himself to relax slightly, now that the interview was going so well. He said, "Thank you for telling me, Your Highness. Are you willing to show me the access to these places?"

Lakshman Singh shrugged. "Now that you know they exist, I see no reason to make you tear down my home to find them. Yes, I'll show you."

Vijay happened to glance at Kaushalya. She was watching her father, and her expression was not at all what Vijay would have expected. She bore a look of....surprised amusement? She realized Vijay was looking at her, and her face quickly sobered.

What, wondered Vijay, is going on?

The Maharaja took another puff on his cigarette and said, "You'll need some lanterns or electric torches."

"I'll get some," said Ranjit.

Vijay felt a sense of anticipation as he waited with the others for Ranjit to come back. Could the treasure be only minutes away?

Ranjit returned with two flashlights. Lakshman Singh snuffed out his cigarette in the ashtray, rose, and said, "This way." Vijay followed out of the study and down a hallway, toward the kitchens and service area.

After Vijay came Kaushalya and Ranjit Singh. Last came Shiv. They took a couple turnings in the hallway. Then Lakshman Singh stopped at a doorway. At a nod from him, Shiv brought forth a key ring and unlocked the door. A stairway led to a lower level. They descended the stairs and walked along another hallway. Lakshman Singh stopped at a door. "Here," he said. The old servant unlocked the door. Inside was a small storeroom. A large cabinet with open shelves stood against the far wall. On the shelves sat several boxes. "Maybe you can move that shelf unit," said the Maharaja.

Ranjit and Vijay shoved the cabinet aside, exposing a small, low door. Shiv unlocked it and jerked on the handle. With a creaking of old hinges, the door swung open, scraping the floor. A musty, dank odor came from the darkness within. Vijay took a torch from Ranjit and shined it into the opening. The light revealed a narrow, low, windowless passage way with rough masonry walls. The tunnel ran only a short distance before turning a corner. Small pieces of rubble littered the uneven floor, and several old earthen pots stood just inside the doorway.

"I owe you at least a warning," said Lakshman Singh. "A couple of cobras have been seen in there."

Vijay tried to remain calm. "Cobras?"

Lakshman Singh shrugged. "There are small openings to the outside which can give them access. They often frequent dark holes such as this, you know."

Vijay knew. He'd had an uncle killed by a cobra bite. The snake had been in a darkened storage room at the rear of a house in their own village. He glanced at the Maharaja, who appeared amused at their dilemma.

"Let's call for a snake charmer," suggested Ranjit. "To coax them out." Vijay shot him a look of irritation. He strongly doubted snake charmers could do such a thing. They were mainly entertainers and purveyors of herbal medicines. He had seen them capture snakes in fields near his village for use in putting on shows, but the snakes that were captured had come out of their lairs on their own, not as a result of anything the charmers had done.

Vijay opened his mouth to say a snake charmer wasn't necessary. At that moment, he heard a rustling among the rubble. He quickly stepped backward and shone a light into the tunnel. A huge rat shot down the passage and disappeared around the corner.

"We've just sent the snakes part of their dinner," said the ex-ruler, his face sober. "Summoning a snake charmer may not be such a bad idea. I've seen it work before."

Now that the Maharaja had supported the notion, Vijay hesitated to reject it; he didn't want to risk insulting His Highness by disparaging the idea. He glanced at Kaushalya Kumari. Her lips were fixed in an amused smile.

Dammit, he needed to make a decision. He told Ranjit, "See if you can locate a snake charmer." The words sounded silly to him even as he said them, and he mentally kicked himself. He then wanted to tell Ranjit not to do it after all. But having given his order, he hesitated to immediately retract it, which would embarrass himself in front of both the Maharaja and the princess.

"I'll ask around," said Ranjit. Vijay quietly sighed as he watched his friend leave. The matter was decided. Maybe the cobras *would* respond to the snake charmer. Some people did have mysterious ways with animals.

He debated about whether to attempt to search the passage immediately, even though there was the risk of encountering the snakes. After all, there could conceivably be a treasure vault just around the corner, piled high with riches. He had no weapons with him, though he could probably borrow a stick or a sword or maybe even a gun from the Maharaja. But he saw his dying uncle in his mind. It was not at all a pleasant memory. He asked the Maharaja, "Are there any other entrances?"

"None that I'm aware of," said Lakshman Singh. "I believe

the others are all permanently closed off."

Reluctantly, Vijay said, "Then let's close this one until we can deal with the snakes. After you've locked the door, I'll put a seal on it so no one can gain access without our knowing."

With much difficulty Ranjit located a snake charmer in an outlying village. Ranjit took the jeep to collect him and immediately brought him to the palace. Waiting with Vijay were the Maharaja and his daughter. The snake charmer strode in jauntily, bearing a wooden flute, a stick with a forked end, a big, rolled cloth bag, and a broad smile. His face was weathered from the many years seated in the sun as he waited for customers to entertain, and his full white beard contrasted with skin burned almost black. He wore a loosely wrapped turban, a *dhoti*, a frayed shirt, and *chappals*.

It had quickly become clear the man's English was limited to the few words needed to coax money from tourists, so Vijay explained the problem to him in Rajasthani.

"I'll do my level best, sir," said the man, a light of good humor in his bloodshot eyes. "But whether the snakes come out will be as God wills." He grinned broadly. "You must pay me regardless."

Vijay gave a nod of agreement, and managed strained smile in return. "What will you do if they do come out?"

The snake charmer spread his arms wide and said as if for the benefit of a large crowd, "Why, sir! Of course I will capture them and put them in this bag. Unless your honor has some other desire for them?"

"That will be quite satisfactory," Vijay said dryly. He sensed the man was probably a charlatan, but it was difficult not to like him.

The snake charmer added, as he had obviously intended all along, "My payment of course is doubled if I capture one. And I'm sure your honor will be generous with baksheesh for each snake beyond the first."

Vijay glanced quickly at the Maharaja and at Kaushalya Kumari, who were both clearly amused. He now strove to contain his annoyance. The matter was getting out of hand. He nodded curtly. "As you wish."

Everyone gathered round as Vijay removed his seal from the door, which old Shiv then unlocked and pulled creakingly open.

"May I use your light?" the snake charmer asked. Vijay handed him an electric torch. The man shone it down the tunnel. After a moment, he shrugged. He returned the torch to Vijay. The charmer squatted on the floor in front of the door, took his flute, applied it to his lips with a theatrical flourish, and began playing, his body swaying with the music. The onlookers edged away, just in case.

He played. And played. The slow, haunting tune drifted upward through the wing of the palace. The Maharaja smoked. The tax officers and the princess sipped *chai*. After more than an hour, Vijay wondered whether to tell the man to stop. But they had gone to considerable trouble to get him here. Unlike Vijay, the snake charmer showed no sign of growing weary. His body still undulated as he played. Vijay beckoned to Ranjit. "I'm going to go check on matters upstairs. You can let me know if any snakes come out."

Ranjit gave a wry smile of resignation and nodded. "Right." The melody followed Vijay up through the hallways.

For three more hours the snake charmer played. No cobras appeared.

Vijay returned, watched for a couple minutes, and told him to quit. The man gave a nod, stopped playing, and rose. He shrugged and said with his ingenuous smile, "As I told your honor, it would be as God wills."

Vijay sighed. "Yes. No matter. You'll be paid all the same." He stared at the dark entry to the tunnel. He assumed that he himself should be the first to enter it. He looked at Ranjit. "Are you joining me?"

Ranjit shrugged, and smiled wanly. "I can't have you discover the treasure all by yourself." Vijay glanced at Lakshman Singh, trying to discern by the Maharaja's reaction to the mention of the treasure whether or not it was indeed hidden here. The ex-ruler's face was impassive, except for a possible hint of something like amusement in his eyes.

Vijay held a lit kerosene lantern in one hand, and the snake charmer's forked stick in the other. Stooping under the low ceiling, he slowly edged his way in. Ranjit followed with a electric torch and a *lathi*, a heavy stick with an iron-tipped end of the type favored by the police.

Step by step, bent over, they worked their way down the passage. It was considerably cooler in the tunnel than outside.

A sudden rustling by his feet made Vijay start and then freeze. A rat shot down the passage. Somehow, thought Vijay, the rat had escaped being eaten by any snakes. Did that mean there were in fact no cobras?

Heartened at least a little, he moved further down the tunnel. He reached the corner. Cautiously, he shone the lantern around the bend. Another passage, a much longer one. It seemed clear of any debris that could hide a snake. He carefully, slowly, moved down the tunnel. Another corridor branched off. Vijay memorized the turnings, although they were not yet complicated. His back was beginning to ache from having to stoop for so long.

Ranjit said in almost a whisper, "That looks like it must end at about the outer wall of the foundation. And the other passages seem to be mostly under the living quarters."

Vijay looked about, trying to get his bearings. "I think you're right."

They continued on down what seemed to be the principal passage. Vijay stopped at an alcove. A short, narrow flight of steps led upward, but they halted at what appeared to be a bricked-in doorway. From the dust and cobwebs it was clear no one had been there in years.

"Could this be the entrance to a vault?" Ranjit asked.

"Maybe. Let's keep it in mind for another look later." They continued down the main passage. It turned to the right, and there was another small stairway similar to the one they'd checked previously. Some large plumbing pipes exited the wall and then disappeared again into the masonry.

Something about the arrangement made Vijay stop and think. This network of tunnels seemed far too extensive to be designed simply as a hiding place for wealth. Did it have some other purpose? Maybe an escape route? But the palace had been built long after the region was at peace.

He stared at the iron pipes. "Dammit!" he suddenly exploded, as he realized the reason for the passages. "Bloody hell!" He straightened, hit his head on the ceiling, infuriating him all the more. He turned, shoved roughly past Ranjit, and stomped back the way they had come.

"What is it?" Ranjit called. "The snakes?"

Vijay did not reply. He was too bound up in his fury.

"Vijay!" called Ranjit from far behind him. "Did you see the snakes?"

Vijay stormed out the access door, past the startled ex-ruler and his daughter, the snake charmer, past Shiv.

Ranjit shouted, "It must be the snakes!" He dashed after Vijay.

The snake charmer, too, looked alarmed. The Maharaja and his daughter exchanged puzzled glances. Lakshman Singh shrugged, and the two followed at a walk.

Vijay charged up through the palace and out the nearest door. In the harsh glare of sunlight, he stood, breathing hard. How dare they pull a stunt like that!

He remembered—with outrage—Kaushalya Kumari's amusement over their searching the "secret tunnels."

The tunnels that were made in the days before flush toilets were common in palaces. In the days when Vijay's ancestor Untouchables, unseen, would quietly creep from the hidden passages into the bedrooms at dawn and carry out the chamber pots to be emptied.

Ranjit followed him outside, and Vijay angrily told him what he had realized.

Ranjit laughed, a bit uneasily. "I *thought* they were being too cooperative." He eyed Vijay. "But why did you leave so fast, without telling me the reason? You scared hell out of me."

Thinking, Vijay stared at him a moment. "Sorry. I just got furious when I found they'd tricked us."

Ranjit shrugged. "I can't blame them too much. Look what we're doing to them. And so far nothing's even turned up to make it worthwhile." He examined Vijay. "You've been spending a great deal of time with the lovely princess, though. I'd guess you're probably growing rather fond of her and didn't expect she'd enjoy fooling you." Vijay glared at his friend and said, "Mind your own damn—" He caught himself. After several seconds, he looked away and said, "Sorry again. This whole matter is getting on my nerves."

At least Ghosali hadn't been present to enjoy Vijay's humiliation. Neither Ranjit nor Shanta Das would say anything about it, so the snobbish Bengali Brahmin might never find out. Vijay thought for a few moments. At last, he said, "I need to go visit the fortress again."

"Mr. Singh!" Kaushalya Kumari called from behind Vijay as he neared the jeep. Reluctantly, he turned and waited for her.

"What is it?" he asked, assuming an abrupt, officious manner.

"Mr. Singh, I'd like to apologize." He saw that the expression in her eyes seemed genuinely abject. "Please don't take it personally. My father has always loved practical jokes. I'm sure it was too much for him to resist when he saw the opportunity. Needless to say, I felt I couldn't interfere with him."

Vijay examined her. He was certain she'd taken more than a little pleasure in the joke, too. But it would be graceless to say so. "I understand, Princess," he said, waving his hand to dismiss the matter as if it were of no consequence.

She nodded, turned and strode back into the palace, her scarf flowing gracefully behind her.

Naresh Singh, the ADC, appeared at the top of the steps and called to him: "Mr. Singh—telephone call, sir. From Delhi."

Vijay struggled to suppress his panic at the thought that the aide might recognize him. "Thank you," he said, and hurried up the stairs, his gaze downward. Half holding his breath, he followed the ADC to the office. "On the desk," said Naresh Singh.

Vijay picked up the phone and answered in Hindi, "This is Vijay Singh." He tried to keep his face turned away from the aide-de-camp. To his relief, Naresh Singh promptly left the room.

"Who is this?" demanded an authoritative voice.

"Vijay Singh. Did you wish to speak to me?"

"I wish to speak to the director *sahib*! Prasadji!"

"Prasadji had to return to Delhi. I am in charge here now. May I help you?"

"This is Dev Batra. Why is Director Prasad no longer there?"

"His father has died."

There was a moment of static-laden quiet on the line. Then: "Oh. And who are you?"

"Vijay Singh. Income-tax officer. Now in charge of the search."

"Where is Ghosaliji?"

"He is at the other search place." So Ghosali really must know Batra....

Another silence. Then: "But you are leading the raid now?"

"That's correct sir. How may I help you?"

"I want to know what's happening. Have you found anything?"

"Not yet, sir. We're working hard at it."

"Did Prasadji tell you I want results?"

"Yes, sir. We're doing our level best."

"I gave Director Prasad one week. You've had what—three days?"

"Uh, yes, sir. This is the third day."

"Find something, Mr. Singh. And report to me when you have."

His gut tightened. "Uh, yes, sir. I'll certainly telephone you as soon as we've found anything."

Batra broke the connection. Vijay took a deep breath, put the phone back in place. Nothing like more pressure. He realized he'd better leave the office before the ADC returned, so he hurried out of the palace.

As he was about to step into the jeep, Shanta Das approached him. "Sir," she said, "may I make a suggestion?"

He stopped and faced her. "Of course." He couldn't help but notice her attractiveness again. Somehow a softer, more subtle beauty than that of the princess, yet still quite appealing.

Shanta seemed hesitant, but she said, "It will take quite a few days to search the fortress more thoroughly. It's so large, and given that we haven't yet found any clues to a hiding place, we'll be depending to a large extent on luck." She hesitated, her eyes on his, as if reluctant to continue.

"Go on." He gave her his full attention and an encouraging smile.

"Well, it seems to me that if we try to think as the people themselves might have when they hid the treasure, we might narrow the search considerably, and maybe revise the priorities for the areas to look at. Maybe even think of some places that wouldn't otherwise have occurred to us."

Vijay tried to remain patient. Everything she'd said was obvious; in fact it was the approach he'd already begun. "Of course," he said, trying not to show his irritation. "That's exactly what I intend."

"I'm sure you do, sir. I've admired your ability ever since I've come to work in the department. But I wonder if you've thought of taking a more historical approach to it. The princess seems so knowledgeable about the past of this area and her family. The Maharaja is, too. If you could find out more details about their family's history, you might gain some insights as to if there really is a treasure. If so, when was it acquired, and by whom? Then you might be better able to put yourself in the place of the ruler at the time, or his treasurer or whoever. You could better imagine who it was who hid the wealth." She paused, searching his face. Seeing she now had his interest, she went on, "Why did they hide it, rather than leaving it all in the official treasury in the fortress? Who were they hiding it from? Robbers? Invaders such as the Marathas? Maybe from stronger powers, such as the Mughal Emperors or the British? Or maybe even other members of their own family? If we knew who they were hiding it from, that might give us a clue as to where it could be."

Vijay stood entranced; it seemed an excellent suggestion, but now that it had been stated, it was also obvious. Why hadn't that specific approach occurred to him before? Because he rejected his own past, which was tied so much with Mangarh? He smiled at her with new respect. "It's an excellent idea. But how will we get the princess to cooperate? So far, there's been no real risk of her help leading us to any secrets. She might be less willing if she saw we might be able to get somewhere with her information."

Shanta said carefully, "You could use the same argument you did with getting her father to show you the...tunnel."

Vijay flinched inwardly. That was a sore spot. After a moment, he said, "I'll talk to them first thing in the morning."

Kaushalya was present when Vijay made the request to her father in the Maharaja's study. The income-tax officer's audacity in asking for her help surprised her, even though he was courteous enough to suggest she and her father might want to discuss the matter alone.

When they were by themselves, Lakshman Singh said thoughtfully, "The faster they get their job done, the sooner they'll leave. And they could destroy a great deal of the fort if they demolish areas indiscriminately." He looked at Kaushalya. "Do you agree?"

She was pleased he wanted her opinion, but she found herself uncharacteristically indecisive. "I'm not eager to help them, Father," she said hesitantly. "They'll use everything they can against us. On the other hand, if it keeps them from tearing up our property, maybe it's worth it."

"It may very well do that. And don't assume you'll give them anything really useful. In fact, you may divert them...." his voice faded off.

"Daddyji! Does that mean you'd be using me to lead them away from something they shouldn't find?"

He grinned slyly. "Not exactly. That would assume there is indeed some place I don't want them to look. I'm not admitting such a thing. But it might be useful if you could keep them occupied in relatively harmless ways."

"So," said Kaushalya with some satisfaction, "if there *is* indeed a treasure, you don't think the historical approach will work to find it."

He was still smiling mildly. "Or maybe it might work, but it will take so long they'll give up."

Kaushalya tried to control her frustration. "They're not stupid, Father. Don't underestimate them just because they fell for your little prank."

He sobered some. "I'll try to remember that." They sat in silence for a minute or so. Then Lakshman Singh said, "You've spend considerable time now with Mr. Vijay Singh. What do you think of him?"

Kaushalya glanced sharply at her father. Why did he ask? And why did she feel reluctant to answer? She composed her face and said, "He's good at his job. I was surprised at his approach—I get the feeling he's trying not to make the raid harder on us than he has to. Beyond that, I'm not sure what to think. He's Rajput, you know, and from this area." She wasn't sure why she added the last pieces of information, other than to show the irony of a Mangarh Rajput directing a raid on other Mangarh Rajputs. It was too bad, in a way, that he was an adversary. Otherwise he might well be the type of person they would invite to dinner.

She stopped herself. Why was she thinking of him that way? Just because he was the same caste? He was still their enemy!

Her father was looking at her closely. The corners of his lips were curling in amusement at something. He asked, "Rajput, is he? Did Singh ever mention anything more about his background?"

Kaushalya, still puzzled over his questions and her own reactions, replied, "No, not that I recall. Why do you ask, Father?"

A smile flickered across his face. "Oh, no reason. I just wondered."

"Did you know of him when he lived here?"

That mild smile again. "I can't say I ever met him."

Kaushalya sensed her father wasn't telling her everything, and that he had some purpose in his questions. But she also knew he wouldn't tell her more, at least not now. She asked, "Father, assuming for the moment there were something to find—I'm just being hypothetical, mind you—how badly could it hurt us if they found it?"

He appeared to be considering, no longer smiling. "Kaushi, I'm still not admitting there is anything. If there were, how badly it hurt us would probably depend on what it was they found."

"Father, you're being evasive even hypothetically! If there is something that could hurt us, why not tell them where it is? The penalties would probably be less if we confess. They'd just assess a tax liability, and then we'd get rid of them!"

Her father still appeared thoughtful. At last he said, "They'd think I was giving in too easily, that I was still holding something out on them." He again smiled at her. "Besides, I rather enjoy watching them hunt."

Exasperated, Kaushalya thought a moment. "Father," she said after a time, "Maybe I can understand, at least a little, your playing games with them. But why with me? I could protect our interests better if I knew what I was protecting!"

He patted her shoulder. "I have my reasons, Kaushi. You'll have to trust that I have the best interests of our family at heart. And Mangarh state."

She felt like retorting: There *is* no more Mangarh state! There hasn't been since 1948! But she didn't say it, and after some time she sighed. "All right. I'll help them." She looked sternly at him. "I hope you're doing the right thing, Father. I have no way to judge."

At last the searchers had finished in the Bombay house, and Mahendra arrived in Mangarh. Kaushalya felt relieved to have her older brother present. She often disagreed with him, and his impulsiveness and excitability frequently made her uneasy. But at least she had another ally against the tax raiders.

As the current Member of Parliament from Mangarh, like most politicians he arrived home with an entourage of several hangers-on and constituents hopeful for favors. She got him alone as soon as she could. They sat facing each other in the big, high backed wicker chairs on the veranda outside his apartments. "Brother," she said, "Father won't tell me anything. How am I supposed to help if I don't know whether or not we have anything to hide?"

Mahendra was handsome, and overweight just enough to look fashionably prosperous. Many people compared his appearance to one of the currently popular Hindi film stars. He frowned, pressed his lips tightly together, and lit a cigarette. Obviously reluctantly, he said, "Father's always kept things close to his chest. Frankly, he hasn't told me if we have a treasure, either."

Kaushalya's jaw dropped as she stared at him. "But you're his only son now!"

Mahendra spread his hands in a gesture of futility. "You know he and I haven't been getting along well. He tells me it's a tradition for the ruler of Mangarh to leave sealed instructions for his heir. He says he'll follow that tradition. Beyond that, he won't tell me anything." He gave a wry smile. "Apparently I have to wait until he dies to find out."

Kaushalya chewed on her lip as she absorbed this. At least she no longer felt quite so discriminated against. "I think he is hiding something," she said finally. "I don't know if it's wealth, or something else."

Mahendra shrugged, and she was reminded of her father's similar habit of gesture. He drew on his cigarette and said, "I think so, too. I'm annoyed he won't tell me. But I haven't a clue as to what he's doing." He abruptly stood, went to the decanter placed on a nearby table, and poured himself a Scotch. "Bloody hell!" he said. "This search is all his fault. If he didn't spout off all the time about the Prime Minister, it wouldn't be happening."

Kaushalya couldn't really disagree, but she wished Mahendra wouldn't be so vociferous in his criticism of their father. They sat silent for a time. Eventually, she asked, "What do you think of my answering the tax people's questions about our properties and history?"

Mahendra thought for a few moments, scowling. Then: "It would help if we knew whether there's anything for them to find. If they discover hidden assets, there'll be a lot of publicity. It could hurt my standing in the party."

"But we don't know if there's a serious risk of them finding anything. I guess we have to assume Father knows what he's doing." "I wish I had that much confidence in him." Mahendra finished the Scotch, poured another. He shook his head. "I don't approve of helping our enemy. But if it keeps them from tearing down walls and digging holes all over, maybe it's worth it. I suppose they could get most of the information from other sources anyway if they really wanted to. But that would keep them here longer. And if we seem honest and open, maybe they'll conclude we don't have anything to hide." He again shrugged. "Let's cooperate with them—for the sole purpose of getting rid of them as fast as we can. And dammit, I hope Father hasn't gotten us all into a spot we can't get out of."

Shanta Das stood with Vijay Singh and Kaushalya Kumari in a large, windowless storage room near the office in the newer palace. Piles of dusty, cloth-wrapped record books crowded the wide deep shelves of masonry, as well as the floor.

Shanta was pleased Vijay Singh had asked her to help look for clues to the treasure by exploring the ruling family's history. Of course, she had been the one who suggested that approach, and she knew she had a quick mind.

She had noticed that the hot weather and the worries of supervising the search were affecting Mr. Singh. He was uncharacteristically tense and edgy, and his eyes looked red and tired, like he had not been getting much sleep.

Shanta had the distinct impression Vijay Singh was quite taken by the princess. That was certainly understandable. Of course, he was quite handsome himself, as well as generally pleasant and considerate. Shanta could almost wish she herself were a Rajput, so he might conceivably be a match. But in reality it was highly unlikely such a man would marry so far beneath his caste, especially someone from the Untouchable shoe makers of Agra. An alliance like that would cause tremendous problems with both of their families and with fellow caste members.

"You said you wanted to know some of my family's history," Kaushalya Kumari was saying. "A lot of it's here, everything from the household accounts to the forest department records."

Today the princess wore a peach colored *shalwar kameez* that went well with her relatively light complexion. Shanta always wore saris and had never tried one of these tunic-and-pants outfits of Punjabi origin, which so many of the younger, more sophisticated women had adopted. The princess looked terrific in it, and it appeared practical besides. Although a *shalwar kameez* was not quite as graceful as a sari, the long, semi-transparent *dupatta* or scarf did add a feminine touch and flowing lines. Shanta was a good seamstress, and she resolved to sew one of the outfits when she returned to New Delhi. Maybe a green one, a color she knew looked good on her, with some embroidery on the front.

She realized she'd better concentrate on what Kaushalya Kumari was saying: "Many of the less valuable files and ledgers are also in storerooms in the old fort. Quite a few of those have been damaged by white ants. Where would you like to start?"

Vijay raised his eyebrows, and scanned the overflowing stacks. It would take months, possibly years, if he were to try to go through them. Obviously such an undertaking was out of the question. "Maybe you could summarize things, Princess. Perhaps start at the beginning. When do you first have knowledge of your ancestors?"

Kaushalya Kumari tossed her filmy scarf over her shoulder and replied, "Our lineage is said to go back to the time of the heroes of the *Mahabharata* and the *Ramayana*. Our *charans*, our bards, say we're descended from Lord Rama's brother, Lakshmana. If it's true, our clan must have been founded sometime between 600 and 900 B.C.E. Our family has been here ever since a collateral line of our early ancestors conquered the Bhil tribals and took over the land." She smiled drolly. "Of course, we have no proof going that far back, only a genealogy list. Our people were apparently ousted from Mangarh sometime in the seventh century. Then they retook it again a couple centuries later with the help of the Bhils. The first historical event with a definite date was when our ancestor Raja Man Singh fought at Prithviraja Chauhan's side against the Muslim invader, Muhammad of Ghur, in 1192."

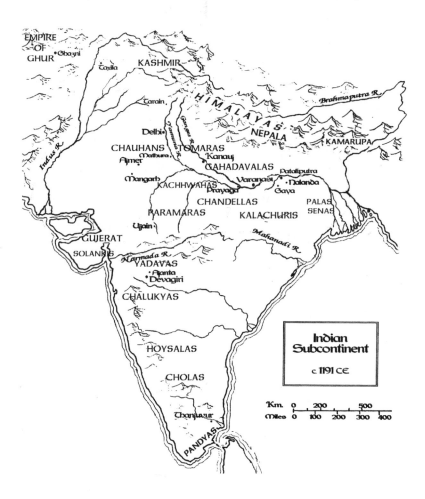

EMPIRE
OF
GHUR •Ghazni
Taxila
KASHMIR
Tarain
Indus R.
HIMALAYAS
Brahmaputra R.
NEPALA
Delhi•
CHAUHANS •TOMARAS
Ajmer• •Mathura Kanauj
KAMARUPA
Mangarh
KACHHWAHAS
GAHADAVALAS
Varanasi Pataliputra
•Nalanda
CHANDELLAS Prayaga •Gaya
Ujjain • PARAMARAS
KALACHURIS
PALAS
SENAS
Mahanadi R.
GUJERAT
SOLANKIS
Narmada R.
YADAVAS
•Ajanta
•Devagiri
CHALUKYAS

HOYSALAS

CHOLAS

Thanjavur

PANDYAS

Indian
Subcontinent
c. 1191 CE

Km. 0   200   500
Miles 0   100 200 300 400

Bride's Choice

1

Kanauj, northern India, in the winter of 1191 CE

The sun spilled over the walls of the garden, painting bright highlights among the branches of the *pipal* and mango trees outside the women's quarters of the royal palace. As she rose from her daily massage, Princess Samyogita's skin glowed warmly from the sandalwood paste and saffron. Her maids wrapped the long, wide strip of fine silk around her hips and arranged its folds.

The princess was selecting the gold jewelry to wear for the day when her younger sister Lakshmi ran into the apartments. Samyogita was amused at seeing that Lakshmi wore a blouse, as well as a skirt. The fashion of wearing clothing on the upper body had come relatively lately from the lands of the *mlecchas*, the foreign invaders of the Muslim faith who had caused so much trouble with their raids in recent years. No doubt all the women would be wearing the blouses before long. But she herself would refrain as long as possible.

"Did you hear?" Lakshmi asked breathlessly. "Prithviraja Chauhan defeated that *mleccha*, the Sultan of Ghur!"

Excitement coursed through Samyogita. She exchanged a quick glance with her maid and mentor Chitralekha, who shared her secret. The old woman let a smile curl the corners of her lips. Samyogita tried to act calm as she asked, "Oh? Where?"

"Some place called Tarain," replied Lakshmi. "Do you know where that is?"

"It's a long way to the west, near the Chauhan fortress the Sultan seized."

"You know so much!"

"I've studied it all. You could do the same." Her attendants were attaching the necklace and the earrings, and Samyogita relished the feel of the cool, hard metal in contact with her soft skin.

"Why should I bother?" asked Lakshmi.

"So you can help your husband rule some day." Ever since their mother had died three years ago, Samyogita had felt responsible for ensuring Lakshmi was raised properly, and she often gave advice that she hoped was helpful.

Lakshmi's eyes went blank for a moment, then regained their liveliness. She returned to the subject that had brought her. "I bet Father will be angry that Prithviraja won *another* victory!"

Samyogita smiled. "Yes, I'd love to have seen his expression when he heard!" Their father Jayachandra, King of Kanauj, ruled the Ganges plain all the way east to Prayaga. He saw the daring exploits of his cousin Prithviraja III, King of Ajmer and Delhi, as an intolerable challenge to his own position as the most powerful ruler in the north.

"Wouldn't it be exciting if Prithviraja could come to your *svayamvara?*" Lakshmi asked, her eyes shining with enthusiasm, as if the contest would be for herself rather than her sister.

Months ago, when Samyogita had turned sixteen, Jayachandra announced he would hold a *svayamvara*, a Bride's Choice, for her. Eligible men from Rajput royal families were invited from all over north India to come to Kanauj. After an opportunity to observe the princes in various contests of skill and to consider their relative merits, Samyogita would place a garland around the neck of the suitor she had chosen to be her husband, normally the man who had excelled in the contests.

She replied casually to her sister, "Yes, it would definitely be exciting if he came." She was not yet ready to tell Lakshmi what Prithviraja himself had communicated.

"Did you think he was handsome when we saw him on his visit?"

Indeed Samyogita had.

The visit was over three years ago, but Samyogita had thought of it every day since. Prithviraja Chauhan had already been famous for his many exploits. Although bards tactfully didn't sing of him in Jayachandra's palace, gossip had prepared the court for his arrival. She vividly remembered watching from her balcony and seeing him arrive on his elephant, one of dozens in his procession. "He's quite handsome," Chitralekha had observed. "So the legends are true in that regard."

Samyogita was enthralled: the way he carried his head, the proud arch of his nose, the brightness of his eyes, the strength evidenced by his massive chest. She thought of the many stories she had heard about Prithviraja. He was not only a great warrior; as King of Ajmer and Delhi he was a true father to his people. It was said he never refused to see a petitioner, day or night, no matter how poor the person or how low his status. Samyogita thought that was wonderful. What a contrast to her father, who set aside only an hour in the morning for audiences with his subjects! And whether or not a person got to see her father usually depended on the sizes of gifts the petitioner gave the King's officials. She had no opportunity to actually speak with the famous visitor. But she listened from behind the latticed stone screens piercing the walls of the audience and banquet halls, and she heard his strong, resonant voice in conversations with her father. By the time Prithviraja left after a week, Samyogita confided to Chitralekha that she yearned to be his wife when she came of age.

In the ensuing three years, on her visits to the small temple of Lord Shiva at the edge of the palace compound, she often prayed that Prithviraja Chauhan would one day be her husband. Samyogita's favorite pastime was her painting, and when she felt her skill had evolved enough, she rendered a portrait of Prithviraja, based on her memories. Occasionally, she would dismiss her maids for a short time, and she would remove the painting from its hiding place and gaze at the image, wondering what life might be like with such a handsome, heroic man.

She decided there were sound reasons for marrying the Chauhan King, in addition to her personal desires. She listened carefully to Chitralekha and absorbed much of the old woman's practical approach to life's challenges. She often overheard the conversations of her father and his advisors, and of the women in the ladies' wing, discussing the wars and alliances of the current Rajput rulers. Samyogita consequently formed a strong sense not only of her own *dharma*, but also of the ever-changing relations between the various major kings of Aryavarta.

She thought of how Chitralekha, in one of their quiet, private conversations in the garden pavilion, had questioned Samyogita's making up her mind about a husband at so early a time, especially since her father so hated Prithviraja Chauhan. Samyogita had looked solemnly at her mentor. "Eventually," she said, "Father and Prithviraja will war against each other. They both want to be Emperor of all of Aryavarta."

Chitralekha nodded, smiling encouragingly at Samyogita's demonstration of learning and thought. "They should never fight that war," Samyogita said firmly. "My father and Prithviraja's forces are too closely matched. Even if one wins a clear victory, both kings will be weakened. That would make each more vulnerable to conquest if the other kings should form an alliance against them. And the *mleccha* Sultans might also take advantage to invade and conquer."

"I can't disagree," said Chitralekha, obviously impressed. "You think your marriage to Prithviraja would change that?"

"Joining the two houses should make my father much less likely to attack Prithviraja. And"— she smiled at realizing she probably sounded boastful—"I think I might be able to influence Prithviraja not to war against my father. So in the long term, both kings would end up stronger."

Chitralekha had said admiringly, "You've gone far beyond anything you've learned from me. And at such a young age! I think you'll be a true asset to the prince you marry."

Unfortunately, because of Jayachandra's jealousy toward his rival, Samyogita still didn't dare express her yearnings openly to anyone besides Chitralekha. Not even to Lakshmi, who might carelessly let the information slip out.

"Prithviraja has several wives already, of course," Lakshmi was saying.

"Naturally," Samyogita replied absently. She was only slightly concerned about that fact. She had long ago decided to devote herself to becoming Prithviraja's favorite. It seemed likely to her that after she went to live in his palace, she could gain influence with him by her beauty and charm, and she could then use her intelligence to aid him in being an even greater and wiser ruler.

The maids encircled her lower waist with the heavy *mekhala*, the jeweled silver girdle. Since it was a chilly morning, she allowed them to drape a gold-embroidered shawl around her otherwise bare upper body. She wondered how Prithviraja would fare in the contests at the *svayamvara*. He must be almost thirty years old now. Most of the princes would be younger, which might give them a slight edge in strength and speed. But surely Prithviraja's greater experience would compensate for any lack of youth. And thirty was not exactly ancient; her own father was nearly twice that age and was still vigorous.

Lakshmi was saying, "It's really too bad Father would never invite him. Father hates him too much."

Samyogita tensed. "Don't be so certain about that!"

"Oh—you think Father *did* invite him?"

Samyogita replied more confidently than she felt: "Father was supposed to invite *all* the eligible kings and princes." She glanced at Chitralekha, who gave a slight shrug.

Although Samyogita had never dared to ask her father, she nevertheless managed to receive an indication that Prithviraja was in fact coming. With Chitralekha's aid, Samyogita had secretly encouraged Prithviraja to compete by sending him a message: *"There can be no doubt of your victory in my svayamvara, as in everything else you attempt."*

She was thrilled when the reply was smuggled to her two months later: *"There can be no doubt that the prize of the svayamvara is the most valuable in all of Aryavarta, and one I would eagerly accept."* Samyogita reviewed the wording of Prithviraja's message in her mind and was again distressed that he had not *specifically* promised to come—that had just been the way she interpreted his words. He'd certainly *implied* he would come, though, hadn't he?

But what if her father *hadn't* actually invited Prithviraja?

She realized she had let her fear about hearing the wrong answer discourage her from asking her father the question for far too long. "I need to go," she said. "I'll see you again later today." She evaded her sister's look of surprise and, anklets jingling, strode from the apartments, accompanied only by the always present Chitralekha. They left the women's wing of the palace and padded down the corridors of cool stone to the King's small private meeting hall.

Standing next to the Rajput guards by the doorway was the minister in charge of construction, waiting for an audience. She recognized the two men who accompanied him, bearing rolled up drawings, as master stone carvers. Samyogita edged inside the door, and she saw that her father was conducting business with two of his other ministers. Jayachandra sat on the thick carpets, leaning against the richly embroidered bolsters. She caught a few words of her father's conversation, and as the subject strongly interested her, she eased closer.

Jayachandra, his elegant mustache and beard gone entirely white, was disagreeing with the two counselors. "I'll worry about the *mleccha* when he comes, if he ever does. If Prithviraja Chauhan can defeat him, surely I can, too!"

"An alliance with the Sultan wouldn't necessarily suggest weakness on your part, Your Majesty," said one of the ministers. "It could be a clever move. It could strengthen your position considerably if you were able to convince the Sultan to make war against one of your own enemies—instead of you."

Jayachandra looked toward the door and saw Samyogita waiting. "Maybe. I'll consider it a while." He waved a dismissal.

When the ministers had made their obeisances and left, Samyogita approached her father. He sipped his wine and smiled at her, but she saw caution behind the smile. "What can I do for you today, my dear?" he asked.

She seated herself in front of him, arranging her legs on one side and smoothing her skirt for a graceful appearance. "I wondered about the plans for my *svayamvara*, Father," she said casually, "since it's only a month away."

Jayachandra shrugged. "My ministers assure me everything will be ready on time. All you have to do is be there and look beautiful, which won't be difficult."

Samyogita smiled to acknowledge her father's compliment. "All the invitations were accepted?"

"Mostly. One or two princes were too occupied in their wars."

"Including Prithviraja Chauhan, I suppose," she said offhandedly.

"Prithviraja Chauhan?" Jayachandra's eyes narrowed. "You don't think I'd invite that vulture? If it weren't for him, I'd rule of all of Aryavarta by now!"

Samyogita stopped breathing, her mind numb. Eventually, she realized she must say *something*. "I'm sorry, Father. I assumed you'd sent an invitation to every eligible raja." She was surprised, and relieved, at how calm she sounded.

"You should have known I wouldn't invite *him*! That scavenger will never visit my palace again."

"Of course." She thought furiously, and asked cautiously, "But aren't you concerned that people might say you didn't invite him because you're afraid of him?"

"*Afraid* of him?!"

She straightened. "Oh, *I* know you're not afraid of him, Father! But I wonder what some of the other rajas might think. If you asked him, he might not come anyway, and then everyone would say *he* was afraid of *you*."

Her father scowled. "If I'd invited him and he refused, everyone would see it as an insult to me. No, better not to ask him at all."

She raised an eyebrow. "Isn't that an insult to *him*?"

Jayachandra smiled smugly. "Of course. At least, I hope it is. What of it?"

She leaned toward him, and with a smile she hoped would soften him at least a little, she asked, "Wouldn't it show you were more generous of spirit if you invited him, even though everyone knows you dislike him? It would show you don't let petty jealousies control you."

He stared at her. At last, he said, "That upstart has thrust himself into battles and treaties he had no concern with, and now he stands in the way of my future conquests. You consider that a mere petty jealousy?"

She shrank almost imperceptibly away from him. "Of course not, Father. I merely meant it was possible some others might mistakenly see it that way." She smiled coyly, again leaned toward Jayachandra, and said that for which she had been preparing him: "Wouldn't it be evidence of your supremacy if he came? Invite him secretly, Father. If he refuses, no one else would need to know. If he accepts and comes, it will show he's hesitant to insult you by refusing. And maybe that he respects your prestige as being higher than his own." As Jayachandra's forehead furrowed in thought, Samyogita felt pleased with her cleverness.

She added, as extra weight, "The mere fact that he'd receive his invitation so much later than all the other princes is an insult in itself! He'll be so angry he won't know how to handle it. It would be much more effective than simply ignoring him." She settled back, anticipating a positive response.

Her father was looking out beyond the pillars of the entry, where the ministers, the stone carvers, and others wanting an audience still waited. Then a smile crossed his face, a smile out of all proportion to her suggestion.

"I'll show them how little I fear that bandit!" he said. "But *not* by inviting him."

Her whole being sank. Mouth dry, she asked, "What do you mean?"

Jayachandra laughed heartily. "Oh, you'll see. He'll be here, all right. But in a way no one expects!"

"I—I don't understand, Father."

Jayachandra again laughed. He waved a hand, dismissing her as he had the ministers. "You will, my dear. I'm glad you came—otherwise I'd never have thought of it!"

2

Samyogita tried desperately to guess what her father's plan might be, but she reached no conclusion. That afternoon she led Chitralekha to their usual place in the garden. She stood beneath the ancient *pipal* tree, too filled with anxiety to sit still on the bench in the pavilion. "How can my father be so certain Prithviraja will be at the *svayamvara* without an invitation? And what could he mean when he said Prithviraja would be there *in a way no one expects*?"

Chitralekha shook her head. "Surely His Majesty would never try to kidnap Prithviraja and bring him here by force."

"No. That would be impossible. And I'm sure Father wouldn't do anything so dishonorable as having Prithviraja killed and bringing his head here to display it." She stared vacantly toward her father's audience hall. "Still....I wonder if I should warn Prithviraja to be on guard."

"On guard against what?"

Samyogita did not know.

In the days that followed, she twice went as far as the door of her father's audience hall, intending to swallow her pride and insist that her father tell her what he'd planned. But each time she hesitated, and then she turned back, doubting Jayachandra would spoil his fun by telling her. All she would accomplish would be to infuriate her father if he realized the extent of her interest in his rival.

As the days turned into weeks the uncertainty wore at her. Her temper became short, so she had to concentrate to keep it controlled. Once she even snapped at Lakshmi's well meaning attempts at conversation, and she later had to apologize.

At times in her daily visits to the Shiva temple, as she participated in the worship of the *lingam*, she often felt the power of Lord Shiva flowing through her and vitalizing her, but she saw no evidence that her prayers as such were answered. The only activity that calmed her nerves was her painting; it captured her attention so completely that she could lose herself in it, unaware of the passing of time, for an entire morning or afternoon. She loved trying to capture on her boards the gracefulness of palm fronds or the complexities of a banyan tree's roots. When she wanted a challenge, she painted yet another portrait of Chitralekha and of Lakshmi.

The *svayamvara* would be the most important event celebrated in Kanauj in many years. During the final week before its opening, workmen labored throughout the nights as well as the days to decorate the city and the palace. The air reverberated with the sounds of the carpenters' hammers as they built additional viewing stands for the contests in the arena—and the *mandap*, the pavilion for Samyogita's marriage ceremony.

For several days, the guests and contestants had been arriving: Rajput kings and princes from virtually all the leading clans. Samyogita instructed a maid to watch and to inform her as each entourage appeared, so she would know if Prithviraja came. Then the opening day of the *svayamvara* arrived, and still Samyogita did not know what to expect.

Prithviraja had not appeared in Kanauj. There was still a possibility he might arrive late. But what if he didn't? Must she forever give up all the dreams and plans she had nourished for so long? A future life that did not hold Prithviraja Chauhan as her husband had become inconceivable.

She was filled with anxiety as her attendants clothed her elaborately in new embroidered red silk. She felt heavy under the weight of so many pieces of her finest gold jewelry. Although the actual marriage ceremony was five days away, she was dressed almost as she were already a bride on her wedding night, laden with bracelets, anklets, hair ornaments, *mekhalas*. Her lovely breasts could scarcely be seen under the long rows of gold and pearl and diamond necklaces, which flattened them under their weight anyway. Her attendants had been wary of her in recent weeks due to her preoccupation and irritability, so there was an audible sigh of relief in the room when she nodded approval after examining her appearance in the mirror.

It was time to leave for the festivities. Outside her apartments, she joined her father's three queens, who led the way. An excited Lakshmi accompanied Samyogita, and the women's principal attendants all followed.

As her entourage approached the doorway of the public audience hall, Samyogita saw the culmination of the elaborate preparations for the festivities. The hall had been enlarged by extending its sides with even more and bigger canopies than usual. Bright colored banners hung everywhere, and the sound of orchestras filled the air, mingling with the scent of sandalwood incense. Off to the right she saw the large wood and cloth *mandap*, the temporary pavilion that had been newly constructed for the actual wedding. The marriage ceremony would be held immediately after the contests, as soon as she selected her husband. The approaches to the audience hall were lined with rows of bright standards and a file of guards: her father's warriors in their finest battle dress. By the doorway itself stood a new statue of a soldier in armor, spear in hand, guarding the entrance.

As Samyogita waited at the door, under the shelter of the spreading canopies, the music stopped. The conches sounded a great fanfare, and she entered the pillared room. For the first time, she saw the many suitors, lined up with their retainers along the side of the hall. Then she lowered her eyes to appear appropriately modest and submissive. A smile tore at her lips at such a thought. She felt everyone watching her; most of the contestants were seeing her for the first time.

Her face grew warm and her breath quickened. All of these powerful and famous men were here solely for one reason: to win *her*. Despite her concern over Prithviraja's absence, the moment was thrilling.

The Prime Minister came and escorted her to her father's low, cushion-strewn throne. After making her obeisance, she arranged herself on a smaller platform throne, facing the assembled princes. The other queens seated themselves on either side.

Trying not to let her satisfaction in being such a coveted object of so many men appear obvious, she kept her eyes lowered as the suitors were presented one-by-one: Bhana, Prince of the Yadava dynasty of Devagiri in the Deccan. Chandraraja, son of the Governor of Delhi, of the Dahima Rajput clan. With her gaze focused at the stone paving of the floor, she saw only the feet and lower legs of her suitors clearly; above the knees she could gain merely an indirect impression.

Man Singh, the tall ruler of the Pariyatra Rajputs of Mangarh stood before her. So far, the other princes had immediately returned to their places in the hall. But Man Singh made no move to leave. She felt his eyes examining her. A wave of subdued laughter swept through the onlookers at the Mangarh Raja's boldness. Unable to resist her intense curiosity, she let her eyes flick up to meet his, then back down. She saw an expression of amusement, as if he had peered into her thoughts and was smugly satisfied he had drawn her attention.

In spite of her lack of serious interest in anyone other than Prithviraja, she was annoyed. How dare the Mangarh ruler deliberately toy with her before such an assemblage of royalty! And he risked insulting her father at the same time. The Mangarh prince was a vassal of Prithviraja's, and perhaps he felt protected by the fact that he owed no obligations to King Jayachandra of Kanauj. Or maybe Prithviraja himself had incited Man Singh's actions to demonstrate a complete lack of fear of Prithviraja's rival kings. Samyogita did not risk glancing at her father's face to see how he reacted. Meanwhile, Mulraj II, the King of Gujarat, and his elder half brother, Bhima, presented themselves before her.

But where was Prithviraja? Even if he had somehow managed to slip into the hall in disguise, she was sure she could not miss him. She laughed inwardly at the thought—how unlikely that he would conceal himself, rather than boldly dominating the gathering.

The introductions continued. Samyogita noticed three of the courtiers whispering to each other, smiling broadly as if sharing some secret joke. Then it happened again, with a group of four other nobles. What could the banter be about? Surely there was nothing in her own dress or demeanor to cause mirth! Several times she saw spectators look with expressions of amusement toward the main doorway. They seemed unconcerned about whether or not their host, the powerful Maharaja of Kanauj and Benares, saw them or not. So the joke was not at her father's expense, nor was it anything he would disapprove of. What could it possibly be?

The end of the introductions came. Still no Prithviraja. Her pride at being the object of so much attention had worn off, replaced by renewed anxiety. Could he be late arriving? That was unlikely. He'd had more than enough time to travel to Kanauj.

She felt trapped, and her anger grew. She was a prize in a contest; nothing more. It was time for her to leave the hall; the contests would formally begin the next day. She rose from her seat and followed the queens from the assembly. She did not so much as glance at the powerful kings and princes who had come to win her hand. She knew her obvious indifference would displease her father and irritate his guests, but she did not care.

Walking toward her apartments, her mind in a turmoil, she became aware of what her little sister was saying: "—a terrible thing to do. He doesn't deserve it, even if his *is* our enemy!"

"What?" Samyogita asked numbly, forcing her attention toward Lakshmi.

"Haven't you been listening? Doing that to Prithviraja!"

Samyogita froze. "Doing *what*?"

"That statue, *of course!*"

Samyogita tried to make sense of what Lakshmi was saying, to not betray her ignorance. She was annoyed at herself for missing something everyone else knew, and at Lakshmi and her maids for not informing her earlier. "What about it?"

"Prithviraja's statue by the door! You didn't even see it? Father insulted Prithviraja in front of everyone by putting a statue of him there dressed as a doorkeeper!"

The occupation of doorkeeper was low caste. Samyogita's anger grew as Lakshmi went on, "I didn't know who it was until someone told me. But the rajas and nobles must have recognized him right away. Didn't you see them all laughing?"

Samyogita twisted toward the statue, her fury near bursting. She quickly took in the appearance of the broad chested figure. It was, indeed, a likeness of Prithviraja, much as she remembered him: handsome, with an arched, prominent nose and the flowing mustache worn by Rajputs. His eyes seemed somehow different from those she remembered, but she could not quite place just why.

Tears came. She whirled about and marched toward her rooms. There, she ordered the attendants who were about to undress her to leave; everyone except Chitralekha. She strove to control her voice, so she could not be overheard by the servants who would quickly spread gossip. "How could Father do such a thing?"

Chitralekha quietly shook her head, reluctant to say anything critical of the King even in private.

"Prithviraja will never forgive such an insult!" said Samyogita, her eyes most at the same time as they flashed in anger.

"Probably not," said Chitralekha with a sigh, her own eyes dull with sadness.

Samyogita blinked at her tears, and let free her fury: "How can I ever marry Prithviraja now? Father has made it impossible!"

Chitralekha again sighed, and she shook her head.

Late that night, when the vast courtyard was deserted, Samyogita slipped out in the cool air to look at the statue more closely. The sculpture, insult though it was, had been masterfully carved. Chitralekha held a coconut oil lamp near for her to examine the face. "How could I have walked by, twice, and not recognized him?" Samyogita whispered. She tried to imagine what it would be like to run a finger along the side of his cheek, to finger the lush mustache....

She stepped back for an overall impression. The King of Ajmer and Delhi stood stiffly erect, his stance reinforcing the impression of a proud ruler. But there was that something about his eyes. He was looking slightly to the side, with a puzzled furrow just starting to crease his brow. As if he had suddenly realized he was the object of a joke.

Samyogita clenched her small fists and fixed her lips tightly, striving to control her growing anger. She stepped further back, while Chitralekha remained holding the lamp by the statue. She examined the face for some time, bitterly annoyed at the expression the sculptor had given the great warrior at her father's direction.

Her bare feet had grown cold from the paving stones. Even in the heat of her wrath she shivered in the coolness, and she tightened her shawl around her shoulders. Eventually, she turned and went numbly off to her bed. Lying there, she cried for what might have been.

The next day, in the great hall, Samyogita made an effort to thrust aside her feelings. After all, as she had been repeatedly told from an early age, her *dharma* as a Rajput princess was to do as her father desired. Her own preferences were of no importance, so matter how much she might wish otherwise. So she tried to force herself, as her duty required, to become interested in the five days of contests. After all, she was compelled to choose one of the entrants, presumably the winner, as her husband. She snorted quietly to herself at the irony that only opportunity she truly had to exercise *her own* choice was to make a selection she cared nothing about.

She watched as Man Singh of Mangarh, tallest of the contestants, haughty in bearing and wearing an amused smile as if he did not truly take the proceedings seriously, won the archery competition. As he was declared the victor, he looked at Samyogita with confident smile, as if challenging *her* in some way. She was annoyed by his brashness, but also slightly intrigued.

The next day, she watched Man Singh closely as he fought in the important swordsmanship contests. She momentarily found herself caught up in the clashing of metal against metal, the danger of injury even with blunted swords. Man Singh's long arms gave him an advantage with the sword, but he was also fast, appearing to instinctively anticipate his opponents moves. He won this event also.

Could *he* be the one she should choose? She wanted her husband to be strong, a man everyone would envy and respect, and Man Singh might well qualify. However, as one of Prithviraja's vassals, his status in the rankings of princes was lower than she preferred.

The third day, Mulraj of Gujarat won the equestrian events. He, at least, was already a king. Powerful, young, not unattractive, he might be a possibility. She was troubled that he did not enter the sword fights; possibly he felt it was beneath his dignity as an important ruler. In spite of his many attributes, he did not stir her.

On the fourth day, she found the wrestling exciting, with the flesh-on-flesh contact, the straining of hard muscles threatening to burst forth from gleaming taut skin. But the brawny winner, a Chandela prince, appeared to seethe with anger and to use the wrestling as an excuse to brutalize his opponents. She imagined him using his strength to force her compliance in bed, and she shuddered. She wanted a forceful, manly husband—but not one who would batter and bruise her.

The final day, Man Singh of Mangarh won yet another contest, javelin throwing from elephant-back.

The competitions ended. Jayachandra declared a pause in the proceedings to give his daughter time to decide, and also to maintain the suspense among the guests.

With Chitralekha, Samyogita strode back and forth in the garden outside her apartments. "How can I possibly choose?" she asked in frustration, her voice low so as not to be overheard. "Nobody *clearly* won! Besides, I don't want to marry *any* of them!"

Chitralekha stared at her. "You have no feelings at all about any of them?"

"No!" She continued pacing. Eventually, "Well...I suppose maybe a little...."

Chitralekha waited.

"Bhana of Devagiri is handsome. He seems to be quite charming," Samyogita said tonelessly.

"He did well in every event," said Chitralekha, with no expression. "Even though he wasn't actually the victor in any."

Samyogita resumed pacing. After a time, she said, "Chandraraja of Delhi is young and good-looking. Fair-skinned, too. He placed near the top in all the contests." She spoke with no enthusiasm.

"He might not be a bad choice," said Chitralekha.

"But he's only the *son* of one of Prithviraja's vassals. His status is even lower than Man Singh of Mangarh."

"True."

Samyogita stood, facing Chitralekha. "Man Singh was definitely one of the best in the contests."

"Indeed he was." "He rules his own kingdom, even though it's small and he's a vassal of—" She swallowed. "Of Prithviraja." Chitralekha gave a nod.

Samyogita tried not to let her mind dwell on Prithviraja. "But Man Singh is so...so arrogant! Did you see the way he looked at me sometimes? Like I was some plaything he could either take for himself, or forget about without a thought."

"Don't *all* princes take what they can for their amusement? He's a king, after all."

Samyogita sighed. It was true. She turned her thoughts to the remaining choices. "Mulraj of Gujarat seems the only other likely one. He's a king, too. He didn't do badly in the contests....But I just don't find him interesting."

"So," said Chitralekha. "Is it Bhana, or Chandraraja, or Man Singh?"

Drained from weighing such a heavy matter, Samyogita let herself slide onto the pavilion's cushioned bench. Man Singh's face— amused, maybe disdainful, but still attractive and intriguing—kept returning to her thoughts. But he was not the one whom she had fixed her intention upon for the past three years. "I just don't know what to do," she whispered.

The excitement was tangible in the air as all assembled in the great audience hall in the evening for the culmination: the Bride's Choice. Samyogita approached the hall slowly and deliberately. She again wore brilliant crimson bridal clothing. The soles of her feet flashed red from the painted lac. Rings gleamed on her toes. The golden bells surrounding her ankles tinkled with each step. The enormous quantities of gold jewelry and precious gems sparkled on her head, her neck, her arms, her hands.

She saw that the Brahmin priests had lit the sacred fire at the marriage pavilion, expecting the ceremony to be only hours away. She deliberately did not look at the statue of the door keeper as she padded by, her entourage of women trailing after her. She would not give anyone that satisfaction, even though no one but Chitralekha knew of her passion for Prithviraja.

She bent, touched her father's feet, then stood. Jayachandra handed her the garland to award. She smelled the fragrance of the jasmine. The moment she dreaded most had come. She turned to face the suitors. The orchestra ceased playing. The hall fell silent. Samyogita surveyed the assembled princes and rulers. Her consternation grew so it was almost unbearable. Her frustration mounting, still not knowing what she would do, she examined the expectant faces.

Should she choose Man Singh of Mangarh? With his unusual height and his challenging, amused gazing at her, he was difficult to ignore as he towered above the line of other princes. But he seemed so confident of being the one. Maybe she should choose another, just to show him how inflated was his self-opinion.

She seethed in frustration. She raised the necklace of flowers, tempted to cast it to the floor as she screamed her defiance. She would not do that, of course, but she had the odd feeling that she would not know who would be her husband until her hands had, somehow of their own volition, garlanded one or another of the contestants. She hated being in such a position, of being forced to try to decide which prince was least objectionable.

Then, in an instant, her choice became clear. She could not predict the outcome of her selection. She was taking a wild gamble, more likely to fail miserably than to succeed, but it was the sole alternative that held even a slight hope. She smiled grimly. Holding the garland carefully with both hands, she strode toward her choice. Only the jingling of her anklets and bracelets broke the stillness in the huge room.

She heard whispered, puzzled, exclamations as the crowd saw the direction she headed. She was unable to resist a quick glance at Man Singh of Mangarh to see his expression as he realized she had not chosen him. She expected him to be surprised, maybe annoyed, at her rejection. Instead, she was startled to see that his eyes showed dejection, even hurt. She had no time to consider the meaning.

She reached the door, and pandemonium broke out in the hall. Her father was among those who had a clear view through the doorway as she calmly placed the garland around the neck of the statue of Prithviraja Chauhan.

3

Samyogita continued toward her apartments, aware that she was alone. None of the women of her entourage had dared follow. She trembled in reaction to what she had done. Her father, as well as the contestants, would be outraged. He would never forgive her.

But in fact, she thought, her action was not so scandalous. After all, how could she honor one contestant over the others when there was no clear winner? And her father's using the sculpture to insult Prithviraja was in such poor taste. Garlanding the statue was a step toward peacefully resolving the two kings' rivalry. The other kings just might put pressure on Jayachandra to go along with her choice. The odds were against it. But she just might, after all, end up being given to Prithviraja as a bride.

She had almost reached the doorway when she heard the heavy

footfalls of running men, the clattering of weapons against armor. She forced herself to appear calm, tried to bring her trembling body under control, and she turned to face the squad of her father's soldiers who came to a halt before her.

"A thousand pardons, Highness," the commander said. She recognized Baluka, one of her father's senior guard officers. His eyes would not meet hers as he bowed, then straightened and said: "The King commands us to escort you immediately to the Lal Niwas."

"And if I don't come willingly?"

The officer said in a weary, reluctant tone, "I'm very sorry, Highness. We're ordered to take you there anyway. And to see that you're confined to your apartments."

Although the small fortress-like palace near the city wall had occasionally housed high ranking prisoners in the past, the Lal Niwas smelled of bats and urine. The uncleaned floor of the corridor felt damp and gritty on the soles of her feet. As she entered her room, with its dank odor of dust and mold and bird droppings, there was little doubt that the structure was now a prison, not a palace. Although the apartment had once been elegant, it had been neglected during the many years of disuse.

A guard stood outside her doorway to ensure she did not leave. It felt so odd to be alone, except for the guards. Never before in her life had she been away from Chitralekha, and from the presence of other women. Surely her father would send her servants! But what if he didn't think to? No one else would dare suggest it, or to do it on their own. She might be alone for days!

The night grew cool, and she did not have adequate bedding. She saw no way to cover the open window, which overlooked the enclosed courtyard three stories below. Still dressed in her wedding finery, she wrapped her shawl around her and huddled in a corner, digging her bejeweled, red-bottomed toes into the dirt, futilely trying to warm them.

After what seemed like many hours, she heard voices in the hallway. There was a short pause, and the door creaked open. In the dim lamplight, she saw a familiar face. "I hoped you would come!" she cried happily. Chitralekha carried an oil lamp in one hand and a bundle of blankets in the other. The maid looked around the room with distaste. "Your father's anger is understandable," she said. "But this is disgraceful! I'll see about getting everything changed in the morning."

"Did my father have you sent here?"

"No. He's so furious, I'm sure he has no thought for your comfort. I came on my own. I knew your guards would realize you needed someone, and I look harmless."

After a moment, Samyogita said quietly, "I'm glad you came."

Chitralekha scowled at her. "That was a foolish thing you did. No good can come of it."

Samyogita looked away. Her shoulders slumped. "No doubt, you're right," she murmured. She returned her gaze to the old servant. "But it was the only way I could think of to give me any chance at all to marry Prithviraja."

Chitralekha wearily shook her head. "You meant well. Still....Your actions will never be forgotten! They'll be talked about for generations."

Samyogita considered this. She sighed. "Maybe so. But by marrying Prithviraja, I might have been able to help both him and my father. And the people they rule."

The old woman shook her had sadly. "Possibly. It's still your duty to respect your father's decision."

Samyogita again sighed. She said in a low voice, "So I've been told many times."

Chitralekha assisted her in removing the many items of gold jewelry Samyogita still wore, and tied them into a bundle in a shawl. Then the two women settled in for the night as best they could.

It seemed to Samyogita that sleep would never come. But she knew she had somehow dozed off when she was suddenly awakened by the creaking of the door. She opened her eyes; the only light came from a lamp in the hall. She saw a heavily built, armed man silhouetted in the doorway. "What do you want?" she demanded, assuming it was one of her guards.

"Princess Samyogita of Kanauj?" the man asked peremptorily, in a voice that was resonant and confident.

"Yes, of course! What are you doing in my room?" The lamplight glinted on the unsheathed sword in his hand, and she felt a stab of fear.

He strode toward her and boldly announced: "I've come for you!"

Chitralekha was now awake also. "What's the meaning of this?" the maid cried. "How dare you disturb Her Highness at such an hour?"

The man gave a hearty laugh. "Because she's going to marry me. I came to claim my prize from the *svayamvara!*"

His voice was vaguely familiar. Samyogita peered into the shadows, trying to discern his face. Which of the contestants was he? And how did he dare to come here? He turned his head slightly, and in the dim light from the hall Samyogita could at last make out his features. She gasped.

It was Prithviraja Chauhan.

Too stunned for words, she stared, her mouth open.

The King grinned. He took firm hold of her arm. "We must move fast, before we're discovered."

She stood rigid in his grasp. "How—" Her voice was high with agitation and disbelief.

He laughed. "I'll explain later. We need to hurry."

"But—where?"

"Ajmer. We'll be married there." His confident voice held no doubt of her compliance with his will. He guided her to the doorway.

"Highness!" said Chitralekha urgently. "Are you sure you want this? Your father will disown you forever!"

Samyogita hesitated, resisting the strong hand on her arm. Her hope of helping avoid an eventual war between the two kings now appeared doomed. But even if she remained in Kanauj, she doubted her father would ever pardon her. And he would probably force her to marry one of the contestants.

"You'll want your maid with you," Prithviraja said, again with total assurance.

There was no time for thought. Still uncertain, she let the strong hand lead her from the room while her mind struggled to weigh the options. She looked back and saw Chitralekha, wide eyed, gaping after them. They stepped over the legs of one of her guards, bound and gagged, leaning against the wall. As they rounded the corner, she saw two more guards tied securely to a pillar. "We surprised them," Prithviraja told her matter-of-factly.

For a moment, she hesitated. Only half willingly, she allowed Prithviraja to drag her along the hall, then down the narrow stone stairs. If she left with him she would be utterly cut off from all she had ever known, with no visit home ever possible! She would probably never see her sister Lakshmi again. Did she really want that? Long before, she had come to accept that most royal brides had little contact with their previous families, but any visit back to Kanauj would be utterly impossible for her now.

Still, forced to decide quickly, she made her choice. While this was not the way she preferred to leave her home, it was certainly thrilling! An abduction such as this would give the bards material for countless legends and songs.

Suddenly, she felt another stab of worry. Would Chitralekha come? She glanced back and was reassured to see her servant hurrying after them, carrying blankets and the shawl with the bundle of jewelry. Samyogita lifted her chin, and increased her pace to keep up with Prithviraja.

In the courtyard, several men waited with horses. "Do you ride?" asked Prithviraja, his voice quieter now that they were outdoors where they might be overheard.

"Of course. I'm Rajputni! Just give me the horse."

He again laughed. He hesitated an instant, then his smile broadened. "I changed my mind about your riding your own horse. It will be more fun this way!" He sheathed his sword, seized her by her waist, and hoisted her onto a mount. Before she could catch her breath, he was behind her on the same animal, his arm around her, holding her tightly to him. Samyogita dug her toes into the horse's warm sides to help secure herself.

Prithviraja led the way, his horsemen clattering after, one of them holding Chitralekha. It seemed to Samyogita that the hooves made considerable noise. How could they ever escape? The city gate would be closed for the night, and guarded.

But as they approached the portal, two waiting men quickly swung it open, and the horses thundered through. Prithviraja must have bribed the guards—or replaced them with his own men. They swiftly left the city behind.

On through the coolness of the night they rode. She was aware of herself cradled, virtually surrounded, by the man close behind her. Never had she touched a man other than her father, much less so intimately! Since they weren't yet married, it seemed scandalous. Yet, it was wonderful. She felt the warmth of his breath by her ear, the security of his encircling arms, the press of his lower body against her own.

Behind the clouds, the moon provided just enough illumination. As they sped through the darkness of a forested area, Samyogita saw dimly that a large number of other horsemen had joined them. They streaked across the Doab, the flat region between the Ganges and the Yamuna, splashing through small rivers, skirting walled towns, galloping through sleeping villages where dogs barked in alarm.

At one spot, they stopped to exchange their tired mounts for fresh ones which awaited them, and to refresh themselves with wine. Samyogita hurried to Chitralekha, who was sipping at her own drink, and asked, "Are you all right?"

The maid replied in voice surprisingly strong, "These old joints will be sore for a while, but I'll manage."

Samyogita returned to Prithviraja and asked a question that had puzzled her. "How did you get to me so fast?"

He laughed heartily in the manner that was becoming familiar. "A spy sent word of the statue as soon as your father gave the order to the stonecarvers. I knew then what I must do."

"But how did you get into Kanauj with no one knowing?"

He finished his wine, handed to cup to an aide. "I and my men disguised ourselves as horse traders. We split into small parties to travel, and when we camped in the forests near Kanauj. But I confess I wasn't sure how I'd get into your father's palace and take you out. You made it easier by being in that prison near the wall!"

They remounted and sped onward. Despite her weariness, she was aware of Prithviraja's huge chest against her back, her hair brushing his face. This was her future husband, she reminded herself, and she felt a new stir of excitement. Determined to be a worthy queen for him, she straightened herself, gripped the horse's belly more tightly with her icy toes.

***

The marriage of Prithviraja III Chauhan and Samyogita—possibly mythical—would be brief. Within a year, Muhammad of Ghur again invaded. This time, Prithviraja was defeated in the second battle of Tarain. Although given the chance to continuing to rule Ajmer as a vassal, Prithviraja is said to have been executed after he failed in an effort to assassinate the Muslim conqueror.

According to legends, Samyogita threw herself upon her husband's funeral pyre, perishing in the flames in the rite of sati. *Her earlier encouraging words to her husband lived on, recited by bards to inspire countless Rajputs in future centuries:*

"Oh Sun of the Chauhans, no one has drunk so deeply both of glory and of pleasure as you. Life is an old garment—what does it matter if we throw it off? To die well is life immortal!"

Prithviraja's defeat in 1192 C.E. is often considered a major turning point in the history of the subcontinent. With the destruction of one of the strongest native monarchs, who also had blocked major access routes, the invaders prevailed over the majority of the remaining Hindu and Buddhist kingdoms. The newcomers were often aided by the rivalries of the native princes among themselves, with their consequent frequent reluctance to join in a common defense.

The Muslim rulers' empires would dominate the region for centuries, until eventually supplanted by the British.

The
Mangarh Treasure
Six

11

Mangarh, the Bhim Bhawan Palace, 1975 C.E.

Kaushalya Kumari put on her reading glasses, pulled a folio from the shelf and carefully unwrapped the cloth that held it. "Many of these paintings," the princess said, "are illustrations of episodes in the life of Lord Krishna. As you know, that's a common theme for the miniature paintings and the murals done in the Rajput courts. A lot of the paintings are also *ragamala* themes—paintings of the seasons, to evoke a particular *raga* or mood."

"These must be extremely valuable," said Shanta Das.

"Quite," said Kaushalya Kumari. "Unfortunately, many of them have disappeared over the years. My father says he remembers stacks and stacks of the miniatures. Now there are just these few folios left. I suppose some were sold, but I've never been able to find the records. Some of them were loaned out to scholars and never returned. A couple are in the Victoria and Albert Museum in London. I hope to try to get them returned some day. Others were probably just stolen. But of those remaining, these are of most interest: the scenes of the lives of the rulers—portraits, festivals, hunts, a couple of war scenes."

She placed one on the table before them. "This is a portrait of Maharaja Hanuman Singh, painted around 1600. We consider him probably the greatest of our ancestors, both for his political skills and for his patronage of architecture in Mangarh. So far as I can determine, the painting was done by his senior wife, one of my great-great-great grandmothers (I'm not sure just how many 'greats' should be in there). I like to think maybe I inherited my artistic interests from her, rather than from the subject of this next one."

She showed them another. "Maharaja Madho Singh in procession, returning in triumph from a war, around 1700 or earlier. He was quite an art patron and had a large *atelier*, so many miniature paintings are of himself."

"Such detail!" exclaimed Shanta.

"It's exquisite," agreed Vijay, wondering if a 1700s scene could hold any clues still relevant roughly three hundred years later.

"And this," said Kaushalya Kumari, "is Madho Singh himself." She displayed a small portrait in profile of a rotund, richly dressed, proud man.

"He looks rather heavy," said Vijay.

"'Fat' is the word," said the princess. "He's that way in every portrait." In the rendering, Madho Singh held a large gem up before his face with his thumb and forefinger, and he was peering at the stone. "This particular pose is stylized," she said. "You've probably seen similar ones of the Mughal emperors or other Rajput kings, usually holding a flower up to gaze at. It's intended to show that the ruler is a patron of beautiful things. Also that he's the flower of his people, who should gaze upon him with the same reverence."

"But he's holding a gem, not a flower," said Vijay. "It looks like a large diamond, possibly."

Kaushalya Kumari stared closely at the miniature as she said, "Madho Singh was notorious for his greed. He loved bringing loot home. I suppose that's why he wanted to be shown with a jewel."

"So this was around 1700?" asked Vijay.

"Thereabouts."

"I don't suppose the diamond is still here?"

The princess removed her eyeglasses and looked at him as if uneasy. "I've never seen it. The bards tell a tale of a big diamond, the 'Star of Mangarh.' But it must have disappeared long ago. Sold or stolen or whatever."

"I see." He furrowed his brow, as he remembered hearing a story as a child about the legendary "Star of Mangarh" diamond. How could such a fabulous gem simply disappear? Vijay said, "Would you come with me, please? I'd like to ask you about something else."

Kaushalya Kumari oversaw the securing of the strong room, then she followed him and Shanta Das to the front reception room, off the palace's entry hall. There they stood before a huge European-style oil portrait of a proud, mustached, bearded man of late middle age. The brass plate on the bottom of the wide gilded frame read, "Maharaja Bhim Singhji. 1870-1936." The former ruler was depicted in his ceremonial finery, and he wore a number of medals. Jewels sparkled on his turban, around his neck, on his chest, on his fingers.

Vijay asked the princess, "Your grandfather, if I'm correct?"

"Yes."

"I'm interested in the gems he's wearing. They're pictured in convincing detail." Vijay watched her closely, and he saw her eyes grow wary. He'd been sure she'd figure out quickly what he was after. He continued, "I've compared all the jewels in the portrait with the tax returns and with the inventory of the strong room. There are at least three items missing. The large stone in the turban ornament appears to be an emerald. Do you know where it is now?"

Kaushalya Kumari put on her eyeglasses, looked carefully at the painting. She moistened her lips with her tongue, and turned back to Vijay. "I've no idea—I don't think I've seen it. I've never really thought about it. I've heard of a large emerald the family used to own. But so many things were lost after Independence, or sold over the years."

"And the necklace of five strands of large pearls?"

She shrugged; her large eyes seemed innocent behind the lenses. She smiled as if embarrassed at her ignorance. "The necklace was known as 'the Mangarh Pearls.' I'm sorry, but I've no idea what's happened to it. You should ask my father."

"The rings...that one appears to be a huge ruby. Almost too big to be on a ring."

She examined it, then again shrugged and smiled. "I'm not much help. I remember hearing as a child that my grandfather owned a big ruby ring. It was called 'the Blood of Shivaji.' But I'm sure I've never seen it. It must have been sold long ago."

Vijay was silent a moment. Then he said, "These items must all have been uniquely valuable. One might say they're the type of jewels that acquire a reputation or a legend. People talk about them and who currently owns them. In this case, I assume the gems may have been part of the state jewels of Mangarh. So there must be some record of their whereabouts."

"I would think so too," Kaushalya Kumari said slowly. "Maybe we'd better ask my father."

"I really can't tell you where they are," said Lakshman Singh, his face expressionless. "I wore them at my consecration ceremony, when I was confirmed as ruler in 1936. But I haven't worn them since."

"You don't know where they are now, sir?" asked Vijay, incredulous.

"As I said, I haven't seen them in a long time. I've never been particularly interested in jewelry." The ex-ruler's face remained unreadable.

Vijay could not believe anyone could be so casual about property worth *lakhs*, maybe *crores*, of rupees. He said, "I've seen the listing of items, including state jewels, that were turned over to the new government at the time the Rajasthan Union was formed. These particular gems weren't included."

Lakshman Singh abruptly smiled. "Undoubtedly they weren't included because they were my family's personal property, not part of the state treasury. But a few years before my state was merged into Rajasthan, there were some officials, including my chief minister, who were found to have embezzled a great deal of money. They were dismissed from my service. They may well have stolen jewelry, as well as cash. We have no way of knowing now."

Vijay digested this. "When was this, sir?"

"Oh, the early 1940s. Probably about 1940, as I remember."

"The 'Star of Mangarh' diamond was among those that disappeared?"

Lakshman Singh shot a quick glance at him. "You really need to be asking someone else."

Vijay found it almost impossible to believe the Maharaja could be so ignorant of such a major gem. "There must have been records of the jewelry. Inventories. Where are they located?"

Lakshman Singh waved a hand airily and again smiled, as if amused. "Really, Mr. Singh. I had administrators who handled those types of details. Do you think I conducted my own inventories?"

"Of course not, Highness. But I thought maybe you could tell me where the records are kept." The ex-ruler shrugged. "When my state was merged with the Rajasthan Union, most of the official records were taken in custody by the government of the new state. I think they're housed in Jodhpur. Many of my less important personal and family records were kept in storerooms in the fortress. The rest are in various rooms in this palace. I believe my daughter has shown them to you."

"Yes, sir. Without some guidance by a knowledgeable person, though, it would take a long time to find the relevant documents."

"No problem, Mr. Singh," said the ex-Maharaja. "I'll have my ADC help you. He knows more about the records than anyone else alive now." He spoke to Shiv in Rajasthani: "Bring Nareshji, at once."

Vijay swiftly tried to compose himself. He'd walked right into this one. Could he avoid a direct meeting with Naresh Singh by assigning someone else to talk with the ADC? Yes, that was the answer. He'd get Shanta or Krishnaswamy to do it.

But Shiv had already left to get the aide-de-camp. Vijay searched for an excuse to leave quickly, before Naresh Singh appeared.

Too late. The ADC hurried in. "Naresh," said the Maharaja, "Mr. Vijay Singh needs your help. Show him whatever he asks for."

"Yes, Highness." Naresh Singh turned to Vijay. "Shall we go to the office, Mr. Singh?"

No hint of recognition so far. "Of course." Vijay tried to act casual, unconcerned. To the Maharaja, he said, "Thank you, Your Highness."

"Don't mention it, Mr. Singh."

Vijay and Shanta followed Naresh Singh. Vijay tried to think of a good reason to send Shanta away, so no one else would be present if Naresh Singh recognized him and accused him of false claims. But they were already at the office, and it would be awkward to dismiss Shanta at this point. At least she was probably the best member of the team to have present: as an ex-Untouchable herself, she should be sympathetic to any disclosures, and he could probably convince her to keep the matter to herself.

It would still be extremely embarrassing—and risky to his career—if a mention ever got to others on the team, whether from Naresh Singh or the princess or the Maharaja. Naresh Singh waved them into a couple of chairs and seated himself behind the desk. "Now, how can I help you, sir?" His narrow face watched Vijay, waiting.

Vijay quickly explained what was needed. Only part of his mind was involved in stating the request; the other part was caught up in anxiety. Somehow, he managed to sound coherent.

Naresh Singh sat in thought for a time, frowning. "Inventories of jewelry, from the 1940s? I have to confess, I have no idea whatsoever of where they might be. I've only been in my current position the past five years. I've had no occasion to look for any records from so long ago."

"Could anyone else know of them?"

Singh considered for a few moments. "Maybe Balendra. He's the clerk who keeps all the account ledgers. Been here for decades. But he's on a long leave to his home village. His wife's quite ill. Anyone else who might have been familiar with them is likely to either be dead, or moved elsewhere when the old Mangarh state government was dismantled. I sorry—I can't think of anyone else at all. But of course, you're welcome to look for yourself. I can show you the places where most of the records are stored that we still have."

"Thank you. We'll think about it." Vijay rose to leave. The sooner away from him, the better.

Then it came: "I say," said the ADC. "Have we met somewhere before? You look familiar."

Vijay tried to suppress his panic while appearing appropriately surprised and ignorant. "I don't believe so. I'm sure I'd remember if we'd met."

"You're from Delhi?"

"That's right, for the past fifteen years or so."

"I'm probably mistaken, then. I spend little time in Delhi, myself. Still, I'm usually good at remembering people..."

Vijay gave a strained smile. "I must have a common looking face. People are always telling me they think they've seen me before."

"Well. As I said, I'm sorry I can't be of more help. But let me know if I can do anything more."

Vijay nodded, and he and Shanta left. He let out his breath in great relief. Shanta had been silent throughout the meeting. As they exited the Bhim Bhawan, she said, "Sir, since you're from Mangarh, couldn't he have seen you around here, rather than in Delhi?"

Vijay tried not to show his discomfort. "I suppose that's possible." He added lamely, "I didn't think of it at the time, since I haven't lived here in so long."

Shanta said no more. His burden at least temporarily lightened by escaping exposure so far, Vijay went to telephone Prasad about the problem in locating the relevant records. On the poor connection he had to strain to hear Prasad, who was saying, "After independence many rulers shipped assets to Europe and other places, Vijay. Maybe that's what happened here."

Vijay shouted to make himself heard: "Or maybe they really were stolen."

Prasad said, "We could subpoena the whole lot of the records and assign a bunch of inspectors to go through them. That could take weeks—" The connection broke, and Vijay heard only static.

He sighed, contacted the operator to re-ring Prasad, and hung up to wait. In five minutes or so, the phone rang, and soon he was again talking with the Deputy Director. This time the connection was clearer. Prasad resumed, "Even if we had the records, Vijay, it could take a long time. We still might not find anything. Maybe we should give up that approach."

Vijay sighed. "I'd rather try something else."

"I hope you find something good. Dev Batra phoned again—asked if you had my confidence, or if Ghosali would be a better choice to head the team."

God!

"I told him you'd succeed if anyone could," Prasad continued. "Still..."

"Thank you, sir. We're doing our best."

Not since the search had begun had he felt so discouraged about the lack of progress. Hoping for inspiration, he walked with Ranjit through some of the back corridors of the Bhim Bhawan Palace. He seemed safely away from another encounter with Naresh Singh here, so far from the office. They climbed a stairway, ending up on the wide, flat roof, exposed to the glaring sun.

It wasn't out of the question that a hidden storage vault could be accessible only from the roof. Vijay scanned the area, on the chance he might see some clue his team had earlier missed. He saw nothing unusual regarding the structure of the roof itself, but on the far edge, by the parapet, stood a telescope on a portable tripod. By it sat what appeared to be a much larger instrument, mounted on a concrete pedestal and covered by a tarp.

Vijay and Ranjit walked over to the instruments. Ranjit said, "His Highness must be interested in astronomy."

"Apparently."

Ranjit's affinity for gadgets and machines of all kinds asserted itself. He immediately untied the ropes on one side of the canvas, and Vijay helped him pull it back to reveal the big telescope.

Its tube was a foot and a half or so in diameter, aimed at a slight angle above the horizon. "This looks like a reflector-type telescope," said Ranjit. "It uses a big mirror at the bottom of the tube to gather the light and reflect to the eyepiece near the open end. See how it's mounted with that counterbalance weight? The tube can rotate around an axis, so it compensates for the earth's turning. The telescope can always stay pointed at whatever object you're looking at."

They pulled a round plastic cover off to reveal the open end, and looked down through the tube at the reflection of their faces in the mirror at the bottom. "Obviously nothing hidden here," said Ranjit. He stepped away and indicated a small cylindrical projection on the outside of the tube. "The eyepiece goes in here. But it must have been taken off."

Vijay thought about how he had so often watched the stars at night when he had lived in the village. With no artificial lights to illuminate the sky and compete with them, the stars had shone brilliantly. He wondered what it would be look to look at them through an instrument as large as this. They replaced the end cover and put the tarp back on.

"This other telescope must have been used quite recently," Ranjit said, gesturing toward the smaller one, "or it would have been taken in or covered."

Vijay nodded; dust would accumulate quickly on the lenses if an instrument were left exposed to the air. Plus, the sun would heat the metal enough to sear the skin upon touch. The smaller telescope pointed not at the sky, but rather toward the old fort.

"This one's a simpler design," said Ranjit. "See how it has a big lens instead of a mirror? The light goes straight through the tube from one end to the other." He bent and peered through the eyepiece on the smaller end of the tube. After a moment, he shrugged, and moved away.

Vijay looked through the instrument. The telescope was aimed at a facade of the palace living quarters of the old fortress, and the windows and balconies and walls showed clearly, though shimmering and distorted by the hot air currents above the town.

Attractive architecture, but not a subject to watch for a long time. Vijay straightened, took his handkerchief and wiped his forehead. The masonry roof was radiating heat as if it were an oven. "We'd better get out of the sun," he said.

They walked toward the stairway. A sudden thought occurred to him. "I wonder," Vijay said, "if someone has been using that smaller telescope to watch our men search the fort."

Ranjit raised an eyebrow. "Possibly. If so, it could mean someone's worried about what we're doing there."

"I wonder who. His Highness? The Princess? Maybe the ADC, or old Shiv?"

"It could be any of them."

"Let's tell our people to check up here from time to time, maybe find out who it is. And what the telescope is being aimed at."

That night in the *dak* bungalow, while they were waiting for dinner, Vijay kept trying to think of new strategies. For the other team members, the search seemed to have settled into something so routine they weren't even talking about it. Ghosali was pontificating to Krishnaswamy about how Hindi shouldn't be the official national language because it was spoken only in the north, and by less than half the population of India.

"Then what should we speak?" asked Krishnaswamy, placing his Limca bottle carefully on the table. "English, as we are this very minute? It's the *de facto* national language anyway. Or," he smiled to show he was jesting, "would you prefer Bengali?"

Ghosali said in all seriousness, "Bengali would not be a bad choice. Granted, it is a minority language. But Bengalis are noted intellectuals. Tagore won India's only Nobel Prize for literature. Satyajit Ray is the only film maker widely recognized outside of India. The list could go on and on."

"And, of course, *you* speak it, sir," said Krishnaswamy.

Ghosali gave a slight shrug. "So I do." He took a drink from one of his water bottles. Vijay wondered if the supply would last the duration of the search.

"Maybe Tamil should be the national language," said Krishnaswamy. "There are many worthwhile Tamil works of literature, too."

"I wouldn't know," said Ghosali. "But you do not seem to take the matter seriously. Don't you realize that Tamils will be at just as much of a disadvantage as Bengalis for obtaining government positions and university educations?"

"So English must be the national language. More Tamils speak English than speak Hindi."

"It's the language of colonial overlords!"

Krishnaswamy shrugged. "Then Hindi's the only realistic alternative. The Constitution says Hindi, and the Official Languages Act says so. I'm not happy about the fact, but there you are. I'm not going to set fire to myself in protest like those Tamil demonstrators did several years ago."

Vijay had heard the arguments far too many times. He considered the issue incapable of reasonable solution; millions and millions of people would be dissatisfied no matter what the outcome. For now, English was the language in use because it was already so widespread, especially in government and commerce. But the Hindi lobby had virtually won, because Hindi speakers were the largest voting bloc and it was simply unacceptable to have a language originally imposed by foreigners continue in use with official sanction.

Ghosali changed the subject. "Did you see those carved hand prints by the inside gate at the fort?" he asked Krishnaswamy.

"Yes, sir."

"You know what they're for, do you not?"

"Something about women who were *satis*, I believe."

"Correct!" said Ghosali. "Each of those hand prints was by a Rajput royal lady who burned herself on her deceased husband's funeral pyre. What dedicated devotion! A pity it had to be outlawed."

"Now just a minute," said Mrs. Desai. "I must disagree."

"But of course! What else can be expected from a woman?" said Ghosali.

Shanta Das said, "You mean you would like to see the practice reimposed even though the women who would have to carry it out may not agree with it? I'd wager that *sati* is one Rajput tradition Kaushalya Kumari is glad to see abandoned."

Ghosali glanced at her, then looked away. He scowled. Vijay wondered if Ghosali were annoyed at being challenged by a young woman, or by an Untouchable, or both. At last Ghosali said stiffly, "That's precisely the problem today. People are no longer willing to sacrifice for the greater good of the whole. Our entire society suffers when women withdraw from doing their duties to their husbands. I ask you, what kind of example do they set for their own children?"

"That was a barbaric custom!" said Mrs. Desai.

"A time honored one," said Ghosali, "which lasted for thousands of years." He inserted his pipe in his mouth and looked about, as if daring anyone to dispute him.

No one bothered. They all were staring at their drinks or their hands.

12

26 June 1975

Bhajan Lal drove Kaushalya and Gopi out of the palace grounds in the eight year old blue Bentley that her father so often used. Kaushalya would have preferred to do the driving herself, as she did in Delhi or Bombay, with only Gopi for companionship and help. Her father had prohibited that here. Many people in Mangarh, including, to some degree, Lakshman Singh, still considered it improper for a high-born woman to expose herself to public view. And not many years ago, of course, robbers often ambushed lone travelers.

But bandits no longer roamed the hills, and after years of persistent effort Kaushalya had succeeded in getting her father to acknowledge that in these modern times it was reasonable for her to go out in a motor car—so long as she was driven by a relative or by a trusted servant such as Lal. And so long as at least one other woman accompanied her for propriety's sake.

Small, gray haired Bhajan Lal had served the Mangarh royal family ever since he was a child, as had his ancestors, who had been elephant drivers before most of the elephants were sold. Lal had been Lakshman Singh's personal driver for many years, but the ex-ruler preferred to take the wheel himself except in formal processions. So most of Lal's driving involved running personal errands for the family or taking Kaushalya around when she was in Mangarh.

They first drove to a large old house near the edge of the newer portion of town. A white sign on it, with a red cross, read, "Dr. Savitri Chand, Medical Clinic."

Kaushalya and Savitri Chand embraced warmly; around fifty year's age, the doctor was the aunt of Kaushalya's closest friend Usha. She also served as one of Kaushalya's favorite confidantes.

"What is happening with the income tax raiders?" asked Dr. Chand. She was slender and the bone structure of her face was elegant; Kaushalya thought her a beautiful woman except for a typical somberness of expression. Unusual for an Indian woman, she had never married. It was said that Savitri Chand had some terrible ordeals at Partition in the Punjab when her family lands suddenly became part of Pakistan.

"So far they're mainly a nuisance, Auntie. I seem to have fallen into the role of being the one to help them, sort of the family's representative. I even went with them to the Harappan site and the *stupa*. Father somehow stays mostly above it all and doesn't seem particularly worried."

"I suppose he's the one who should know."

"He even played a trick on the raiders—let them think the tunnels for the latrine sweepers were hidden treasure vaults!"

Savitri Chand gave a rare smile. "Still," her face again became sober, "it must be an extremely trying time for you and your father."

"The raid is definitely a distraction. I hope it doesn't go on much longer."

Kaushalya turned to another purpose of the visit. "I'm on my way to Guruji's. On the route I need to visit a little girl with conjunctivitis, but I'm out of the salve."

They went to the dispensary where Dr. Chand unlocked a cabinet and gave Kaushalya a box of the small tubes. "If you're not careful, Kaushi, you'll end up a medical doctor instead of an art historian."

"If you'd just get around the villages, I could concentrate on my art." It was their usual small joke; everyone knew Savitri Chand regularly made the rounds with free medical help, but the needs were more than she could keep up with.

On the way into the hills Kaushalya thought about Guruji. She hoped for a private meeting with him, and she had left at a time so she should arrive shortly after the guru's morning prayer and meditation periods had ended.

Gopi interrupted her thoughts, "Highness, that one tax man seems unusually kind to you."

Kaushalya glanced at her. "You mean Mr. Singh?"

"Yes. And he watches you sometimes when you're not aware."

Kaushalya laughed lightly. "He's probably trying to see if I'm telling the truth."

Gopi sniffed. But she smiled as she did so. "I doubt that's the only reason."

Kaushalya looked out the window at a passing camel towing a cart. She knew men found her attractive. She briefly wondered if there was any way that could be used to advantage with Vijay Singh. Probably not; he seemed the type of man unlikely to let personal feelings interfere with performing his duties. "Anyway," she said, "it can't hurt to have him as sympathetic as possible to us."

Kaushalya had Lal stop at the village so she could deliver a tube of the eye medicine for the child she had mentioned to Dr. Chand, a three year old Chamar girl with an eye infection. Kaushalya enjoyed the lower caste villagers, with their generous hospitality, their direct, simplified way of looking at matters. At first the women had been shocked that a Rajput princess could be traveling unprotected, out of *purdah*, out in the view of strange men. But Kaushalya always was accompanied by Gopi or by an aunt or a girl friend, and she took care to wear the traditional Rajput *kanchli kurti* and to modestly hide her face from the men with her veil, just as the village women did. So their uneasiness about her had quickly changed, first to curious interest and then to acceptance.

The quiet existence of the village seemed so far removed from the world of income tax raids. She only wished she were in a position to do much more to help them break out of their poverty and to improve the lack of sanitation which led to so much disease. After taking a glass of tea with the women, she continued on her way.

It took ten more minutes to reach Guruji's ashram in its wooded gorge high in the hills. The place had been holy for as long as human beings had lived in this region. A small natural cave in the hillside had been the home of meditating *rishis* for many centuries, and traces of paintings on its walls showed that even earlier it had been used for ceremonies by prehistoric tribals.

A thousand or more years ago, Buddhist and Jain monks had enlarged the cave and carved a series of a half dozen small living chambers out of the rock. But the stone was too crumbly to be ideal for dwellings, and after some cave-ins the rooms had been abandoned. Now doors of roughly-hewn timbers barred access to all but the one ancient natural cave.

In the early 1900s Guru Dharmananda's own spiritual mentor had built wooden huts in the style of the local Bhils. His small but steadily growing following of disciples later donated funds to construct more permanent buildings of stone and brick. When the old master ascended to a higher plane of existence, Guru Dharmananda succeeded him. By the time Kaushalya's father became a follower, the ashram was virtually a tiny village. Now that Kaushalya, too, came here once or twice a year for a week's retreat, there were a number of tiny and basic but comfortable cottages.

The guru's American secretary, Peter Willis, hurried out to meet her with folded palms. "Welcome, Your Highness! We're honored! We've been expecting you of course, but not quite so soon." A slender, dark haired, bearded man of around thirty, he had always seemed in awe of her, eager to please, a characteristic she had noticed with puzzlement about many Americans in general. For a democratic society, they often had an odd admiration for royalty, even ex-royalty. Kaushalya was sure the guru would prefer that all visitors to the ashram be treated equally.

"Will Guruji be free to talk?" she asked.

"I'm sure he'll be available for you, Princess. Please, come right this way. The morning meeting is almost finished."

Lal and Gopi followed as Willis led Kaushalya to where Guru Dharmananda sat on a mat, framed by the arched roots of the magnificent banyan tree, facing a couple dozen ashram residents. Although the morning was already hot, the ancient tree was huge enough to shield the entire group from direct sun. The guru, dressed in his usual white robe, was addressing the gathering, but from his glance and quick smile sent in Kaushalya's direction, she knew he had seen her and would speak to her eventually. She sat on one of the vacant mats scattered about in the shade, and listened. Lal and Gopi seated themselves also.

Now in late middle age, with the light complexion of a Brahmin from the northern hills, and balding, with grey-flecked hair and beard, the guru was of medium height and build. Due to the large numbers of visitors from abroad, as well as from other regions of India, the language most often used in the ashram was English, which the guru spoke fluently from his medical education in London as a young man. His gentle voice easily carried to the entire gathering: "This is the law of karma—as Jesus Christ said, 'we reap what we sow.' Each of our actions, no matter how small, casts a seed in the ground. We will harvest what grows from each seed. Often the harvest comes in this same lifetime, but sometimes in a future incarnation.

"Some obvious examples of results from undesirable actions: if we eat too much fattening food, we will grow fat. If we drink too much alcohol or smoke too much tobacco, we cause our health to decline. If we commit adultery, we cause hurt and anger in our marital partner and ruin what could be a happy union."

The guru gave a gentle smile. "But the opposite is also true. Sowing good seeds results in a healthy, abundant harvest. If we take good care of our body, usually it will remain healthy and strong for us. If we make others happy, their happiness will reflect back on us and enrich our own lives." He looked about. "Questions?"

A middle aged European woman seated immediately before him asked, "But why do so many evil people seem to prosper, Guruji? I know a man who got rich by destroying some beautiful natural areas to build housing developments. He even cheated the home buyers by using poor materials where they wouldn't show. That's only one example. I don't support doing evil, but I'm convinced it does pay!"

The guru looked over the gathering. "Would anyone care to reply to Emily?"

A young Indian man said energetically and rapidly, "The evil man may be prospering now, but in his next lifetime, his karma may dictate that he is reincarnated as an animal whose forest home is destroyed by some other thoughtless developer!"

"Or," said an elderly European man with a German accent, "in another lifetime he may buy one of the very houses he built so poorly, and have it fall down on his own head."

Mild laughter rippled through the group. An attractive Indian woman said in a pleasant voice, "Guruji, there is so much corruption in our government, with the evil persons seeming so successful. Should we merely let their karma work itself out, so that maybe they will get their just rewards in a future lifetime? Or should we try to bring them to justice as soon as possible?"

Kaushalya instantly thought of the income tax raid, which was almost certainly motivated solely by political reasons. It was one aspect of corruption: using the power of political office to torment citizens just because they opposed the current government's ways of doing things. The guru slowly moved his gaze from one person to another. Directing a question at the group in general, he said, "When do circumstances demand that we step in and try to change an unjust situation?"

The young Indian man spoke again: "I think we each have a duty to act when we see a situation needing correcting. Karma does not have to operate solely on its own. There is nothing wrong with hurrying it along!"

More laughter. "Besides," said the young Indian woman, "we can build up good karma as well as bad. When we do a good deed, such as working to correct an unjust situation, that will bring us good karma and good results."

Kaushalya said, "I think our good deeds will build up good karma if our motives are pure and charitable. But if we act largely out of self interest—because there's some sort of personal gain involved, or because we think our work draws attention and admiration from others, or because it puts us in a situation of wielding influence over other persons—then I think that our good karma will reflect our motivations and be somewhat diluted." She let her head covering drop to her shoulders, as she went on, "For example, I belong to the Indian Ecological Society because I think our country's future well being depends on protecting the natural environment. But I have to admit my motives are mixed. I selfishly enjoy experiencing the beauty of a lush forest or peaceful river much more than seeing a big dam or an industrial development."

The disciples were listening to the newcomer with obvious curiosity. When she had finished, Guru Dharmananda took advantage of the pause to conclude, "I think Kaushalyaji has a wise point, one that can apply to *all* of our actions. Are we acting mainly out of selfish desire, to further our own convenience or pleasure? Or are we acting from love, to serve the higher power that is a part of each of us, that connects us, and makes us all one with each other? Let us think on this, until we get together again this evening." He looked at Kaushalya, and gave a nod.

The audience was rising, and leaving. Kaushalya came forward, bent and touched the guru's feet. Although he did not require the traditional gesture, she did it out of custom and respect. She straightened and was met with the warm depth of his brown eyes—and felt as if she were in contact with his soul. As always, she sensed that he acted out of genuine, unselfish Love. When she was engaged in conversation with Dharmananda, it was a direct conversation between their essential spirits.

"I heard about your income tax raiders," he said gently. "Please sit, Kaushi."

She lowered herself to the ground. "Guruji, I have to postpone my stay. I don't know when the search will end, and I need to be there."

His eyes took on a look of concern. "The Income Tax Department is looking for the treasure that was supposedly hidden in the old fort?"

"Yes. But they're searching almost everywhere, it seems."

The guru peered at her intently. "Almost everywhere?"

"Yes, the Bhim Bhawan, the Moti Mahal, even archaeological sites."

"Archaeological sites?" She thought she caught a quick flicker of concern cross his eyes. He appeared lost in thought for a few moments. Then, he asked, "How is your father taking it?"

She shrugged. "Quite well under the circumstances. He doesn't seem to let it bother him much." She told him about the trick her father had played on the raiders with the tunnels for the latrine sweepers.

The guru chuckled, and amusement lit his eyes. "Your father does like his jokes." He again turned sober. "How are you yourself managing, Kaushalya?"

She hesitating, thinking. At last, she said, "I'm not sure. Naturally I don't like the raiders poking around our home and property. I'm put in the position of answering their questions about our clan's history, even showing them around. Both so I can keep an eye on them and so we can get them out of our hair as soon as possible. But I'm not comfortable helping them. It's as if I were betraying my family when I give the tax people information."

He sat quietly looking at her for a time. Then he asked, "Do you think you're actually harming your family by helping them?"

She frowned, chewing on her lower lip. "I'm not sure. I just don't know! My father won't tell me or my brother if he's hiding anything or not. So how can I know if I'm giving away information I shouldn't?"

He nodded. "I see your difficulty. What alternatives do you have?"

Kaushalya shifted uneasily. "It seems I have little choice but to trust my father. He's head of the family, after all. If he chooses not to inform me fully, then I'm hardly to blame even if I do unknowingly reveal something better left unsaid. He must be aware of any risk, and he must have decided it's not cause for serious concern."

Dharmananda again gave a nod. "Well said."

Kaushalya grinned wryly. "So why does it continue to bother me so much?"

He returned her smile. "Because you're conscientious. Loyal to your *dharma*. You want always to do the right thing."

She furrowed her forehead, and nodded vigorously. "That's me."

She had an odd impression the guru knew more than he was revealing about her situation with the tax raid, and she briefly wondered if her father might have consulted him recently without her knowledge. However, Dharmananda apparently did not intend to say anything further.

She let out her breath. Surprisingly, she felt better. She rose, touched his feet once more. "I'm grateful, Guruji."

"Please be sure to let me know, Kaushalya, if there's anything I can do to help."

She nodded, flashed a tight smile of thanks, and left.

She therefore missed hearing when Peter Willis, only minutes later, hurried to the guru to tell him about the announcement on All India Radio.

13

On the drive back to Mangarh she thought more about the tax raid. What a nuisance! It totally distracted her from her work, and it had even forced her to postpone her retreat at the ashram.

Still, oddly, she realized that she almost liked explaining her family and its heirlooms to the tax officers. She had never before had a chance to do that with anyone in such detail. They seemed so attentive and interested that she sometimes almost forgot their motives.

Maybe under other circumstances the bright and pleasant Miss Das could even have become a friend. Kaushalya thought of Gopi's comments about Mr. Singh. So what if Gopi's observations were true? The man was still an antagonist.

When the Bentley reached the wide area in front of the palace, she immediately saw that something unusual had occurred. Servants stood about in front of the main steps, talking animatedly with each other. The conversations ceased as they saw her arrive. Shiv, at the head of the steps, quickly ducked in the door, out of sight.

Kaushalya's first thought was that the tax people must have found something important. She stepped from the car just as Shiv reappeared with Naresh Singh. "What is it?" she called to them as she rapidly climbed the steps.

Naresh had a dazed look in his eyes, and Shiv hung back as if ashamed of something. "Princess," said ADC, "I—Your father. His Highness. He's been arrested!"

"What!"

"The police came while you were gone. They let him finish his prayers, but then they took him away!"

"How could they do such a thing!"

His eyes shifted away. "They didn't give much of a reason. Something about state security."

"What nonsense! They have to say what he's been arrested for!"

Naresh Singh hesitated, and asked, "You heard Mrs. Gandhi's announcement?"

"No. What announcement?"

"The Prime Minister said the President has declared a state of emergency—I think His Highness' arrest is somehow related to that."

"'State of emergency!' Whatever for?"

Naresh Singh held his hands open helplessly. "I'm not sure. Something about internal threats to the nation."

"Threats? What threats? Where did they take him?"

"I asked, but they wouldn't tell me."

"What! Didn't anyone go along with him? Where's my brother?"

"He's inside on the telephone trying to find out what's going on. He tried to follow, but the police wouldn't let him—they said they'd arrest him, too, if he interfered."

Kaushalya stormed in. She found Mahendra in the palace office talking loudly on the phone. His eyes met hers, and he motioned her to wait. "How can you not know where he's being taken?" he all but shouted into the mouthpiece. He listened a moment, then said abruptly, "You'll hear from me later!" He smashed the receiver into the cradle.

He said to Kaushalya, "You know?"

"Why would they do such a thing!"

"All the police will say is some section under MISA—the Maintenance of Internal Security Act. Our beloved Prime Minister has somehow convinced the President to declare a state of emergency. That law authorizes persons who are security threats to be arrested and held."

"Father a 'security threat?' That's ridiculous! Held how long?"

"I'm trying to find out."

"I assume you've called a lawyer?"

"I phoned Surendra Dutt, and he's checking with the police

now." Mahendra looked pointedly at her and said, "I had a call from a friend in Delhi who's active in our party. He said all the major opposition leaders have been arrested—Jayaprakash Narayan, Morarji Desai."

Kaushalya gasped. "JP and Desai both!" The two were so famous, so prominent—revered leaders of the movement for independence from Britain. She sank into a chair. "I can't believe this is happening!"

Mahendra continued, "A lot of others were arrested, too. So Father won't be alone, wherever they're taking him." He slowly shook his head.

"What must Daddyji be feeling now! Arrested—in his own home! How did he take it?"

Mahendra said slowly, as if still stunned, "Quite well, actually. Of course, he was surprised. But it would have been beneath his dignity to protest too loudly. One of the policemen even apologized to him—said they were only carrying out their orders."

She slumped in the chair. She had a strong urge to jump in her car and chase after the police. But she realized, reluctantly, it would be futile at this point. The lawyers would let Mahendra and her know what could be done to help. "I'm worried about his health. I hope we can get him out on bail right away."

"We should be able to. So far as I know, our 'Empress' hasn't closed down the courts."

"What's our country coming to?" Kaushalya asked rhetorically. "First a tax raid, now this. And that 'emergency.' I wonder if any of this would have happened to us if Father had been in Congress instead of the opposition."

"I doubt it. Kaushi, I need to make more phone calls so we can help Father. Why don't you check on our tax people? See if you can learn anything from them."

She glanced at him in surprise. "You think they had something to do with Father's arrest?"

He flung a hand into the air. "I don't know. But it's quite a coincidence—the tax raid and the arrest at the same time."

Anger welled up within her. "I'll find out!"

"Most of them are probably at the fort. I'll telephone you there if I learn anything."

Always before, she had told the driver to park the car at the bottom of the hill. Jeeps were designed to withstand roads as rough as the cobblestones leading up to the main gate; Bentleys weren't.

Today she didn't care. She ordered Lal to go straight to the top. The car roared as, in low gear, with Gopi beside her, it bounced up the hill, jarring her spine despite the deep cushioning in the seats, and shot through the open gateway. She saw income tax officer Singh talking to some of his people, including Shanta Das. Nearby Airavata the elephant fed, unconcerned with such mundane affairs as those which troubled human beings. The car stopped, and Kaushalya stepped out.

The officer saw her, dismissed his people except for Miss Das, and walked toward her. "Princess," he said, "I'm so sorry about what happened with your father."

A part of her mind recognized that he seemed sincere. But another part said tartly, "Is this how you put more pressure on us to cooperate with you, Mr. Singh?"

He froze in place. "Princess, I—"

"Are you people feeling frustrated at not finding anything, so it's time to twist our noose a little tighter?"

"I assure you, we—"

"Can you really assure me, Mr. Singh, that your superiors in Delhi had nothing to do with my father's arrest? I doubt it!"

Vijay Singh had held his mouth open; now he closed it. She stood there, every angle of her pose a challenge to him. He appeared to be thinking. At last, he said quietly, "No, I can only speak for myself right now. I can't make any assurances for my superiors in Delhi."

She felt the tears in her eyes. But she blinked at them and continued to hold her head high. They stood facing each other awkwardly, while Miss Das stood off to one side. Eventually, Vijay Singh said, still quietly, "You have a lot on your mind this morning, Princess. I'm glad to have you remain here if that's your wish, but I won't trouble you with questions today."

The next few days, Kaushalya all but forgot the income tax people in her anguish about her father. Incredibly, Mahendra and the lawyers had not even been able to locate where the police had taken him, much less bail him out. Under the State of Emergency, the government had immediately begun censoring the press, so there was no information from the newspapers or radio. Mahendra learned from a friend that huge numbers of detainees had been confined in Delhi's notoriously terrible Tihar jail, but other, smaller groups, had been taken to additional prisons. Jayaprakash Narayan was rumored to have been taken to a place of detention in the Punjab.

But most people Mahendra called were evasive. "I can tell they're afraid," he told Kaushalya. "They're worried that they may be arrested themselves if they tell us too much."

Kaushalya shook her head in disgust. "We threw out the British and replaced them with this?"

"One of my friends even suggested we shouldn't use the phone, in case it might be tapped!" He frowned. "I'm not so sure he's wrong. I think I've noticed even more noise than usual on the lines."

Kaushalya pondered the implications.

Apparently," Mahendra said, "Dev Batra may be the one most directly responsible for Father's arrest." He shook his head sadly and cast a doleful look at her.

"Dev Batra? Who's he?"

"He does dirty work for the party leaders. Unfortunately, he hates me as a result of a run-in we had last year. He's the last one I'd approach for help in getting Father released."

Kaushalya stared at him a moment. "Then why don't I talk with him? He's never met me."

"Absolutely not! You stay as far away from him as possible. He's dangerous."

"How so? I don't understand."

"He can't be trusted. He'd try to...use you for his own ends. He might promise to help you in exchange for your giving him something, but then he'd double cross you."

"But isn't he at least worth a try?"

"No! Forget I even mentioned him. It's out of the question."

She started to protest, but seeing she would get nowhere with Mahendra, she bit back her words. Maybe she could pursue the matter later.

Meanwhile, they could only hope that extra consideration would be given because of Lakshman Singh's position as an ex-ruler, and because of his age and ill health. Kaushalya could not rid herself of the feeling that at any minute her father would be delivered to the palace by police apologizing profusely at the terrible mistake that had been made.

She wished she had someone to talk with about it, besides Mahendra and other family members or Gopi. She had many relatives and many acquaintances, of course. But she had few friends to whom she felt she could bare her soul. Her confident facade hid an inner reticence hardly anyone suspected, and her preferences for solitary pursuits such as her art history studies and her own drawing and painting meant she often avoided the long visits and chatter that Indians were so fond of.

Of her two best friends, it was impractical to reach Susan Peterson, halfway around the world in Seattle. Kaushalya thought of telephoning her other confidante, Usha Chand, in New Delhi. But a lengthy, intimate conversation of the type she needed was seldom satisfactory over the long distance lines where one often had to shout to be heard.

She rang up Dr. Savitri Chand, the "auntie" whom she felt closest to in Mangarh. But she was informed that Dr. Chand was "out of station" today, off somewhere in the hills providing medical care for some of the more remote Bhils.

Mahendra's voice carried loudly down the hall. Kaushalya entered the office, where he and Naresh Singh were seated before some open account ledgers. "How could he let things get to such a state?" Mahendra shouted. He slammed a ledger shut, stood and strode to the wall, then back. At last he noticed Kaushalya. He stopped. "Did you know about any of this?"

"What?" she asked, puzzled.

"We're almost bankrupt, that's what!"

She took a deep breath. "Whatever do you mean?"

"Naresh just showed me the books. Our expenses have exceeded income every year since 1948! I knew it might be bad, but Father always shrugged me off whenever I asked him about it."

She sat down, feeling faint. It was all too much, on top of everything else. "It's really that bad?"

"Father's been drawing down the bank deposits and selling investments every year! Unless we sell some gold, we've hardly enough cash to make it until the income from this year's crops comes in."

"But—isn't there almost half a *lakh* in the strong room?"

"Do you know what our expenses are?"

"Not really."

"Look!" Mahendra thrust a book in front of her. "We've got wages for all the Bhils and the entire palace staff, and the pensions for everyone who's retired and the families of those who have passed on. Repairs to buildings. The houses in Delhi and Bombay. Taxes. The charities are mostly paid from the trusts, but income's down there, too. And now we'll have attorneys' fees, and maybe bribes, for trying to get Father freed!"

Kaushalya shook her head. "Why wasn't Father more worried if it's so bad?"

He threw his hands into the air. "How should I know? He must be losing touch with reality."

"What about all our assets? The land, the buildings, houses, cars."

"Except for the rental income from farm land, everything else is a just a big drain on us for upkeep! We could only get cash if we sold something. Or pledged it as collateral for loans. Are you really ready to sell your ancestral property? This palace, or the fortress you love so much? We'd be lucky to get ten percent of the value on them anyway."

"I still think we should turn parts of both places into hotels. That would bring in money from tourists."

"Do you have any idea how much it would cost to modernize enough of the fortress? Anyway, Father doesn't like the idea."

Kaushalya looked from Mahendra to Naresh, and back again. "Could—could Father have been relying on the treasure to make up any difference?"

Naresh started to speak, but Mahendra cut him off. "Treasure? *What* treasure? I'm convinced now there isn't any! Naresh doesn't know anything about it. Even Father's never claimed it exists. I just don't think it's there."

"According to tax officer Singh," Kaushalya said, her voice deliberately calm to try to quiet Mahendra, "the raiders have been given one more week to find it."

Mahendra scowled. "What happens if they don't?"

"I'm not sure. Apparently some big men in Delhi will be extremely unhappy. They may increase the pressure on us even more."

"How could they do that? Arrest you and me?"

She winced. "I hope not. I don't know."

14

On the evening of the third day after Lakshman Singh's arrest, Mahendra said, "We aren't getting anywhere here on freeing Father. We need to go to Delhi. That's where the decisions are being made about running this 'emergency,' including what happens to the political prisoners. I'm thinking of leaving early in the morning."

By this time Kaushalya was ready to do anything; anything that meant real action as opposed to mere waiting and futile telephoning. And going to Delhi meant visiting Usha Chand, her best friend of her own age and Dr. Savitri Chand's niece. She said, "If we get there early enough, we can contact a few people at their homes in the evening, and then start visiting offices the next day." She thought about whether there was anything to take care of before they left.

The income tax people! She had again forgotten them. "What about our tax raiders?" she asked Mahendra.

"We'll have to ignore them for now. Naresh and Shiv and the Bhils can keep an eye on them and let us know if they get too carried away."

She thought of officer Vijay Singh. He seemed careful to observe the legalities, even to be as considerate as the circumstances allowed. She doubted that with him in charge the searchers would do anything too outrageous.

She asked, "Why don't we take the Bentley and have Lal drive us?" Mahendra was even a worse driver than her father. He drove his jeep as if everything else on the road were an enemy to be either outflanked or destroyed, as a number of dents—and accidents—attested.

Mahendra shot her a look of annoyance. "There's no need. My jeep will do fine."

"It rides so hard. Gopi and I'll be jarred to pieces by the time we get there."

"I know you don't like my driving. Let's take the jeep, but we'll trade off at the wheel."

Kaushalya resigned herself to the unsatisfactory compromise.

Mahendra's two periods of driving made her nerves feel like broken glass. Lorry traffic was increasing noticeably every year. With only a single lane of paving most of the way to Ajmer, she almost constantly found herself facing the front of a rapidly approaching tower of truck stacked high with cargo. Mahendra seemed to like taunting the behemoths; it was roughly the equivalent of a bicyclist pedaling full tilt toward a straight-on confrontation with a charging elephant. When the "T" of the Tata emblem on the front of the lorry had expanded to virtually (in Kaushalya's eyes) fill the jeep's windscreen, Mahendra would at last swerve to the shoulder. The truck, still in the center of the road, would roar past only centimeters away.

She glanced back a couple of times at Gopi, who was sitting stiffly erect, forehead creased, lips pressed tight.

Finally, a lorry almost scraped the paint off Gopi's door. When Kaushalya had regained control of her breathing, she asked, "Why don't you just let them have the road? Why play their game?"

He looked at her and laughed. "It must be the Rajput in me. It's a sport. We can't hunt much anymore with all the wildlife endangered, and I've never been good at polo. What games are left? Only politics, and playing chicken on the highways."

She shook her head and looked away. "You're crazy."

"Are you saying you want to drive already?" he teased. "We've hardly covered any distance at all."

"Anything's better than your own driving!"

The roadway ahead was partially blocked by a string of bullock carts. "Hang on," Mahendra said. She braced herself against the dashboard as he plunged the jeep down the three foot embankment and raced along the bumpy edge of a field. Past the obstruction, he tore back up the bank and onto the road, just in time to swerve out of the way of another overloaded lorry.

"God!" exploded Kaushalya. "You *are* crazy!"

The jeep skidded to a stop, in the center of the road. "All right. It's your turn."

She sat paralyzed for a moment, trying to calm herself.

He opened his door and stepped out. "Better hurry," he said. "There's a truck coming up behind us really fast."

"God!" she said again, and threw herself into the driver's seat. "Get in!"

He took an agonizingly long time. She fumbled as she frantically adjusted the rearview mirror so she could see behind.

No truck.

He grinned at her as he climbed in. "Just kidding."

She let out her breath at the same time she let out the clutch. "Sometimes, I think I hate you."

They arrived in Delhi, weary, hot, and filthy, when the evening rush hour traffic was at its peak and the heat was also intense. Kaushalya was again at the wheel as they drove to Mangarh House. She breathed deeply in relief when they entered the driveway, where Amar the old *chowkidar* came to stiff attention by the gate he opened in response to their horn. The large bungalow was set in a secluded, tree shaded garden in the pleasant residential area between India Gate and the diplomatic enclave. After settling into the house and bathing, Kaushalya telephoned Usha Chand.

Usha quickly offered her sympathy concerning Lakshman Singh's arrest. Abruptly, the connection was cut off, and Kaushalya heard clicking on the line.

When they reestablished contact, Usha's voice sounded faint, as if coming from a far distance. "Let's meet in the morning," Usha shouted. "The southwest corner of Tughluqabad. Say, nine o'clock?"

Tughluqabad? Kaushalya was puzzled. The ruins were several kilometers away from either of their two houses. "I'll be there," she shouted back. "Nine a.m."

Mahendra began telephoning friends and acquaintances who might be willing to use influence with the government. Following several calls, he said angrily, "It's as if everything has changed overnight! No one will risk committing themselves for fear of offending those in power. And I can tell they're worried about the phones being tapped."

Kaushalya thought of the broken connection with Usha, of the clicking on the line. But the phones were so unreliable anyway, she was reluctant to assume these particular problems were due to more mischief by the government.

"I'll try to make some appointments tomorrow," said Mahendra.

"I'll see what I can do, too," Kaushalya said.

"Just be cautious. It might be a good idea to check with me before you actually meet with anyone."

Kaushalya stifled her annoyance at his assumption that she needed any oversight. She already knew he would not approve of what she had in mind.

Delhi seemed even hotter than Mangarh. The study in the house was not air conditioned as were the bedrooms. Barefoot and wearing a loose, pastel blue cotton dress, Kaushalya was again telephoning while Mahendra visited politicians and bureaucrats.

She succeeded in obtaining the number of the person who seemed most likely to have the influence needed. She phoned his quarters in the Ashoka Hotel at eight-thirty, a likely time to catch him after he had breakfasted but before he left for any meetings. A sleepy sounding assistant told her that Dev Batra was unavailable and that she should try later in the day.

Taking the old Jaguar sedan their father kept in Delhi, she left for her meeting with Usha Chand. For the first time in ages, she was out by herself, with Gopi off to visit a friend. Kaushalya first drove east through the residential area. Was it her imagination, or was there less traffic than usual on the streets?

She passed a police check point. The rifle-bearing, khaki-uniformed policemen watched her as she went by, and she felt uneasy. She could not remember ever seeing anything similar in New Delhi.

She reached the Mathura Road and turned south, passing the complex surrounding the domed tomb of Shaikh Nizamuddin Auliya. Soon the buildings thinned out, and the road cut across sun scorched, dusty scrub land, dotted here and there with ruins. Eventually the massive stone ramparts of Tughluqabad appeared. Kaushalya cruised slowly along the western side until she spotted Usha, dressed in a pink *shalwar kameez*, waiting by her motor scooter under the shade of a *neem* tree. Kaushalya parked next to her.

When Kaushalya opened the car door, Usha rushed to her and they clasped each other in a warm embrace. "You look good," Kaushalya said, when they had pulled apart.

The slender, attractive Usha smiled, but concern shone in her eyes. "I was so sorry to hear about your father!"

Kaushalya looked away, and nodded. At first she had been surprised at Usha's caution in meeting at such an isolated location. But then Kaushalya realized that with Lakshman Singh raided by the income tax authorities and imprisoned, Usha could actually be considered loyal and courageous in agreeing to meet at all.

They sat side by side on a large, flat rock, fallen from one of the crumbling buildings. Kaushalya gazed above at the towering stone walls. She wished she hadn't come here; the grim fortifications added to the atmosphere of oppression. These ruins had always affected her this way; it was quite a different feeling from the old structures scattered about Mangarh. The remains of seven former capitals graced the Delhi area, and she felt little affinity for any of them, except perhaps for the Qila Rai Pitora, the ruins of Prithviraja's walled city. The others were all sites from which foreign regimes had imposed their rule on the native kingdoms. Modern New Delhi seemed little different, even now that it was run by the natives themselves.

She stared out at the marble domed tomb of Ghiasuddin Tughluq. Surrounded now by fields, it was said to once have been an island in an artificial lake. It was amazing how a place could change so much over time.

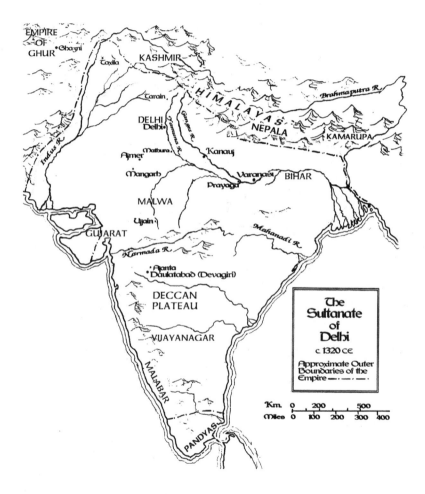

EMPIRE
OF
GHUR   •Ghazni

Taxila

KASHMIR

Tarain

HIMALAYAS

Brahmaputra R.

NEPALA

KAMARUPA

DELHI
Delhi

Indus R.

Ganges R.

Yamuna R.

Ajmer

Mathura

Kanauj

Mangarh

Varanasi   BIHAR

Prayaga

MALWA

Ujjain

Mahanadi R.

GUJARAT

Narmada R.

Ajanta
•Daulatabad (Devagiri)

DECCAN
PLATEAU

VIJAYANAGAR

MALABAR

The
Sultanate
of
Delhi
c. 1320 CE

Approximate Outer
Boundaries of the
Empire ———

Km.   0   200   500
Miles 0   100   200   300 400

PANDYAS

The Price of Nobility

1

Amir Ali Surajuddin Aruzi gradually became aware of the high pitched voice of his eunuch Ishaq: "Master! Please wake up!" Ali fought the intrusion for a time, trying to retreat back into the comforting unconsciousness.

Eventually, he realized Ishaq would not be so insistent unless the matter were urgent. Ali sat up, held his head in his hands, and strained to clear his mind. It seemed as if he'd barely had time to fall asleep. "What is it?" he asked, his mouth foul tasting from last night's wine.

The plump, middle-aged slave took a step backward and bowed deeply. "So sorry to disturb you, Master. Your father wishes to see you immediately."

"Already?" Ali rubbed his scratchy eyes and glanced toward the window. The morning sun was still low, so indeed he had not been in bed long.

"Yes, Master. His honor says it's urgent."

Ali rose. Ishaq beckoned, and two slave girls entered. One helped their master into an embroidered pink robe, while the other offered a basin of water and a towel. Ali washed quickly and rinsed out his mouth, but he waved away the girl who held his tall *kulah* cap, as he would not yet be seeing visitors or leaving the house.

Ali walked through the ornate, arched doorway to the pillared balcony. He narrowed his eyes at the sudden brightness. Already the morning was growing hot. He descended the exterior marble stairway to the garden, where slaves were sweeping the paths and dismantling the tents and awnings erected for last night's huge affair. The monsoon was expected any day, and the tents had been a precaution against a possible deluge. From the kitchen came the sounds of the staff scouring the hundreds of pots and plates. The scents of spices and roasted meats still lingered faintly.

It had been a memorable party—the dancers and musicians at the beginning, when the evening was still uncomfortably hot; the long, leisurely dinner at which almost a thousand guests had feasted; the quiet after-dinner political discussion with his friend, Ziauddin Barani, in a secluded corner of the garden, when the jasmine-scented night air had at last lost enough heat to be comfortable; and the concluding highlight just before dawn: the recital of a lyrical love poem by the greatest poet and musician of the age, Amir Khusrau.

Ali found his father ready to leave the house. The white-bearded nobleman, whose exalted rank of *malik* placed him only a single step below the great *khans*, wore an elegant robe embroidered in gold thread, with a matching *kulah* cap. Probably his father had not had time to go to bed at all; no matter how late when the last of the guests left, Malik Mahmud Aruzi would not have missed his *fajr* prayer at sunrise. The *malik* seldom consumed wine himself, since the drinking of alcoholic beverages was prohibited by the Qur'an and strongly frowned upon by the conservative theologians of the *ulema*, with whom he must remain on good terms. Still, as Ali greeted his father, he saw that the *malik's* eyes, normally notable for their liveliness, were reddened with dark bags beneath; he looked as if he were feeling all of his seventy-five years after the night-long affair.

Mahmud said to the servants hovering about: "All of you, leave!" The domestics disappeared from sight. In a household with such a large staff there were certain to be spies, and Mahmud lowered his voice so no one could overhear. "Khusrau Khan killed Mubarak last night, in the palace, while our party was going on."

"So he felt confident enough to act!" Ali exclaimed, suddenly fully awake. The *Wazir*, the Prime Minister himself, had assassinated Sultan Qutbuddin Mubarak Shah, and seized power!

Ali struggled to comprehend the implications as his father continued, "Khusrau's summoned all the ministers immediately. He no doubt wants us to confirm him as the new Sultan. I'm going there now. You must take charge of the family."

Mahmud Aruzi held the high post of *sadr-us-sadr*, chief *sadr*, the minister in charge of religious matters. Subject only to the authority of the Sultan personally, Mahmud was responsible for enforcing the *sharia*, the Islamic religious laws. And—at least as importantly—he oversaw the management of religious endowments, appointed the leading *imams* or priests, and he disbursed grants and stipends to scholars, priests, and other Muslim holy men.

Mahmud had done so well at balancing the opposing interests he supervised that he had been retained during the rules of four successive Sultans, including even the long reign of the great Sultan Alauddin Khilji. But what a Sultan gave, a Sultan could abruptly take away. Ali's mouth had gone dry. He cleared his throat and asked, "How do you think Khusrau views you now, Father?"

Mahmud toyed fretfully with his beard. "I wish I knew. But if he knows I supported the earlier attempt to kill Mubarak, he may think I also favor his own move."

Ali's stomach still became queasy whenever he thought of how precarious the family's position had been after the previous assassination plot failed. Sultan Qutbuddin Mubarak had begun his rule well, but Khusrau Khan, as his trusted adviser, had deliberately undermined the inexperienced young Sultan by steering him into a life of debauchery unparalleled even in the Sultanate. Eventually, Mubarak had offended virtually everyone in the nobility. Not only had the Sultan appeared at court dressed as a woman, he had encouraged his slave boys and dancing girls in such unbelievably outrageous behavior as soiling their own clothes in public in the audience hall.

Several of the outraged nobles, with Ali's father as a supporter, had conspired to overthrow Mubarak. The Sultan had discovered the plot and executed the known leaders, their associates, even their children. Mahmud and Ali had gone through a time of intense anxiety. Somehow, Mahmud had escaped being implicated in the plot. But he and Ali had been on edge ever since.

"—Still," Mahmud was saying, "I can never be sure if anyone's poisoned Khusrau's ear against me. So you'd better get the family ready to leave, in case I don't come back."

Ali gave a stiff nod. If his father didn't return, it would be his own responsibility to get their family to safety. "Should I take the women and children away now, just in case, Father? There may not be time later."

Mahmud hesitated; he again fingered his beard, but then dropped his hand as if he had realized he was revealing his trepidation. "I thought of that," he said finally. "But I don't want it to appear we're guilty of anything. It could look bad if someone reported their leaving to Khusrau Khan. Anyway, I'll try to send one of my men with as much warning as possible."

Ali, tight-lipped, again nodded. "I understand, Father." The old man slipped on his gold-embroidered sheepskin shoes, and Ali walked with him to where Mahmud's entourage waited in the outer courtyard.

Upon Mahmud's appearance, the orchestra which would accompany him began playing.

Ali had a sudden thought. "What about the alms, Father?"

The *malik* had become famous for his generosity to the poor. Every morning he took a sizable purse and distributed coins to waiting supplicants as his procession went through the streets, until the sum was exhausted. As a small child Ali had sometimes accompanied his father on these rounds. From an early age he had learned that sharing with less fortunate persons should be done out of empathy and a sense of fairness, not merely as a requirement imposed by Islam. As soon as he had acquired a government post with an income, Ali, too, had begun donating his wealth, although on a smaller scale than his father, and not quite so early in the mornings.

Mahmud replied, "I think those who rely on me for their daily food are at least as important as the new Sultan, don't you? I'll share with them as usual on the way to the palace. The small delay won't matter." Mahmud seated himself in the palanquin and nodded at the servant heading his entourage. The musicians, the five hand-led horses, and the six standard bearers permitted to the rank of *malik* preceded him out the gate. Before and after Mahmud's palanquin came the body-guards and the other servants.

"Allah be with you, Father," Ali said quietly to the retreating procession.

He was glad he himself had no matters requiring him to appear in court today. Ali held the rank of *amir*, and the post of city magistrate. This and his father's own prestige placed him well up in the middle ranks of the nobility. He always felt grateful that the position afforded him the opportunity to do a great deal of good—ensuring that every disputant who appeared before him for judgment was treated justly, and dispensing charity to the poor and needy when appropriate.

But it could all be lost in an instant at a Sultan's whim. Ali turned to Ishaq, who had stood by awaiting further orders, and said, "Go tell my father's women to prepare in case they have to leave." Although Ali's mother was deceased, his father had four other wives and thirty-three concubines. "You get the horses and carriages ready. I'll see to my own women."

Ishaq's eyes were wide with anxiety. "Master, are we in serious danger?"

Ali shook his head. "There's no way to know. But," he looked pointedly at the eunuch, "you know what our last Sultan did to his opponents and their households. We must be prepared."

Ishaq turned and hurried toward the women's quarters.

All morning, the huge house near the western wall of Delhi echoed with the muffled sounds of preparations for flight. Of Ali's own two young wives, Halima, pretty with a heavy, rounded figure, wearing the typical loose drawers and scarf of Muslim women, took the news with outward calm. "I'll see that the servants get as much done as possible." Only the worry in her eyes betrayed her true concern.

Stunningly beautiful, slender Ayesha, dressed similarly but in brighter colors, was fearful in spite of Ali's attempts to reassure her. "You're quite safe, *inshallah*, God willing," he said. "It's just that we're being careful."

She broke into tears. "Why must we always be in danger?" she asked between sobs.

"We're *not* always in danger!" Halima snapped. "Stop your crying right now and see to getting your jewels packed!"

Ayesha sobered, hurried over to her pet parrot, Gulam, and beckoned to a slave girl, ordering her to be sure to bring the bird if they had to leave.

Ali slipped away. Ayesha could be trying at times. Halima could be brutally blunt, but thanks be to Allah that she was so practical.

Ali hastily walked through the living quarters of the magnificent house built by his grandfather, and glanced about each room. It was unbearable to think that he could lose this home, which he had always loved so much. Still, he must be prudent and force himself to at least plan for the possibility. If the family should have to flee, they could not begin to take with them everything of value. The gold, silver and jewels were being gathered and loaded into the guarded carriages. There was a surprisingly small amount of that type of wealth, since a nobleman had to expend virtually all his income on maintaining his extensive household and on the lavish gifts, entertainment, and charitable donations expected of him.

Of the other valuables, Ali wondered if he could take anything else. He looked around the huge banquet hall. It was sparsely furnished except for the rich carpets and hangings, which would have to stay due to lack of room in the carts. He walked down the hallway to the library, with its comforting slightly musty odor, and he eyed the rows of precious manuscripts lining the walls. He would miss the many books if he had to flee.

He stepped through a pillared archway onto the terrace and looked out over the gardens: the big banyan tree, the mango orchard, the orange trees, the marble watercourse bisecting the courtyard. All this, too, would be painful to leave.

He thought of his spiritual master, the great Sufi saint, Shaikh Nizamuddin Auliya, who cared nothing for material wealth and lived a live of austerity. The *shaikh* often advised his followers to have as little contact as possible with the Sultans and their self-serving officials. Ali greatly admired the saint, and he frequently pondered the fact that he himself was so firmly attached to his own wealth, home, and position. Personally, Ali found the constant intrigues of the Sultan's court extremely distasteful. But he also knew that his own family's wealth and position had been utterly dependent upon his father's enduring ability to succeed at those very same manipulations of power and influence.

Ali wished his father would send some word. Had Father been demoted? Promoted? Imprisoned? Executed? There was simply no way yet to know Khusrau Khan's true feelings.

From over the walls he heard a clatter of horses' hooves on the cobblestoned street. Ali tensed as the riders drew near. It could not be his father, for the *malik's* procession was limited by the speed of the palanquin, the most comfortable mode of travel for a body that was developing aching joints. The horses halted, and Ali hurried up the stairs to look from a second floor window. Could the new Sultan have sent soldiers already to seize the Aruzis?

He let out his breath in relief as, outside on the street, he saw Ziauddin Barani dismounting, accompanied by the nobleman's usual retinue of bodyguards and servants. Ali went down to meet his friend. Zia's wide-nosed, large-jawed face was attractive in a way that was quite in contrast to Ali's more delicate handsomeness. Zia's eyes, though reddened from lack of sleep, were penetrating and observant as always, and they darted about to assure there were no likely informers in earshot. He asked Ali, "Did you hear what Khusrau's men did after they killed Mubarak?"

"Not in detail, no—"

Zia said, his eyes blazing, "His men—mostly Hindus—invaded Mubarak's harem! They killed and raped many of the women, and murdered all three of Alauddin Khilji's sons!"

Ali felt his face turn pale. He said dryly, "It seems Khusrau's effectively eliminated all rival claimants to the throne."

"How can any of the nobles support him after that? It's bad enough that he's an infidel!"

Ali frowned. "Khusrau did convert to the Faith, after all. So I wouldn't necessarily assume his interests are opposed to ours in that regard. But certainly I wish he would moderate his conduct."

"Doesn't it bother you that he's so low-born? It's disgraceful we should have to submit to him. Your own lineage goes back almost as far as mine—can you really accept him as Sultan?"

Ali struggled with whether or not he agreed with Zia's concern. A hundred years before, Ali's own grandfather had been taken prisoner as a child in Samarkand by Genghis Khan's Mongol raiders and sold as a slave. But he had eventually been purchased for the Delhi household of the Sultan Shamsuddin Iltutmish, a former slave himself. The Turks permitted their slaves to rise as high in rank as ability would carry them, and Ali's grandfather had eventually become one of "the Forty," the elite group of nobles who held the high leadership posts in the Sultanate. Ali's father, and Ali himself, had built upon this foundation. Now few could surpass the Aruzis' position in the Turkish nobility of Delhi.

Ali sighed. "I suppose I can accept Khusrau Khan if I have to. Remember, you wanted Mubarak removed, just as I did. Whatever we think of Khusrau, he did do the job where others failed."

"Still," Zia said in disgust, "I don't see how I could accept a post under him, even if it were offered."

Ali smiled in irony. "At least the Sultans provide you with topics for your writings."

"True. Unfortunately that's not nearly as good as a position at court." Quite unlike Ali, Zia had been eager to get as close as possible to the center of power, preferably to be a courtier of the Sultan himself. But so far he had been thwarted in those hopes despite being an able scholar and a charming, witty conversationalist from a fine family. Meanwhile, he kept a record of the happenings at the court, which he hoped would some day bring him renown as a chronicler. Zia now looked at Ali speculatively and said, "I assume your own post should be secure."

"*Inshallah*," Ali said, more casually than he felt. "I'm far enough from the Sultan's court myself that Khusrau probably doesn't know I exist. But I'm still awaiting word from my father as to how we'll fare."

"I should think Khusrau would be glad to have him. Your father's a good liaison with both the *ulema* and the nobles."

Ali looked in the direction of the Sultan's palace. "I sincerely hope Khusrau feels that way."

Zia became less serious. "A truly great party last night! I've never seen our superb poet in better form!"

"Yes, he's unbelievably good. Although I confess I had difficulty following him toward the end. My fault, not his. I was having trouble staying awake after so long."

Zia eyed him with amusement. "You did seem as if you'd had a little too much wine, my friend. Do you remember Ishaq helping you to your rooms?"

Ali's face grew warm. "Ishaq had to help me?"

Zia laughed. "No, no. Just teasing you!" He turned to leave. "I must go. Will I see you at the *khanqah* tomorrow?" As members of the inner circle of Shaikh Nizamuddin Auliya's disciples, they often met in the morning at the Sufi saint's monastery.

"God willing, I'll be there," Ali replied. Assuming he wasn't fleeing for his life, or already dead.

Not long after the post-noon *zohar* prayers, the approaching sound of Mahmud's orchestra announced his return. When Ali hurried out to meet the procession, he could tell from his father's relaxed face and animated eyes that they had survived the crisis.

Mahmud nodded to the leader of the musicians to silence them. When the music stopped, he said to Ali in a voice again confident, "I'm confirmed in my office." Filled with renewed energy, he climbed from his seat and led Ali into the garden, where he waved off the servants and said quietly, "Khusrau had obviously planned this for some time. He knew just whom he would remove and whom he would retain. Of course, it remains to be seen how much of a favor he did us by keeping me!"

Ali replied thoughtfully, "Everyone says he converted to the Faith only to advance himself. And most of his supporters are Hindus. So maybe he'll leave you free to run your department as you wish."

"That's my hope. But I disburse a great deal of money. Sultan Khusrau might well decide he has better uses for it than furthering Islam."

"He still needs the support of the Faithful, and the nobles. No one is better than you at keeping on good terms with all the conflicting interests."

"That's probably why Khusrau reappointed me," Mahmud said. "God willing, I'll keep him satisfied."

2

The monsoon arrived, bringing cooler air that was most welcome. At first the downpours flooded Delhi's streets, but eventually the rains moderated, and the drains were able to handle what fell.

During a quiet period between storms, Mahmud led Ali into the garden of their home, where they were certain to be safe from being overheard by any of the Sultan's spies. Servants placed dry pillows on a wet stone bench and then left. Mahmud reached inside his robe and withdrew a letter which he handed to his son.

Ali read it quickly, then again, more slowly. His stomach tightened into a knot. At last, he said, "So Ghazi Tughluq wants your support in overthrowing Sultan Khusrau, Father."

His father's eyes, their liveliness subdued by the weight of the decisions he must make, shifted away. His hand toyed with his beard in the habit he'd acquired in the past year. He said quietly, "Yes. I much prefer him to Khusrau as Sultan. But we must be certain to back the winner. It does us no good to support a cause, however just, if it loses."

Ali thought hard. Many of the Turkish nobles remained outraged at Khusrau's men ravishing and killing the royal women and assassinating the three young sons of the former great Sultan Alauddin Khilji. And Ziauddin Barani was certainly not the only one who considered Khusrau, as a non-Turk, to be a usurper. Recently word had spread that the Turkish noble Ghiasuddin Tughluq, governor at Dipalpur in the Punjab, had refused to recognize Khusrau as Sultan and was quietly gathering support before openly contesting the throne. Tughluq was a popular general who also held the post of Warden of the Marches, the military commander charged with guarding the Sultan's territories from the Mongols and other invaders from the northwest. He was called Ghazi ("Slayer of Infidels") Tughluq for having successfully repulsed the feared Mongols on numerous occasions.

Ali's father faced a serious dilemma. Should he support Khusrau—who was, after all a non-Turk and whose sympathies with the teachings of the Prophet were suspect; or should he support Ghazi Tughluq—like himself a Turkish noble who held steadfastly to orthodox Islam?

"How can we know who will win, Father? Ghazi Tughluq is a good general, but Khusrau also led successful military campaigns."

His father was staring vacantly at the marble water channel, .full now from the rains. A drizzle began to fall, generating hundreds of small circular ripples on the otherwise placid surface. He took the letter and slid it back into his robe to ensure the ink would not run. "We can't be certain," he said, his voice gone weak. "I'm sure Ghazi Tughluq is the better general. Anyone who can defeat the Mongols every time has to be good."

"So we should back him then, Father?"

His father sighed. "Probably."

Ali stared through the falling mist to the pillared arcades of the house he had been raised in. He had always hoped it would be home to his own sons and their descendants to the end of time. However, yet again, not only the elegant house, but their very lives, could be lost if they made the wrong decision. He asked hoarsely, "What will we do if the Sultan finds out?"

His father looked away. "Perhaps we should support him, too."

Ali thought for a time. It was not uncommon to attempt to appear to favor both adversaries in a power struggle. Occasionally the effort worked out well, convincing both sides. Sometimes, on the other hand, the eventual victor was not fooled, and when his position was secure he punished his supposed "supporter." Perhaps more often, the victor was not fooled but chose to ignore the duplicity in order to enhance his position with as much apparent support as possible. "How would you go about it, Father?"

His father said slowly, "I'll send a reply to Tughluq agreeing to support him. Then I'll show *this* letter—" he pressed his chest with a hand "—to Khusrau, to convince him he can trust me as his own supporter."

Ali nodded thoughtfully. "Khusrau is probably so desperate for support now that he can't afford *not* to believe you."

The rain began to fall harder. Mahmud boosted himself slowly to his feet, and the two hurried silently to the shelter of the house.

Ali could not read Mahmud's face when the *malik* returned from the private audience with the Sultan. His father merely nodded, and beckoned toward the garden, where the sun shone through a break in the clouds. Alone there, Mahmud said with a frown, "I think the meeting went well overall."

Ali raised his eyebrows; clearly his father retained some reservations about the outcome. Mahmud resumed, "I assured Khusrau of my continuing support and handed him Ghazi Tughluq's letter. I told the Sultan I wanted to ensure he knew what Tughluq was doing, since the Ghazi undoubtedly contacted other nobles also. The Sultan read the letter and said it was most interesting. Then he asked me what I intended to do about it."

"And...?"

"I told him I planned to ignore it; that the uncertainty of no response would likely be disconcerting to Tughluq. Then"—his forehead wrinkled in worry—"this is the part I'm most concerned about:

Khusrau said he'd like to show the letter to an advisor, and that he'd return it to me on my next visit. I couldn't think of a convincing reason to insist I keep it. So I left it with him."

Ali thought for a time, then said, "Naturally, it would be better to have kept control of the letter. Still, I suppose it's unlikely any harm will come from leaving it, Father."

"Probably not. Still...I'd have preferred to keep it. Well, the matter is in God's hands, praise be to Him. Allah has been merciful to us for many years."

So far as Mahmud could discern, he continued to be a trusted minister of Sultan Khusrau Shah. The new Sultan, worried that Ghazi Tughluq would attack when the monsoon season ended, attempted to purchase the support, and the prayers, of several popular religious leaders through large gifts of money. It was Malik Mahmud Aruzi, as chief *sadr*, whom the Sultan charged with disbursing the funds to the holy men.

Most of the donations were in the huge amount of three *lakhs*, three hundred thousands, of *tankas*. But the ruler allocated five *lakhs* to the famous Sufi saint, Shaikh Nizamuddin Auliya—an immense gift even by the standards of the Sultans.

As a disciple of the *shaikh*, Ali was personally pleased by the gift. The morning after the donation was announced, he arose in the damp predawn and set out for the *shaikh's khanqah* in the nearby village of Ghiaspur, after first obtaining the purse of coins from Halima to be used in the daily alms-giving. Because a light rain was again falling, he decided to ride in his two wheeled carriage rather than his usual method of travel by horseback. As expected for an *amir's* entourage, his three standard bearers and two men hand-leading horses preceded him, so the procession moved at the pace of a fast walk.

Supplicants, many of whom would likely starve were it not for Ali's regular daily gifts to them, approached his carriage, bowing and making gestures of deference. Ali handed the usual coin to each. He gave to one of his regulars, a man with matted hair and a ragged loin cloth and glazed eyes, who always mumbled to himself, appearing lost in a world that no one else could see. He gave a coin to an old, stooped, emaciated widow who had no other means of support. He gave to an orphaned little boy with big, wide eyes and a tiny sister in tow. He gave to an aged leper man who could barely hold the coin between the two stumps of his hands. He gave to a dirty, raggedly dressed woman with three small dirty, naked children.

On and on he gave, until the purse was exhausted. He always wished he could give more, as the needs were so huge, but one must be realistic. It had been a welcome relief to him when Halima had taken upon herself the duty of keeping his accounts and parceling out an appropriate amount for charity each day.

Ali's route took him northeasterly across the central part of the city. Smoke from cooking fires hung in a low haze. At wells along the route, men who had just risen from their beds were clearing their throats and rinsing out their mouths and pouring pitchers of water over themselves.

Ali was passing the great Quvvatal Islam Mosque when the *muezzin's* call to prayer came from the broad, towering red sandstone minaret, the Qutb Minar. Ali therefore halted his procession outside the mosque and entered on foot by the eastern gateway. The rain had stopped. After his ablutions at the basins, with several hundred other men he spread his prayer carpet on the smooth, wet paving stones, and stood facing west toward Mecca. In unison the men knelt, touched their foreheads to the carpet, stood again, all as prescribed for the prayer rituals.

At the conclusion of the worship, Ali stood and looked about the mosque. He had always been impressed by the carved inscriptions on the structure and by the magnitude of the adjacent giant tower. Over the heads of the other rising men, the low sun shone through a break in the clouds on the Qutb Minar, turning it a glowing rose hue. The famous iron pillar in the courtyard, said to be more than a thousand years old, glistened. But he must not linger.

He reentered his carriage and drove across the remainder of the city, then out the main gate in the massive northern wall. In the less populated suburbs on the Ghiaspur road, his entourage passed first one, then another, of the raised platforms with thatched roofs and adjacent wells, built by wealthy admirers of Shaikh Nizamuddin Auliya for the convenience of visitors who needed to pause along the way for their ablutions and prayers.

Ali turned eastward to the village of Kilukhari, near the Jumna River, where he knew he would find his friend Ziauddin Barani since it was still early morning. Barani kept a number of slave girls and entertainers in the house in Kilukhari, and it was here that he usually spent his nights in revelry. For the sake of appearances, he kept a more respectable home in Ghiaspur for his wives and children, near the saint's *khanqah*.

The Kilukhari house was behind the village's mosque in a maze of alleys which were a mess of mud now from the rains. Ali was always perturbed at how rundown the house appeared. How, he wondered, could his friend, otherwise so well cultured, enjoy such squalid surroundings? He dismounted and pounded on the door.

Zia's bare head poked out an upper window. "*Assalaam aleicum.* I'm just coming," he called. Soon he appeared at the doorway. His *kulah* was now in place, but his eyes were dull and red from whatever entertainments had filled the night. At Ali's invitation he climbed stiffly into the carriage and sagged onto the seat for the short ride northerly to Ghiaspur.

Ali grinned. "You look fresh and well-rested this morning."

Zia's penetrating eyes shot him an irritated look, then he relaxed and laughed. "How could I waste time on sleep, when I might miss out on a pleasurable experience? You could do with a little more fun yourself, my friend. You've been looking altogether too solemn lately. I have a new slave girl from Bukhara who might be refined enough for your tastes. You'd swear she had two tongues in her mouth. And you'd be amazed at what she can do with her feet!"

Still smiling, Ali shook his head. "My wives distract me enough." Zia regularly tried to tease him into joining his nights of sensual delights. Ali didn't take him seriously and didn't mind the joking.

"Anyway," said Zia, "don't I deserve some consolation, since I've had no opportunities for advancement at the Sultan's court?"

Ali shrugged. "Who am I to say? Regardless, maybe we'll see a change of Sultans soon, and your chances will improve."

Zia nodded and straightened. "I've been hoping for days that Malik Jauna would come to the *khanqah* when we're there. It can't hurt to cultivate him a little." Zia lowered his voice, even though it was unlikely he'd be overheard in the carriage. "I'm guessing Ghazi Tughluq's army will be here when the rains end. Allah surely has to be on Tughluq's side, not on that of a false believer. I've offered the Ghazi whatever help I can give. And it can't hurt to befriend his eldest son. Hopefully Jauna will remember me when his father becomes Sultan. And Jauna might even become Sultan himself, one day when his father dies."

Ali smiled at the blatant, though understandable, opportunism. "You're assuming a lot. But I imagine a lot of men are trying to get Jauna's attention now."

"All the more reason for me to get noticed early myself."

Ghiaspur village permanently housed many of Shaikh Nizamuddin Auliya's numerous disciples, as well as providing temporary lodgings for many of the visitors from afar. The *khanqah* itself had grown into a large, sprawling, haphazard collection of mud buildings clustered around the court where the Auliya received his visitors.

Ali and Ziauddin Barani dismounted from the carriage at the entrance to the courtyard. Despite the rains, the yard, dominated by a huge banyan tree, was crowded as usual with persons waiting to see the saint. Ali and Zia had to press through the edges of the throng in order to make their way to the pillared hall with its small meeting rooms, and from there to the *shaikh's* adjacent, simple, thatch roofed living quarters.

The saint had not yet emerged for the day, but present were several of his other leading disciples, including the famous poet Amir Khusrau and the poet Amir Hasan. And also there, as Zia had hoped, was Malik Fakhruddin Jauna, eldest son of Ghazi Tughluq. Ali was amused at how incongruous the rude physical surroundings appeared as a setting for such an illustrious group.

Zia smiled fleetingly at Ali and led him to where Jauna sat near the two poets. Amir Khusrau and Amir Hasan greeted them both warmly, but Ali sensed an unexpected coldness emanating toward him from

Malik Jauna. He had never quite felt comfortable around the young noble. Although the *malik's* demeanor was superficially affable, Jauna had a quick temper. He was a brilliant scholar and conversationalist, but Ali felt the man lacked a sense of restraint, of balance, in his judgment, tending at times to take extreme positions when some middle attitude might be more appropriate.

Another rain shower began, and after the exchange of greetings, Ali and Zia sat on the driest of the remaining spots on the mud floor. Malik Jauna's aloof eyes narrowed as he spoke to Ali: "I understand, Amir Aruzi, that you recently heard a case in your court concerning a debt of one of my servants."

Ali noticed that Zia was frowning slightly. No doubt Zia would have preferred the *malik* to focus upon himself rather than on Ali. "Yes, that's true, sir."

"I also heard," said Jauna, "that you adjudged the debt a valid one, but you paid it yourself."

Discomfited, Ali shrugged. "It was nothing. As I recall, the defendant had some large expenses due to his parents' illnesses."

"You should have told him to petition me for help. He's in my household after all."

When Ali had weighed the matter in court, he had been unsure whether Jauna would be more likely to help the servant or to punish him. But now Ali quickly replied, "Of course, sir. Please accept my apology. I meant no offense. I realize you would have been most generous with him if he'd come to you. It simply seemed more convenient to pay the amount myself, rather than troubling you, since the sum was so small."

Malik Jauna stared at him for a time. Abruptly, instantly, his eyes lost their coldness, and he smiled at Ali. "I understand," he said. "Still...it's to your credit that you paid it at all. It's not a requirement of your position as magistrate that you pay the debts of those who appear before you."

Ali again shrugged. "Naturally, I don't do it in most cases. But our *pir* teaches us to be charitable as well as just."

Jauna nodded agreeably. "Of course."

Zia, at last bringing himself to Jauna's attention, interjected smoothly: "I always admire the way my good friend Ali Aruzi strives to put the teachings of our *pir* into practice."

"I'm sure," said Malik Jauna, sounding entirely sincere, "that we'd all do better if we followed Amir Aruzi's example."

"Please stop," said Ali, embarrassed. "I'm continually unhappy with myself for not being able to better follow the Auliya's practices."

"It's difficult," said Jauna, "for any of us to emulate such a true saint."

"Indeed," said Zia, nodding vigorously.

Ali moved slightly to avoid a growing pool from a tiny stream of water that was slowly eroding a section of the mud wall. Eager to shift the conversation away from himself, he said, "We really ought to convince our *pir* to allow us to rebuild the *khanqah*."

"Haven't many disciples tried numerous times?" asked Jauna. "I sometimes think he uses discomfort as a test to discourage followers who aren't seriously committed to him."

"Then," said Zia with an ironic smile and a gesture taking in the group, "all of us have again and again truly demonstrated our commitment."

"Indeed, we have," said the *malik*, turning his attention toward the entrance, where the Auliya himself had abruptly appeared.

Shaikh Nizamuddin Auliya was nearing ninety years of age, but he still kept a vigorous routine. Ali saw that the white-bearded saint's eyes were, as usual, tinged with pink from staying awake most of the night for study and prayer. He nevertheless radiated an aura of bliss, with a loving smile that seemed to envelop his entire person.

Amir Khusrau, with a short, contoured beard streaked with gray and a pointed horizontal mustache, had been quiet during the exchange between Malik Jauna and Ali and Zia. Now his eyes warmed, and he greeted the *shaikh* by reciting one of the spontaneous verses for which he was famous, making fun of the saint's obvious weariness:

> *You look sleepless and tired;*
> *In whose embrace did you pass the night?*
> *For your drowsy eyes have still*
> *The traces of tipsiness.*

Khusrau finished by closing his eyes most of the way and inclining his head forward to mimic someone nodding off to sleep.

The Auliya smiled and joined in the laughter. All knew he was a strict celibate. "Ah, Khusrau," he said. "What would I do without my favorite Turk to lighten my days?" He composed a verse himself:

> *Khusrau, like whom few men have written poetry*
> *or prose*
> *Is certainly the king of poesy's realm.*
> *He is our Khusrau...*
> *And God himself is his helper.*

The verse met with the approval of even the fellow poet Amir Hasan. Everyone liked Amir Khusrau, whom Shaikh Nizamuddin Auliya was probably fonder of than any other living person.

Soon the conversation turned to Sultan Khusrau Shah's large donation when a disciple questioned whether the *shaikh* should keep the money. The saint turned to Ziauddin Barani. "What does my young scholar suggest?"

"I think you should refuse the gift, *pir*. Is it good to take such a large sum from the Sultan? Won't it look as if you're supporting him?

And Sultan Khusrau Shah is an infidel, no matter what he now claims."

"Now, now, Zia," the Auliya chided. "I detect both too much pride and too much dislike in your voice. I teach humility and love. You must learn to be more loving, Zia."

Ali suspected that Zia stated his position against Sultan Khusrau so strongly at least partly in the hope of favorably impressing Malik Jauna. But there was also the distinct possibility that Sultan Khusrau might have a spy present, in which case Zia could be endangering himself. Clearly Zia was gambling that Tughluq would win, and quite soon.

An aged, long-time disciple said, "*Pir*, you've refused to meet with any of the Sultans. And you've always counseled us to avoid politics as if it were a deadly poison. Mightn't it be better to avoid touching the funds?"

The saint turned slightly, and his eyes focused on Malik Jauna. Jauna's situation was especially peculiar in that Sultan Khusrau Shah had retained him in the important post of Master of the Horses, apparently hoping to influence Ghazi Tughluq to drop further opposition. Now the *shaikh* asked with an amused smile, "Does the Master of the Horses care to state his views in the matter?"

Malik Jauna sat silently for some seconds. He then replied, "It is always proper to accept charity, sir. However, it might be well to take your time in distributing the funds, in case any change in circumstance might require their return to the treasury."

The *shaikh* raised an eyebrow, and then slowly nodded. This time Ali approved the wisdom of Malik Jauna's advice. Jauna was clearly warning that if Ghazi Tughluq became Sultan, the new ruler might consider Khusrau Shah's disbursements from the treasury to be invalid and demand the funds back.

The Auliya turned with a twinkle in his eyes to Amir Khusrau and Amir Hasan. "What do my two poets advise?"

Amir Khusrau said in his smooth, melodious voice, "Hasan and I have discussed the matter, your honor. We see no harm in receiving a donation from the Sultan. Charity is charity. Everyone knows you don't care for wealth yourself. Take the money and give it to the poor. You can do much good with it."

The saint's gaze traveled around the circle and stopped at Ali. He said, "Amir Ali Aruzi. Your father will disburse the gift. Did you have any influence on his decision to make the grant?"

Surprised, Ali replied modestly, "None whatsoever, your honor. Of course, I speak of you often to my father. I don't think he views you unfavorably, even though his own views are more in line with the orthodox members of the *ulema*. But I believe the grant was the Sultan's own idea."

"Should I accept it?"

Ali felt uneasy at being asked for his views by a famous man of God, a man so saintly, so pure. "I wouldn't presume to advise you, *pir*. I come to learn from *you*, not you from me."

The Auliya's eyes again twinkled with pleasure. "It's good to see such humility, Amir Ali. I wish more of my followers demonstrated the virtue to such a degree. Still, I want to know your feelings on the matter."

Ali struggled to marshal his thoughts. He said, "*Pir*, I feel it would be ungenerous to turn down the gift. It would be treating the Sultan as if he were unworthy, while you teach that all men are worthy in God's sight. And as Amir Khusrau points out, you could do considerable good with so many *tankas*."

The saint nodded, and listened to more views. He then fell silent for a time before announcing, "I intend to accept the gift. It will be of great benefit to the needy."

"Will you pray for Sultan Khusrau Shah as he expects, sir, in exchange for the donation?" asked the poet Amir Hasan.

Shaikh Nizamuddin Auliya smiled as he asked, "Why not? I sell amulets to all who ask for them, so why not prayers, too?" More seriously, he added, "The Sultan is *always* in my prayers."

Ali noted that the Auliya had prudently not said he prayed for "Khusrau Shah" in particular, merely that he prayed for the "Sultan," whomever that might be. He had thus said nothing to indicate whether or not he endorsed Khusrau Shah's reign as Sultan as legitimate.

The dampness from the floor had now seeped entirely through Ali's robe. There were definite disadvantages in following even so illustrious a saint.

3

Three months later

"A cold day, Father," Ali said, as they approached their waiting palanquins to leave for the Sultan's palace, where there was now yet another new ruler—Ghazi Ghiasuddin Tughluq. Ali had thought his wool robe and his *kulah* cap would keep him warm, but the winter wind bit straight through the fabric. "Will you be all right?"

Mahmud was pale and weak from the fever that had plagued him ever since the monsoon season; he therefore had asked his son to accompany him in case he needed assistance on the important occasion. He turned sunken eyes on Ali. "I think so. Let's just hope our new Sultan's response to my report won't be frigid, also."

Ghazi Ghiasuddin Tughluq's army had marched in the autumn and defeated Sultan Khusrau Shah's forces near Delhi. Soon afterwards, Khusrau was captured and killed. The Turkish nobility of Delhi had been delighted to confirm Tughluq, one of their own, as the new Sultan. Tughluq moved quickly to appoint Turks to most of the high positions in his government.

Malik Mahmud's strategy of seeming to support both factions

appeared to have succeeded; the new Sultan retained him in the high rank of *malik* and as chief *sadr*.

However, Sultan Ghiasuddin Tughluq was worried about the condition of his treasury, after four consecutive short reigns of Sultans who had been concerned primarily with defending their grasps on the throne, rather than with efficiently administering their governments. Tughluq had ordered Khusrau Shah's huge charitable grants canceled, and he gave Mahmud Aruzi the difficult and embarrassing task of asking the recipients to return the funds. Now, Malik Mahmud had been summoned to the Sultan's palace to report on his efforts.

As customary, at the outer gate of the red stone "Palace of a Thousand Pillars," the blaring of trumpets announced the arrival of the great *malik*, and at the second and third gates the officials greeted Mahmud Aruzi obsequiously.

Ali's own visits to the palace had been rare, as he much preferred. He now found himself shivering in the coolness even in his fine wool robe as they waited at the entrance to the many-columned audience hall. Between the silk hangings by the door, the red sandstone wall was so highly polished as to be mirrorlike, and he was aware of their reflections, looking small in such a vast room. Ali was unprepared when his father bent near to him and whispered, "I don't like the feel in here. Men are less respectful, and they don't meet my eyes."

Already tense over the uncertainty of what would occur at the audience, even though he would not be an active participant, Ali momentarily stopped breathing and went rigid. Over many years of experience at the palace, his father had developed an instinct for quickly sensing the mood of the Sultan, and of the ruler's officers, who took their cue from the attitude of the Sultan himself.

The *Hajib*, the Head Chamberlain, called Malik Mahmud forward. Ali remained at the rear of the hall, but realizing his family's future could well be at risk, he observed closely. The peacock feathers on the Chamberlain's gold cap dipped up and down as the official led Mahmud onto the polished marble floor to the proper spot for his obeisance.

Sultan Ghiasuddin Tughluq, a grim faced man in his sixties wearing a tall, jeweled *kulah*, sat cross-legged on the low throne. Behind the Sultan stood bodyguards with naked swords poised and ready. Before him sat his *Wazir*, or Prime Minister, and the secretaries and clerks.

As etiquette prescribed, Mahmud knelt and touched his forehead to the floor in the posture of prayer. He rose, and advancing toward the Sultan, bowed three times. Finally he handed his written report to the *Barbak*, the Master of the Rolls, who passed it up to the Sultan.

Ghiasuddin Tughluq, a scholar as well as a general and an administrator, briefly examined the papers and then stared icily at

Mahmud. The Sultan said, "So two of the recipients had declined their grants and never received any funds. Three recipients held the funds without using them and have now returned them at your request. But Shaikh Nizamuddin Auliya claims he no longer has so much as a single *tanka*?"

"That's correct, Your Majesty," Mahmud replied. "He insists he has given the entire five *lakhs* to charity." To Ali, still at the rear of the hall, his father's voice seemed strong despite his illness—a mixture of just the right amount of humbleness and obsequiousness with confident authority.

Tughluq never removed his gaze from Malik Mahmud's eyes. "Five *lakhs*. That's a lot to give away so quickly."

"He says there are a great many poor and needy, Your Majesty."

"Hmmph. Does he at least apologize for not having anything to return to me?"

"Your Majesty, when I requested the Auliya to return the funds, he replied, 'It was God's property and it went to God's charity.'"

Tughluq frowned. An orthodox *sunni* and a strong supporter of the conservative theologians who dominated the *ulema*, he had no liking for the Sufis, despite his son being a follower of the Auliya. "I am not pleased. How do we know the *shaikh* has actually given away all the money?"

"There's no reason to doubt him, Your Majesty. His own life of poverty is known to everyone."

The Sultan shook his head, his mouth grim with distaste. "So are his all-night dancing parties, which he claims bring him closer to God." Tughluq fixed Mahmud with a piercing glare. "In exchange for the money, did he pray for Khusrau to win against me?"

Mahmud said levelly, "I'm told he prayed for an outcome favorable to Allah, Your Majesty."

"Hmmm...wise of him. Or clever. But the issue is a large sum of money. Summon him here. I'll question him myself on the matter."

Mahmud hesitated a moment, then replied: "With all respect, Your Majesty, the Auliya has always refused to come to the court of any Sultan."

Tughluq pressed his lips together tightly, then said, "I've heard this said of him before. So it's true—he'd refuse a direct command?"

Mahmud nodded. "Most probably, Your Majesty."

"Naturally, I can order him seized."

"Indeed you can, Your Majesty. But if I may presume to advise you, I fear it would be an unpopular move. The *shaikh* is so well respected—almost worshiped—by many of the nobility."

The Sultan was scowling, his eyes flashing in anger. "I'm not used to having my commands refused. By anyone, saint or otherwise!" He was silent a moment. Then: "You disbursed the grant yourself, did you not?"

"Yes, Your Majesty. But under the orders of the Sult—of Khusrau."

"Still, it's your department. It is your responsibility to administer the grants."

Mahmud nodded. "Yes, Your Majesty."

Ali, observing from the rear of the hall, strained to hear every nuance and to read the Sultan's expression. What was Ghiasuddin Tughluq leading up to?

"Did you recommend against the grant?" asked the Sultan.

"No, Your Majesty, I—"

"—Then it was with your approval."

"I suppose it could be said so in a way, Your Majesty. However—"

"—The money must be returned to the treasury. You know I'm planning to build a new capital between here and the river. I'll need the funds for that. How do you suggest I recover them?"

"I—I've no idea, Your Majesty. It *is* such a large amount...."

The Sultan sat quietly for a moment. Then he beckoned to his chamberlain, who stepped forward and handed a piece of writing to Mahmud. "Do you recognize this?"

Ali went numb. It couldn't be. Not the letter his father had received from Tughluq months ago, asking for support against Khusrau. The letter that had been shown to Sultan Khusrau as a demonstration of loyalty, and which Khusrau had kept for examination—but had never returned.

"This was found among the usurper's papers," Sultan Ghiasuddin Tughluq said. "How did it get there?"

Mahmud barely hesitated before he replied, "An enemy of mine must have found it, Your Majesty! I worried when I realized it had disappeared—I had intended to destroy it. It must have been stolen by someone spying for Khusrau. I'm mortified, Your Majesty!"

The Sultan looked at him suspiciously. "Perhaps." He appeared to think a moment. "Well, no matter." His eyes fixed on Mahmud. "I've decided I have need of your services in a new capacity, Mahmud Aruzi. You will assist the *qazi* of Delhi in whatever way he requires. Naturally, you will no longer need the rank of *malik*, or its revenue endowments. The rank of *amir* should be sufficient for your new post. You may go."

Ali stifled a gasp. He watched his father stand stiffly for a time. Then Mahmud bowed. He backed away, turned and walked with across the vast chamber, somehow maintaining his dignified demeanor. In seconds, the Sultan had stripped him of his office, his rank, and most of his wealth.

The new position was at roughly the same level as Ali's. It was a rank of respect, but certainly not in comparison to the high status Mahmud had enjoyed for so many years. How, Ali wondered fleetingly, would Mahmud fare with his high ranking friends after such humiliation? Assuming, of course, that they still felt him worthy of notice.

A position in the Sultan's administration was always precarious, but Ali had believed his father to be an expert at survival.

He was relieved to see that despite the immense blow on top of feeling ill, Mahmud managed to stride from the hall as if the Sultan's action had been of no import.

4

Though Ali had not been personally demoted, he naturally was stunned at his father's sudden loss of station, which would so profoundly affect the entire family. While their palanquins bore them home, half of Ali's mind tried to consider the implications, at the same time as the other half worried about Mahmud. His father had not thought to order his musicians into a more appropriate silence, or to tell his six standard bearers that as an *amir* he was now entitled to only three, or his five horsemen that he was now entitled to only two.

When they arrived at their house, Mahmud climbed weakly from his conveyance. Then, seizing control of himself, he strode in past the doorkeepers. Ali followed, trying to maintain his own appearance of composure.

Once in the relative privacy of his quarters, Mahmud slumped and stood with a vacant look in his eyes. Afraid Mahmud might fall, Ali quickly grasped a slender arm to steady him. "Why not sit down, Father?" he urged in a soothing tone. "That fever you've had, on top of everything...."

Mahmud did not reply.

"Father?"

Mahmud sluggishly turned his head to look at his son.

"Let's sit down, Father." Ali gently guided him out to the garden.

They sat on a hard, cold stone bench. "Only an *amir* now," Mahmud said slowly, wonderingly.

"I'm sorry Father."

Mahmud sat slumped over, glassy eyes staring at the neatly raked gravel path. "An *amir*. After so long."

Ali said nothing, but his mind raced, still trying to comprehend the implications of the sudden change.

"How can I give alms now to all those people who rely on me? So many will go hungry now."

"I'm sorry, Father. We'll have to hope that Allah in his mercy will somehow provide another way for them."

"I always tried to an agent of Allah's mercy, you know. But now, I've failed Him."

"We'll still give to some who are in need, Father. Just not so much to so many, unfortunately."

Mahmud fell silent. He looked so pale, so weakened, that after a while, Ali suggested, "Why not rest in your bed for a while, Father?"

Mahmud did not respond. Ali beckoned Ishaq over, and the two urged Mahmud to his feet and then assisted him up to the bedchamber. Mahmud did not object.

Ali sat by his father's bed for a time. Mahmud turned tormented eyes to him and said in a voice heavy with resignation, "I'm getting too old anyway. Otherwise I would never have been so foolish as to leave that letter in the palace for so long."

"There was probably nothing you could have done about it, Father. At worst, it was an oversight, that's all."

Mahmud closed his eyes, and he lay limply on the bed.

Ali sat for a time, watching his father's chest rise and fall. He desperately needed to talk with someone. He knew he should discuss the matter with his wives, and with his father's women also. But should he leave his father at such a time?

He felt certain Mahmud had fallen asleep, so at last, able to sit still no longer, he said in a half whisper, "I'll be out for a time, Father. You can send for me if you need me."

Mahmud gave no sign of hearing.

Ali decided the talk with the women could wait; he didn't feel up to it at the moment. He said to Ishaq, "I'm going to visit the Auliya. Let me know immediately if you think Father would like me back."

When he arrived at the *khanqah*, the saint was resting in private, so Ali sat in distress and waited. He knew the *shaikh* would not mind being interrupted on such a matter, but he could not bring himself to disturb the great man.

Not long after Ali's arrival, Ziauddin Barani appeared. Zia immediately took on a look of sorrow. "*Assalaam aleicum*, peace be with you. I just heard about your father. I thought I might find you here. Can I do anything to help?"

Ali looked away and shook his head. "Nothing I can think of. I'm grateful for your concern."

Zia nodded solemnly and lowered himself to the mud floor. "How is your father taking it?"

Ali shrugged and summoned the strength to say, "As well as one could expect. It was a hard blow."

The poet Amir Khusrau appeared in the doorway. He saw Ali and seemed to hesitate, then he walked over. His elderly face looked saddened. "I've heard about it," he said simply. "Your father was one of my best patrons. Can I help in any way?"

Ali strained to focus his thoughts. Amir Khusrau was the ultimate courtier, who adeptly remained on good terms with virtually everyone—including, undoubtedly, the new Sultan. Should he ask the poet's help in getting his father reinstated?

No, it would be presuming too much to put Khusrau in such an awkward position. Anyway, Sultan Tughluq had known exactly what he was doing and would be highly unlikely to change his mind. "I'm grateful for your kind words," he replied with a doleful smile. "I appreciate your offer, but I think we will manage well enough."

Amir Khusrau slowly shook his head. "Ironic, isn't it, that your own *shaikh* should be involved in an affair that affects you so adversely?"

Ali nodded. "I thought of that. But I think the Sultan intended to remove my father anyway. The grant to our *shaikh* merely furnished an added excuse."

"Possibly." Khusrau sat nearby and fell silent. He naturally would not openly criticize the Sultan's action, for fear one of the ruler's many spies might overhear.

Soon the Auliya appeared, looking refreshed from his rest. "Khusrau!" he said, beaming in delight at his favorite follower. "And Ali Aruzi." His face became more solemn. "I fear I've caused you a great deal of trouble."

Ali prostrated himself before his *pir*, and then sat up. "It would have happened anyway, your honor," he said, resignation in his voice.

"Perhaps." Shaikh Nizamuddin Auliya sat quietly, examining Ali. "Still," he said, "you are troubled. For your father, your family, yourself."

"Yes, sir. I've tried to think of your teachings about the unimportance of material things. I think of how little you yourself eat at your simple meals, of how few goods you require. But I've grown used to so much. It's hard to give any of it up."

The *shaikh* nodded. "You're very attached to your comforts, your status. I've often warned of the precariousness of such positions as your father's. This is one of the reasons I myself avoid the company of Sultans. One moment a man is at the top of the world, the next moment he unknowingly irritates the Sultan and finds himself at the bottom—or worse." He smiled. "Better, perhaps, to have less in the first place, so you have less to lose."

Amir Khusrau said in an attempt to lighten the mood, "Not everyone can be an Auliya, your honor, and be supported by the donations of the faithful!"

"And not everyone can be a famous poet, with *tankas* showering into his lap from all sides!" Shaikh Nizamuddin Auliya again looked at Ali. "Just how serious is your situation?"

Ali hesitated. Then he said, "I'm not yet sure, your honor. One of my father's greatest worries—mine, too, of course—is that so many people who were fed though his alms will likely go hungry now.

The *shaikh* smiled gently. "We have to trust that Allah will provide in another way for all the poor who depended on your family's charity. What about your home? Will you be able to keep it?"

"I think we'll be able to hold onto our house if we sell our other properties. We'll have to get rid of many of our slaves and servants, though. I don't see how my father can keep so many women now. And we won't be able to entertain as before."

"There are thousands of people eating the food from our kitchen who would still greatly envy you."

"I know, sir." He strained to put on a slight smile. "I try to remind myself of this."

Shaikh Nizamuddin Auliya looked at Ali with tolerant understanding. "You are one of my most promising disciples. Already you have the humility that I must work so hard to instill in most of my followers. And you have that sense of fairness and generosity that makes everyone eager to go to your court to obtain justice." The Auliya was rising to his feet. "Time for my prayers at the mosque." He again smiled gently at Ali. "I will pray for you. Don't hesitate to talk with me whenever you feel the need—whether day or night."

Ali felt a warm glow at the *shaikh's* generous offer. This great man who had consistently refused to talk with any Sultan had freely offered to help him, Ali, at any hour. In the reassuring comfort of the saint's presence, Ali's problems already seemed less urgent.

What little free time he now had, Ali spent at the *khanqah* of Shaikh Nizamuddin Auliya. He needed the tranquility, the atmosphere of spirituality, to balance the solemnity that had fallen over his household.

"How is your father's health?" asked Zia quietly some weeks later as they awaited the saint's appearance.

Coming from most men, such an inquiry would be merely an expected ritual courtesy. But Ali could tell Zia was sincerely concerned. "He seems to be taking it surprisingly well," he replied. "Fortunately he's over that fever and is able to oversee selling some properties. The hardest part is having to cut back so much on his donations and dismiss so many servants. I've been working with him on it all."

Zia sighed. "A difficult situation."

"I'm grateful for Halima—at least I never have to worry myself with the day to day details of running our household. She's marvelous at keeping the servants in line."

"But you often look so serious now. Why not come to my Kilukhari house tonight for some fun? I have a new slave girl from Samarkand. She's *almost* a virgin. Might be just what you need."

Ali gave a wry smile. "I fear I don't have much time for frivolous pursuits."

Zia gave a mock sigh. "You've never been much given to them, anyway. Despite my efforts to lead you astray."

Ali laughed lightly. "I suppose not. Still, I do miss the parties my father gave, and access to the court gossip." He hesitated, and added, "I'm glad we're still friends. So many others don't think I'm worthy of notice, now that I don't have a father in a high position."

Zia raised his eyebrows in seemingly genuine surprise. "How could I not continue our friendship? You are one of the few persons I truly trust and admire! Everyone else is like me—interested only in what advances their rank or wealth or pleasure!"

"You aren't solely interested in those. And I doubt I'm really worthy of anyone's admiration. But I'm still glad of your friendship. And," he grinned, "not solely because one day your chronicles about our Sultans will make you famous."

Zia groaned and shook his head. "I hope my future greatness doesn't depend only on my writings. But I certainly am making no progress in being noticed by Sultan Tughluq!"

Ali became worried when the *shaikh*, also, faced a crisis. The Sultan summoned the saint before a tribunal to defend the Sufi's *sama*, or music recitals, against charges by numerous orthodox members of the *ulema* that the sessions violated religious law.

The Sultan's son and heir to the throne—formerly Malik Fakhruddin Jauna, but now given the title of Ulugh Khan, or "Great Khan" by his father—still considered himself a disciple of the Auliya. However, the prince's visits to the *khanqah* were now rare, at least in part because he spent many months leading military campaigns for his father. Before Shaikh Nizamuddin Auliya's appearance at the palace, Ali asked his *pir*, "Sir, do you think Ulugh Khan might intercede with the Sultan on your behalf?"

Shaikh Nizamuddin Auliya dismissed the thought with a light wave of his hand. "The matter is of little importance. Ulugh Khan has many more pressing concerns. I'm quite willing to leave the judgment in Allah's hands, praise be to His name."

To Ali, it was unthinkable that the crown prince would not actively do everything possible on behalf of his *pir*. But then, Ali had never felt quite comfortable with the prince's manner of thinking. Many of Ulugh Khan's conceptions were brilliant, but it seemed to Ali the ideas often lacked practicality. Sometimes they were so abstract as to be almost incomprehensible to anyone else. He could not help but wonder what kind of a Sultan the Ulugh Khan might one day be.

Another aspect of the coming tribunal bothered Ali. "*Pir*," he said, "I've often wondered why so many of the *ulema* continue to insist the holy laws condemn our music recitals. You've taught that the Qur'an doesn't condemn music or dancing—that music can be either good or bad, depending on how it is used."

The saint replied with a sad smile, "In large part, the charges are wishful thinking by those who prefer to live a joyless existence. They get their satisfaction from adhering to severe rules. The stricter the rules, the more virtuous these persons feel. Hence, the more they think Allah will exalt them over their fellow men."

"It seems the exact opposite of the humility you yourself teach, sir."

"Perhaps. But it is not our place to judge these men—that is God's prerogative. I know only that Allah, praise to Him, could not possibly object to the feeling of ecstasy, of closeness to Him, that I get from the music of our poet Khusrau and others at our *samas*."

Ali thought of the most recent *sama* he himself had attended, only two nights previously. Amir Khusrau had sung one of his Persian compositions in praise of God:

> *Oh thou, beyond all comprehension*
> > *How can my thoughts ever reach to Thee?*
> *Or my vain intellect understand*
> > *Thy attribute or quality?*

> *And over the great creation stands*
> > *The spaceless pillar of Thy might.*
> *My soul a feeble, wingless bird,*
> > *How shall it climb that endless height?*

Ali, like the other listeners, had been caught up in the rhythm and flow of Khusrau's voice. As the poet continued from verse to verse into the lateness of the night, the hypnotic quality of the sound had transported Ali into an experience of exaltation, of blissfulness, in which he had felt closer to God than at any other time he could remember.

> *A thousand martyrs like Hussain*
> > *Have perished in the endless strife,*
> *Yet human lips have never touched*
> > *Thy water of eternal life.*

> *And day and night Thy light doth shine*
> > *Upon the throne of human heart,*
> *Although our intellect never can*
> > *Thy vision to our eyes impart.*

> *To earnest, humble pilgrims come*
> > *The words of mercy from Thy seat;*
> *Khusrau, to idol-worship given,*
> > *Can but Thy outward symbols greet.*

Ali had sat and watched as many of the listeners formed a circle and danced around the room for hours, swaying their bodies to the rhythms, their faces lit with an ecstatic glow, until they had at last collapsed in exhaustion.

Like Khusrau, Amir Hasan and other singers possessed this ability to capture their Sufi audiences and bring the followers nearer to Allah. To participate in such a *sama* was to transcend the material world and be elevated to the pure realms of the spirit. Ali did not see how such sincere worship of the divine could possibly be ruled immoral.

He felt both gratified and vindicated when, several days later, with the help of a prominent visiting religious scholar, Shaikh Nizamuddin Auliya successfully defended his practices against a conclave of several hundred conservative theologians. The Sultan dismissed the charges, but everyone knew that most members of the *ulema* were still far from satisfied.

Ali's own father, always orthodox in his beliefs, had become even more strict in his personal life, devoting more time to prayer and fasting. One day, he told Ali, "The Qur'an says, 'Nothing will befall us except what Allah has ordained.' I think I must have failed God, and he punished me for it."

"What ever do you mean, Father?"

"It was my duty as chief *sadr* to enforce the laws of Islam. I failed to do so, and God removed me."

"But Father! One reason you were in office so many years was that you performed your duties so well. Everyone thought so."

Mahmud sadly shook his head. "Not the *ulema*. The *imams* were always urging me to bring the Sufis to trial for their heresies and the dancing and singing parties, yet I gave funds to them. And I knew I violated the *sharia* myself when I served wine at my parties."

"Father, God is loving; he's not interested only in punishing. You know that Sufis' dancing is only a way of getting closer to God. By including Sufis when you allocated funds, you included those who worship through love, in addition to those who worship mainly by observing the laws. That's exactly what Allah must want."

Mahmud sighed. "Maybe you're right. But if so, why did Allah bring about my removal?"

Ali said, "I don't know Father. It might have been to make us feel more humble, to help us see we aren't really so far away from any of the beggars we give alms to."

Mahmud thought for a time. Eventually he said, "That's possible. I must pray on the matter some more."

The next four years of Sultan Ghiasuddin Tughluq's reign passed with relative quiet in the household of Ali and his father. But Shaikh Nizamuddin Auliya's health began to decline, slowly at first, then gradually accelerating. Where he had formerly walked the distance to the Kilukhari mosque every day for his afternoon prayers, the saint began riding a mare. After some months, mounting the horse came to require too much effort, and the saint was forced by his ever-diminishing strength to allow himself to be carried in a palanquin.

Eventually, to the consternation of Ali and the multitude of other followers, the Auliya became so weak that he could do nothing beyond lying in his bed. Ali, whose official duties required only a few hours each day, divided most of the remainder of his time between attending the bed of Shaikh Nizamuddin Auliya and keeping his own father company.

Unexpectedly, after ruling five years, Sultan Ghiasuddin Tughluq was killed in the collapse of a wooden pavilion constructed by his son, Ulugh Khan, who had earlier been known as Malik Jauna by Ali and Zia. Some suspected the accident had been planned by Ulugh Khan, who was perhaps impatient to succeed to the throne. In any event, Ulugh Khan immediately became Sultan Muhammad bin Tughluq.

As an *amir*, Ali felt compelled to join the other nobles in the funeral procession for Ghiasuddin Tughluq. The former Sultan's body had been brought from the site of his death at Afghanpur, several miles to the southeast, to the palace within the massive stone walls of the newly built fortress of Tughluqabad.

Like the other mourning nobles, Ali wore a torn robe. Like the others, he walked barefoot and periodically bent to the roadway to take dust which he tossed on top of his head. But he found it impossible to feel true sorrow at the death of the harsh old man who had demoted Mahmud Aruzi and consistently opposed Shaikh Nizamuddin Auliya.

The day was unusually cool and overcast even for winter. Ali's tender soles were unused to walking so far unshod. Even though the cobblestones had been thoroughly swept clear of small rocks and other debris, the paving felt icy. So he was glad the procession had a relatively short distance to walk: out the southern gate of the fortress, and over the causeway to the site of the tomb in the center of the lake.

The mausoleum was appropriate for a warrior king such as Tughluq—a tiny island castle, its grey walls matching those of the nearby fortress city and the dark mood of the lake and sky. Ali was far enough back in the procession that the site was already crowded when he arrived; there was barely room for him within the gate. Even if he had wished to do so it would have been almost impossible in the crush of bodies to approach the sepulcher itself, a small building with slanting walls of red sandstone and white marble, crowned by a glistening white marble dome. Ali could not see the actual interment, and he could barely hear the recitals of the *Fatihya*, the first book of the Qur'an.

Ziauddin Barani, since he lacked an official appointment, was even further back in the procession. But afterwards, as the mourners dispersed after returning over the causeway and reclaiming their shoes, he spotted Ali and joined him. They walked northwesterly along the base of the fortress walls to where their conveyances waited. A misty rain had begun to fall, and Ali's expression was glum, as befitted the setting and the occasion. Zia, however, could scarcely contain his exuberance. He immediately exclaimed to Ali in a whisper, "We now have a Sultan who knows us personally! Our own advancement is much more likely!"

Ali glanced about to ensure no one in the crowd could over-hear. "I have reservations about that possibility," he replied in a low voice. "He can be generous to his friends. But his temper's quick. I wouldn't like to be an official who unknowingly offended him."

"I'll take my chances," said Zia. "He's an enjoyable compan-ion—a brilliant conversationalist on almost any topic. What he needs are good advisors. I wouldn't mind being one!"

Ali managed a smile. "Then I wish you well. You've waited a long time."

5

At the age of ninety-five, Shaikh Nizamuddin Auliya died. Ali assisted in the burial rites and even had the honor of helping carry the saint's bier for a short distance on the way to the tomb.

Amir Khusrau was away from Delhi at the time and learned about his *pir's* death upon returning. The heartbroken Khusrau himself died only a few month's later. As both the saint and the poet had wished, Amir Khusrau was bur-ied adjacent to the tomb of the Auliya.

The *shaikh* had desig-nated another Sufi saint, Maulana Nasruddin, as his suc-cessor. Nasruddin and other lead-ing disciples continued to oper-ate the *khanqah*. But it had been the glowing personality of Shaikh Nizamuddin Auliya himself which had attracted Ali, who con-

Shaikh Nizamuddin Auliya's Tomb

tinued to feel a profound sense of loss. He now spent less time at the *khanqah* and more at home with his father and the rest of the family.

Halima and Ayesha both were clearly pleased to have more of his attention. Halima, who was easily capable of running their part of the household on her own, consulted him more and more often. She somehow, without causing him to grow annoyed, drew him into the details of purchasing food and disciplining servants and paying wages. One evening, he realized he had not thought about the *shaikh* all day, not even at prayer times.

"Your distracting me is working," he told her with a smile as he sat at the edge of her bed."

"Whatever do you mean?" she asked, the corners of her mouth twitching, and her eyes bright and warm. "You know I'm always glad to have you with me and to have you ease my work."

"But you can get along fine on you own. You're deliberately

helping me get involved with household matters so I'll forget how much I miss my *shaikh* and not think about how much our family's fortunes have fallen."

She smiled impishly. "And has it worked?"

"You know it has."

She drew him to her and murmured in his ear, "Then show me some appreciation."

He did.

The months passed, and Ziauddin Barani did not receive his hoped-for appointment from the new Sultan. "I don't understand," Zia told Ali late one evening as they rode together in Ali's carriage to the *khanqah* for a *sama* celebration. "I've sent him presents, even asked for an audience. But it's as if he'd never known me. And my family is just as noble as his own!"

Ali shrugged, though it was doubtful Zia could see the gesture in the darkness. "Who knows what goes on in the mind of a Sultan? Better take the advice of our *pir*—stay as far away from him as possible. You have all you need. Wealth, friends in high places, prestige enough. Why risk it all?"

"Because the Sultan's court determines the course of our world! I want to be at the very center of it!"

The carriage wheels jolted over some obstacle in the dark road, causing the two men to grab for balance. When the more normal smooth creaking sound resumed, Ali replied, "Yet, you also followed the Auliya. What did you make of his constantly telling us that worldly power is unimportant?"

Zia said, "I know he said all those things. But it was his strictness in fasts and prayers and constantly reading the Qur'an that attracted me to him. And, of course, his own prestige."

Ali slowly shook his head. "My friend, you've missed the entire core of his teaching. You're looking only at the outside appearances of his worship. It was love that he really taught. Love of God, but just as importantly, love of other men."

Zia laughed lightly. "Maybe. But love doesn't purchase me a high appointment."

After a short silence, Ali asked, "What do you think of our Sultan's scheme for moving the capital to Devagiri?"

Zia was quiet a moment before answering, "The territories in the south can be administered more easily from a capital in the Deccan. Devagiri's more centrally located than Delhi. It's also not so easy for the Mongols to attack."

"If you were attached to the Sultan's court, you'd have to move there with him. It's seven hundred miles south!"

Again there was a short silence before Zia replied, "Delhi is a truly great city. Naturally I'd prefer to stay here. But the center of the empire follows the Sultan. I'd gladly go wherever he does."

Ali shook his head in amusement. "You're welcome to it. Personally, absolutely nothing would influence me to move so far away."

Sultan Muhammad bin Tughluq continued with his scheme for another capital in the south. In the pleasant weather of winter, Muhammad bin Tughluq himself moved with his court to the new capital, which he renamed Daulatabad.

Ali discussed the matter with his father in the garden on a fine, sunny day. "The Sultan seems to assume the nobility won't mind such a move," Ali said. "That's probably true for some of those officials directly attached to the court, who are used to following the Sultan in tents wherever he travels. But most of the nobles hate the idea of leaving the homes of their ancestors, just as we would. And the very thought of giving up Delhi for a town that hasn't yet been built, in a strange region!"

Mahmud had grown thinner and more fragile, and though he still followed events at the court, he was far less involved with them. "In a way, then," Mahmud said after a time, in his hoarse voice, "maybe it's as well that I lost my position at court. Otherwise, I might be expected to move, too. Then you'd have to decide whether to come or stay here."

Ali sighed. "So maybe Allah was looking out for us after all. Although it didn't seem that way." His gaze moved about the garden. With the reduced staff, it was not so neatly kept as previously. Leaves that had fallen from the trees the previous day had not yet been removed from the watercourse or from the paths. At one time Mahmud would not have tolerated the gardeners being so lax.

"About the only good thing I can say about the move," said Ali, "is that the Sultan has planned every detail. He's ordered shade trees to be planted and wells dug along the entire length of the route between here and Daulatabad. And he's allocated huge sums of money to purchase the Delhi homes of those who are to go with him, so they'll be able to build new houses as soon as they reach there."

"I suppose that's some consolation," said Mahmud.

"A little. But it wouldn't be enough for me. I want to live *here* the rest of *my* life."

To the great annoyance of the Sultan, most of the nobility felt as did Ali, and they did not even deign to consider the possibility of such a major relocation.

The infuriated Tughluq issued a sweeping command directing that all nobles and officials above the lowest clerical levels move to Daulatabad at once.

As soon as he heard of it, Ali hurried to speak of the matter to Mahmud in the garden where they spent so much of their time: "The order clearly includes both of us, as *amirs*! How can it be?"

Mahmud slowly shook his head, tiredly. "This Sultan is as

arbitrary as his father was. Maybe worse."

"And the hot season is coming! The journey takes months. The last part of it will be when the heat's at its worst! Can you imagine women, children, old people traveling in the Deccan at such a time?"

Mahmud again shook his head. "Not good. Not at all good."

"But what shall we do, Father? The Sultan's order includes *us*!"

Mahmud's eyes again took on the sad look that had become so familiar. "I fear you have no choice but to go to Daulatabad," he murmured in a voice so quiet Ali could barely hear. "It doesn't pay to irritate a Sultan."

"This is my home, Father! With you! And I love our house!" Ali gazed at the water course and the orchard. Even with inadequate funds for maintenance, it was far more attractive than some raw, dusty place in the Deccan could be.

Mahmud said, "I'm too old to go, even if the order includes me too. I'll chance staying here. I have little more to lose. But you must leave. You may even have an opportunity to rise to a post as high as my own former one."

Ali shook his head. "I wouldn't want to, Father. It's too precarious. Anyway, I've decided. Delhi is my home. With you and the tomb of my *pir*. I intend to stay."

Ziauddin Barani missed the mandate to relocate, as he was away for an extended time while he accompanied one of the *khans* on a military campaign. Many of Ali's other acquaintances felt they had no choice but to obey the order. Once a week for the following three weeks an official caravan left Delhi for Daulatabad, each containing thousands of people including the nobles' families, servants, and slaves, and their belongings.

However, it quickly became obvious that many men felt just as did Ali, and that they had no intention of leaving Delhi. The Sultan's officers in charge of the move decided they had no choice—the Sultan had issued a command. If it were not obeyed willingly, then force must be used to ensure compliance. Early on a morning a month after the Sultan's order had first reached Delhi, a squad of ten soldiers appeared at the entrance to the Aruzi house.

The young *sar-i-khail* who led the unit wore the usual officer's belted gold-embroidered gown and a turban folded to form four corners. He dismounted from his horse. With no further courtesies after the "*Assalaam aleicum*," he told Ali apologetically, "His Majesty Sultan Muhammad bin Tughluq has commanded that the Amirs Mahmud Aruzi and Ali Surajuddin Aruzi move at once to Daulatabad. I am charged with enforcing that command." He stiffened and said more firmly, "I can give you until midday to vacate your house, sir. The caravan to which you've been assigned leaves at first light tomorrow, so you will have to spend the night at the departure point outside the

Mandu Gate."

Ali's mouth had dropped open; his eyes were wide with dismay. At last he managed, "By midday? That's absurd. How do you expect us to ready our entire household in a few hours?"

"We have our orders, sir. That's more time than many men have been given. You were allowed more because you have so many persons to move."

"What happens to our house?" asked Ali in outrage.

"I assumed you knew, sir. The Sultan has authorized fair compensation, to be paid upon your arrival in Daulatabad."

"This house was built by my grandfather!" Ali moved aggressively toward the officer.

The man retreated a step, then stood firmly. "I'm sorry, sir. I have no choice."

"It takes funds to travel! We'd have to buy more vehicles. We have only a few palanquins, some horses, three carriages—and one of those needs repair before its usable."

The officer said quietly, "The question has arisen before, sir. Our instructions are that those who do not have conveyances must walk."

"Walk! Almost four hundred *kroh*?" Ali shouted.

The officer took another step toward the street. "Sir, I'm informed the Sultan feels he gave adequate advance notice. Those who did not heed it are not in a position to complain. And now, sir, I must notify the others on my list, who'll have even less warning than you. I'll return at midday to ensure compliance with the order."

Ali stood staring as the officer remounted and led his men at a gallop down the street. After a time, he turned and looked into the interior of the house. Disobeying such a direct order appeared impossible. He must resign himself to leaving. And of course his own wives and slaves must come with him. But what about the rest of the household? His father? Where to begin, with so much to do in such a short time?

He shouted for Ishaq, who would spread the word to Halima and the others in the house. Then he went to the garden, where he knew he would find his father.

Mahmud showed no emotion when Ali informed him. "I told you before that you must go," Mahmud said. "But I will stay."

"I can't leave you alone, Father. And you were specifically named on the Sultan's list."

Mahmud shook his head. "What can they do to me? I'm an old man now. Anyone can see traveling so far would be hard for me."

"In that case, I won't go either. I can't live seven hundred miles from you." He doubted that if he left on such a long journey he would ever see his father again. Mahmud could not have many more years to live.

Mahmud gave Ali a strained but loving smile. "I'll miss you, of course, son. *Inshallah,* the Sultan will realize his mistake and rescind the order. But you shouldn't endanger yourself now by staying. I have plenty of servants and women to take care of me. And not all the doctors will move to Daulatabad."

Ali hesitated, feeling the press of time. He said finally, "Then you must hide, Father. If they find you here, they'll force you to go."

Mahmud said placidly, "I'll stay where I am. If it's Allah's will that I remain, the soldiers won't remove me."

Ali stared at his father for a time, and then looked at the house. It was an impossible situation. He must not go, and yet he must.

He reluctantly decided he should at least make a quick check of the preparations being made for the move. He could try to reach a more definite conclusion while he did so.

The household was in chaos. Servants had begun loading belongings into the carriages, only to be told by their supervisors to remove them to leave room for the women, too. The matter was complicated by the fact that if Mahmud should be forced to go, his own women would also come.

Halima was calmly but urgently directing the servants attached to Ali's portion of the household. Ayesha wanted to take her parrot, Gulam, and was trying to put the cage into a carriage. "You can see there's no room," Halima said patiently. "We can't take any of the other animals, you know."

Ayesha burst into tears. "But I love him!"

Several servants were standing with other items requiring decisions. "Take him!" said Halima. "If anyone questions it, he's a member of the family."

Ayesha brightened.

Ali gave Halima a grateful nod as he hurried past.

He knew from helping oversee the accounts that there was little silver or gold remaining, maybe not enough to last until the end of a long journey. Ishaq had run off to hire additional palanquin bearers. He now reported that he had been unable to find any willing to undertake such a long journey, especially on such short notice. The household itself had enough bearers for only one palanquin, since they must have at least two shifts to spell each other off.

"If my father comes, he'll have the palanquin," Ali said. "I'll ride my horse. You and anyone else who can ride may use the other three horses. The older women must have the carriages. Everyone else will have to walk—or else stay behind." He thought a moment, then added, "I'll free any slaves who decide to stay and give the servants who remain an extra payment." Even as he spoke, every part of him resisted the idea of going.

Ishaq hesitated, then nodded and left to make the arrangements.

Ali's thoughts churned turbulently. Shortly after the midday prayers the soldiers returned. The vehicles were loaded, but Halima and Ayesha and the other women were still trying to determine what to leave and what to take.

"We can't allow more time," the officer told Ali. "You must all come now. Is your father also ready to leave?"

Ali said firmly, "None of us is going. I'll stay here and appeal to the Sultan." He was sure he would be taken into custody, but he simply could not leave.

The officer took on a look of exasperation. "Sir, I thought I made the command clear. I have orders to put you in the caravan—willing or not. And your father."

Ali said desperately, "My father isn't well! He'll come as soon as he feels better. But it could kill him to travel now."

"Sir, there are no exceptions to the Sultan's edict. Even for illness. Your father must come. *Now.* I'm sure there will be physicians in the caravan."

"The Sultan wants him in Daulatabad *alive!*" Ali shouted. "What good will it do if he dies along the way?"

The officer turned and said to two of his men, "Find the elder *amir*. Help him if he needs it, but he must come at once."

So they brought Mahmud, who did not resist. His face was drained and expressionless.

On the way through the streets to the Mandu Gate, Ali saw two of the lepers who had long relied on his and his father's daily alms-giving. The beggars watched him leave with questioning, confused looks in their eyes. How would they, and the many other regular supplicants, now feed themselves?

The hastily assembled caravan had been ill-organized for so many people, especially nobles used to comfort, and for their women who had seldom seen the outside of the harem walls. At first, Ali and the other nobles complained vociferously to each other, but resistance was useless in the face of the armed soldiers who accompanied the caravan both to enforce the move and to guard the travelers from any dangers.

They had not gone far on the first day when it became obvious they were headed away from Delhi southwesterly on the Ajmer road, not on the main trunk highway that went almost due south through Agra. In response to puzzled inquiries, the migrants were informed that the previous huge caravans to Daulatabad had stripped the more direct route of fodder and food. The change in route meant the journey would take longer, but it should be easier to obtain provisions along the way.

The caravan halted briefly for prayer at the prescribed times, as well as for meals. Of the Aruzi wives, Halima took everything with calm acceptance, but the others objected indignantly at every opportunity. At camp that first night along the road, inside the tent, Ayesha said, "There's scarcely any water. How am I supposed to bathe? And this tent! It's so small and hot!"

"We can't do anything about it," said Ali. "I think you should try to get used to it."

"How can they do this to us?" shrieked Ayesha, stroking her parrot.

Ali, weary, sweaty, and dusty himself, did not bother to answer.

Halima said, "We'll manage. Others have."

"And we have to wear our *chadars* and veils all the time," said Ayesha. "It's so hot in them."

"Again," said Ali, "I think you had better get used to it." Unlike in the women's quarters of the house, here the women had to go veiled to protect themselves from being seen by strange men.

He left the tent and summoned Ishaq. "Is there any way we can get more water?"

"All the wells nearby have been drained dry, Master. And servants are waiting to take any water as soon as there's enough to get some in their buckets. I've made sure we always have servants there, too."

"No rivers nearby, then?"

"Not with any water in them, Master."

"Then it seems we're doing all we can."

"Yes, Master."

Ali returned to the tent. He doubted he would sleep much that night despite his exhaustion.

By the end of the following day of travel, sheer weariness diminished the complaints to less frequent, quiet mutters.

The family took its evening meal in the darkness, with only a single oil lamp for illumination. "You need to check on your father," Halima whispered to Ali after they had eaten. "I've heard he's been giving most of his water to others, saying they need it worse than he does."

Ali sighed. "That does sound like something he'd do. I'll go to him." He went through the dimness to where Mahmud was lying on a string-webbed cot. He squatted next to the bed and asked quietly, "Father, are you drinking enough water?"

"Oh, yes." Mahmud's voice was weak.

"I've heard you've been giving some to others. But you need it yourself. With all this dust and the strains of traveling, you should do everything you can to help stay well."

For a few seconds, Mahmud was still. Then he said, his voice an unsteady, hoarse whisper, "Allah will keep me well if he wishes. We should be generous to others who need more than ourselves."

"You've always been generous, Father. But I worry when you I hear you aren't drinking enough."

"No need to worry. I think Allah's plans for me don't include finishing this journey anyway."

"Father, please don't talk that way! We'll need you in Daulatabad."

"I'd like to sleep now," came the raspy murmur, trailing off to nothing.

"Yes, Father," Ali whispered. He remained a short while, then went to his own bed.

Each day grew successively hotter as the season progressed. The dust generated by the caravan covered everyone and everything. It choked throats and plugged nostrils. Before the caravan even reached Ajmer people began falling—and dying—from exhaustion, heat, thirst, sometimes hunger. Even Ishaq and many of the other slaves and servants were unused to so much walking.

Ali continued to urge his father to drink plenty of water. Mahmud would appear to comply if Ali were with him, but he would refuse both water and food whenever Ali wasn't present.

Among the travelers in the caravan were the poet Amir Hasan and two of Shaikh Nizamuddin Auliya's most prominent disciples, Shaikh Fakhruddin Zarradi and Shaikh Burhanuddin Gharib. Amir Hasan had anticipated the move and readied his household for it, so it was not quite so burdensome to him in spite of his advanced age. The two Sufi saints were ascetics who were used to living with few material goods; although weary, they seemed less affected by the move than most, and they spent much of their time assisting the other travelers in whatever way they could.

Ali had often noticed Shaikh Burhanuddin Gharib back at the *khanqah*. The *shaikh* was a scholarly man of about fifty years in age, with kindly though sorrowful appearing eyes. He had quietly gone about overseeing much of the work that needed to be done at the *khanqah* and counseling persons in need, but he usually remained in the background. Now, although the saint was no doubt as fatigued as everyone else from the unaccustomed travel, Ali saw him helping older persons who needed aid in walking, or comforting those who were ill, or ensuring people who ran out of food were fed.

Ajmer was left behind, and the caravan traveled parallel to the foothills of the Aravalli mountains. Not far from the town of Mangarh, almost in sight of the elephant cliff landmark and the fortress, Mahmud Aruzi died.

Ali had examined his father at a rest halt, and he seemed to be asleep in his palanquin. The next time Ali checked, Mahmud was dead.

Ali blinked away his own tears and shoved aside his grief while he did his best to console his father's wailing wives and other women, some of whom seemed most distressed over not having brought along any garments of blue, the color of mourning. He was granted permission for the household and the family's friends to lag behind the rest of the caravan until after the important third day rites.

Shaikh Burhanuddin Gharib approached as Ali was looking about for a grave site near the dusty road. "*Assalaam aleicum.* A difficult time," said the *shaikh*, his eyes even more mournful than usual. "Your father was always such a man of integrity. I'm sure Allah will have a special place for him in paradise."

"Yes," replied Ali. "But I'd also like to find a suitable spot for his temporary earthly home, much as I hate to have to leave him here. This is so remote from Delhi!"

The saint nodded, his eyes soft with sympathy.

"I wish the Sultan were here," said Ali bitterly, "to see for himself what he's done."

After a time, the *shaikh* said, "Allah must have a reason for allowing it, difficult though it is for you."

Ali frowned. "Maybe," he said doubtfully. Eventually, he asserted, "I still must find a grave site for now. Possibly under that mango tree? It's isolated enough, I should think no one should object to a grave beneath it."

The *shaikh* walked over to the shade of the tree and stood silently for a time. The mango tree would normally be heavy with fruit in this season, but the many people of the caravan had even stripped it of most of its lower leaves. "Yes," the saint said at last. This place has the right feel about it."

Ali said, "Naturally, I hope to rebury my Father in a fine tomb in Delhi when I return there, *inshallah.* But I have no choice but to leave him here for now."

"Indeed," said Shaikh Burhanuddin Gharib. "However, you may eventually find there is no need to remove your father to Delhi after all. I think this site is one that will house him well through the ages until the Day of Judgment."

Ali resisted such a thought, but gave the necessary orders for the burial. Under Ishaq's direction, slaves dug a grave in the rocky, dust-strewn soil. Ali purchased small rock slabs from a local stonecutter, and he had the grave lined and capped with them, and a temporary marker installed. He supervised the interment, and everyone then gathered and listened to the reading from the Qur'an.

Servants went into Mangarh and returned with jasmine blossoms to sprinkle over the grave and orange branches and fruits to place upon it. On the morning of the third day after Mahmud's death, the household and friends again assembled around the burial site. The mourners seated themselves upon carpets and cloths spread on the ground. The men recited from the Qur'an, and then the *imam* read an elegy and prayed for Allah's blessings on the departed spirit.

While the mourners prepared to resume their journey and overtake the rest of the caravan, Ali lagged behind to bid farewell. He slowly reached high up and picked a single, dust-covered leaf from the tree to take with him. Mahmud had been a loving father, and in many ways a great man. If he had died in Delhi, especially when the family's fortunes were at their height, Mahmud would have been buried beneath a fine structure with a lovely dome atop it.

As he stepped from beneath the tree into the sun's hot blast, Ali felt an intense fury at the Sultan who had been responsible. How, he wondered, could Muhammad bin Tughluq expect an efficient administration if his officials were men such as himself who now hated their ruler and who did not even want to be in the new capital?

"Perhaps," said Shaikh Burhanuddin Gharib, who had quietly come near, "you can return some day and build a tomb here befitting your father."

"A tomb here?" asked Ali, looking once more at the tree and the grave beneath it.

"Why not? In Delhi, a tomb would be only one of many monuments. Here, it would be noticed by everyone who passed, and an important landmark for travelers and local residents alike." The *shaikh* added more solemnly, "Many people might pause here to meditate and pray."

"Possibly," said Ali after a time, impressed by the saint's words, but far from convinced he wanted to leave his father's remains in such a remote location.

With the hot season at its most unbearable, the caravan traveled mainly at night and halted during the hours when the sun was at its most intense. Still the journey was miserable and seemingly interminable.

Ali withdrew into a world of numbness. Almost all that had been dear to him had been taken. He still had Halima and Ayesha and his concubines, but now, when they and he were perpetually hot, sweat drenched, and dirty, weary to the point of exhaustion, they could not even be a source of sensual solace. Although Halima did her best to keep the women organized and cooperative with one another, their well-being was a constant worry to him.

Shaikh Burhanuddin Gharib greeted Ali every day and regularly walked with him a short time. But the saint waited until Ali himself was ready to engage in conversation about the ordeals that had befallen the Aruzi family.

"How can Allah permit rulers to treat their people in such a way?" asked Ali on a day two weeks after his father's death, after the caravan had halted for the night prayers.

"The Sultan himself must eventually submit himself to be judged, just as must the most humble of his people," said the *shaikh* calmly. "And I think the laws by which he will be judged will be quite strict."

Ali thought about this. "So much misery," he said, gesturing at the other travelers. "And it seems so unnecessary."

"Some of us are given heavier burdens than others," acknowledged the *shaikh*. "I think we can only submit to whatever is God's will, and help as best we can to give courage and support to each other in bearing those burdens."

Ali nodded, not yet entirely satisfied, but comforted in a small way by the serene assurance of the saint.

The travelers set out once more, in the manner that had become routine, and which was to be repeated again and again. Long day after long day of heat and dust. Week after week.

At last, the caravan crept over the crest of a range of stony hills, and through the distortion of overheated air the travelers saw a distant, massive, cone-shaped rock on the horizon: the fortress of Daulatabad. Except for Mahmud, Ali's entire family and entourage, and even Ayesha's parrot, had survived the journey.

As they approached, a layer of smoke from the many cooking fires hung low over the plain, mixing with the haze of stirred-up dust. The sounds of hammering and sawing came from the many construction sites. A line of creaking bullock carts carrying stone blocks crossed their path.

Ali was surprised to find a well-organized reception for the huge mass of arrivals. An official immediately took him and his household to temporary lodgings in a tent city on the outskirts of the town. Another official promptly paid Ali compensation for the Delhi mansion in an amount which was almost a fair one for the value of the property. Yet another agent provided Ali with a large plot of land on the southern fringe of the new city on which to build a house. Still another official provided him with an order from the Sultan detailing him to duties similar to those of his old magistrate's position in Delhi.

With so much new building underway, Ali at first found it impossible to hire workmen. Gradually, carpenters and masons and stonecarvers arrived from other regions in response to word that a large amount of work was available, and Ali made his arrangements. But construction proceeded slowly due to the shortage of sufficient building materials in a time of such unprecedented demand.

Frequently, dust from the construction areas blew into the temporary tent housing, emphasizing that this land was not yet ready to be called home. Except for Halima, the women complained constantly at first, but they eventually realized there was little that could be done, and the complaints turned into frequent but minor arguments and bickering. Despite Halima's efforts to find ways to lighten his spirit, Ali performed his duties, both public and private, with the joylessness of a slave who had been sold into captivity in a foreign country.

For two years Sultan Muhammad bin Tughluq shuttled back and forth between Daulatabad and Delhi, in effect considering himself as having dual capitals. Then, when he again moved his court to Delhi, he did not return to Daulatabad.

The ruler had found that it took more than a Sultan's wishes to make a new capital. His administration suffered from so many of the nobles doing their jobs sullenly, having never resigned themselves to life permanently away from Delhi. Communications with the rich northern portion of the empire and with the culturally important Islamic countries to the west were more difficult from the Deccan.

Although he did not openly announce the fact, in effect the Sultan quietly abandoned his idea of a capital in the south. But he made no provision for those nobles not attached to his court to return to Delhi, and he did not cancel his order commanding them to reside in Daulatabad.

Almost a year after the Sultan's departure, Ali and his dependents moved into the new house. No trees or shrubs graced the stark garden. The town itself had a raw, new look. And outside the walls of the surrounding fortifications, the vast, sparsely populated Deccan plateau seemed a strange land, with little to offer a former resident of a great city.

6

Seven years later Sultan Muhammad bin Tughluq returned to Daulatabad to levy troops and supplies before proceeding onward to suppress a revolt in the province of Ma'bar. Accompanying him was a recently appointed courtier, Ziauddin Barani. Ali immediately extended an invitation for his old friend to visit.

The two embraced enthusiastically when Ali met Zia at the door. Then, they stepped apart and examined each other. Ali saw that Zia was heavier, but otherwise he appeared much the same. "So you finally got your appointment from the Sultan," said Ali.

Zia smiled broadly, his eyes even more energetically piercing than before. "It took ten years. But I'm now one of his closest companions. I go with him everywhere." Except for his manservant who accompanied him inside, his entourage waited outdoors while Ali led him through the house to the inner courtyard. Zia glanced about. "You seem quite adapted to life here."

They stood under the arches overlooking the garden. "I planted that mango tree myself," Ali said. "And the orange trees. They're not large yet, but the fruit's delicious."

The night was cool, so rather than remaining outdoors they went into the modest banquet room. Ali sent for his three small sons—all by Halima—and proudly introduced them to Zia: "Mahmud, my eldest. Next is Hasan. And the youngest is Ahmad."

"Such handsome young men!" said Zia. "And I just happen to have brought something from Delhi for each of you." His manservant held a large bag, from which Zia took three parcels, handing one to each of the boys. "The latest toys from the craftsmen who serve the Sultan's children," said Zia.

"How kind of you," said Ali.

The delighted boys exclaimed over a miniature carriage, a camel with legs that moved when it was pulled, and a small model of a fort with tiny elephants in it. "You may say goodnight to your Uncle Zia now," Ali told his sons. When the farewells were completed, a servant led the boys from the room.

The two men washed and seated themselves at the dinner cloth. As the servants under Ishaq's direction began bringing the dishes, Ali said, "I thought of inviting other guests, but I wanted the two of us to have time for conversation."

"Good—I don't know when I'll be able to get away from the Sultan again," Zia said. "He wants me with him constantly." He peered at Ali, and announced, smiling with mock modesty, "I have it on very good authority that the Sultan intends to grant everyone in Daulatabad permission to return to Delhi." Awaiting a response, he watched his friend.

Ali was thoughtful, vacantly staring over his friend's shoulder. Eventually, he sighed. He said quietly, "I always considered Delhi my home. I'm told our house there is still empty. But the area around it is said to still be almost deserted. Apparently it never recovered after the Sultan ordered everyone to leave. My *pir* and my father are both gone." He looked at Zia and smiled. "Many of our old acquaintances are here. Amir Hasan and I are quite friendly. Shaikh Fakhruddin Zarradi left for a pilgrimage to Mecca, but Shaikh Burhanuddin Gharib's *khanqah* outside the walls has become well known. Many other Sufis have settled nearby."

He stopped talking, but as he clearly was not finished, Zia waited. After a time, Ali continued, "Almost without realizing it, I've grown accustomed to living here. You saw yourself Daulatabad is now a thriving city."

"Hardly comparable to Delhi."

"Of course. Still—" Ali gestured about. "My house is comfortable. My garden is developing well. I also took a third wife. And Halima has borne me three sons I adore. Daulatabad is their home. We often go on picnics to the Ellora cave temples. Even to the Ajanta caves once every year or two to see the magnificent murals."

"So you don't want to leave?" Zia sounded incredulous.

Ali smiled grimly. "One long move was sufficient for my lifetime."

Zia said, "You've no doubt heard that the tomb of our saint has become a famous pilgrimage site. Hundreds of people go there every day for their devotions. And every year many thousands come for the festival in his honor."

Ali gave a nod. "I hope to go on a pilgrimage there myself, one year soon."

Zia sat silently for a time, curiously examining him. Finally, he asked, "How do you feel about the Sultan, after the trouble he caused you?"

Ali sighed. "I was furious at him for a long time. I probably still am, a little. But I had many discussions with Shaikh Burhanuddin Gharib at his *khanqah*. I think I learned to accept what I couldn't change. I eventually decided as long as I was here, I might as well do my job as best I can." He added with satisfaction in his voice, "The cases I judge are mostly small ones. But men come to me for justice. I try to be fair, to always give them the best result I can."

Zia seemed lost in thought for a time, his eyes losing some of their animation. Then, he said, "I see. Well, you always were extremely fair and compassionate in handling the matters that came before you."

Now Ali said, "It appears being the Sultan's confidant appeals to you."

"You know it's what I always wanted." Zia fell silent, and to Ali's surprise, he abruptly appeared troubled.

"It must be difficult at times," said Ali.

Zia did not respond at first. Then, he said in a low voice, "It does have drawbacks." His eyes met Ali's. "I sometimes tire of being at his call so constantly. Of having to be so careful of what opinions I express."

"I assume he doesn't tolerate much disagreement," Ali said dryly.

"It depends on his mood. There are times I should probably tell him I disagree. But I never do." Zia suddenly seemed despondent, and Ali wondered if he should change topics. However, Zia continued, looking downward, "Oh, he's the most generous man I've ever known. He'll give anything to someone he likes, appoint him to the highest post anyone could want. But he also seems to delight in spilling blood. He'll order men executed at the slightest excuse, including men he was friendly with moments before."

"I always assumed being a courtier *would* be precarious."

Zia smiled tightly. "More so than I realized, and I thought I knew all about it. But there's little danger so long as he's sure of one's loyalty." He lowered his voice: "I think we should talk of other things. I shouldn't chance being overheard."

Less than a week later, a summons came directing that Amir Ali Surajuddin Aruzi appear before Sultan Muhammad bin Tughluq.

Ali's stomach began to churn. There had been safety in his anonymity—it was dangerous to come to the attention of the Sultan. Could Zia be responsible? And if so, why would he have put Ali at risk?

Ali wore his most elegant clothing, a green brocade robe and white silk *kulah*, to the Sultan's audience hall. When he entered, he saw Zia standing at the far end among the other nobles in attendance. Zia's eyes met his own fleetingly and seemed to speak reassurance.

The *Hajib* called Ali's name and led him forward. Sultan Muhammad bin Tughluq sat leaning against his cushions on a raised dais covered with a white cloth. Behind him stood the ever-present bodyguards with drawn swords. Ali made his obeisance before the man who had caused him so many difficulties, who had hastened his father's death. The Sultan said kindly, "Welcome. It's been many years since I saw you in the *khanqah* of our *pir*, may God sanctify his tomb."

"Yes, Your Majesty, may the peace of God be upon our *shaikh*." Ali strained to keep his voice neutral.

The Sultan's face appeared pleasant, not at all stern and harsh as Ali had imagined. Tughluq said, "Our *shaikh* was a great saint. I miss him terribly. I often wish I could call upon him for his wisdom."

"I often wish the same, Your Majesty."

The Sultan said, "I understand the move here—when was that? Ten years ago? So long! I understand the move caused you difficulties and inconvenience, and that your father—may God sanctify his tomb— died on the journey. Please accept my sincerest apologies. My officers were overzealous. It was all most unfortunate—a mistake I'd like to put behind me."

Ali stood, uncertain how to respond. He nodded. "I understand, Your Majesty, and I'm grateful for your regrets."

"Good. You've no doubt heard I'm allowing everyone who wishes to return to Delhi. But I'm told you now prefer to remain in Daulatabad."

That information *must* have come from Zia. Ali wondered in anxiety what the Sultan could be leading up to. "That's my preference, Your Majesty."

"I also understand you've been performing your magisterial duties in an exemplary manner. Just as you did back in Delhi."

The perplexed Ali could only reply, "I'm honored by your approval, your Majesty. I do my best."

The Sultan said, "You're no doubt aware that the position of *qazi* of Daulatabad is vacant. I need someone I can trust. Someone I have confidence in. I hereby appoint you to the post." Tughluq turned his head and nodded to the *Barbak*.

The *Barbak* told the astonished Ali, "The position carries with it a *mahararibi* robe." This was a prestigious garment with the image of an arch on front and back. "Also a horse with bridle and caparison. And an annual salary of twelve thousand *tankas*."

Ali stood stunned. *Qazi* of Daulatabad, chief judge of the province. "I'm overwhelmed at such an honor, Your Majesty," he managed to say to the Sultan.

"Long overdue," Tughluq said warmly. His expression then changed instantly, and his tone. He gave Ali an intent look and said bluntly, "I expect that as *qazi* you will administer justice completely fairly, no matter who the litigants may be."

Ali, even more puzzled, replied, "Of course, Your Majesty."

"No matter who the litigants may be!" the Sultan repeated. "All persons who come before you must be equal in your eyes, just as they are in the eyes of Allah, praise be to Him. *All* persons."

Ali could only nod and repeat, "Of course, Your Majesty."

Tughluq waved his hand in dismissal. Ali numbly backed away the prescribed distance, and turned to leave. He saw a look of consternation on Ziauddin Barani's face. Had Zia not been aware of the appointment after all?

It was most strange. Ali would have expected such an important position as chief judge to go to one of the elder members of the *ulema*, one more orthodox in belief and practice. But Tughluq himself had been a Sufi. From the remark the Sultan had made about Shaikh Nizamuddin Auliya, maybe he was still sympathetic to the Sufis. However, it was also odd that the Sultan put so much emphasis on a concept that was implicit: treating all persons fairly. Naturally a judge should treat everyone equally. That went without saying.

The *Barbak* abruptly stood before him at the exit to the audience hall and handed him the folded robe of honor. And an official writing: "Your first case as *qazi*, to be heard tomorrow."

A case already! Matters were moving almost too quickly to comprehend. He left the hall.

Since the dispute was to be heard the next day, Ali decided he'd better get a quick idea of what it was about. The courtyard was pleasantly warmed by the winter sun, and he looked about and saw a vacant stone ledge on which to sit. He placed the robe beside him, seated himself, hurriedly read the summary of the case.

A chill swept through him.

The defendant was accused of striking the complainant without cause, resulting in bodily harm. Ali was not familiar with the man bringing the complaint—Nasiruddin bin Malik Mall.

But the defendant was Sultan Muhammad bin Tughluq.

Ali immediately sent word for Ishaq to take the family from the city, and to travel to the Ajanta caves to hide. Although the caves at Ellora were closer, the ones at Ajanta would be more secure as a refuge from the very fact of being more remote.

The remainder of the day he anguished over the unparalleled situation in which he found himself. He visited the *khanqah* to seek Shaikh Burhanuddin Gharib's counsel. Untypically, he requested a private audience with the *shaikh*, and he was led into the saint's simple, mud walled living quarters. There he outlined his predicament.

"A difficult dilemma," acknowledged the *shaikh*, his sorrowful eyes fixed sympathetically on Ali. "Do you feel the Sultan meant what he said about treating him the same as any other defendant?"

Ali frowned as he reviewed the audience in his mind. "The Sultan emphasized it a couple of times. But I don't know if he was sincere. And even if he meant what he said, what if he changes his mind in the meantime? He can be incredibly brutal to those who displease him."

"It seems to me," said the *shaikh*, "that the Sultan gave you a command which you'll ignore at your peril. Maybe you should have faith that even such a man as he can be honorable in some ways."

Ali thought for a time.

"You always strive to be completely just in your decisions," said the saint. "To do what is right. Isn't that so?"

Ali nodded. "I do, of course."

"And what is the just way to proceed when a case comes before you?"

"To treat both litigants fairly, naturally. To set aside my personal feelings, except for a desire to help the parties reach the best resolution of their dispute."

The *shaikh* smiled. "Have you answered what you need to do tomorrow?"

Ali drew a deep breath. "I believe so. I think I can face the consequences of angering the Sultan, so long as he doesn't order too many horrible tortures before I die. But I dread the possibility of leaving my family unprotected and without income."

"I'd do my best to see your household was provided for, in whatever small way I could," said the *shaikh*. "And I'd ensure that my disciples aid your family. It would not be the same as having you, of course, but it's something."

Ali nodded, and slowly rose to leave.

"You'll be in my prayers," said the *shaikh*.

Ali smiled weakly. "I think I'm seriously in need of them."

That night an anxious Ziauddin Barani visited Ali at home. "*Assalaam aleicum*. I can only stay a moment," Zia said hurriedly, his eyes darting about as if expecting to see one of the Sultan's spies. "I want to tell you how sorry I am. I recommended you to the Sultan as the new *qazi*." He gave Ali a distressed look. "But please believe me—I had no idea you would be hearing a case involving the Sultan himself!"

Ali nodded numbly. "I believe you." They stood for a moment in uneasy silence. Then, Ali asked, "Do you have any advice?"

Zia shook his head, his lips pressed tightly together. "I don't know what to suggest. I've heard that once before the Sultan did submit himself to a court. The judge ordered a monetary fine, and the Sultan paid it promptly. So far as I know there were no repercussions on the judge."

Zia started to open his mouth, hesitated, then added, "That was a few years ago. Since then, the Sultan has become more, uh, unpredictable."

Ali was still awake, wrapped in blankets against the chill, when the sun rose into a clear sky. Although he was relieved he'd had time to send his family to safety, he missed them terribly. He would have especially welcomed Halima's understanding comfort and wise advice. The thought that he might never again see any of them in this life was almost unbearable.

The morning remained cool as he rode his horse to the courtroom, accompanied by his small entourage. He had not yet added the numbers of attendants that went with his new position of *qazi*. But then, he thought, maybe after today he would have no need of them anyway. Halima had left a purse for him containing the usual daily allocation, and he distributed the coins to the supplicants who awaited his passing every day: several widows of varying ages; some old men; a few orphaned children; a leper; a couple of young men too crippled by injuries to work; numerous others.

He hoped he would still be able to help them tomorrow.

As he entered the building and approached the courtroom, all talk among the staff and hangers-on stopped. He was met with the expected obsequiousness, but eyes avoided his, and everyone had become silent.

Ali strode into the courtroom and mounted the dais. Curious onlookers, all members of the nobility, filled the chamber, but the hum of conversation died almost instantly. As his gaze swept the room, faces turned away. Only Ziauddin Barani met his eyes for a moment, before looking down.

Maintaining his customary judicial expression of calm receptivity, Ali took a deep breath and signaled his readiness. The *amir-i-dad*, the official charged with summoning the defendant in all cases involving high nobles, led in the Sultan.

Muhammad bin Tughluq had arrived unarmed and unattended, like a commoner. Ali instantly rose to his feet, as did his two assistants. But the Sultan waved them back to their seats, and instead he saluted the *qazi*.

Ali quickly called the complainant as the first witness. Nasiruddin bin Malik Mall was a robust young nobleman. The unevenness of his voice betrayed his anxiety, but he testified boldly, his words reverberating harshly in the room: "Your honor, five days ago I was attending His Majesty the Sultan. Two brothers were brought before him, and he ordered them executed immediately—by being cut in two in the middle. I suggested they should not be killed, and His Majesty grew angry. He grabbed a rod and struck me with it. Then he ordered me to leave his sight. I was bruised on my left arm and shoulder when he struck me. I can exhibit the bruises if you wish, although they now are fading."

"Perhaps later." In the hushed chamber, Ali's own voice sounded loud and discordant to him. He sat thinking. He glanced briefly at the Sultan, whose face was bland but attentive. Eventually, Ali asked the complainant, "What was the reason for His Majesty ordering the execution of the two men?"

"Your honor, the brothers were from Farhana, where they were quite notable. They had been serving the Sultan for many months, but they wanted to return home. They knew he would not permit it, so they tried to sneak away at night. Someone informed the Sultan of their plans. He had them seized. Before they died, he ordered that the informant be granted all their property."

Ali carefully considered. It was common to give the informer the property of the persons executed, but certainly the executions themselves seemed extreme in this case. "Do you have other witnesses?" he asked.

"Many, your honor. But they are afraid to testify. And I think they might not speak the truth even when they came, out of fear of the His Majesty."

Ali stroked his beard. "I see." He looked at the Sultan. "The defendant may now testify."

Muhammad bin Tughluq said, simply and humbly, "Everything the complainant says is true, your honor. I await your judgment."

"You have nothing further to add?"

"Nothing, your honor."

Ali tried to maintain his composure. The Sultan was inviting whatever punishment he might award! In his mind Ali quickly reviewed the Qur'an; the *Hadis*, the traditions and teachings of the Prophet; the *Ijma*, the various precedents decided by Muslim jurists construing the law. There was considerable room for his own interpretation in this particular matter.

He felt he knew what his decision would be in the case of normal litigants. He carefully weighed it. Had he been influenced at all by the fact that the defendant was the Sultan?

He felt nauseous. He was sweating profusely. Could he really impose such a judgment?

At last, he faced Muhammad bin Tughluq and said, "My decision is this. I find that the complainant was struck by the defendant without just cause. I therefore find in the complainant's favor." He heard the intakes of breath throughout the courtroom.

He continued, "As punishment the defendant shall receive twenty-one strokes of the rod, to be administered by the complainant after the *zohar* prayers."

The Sultan's expression remained calm, but the audience gasped as a whole.

Ali hastily added, "However, if the complainant agrees, the defendant can instead pay a cash indemnity of five hundred *tankas*."

"I will never agree to only money!" the young nobleman said quickly. "The defendant struck me, and he deserves to be struck himself."

The assembled onlookers' faces registered stunned dismay. Ali—who had been almost certain the complainant would accept the cash indemnity rather than putting his own life at further risk—searched desperately for an alternative. He saw none.

"Then my judgment stands," he said.

*

As he awaited developments, Ali felt as if he were a man already condemned to death.

In the afternoon of that same day, he received word that Nasiruddin bin Malik Mall had indeed administered all twenty-one strokes of the rod. He had struck the Sultan so hard that the ruler's cap had flown off.

Ali expected to be seized at any moment, or at the very least to be removed from his new position as *qazi*. The post had been granted seemingly at whim; it could be taken from him in the same manner. The other nobles, clearly uncertain of his status, were avoiding him.

Ali's new position required him to stand in regular attendance with the other high officials at the Sultan's court. Each succeeding day, he surreptitiously examined Tughluq's face, trying to discern the Sultan's mood, to determine if today would be the last day of his own life.

But Muhammad bin Tughluq paid him no notice whatever.

The days passed.

Finally, the Sultan left Daulatabad to fight the rebels in Ma'bar. Ali remained untouched by the Sultan's retribution.

The nobles who had been avoiding him cautiously resumed their previous friendliness. The young nobleman who had thrashed the Sultan remained in Daulatabad, admired for his courage by everyone. But he was also thought by most to be an outspoken, reckless, fool.

Ali recalled his family to the city from the Ajanta caves. He worked conscientiously at his new position. He was scrupulously fair, and he quickly gained a reputation as an outstanding chief judge. But always, he felt an underlying insecurity. The capricious Sultan could punish him at any moment.

Many nobles of Daulatabad revolted against the Sultan in the following year under the leadership of a *malik* who was the son of the governor. Ali carefully avoided taking sides.

The revolt failed, and the Sultan replaced the governor and many other officials.

But he did not dismiss the *qazi*. When the Sultan was in Daulatabad he did not even seem to take particular notice of Ali's attendance in the audience hall.

Like the other nobles holding ranks under the Sultan, Ali continued to receive a twice-yearly gift of a robe of honor from the ruler. To all appearances, the Sultan had forgotten the incident in the *qazi's* court. Eventually, Ali came to feel reasonably secure, reasonably confident about his own future.

After the end of the next monsoon season, he made the long journey to his father's grave at Mangarh. Shaikh Burhanuddin Gharib still counseled that the body should remain where it rested. Although Ali had not firmly decided on what he would do when he arrived, he carried sufficient funds to remove his father's remains and construct a tomb in Delhi, where he planned a pilgrimage to the shrine of Shaikh Nizamuddin Auliya.

He and his entourage arrived at Mangarh at sunset, and not wanting to continue in darkness past the town to the site of his father's grave, he ordered their tents pitched outside the town walls in the wooded grounds designated for travelers. This was an area ruled by a Hindu Raja, with no apparent Muslim population of any size, so there were no minarets from which the muezzins called the faithful to prayer. Ali estimated the proper time for the *maghrib* prayer as best he could, and he led his party in the rituals.

He awoke before dawn, and at *fajr* prayer time the sun was turning the stone walls and towers of the fortress high above the town a glowing orange. It was still cool, with mist hovering above the river valley, when he arrived with his entourage at the mango tree beside the road.

He was surprised to see several persons gathered at the site. The stone slab atop his father's grave was covered with flowers and fruits, and a woman was prostrating herself before it. A man knelt at the grave in prayer. A couple of men who appeared from weathered faces and simple garments to be farmers squatted nearby. An old man in tattered clothes stood near the trunk of the tree, with a proprietary air about him. Birds chattered loudly in the upper reaches of the tree. Hundreds of tiny shreds of cloth were tied to the branches of some bushes behind the grave site.

Ali doubted he could make himself understood by most of the local people, who spoke their own dialect. But a well-dressed elderly man with a thin, kindly looking face, accompanied by two servants, had arrived on a horse and had apparently halted to watch. "Your pardon, sir," Ali said in Persian in a low voice. "Do you know why these people are gathered here?"

"*Assalaam aleicum.* This is the grave of *pir* Mahmud, a Muslim saint," the man replied, in crude but understandable Persian. "It's said he's responsible for many miracles. Wives who have been unable to bear children have been coming here to pray that they will give birth to sons." He gestured toward the bushes. "Most of those pieces of cloth were tied there by those women. I'm told funds are being gathered to build a stone shelter over the grave. This man," he gestured toward the old man standing by the tree, "has assumed responsibility as caretaker."

Ali stood dumfounded at what he was observing.

After a time, he went to kneel beside the others and to commune with the memory of his father.

Ali saw to the erection of a fine domed tomb over the grave. While the construction was under way, he visited Delhi. He was shocked at how the city had changed as a result of Muhammad bin Tughluq's fiasco. Whole neighborhoods were uninhabited and decaying. His old

Tomb of Pir Mahmud

family home was only a shell, home to several families of poor people who had taken over the ruins, and to bats and squirrels and monkeys.

The population of beggars in the streets was at least as large as he remembered. He half expected to see at least a few familiar faces among them, but for whatever reason, he recognized no one.

He spent considerable time at the tomb of Shaikh Nizamuddin Auliya and the adjacent grave of Amir Khusrau. He was pleased that the site was such a bustling destination for pilgrims, reminiscent of what had happened at his father's grave, but on a far larger scale.

He returned gladly to Daulatabad. On quiet evenings as he sat in his garden, enjoying the scent of the blossoming trees, he would sometimes think of his own grandfather, of how the man who had been taken as a slave by Mongol raiders had adjusted to changing conditions. Of how that ancestor had ultimately risen to be one of the ruling powers in the Sultanate of Delhi. Of how that man's son, Mahmud, and his grandson, Ali, had received the benefits of his efforts.

Ali, too, had been forced by circumstances to move and start anew. He had survived, and he had prospered. That was almost a miracle, for which he was grateful every day to Allah. Maybe, he thought, he also was laying foundation upon which his own sons and their descendants would build.

***

Almost seven centuries after his death, the mausoleum of Shaikh Nizamuddin Auliya continues to be a major pilgrimage site for both Muslims and Hindus. Each November an Urs or festival in the Shaikh's honor is held at the shrine. The present custodians of the site, the pirzade, claim descent from the Shaikh's relatives and disciples.

Amir Khusrau's fame as a poet endures, and many credit him with the invention of that popular musical instrument, the sitar. His tomb shares the same complex as the Shaikh's, and an annual festival is also held in his honor.

Ziauddin Barani is said to have died destitute despite his success in later life as a courtier, but his writings remain a principal source for information about the Sultans during the period in which he lived.

The ruins of many of the buildings constructed by the Tughluq Sultans are major monuments in the Delhi area. Far to the south in the Deccan Plateau, the remains of the fortress of Daulatabad, although mostly in ruins, are still impressive.

The
Mangarh Treasure
Seven

15

"I just don't know what to do," Kaushalya said. "I have a possible lead, but I've no idea if anything will come of it." She became aware of the tears in her eyes and rubbed at them, embarrassed. She was so unaccustomed to showing weakness.

Usha put an arm around her. "It must be horrible. Is there anything I can do?"

Kaushalya shrugged. "I feel so helpless. Mahendra's contacting everyone he can think of. Our lawyers say they're doing all they can. It still seems like I should be doing more. Only I don't know what. If I were in jail, Father would be making waves all over. He'd probably even lead our Bhils on a raid to get me out!"

"Yes, but it's different now." Usha gave a strained smile at the thought of the Bhil guards storming a prison. "You need to be careful. It won't do your father any good if you get arrested yourself."

Kaushalya sat motionless for a moment, then nodded.

Usha looked into her eyes and said, "I'll ask my father if he can help. But so far the police don't seem to be releasing anyone arrested under the Emergency."

"So I've heard." How ironic, thought Kaushalya. Usha's father Ashok Chand was a former Congress Party minister who had been imprisoned by Lakshman Singh in the old days for agitating in favor of reforms in Mangarh. And now she hoped he might help get Lakshman Singh freed from arrest!

Kaushalya asked, more for something to say than out of interest at this time, "What's the IES doing? I've been so out of touch."

"We've suspended activities for the moment," said Usha, treasurer of the Indian Ecological Society. "Everyone is too worried about being arrested."

"But what about the conference on deforestation? Isn't the society still sponsoring it?"

Usha looked away. "We've canceled it. Pratap Singh and I didn't want to give up so easily. He spoke quite eloquently at the meeting at my house. But we were outvoted—everyone else felt it was too difficult to know where we stand with the government."

Kaushalya could imagine the scene, from the IES meetings she'd attended herself. Pratap Singh, whom she had known from childhood because he was the son of the ex-Maharaja of Shantipur, had a quiet manner, but he never hesitated to voice his opinions. Kaushalya admired his flair for drawing cartoons lampooning the government's corruption and stupidity on environmental matters. "I wish I'd been there to help you and Pratap." She smiled a wry, distorted smile. "But I've had other things on my mind."

Usha nodded. "Most people at the meeting felt too many 'big men' are making too much money from illegal timber cutting. The Forestry Department hierarchy has to be involved in it. And right now it seems so easy to offend the government without even trying!"

"So we've found," said Kaushalya dryly.

"You can't be getting much done on your thesis."

Kaushalya shook her head, her gaze on the dusty ground. "I'm afraid the Ajanta Cave murals aren't foremost in my mind right now." Never in her life had she felt so demoralized. Whatever had happened to the world's most populous "democracy"?

She asked Mahendra, "Why not give Dev Batra a try? The worst he can do is say no to us."

"No, no! I told you he doesn't like me." Mahendra shook his head vigorously. "The feeling's definitely mutual. I need to find a way to work around him, not meet him head on."

"Then why don't I try approaching him?"

"Absolutely not! I told you—he's not to be trusted."

"But if I'm careful?"

"Don't you understand? This man preys on women! He'd promise to help, but only if you...went to bed with him. Afterwards he'd forget all about you."

"Oh!" She realized now why Mahendra had been so adamant. But if she were careful, knowing the risks, wasn't the avenue worth pursuing?

When Mahendra had left the house, she thought a bit. She still saw no realistic alternatives.

She at last connected with Batra in the Ashok Hotel. On the telephone, he sounded more agreeable than she had expected. "Yes, Princess," he said. "You may know I am acquainted with your brother.

He and I have disagreed in the past, but naturally, I do not hold that against yourself. Perhaps we should meet in person. I find it more conducive to business to be face-to-face."

"Do you think you'll be able to help?" she asked, hoping to get at least a preliminary commitment. She wiped sweat from her forehead. The hot breeze from the ceiling fan fluttered the papers on the desk but did little to cool her.

"Quite possibly, Princess. I pride myself that I do have friends in high office." His voice resonated with confidence. "Shall we say 3 o'clock, at the Ashok Hotel? I have a suite I often use for meetings."

Kaushalya scribbled down the room number he gave her and glanced at her wristwatch. It was just before 1:00, so there was plenty of time. But she hesitated in her reply. It seemed odd, especially for a woman, to be meeting him at a hotel. Maybe Mahendra was right about the man. However, he sounded as if it were an everyday occurrence to conduct business there. And he was the first one who had offered any real hope of helping free her father; she could hardly risk offending him at this point by suggesting an alternative place which might be less convenient for him. The ceiling fan lifted the piece of paper in the air. She snatched it, put it down firmly and set a paperweight on it. "I'll be there."

"Shall I send a car for you, Princess?"

The offer took her by surprise. "There's really no need—I'll take my own car."

"*Accha.* I look forward very much to meeting you, Princess." He seemed almost overly courteous for someone with influence, she thought. "Three o'clock then," he said, and hung up.

She uneasily replaced the receiver in its cradle. She wished there were someone to accompany her. Mahendra was clearly not a possibility. Anyway, whenever she was away from Mangarh and its conservative inhabitants, especially in the bigger cities such as Delhi and Bombay, she often went places unaccompanied. She would take Gopi along this time, just to be safe. She thought of making more calls, but the urgency for them seemed to have diminished. If Dev Batra could help, there might even be no need for further telephoning.

She went to her bathroom, stripped off her sticky dress and underthings, and poured bucket after bucket of tepid water over herself. She dressed in a *shalwar kameez* for the meeting. Finally, she applied a pale lipstick and slipped into white high heeled sandals.

She and Gopi left the house. Outside, the heat hit her hard, even in the shade of the big trees around the bungalow. The door handle of the Jaguar had been in the sun, and it burned her fingers when she touched it, causing her to jerk away. She stood thinking as she rubbed her hand, absently watching Amar the *chowkidar* hurrying to open the gate for her. Hopeful as she was about the meeting, she was distinctly uneasy.

It took only a few minutes to drive to Chanakyapuri, the nearby diplomatic enclave. On Prithviraj Road she and Gopi passed another police checkpoint, but the bored-looking officers never glanced at them.

With the possible exception of the older Imperial which had been favored by the elite in earlier years, the Ashok was New Delhi's premier hotel. Although the huge complex was not unattractive, as an art historian Kaushalya had always been mildly irritated at the attempt to graft the style of a 16th Century Mughal palace onto a sleek modern structure—especially when the hotel was named after a 3rd Century B.C.E. Mauryan emperor. But no one had consulted her on the matter, she often wryly reminded herself.

Today she was oblivious to the architectural and decorative inconsistencies, including the lobby's giant chandeliers reminiscent of frozen waterfalls. She led Gopi straight to the elevators. On the fifth floor Kaushalya searched down the gray-carpeted hall until she spotted the shiny brass numerals she was looking for. She knocked on the dark wooden door. A short, pudgy, smiling man answered it almost immediately. "Kaushalya Kumari?" he asked in a high pitched voice. He then looked beyond to stare at Gopi, apparently surprised to see an additional person. His glance returned to Kaushalya and he said, "Please come in, Princess. Batra *sahib* is expecting you."

They entered a large room with a couch and some armchairs grouped around a coffee table. A old man and a young one in his twenties were sitting on the couch, and a middle aged woman, heavily made up, occupied one of the chairs. Two young men in white *khadi* or homespun were standing by a door. A fairly typical collection of the supplicants and hangers-on to be expected around any person of influence, prestige, or wealth.

"Please sit," said the man who had shown her in. He moved lazily to a bar. "Something to drink while you wait, Princess? Rum, Scotch, vodka...? All are imported, of course."

Kaushalya sat in one chair and motioned Gopi to the remaining vacant one. "Nothing, thank you." While alcohol might help calm her nerves, Kaushalya had little tolerance for it and did not want to get light-headed or dizzy.

She looked around at the room. The drapes had been drawn back from the window wall to reveal white French doors opening onto the balcony outside. Here and there were several items apparently removed from old buildings: three matching carved wooden corbels or roof supports in the shape of horses' heads sat on the floor; an arched, intricately carved wood double doorway inlaid with brass leaned against a wall.

A door was partly open into an adjoining room, and she heard male voices in conversation, but could see little except for a man's back. One of the voices, deep and resonant, gave the clear impression of being in command.

"I can send for *chai*, if you'd prefer," said the assistant to her in his high voice. His ingratiating smile never left.

"No, thank you. I'm fine." Something about him made her uneasy, but she couldn't discern what it was. He gave the impression he flowed when he walked, rather than stepping. It was as if underneath the facade of amiable casualness, he was something else....

He stood by the couch, staring at her, the smile on his face. Avoiding his gaze, and those of the other waiting persons, Kaushalya's attention was drawn to a small table against a wall, on which stood a silver-framed photo, draped in a garland of fresh marigolds. The photograph was of Swami Surya, the holy man with a jet-set lifestyle who was revered by many celebrities. The Swami smiled broadly, as if delighted with everything about him.

She next examined the carved doors and frame that sat leaning against the wall. They were an outstanding example of craft that had virtually died out. "What lovely doors," she said. She spoke partly to ease the silence, but it might also be helpful to have the assistant favorably inclined toward her when she tried to influence his boss to aid her father.

"For the new farmhouse Batra *sahib* is building," said the man.

"I see."

Silence. Kaushalya asked, "And the corbels?"

"The same. For some years now Batra *sahib* is collecting items to furnish the house."

Kaushalya nodded. "It must be a very fine house."

"Very fine. Very large. Even is having air conditioning. Batraji's family lost their ancestral home at Partition. He is determined to replace it."

"I see. Is the house near to Delhi?"

"One hour's drive only."

Three men came from the adjacent room and exited into the hallway. "Batra *sahib* will see you now," the assistant said to Kaushalya. He flowed into the adjoining room. She and Gopi followed.

A large framed, overweight man of around thirty years in age slowly rose from a big armchair. He wore *khadi* like a great many other Congress Party adherents, but the cloth was so finely woven it appeared luxurious. Dev Batra appraised Kaushalya a moment with bright, shrewd eyes set in a round face with a long, arching nose. She felt a vague unease, as if he were somehow peering into her, weighing her soul, judging whether or not she could be useful to him.

He pressed his palms together in greeting and said in a voice full of charm, "Welcome, Princess. Please sit. Your brother failed to mention having such a beautiful sister. Did Gulab offer you refreshment? Good. I'm told you are a painter and a student of art history. I am somewhat of an art collector myself, so we share an interest."

His knowledge of her artistic passions disturbed her. She had not mentioned them on the phone—so he had found out from some other source. And in only two hours.

Batra said, "You should be quite interested in the furnishings I am acquiring for my house. See these hangings?" He lifted a length of finely woven, richly colored red and brown fabric, inlaid with tiny round mirrors. "What is your opinion of them?"

"Very nice," she murmured, pretending to look carefully at the cloth. "Where did you find them?"

He gave a wave of dismissal. "I admired them on a wall, and my host insisted I take them." He waved toward the other room. "Those corbels. Another gift. From a friend showing his appreciation for some small help I was able to give him."

He put his hand on a carved door frame leaning against a wall. "This doorway matches others taken to my house site. As a favor to me, the Public Works Department condemned and demolished an old *haveli* that was in the way of a redevelopment I sponsored."

"It's a shame to have to destroy the old to make way for the new."

The smile left his face. He raised his eyebrows. "I'm sure that's sometimes the case. However, don't you think old buildings are often impractical, unsuited to modern needs with their lack of plumbing or wiring, their continual need for repairs? I say, better to clear away the old and build afresh. But parts of the old buildings can have some worth if they are salvaged for use in the new. Much less expensive than hiring artists and craftsmen these days. And you may know there is now a growing market abroad for such artifacts."

His gaze lingered on her face, and he said, "I can show you more of my collection later. We can discuss our mutual art interests at length then. Now, then, you have a problem involving your father, Princess."

Kaushalya adjusted the drape of her *dupatta* over her shoulders as she tried to compose herself. Still a bit unnerved by his prior knowledge of details about her, she was also annoyed at his dismissal of the value of older buildings, the structures she herself so often admired and loved. And the idea of exporting portions of India's architectural heritage to other countries was outrageous.

When Batra had lowered himself into his big armchair, she repeated what she had said over the telephone about her father's arrest. He listened, staring into her eyes, his brow wrinkled and his fingers pressed together in a steeple. She ended, "And our lawyers can't even find where my father's been taken!"

He remained staring at her, his fingers forming the upside-down V. After a few moments, he said, "There have been a great many arrests. It takes time for the police to process them all."

"But as I've told you, he's in poor health. What harm is there in at least letting us know where he is?"

Dev Batra did not answer immediately. He blinked his eyes, then continued looking into her own. She had to concentrate to keep her customary poise under the bold examination.

Then he smiled, although the smile did not fully reach his eyes.

"I'm sure I can be of help to you, Princess. But first I must make some inquiries. Meanwhile, I've heard so much about you, and I like what I hear, as well as what I see. Perhaps you could join me for dinner this evening, and we could become better acquainted? Maybe go to a club or two afterwards?"

Kaushalya had prepared herself to some extent to meet a man of his reputation. But the immediacy of the invitation still took her by surprise. Thinking quickly, she replied, "I regret that my brother expects me for dinner. We're having friends over."

Batra shrugged and smiled tightly. "Another time soon, then, I hope. I could uh...be of more help to you if I became better acquainted, Princess."

She hesitated, gave a quick nod.

"You must be aware, Princess," said Dev Batra, "of certain realities."

She tensed and waited.

"You have asked me to put my position at some risk to obtain the results you wish, Princess. To get results I must make inquiries. I may appear to be taking more than a casual interest in your father. I unfortunately have enemies, and they may try to make it appear I have become sympathetic with the government's opposition."

"I see that those inquiries could be awkward, Mr. Batra. I very much appreciate your efforts."

"I hope we can become good friends, Princess. I will do anything to help my friends."

She drew in her breath, wondering how to reply.

He asked, "Your woman does not understand English?"

Puzzled, Kaushalya glanced at Gopi. "Almost none."

He smiled rigidly. "Even so, Princess, it is difficult to talk about these matters when there are others present who might repeat what we say to, uh, unfriendly ears. Next time we must meet alone. We can then more readily discuss these confidential government matters."

Again, she was uncertain how to respond.

"Perhaps," he continued, "you would care to meet me here again at about ten o'clock tomorrow morning. I will see what I can do in the meantime about your father." His lips tightened into the smile again. "You must put your faith in me."

She allowed herself to relax, just a little. "I'd be very grateful, Mr. Batra." Kaushalya rose, gave the scarf a tug to adjust its fall over her shoulders. Gulab appeared to usher her and Gopi to the door.

Kaushalya hesitated there a moment. Then she turned and said hoarsely, "I'll be here tomorrow at ten, Mr. Batra."

As they were walking down the hall, Gopi said, "He's not a good man. I can tell that even without speaking English. You should be very careful, Highness."

"I intend to be."

*

"You saw Dev Batra?!" shouted Mahendra when she told him of the meeting, before she could relate its outcome. "I specifically told you not to!"

"I did it only for father's sake!"

"Did he—did he try to do anything to you?"

"With Gopi there? Of course not."

After a few seconds, more calmly, Mahendra asked, "Did he say anything helpful?"

She had been going to tell her brother she was meeting Dev Batra again, but rather than risk another outburst, she said only, "He's doing some checking. He'll call me when he's found out more."

Mahendra sat scowling. Then, "Oh, hell. Maybe we have to try everything. With Father's health at risk, maybe even his life." Mahendra's eyes were on her. "I'm still afraid he may want something personal from you in exchange. Don't meet him again, not without me along."

"You said he's upset with you. Wouldn't it be better if you stayed away from him?"

"Maybe. But you can't see him without a man along with you."

Kaushalya bristled, but said nothing.

Mahendra said, more gently, "I just don't want you to take chances with someone like him." He reached for the Scotch.

The next morning, wearing another *shalwar kameez*, Kaush-alya again waited, with Gopi beside her, in Batra's suite at the Ashok Hotel. The door into the room where Batra held court was closed this time. Such an observance of privacy was unusual for India. But soon the door opened, and a corpulent, middle aged man hurried out, a scowl on his face.

Gulab, lazily smiling, appeared and stepped back, indicating for her to enter. She noticed that in his hand he held a folded pocket knife. It was folded, but it was by far the longest she'd ever seen. Dev Batra sat in his big chair, a drink in his hand, a cigarette in his lips. He smiled, set down his drink, and rose. He placed the cigarette in an ashtray. "Princess!" His smile turned to a frown. You still have your companion, I see." He waved them to a spot on the couch.

Another man, tall and solid looking, with wild, bushy hair, stood by the French doors to the balcony; he watched Kaushalya with black, penetrating eyes. She was aware that Gulab was casually tossing his big knife from hand to hand. She again breathed in deeply. She did not like the situation, even with Gopi present.

A smile curled the corners of Batra's lips. "Would you like a drink? Some Scotch or brandy? No?" He motioned to his two companions, who swiftly left the room.

"What have you found out about my father, Mr. Batra?" she

asked abruptly.

"I do have news. I assure you he is quite safe and in good health."

"That's wonderful! Where is he?"

"It was hard work to obtain this information, Princess. I spent much of the night and morning on the telephone. You know how frustrating that can be."

"Yes, I see that it must have been difficult. I'm most appreciative. But where is he?"

Batra took on a look of concern and sympathy. "He's in Tihar, Princess."

She almost fainted when she heard the words. Tihar! The very name of the Delhi prison carried a sound of horror. A place where hardened criminals were held, reputedly under some of the most unhealthy conditions.

Batra lowered his voice. "However, I assure you I'll do what I can to ensure he gets the best possible treatment. You must stay in frequent contact with me, Princess. Then I can keep you informed as I get more information."

"Is there any way I can see him?"

"I am going to inquire about that very matter. Maybe if you could have dinner with me tonight, by that time I will know the answer."

She shrank from the thought. Even aside from his reputation, and the fact she did not find him in the least attractive, it would not be appropriate for her to accept such an invitation from a man. "I really can't, Mr. Batra. I must apologize, but I've already accepted an invitation with friends. Perhaps I could phone instead?"

Batra's smile turned into a definite frown of displeasure. "I just remembered, Princess, I am expected at Safdarjang Road this afternoon. I'll do my level best, but regrettably I'll have little time to spend on your matter today. However, if you could have lunch with me here at the hotel tomorrow?"

'Safdarjang Road' obviously referred to the Prime Minister's residence. Kaushalya wrestled with the predicament. Batra was sending the message that he expected her company in exchange for his inquiries on her behalf.

True, he had only asked her for "dinner" or "lunch." When she was attending university in America she had occasionally accepted similar invitations, from young college age men. Still, that was there. In Mangarh, even being in the same room with Batra, as she was now, would be scandalous. Among a particular set of the Westernized "elite" in New Delhi, agreeing to such a lunch would probably be considered within reason for a progressive young woman. But even in Delhi, there were numerous persons of more traditional views who might see her with Batra and whisper. Gossip could get to Mahendra or to other relatives and family friends.

And of course Batra wanted much more from her than companionship at a meal. The only reason she was even considering the possibility was to help her father. And her father definitely would not approve. "I'm sorry, Mr. Batra. I can't accept such an invitation. In fact, I probably shouldn't be here with you in the room now. My family is quite traditional and wouldn't understand. It's nothing personal." She rose to leave.

"Princess," he said, his voice now cold, "if you want help with your father from me, you must be more friendly."

"I don't mean to be unfriendly at all, Mr. Batra. But you must realize my circumstances. I simply cannot accept invitations with you alone."

He stared at her. Then he gave a shrug. "Well, Princess, call me if you change your mind. Meanwhile, of course I'll try to give some attention to your father's situation, but unfortunately I do have many other pressing matters."

She absorbed his meaning, then gave a nod, and she and Gopi left. "How horrible!" Gopi said. "Even though I couldn't understand most of that man's English, I could tell His Highness is in Tihar. Who would have thought such a thing could ever happen?"

"I know. It's hard to believe it's real."

In the car, Gopi said, "Dev Batra is a most unpleasant man. I could tell he wanted to manipulate you. You were right to refuse him."

"I know. But he won't be much help to Daddyji since I'm not cooperating."

16

When Kaushalya informed her brother that their father was in Tihar jail, Mahendra was so glad to have the information, horrible though it was, that he had forgiven her for lying to him about the second meeting with Dev Batra. But when she and Mahendra tried to visit their father at Tihar, they were turned away at the gate of the massive complex.

She hadn't dared mention Batra's threats or his insistence on seeing her again. She tried hard not to think about that particular menace. Surely there had to be other ways to help her father, other men with influence who wouldn't be so impossible to deal with.

At Tughluqabad again now, Usha Chand lowered herself to the quarried stone, in the shade of the *neem* tree. Kaushalya sat, too. "I found out Daddyji's in Tihar," Kaushalya said.

"No! How terrible!"

"Dev Batra told me."

"You actually saw Dev Batra?" asked Usha with a frown.

Kaushalya nodded. "Twice. Only because he said he'd help me."

Usha slowly shook her head from side to side. "He's a dangerous man. Try to avoid him if at all possible."

"At least I found out where Daddyji is."

"Tihar." Usha stared at the ground, drew in the soil with her toe. "I wish I could suggest a way to get him out." She looked at Kaushalya. "I'll ask my father again."

They sat still for a time. Kaushalya once more thought about Batra. She needed to confide in someone. And Usha was her best choice. "Dev Batra hinted he won't help any more if I don't...spend some time with him."

Usha's eyes were wide. "You mean—Batra wants you to, uh, date him?"

"It looks that way."

Usha sat speechless, still staring at her. Then, she asked, "You won't do it, will you?"

"I intend to only see him to the extent I have to. But I can't help but think—I mean, if I can help Daddyji, is it my duty, no matter how I have to go about it? What if he dies in jail, when I might have been able to save him?"

"You know your father wouldn't want you to help him that way! He'd be shocked and outraged if you did."

"I know. But I still can't help but wonder."

Usha slowly shook her head, smiling gently in understanding. "You always feel it's your duty to help change everything, make everything better. But there's only so much one person can do. You didn't put your father in jail, and you probably can't get him out by yourself alone, much as you want to."

Kaushalya sighed.

"Why don't you come speak to my father?" Usha asked again. "Maybe he can at least suggest something new to try."

"You don't think he'd mind? A lot of people are avoiding us now."

"He wouldn't mind. He'll be glad to help all he can."

"I'd like you to come with me for this appointment," Kaushalya told Mahendra. "It's with Ashok Chand."

Mahendra stared at her. "So we actually have to ask *him* for help."

Kaushalya looked down, absently twisted her bracelet. "I felt we had little to lose. Usha was glad to arrange it."

Mahendra said, "He's always been quite cordial to me—I really think he's never held a grudge against Father. I doubt I could be so noble about someone who put me in jail for a large part of my life."

"Nor I," Kaushalya said, shaking her head wonderingly. "I know Father feels Ashok Chand was even fair when he negotiated dividing the assets when Mangarh was dissolved as a state." She gave a tight grin. "It's my turn to drive. Besides, I know where Chands live, and you don't."

*

Kaushalya parked the Jaguar in the driveway behind a blue Ambassador. For a former minister in the central government it seemed to Kaushalya that the one floor bungalow was quite modest; it could have been the house of any moderately prosperous middle class person, with trees shading the small walled front and side gardens.

Ashok Chand answered the door himself, his smile showing the gap where he had lost a front tooth to a police *lathi* during a demonstration long ago. Chand wore round-lensed glasses and was clad in white *khadi*. "Come in, come in," he said in the Mangarh dialect of Rajasthani. "You're most welcome, *Rajkumar, Rajkumari.*"

He didn't look at all like a national hero, Kaushalya thought. Ashok Chand had become a celebrity when, during the Partition violence of 1947, he happened to be on a train that was abandoned by its driver in the Punjab. Fearing Muslim attacks against the Hindu and Sikh passengers, Ashok Chand personally took the controls of the locomotive. Despite never having been on a footplate before, he drove the train over fifty miles to safety across the new border into India.

Usha appeared behind her father and greeted them. When they all entered, Chand gestured to a bespectacled young man of medium height who was standing in the middle of the living room. "You surely must know Pratap Singh."

Kaushalya's spirits lifted some at the sight of Pratap, such a good family friend. "Of course," Mahendra was saying. "So good to see you again, Pratap."

"The pleasure is all mine." Smiling, Pratap pressed his palms together and nodded to both of them.

Kaushalya told Mahendra, "Pratap and I share Usha's interest in the Indian Ecological Society, you know."

"Ah, good!" said Ashok Chand. He shifted into English, seemingly without noticing the fact: "Please be seated. Pratap has been helping me with some scientific advice regarding a lawsuit I've filed opposing the Khari River dam project. You know he's an expert botanist. He's telling me about the species that might be affected by the flooding if the dam's built. And we've been talking about the deforestation of the Aravallis. But your business is even more urgent. Do you mind if he stays while we discuss it?"

"Not at all," said Mahendra.

"Of course not," said Kaushalya.

"I was so sorry to hear about your father," said Pratap solemnly. "Is there anything I can do to help?"

"Thank you," said Kaushalya. "Only if you've got influence with Sanjay Gandhi or his mom."

Pratap grimaced. "I'm no help at all there. If anything, they probably think I'm a troublemaker."

Ashok Chand said, "They probably feel the same about me. But I'm still a Congresswallah—although an old one with somewhat dated ideas—so they tolerate me. How can I help you and your father?"

Mahendra related the tale of Lakshman Singh's imprisonment. Somewhat sheepishly, he concluded, "I hope you don't think us too brash in coming to you, sir, considering our father's treatment of you in the past. And considering that I've been in opposition to the Congress. But most people won't even talk to us now, much less help. We thought maybe...." He did not finish the sentence.

Ashok Chand smiled reassuringly. "I'm flattered you thought of me. Of course I'll do what I can. I hold no grudge against your father for his imprisoning me—he wanted to do what was best for his state, and he thought I was a danger to it. We've had many disagreements, but we've respected each other as men who try to do their duty. He was quite cooperative when I worked as Regional Commissioner with him to wind up the affairs of Mangarh state, even though I know it was a traumatic period for him."

"I respect you, sir, for being so large-minded," said Mahendra. "Especially in a time such as this when it may be risky."

Ashok Chand shrugged and again smiled. "Considering the risks I've taken in the past, the dangers to me now seem relatively mild. Anyway, I've survived jails before. I could do it again if needed. What specifically would you like me to do?"

"Well, sir," said Mahendra, "we have reason to think the orders to arrest my father came all the way from the top. We won't ask you to try to change their minds—that's putting you on the spot altogether too much. But if there's anything you can do to get us a meeting with the Prime Minister, or even her son, we'd be most grateful."

Ashok Chand nodded. "I wouldn't hesitate to ask that they release your father if I thought I had enough influence to get results. But there have been so many other arrests, and so far I don't know of anyone being set free. I think it's better if I merely bring the matter to their attention and try to get you a chance to argue your own case."

"We certainly understand and agree," said Kaushalya.

"I know the Income Tax Department is also searching your properties," said Ashok Chand. "This must make it a doubly trying time for you."

Mahendra inclined his head. "It doesn't help matters."

Kaushalya felt embarrassed at the irony: if indeed her father had concealed some wealth, it would have been Ashok Chand from whom he originally hidden it, since Chand had supervised the division of assets when Mangarh state was merged with Rajasthan. She said, "At least the man leading the raid seems to be a person we can deal with."

"May I ask his name?" said Chand.

"Vijay Singh. He's from Delhi now, although I think he came from somewhere near Mangarh originally." She saw an odd look in

Ashok Chand's eyes, and asked, "Do you know him?"

Chand gave a mild smile. "In a way. But it's been years since I've seen him." Ashok Chand fell silent, and it was clear he did not intend to add more about Vijay Singh. At last, he did say, "There's another aspect to your father's arrest, and possibly to the raid, you may not know about."

"Yes?" responded Mahendra.

"Indiraji once visited Mangarh with her father when *he* was Prime Minister. I was there at the time. His Highness went away from Mangarh to avoid receiving them. I never heard Nehru himself mention the incident, but I know Indiraji felt insulted. I doubt she's forgotten it."

Kaushalya and Mahendra exchanged glances. "That doesn't sound good," said Mahendra.

"It may be an added complication," agreed Ashok Chand.

Mahendra rose, as did Kaushalya. "Thank you so much, Mr. Chand," she said warmly.

"Not at all, Princess. I only hope we succeed. These are difficult times."

"Best of luck," Pratap Singh said to them. "Let me know if I can do anything. Anything at all."

"We will," Kaushalya told him gratefully.

"Before you go, you might appreciate seeing Pratap's latest cartoon," suggested Ashok Chand.

Pratap smiled as he withdrew the drawing from a folder and handed it to Mahendra. Mahendra examined the cartoon, laughed heartily and passed it to Kaushalya.

It showed Indira Gandhi being fitted for a sari by a tailor, who wore a ball and chain. On the sari was lettered "INDIA'S CONSTITUTION." The caption below the cartoon said, "Better shape it to fit my figure, Buster!"

Kaushalya chortled, trying to keep from whooping with unladylike loudness. "It's perfect," she said, as she handed it back to the pleased Pratap Singh.

She made no objection to Mahendra driving back to their own house; it was a short distance. When they were in the car, she said, "What a fine man Chandji is! He's such a contrast to the Congress politicians now who'd never think of doing anything that might put their precious privileges at risk."

"He's from a dying breed," Mahendra said, as he sped backwards into the street, seeming oblivious to whether anyone might be in the way.

Kaushalya cringed, thankful to hear no crashes or screams. "I wonder why certain times seem to bring out the best, and others the worst," she said. "There were so many great leaders at the time of Independence—Mahatma Gandhi, Nehru, Patel, Rajaji, Balwant Singh Mehta. Chand is one of the few still left. Outside of those who are in jail, of course, like Jayaprakash Narayan. We might disagree with some of them, but they had integrity and courage. There was no doubt they had the best interest of the people at heart and would sacrifice anything for their country."

The tires squealed as Mahendra tore around a corner. "I'm glad for Pratap's support, too," he said. "With so many friends avoiding us, it's nice to have somebody who's sympathetic."

Kaushalya gave a nod as she braced a hand on the dashboard to avoid being thrown about. "He goes about things quietly. But he sees what needs doing and he acts on it."

Amar could barely pull the gate open before Mahendra shot into their driveway and slammed on the brakes. "Well, back to the telephone."

17

New Delhi, 4 July 1975

"We've done it!" Mahendra said, his face flushed with excitement as he hung up the phone. "We have an appointment with the Prime Minister for 10:15!"

Kaushalya glanced at her watch. "We've barely time to make it there! How did you get one on such short notice?"

"Ashok Chand's work, I'd bet. Apparently she decided to cancel a batch of appointments she'd already scheduled."

Kaushalya ran to check herself in the mirror. No time to change into a sari; at least her *shalwar kameez* looked presentable.

Mahendra was already waiting in the car with the motor running. As soon as she climbed in, they sped out the driveway, almost hitting Amar, who was a fraction of a second slower than usual in leaping out of the way after swinging the gate open.

Thoughts of the upcoming meeting with Indira Gandhi crowded even her fear of Mahendra's driving from her mind. Kaushalya had met the Prime Minister before on a couple of social occasions, and also the PM's father, Jawaharlal Nehru, when *he* was Prime Minister, but they could hardly be said to be acquaintances.

Indira Gandhi often impressed people as personable and even feminine. But it was said she never forgot a slight and never missed an opportunity to get even. Kaushalya felt certain the PM was deeply concerned about the many serious problems facing India and had the intelligence to grapple with them competently. But Mrs. Gandhi insulated herself from those problems with advisors who often gave bad counsel, with self-seekers more concerned with promoting their own advancement than with advancing the cause of the country they supposedly served.

It was only a couple of minutes to the South Block, the huge

Lutyens-designed building housing the Prime Minister's offices, among numerous others. Several officials waited in the PM's outer room; some looked bored, as if they had been there a long time. Promptly at 10:15, a male secretary ushered Mahendra and Kaushalya into the inner office.

Kaushalya knew that Indira Gandhi could turn on the charm when she wished. Today, she apparently didn't wish. Wearing an immaculate yellow sari, she seemed tired and preoccupied. To Kaushalya it appeared that the famous gray streak at the front of the Prime Minister's hair was more prominent now than in the last press photographs.

Indira Gandhi had on her reading spectacles. She remained seated behind her gigantic desk, the same one that her father Jawaharlal Nehru had used. His photograph hung on the wall. As on the few previous occasions when she had seen the leader in person, Kaushalya was surprised at how small, almost tiny, the woman was. After initially glancing up over her glasses at Mahendra and Kaushalya, Indira Gandhi lowered her hooded eyelids and fixed her gaze down on her papers. "Well?" she asked.

"Madam Prime Minister," said Mahendra, his voice hoarse, "we're here to see about getting our father released from police custody. So far as we know, he's been charged with no crime. And as an ex-ruler, he should certainly be eligible for bail—obviously he has no intention of leaving the country. His entire life is here. We'd very much appreciate your help in getting him freed."

Indira Gandhi had been looking down at her desk the entire time, as if examining the papers on it. She scribbled something on one of the documents. Frustrated at not having their cause given more pointed attention, Kaushalya sensed already that the outcome of the meeting would be unsatisfactory. Still without looking up, the Prime Minister said, "He was arrested for violation of currency laws. There was undeclared foreign cash found in his premises."

Mahendra glanced quickly at Kaushalya; this was the first either of them had heard of a reason for the arrest.

"But Madam, any amounts he had must have been quite small! He hasn't even been abroad in years!"

Indira Gandhi at last raised her head and fixed him with a stern gaze. "We're quite strict now in the matter of this type of violation. However, I'll instruct that the appropriate authorities give his case every consideration."

She returned her attention to her papers; again she scribbled on one of them.

"Madam, we haven't even been able to see him yet. Can't we at least have a visit? Or bring him some clothes and food?"

Indira Gandhi looked at him, but did not appear to actually focus her eyes. "The jails have rules about these things. I'm sure the superintendent will be fair with you." Her shoulders stiffened and she bent her head to look back down at her desk top.

The secretary moved forward; the interview was over. Kaushalya could not stand for such a brush-off. "Madam Prime Minister," she said.

Indira Gandhi looked up; having dismissed the visitors, she obviously expected nothing further. Kaushalya momentarily found herself without words. What could she say that could possibly change the PM's mind? And speaking so bluntly as to offend the lady would not help Lakshman Singh's cause.

"Madam," said Kaushalya quietly, "quite a number of your own family members spent time in prisons as a part of India's freedom struggle. You were in jail yourself. You must have missed your father terribly when you were separated. I miss mine. He's old and in poor health, and from what I've heard of Tihar, conditions there are probably even worse than the jails the British used."

Indira Gandhi had been staring at her. The Prime Minister nodded, expressionless.

Frustrated at the lack of a stronger response, Kaushalya added, "May we at least have a doctor see him?"

"Why not?" said the Prime Minister brusquely. She returned to her papers.

Kaushalya persisted: "So we can tell the superintendent you've instructed him to let our doctor see my father?"

"*Miss Singh*," said Indira Gandhi in an irritated tone, her stare icy, emphasizing the words to show she did not recognize any honorifics for royalty. "I understand your concern about your father. But the superintendent runs his jail without any help from me. I suggest you talk with him and leave me out of it."

The secretary ushered Kaushalya and Mahendra from the office.

"Bloody hell!" said Mahendra when they were on the stairway, out of hearing of anyone in the office. "She had no intention of hearing our side. She only met with us to satisfy Ashok Chand."

Kaushalya had angrily concluded the same. "Father was arrested because he criticized her. And because she feels he snubbed her that time long ago. Not for foreign exchange violations."

Mahendra sighed, and said wearily, "We'll keep on trying. Maybe *someone* in this government will be ashamed of what they're doing." He looked over at her. "Your appeal to Madam was well put, Kaushi. It might have worked with someone else. Maybe even with her at another time. But not now. She's too afraid if she shows any weakness her power might collapse."

"Like most tyrants," said Kaushalya, still furious.

"Maybe so," said Mahendra, eventually.

18

Mangarh, 7 July 1975

At about an hour before sunset, Vijay drove to the old fort. Ascending the hill, the jeep met Airavata, who was being ridden down for his daily bath in the river below. Just as the jeep stopped in the courtyard, the timekeeper rang his big gong. Several of the ever present gray langur monkeys scampered along the wall. As usual, the pigeons fluttered from Vijay's path as he crossed the courtyard.

The workmen under Ghosali's direction had cleared the rubble in the tunnel entrance by the old treasury in the upper level of the fortress, and Ghosali and Krishnaswamy had then investigated the passages. "Unfortunately we have found absolutely nothing of interest," Ghosali told Vijay. "They are simply foul smelling old tunnels that go from nowhere to nowhere."

"I'd still like to look at them," Vijay said.

Ghosali sighed. "I thought you would. Perhaps Krishnaswamy can show you. I've had quite enough of dark passages."

Krishnaswamy grinned and his eyes brightened at the chance to show off his explorations. The Bhil guard captain Surmal watched closely, but did not follow, as Krishnaswamy lit a kerosene lantern and led Vijay down the narrow stone stairway descending from the opening that had been cleared of debris. A tunnel hewn from the solid rock soon branched both right and left.

Krishnaswamy held the lantern toward the right hand branch. "This is the longest one, sir. It goes in a straight line to the back of the hill." The tunnel was high enough to walk in without bending over, but only barely, and Vijay felt uncomfortably confined as he followed Krishnaswamy, their footsteps echoing harshly from wall to wall. The air smelled musty, although it was refreshingly cool in comparison to the furnace outdoors. Occasionally a fragment of stone crunched underfoot on the uneven floor.

Krishnaswamy slowed for a moment to say, "We looked for possible hidden chambers or additional openings off the tunnels, sir, but we couldn't spot anything."

Vijay nodded, and they continued. Vijay eyed the rough walls and ceiling and he moved along, but he saw no irregularities that might indicate a concealed exit. The passage continued for a few hundred feet and then ended abruptly. A doorway to the right led to another narrow stairway.

"We had to clear away some more rubble here," Krishnaswamy said. He raised the lantern higher, and Vijay saw that the stair steps continued to the very ceiling. Krishnaswamy climbed to where he could reach an iron hook, which he grasped, using it to pull aside a stone slab overhead, revealing daylight. The two men climbed through the opening, and Vijay saw that they were inside a tiny, open-sided temple, consisting of a stone roof supported by a pillar at each corner. On top of the slab which had covered the exit sat a Shiva *lingam*.

"Maybe an escape route, sir?" suggested Krishnaswamy.

"Most likely." Vijay looked out over the landscape, away from the town. There was little to see through the shimmer of heat, other than a path that angled down the hillside, leading away from the shrine. The *lingam* was dabbed with red paste, and flowers had recently been draped on it, indicating that someone still worshiped here.

"Let's see the rest of the tunnels," said Vijay.

They again descended underground and returned the way they had come. Vijay again carefully watched for signs of a concealed doorway, or any thing that might indicate a hiding place. He saw nothing suspicious.

Near the old treasury, another passage continued in approximately the opposite direction, angling downward. After a few hundred feet it ended at a wooden doorway. Unoiled hinges creaked as Krishnaswamy shoved open the door. In the shadows a small animal, most likely a rat, scampered off.

They ascended a stairway, along which a wooden ladder lay against the wall. At the top, Krishnaswamy removed a bar and opened another wooden door. They stepped out onto a narrow ledge in a recess by a tower in the wall of the fortress. The town of Mangarh lay below, simmering in a haze of hot air. Above the city, kites circled lazily. Vijay looked over the ledge to the rocky soil, perhaps a dozen feet down.

"The ladder on the stairs was probably used to get to the ground, sir," Krishnaswamy said.

"Right. So I suppose this could have been another escape route, or maybe just a way to enter the fort secretly."

"It appears that way."

Vijay pondered what he had seen. "These tunnels are interesting," he mused. "But like you, I didn't see any obvious hints of a hiding place."

"No, sir." Krishnaswamy looked down, as if dejected by the failure.

"Well, your work wasn't for nothing, you know. You've eliminated some likely possibilities, so we can concentrate on other areas."

"I suppose that's true." Krishnaswamy nevertheless was clearly disappointed. Vijay, too, was beginning to feel as if the search would go on forever.

When they returned, Kaushalya Kumari waited with the Bhil guard captain. Ghosali stood by looking glum. Her eyes flashing, the princess said, gesturing toward Ghosali, "Mr. Singh this man is outrageous. I protest having him here!"

Vijay frowned. "What are you referring to, Princess?"

"Captain Surmal tells me that this officer tried to bribe him!"

Vijay stared coldly at Ghosali. "Could this be true?"

Ghosali shrugged. "These guards obviously know where the treasure is hidden. How else could they protect it? Given their loyalty to His Highness, they were hardly likely to volunteer the information. I thought offering some money might buy us at least a hint that would speed the search considerably."

"You know that's against regulations! Any attempts to make a deal in exchange for information have to be approved higher up."

Ghosali's lips curled into a tight smile. "This case has more high level attention than most. I assumed that so long as I got results, no one would give me a hard time about stretching the rules a bit. Anyway, I didn't succeed." He looked pointedly at the Bhil captain. "Not this time, anyway."

"Don't ever do that again!" said Vijay.

Ghosali opened his mouth as if to argue. Then he again shrugged, gave a nod.

Vijay turned to Kaushalya. "I sincerely apologize, Princess. I'll see that the incident is reported to my superiors. If anything like that happens again, please let me know right away."

Kaushalya nodded, tight-lipped, eyes hard. She turned and marched off, the Bhil following.

Vijay glared at Ghosali. "Whatever possessed you to do that?"

Ghosali's again smiled. "You're just upset you didn't try it yourself. I know you've thought of it."

"What nonsense!"

The smile vanished. "Look, Vijay—we haven't found a thing. It is foolhardy to continue blindly digging here and there in the hope we might get lucky, when every one of these Bhils knows exactly what is hidden and where. We just have to keep after them until one of them tells us."

"You leave them alone. They have their rights."

Ghosali shrugged, turned, and strolled away.

Vijay sighed in frustration. Part of what Ghosali said had to be true. The Bhils did know. But there was no legal way to get them to tell.

19

With the ex-Maharaja arrested, Kaushalya Kumari and her brother claiming no knowledge, and the Bhils uncommunicative, Vijay decided to try other persons who could possibly know something about the hidden wealth. He made an appointment with the Thakur of Baldeogarh, and he drove there in the jeep.

Typical of so many villages in Rajasthan, the hilltop castle dominated the town of Baldeogarh below. This fort was not so lofty as that of Mangarh, and it was considerably smaller. But it was still impressive with its high crenelated stone protective walls interrupted by semicircular bastions. Domes and balconies and cupolas crowned what were obviously the living quarters of the palace.

The jeep roared up a cobblestoned incline and through a large gateway. Except for langur monkeys scampering along the base of the wall, no activity was evident in the large open area, so Vijay directed Akbar Khan to drive across it and through the next gate, which was flanked by painted murals of howdah-bearing elephants.

There they entered a smaller courtyard. Ahead hung a marble-pillared balcony, and beneath it another doorway surrounded by murals. A tall, thin man of late middle age, dressed in white shirt, brown trousers, and *chappals*, appeared from the door. When Vijay stepped from the jeep, the man folded his hands in greeting. "Welcome. I am Rajendra Singh. I was expecting you."

Vijay returned the salutation.

The ex-lord of the village led Vijay through a much smaller courtyard to a small, octagonal-shaped balcony overlooking the valley. "May I offer you a drink? Some Scotch? Iced coffee? Or perhaps *lassi*? *Lassi* always tastes good on such a hot day." A young male servant stood waiting.

"*Lassi* would be good, sir."

With the drinks in hand Vijay stated his business of searching for undeclared wealth in the properties of the ex-Maharaja. He ended, trying to be as tactful as possible, "I know that for centuries you and your ancestors have been principal *sardars* in Mangarh State. I thought that you might be able to give me a somewhat different perspective on any wealth that the ruling family has acquired, and maybe even some suggestions as to where we might look."

Rajendra Singh sat looking at Vijay for what seemed like a very long time. At last, he said, "In the absence of a warrant, Mr. Singh, I can't help but wonder about the propriety of my helping you against a fellow Rajput of my clan. Especially when he's been arrested and is therefore not available to defend his interests."

Vijay said, "I understand your reluctance, sir. I can only say that the lost revenues from concealed wealth hurt everyone else in the form of higher taxes. If there's any hidden treasure, we'll probably find it eventually. Having to search longer just makes it more difficult, and costs the taxpayers more money." He took a sip of the *lassi*. He felt more than a little hypocritical making that type of appeal under the circumstances, when so much of the reason for the search was obviously political.

Eventually Rajendra Singh said, "You may have come to me because you've heard that historically there were some conflicts between my branch of the family and His Highness' branch."

"I had heard a mention of such a rift," Vijay admitted. He did not say that the quarrel was the main reason he had thought Rajendra Singh might be willing to help.

"At one time," the Thakur of Baldeogarh said to Vijay, "the division between our clan's branches was deep indeed. My line has even been barred from ever sitting on the throne of Mangarh, right up to the present day."

He watched Vijay, apparently waiting for a reaction. "I've heard that, too, sir," Vijay acknowledged.

"But His Highness and I are now on quite good terms. The rift occurred centuries ago, between two brothers, Hanuman and Baldeo. Hanuman was an ancestor of the present His Highness. Baldeo was my own ancestor, for whom this fortress is named."

HIMALAYAS

PUNJAB
Lahore

Chenab R.
Ravi R.
Indus River

AKBAR'S

EMPIRE

Delhi
Jumna River

Bikaner

(RAJPUT

Jaisalmer

KINGDOMS)

Agra

Amber   Fatehpur
Sikri

THAR   OR   Jodhpur   Merta Pushkar
GREAT   INDIAN   Ajmer
    DESERT   *Khari R.*

ARAVALLI RANGE

Chambal River

Betwa R.

SIND

Mangarh
Banas
Amargarh   Bundi
Haldighati   Kota

Chittorgarh
Udaipur

MALWA   Ujjain

GUJARAT

Narmada River

KANDESH

Tapti River

BERAR

Ajanta

Daulatabad

ARABIAN SEA

AHMADNAGAR

DECCAN
PLATEAU

BIJAPUR

(HINDU EMPIRE
OF VIJAYANAGAR)↓

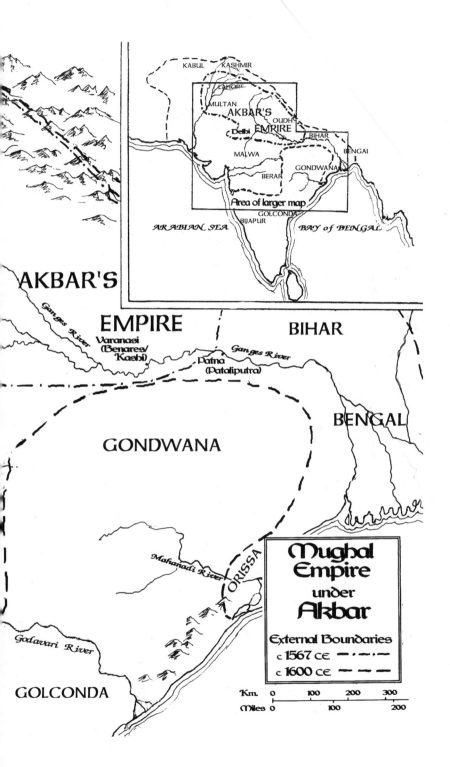

AKBAR'S

EMPIRE

Varanasi
(Benares/
Kashi)

BIHAR

Ganges River

Patna
(Pataliputra)

BENGAL

GONDWANA

Mahanadi River

ORISSA

Godavari River

GOLCONDA

**Mughal
Empire
under
Akbar**

External Boundaries

c 1567 CE — · — · —
c 1600 CE — — — —

Km.   0   100   200   300
Miles 0   100   200

Inset map:

KABUL   KASHMIR

LAHORE

MULTAN

AKBAR'S
EMPIRE

OUDH

Delhi

BIHAR

MALWA

BENGAL

GONDWANA

BERAR

BERAR

Area of larger map

GOLCONDA

BIJAPUR

ARABIAN SEA

BAY of BENGAL

Saffron Robes

1

"A wall may fall, but a Rajput stands firm."

—Rajput war proverb.

Chittorgarh, Mewar State, 30 November 1567 C.E.

Raja Hanuman of Mangarh doubted that he and most of the thousand others he had brought would leave alive. He watched as two of his Rajput retainers set their shields on the ground. Encumbered by their heavy quilted coats, they stiffly knelt to press the palms of their hands on the stony soil. The sappers who labored for the Mughal Emperor Akbar's besieging army were burrowing beneath the foundations of the two towers flanking Chittorgarh's northern gate, and soon the tunneling would be close enough for the fort's defenders to feel the vibrations.

"Nothing yet, *Annadata* (Giver of bread)," Shyam eventually said to the Raja. He stood and retrieved his buckler from the ground.

"I can't be sure," said Kesari, the youngest of the Rajputs present. "I may feel something, but it's too faint to tell."

"It's just your heart thumping with fear," joked the deep rumbling voice of Ajit, the huge Thakur who was the Raja's chief military commander.

Raja Hanuman and the others of his entourage laughed, but he sensed an element of bravado in their mirth. He said levelly, "I'd guess two weeks, three at most, before they blow the explosives."

"We'll be ready," said Ajit.

"Of course," responded Hanuman. As usual, his face did not betray his worry. Although he and the troops he'd brought from Mangarh would ferociously defend the likely breach in the fortifications, the Pariyatra Rajputs were badly outnumbered.

Hanuman often wondered if he would ever again even see his beloved Mangarh: the ancient fort where he'd spent his childhood, where he hoped to construct a magnificent new wing to the palace, with views over the picturesque walled town far below; the forested hills where he and his Rajputs went riding and hunting, just as the legends said Lord Rama and his brother Lakshmana had done in the same places long ago; the valley where he hoped to dam the river and create a beautiful lake with a small, gem-like summer palace on its shore.

Hanuman bent back his steel-helmeted head to look at the overcast winter sky, where the vultures circled through the haze of smoke from the funeral pyres. The fires blazed almost continually, burning the earthly forms of the most recent of Chittorgarh's defenders to die from artillery or sniper fire. And always the big birds were overhead, waiting for opportunities to feast on casualties of the siege.

The Raja heard a cannon ball smash into the top of the fortress wall, and he turned to see masonry and dust fly. Men screamed. Hanuman rushed up the stone steps, his entourage close behind. On the walkway several Rajput warriors were already trying to help their injured brothers. The *vaidyas* and their assistants ran to administer medical aid.

The cannon ball had shattered the curved edge of a merlon and torn through a group of defenders, scattering flesh and bones. One man clutched at where his arm at been and found only pouring blood. Another lay sprawled on his back, missing part of his side and stomach. Yet another, blinded by flying fragments of stone, confusedly held a hand to face and found only warm, wet, softness.

"All four are Lord Govinda's men?" asked Raja Hanuman.

"Yes, *Annadata*," said Ajit.

The Raja shook his head, frowning. "I ordered that everyone on the walls space themselves out enough so this can't happen."

Ajit scowled. "They knew your commands, Highness," he rumbled. "I've repeated the orders often enough myself.'

"So why..." Hanuman realized the question was useless and closed his mouth. The men had paid heavily for ignoring their instructions. At least two would join today's funeral pyres.

A musket ball struck the edge of another nearby merlon with a *whack* and ricocheted off. Tightening his gut to suppress his instinct to

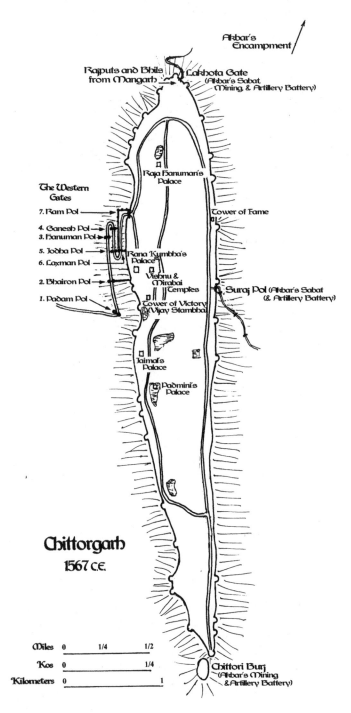

Akbar's
Encampment

Rajputs and Bhils
from Mangarh

Lakhota Gate
(Akbar's Sabat,
Mining, & Artillery Battery)

Raja Hanuman's
Palace

The Western
Gates

Tower of Fame

7. Ram Pol
4. Ganesh Pol
3. Hanuman Pol
5. Jodha Pol
6. Laxman Pol

Rana Kumbha's
Palace

Vishnu &
Mirabai
Temples

2. Bhairon Pol

Suraj Pol (Akbar's Sabat
& Artillery Battery)

1. Padam Pol

Tower of Victory
(Vijay Stambha)

Jaimal's
Palace

Padmini's
Palace

Chittorgarh
1567 C.E.

Miles   0   1/4   1/2

Kos   0   1/4

Kilometers 0   1

Chittori Burj
(Akbar's Mining
& Artillery Battery)

quickly leave, Hanuman slowly looked around, assuring himself none of the others of his party had been hit. He noticed that his younger brother Baldeo's face was purple with anger at yet another loss of men with no good way to retaliate. Baldeo's increasing questioning of Hanuman's handling of the defense had become almost as much of a problem as Emperor Akbar's siege.

The bard Dwarka Das, always alert to material to incorporate into the epic he was composing, had been watching Raja Hanuman with satisfaction. Here was what a Rajput king should be: confident-appearing, intelligent, dedicated to the welfare of his clan and his soldiers, a capable horseman and swordsman, admired by his warriors, even a patron of architecture. The Raja had the light skin, the high forehead, the long slender nose of the Pariyatra clan. If only Hanuman had sired an heir. But hopefully that would come in time—assuming the ruler survived the siege.

Words now came to the bard:

As a cloud pours its rain upon the earth,
So did Akbar pour his barbarians over the land.
But the goddess of Chittorgarh rested,
Relieved that the mighty king Hanuman
Championed her defense against the horde
Who bayed at her feet like a pack of jackals,
Eager to seize hold and drag her to her knees.

Dwarka Das felt gratified to be present at a place where such a glorious struggle was occurring before his eyes. Chittorgarh was not only the capital of the Rajput kingdom of Mewar, it was one of the greatest fortresses of India. The city lay seemingly secure atop its steep sided, boat-shaped ridge over half a mile wide and more than three miles long, all of it protected by the well-built wall and bastions around the entire edge of the flat top. But Akbar was determined to force the Rajput states to acknowledge him as their overlord, and a key element in his strategy was capturing Chittorgarh. The army he commanded in person completely surrounded the fort, and the Emperor was determined to press the siege until the defenders either surrendered or were crushed.

Maharana Udai Singh, ruler of Mewar state and Chittorgarh, had earlier forced the smaller neighboring state of Mangarh into an alliance. When Akbar marched to invade Mewar, Udai Singh had demanded that Raja Hanuman bring Mangarh's army to help defend Chittorgarh. Hanuman's duty was to protect the small but important Lakhota Gate at the north end of the fort.

The Raja moved to another merlon. Careful to keep behind its protection, he gazed down through the slit in the middle at the beast that menaced him and his men. The gigantic snakelike monster of timbers and mud and hides was creeping ever closer to base of the fortress wall, and it would eventually be the main threat to any defenders who might survive the earlier attack when the mines were blown.

The men of the Raja's retinue had gathered along the walkway on either side of him—Ajit; Dwarka Das; the several Rajput retainers of varying ages dressed for war with helmet, shield, and sword; the umbrella and flywhisk bearers; assorted other servants and hangers-on. And, of course, Baldeo, with his own smaller entourage. Hanuman was satisfied to see that the men had all spread themselves apart more than normal. Maybe today's lesson had been learned.

Hanuman sweltered in his quilted coat, and beneath his helmet his head perspired. He watched a Bhil archer, more comfortably clad in only a loincloth and white turban, take aim through the slit in one of the merlons and let fly an arrow at a steep downward angle.

On the plain almost four hundred feet below, a workman clutched his chest and tumbled backward to the ground. The Raja turned toward Dewa, the Bhils' elderly chieftain, who smiled at him. In other circumstances Raja Hanuman would have been appalled at shooting an unarmed laborer. He now nodded approval and said, "Well done, Chief. I'm told your men killed almost a hundred workmen again yesterday."

The tribal's grin broadened. "I shot one myself, *Annadata*. I would have hit more, but my eyes are not so good as they used to be."

"Still, at such a distance! Your bows are doing as well as our Rajputs' muskets," Hanuman said with a fond look at the small, gray-bearded chief, whose people the Rajputs had conquered centuries before.

Hanuman turned back to the ingenious *sabat*, scrutinizing it for the thousandth time, trying to discern some way to slow its progress, if not destroy it. The enemy's zigzag, above ground tunnel was being constructed of thick, mud covered walls, with a roof of planks, surmounted by battlements. Rectangular screens of hides partially shielded the laborers as they worked on the new portions.

Even while building continued, Akbar's soldiers hid behind the fortifications atop the completed parts while shooting upward at Chittorgarh's defenders. When the *sabat* reached the base of the fort, the enemy sappers would use its protection to tear or explode a huge hole in the wall. Then, under complete cover, the attackers would ride their horses and elephants through the tunnel, directly into the fortress.

And the gate Hanuman's troops defended faced only one of the *sabats* the enemy was building; another *sabat* threatened the fort's eastern gate. With his own passionate interest in construction of all types, it was disconcerting to Hanuman that he could devise no way to defeat the ingenuity of the Mughal engineers.

"Even killing a couple hundred workers a day doesn't slow them," grumbled Ajit, a scowl on his ugly, pockmarked face. "The way those layers of mud absorb the impact, our cannon are almost useless. It's hard to aim them down at such a steep angle anyway."

"I'd still estimate about ten to twelve weeks to completion, at the rate they're going," Hanuman said.

"That's my guess, too," said Ajit. "Plenty of time for us to recover after we've repelled the assault when the mines are blown."

Hanuman gazed in frustration at the structure and nodded. He turned to his bard and advisor, Dwarka Das. "Any new suggestions, *charanji?*"

Dwarka Das was a lazy-seeming, chubby man. His droopy eyelids and languorous movements always gave the impression he was half asleep. But he missed nothing. With his keen, clever mind, he was Raja Hanuman's closest and most trusted confidant. Dwarka Das replied in his hoarse voice, "Patience, *Annadata*. As you said, it will be weeks before the *sabat* is finished. Much can happen before then."

Hanuman gave a curt nod. Dwarka Das firmly believed that most difficulties could be outlived if one had the patience to wait. Hanuman was not sure he agreed in this case.

Baldeo, short and muscular, with a heavy-jowled, dark-complexioned face, said bluntly to his brother the Raja, "We need to attack. Now! The longer we wait, the harder it will be to destroy that devil's work."

Raja Hanuman glanced quickly at Baldeo and saw that the warrior's eyes blasted frustration and rage at remaining confined in the fort while the enemy's artillery and sharpshooters steadily reduced the defenders' numbers. "You know the problems with attacking such a huge force," Hanuman replied. "Anyway, we've been ordered not to try anything like that without permission."

Baldeo snorted, a notable lack of courtesy given that Hanuman was the ruler of Mangarh.

Hanuman said coldly, "We can discuss it in council tonight."

His brother made no response. Hanuman stared at him a moment longer, then faced away. He had ordered Baldeo to accompany him on the daily inspection tours primarily to keep watch on him and, hopefully, to know what the man was thinking. Hanuman turned to look within the fortress.

In the mango orchard a short distance away, smoke rose from the campfires of Baldeo's small troop of cavalry. Among the trees and tents, the horses stood tethered. For several days, something had not seemed quite right there. Baldeo's camp had been a little too quiet, and his men had been keeping too much to themselves. Only yesterday, Hanuman saw a bird flutter upward from behind his brother's tent and speed toward the north. It was quite possibly a carrier pigeon. If the bird was indeed bearing a message, to whom would Baldeo be trying to communicate? Someone in Baldeo's own fort in Mangarh territory? Or maybe a neighboring ruler, a rival of Hanuman?

The wind had shifted, and it brought fine ashes and the odor of burning flesh from the funeral pyres. Hanuman turned away; he would consider the matter of his brother again later. For the moment, there were the problems of the mines, and of the *sabat*. He moved along the

walkway toward the gate tower. Shields and swords rattling, his retinue trailed in his wake.

Hanuman carefully scrutinized those of the fort's defenders
who were under his command. To his right, the Bhil archers in their
loincloths and bulky turbans manned a couple hundred feet of wall; to
the left, Rajput musketeers clad in quilted coats and steel helmets guarded
the gate itself. At least the men were spacing themselves out properly
now.

Another enemy musket ball rent the air scarcely a hand's breadth
away from Dwarka Das. The bard reflexively jumped backwards, and
fear flickered momentarily in his eyes. But after quickly glancing about
in embarrassment to see if anyone noticed his lapse, he reassumed the
slight smile that always gave the impression he was enjoying some
secret joke. Dewa the Bhil pretended not to have noticed; the danger
was routine whenever someone was on the parapets.

Hanuman strolled over to assess a section of wall that his own
workmen had repaired before daybreak. His face darkened as he extended a hand, grasped a rough, irregular block of stone. The rock had
been incorporated into a crude mending job done as quickly as possible, by the light of shielded torches to minimize the dangers from
snipers. To a man who loved to build in stone, one of the worst aspects
of a siege was this destruction by the enemy's artillery. The graceful
curves of two adjacent merlons had been merged into a single uneven
mass of undressed rocks. Hanuman decided the repairs were solid enough
for the moment, but they definitely offended his sense of aesthetics.

The Raja moved off, his entourage following, and he led them
up the steps to the gun platform atop the right-hand gate tower. Akbar's
artillery had pounded the semicircular bastion, but overnight the workmen had filled in the gaps in the parapet and re-leveled the surface.
Once again, Hanuman was annoyed at the unsightliness of the recon-
struction.

The four wooden wheels creaked as men strained to position a
new cannon, replacing one that had been destroyed. But the cannons on
the bastions were under the control of Jaimal, the overall fort commander, so Hanuman did not linger to watch the sweating crew mount
the gun.

Taking care not to unduly expose himself to enemy sharpshooters, he gazed down at the plain to the north. The Mughal encampment
stretched as far into the distance as he could see. Even this late in the
morning he smelled smoke from the enemy's thousands of cooking fires
lingering in the air. There was a lull in the artillery barrage, and he
clearly heard the shouts of men down below.

Akbar's army was big—the best estimates were over fifty thousand fighting men, and perhaps five thousand laborers. Still, the fort
itself was so large and strong-walled, so high above the surrounding
flatlands, so well supplied with water and food stores and arms, that
even though it only had eight thousand defenders, it gave many a feel-

ing of invulnerability. Hanuman knew better, and despite his appearance of calm, he was annoyed at himself. He had not anticipated a number of crucial factors: the size of the army Akbar would bring, the extent of the siege train, the cleverness of the enemy engineers, or Akbar's fierce determination.

As a result of his own miscalculations, Hanuman had brought most of his army, as well as many of the men's families, to be trapped in his neighbor's fort. Had he known how determined the Emperor would be to take the city, Hanuman would have devised some way to avoid the treaty obligation to help defend Chittorgarh.

It was not that he feared death. Raised in the Rajput tradition, he expected death in battle rather than dying in bed. But he worried about his clan. The invulnerable-appearing fortress of Chittorgarh had fallen twice before to other tenacious Muslim invaders with huge armies. The First Sack of Chittor had been two hundred fifty years ago, when the Sultan of Delhi, Alauddin Khilji, besieged the fort and ultimately overcame the defenders. The Second Sack was only thirty years ago when Bahadur Shah of Gujarat had blown the walls with explosive mines and defeated the Rajputs.

Each time the battle had concluded with the rite of *jouhar*. The Rajput defenders built huge fires into which their women hurled themselves to avoid facing dishonor at the hands of the foreign conquerors. The men then donned their saffron robes, threw open the gates of the fortress, and rode out to battle the attackers until all the Rajputs had perished.

If the fort fell once more, the defenders would again follow tradition. Hanuman's two wives would burn themselves in the garden of the mansion where they were staying, and he and the other warriors would fight to their deaths. It was likely that the Pariyatra Rajput clan would be virtually eliminated in the *jouhar*.

Ironically, at the request of his council of chiefs, Maharana Udai Singh himself had left to hide in the hills, leaving his capital to be defended by his subchiefs and by allies such as Raja Hanuman. So if Chittorgarh fell, Udai Singh would still survive to challenge Akbar's claim of supremacy over Mewar.

A puff of smoke rose on the plain, and a cannon ball smashed into the side of the tower, jarring the stone floor underfoot. From several enemy gun emplacements came more smoke and the booms of artillery. The barrage was resuming. Hanuman saw no point in lingering in the dangerous position. He descended the steps to the ground, his retinue and Baldeo following. He walked to where giant Chanchal, his favorite elephant, waited patiently, a ladder against the animal's side. The ruler patted the bristly coarse skin on Chanchal's trunk. Hanuman beckoned to an aide, who produced a lump of *gur*, which the Raja took and held out to his friend. Chanchal seized the raw sugar with the tip of his trunk and quickly thrust it into his huge mouth.

"Not much to eat for someone as big as you!" Hanuman told

the elephant. He turned and climbed the ladder to the howdah. The mahout astride the elephant's neck was watching as Hanuman seated himself and gave a nod. Ankle bells jingling, Chanchal obediently lumbered off at the mahout's command.

From the height of the howdah, Hanuman looked over at the small tower-flanked portal, barred now and reinforced with extra timbers and boulders. He thought about the legend related by the bards, which said that the Lakhota Gate had achieved its name because a *lakh* of men had died defending it in an earlier battle. *A hundred thousand men.* Allowing for the poets' exaggeration, that was still a high number of casualties. How would the Mangarh Pariyatras fare, with fewer than *one* thousand defenders?

2

Although built a century before, Hanuman's three-story stone mansion at Chittorgarh appealed to his own taste in architecture. The first requirement for a palace was protection from attack, but once that necessity was taken care of, the designers should concentrate on beauty and interest. The ground floor of this mansion was a plain oblong box for ease in defense, but the two upper levels were ornamented by domes and by small roofed balconies overlooking walled gardens and the lake.

The war council of the Mangarh chiefs met in the courtyard, where oil lamps glowed and torches blazed against the darkness of the cool winter night. Smoke from the funeral pyres hung in the air. The odor was so common now, Hanuman scarcely noticed.

He sat on the *gadi*, the cushions representing the seat of power of his clan, under the red royal umbrella. Tradition fixed the placement of every person present, as well as which men had the privilege of being seated, as opposed to standing. In the shadows behind Hanuman stood a male aide with the white oxtail flywhisk, and yet another held the fan of peacock tail feathers. Another attendant bore Hanuman's sword, still another held the Raja's shield. By Hanuman's special order, the bard Dwarka Das was entitled to be seated, in a position slightly behind the ruler and to the right—conveniently placed in case the ruler wanted advice.

Their turban jewelry sparkling and gleaming in the flickering torchlight, the eight *sardars*, the chiefs of the clan, sat in two rows flanking their king, with the more senior nobles on the Raja's right. At Hanuman's left hand sat the Bhil chief, Dewa, a blanket around his shoulders against the night air.

Seated with the *sardars*, his face often in the shadow cast by a stone pillar, was that constant source of annoyance to Hanuman—his younger brother Baldeo. Baldeo had always been envious of Hanuman, who inherited the throne three years ago at age thirty-four upon the death of their father. On his deathbed, their father had spoken privately to Hanuman, telling him quietly but in earnest, "If anything should happen so you are unable to rule, Baldeo still must never be Raja. He fights well, but away from the battlefield he has no sense of honor."

The traditional Rajput courtesy prevented overt displays of hostility between the brothers. But Hanuman knew Baldeo would gladly oust him from power if a way could be found, such as obtaining the help of armies from neighboring rulers. So Hanuman kept himself informed of Baldeo's activities. And although he doubted Baldeo would go so far as to try assassination, at Dwarka Das' urging, Hanuman had reluctantly ordered extra care to guard his own food against poison.

Tonight, after Hanuman opened the assembly, Baldeo was the first to speak. He leaned forward so his face was in the full glow of the torches. His voice, deep and loud, carried not very subtle criticism of Hanuman. "Brothers, we came here to help Rana Udai Singh defend his capital. Then we find the Rana is not even here. He's hiding in the hills, while we—who are not even from the same clan—defend his city! Back in Mangarh I questioned our duty to come to Chittor. Now I question our staying here. If we are to remain, let's at least engage the enemy."

A murmur of agreement came from two of the *sardars*. One was the young Thakur Govinda, who was loyal to Hanuman in general, but who was swayed by almost any impassioned oration.

The other was Karan, a sullen, heavyset thakur fifty years in age. The *sardar* was Hanuman's chief rival for power in the clan, even more so than Baldeo, due to the fact that he held lands greater in extent than those of the Raja. Karan seldom challenged Hanuman outright, but he did whatever he could to encourage the split between the two brothers, apparently in the hope that if they somehow destroyed each other he might be able to gain—or at least control—the *gadi* himself.

Wondering where his brother was heading, and remembering the possible carrier pigeon flight, Hanuman replied, "We all know that by our treaty Rana Udai Singh had the right to demand our help in defending his capital." Although Hanuman wasn't entirely sure he agreed with the decision, he continued, "It makes sense for the Rana to retreat to the hills. His clan's council of chiefs insisted on it. Then even if Chittorgarh falls to the enemy, the Rana can continue to hold out against Akbar and insist that Mewar is still independent."

A cool wind swept across the courtyard, and the flames in the lamps and torches leaped and flickered. Baldeo leaned forward to speak again, his eyes gleaming in the wavering light. "I ask, why should Chittorgarh fall? We have the strongest fortress in the land, with eight thousand defenders, most of them Rajputs!" There came another small murmur of agreement.

Hanuman spoke, reminding his chiefs of the fact every Rajput knew. "Chittorgarh has fallen twice before." He added pointedly, "Each time, the enemy was determined, and far superior in numbers. Just as Akbar is now."

Baldeo spoke, his powerful hands gesturing broadly, "Then why are we hiding behind the walls like scared sheep? This isn't fighting. Our Bhils, with only a hundred among them, have killed more of the enemy than all eight hundred Rajputs from our clan!" Eyes turned toward the Bhil chief Dewa, who smiled with satisfaction. But Baldeo was continuing, "If we have to be here, the least we can do is raid the enemy's camp!"

The cool wind again blew through the gathering. Hanuman replied, controlling his annoyance with effort, "The enemy's watching every gate. We'd be attacked before we entered their encampment. We would kill a few of them, but they would soon overwhelm us. We'd be throwing lives away needlessly."

Baldeo said, "Brother, I fail to see the point in sitting here waiting. We're like cattle in a pen!"

More murmurs of agreement. "We can't even go out hunting!" said young Thakur Govinda petulantly.

"We all miss hunting in our own hills," Hanuman acknowledged. "But the longer the siege goes on, the more likely Akbar will tire of it and come to terms."

"And if he doesn't?" Baldeo's eyes were glaring at Hanuman in challenge.

Hanuman struggled to appear unmoved by the breach of traditional Rajput courtesy. Disagreements must always be voiced in a friendly manner—especially when arguing with one's Raja. He replied in a level voice, "When the Emperor finally launches his assault, if we've conserved our strength, we can put up the strongest possible resistance."

Baldeo shook his head long and hard in disgust. He said, "More likely, we'll have grown so lazy he'll kill us all in our sleep. *Bhai*, we must raid the enemy's camp! As long as we're here, we might as well bloody our swords on them. I request permission to lead the raid myself."

Hanuman had half expected this, given Baldeo's impatience. Still Baldeo must have known what the answer would be. What was the real reason for the demand? Hanuman wished he had better information as to what was occurring in his brother's inner circle. His spy among Baldeo's men had proven unreliable. Hanuman realized he should attempt to recruit another agent in Baldeo's camp. Although irritated at his brother's tone and at the strongly implied criticisms, Hanuman remained outwardly calm as he replied to Baldeo's request, "No, *Bhai*. Raja Jaimal and the other commanders have agreed—no raids, unless we see a definite need."

Still trying to discern Baldeo's real purpose, Hanuman scrutinized his younger brother. But in the ever-changing glow of the lamps and torches it was even more difficult than usual to read Baldeo's face as he said, "We are all concerned about the *sabat*. But we've done nothing. I'll lead a party to destroy it!"

Hanuman responded evenly, "You know that's been considered, Brother. The *sabat's* too big and too solidly built. You'd be killed before you could seriously damage it. Our clan would be deeply hurt by such a loss."

Baldeo said with sarcasm, "I appreciate Your Highness' concern for the welfare of myself and my men. But we're surrounded by those *mleccha* Turks. All we do is shoot at them from behind our walls! Isn't there a need for more?"

Ajit, seated at Hanuman's right, now spoke, his voice rumbling from his great frame, "Not when it's bound to fail, Baldeoji."

Baldeo said, "With all respect to Lord Ajit, our Rajputs will kill ten of them for every one of us! I don't consider that failing."

Ajit said, "I do, when there will still be fifty thousand of those monkey-faced barbarians left here after all our Rajputs have gone to heaven!"

Karan, Hanuman's other principal rival, slowly shook his head, the diamonds in his turban sparkling in the light of the flames. "*Annadata*, maybe it's indeed a mistake to merely wait out the siege. We're giving the enemy time to gather even more strength. A bold action such as Baldeoji proposes might be evidence to the Emperor of our determination."

As the discussion progressed, it was clear five of the *sardars* and Dewa agreed with their Raja, regretfully, that a raid was not prudent. But the vocal minority of Baldeo and Karan and Govinda argued for action no matter what the result.

"We'll continue our discussion on another day, brothers," said Hanuman at last. He passed the *paan* to his chiefs, signaling that the meeting was concluded.

Except for Ajit, the nobles left, most of them sullen and mumbling to each other.

The Raja thought for a few moments. Baldeo was not only a bold warrior; he could be clever and devious. He had to know the request would be refused. So why had he made the demand? "Damn that brother of mine!" Hanuman said to Ajit and Dwarka Das. "What game is he playing?"

Ajit's ugly, pockmarked face wore a scowl. "He's up to something. But what game could there be? He's caged here like the rest of us."

"He may be communicating with someone outside," said Hanuman. "I think I saw a carrier pigeon leave his camp yesterday."

Ajit grunted. "Then he bears watching. But I wouldn't mind a raid myself if there was anything to be gained."

"Nor would I. He knows it's foolishness, though."

"Then maybe he's just trying to annoy you."

"He's succeeding," grumbled Hanuman.

Dwarka Das said, "If we wait and watch, Highness, no doubt we'll discover what's behind his talk."

"Possibly," said Hanuman. "But it worries me when I can't see where he's headed."

"Guard your back, Highness," the *charan* advised.

"I do," Hanuman muttered. "But from what?"

Normally at this time of the evening, Hanuman would retire to his own apartments, and then to those of his women. However, he was too angry at Baldeo and Karan to relax. Instead, he summoned Bajraj, his favorite charger, and he went to the stables with his retainers following: those loyal Rajput warriors of his clan who almost always accompanied and guarded him, whether in battle or not. Bhupendra, the eldest, was around his own age; Shyam, slightly younger; Kesari, the youngest; and Bheron the second youngest.

The grooms had not expected a ride so late at night, so there was a delay while the trappings were put on Bajraj and the retainers' horses. Hanuman fumed at having to wait, but he strode over to the elephants stabled along the wall of the outer courtyard. The odor of the elephants was always comforting to him, and the smell of the smoke from the mahouts' campfire was pleasantly obscuring that of the funeral pyres. At the Raja's approach the drivers leaped to their feet and did their obeisances. Then they hurried to stand with their animals, ready in case the ruler should want to question their care of their charges.

His retainers held the torches high while he went down the line, speaking to each elephant. Fateh, "Victory," looked tired, his eyes dull. "Has he been eating well?" Hanuman asked the mahout.

"Oh, yes, *Annadata*."

Hanuman held out his hand, and his cup-bearer deposited a lump of sugar. Fateh, with the tip of his trunk, picked it from Hanuman's palm and thrust it into his own mouth.

"He's one of our best," Hanuman said to the mahout, who smiled with pride.

Hanuman moved on to his favorite, the magnificent Chanchal. He stroked the elephant's bristly trunk, fed him a lump of sugar also. "How's my good friend?" Hanuman asked the mahout.

"Very fine, Highness. I can tell he's pleased at your unexpected visit."

"Is he? Good!" As Hanuman stroked the animal's trunk, he found his own anger diminishing. He toyed momentarily with calling for the howdah and taking Chanchal out again. But that meant more delay. And what he really needed was to ride furiously and fast. That meant his charger.

Bajraj now waited with the cavalry escort. The Raja strode over, spoke a few words of greeting to the fine Kathiawari bay. Hanuman then mounted the horse, and they sped out the gate and down the road to the south. Ajit and Dwarka Das and the escort galloped after.

Hanuman habitually rode this circuit of the fort's perimeter in the freshness of each morning, before the sun drew the dew from the grass. Tonight, in the moonlight, the road shone a ghostly white.

Hanuman rode hard, enjoying the feel of the horse's muscular body between his legs, the drum of the hooves on the dusty road, the rush of cool air past his face.

Normally he stopped to look at the Tower of Fame, the smaller of the two elegantly sculptured ornamental towers at Chittor, and always he checked the structure for damage from the enemy bombardment. So far, Akbar's artillery had spared both this tower and the other one, perhaps because the buildings had no significant military value. Tonight Hanuman raced by in the darkness. He tore past the eastern gate without stopping to visit the nobles commanding the guard contingent, and without looking at the additional *sabat* the Mughals were building to destroy this spot in the defenses also.

The scent of smoke from the nearby cremation grounds lay strong in the air now, and he could see the glow of the fires as they consumed the earthly remains of those killed during the day by the enemy artillery and marksmen.

Hanuman rode onward, all the way to the southern tip of the fortress, where the enemy were digging yet more mines, as well as constructing an artillery battery on the small hill opposite. He whirled Bajraj about, and, more slowly now so as not to overtire the horses, led his escort north again, but up the western road this time. Past the small lake, past the tiny water palace where the legendary Queen Padmini had lived. Past the mansions of other Rajput chiefs, including that of his friend Jaimal, the fort's overall commander. But he did not stop to disturb Jaimal so late at night.

He slowed and pressed his palms together in respect as he rode opposite the site of the *mahasati*, where in the earlier sieges so many Rajput women had voluntarily perished by fire rather than be captured by the enemy.

He passed his favorite structure at Chittor, the nine-story sculptured Tower of Victory, its pillared balconies glowing high above in the moonlight. Because of the darkness he did not linger to inspect the tower as was his usual habit.

The scent of Bajraj's sweat mingled with the freshness of the night air, free in this spot from the smoke of the cremation fires. Slowing now, Hanuman trotted the bay past the Vishnu and Mira Bhai temples, and the palace of the legendary Rana Kumbha. Past the fort's main gate, the huge Ram Pol. Then back up to the northern end of the fortress, to his own palace.

He had ridden about three *kos*, six miles in all. Feeling better after the exertion, he dismounted and dismissed his escort, bid Bajraj goodnight.

Hanuman bathed, donned fresh robes, and then he went to his women's apartments. Like all Rajput quarters, these were small, and sparsely furnished—carpets and pillows on the floors, some draperies over the doors and windows, a few oil lamps in wall niches, several storage chests.

He first visited his younger wife Champa, who, because she came from the Hara Rajput clan of Bundi, was usually referred to as the "Bundi Rani" or "Bundiji." Although hungry and fiery in their love-making, she had still failed to conceive after almost six years of receiv-

ing his seed almost daily. Bundiji was twenty-two years of age, short, slightly plump, with a sensual mouth and sultry eyes. Tonight she wore a blouse of thin, sheer red fabric that ended just below her breasts, and a red and yellow full skirt. Because of the coolness of the night, she had wrapped a shawl of fine Kashmiri wool around her shoulders.

She gave him a smile that was at once welcoming and coy, and came to him eagerly for an embrace. In his arms she felt soft and warm through the thin shawl. She had bathed in preparation for his visit and she smelled of her customary sandalwood perfume.

As he held her close, his chin pressed into her gleaming hair, Hanuman again wished that he hadn't endangered her, or the other women, by bringing them to Chittorgarh. But it was customary for the household to accompany a vassal performing a lengthy obligation of service to his overlord. And no one had expected Akbar to bring such a massive siege train to Chittorgarh. Now the future of the entire Pariyatra clan was at stake, with Hanuman's wives here, surrounded by a huge enemy force.

Somehow, though, just being with Bundiji, however briefly, renewed him. "Your back is stiff, my lord," she murmured, looking up at him. "You feel like you are carrying all the troubles of Chittorgarh on your shoulders."

He shrugged. "My duties to our clan often weigh on me. It's to be expected."

Her hand moved down to grip his hip and pull him firmly to her. She grinned. "Let me distract you, my lord."

He smiled down. "I'd like nothing better, beloved. But I can't stay this time." Hanuman had slept with her every night for the past week, so he was overdue for staying with his senior queen instead.

Her breasts pressed into his chest. "Are you sure?" The way she said it, she didn't sound the least bit selfish; rather, her voice was full of concern for him. "I know it's not my turn, my lord—I've already had you more than my share. But if I can relax you first...."

The swelling at his groin was hard to ignore. Reluctantly, he pulled away and said, "You'd relax me too much. I need to reserve some strength."

She smiled at him. "Then I'll be thinking about you. And about tomorrow night."

With regret he left her and walked the few steps to the apartments of his senior queen. Although her name was Sarasvati, she was referred to as the "Sisodia Rani" since she was of that clan. He continually felt guilty at not spending more nights with her. But she never complained, and indeed seemed indifferent to whether or not he was with her frequently.

Tonight she wore a transparent shawl over her head, and a blue and silver blouse and long skirt. She smelled of rose perfume. "Welcome, my lord," she said, her voice courteous but somewhat distant. "Are you ready for some wine?"

He never understood why she often seemed unhappy, aside from the fact, of course, that after so many years she too had not provided him with an heir. Short and still slender in her thirty-second year, she retained much of the beauty she had brought to Hanuman as a fifteen year old bride, when he had been pleased to be given a princess from such a prestigious clan as the Sisodias of Mewar. But although dutiful, she had always been restrained, whether in lovemaking or other matters.

In contrast to the Bundi Rani, who liked to lounge about with her women attendants, gossiping and laughing and eating, the Sisodia Rani frequently spent her time in solitary activities. She was intelligent; she had even learned to read, and she wrote poetry and drew and painted. But her smiles often appeared forced.

Hanuman assumed it was because, despite the repeated visits to pray at the tomb of *pir* Mahmud near Mangarh, she had not yet borne children, and that no doubt made her the subject of ridicule among the other women. He still dutifully paid her a brief daily visit, but their sexual encounters had diminished to no more than once every week or two, mostly an obligation in the hope that some day she would yet provide an heir to the *gadi* of Mangarh.

Tonight the two sat on the cushions, and he inquired about her artistic efforts. In addition to his own fascination with building construction and ornamentation, he took interest in the details of painting. The Rani was often reticent about displaying her work to her husband, but the topic was one of the few which she seemed to truly enjoy discussing with him. She showed him a small painting she had just completed on heavy paper of the mansion and its adjacent pool, done in the increasingly popular style of the painters at the Mughal court.

"You've done well at conveying the rounding of the domes," he said. "And the effect of the water in the pool is masterly."

She smiled in pleasure at his appreciation. He continued to examine it for a short time, then set it aside. Because she oversaw the household budget and the quantity of supplies, he took up the topic of Akbar's prolonged attack. "We should continue to use care with the food and water," Hanuman said. "I don't anticipate running out. But if the siege should continue long enough, and the tanks dry up, or the grain stores somehow got contaminated....It's best to be safe."

Her mood again solemn, she nodded and absently fingered the tassel at the end of her long braid. "I'll see that everyone's careful."

There was a long silence. He tried to turn again to a less serious subject. "Besides the painting, what have you been doing to occupy yourself?" he asked finally.

She gave a shrug of indifference. "The usual. I read. I check the kitchen accounts."

"What have you been reading?"

"Some of Mira Bai's poetry."

"I understand much of it was written here at Chittorgarh."

"So I was told when I was a child and visited here." She seemed to realize she was toying with her braid, and she dropped it and gave him a quick smile as if embarrassed at the fidgeting.

Eventually, he took her to bed, where they each did their duty.

3

He left his wife before first light. He bathed, and his own maid, a pretty girl from a Mangarh village, dressed him in a clean white *dhoti*. As was his custom, he then went to the small room which served as the temple of Ekadantji. Hara, the young Brahmin priest, pulled aside the curtain and stood by as Hanuman entered .

Ekadanta was a silver image of Ganesha, the god with a man's body and a single-tusked elephant's head, a little over a foot tall. Referred to as Ekadantji, "Respected One-Tusk," the household god of the ruling family normally resided in small temple in the garden of the palace at Mangarh. But during times of war, Ekadantji went wherever the Raja went. Even if he had not been the patron deity of the rulers, Hanuman would have prayed to him, for Ganesha was the remover of obstacles, the god of good fortune, and virtually all Rajputs paid him homage before setting out for war, or for any other important undertaking.

Now, Hanuman knelt for some time before Ekadantji. On his behalf Hara the priest presented offerings of grain and flowers, and chanted mantras. Hanuman himself prayed for the departure of the besieging imperial troops, and for the strength and wisdom to emulate Lord Rama so that he himself could lead the Pariyatra clan well.

The sky was growing lighter with the dawn. When he left the shrine, Ajit awaited him, along with Hanuman's retainers. The commander came forward like a moving mountain, his steel buckler clanging against his cuirass as he pressed his palms together and bowed.

"*Annadata*," said Ajit, "I wanted you to know as soon as possible— your brother and his men are missing from their posts."

"Missing! Where have they gone?"

"They had vanished when I arrived at the wall this morning, Highness. Govindaji had the night watch. He said your brother slipped out the gate with his men just before dawn. Baldeoji told Govinda he was leaving to carry out some secret orders."

Hanuman muttered, "Secret orders be damned! He went on a raid after all." Baldeo's timing was good; out of all the chiefs who might have commanded the watch, the naive, gullible Govinda was the only one who could have been convinced by such an unlikely explanation.

Ajit said, "I'm sure there's been no fighting anywhere in the enemy camp, *Annadata*. We'd have heard the commotion."

Hanuman thought quickly. "You're right. Then where could he have gone? You're certain he left the fort?" Hanuman absently let his armorer help him into his cuirass and strap on his sword.

"Yes, Highness. I wondered how such a large party could get past the enemy's sentries, even at night, so I questioned Govinda's men. They said they watched Baldeo and his men disappear into the darkness. They heard an enemy picket shout a challenge, and then everything went quiet. There was no sound of fighting."

"That's odd. I'm going to the gate," said Hanuman, striving to control his temper. He thrust his dagger into his belt and grabbed his buckler, and paused impatiently for his armorer to place his helmet on. "I wonder if this is connected with that carrier pigeon," he muttered.

His entourage fell in behind him and Ajit as Chanchal carried the two swiftly to the portal, where the rising sun was turning the battlements of Chittorgarh an orange tinged with rose. The air was still cool, so many of the foot soldiers on the walls wore blankets around their shoulders. Holding matchlocks and bows ready in case a target should present itself, the men peered through the openings in the merlons.

The section of wall assigned to Baldeo's fifty-odd foot soldiers lay undefended, except for a few men Ajit had temporarily posted to fill the gap. Fighting his rising anger, Raja Hanuman descended from the howdah, turned and gazed across the stony open area to the gardens where Baldeo's thirty or so cavalrymen normally picketed their horses under the shelter of the trees. Although the tents were still pitched, no men or horses were about; crows pecked at the ground by the campfire sites, now black and smokeless. So Baldeo's horsemen had indeed left, too.

Hanuman felt a sinking feeling in his gut. He climbed to the top of the right-hand gate tower, where the gun crew was working on repairing a broken wheel on one of the cannons. Hanuman scanned the road, little more than a steep path, that exited the small portal and wound down the rocky hillside.

As usual the enemy workmen were laboring on the *sabat*. Hanuman looked beyond to the Mughal pickets and artillery positions. There was no indication a skirmish had taken place, no sign whatsoever of Baldeo's passage. Beyond, the vast imperial encampment stretched northward for many *kos*. The sea of tents appeared just as it had the day before. Hanuman saw no indication of a raid; indeed, the number of vultures in the sky seemed fewer than usual.

It was most puzzling. He turned to Ajit and Dwarka Das and asked in frustration, "So why did he leave, if he wasn't going to attack the enemy? And how did he get past them without an alarm being raised?"

Everyone was silent, no one daring to raise the obvious suggestion—that Baldeo had made some arrangement with the enemy, and was therefore a traitor. That was almost unthinkable. Eventually, Dwarka Das spread his hands and said, "We'll find out in due time, *Annadata*."

"Whatever the reason," said Hanuman, "he's brought shame on me. On our whole clan. Deserting his post when we're surrounded—who'd have thought it could happen?"

"He's no coward, Highness," said Dwarka Das. "He didn't leave to avoid a battle. I'm worried at what he might have planned. But I can't see what that may be."

Ajit, who often saw plots even where none existed, said, "I'll wager he's going to try to seize Mangarh while you're trapped here inside Chittorgarh."

Raja Hanuman absently stroked his chin as he considered briefly. Since most of the clan's warriors were here at Chittorgarh, Mangarh itself was lightly defended at the moment—by only fifty horse and a like number of foot soldiers under command of his aged uncle, Mahendra. But Baldeo had even fewer. Hanuman replied, "My brother hasn't enough men to take Mangarh by himself. Even if he found a way to deceive my uncle and grab the fort by a trick, he couldn't hold it for long with so few men."

Ajit said pointedly, "Your brother was the only thakur who didn't bring his wives here."

Hanuman nodded, wondering where Ajit was leading.

"So he must have intended all along to sneak away! It would have been too difficult to get his women out, too, without arousing suspicion."

"Maybe," Hanuman said, unwilling to see that fact alone as proof of a devious scheme.

"Highness," Ajit persisted, "if we're all killed in the final attack, and your brother survives because he's not here, he'd be in a position to lead what's left of our clan. Your uncle Mahendra would be the only chief left, and he's too old now to oppose Baldeo."

Hanuman said reluctantly, "Possibly."

Atop the bastions they were vulnerable to being hit by a cannon ball as well as by the enemy marksmen, so he led the party down the stone stairs to the ground, still trying to make sense of Baldeo's actions. Had Baldeo been trying to divert his attention from something else that was occurring, such as the preparations for leaving the fort? Or had Baldeo been trying to mislead Hanuman as to the possible *reason* for deserting his post? If so, what, then, could be the true justification?

Hanuman could think of none that made sense, and he cursed himself for failing to have planted a good spy among Baldeo's men. He straightened his shoulders. He had his clan's army to lead; he could not afford to let the difficulties overwhelm him.

Dwarka Das, although his sympathies lay totally with the Raja, could not help but be pleased at the unexpected twist in the unfolding drama. What grand material for his epic! The words came easily, gifted to the bard from the gods:

> *Betrayed by the treacherous lord Baldeo,*
> *His own closest kin,*
> *The mighty King Hanumanji*
> *Faltered not an instant.*
> *"Brothers," said Raja Hanuman,*
> *"As an orange tree is strengthened*
> *By the pruning of a diseased limb,*
> *So is our glorious clan*
> *Strengthened by loss of a traitor."*

Dwarka Das nodded to himself in satisfaction. A word could be changed here or there, but it was good.

Cheers sounded from further along the wall toward the south, "*Jai Jaimal ki! Jai Jaimal ki!*" A thunder of hooves and a cloud of dust filled the air, and the men loudly welcomed the arrival of the popular commander of the fort, Jaimal Rathor.

Jaimal and the cavalrymen in his escort reined to a stop. A compact, energetic Rajput around forty years in age, Jaimal dismounted, and he and Hanuman enthusiastically embraced. "Come drink some wine with me," said Hanuman, still upset from Baldeo's disappearance.

He escorted his friend into the tent pavilion under a mango tree a short distance from the wall, and invited him to the seat of honor on one end of the cushions. Jaimal, of the Rathor clan of Rajputs, was widely admired for his courage. He had once commanded the fortress city of Merta. But after a valiant defense he had lost Merta to one of

Akbar's armies. He had negotiated a surrender and left to serve Rana Udai Singh, for whom he now fought.

The Chittorgarh defenders had been badly disorganized when the Rana placed Jaimal in command, but he had quickly brought order to the garrison. It was Jaimal who had divided up responsibilities for protecting the various gates and walls, and he who had organized the workers to so efficiently repair the damage from the nightly poundings of Akbar's artillery.

After Hanuman served the wine, there came the customary inquiries as to each other's health, the trading of gossip. Then he informed Jaimal of Baldeo's mystifying desertion.

Jaimal raised an eyebrow as he listened. Then he gave a shrug and said calmly, "You'd have prevented him leaving if you could."

Hanuman scowled. "My face is still blackened. It's a shame on me and our entire clan."

Jaimal frowned and said, "A few men might think so, but not most."

"Even so, I'll have a black robe waiting for him if he ever returns."

Jaimal sighed. "Exile is an extreme measure. Maybe he had a better reason for leaving than you know."

"Nothing justifies leaving one's post without permission. Or explanation."

Jaimal did not reply; it was difficult to disagree with the statement. They were silent for a time, looking out at the gate and its bastions. Jaimal said, "Eighty men, more or less, will make little difference. But I could use another ten thousand."

Hanuman nodded. "Akbar could bring in ten thousand more, but we can't." He knew that Jaimal, a competent general who had been defeated at Merta only because the odds were overwhelmingly against him, often felt frustrated at the likelihood Akbar would duplicate the conquest.

Both men sat for a time in silence, sipping their wine. Eventually, Jaimal asked, "You agree with me that Akbar can likely overcome us?"

"Yes," Hanuman replied. "We'll ultimately lose. We're too badly outnumbered, and we can't get reinforcements or replenish our supplies. If Akbar breaches the battlements with the mines and *sabats* at a number of points, or if he brings in enough large artillery, we won't be able to repair the walls fast enough."

Jaimal sat quietly a moment. He then said, "Even though I'd hate to surrender without a major battle, we must make at least one try to negotiate our withdrawal. The Rana instructed me to hold Chittorgarh if possible, but not at the sacrifice of everyone within."

Hanuman nodded. "Akbar might be willing to call off the siege if he gets enough concessions."

"I'd like you to head our delegation."

Hanuman stared at his friend in surprise. "Why me? I'm only an ally." The majority of Chittorgarh's generals were vassals of the Rana, and although most of them did not rank as Rajas themselves, some of the thakurs held lands comparable in size to the entire Pariyatra domains.

"They don't have independent kingdoms," Jaimal pointed out. "In Akbar's eyes, you're our most important Raja, since you head your own clan. And I trust you."

Hanuman gave a slight nod. After a moment, he replied, "Then I accept." This honor, this expression of confidence, went far toward expunging the humiliation dealt him by Baldeo.

"I'll send a representative to try to arrange a conference with Akbar," said Jaimal. "It's not certain the Emperor will meet with you personally. He has too much pride. You may have to negotiate through his officers."

Hanuman frowned. "It would be better to talk with him directly. If I offered to present myself at an audience, maybe it would flatter him enough he'd agree. I wouldn't insist he receive me as an equal, of course."

"Couldn't that make him think our resolve is weakening, that we're so ready to abase ourselves before him?"

Hanuman shrugged. "He knows he'll likely win in the end. The fact that we're making an offer to capitulate already puts us in the position of pleading with him. But he's also intelligent enough to realize continuing the siege will be costly for him, too. One reason I'd like to meet with him in person is so I can communicate our resolve to fight to the death. If he hears our proposal indirectly through his officers, its strength might be diluted."

Jaimal gave a shrug. "Maybe. I'll see your offer to go to an audience is communicated. We'll try to save as much of your own prestige as possible, even though it is you who are appearing before him."

Before the sun became uncomfortably hot, Hanuman led his retainers and his personal cavalry contingent of a hundred men on their usual morning circuit of the road around the perimeter of the fort. Then, back at the Lakhota Gate, he dismissed his men and invited Ajit and Dwarka Das to his tent for refreshment before bathing to remove the dust from the ride.

They sensed his mood and did not try to engage him in conversation. As he sipped his wine, Hanuman again worried about the real possibility of most of the Pariyatra clan being wiped out if Chittorgarh fell. He worried about what Baldeo had done. He worried about the likelihood that Akbar would attack Mangarh, regardless of the outcome at Chittorgarh. "You realize," he said to Dwarka Das and Ajit, "that we *must* find the keys to dealing with Akbar. He'll destroy our clan if we don't."

"If Chittorgarh falls, you're probably right," grumbled Ajit.

"Naturally, that's our biggest threat, and our problem at the moment. But even if we survive this siege, Akbar will send an army to conquer Mangarh, almost certainly within the next few years."

"Why?" asked Ajit. "We're too small to be a threat to him."

Hanuman sipped at his wine. "The main highway connecting the Akbar's empire with its ports on the Gujarat coast crosses the fringe of our domains."

Dwarka Das said, "True, and the road's not only used by trade caravans. Akbar needs it for his troops, and for Muslim pilgrims on their way to Mecca. The Emperor will want to ensure the highway is controlled by an ally who would never interfere with free passage."

"Can't we just promise him we'll leave all that traffic alone?" asked Ajit.

"We could. I doubt it would satisfy him. Not when we've been allying ourselves with other Rajputs he sees as his enemies."

Hanuman was tempted to direct that opium be mixed with the wine to help calm his anxieties, but he rejected the notion. Although the opium increased courage and alleviated worries, it also interfered with clear thinking.

Unfortunately, clear thinking was getting him nowhere. He said to Dwarka Das, "*Charanji*, tell me again the words that Samyogita said to Prithviraja Chauhan when he knew he must fight the invader."

The bard replied, "Her words were:

Victory and fame to my lord!
O, Sun of the Chauhans, in glory, or in pleasure, who has
*   tasted so deeply as you?*
To die is the destiny not only of man but of the gods:
*   all desire to throw off the old garment;*
*   but to die well is to live forever.*
Think not of self, but of immortality; let your sword divide
*   your foe.*
If you die, I will be your other half hereafter."

Hanuman nodded, and he sat in thought for a while. Realizing only too well that Akbar would probably be his most dangerous adversary, over the years he had learned as much as possible about the Emperor. Dwarka Das had also gathered considerable information from his own sources. Hanuman asked the *charan*, "What do we know about the Emperor that might help me negotiate?"

"The Emperor has many facets," replied Dwarka Das. "He is intelligent and clever. He can be ruthless, or he can be merciful and forgiving. For a Muslim, he is quite tolerant of other faiths. But he sees himself as the ruler over all the lands he can grasp. He believes his god Allah has destined him to rule all of Hindustan."

"He's shown himself willing—almost eager—to make use of Rajputs as his allies," mused Hanuman. "No doubt partly because he sees too many of his own Muslim nobles as possible rivals."

"With good cause. He had to eliminate some of them to secure his throne."

"Indeed."

Dwarka Das said, "His main goal is clearly to subjugate this entire region. He sees subduing the Maharana of Mewar as the most important step in this. Conquering Chittorgarh is a means to that end."

"So," said Hanuman, "if he can achieve his end without destroying all of us, he'd probably be amenable."

"That seems likely."

"What else do we know about him?" mused Hanuman. "He loves hunting, of course."

"He delights in it. He's proud of his prowess, his marksmanship."

"Like Rajputs."

"You've heard how he killed a tiger with one blow of his sword," said Dwarka Das. Hanuman gave a nod. "Maybe you haven't heard the song about him that villagers sing."

"I think not."

Dwarka Das recited:

Akbar is great; Akbar has no fear in his heart;
Tigers and lions tremble at his approach.
He is generous; he is a protector of the poor,
A Messiah come to wipe the tears of the indigent;
His sword is sharper and brighter than the lightning,
His mace heavier and more deadly than that of Rustam;
He is truly the Emperor of the world; the like of him
*   has not walked the plains of Hindustan before.*
We salute him as the greatest of all kings.

"Interesting," said Hanuman after a time. Then, he said, "We know his strengths. What do you see as his weaknesses?"

"I doubt they'll help us, Highness. Women, for one. He's alienated many of his people by having his agents search out the most beautiful and desirable girls—regardless of whether or not they were married."

Hanuman rubbed his clean-shaven chin with a thumb, then absently shaped his mustache with a finger. He said thoughtfully, "The Kachhwaha Rajputs have been able to take advantage of that. But I wonder if it's worth the price. The pollution of offering a daughter to a foreigner with no caste, even if he is a king. I imagine he'd like to acquire a Mangarh princess since our women are so famed for their beauty. But I have none to offer."

Dwarka Das shook his head. "Since the Emperor is still without an heir, he'd be forever grateful for a bride who produced a healthy male child."

"So would I," said Hanuman, sighing.

"Of course," said Dwarka Das with a quick glance at the Raja. "I meant no offense, Highness."

"I take none, naturally. What else interests him? Elephants are obviously a passion."

"Animals of all kinds, Highness. Horses, camels, cheetahs—but elephants especially. You're aware he collects them by the thousands. He's said to know the names of hundreds of them and of their mahouts. He's always looking for prime specimens to add to his stables."

Hanuman frowned. "Maybe I could use that particular weakness to advantage."

"Ah," said Dwarka Das with a nod. "Chanchal."

Hanuman cursed the necessity. Wouldn't another elephant serve the purpose? What about Fateh, who was quite large, too? But Akbar was a true expert. Only the most magnificent of animals would be likely to move him. Hanuman sighed. "Yes. Chanchal."

That evening Hanuman went to the women's apartments to inform his wives of his mission. They had a definite stake in it; if he failed, he would probably die in battle before long, either during the siege, or when the fort fell. And if he died, his wives would also die.

The Sisodia Rani wore a transparent head scarf as usual, this time with a decorative gold fringe. Her yellow orange blouse and *ghagra* appeared to glow in the light of the mustard oil lamps. He told her, "I'm leading the negotiations with Akbar to try to get him to let us withdraw."

His senior wife glanced sharply at him, gave a nod. "I wish you success, my lord."

He said, "I should never have brought you here from Mangarh. But at the time, of course, we never realized how big an army Akbar would bring. Or how determined he'd be."

She shrugged. "It's of no matter."

"It is to me. If we have the *jouhar*...."

"Then we have the *jouhar*."

"I'll do all I possibly can to avoid it, naturally."

She did not respond. She looked out the window, her face unreadable.

"It must not be easy, knowing it may face you."

She said, still looking out over the gardens, her voice low, "*Sati* or *jouhar*. It's all the same. Whenever, and however, you die, I'll also burn."

"But if I succeed with Akbar, the fighting will end. No *sati*, no *jouhar*, either one."

She looked at him again. "Sooner or later, it's all the same. I will do my duty."

He looked down, not meeting her eyes. "I know you will. You're like Sita in the *Ramayana*, always dutiful."

She took a sharp intake of breath. "Yes. I always do my duty. But I wish you wouldn't always tell me about Sita."

Surprised, he asked, "Why not? She's the ideal wife—and I use Lord Rama as my own standard."

"Please, my lord, just don't talk to me about my duty. I'll do it, but I don't want to talk about it."

Puzzled, Hanuman left her and went to the Bundi Rani's quarters. She wore a yellow blouse and *ghagra* as bright as her smile. After her warm embrace, he explained his mission to her, while still holding her in his arms.

His junior wife stiffened, looking up at his face, and her eyes grew wider. "Oh, I hope you succeed, my love! I try not to think about—about—" she fell into silence.

"The *jouhar*?"

She pulled away just a little. "That, or if anything should happen to you. I don't want to think about it! Let's talk of something else!"

Again, Hanuman regretted bringing his women to Chittorgarh. He was sure the Bundi Rani, like the Sisodia Rani, would do her duty if the time came. But she was clearly terrified by the prospect of either *jouhar* or *sati*. He *must* succeed with his mission, he swore to himself.

His wife tossed her head, and her braid flew to the other side. She smiled at him, seeming to have dismissed their peril from her mind, and she led him to where her bed was arranged on the small balcony overlooking the garden.

The distraction, he realized as he lay quietly afterwards in her embrace under the quilts, while the maids served wine and *paan*, was just what he had needed.

4

The elephants' ankle bells jingled loudly, competing with the slow, steady rhythm of the kettledrums signifying Hanuman's status as Raja. Accompanied by two other lords on their own elephants, Hanuman rode the elephant Fateh toward the audience with the Emperor. A contingent of Rajput horsemen and foot soldiers escorted the party; Dwarka Das rode near Hanuman on horseback. At the rear, led by Chanchal, came ten elephants ridden only by their mahouts.

Hanuman's procession left the fort through the principal gate, the monumental Ram Pol on the west. From there, the cobblestoned road slanted downward, hugging the hillside. On the walls a line of defenders watched and cheered.

After a switchback in the road, the delegation passed through the next of the seven gates, the Lakshmana Pol. Then the Jodha Pol and the Ganesh Pol. As Fateh lumbered down the incline, Hanuman reviewed the elaborate defenses. A separate bastion guarded each gate, and cross walls tied the towers into the hillside to prevent their being bypassed by the enemy. The arrangement had apparently achieved its purpose; Akbar had not concentrated his siege on this main entrance. He instead focused his assault on the north and the east and south, on the smaller gates which, although they had less easily-ascended roads, were also less well protected by subsidiary defensive works.

Beyond the outermost of the western gates the welcoming delegation from the Emperor awaited Hanuman. He recognized the five-colored flag and standards of Akbar's Rajput ally, Bhagwant Das, eldest son of the ruler of the Kachhwaha clan of Amber.

Because Bhagwant Das' father had given a daughter in marriage to the Emperor, the other Rajput clans tended to look down upon the Kachhwahas for the alliance with the unclean barbarians. Still, the customary Rajput courtesies must be followed. While thousands of defenders watched from above on Chittorgarh's ramparts, both parties dismounted from their elephants and approached each other.

"Rama, Rama," called Bhagwant Das in greeting.

Hanuman and the other two chiefs responded in kind and embraced the Amber heir. It had been several years since Hanuman had seen Bhagwant Das, and the broad chested crown prince appeared to have put on weight in late middle age. Hanuman could not help but wonder if Bhagwant Das felt any regret at fighting against other Rajputs on behalf of the invading Emperor, but he saw no sign of anything but calm confidence.

With Bhagwant Das was his son and heir Man Singh. Although only seventeen years of age, Man Singh's handshake was strong, his bearing poised. He had a roundish face, a high bridged nose, and the beginnings of a mustache. The young prince's eyes met Hanuman's with a rapid, intelligent, evaluation.

Both parties immediately remounted their elephants. Bhagwant Das led the delegation northerly toward the center of the encampment. Hanuman had been awed by the vast size of the Mughal camp as he examined it each day from atop Chittorgarh's walls. Close up, it was just as impressive.

Water carriers had preceded the delegation and sprinkled the ground to lay the dust. The procession moved slowly along the length of the broad thoroughfare, which was bordered on each side for perhaps two *kos* by the thousands of dust-tinted whitish tents of the camp followers and ordinary soldiers. After the soldiers' sections came the encampments of the nobles with their multicolored striped tents, most of them larger and finer than those used by Hanuman on tour.

The party passed the raised platform where the timekeepers waited to strike the hour on their drums, and where musicians now played. At last they reached the Emperor's headquarters with its tents of solid red. Bhagwant Das led the procession into a long enclosure surrounded by a rope fence, and here the party dismounted.

By the entrance Hanuman was surprised to see a familiar face among the nobles who awaited them.

Baldeo.

Trying to appear calm, Hanuman walked toward his brother. "Rama, Rama," Hanuman said. He extended his hand in observance of the Rajput courtesy which was customary even between enemies. After the slightest hesitation Baldeo gripped Hanuman's hand with his own. Then, rigidly, they embraced and stepped apart.

Hanuman asked levelly, "Why are you here among our enemy?"

Baldeo had been observing Hanuman with a bold lack of expression, but now his eyes shifted away. "I made it clear I won't fight against my own kin. The Emperor accepted that."

Hanuman strained to control his rage. "You have an arrangement with him?"

Baldeo determinedly looked at his brother and said loudly, "I command a cavalry unit. Five hundred horse. But I won't lead them at Chittorgarh."

Hanuman raised his eyebrows. He said with sarcasm, "You command more cavalry than I." He expected a response, but instead came silence. Baldeo gazed at him with a satisfied air. Hanuman wanted to shout, "You've shamed your clan! I wish I had brought your black robe." However, the tradition of courtesy was too strong. Instead, he said coldly, "I wish you well with your new master."

He signaled the others in his party to continue. Imagine—Baldeo fighting with the Mughals. True, the Kachhwaha Rajputs had joined the imperial troops. But in this case, where the Pariyatras as a whole were fighting Akbar, Baldeo had, in effect, already exiled himself from his clan. Maybe the black robe was not needed, other than as a clear statement of the strength of Hanuman's own disapproval of his brother's actions.

It seemed odd that Baldeo had been waiting in such a conspicuous location, almost as if he wanted Hanuman to see him. Or had Baldeo been instructed, perhaps by the Emperor, to ensure that Hanuman would encounter him? If so, why? Was it an effort by Akbar to annoy Hanuman, in the hope his judgment would be clouded so the Emperor would have even more advantage in the negotiations?

There was probably no way to know. Hanuman struggled to dismiss Baldeo from his mind for the moment, to calm himself for the upcoming audience.

Bhagwant Das, who had tactfully pretended to ignore the exchange with Baldeo, led the delegation into an immense, many-roomed tent pavilion, its floor laid with a colorful patchwork of fine carpets. Hanuman guessed its size at eight times that of his own largest tent. A line of servants entered with trays of sweetmeats. At one end of the room, musicians began to play. When the delegation had been seated and served and the pleasantries exchanged, Bhagwant Das said, "The

Emperor will receive you in a moment. If you first tell me your position, Highness, perhaps I can aid your cause at His Majesty's audience."

Trying not to show annoyance at being required to wait, Hanuman responded, "As a brother Rajput, you know Chittorgarh's strength as a fortress is legendary. We're well supplied with both foodstuffs and ammunition. Your Emperor has already lost many soldiers to our marksmen. We can make the siege a long and costly one. However, we prefer to avoid protracted hostilities. I'm authorized on behalf of our fort's commander, Raja Jaimal Rathor, to offer Chittorgarh's submission. In exchange, your Emperor would lift his siege and guarantee the safety of everyone within."

Bhagwant Das gave a slight frown; however, he said, "The Emperor views Chittorgarh as a symbol of Rajput independence. If the Rana submits to him it will set an example for other Rajput rulers. So the sooner the fort succumbs, the better. Naturally, an annual tribute would be required."

"Of course. We're prepared to negotiate the amount."

An aide entered and signaled Bhagwant Das. The Kachhwaha said, "I'll be pleased to recommend such an agreement to the Emperor. I understand he's now ready. Please come with me." As they walked, Bhagwant Das asked Hanuman, "Do you speak Persian?"

"Very little. I've studied it some, but to date I've had no need of it. Of course, our delegation has an interpreter."

"I can translate for you also," Bhagwant Das said. "It will be more in keeping with the dignity of the court."

Hanuman felt reluctant to depend upon one of Akbar's commanders for interpretation, but he saw no diplomatic way to refuse. Later, he would ask his own translator to confirm Bhagwant Das' accuracy.

The Kachhwaha prince led them around a corner to another side of the immense tent pavilion. Within a large, lushly carpeted open walled room, sat a dais with a golden, six sided platform throne on which lay a crimson bolster. Soon, several obviously high ranking nobles entered and took their places on either side.

Drums sounded. The Emperor Akbar, twenty-five years in age, of medium height and build, wearing a brightly striped robe and a golden turban, strode in. Male attendants followed bearing flywhisks and maces.

The preliminary negotiators had agreed that as a Raja and as a representative of the unconquered Rana, Hanuman would not perform an obeisance before the Emperor. However, since Hanuman was not the ruler of Mewar himself, he would remain standing before Akbar as was customary for all in attendance. Everyone except Hanuman quickly bent to touch the ground, then stood and placed the palms of their hands to the tops of their heads. Twice more they repeated the *taslim* as Akbar seated himself on the throne.

Hanuman examined the Emperor's face closely. Akbar's descent from the Turks and Mongols of Central Asia showed in the narrow eyes and thin eyebrows. Except for a tiny mustache, he was clean shaven. Bhagwant Das presented the negotiators, and the Emperor's head tipped slightly to the right while he turned a pleasant but intent look upon Hanuman. Hanuman had the distinct impression Akbar was evaluating him, taking his measure.

When Bhagwant Das had finished, Akbar spoke in a deep, commanding voice, and Bhagwant Das translated, "The Padshah says he has long admired the valor of the Rajputs of Mangarh." In a lower tone, he added, "You may now present your gifts."

At Hanuman's nod, an attendant brought forth a buckler on which two swords rested. Akbar's minister first examined the weapons, then handed them one at a time to the Emperor. Akbar held a sword up to the light, sighted along its blade, and said, "From Mangarh."

"Yes, Your Majesty." Hanuman felt pride that even the Emperor knew of the fame of the Mangarh swordsmiths and could identify the weapons.

The line of elephants came into view and halted in front of the pavilion. "Also from Mangarh, Your Majesty," said Hanuman in an effort at mild levity. He watched Akbar closely. The Emperor focused on the animals, and at the sight of Chanchal, excitement flickered in Akbar's eyes. He rose, and he strode out to look more closely.

The Emperor went straight to Chanchal, walked slowly around the elephant, examining him carefully. Hanuman felt as if he were betraying his best friend. He only hoped the generous gift would sway the recipient. Akbar glanced quickly at Hanuman, and although he had striven to keep his face composed, he suddenly feared the Emperor must see his feelings of regret at the parting.

Without saying a word, Akbar returned and seated himself on the throne. He appeared more jovial, and Hanuman felt certain the gifts had pleased him.

Bhagwant Das outlined the offer of surrender. Akbar listened carefully, then spoke. Bhagwant Das translated, "The Emperor says he's always admired Rajput valor. Some of his most loyal commanders are Rajput. He has no desire to reduce such fine opponents to food for the vultures that are circling overhead in ever greater numbers. He feels your terms are ones he can agree with, assuming the amount of tribute can be met."

Hanuman's hopes rose.

Akbar was saying something else, and his face had assumed a sterner expression. When he had concluded, Bhagwant Das translated, "The Emperor says, however, that his present quarrel is with the Rana of Mewar himself. He can agree to your terms on only one condition: that His Highness the Rana come and present them personally."

Instantly Hanuman's hopes fell. He tried to marshal his thoughts. Could there be any way to avoid this added condition? He said slowly, while Bhagwant Das translated, "As you know, Your Majesty, I am a Raja myself, and I rule an independent clan. I trust that my own word as a Rajput is sufficient bond."

Akbar smiled and replied through Bhagwant Das, "I am well aware of the Pariyatra Rajputs of Mangarh, and of your own honor. I mean no offense. However, Chittorgarh is the capital of Rana Udai Singh, who is chief of the Sisodia Rajputs. He is my main obstacle to pacifying this region. So it is he I must see in person."

Hanuman slowly shook his head. "The Rana will not agree to that, Sire. His pride is too great. He would feel it would diminish his prestige to appear before you."

Bhagwant Das translated. The Emperor gave a slight shrug. He said a few words. Bhagwant Das turned to Hanuman. "The Padshah says he sees no point in further direct discussions. You can talk with his representatives if you wish. He does not want his own time further taken up until your Rana decides to be reasonable."

It was a dismissal, but Hanuman pretended not to realize that. He said, "I suggest as a compromise that the Padshah receive the Rana as if he were an equal. The Rana might than be willing to come to a meeting."

Bhagwant Das translated, and Akbar gave a shake of his head, spoke a few words. "The Padshah refuses," said Bhagwant Das.

Akbar, his head still leaning to the right as it had been throughout the audience, resumed speaking, and Bhagwant Das translated, "I fear we must settle the matter by measuring our swords." His lips still formed a pleasant curve, but his eyes did not smile. "I have heard many tales of how Chittorgarh is a symbol of valor to all Rajputs. At the moment it seems a symbol of defiance to me personally. And every day I am forced to continue the siege, my irritation grows."

The Emperor's voice took on an edge of steel: "I must warn you—I have made a vow to the spirit of my saint, Khwajah Muin-ud-din Chisti, that I will not leave this place until I have conquered it. I will bring whatever troops and equipment I need to speedily accomplish that. I suggest you convey that message to your Rana. I will guarantee safe passage for a messenger to him."

Hanuman stood silently for a moment, trying desperately to think of some way to change Akbar's mind about requiring the Rana's personal submission. But he knew neither ruler would give in on such a point of pride. With great regret he exchanged farewells with the Emperor and left, escorted by Bhagwant Das.

He felt his failure acutely as he remounted Fateh and slowly proceeded out of the huge encampment. He tried not to think of his two wives burning to death when Akbar's hordes made their final assault. And he tried not to think about Chanchal, whose change of masters had apparently accomplished nothing.

Upon returning to the fort, Hanuman at once reported the results to Jaimal, who received the information stoically. Jaimal then said, "We'll send a messenger to the Rana. But I'm certain he'll never agree to come and submit himself."

Both commanders knew the failure of the negotiation likely meant the deaths of themselves and of the thousands of other Rajputs in the fort, men and women alike, and probably many children, too.

That night, Hanuman told first his Sisodia wife of his efforts. She never changed her expression. She said only, "It doesn't matter. Whether soon or whether later, I'll die by fire anyway."

Bundiji's eyes were anxious when he told her. But then she shoved her concerns aside, and said breezily, "Please don't be worried, my lord. I know you did your best as always."

5

The siege continued. Daily, despite the Bhil archers and the Pariyatra musketmen downing large numbers of workers, the *sabat* opposite the north gate crept closer. To Hanuman, its tunnel looked large enough for two elephants to walk abreast, totally protected against fire from the fort's defenders. The Mughal army's own sharpshooters and artillery crews, using the *sabat's* walls for protection, each day moved their positions continually closer to the fort, resulting in ever-increasing casualties to the Pariyatras and Bhils on the Chittorgarh battlements.

The morning of the fifth day following his meeting with Akbar, Hanuman arrived at the north gate to inspect the placement of his men. First, he squatted and, as usual, placed the palm of his hand on the large flat surface of a rock which was exposed above the surrounding thin layer of soil. He felt a faint, rhythmic pounding of the ground.

"They're much closer, *Annadata*," Ajit said.

"Yes." Hanuman tried to keep his expression calm despite his worries. Akbar's miners labored all hours, tunneling into the base of the hill beneath the two flanking towers of the Lakhota Gate. Sometime soon the workers would reach their objective and set their explosives.

The young Thakur Govinda appeared, accompanied by a small, pockmarked man. Govinda made his obeisance and said, "Highness, this man just returned from Rana Udai Singh. As you expected, the Rana refuses to visit Akbar. But there's something else you should hear."

"What is it?"

"Highness," said the messenger, "when I was passing south of your own territories, I saw a body of cavalry—hundreds of horses—pass in the distance, headed toward Mangarh. At the next village I asked who they were. I was told they were led by your brother, Lord Baldeo. Jaimalji thought you should know this."

Hanuman frowned and pulled at his mustache. Why would

Baldeo head toward Mangarh?

Suddenly he cursed, and exclaimed, "I was a fool not to expect it! He commands five hundred horse now! He might have gotten even more from the Emperor! My uncle can't hold Mangarh against a force such as that!"

Govinda asked, incredulously, "He'd attack Mangarh? His own clan's seat?"

Hanuman replied, "He planned it all along! Why else would he desert his post, exile himself from us, unless he thought he could gain something big enough to compensate for the loss?"

Ajit growled, "I knew it! Even if some of us survive the siege, our numbers will be weakened by the battles. We won't be strong enough to retake Mangarh from Baldeo. Especially if the Emperor supports him!"

Govinda said, "We have to stop him!"

Ajit asked, "How? We're surrounded by the enemy!"

"The carrier pigeons!" said Govinda. "We can at least warn Mahendraji!"

"I'll send some," said Hanuman, growing numb as the full realization of Baldeo's treachery sank in. "But it's too late. Baldeo must have arrived at Mangarh long ago."

Govinda said, "Maybe we can break through Akbar's forces at night and retake Mangarh while we're still strong!"

Hanuman replied with mixed anger and resignation, "My brother has at least five hundred horse." Despair threatened to overpower him as he continued, "By the time we broke through the Emperor's men here, we'd be lucky to have half that many. And we'd probably be pursued all the way by Akbar's cavalry."

How could he have let such a thing happen? He'd been an idiot not to make more of an effort to spy on Baldeo. Again, he cursed himself for coming to Chittorgarh.

Eventually, a message from his uncle arrived via carrier pigeon:

Thakur Mahendra Pariyatra to his nephew, Sri Maharaja Hanuman, commanding:

My face is blackened. I regret to inform you I no longer command Mangarh. Your brother Baldeo used his knowledge of our lands to sneak into the city with a force of Mughal horse disguised as our own men. Under the cover of night, he led several companions into the fort by one of the secret passages. He then subdued the guard and opened the gates to allow the troops to enter. They took the entire fort, myself included, by surprise.

Your brother now claims to be Raja of Mangarh by virtue of appointment by the Mughal Emperor Akbar. He

*ordered me to return to my own castle. We have been well
treated after the seizure. I await your further orders.
    I beg to be allowed to extinguish this shame on my
name.*

Hanuman was now a Raja without a capital or even a palace from which to govern.

He again thought, as he had so often lately, of his dying father's wish that the Pariyatras not be ruled by Baldeo. What would Lord Rama do, if he were in Raja Hanuman's place? That was often the question Hanuman asked himself. He always tried to model himself on the prince who was the hero of the great epic, the *Ramayana*, and he held Rama out as the perfect example of an enlightened ruler. Frequently the answer to a question was clear: live in accordance with one's *dharma*, one's duty, in as honorable a manner as possible. Sometimes the answer was not so clear, especially when the future of the Pariyatra clan was at risk. Hanuman beckoned Dwarka Das forward to be seated near him, and directed, "Recite the part of the *Ramayana* leading up to Lord Rama's exile."

In addition to composing poetry himself, Dwarka Das had committed a number of lengthy epics to memory. Included were the tale of Prithviraja Chauhan and his bride Samyogita; vast portions of the *Mahabharata*; and the *Ramayana*. Despite his hoarse-sounding voice, the vitality of his recitations could entrance audiences and move them to strong emotion.

The *charan* now told of how one day King Dasharatha of Ayodhya realized he was getting old and infirm, so he decided to install his eldest son Rama as prince regent. There was much rejoicing in the kingdom, for Prince Rama was loved and admired by all.

However, years before, King Dasharatha had told his junior queen Kaikeyi that he would grant her any two boons she wished. Now Kaikeyi demanded of the horrified king that he banish Rama to the wilderness for fourteen years and install her son Bharata as prince regent instead. The distraught king felt he had no choice but to grant her requests, since once a promise has been given, the moral law of *dharma* requires it must be kept.

When Rama was informed of his exile, he instantly consented to carrying out his father's agreement. Rama's devoted brother Lakshmana insisted on accompanying him into the exile. And Rama's beautiful wife Sita insisted on going into exile also, in spite of the hardships of living in the forest, as a wife's *dharma* is to remain with her husband, for he is her lord.

"Stop for now," Hanuman interrupted." Dwarka Das sat waiting, and Hanuman asked, "Tell me, why it was so important for Lord Rama to fulfill his father's agreement?"

The bard replied, "The well-being of an entire kingdom depends on the Raja's strict following of his *dharma*. That includes always keeping his promises. And a son's *dharma* includes following the commands of his father, so for Lord Rama to have done anything else would have been unthinkable."

Hanuman nodded. He asked Dwarka Das, "You realize our clan may be almost eliminated from the earth if Akbar defeats us here at Chittorgarh."

Dwarka Das nodded, his half smile gone for once. "It's possible, Highness."

"What do you think Lord Rama would do, if he were leading our people instead of me?"

Dwarka Das peered at him, and eventually said, "The same as you're doing, Highness."

"You're certain?"

"Yes, *Annadata*. Lord Rama always did his duty. So do you."

"And my duty is to fight to the death at Chittorgarh, even if it destroys our clan?"

Dwarka Das hesitated only a moment, before replying, "You are sworn to fight for Rana Udai Singh since he requires it of you, even if you have good reasons why you'd rather not. Just as King Dasharatha had to keep his word even if it broke his heart. He quoted from another part of the *Ramayana*:

> *Man is not entirely free;*
> *Fate drives him here and there.*
> *What rises, falls...*
> *Whether you are here, or elsewhere,*
> *Time passes,*
> *Death walks with us, and sits with us.*
> ...
> *The sun rises, and man rejoices;*
> *The sun sets, and he rejoices;*
> *Little realizing he's died a little.*
> ...
> *A river cannot return to its source,*
> *There is no turning back in life.*
> *Only a going ahead—only acts*
> *That should bring happiness and peace.*
> ...
> *This is how a man of* dharma *should act:*
> *He should obey his guru,*
> *He must be true to himself,*
> *He must keep his word.*

Hanuman always felt renewed, inspired, by this portion of the epic. Here were princes who acted as princes should act, doing what was right regardless of the consequences to themselves. He invariably found himself caught up in the role of Lord Rama, as if he actually were Rama, so many centuries ago. But the idea of the fourteen year exile appalled him. Imagine, so many years away from the city one loved, the friends, the family, the lands that had become a part of one! True, Hanuman might well die here at Chittorgarh. But death was acceptable. The idea of such a long exile was almost unthinkable. Consequently he admired Prince Rama all the more. Hanuman stroked his mustache and asked, "What of my father's command that my brother should not rule Mangarh?"

Dwarka Das looked perplexed. At last, he said, "Highness, as usual I counsel patience. At the moment you can do nothing. If you are killed here you can do nothing. But if you survive, then you can act against your brother. That is all your father could expect of you."

Hanuman slowly nodded. He was glad his bard at least agreed with him that there was no other choice at present. He thought a few minutes. Then, he sighed, and said most reluctantly, "Mangarh must wait. We've agreed to help defend Chittorgarh. We can't desert our allies at such a critical time. Especially not after Baldeo's treason."

Daily Hanuman felt the vibrations from the mining grow stronger. And daily he watched the growing numbers of vultures arrive to circle high overhead in anticipation of a feast, and to perch in trees, weighing down the branches while they peered hungrily from atop their long curved necks, periodically flapped their big wings, and waited.

There was no way to know when Akbar's men would blow the charges in the tunnels. As a precaution, Hanuman ordered that only a few lookouts and marksmen man the gate towers and adjacent walls, to minimize injuries if the structures should be exploded without ample warning. He ensured that a large supply of stone and rubble was available to repair the expected breach. Jaimal ordered additional troops to stand by to reinforce the Pariyatras, who would bear the brunt of the assault.

In mid-December, not quite two months after the beginning of the siege, the defenders saw what appeared to be more than usual enemy activity. From throughout the vast Mughal encampment, elephants and cavalry and foot soldiers flowed toward the area opposite the Lakhota Gate, stirring up a haze of dust amidst the ocean of tents. Hanuman repositioned his men to withstand the assault. Although the *sabats* were not yet completed, Akbar apparently thought the mines alone might be adequate to force entry to the fort.

At the direction of Jaimal, priests sacrificed goats at the cannons atop the bastions and anointed the mouths of the guns with the blood.

Hanuman sat astride Bajraj to address his men, who were excited that at last the long wait appeared to be at an end. He ignored the anxiety that permeated his own guts. Well-founded though the fears were, there was no room for them at a time such as this. He took a deep breath. "My brothers of Mangarh!" he shouted. "Remember what we have all heard from childhood. Often they were the first words spoken to us by our fathers: 'A wall may fall, but a Rajput stands firm!'"

His warriors waved their swords and spears and cheered jubilantly, "*Maharaja Hanuman Singhji ki jai!*" "Victory to the Great King Hanuman Singh!"

"I say to you this day," continued Hanuman, "we will hold this gate and this wall, or we will die!"

More shouts, cheers.

"*Ekadantji ki jai!*" shouted Hanuman. "Victory to Ekadantji!" His men joined the call. "*Ekadantji ki jai!*"

Then came the *puja* in which Hanuman's priest, Hara, blessed the swords, the muskets, the bows and arrows, the lances as the men brought the weapons before him. At last Hanuman gathered his chiefs before the gate, and he passed the cup of wine. He personally welcomed its calming effects. Afterwards, some of the chiefs would add opium to their own draughts. The use of the drug had spread rapidly among the Rajputs in recent years. To keep clear judgment, Hanuman would refrain from the temptation.

All day the defenders waited, while the enemy troops gathered on the plain below. The artillery bombardment grew in intensity as the sun crept farther across the sky.

At nightfall the artillery stopped. But Hanuman insisted his men remain alert, spelling each other off to allow time for sleep. Although he himself was now used to little rest, the weariness and tension had brought him near exhaustion. And waiting was difficult. He would peer out into the darkness at the flames of the enemy's campfires, and he would strain to make sense from the occasional shouts of the men far below, wondering if Akbar's troops might be closing in for an assault before daylight.

Dawn came, and in spite of his efforts to keep awake, Hanuman dozed lightly in short fits as he sat with his aides and Dwarka Das in his tent near the bastion.

Abruptly, a tremendous blast and a convulsion of the earth threw him to the ground. Ignoring the pains in his side, he sprang to his feet and peered toward the gate.

To his amazement, the left tower actually rose from its foundations as dust billowed into the sky. Standing transfixed, he watched the tower lift several feet into the air, and then crumble as chunks of stone flew in all directions. He and the nearer of his aides hurriedly ducked behind the trunk of the mango tree for shelter from the flying debris as the remains of the tower began sliding downward, away from the battlements, toward the enemy.

He drew his sword. The attacking troops shouted their war cries as they clambered upward over the rubble and through the hole blasted in the defenses. Hanuman rushed forward and yelled to his men to meet the assault. Amid shouts of "*Jai Ekadantji!*" his men threw themselves at the attackers. Hanuman scrambled into the debris-strewn gap to aid his troops. The men of his personal escort were moving into position on either side to protect him at the same time they fought the enemy.

The air was filled with the clashing of swords, the firing of muskets, the screams of men. For a moment, he debated whether he should mount Bajraj. But so long as the fighting remained at the breach in the walls, the footing was unsure and there would be little room to maneuver the horse.

He tried to keep an eye on the treacherous footing at the same time as he moved swiftly to engage the enemy. Abruptly, a massive warrior was before him, an imperial officer judging from the steel helmet and breastplate. The enemy's sword was beginning to swing. Hanuman instinctively thrust his shield to deflect the blow. The sword struck with a deafening, arm-numbing clang. Hanuman stumbled on a hunk of stone from the tower, barely regaining his balance.

His huge opponent was dark, round faced, with a fierce, intent, determination in his eyes. The man swung blow after blow, each of which Hanuman barely blocked in time, and each of which threatened to cleave through his shield or knock him off his unstable footing.

Hanuman was rated a better than average swordsman, but this opponent was clearly both more powerful and more skillful. Hanuman desperately warded off the blows as he was driven steadily backward on the uneven footing of the debris, toward the fort's interior, away from the outer wall.

Normally, one or more of his retainers would come to his aid, but apparently all were distracted at the moment by their own perils. He again stumbled as he tripped on a piece of rubble. He frantically recovered as an impact jarred his helmet, his opponent's blade glancing off the steel.

Hanuman swung his own sword hard, but his opponent parried, and then the enemy swung again. Hanuman somehow blocked the blow, but his shield arm felt as if it could no longer answer his will. The next blow, or the one after, his shield would inevitably be a fatal hundredth of a second too late.

He now had been driven backward onto the solid earth; his enemy stood on the edge of the irregular landslide of stones that had so recently been the tower. Hanuman tried to suppress his panic and to use the more solid footing to go on the offensive while he still had some remaining strength.

As his desperate sword swing glanced off his opponent's shield, Hanuman slipped on a stone fragment and lost his balance. He was vaguely aware of his enemy swiftly moving for another blow, a blow Hanuman could never block in time, and he was certain he would die.

Then the earth rumbled and shook beneath him.

A second mine! He struggled vainly to regain his footing as the remaining gate tower exploded into flying rock and dust.

He saw the startled look in his opponent's eyes as the ground slid away and the man tumbled backward down the scarp of the hill.

Hanuman scrambled toward safety. Rock fragments rained from the sky. A hunk glanced off his shoulder. Breathing heavily, trying to summon his strength, he again sought the shelter of the tree.

The shower of stones was lessening. Ignoring the pain of his shoulder, he peered through the spray of dust at the breach in the wall. The second blast had apparently collapsed the remains of both towers inward and downward, into the mass of friend and enemy alike.

It had coincidentally saved his life, albeit maybe only for the moment. His workmen were cowering some distance away, obviously afraid of the explosions and the fighting. Weak from the duel that had almost ended his life, Hanuman forced himself to move forward. "Remove the wounded!" he shouted hoarsely to the head of the laborers. "Fill that breach!"

He saw that his retainer Bheron lay crumpled on the ground, helmet off, his smashed head in a pool of blood. Shyam was helping the young Kesari staunch the flow of blood in a badly cut arm.

Hanuman's cavalry, led by Ajit and Karan, were still engaged with several of the enemy who had burst into the fort itself. Hanuman saw Ajit on horseback, apparently uninjured, vigorously swinging his sword into the small throng of imperial soldiers.

The enemy, outnumbered now that no more reinforcements were arriving, at last turned and fled. The Bhil archers sent showers of arrows at their backs, dropping many of the fighters.

Hanuman's shoulder throbbed. He wondered if his collarbone had been broken by the blow from the rock; it felt painfully tender to his touch. He saw that his laborers, exposed in the daylight to rifle and arrow fire from below, were still reluctant to set to work. He moved forward to oversee the filling in of the giant breach before the enemy should decide to try another assault.

Clearly Akbar's miners had erred in setting the Lakhota Gate mines at different times. The enemy might well have broken through had they destroyed both towers at once and then sent enough men through the huge gap.

An aide appeared, sweat stained and bleeding from several cuts. "*Annadata,*" he reported, "a messenger says the enemy set off another mine at the south end. But they were held off there, too. We've won!"

This time, Hanuman thought. He nodded and managed a tight smile.

6

The funeral fires disposed of the bodies of the dead, removing them from the sight of the survivors. Hanuman would miss Bheron, who had frequently told a coarse joke to lighten difficult moments.

Young Kesari would not wield a sword for weeks, maybe months. Hanuman well knew his own good fortune in escaping so lightly; his shoulder gradually ceased to trouble him.

In the ensuing days he felt an increasing concern at the growing numbers of dead and wounded. The enemy artillery continued to pound the fort. The huge cannon the Mughals had cast in their camp smashed apart buildings as if they were toys, tore gaps in the walls so fast the laborers could barely keep up with the temporary repairs. Hanuman continued to lose men, many of whom he had known all his life.

At least every second man wore a bandage of some kind. Everywhere a group was assembled, someone had an arm in a sling or limped from a leg or foot injury. Sheltered under the awnings in the camps were those confined to their beds by more serious wounds, a few of whom inevitably died every week.

Akbar's laborers continued building the *sabats*. Daily the massive covered passageways crept closer to the fort. In the constant exchange of arrow and musket fire, Akbar lost many more men than did the Chittorgarh defenders. But he had far more men to lose, and he could bring in others. The construction on the *sabats* never slowed.

In the fortress, the armorers' hammers clanged night as well as day, and their grindstones honed at swords and spear points, striving to give the defending warriors every possible advantage in the final encounter.

Hanuman's men diverted themselves by throwing dice or playing games of *chaupar*. Some of the younger men who had not been wounded seriously held wrestling contests. Many of the chiefs continued to lament the lack of opportunity to go hunting, their favorite pastime back in the game-rich hills of the Pariyatra homelands. As a substitute, Govinda and several of his men organized contests in which horsemen armed with spears and bows chased after targets dragged swiftly behind other horses. All the Rajput nobles, Hanuman included, took part, a fact which gave the youthful, naive Govinda great pleasure.

One evening, during his perfunctory visit to his senior wife, she surprised him by making a request. "My lord, I've seen the *Vijay-stambha* only from a distance. I'd like to visit it so I can look at it in detail, and possibly paint it."

He examined her. Her face, though thin, was lovely, framed by a transparent white shawl with small purple tassels hanging from the border. He was at first at a loss for words; she virtually never asked him for anything. And the fact that the tower was his favorite structure made it all the more unexpected. But at last he said, "Of course, my dear. I'll take you there tomorrow. I never thought you'd care, or I would have arranged a visit sooner."

She pressed her lips tightly together and looked away, giving him the impression he had somehow failed her by not knowing she might be interested in the building. She's still beautiful, he thought, as he watched her. If only she weren't so remote. And maybe if she were happier she could gain a little weight. What she needed was a son. He just didn't understand why she couldn't conceive after he'd tried so hard for so long.

Because of its height, the intricately sculpted nine story *stambha* was the structure seen first by anyone approaching the fort from a distance. Built by the great Rana Kumbha a century ago, it was said to commemorate one of the Rana's military victories, although it was also an adjunct to the nearby temple of Vishnu. Hanuman was delighted for the chance to show the structure to someone. Few Rajput nobles cared about buildings or sculpture, beyond ensuring an imposing fort and palace for themselves.

Upon alighting from her palanquin, his Sisodia wife slowly backed away, then stood to gaze upward at the *stambha*. Her three women attendants stared at it with her, chattering among themselves about how remarkable it was. Hanuman was pleased that his wife's face showed such interest.

"The narrow waisted appearance is a powerful effect," Hanuman commented, gesturing toward the five middle floors, which were smaller than the two top and the two bottom stories. His wife did not answer, but she stood, her eyes roaming up and down the tower, for some time.

When at last they walked to the base of the structure, he said, "The combination of vertical and horizontal lines complement each other like the treatments on the towers of the best temples, even though the profile is totally different." Unlike temple towers, which normally arched inward to meet at the uppermost point like a symmetrical mountain peak, this tower rose straight and vertical like a giant erect phallus.

"The sculptures are exquisite," she said.

Hanuman nodded. "No surface is left uncarved. I doubt there's a god or goddess who isn't represented somewhere." With his queen and her women close behind, he climbed the stairs to the plinth, the platform on which the tower stood. He entered the doorway, and, careful not to bump his head on the low overhead sections, climbed the narrow winding stone steps to the *stambha's* top floor. There he pointed out to his wife the long inscription by Rana Kumbha concerning the tower and its nearby temple. Although she herself was literate, Hanuman read aloud a portion that summed up his own opinion of the building:

This abode of Lord Vishnu was built by Kumbha. It is beautiful like Kailasa, the high abode of the gods, and full of wonderful things like the Himalayas....

They moved to the railing and looked out at the view from first one portico, then another. They lingered at the balconies that over-

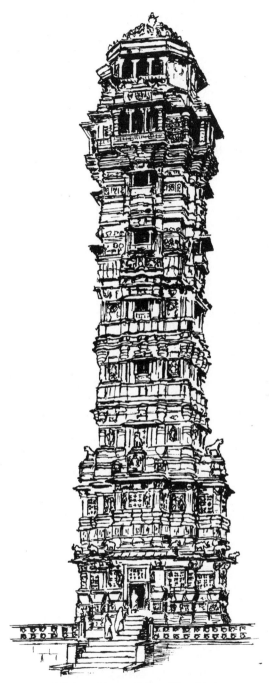

Victory Tower (Vijay Stambha)
at Chittorgarh

looked the city of Chittor in three directions.

But not wanting to be reminded of their peril, they gave only a glance to the western view of the vast Mughal encampment. "Come," said Hanuman. "I'd like to show you something. It's no doubt of little importance, but I find it an interesting detail." They descended to the eighth level and Hanuman led her onto one of the balconies, where four slender pillars supported the overhanging roof. "See here: two of these pillars are clearly of different origin and workmanship from the other two. All four porches on this level are the same way."

She nodded. "Interesting, my lord."

Hanuman said, "The Muslims destroyed tens, maybe hundreds of ancient temples all over Chittorgarh after they captured it the first time. You can see pieces of pillars and statues littered all over the fort. I think the builder of this tower discovered some old matched columns he liked and used them on this level. But he only found eight of them. So he used a pair on each of the four balconies, and had his carvers make eight new pillars to accompany them."

Her lips formed a smile, and she gave a nod.

They spent some time examining the sculptures of the divinities arranged throughout the tower. There were representations of the rivers, the Ganga and the Yamuna. There were the Seasons. The god Shiva and his consort Parvati. The various incarnations of Lord Vishnu. With hundreds of the carvings, it was impractical to inspect them all in one visit.

His wife seemed reluctant to leave, uneager to return to the limited confines of her apartment and garden. "My lord, I'd like to come here again tomorrow and begin my painting of the tower. It's so complex, I'll probably need to return for several days before I've finished."

"Of course. I'll arrange an escort." And Hanuman resolved to make more of an effort to arrange outings for her and the other women.

When they exited the tower, both stood and gazed over the walled garden to the south, their hands pressed together in *mujras*. Neither Hanuman nor his queen commented. The area was where the *mahasati* had occurred thirty years before. It was said Rana Udai Singh's mother had led 13,000 women in burning themselves to death in that *jouhar*.

7

February, 1568

Two months after the failure of the mines, and four months after the beginning of the siege, the *sabats* grasped the feet of Chittorgarh's walls. Soon the final assault would come. Akbar's forces intensified their artillery barrage. For two days and two nights they pounded the bastions and breaches at a number of spots, including near the *sabat* at the Lakhota Gate. Workmen struggled to repair the gaps but were only partly successful.

In the middle of the second night, Hanuman and Jaimal, both nearing complete exhaustion, were supervising the filling of one of the breaches by the Lakhota Gate *sabat* with oil-soaked wood and cotton. The material would be set aflame at the time of the assault to slow the attackers, who would have to dash through the blaze in order to gain entry to the fort.

Jaimal stood near the top of the ramparts, assuming that darkness concealed his activities. But he was dimly outlined by the torches and oil lamps the laborers used to see their work.

A shot rang out from the *sabat*, one of many shots that night. Jaimal fell backward, a spot of blood on his forehead. With many others, Hanuman rushed to the fort commander's side. Jaimal lay on his back, unconscious. Two *vaidyas* examined him; although seriously wounded, he still breathed. The physicians supervised placing him in a litter. Hanuman watched as the bearers carried the commander away.

With such a critical injury, Hanuman knew it was the last time he would see his friend on this earth. He wondered about the implications for the defense of Chittorgarh. Would the garrison still have the enthusiasm to hold out as long as possible? Jaimal had been an extremely popular general, and in many ways he personified the fort's defense, having organized the preparations from the beginning. Because personal loyalties to a chief were so important, and because so many troops were paid mercenaries, battles were often lost when a ruler or commander was killed and his men no longer saw any reason to continue fighting.

In less than an hour word spread throughout the fort that Jaimal was dead and that his nephew Fateh had assumed command. Hanuman sensed that after the past two havoc-filled days, the spirits of the defenders—including his own—were at the lowest point since the beginning of the siege.

It was clear that the Mughals would begin their final onslaught at any moment. Hanuman was almost certain that this time they would overwhelm the defenses, and Chittorgarh would fall for the third time.

"*Annadata.*"

Ajit's voice startled Hanuman. Lost in his thoughts, he had not seen his chief approach through the darkness. "What is it?"

"The *jouhar*," Ajit said. "The Sisodias and Chauhans and Rathors are already starting." His voice was characteristically unemotional despite the announcement of the defenders' imminent dooms.

Hanuman called his *sardars* together in his tent and seated them on the carpet. He passed the customary cup of wine, but there was little time for the usual drawn out conversation. They sat in their traditional spots, dark shapes outlined dimly in the lamplight. Metal clanged against metal as Ajit's huge form changed position.

Hanuman forced his exhausted body to straighten to its full height. He said in a loud, firm voice, "Brothers, we must decide our next course of action, and we have little time. Therefore, before asking for your opinions, I will give you some information bearing on it. I know we will resist the expected assault with all our strength, as the Pariyatras have always done. Many of us will fight to our deaths.

"The other clans will soon begin the *jouhar*. Normally we would share it and die with them. However, I have a pledge to fulfill, one to the spirit of my own father. My brother must not rule Mangarh. I need all of you to help retake our capital from him."

The chiefs shuffled uneasily, surprised by the abrupt announcement which assumed outlasting the siege. Then Govinda blurted with his typical youthful lack of restraint, "But Highness, we're surrounded and outnumbered. How could we survive even if we wanted to? And how would we protect our women from being dishonored by the enemy?"

Ajit asked more bluntly, "Are we all to hide in some hole like rats, hoping the enemy won't find us?"

"You raise serious questions," said Hanuman. "Here is my proposal." He summarized his plan.

Silence followed, broken only by uneasy shiftings of weight. At last, Ajit spoke in his rumbling voice, "Maharaja, I feel we should all fight to our deaths. That's what our fellow clans will do. Do we want them to think us cowards?"

Hanuman had hoped Ajit would speak in support of him. But clearly the warrior felt strongly about the matter. Then Karan's voice came from the darkness, resisting the idea as Hanuman had expected: "The first words we learned from our fathers were the ones you've quoted yourself—'A wall may fall, but a Rajput stands firm.' Would you have us betray our heritage? How can we not fight to the last man, when the other clans are doing so?"

Govinda again spoke, his voice hesitant, "Maharaja, I want to help you. But my men want to fight to the end here. So do I."

"I do also, Govindaji," Hanuman said calmly. "However, I looked to the exploits of the great Lord Rama for guidance. He, too, had to face a dilemma. His decision was that his father's word must be kept at all costs. I must keep to the pledge I gave my own father on his deathbed."

More silence. Then, Ajit said, "I hardly know which path to take. But I think we must support our Maharaja in this difficult choice. If we all die, Thakur Baldeo and his line will rule Mangarh forever. No one will survive to challenge him!"

"I don't like running away," growled Karan.

"Neither do I," said Ajit. "But how can we let Lord Baldeo rule? How can we not support our Raja in keeping his father's pledge?"

"What about our pledge to Rana Udai Singh to defend his fort?"

asked Karan.

"We'll keep that promise," said Hanuman. "Some of us, maybe even all of us, may yet die in battle before dawn comes."

"*Annadata*, your plan has its own risks, even if we agree," said Karan.

"Indeed it does," replied Hanuman. "Nonetheless, it's the best I can think of."

"I still don't like it," grumbled Ajit. "But I'll support our Raja. I only hope the other clans realize why."

Dewa said simply, his face expressionless, "We Bhils have sworn loyalty to our Raja."

Govinda said, "I'll support our Raja. I hope my men will understand."

One by one, the remaining *sardars* gave their reluctant agreement.

Hanuman distributed *paan* to each chief, dismissing them. "You must see to the arrangements for your men and your households."

The chiefs sat a moment longer, then by ones and twos they rose and moved off.

Hanuman turned to Dwarka Das, whose face had been inscrutable. In a way, Hanuman was more concerned with the bard's opinion than with those of the chiefs. Because a *charan* was protected by his traditional immunity, a bard who considered a patron to be cowardly could compose and publicly recite poems in which the patron was mercilessly ridiculed. "How do you feel about my decision?" Hanuman asked Dwarka Das.

The bard gave a tight smile and replied, "There is more than one type of courage. And sometimes it takes more courage *not* to keep on fighting to the death, than to blindly continue, Highness."

"Then I assume that you don't disapprove of what I've done."

Dwarka Das said, "There is the *dharma* of everyday life, and there is a higher *dharma*. Few men realize that. Fewer still can perceive when the higher *dharma* should override the lower. I can't predict the outcome of your decision any more than can you, Highness. But you based it on the highest principles, not merely for selfish gain. So I can't disagree."

Hanuman thought a moment, nodded. It was as much approval as he had any right to expect. The decision was his own, and the consequences were on his own head.

He hurried to his mansion. When he arrived, in the lamplight he saw his senior queen, stern faced, directing the servants at the stacking of logs in the center of the garden in preparation for the huge *jouhar* fire, where she expected to die. A slave girl was pouring *ghee* from a large earthen jar over the wood.

Hanuman summoned his two Ranis to the terrace. His junior wife, too, appeared exhausted and tense. "No one in our household will take part in the rites," he told them. "I'll need you when we return to

Mangarh."

His Sisodia wife's eyes narrowed. She remained silent, waiting for him to explain. Bundiji looked relieved at having her sentence of imminent death lifted. But she asked, "We won't share the *jouhar*, my lord? What will the other clans think?"

"I don't know." He met her eyes. "I hope they'll understand I've pledged to carry out my father's wish that my brother not rule Mangarh. So I must retake the *gadi*. I need both of you for our escape from Chittorgarh."

"Escape!" said his senior wife at last. "You won't wear the saffron, my lord? What about your duty to defend the fort? You want the other clans to think the Pariyatras are cowards?"

It seemed to Hanuman almost as if she was disappointed at the reprieve. Had she truly been that unhappy? He replied, "I'll fight to defend the fort until the last moment. But if I'm still alive when Chittorgarh falls, I intend to leave. You'll come, too."

His junior wife asked, her voice hoarse, "How can we leave when we're surrounded by thousands of enemy?"

Hanuman told them what he had in mind. Bundiji's eyes suddenly glowed with hope. The Sisodia Rani said simply, tonelessly, "If that's what you want, my lord."

"It is." He sent them to begin their preparations. Then he went to his own apartment, of which he had seen little in recent days. His own yellow-orange robe had been laid out on his bed. He fingered the coarse cotton.

His servant girl moved to help him put on the robe. He hesitated. Did he have the right to wear it along with the brave men of the other Rajput clans, when he did not intend to die with them in their final charge against the enemy?

At last, he nodded at his maid and raised his arms so she could slip it over his cuirass. He planned to fight with the other clans until the last possible moment before their mass suicide. He would fight with all his strength, at the full risk of his life.

The saffron robe did not signify only fighting to the death. It signified fighting to death *or* to victory. Perhaps there was more than one way to fight to victory.

He prayed before the shrine of Ekadanta. As Hanuman left for his post at the Lakhota Gate, Hara, the priest, approached to complete his own part of the preparations for the escape.

The air now smelled strongly of smoke, and of burning flesh. In several directions the sky over the fortress city glowed from large fires. But he heard no screams; the only sounds were those of voices drifting faintly up from the surrounding Mughal army. He felt the utmost admiration for the women who could meet their fates with such dignity and quiet. So many Rajput men, no matter how brave, screamed when dealt a painful blow in battle, or moaned in agony when wounded.

He again felt the guilt over his own wives not participating in the *jouhar*. It was as if he were betraying his fellow chiefs, and he hoped they could comprehend his conflicting obligations.

At the Lakhota Gate, Ajit waited on his horse. The saffron robes worn by him and the other clansmen glowed warmly in the torchlight. Only the Bhils and Dwarka Das and the other non-Rajputs wore their usual fighting attire.

Hanuman rode Bajraj back and forth, inspecting the men. He could tell from their eyes, their speech, that many of them had taken opium to help them maintain their valor in the fighting and to ignore the pain from any wounds. He understood why his warriors wanted to use such an aid. Thousands of men and women would die before dawn, and thousands of others would be injured.

He himself could well be one of the dead or wounded. Despite his Rajput upbringing, despite his own experience in earlier wars, he could still feel a knot of the fear, somewhere deep within himself. If allowed to come to the surface, that fear could overwhelm him and turn him into a coward.

From his earliest childhood he had ruthlessly suppressed the fear. That was the way of the Rajput, and especially of any Rajput who would rule others and lead them in battle. But tonight the wine he had drunk was not enough to make him forget his trepidation, or his anxieties over whether or not his plan would succeed. Opium would be welcome, except he did not dare to use it. He needed all his wits available to carry out his intentions.

The conversation of his men was subdued; everyone was too aware of the hundreds of women of the other clans perishing in the flames that illuminated the sky. Hanuman tried not to think about the fact that his own wives would be dying had he not ordered them to live.

The horrible night dragged on as if the gods had decreed there would never be another day. And odors of the smoke and the burning bodies lingered for what seemed a very long time, slowly waning as dawn appeared.

Then the Mughal cannons broke the silence. Hundreds of explosions launched projectiles to smash apart the repair work where breaches had already been torn in the fortifications. The air smelled of the gunpowder and smoke. After an hour, the bombardment ceased.

A mammoth blast shook the earth. Down in the *sabat*, enemy sappers were at last blowing a hole in the wall. Rocks flew as the fortifications crumbled.

Through the dust Hanuman saw the gaping dark mouth of the tunnel into the *sabat*. He and Ajit positioned their cavalry and elephants to face the breach. Immediately behind were massed their foot soldiers, with the Bhil archers on the flanks.

His heart pounded, his breathing quickened as they waited. He forced himself to take deep breaths, trying to calm himself.

An elephant appeared in the gap. "Light the fires!" Hanuman

commanded, his voice hoarse, but surprisingly steady. He tightened his grip on his sword. With torches workmen quickly set the flammable materials ablaze, but much of the fuel had been smothered by debris from the collapsing bastions.

More elephants emerged, stepping carefully through the rubble and the freshly leaping flames. Reaching level ground, the animals charged, trumpeting and shrieking. The flames forced the enemy to divert their course, slowing their charge but not halting it.

"*Jai Ekadantji!*" cried the defenders. The Pariyatra's own elephants sped forward and met their opposition with thuds and clashing of metal.

After the enemy's elephants came the Mughal horse cavalry, and suddenly Hanuman himself was fighting with all his strength. The *sabat* was like a funnel from the underworld, spewing out a hell of men, horses, elephants from the smoking chasm.

Hanuman led first one cavalry charge, then another, trying to deal blows that would slow the enemy onslaught. The din of clanging swords, shouting and screaming men, musket shots, shrieking elephants continued on and on. The flames at the breach were dying down and still the enemy came, jubilant in their fighting now that victory was imminent after so many months.

Hanuman's arm had grown so tired that it seemed as if he could no longer swing his sword. Still the attackers came, wave after wave of them, clambering up through the crumpled remains of the ramparts. Somehow his body obeyed his will and kept fighting, and his voice continued to urge his men to resist the onrush.

The Pariyatra and Bhil defenders reluctantly yielded ground as the sheer weight and numbers of attackers forced them backward away from the walls. Numerous blood soaked, saffron robed figures lay crumpled on the earth, intermixed with the loincloth clad bodies of the Bhil tribesman, to be crushed further into the dirt with each minute by wave after wave of horse cavalry, foot soldiers, elephants.

Suddenly Hanuman had an enemy horseman on both sides, each targeting him. The two swung their swords almost simultaneously. He deflected one with his shield, the other with his own blade. He was aware of yet another enemy moving in behind him, but he could do nothing to defend himself, so furious was the attack by the pair who had already engaged him.

Abruptly, one of his attackers fell, dealt a blow from the rear. Hanuman concentrated on the other, who suddenly withdrew and rode onward, as did the one who had threatened him from behind.

He looked to see who had rescued him. Dwarka Das raised a bloody sword in salute. So even the bard was helping the defense, temporarily giving up his immunity from being attacked. Dwarka Das called to Hanuman, "Highness, the enemy's beginning to assault us from inside, as well as out. The fort is lost."

Aching and bruised from his efforts, Hanuman gave a quick

nod. Continued resistance would be symbolic defiance only, acts of Rajput valor creating legends for the bards to tell of when they related tales of the Third Sack of Chittor to inspire future Rajput warriors. But Chittorgarh now belonged to Akbar.

Hanuman stopped to wipe the blood from his sword and the sweat from its handle. His robe was torn and bloodstained, but surprisingly his wounds so far were minor. He knew he must soon attempt the escape or he would no longer be alive to try.

He passed word to his chiefs to disengage. He glanced about, saw his retainer Shyam lying sprawled on his back, clearly dead. Kesari was helping a limping Bhupendra away from the fighting.

As planned previously, Govinda and his surviving troops moved into position to screen the withdrawal. The other fighters who still survived fled the short distance to their Raja's mansion, helping or carrying their comrades who were seriously wounded.

Hanuman cast a last look over his shoulder just in time to see Govinda tumble from his horse as several enemy attackers overwhelmed him. Hanuman strained to resist the urge to go back to aid the young chief. Govinda would have wanted to die in battle; to all appearances he had won that honor.

At the mansion the women and servants waited in the courtyard. Those Rajput fighting men who were still able shed their yellow-orange robes and gathered around their chiefs. They began binding the arms of the women and servants and children, and of Dewa and his surviving Bhils, and of the non-fighters such as the priest Hara. The two Ranis and the wives of the other chiefs, and the men who were too severely wounded to walk, were packed into several bullock carts of the type used by farmers.

An attendant helped Hanuman out of his own robe, and, because he was known to many of the enemy due to the earlier negotiating mission, another attendant fixed a bandage over Hanuman's lower face as a partial disguise.

He looked about. There were substantially fewer men than he had hoped for. He made a quick estimate of the numbers of Pariyatra fighters remaining. Maybe five hundred, at most. Half the number he had brought to Chittorgarh.

His body felt as if it had been hammered in every muscle and torn in every joint. But he forced himself to somehow summon the strength to remount Bajraj, and to begin to lead the exodus toward the main gate.

A contingent of fighting men arrived bearing a robe-clad body, and cluster of women began to wail. "Govindaji's," said Dwarka Das. "His wife will want to join him." Hanuman gave a sad nod. So the *jouhar* fire would be used after all. He had sometimes been annoyed by Govinda being so easily influenced by the opposition's arguments, but the young Thakur had meant well.

Hanuman and his fighters began marching the others toward

the main gate. They had no sooner left the courtyard when a troop of enemy cavalry appeared, galloping toward them from the direction of the western entrance. Hanuman's men readied their swords, but he said to his troops, his voice roughened from the stress and exhaustion, "Don't fight unless we have to. Remember we're pretending to be their allies."

The imperial officer leading the horsemen reined to a halt. He called out in Persian, asking something about the defenders at the north gate.

Hanuman's stomach churned. What was the man saying? "I don't speak Persian well," he replied loudly. He held his breath. The sweat poured from his armpits.

The officer switched to a Delhi region dialect Hanuman understood. "You've been near the north gate?"

Hanuman hesitated only a fraction of a second before replying, "Not long ago. We captured these people there. Why do you ask?"

"You don't know? The Emperor's offered a reward for the heads of those Mangarh marksmen who've killed so many of our own. Are they still fighting there?"

Hanuman's heart pounded so loudly it seemed everyone should be able to hear it. "So far as I know."

The officer shouted to his men, "Then we're the first!" He spurred his horse, and the troop clattered off.

Hanuman let out his breath. He urged his own men forward. Most of the fighting appeared to be away from their route. But down a side street he saw a small group of saffron clad men, wielding swords and spears, dash forth from a temple into a far larger contingent of Mughal troops. Hanuman did not have to see the end of the clash to know the outcome.

Suddenly an authoritative voice challenged them, speaking in the regional dialect, "What are you doing? Where are you taking them?"

Startled, the weary Hanuman whirled on his horse to see an imperial officer who had just emerged from the gate of the Rana's palace. Hanuman's breath caught. Challenged again, so soon! He was glad he'd thought through the possibilities earlier, before he had to respond under the stress of the actual situation. "Emperor's orders," he called. "We're taking them out to be killed. The Emperor wants as many heads as possible for a pyramid." Sweat ran down his sides as he awaited the response

Sounds of looting came from within the compound. The enemy officer shouted, "Some of those heads are too pretty to cut off. How about leaving a few women for me and my men?"

Hanuman spurred his horse. "You'll find plenty of others here," he called back. "I don't want to disappoint the Emperor."

The officer stood, still watching. Hanuman again held his breath. Soon, they turned a corner and the man was lost from sight.

They were on the main road now, only a short distance from the gate. Hanuman saw two elephants charge a small group of saffron robed fighters. The Rajputs gave way, then tried to clamber onto the elephants to kill the mahouts and the Mughal warriors. The elephants whirled, the swords attached to their tusks slicing off parts of bodies. In seconds, the last Rajput was crushed beneath the giant feet. The elephants moved on, leaving a crumpled mass of orange and red.

Now he could see the Ram Pol, the main gate. A steady stream of cavalry, elephants, foot soldiers poured into the fort from the huge portal. Hanuman formed his "captives" into a single file of marchers and elephants and bullock carts along one side and forced his way against the crush of entering besiegers.

Out through the arch, then down the entry road, against the oncoming traffic: probably even more cavalry and artillerymen coming to loot.

Around the bend at the Lakshmana Gate. Then down to the Ganesh Pol, in ruins now from the Mughal artillery. A work crew was clearing away debris to enlarge the passageway.

Around the next turn. Here they had to wait while a cavalry contingent clattered up the hill.

Down through the next gate, the Hanuman Pol. Then the Bhairon Pol.

One gate to go. Slowly downward through the Padam Pol at last. But the long march through the encampment lay ahead.

Outside the Padam Pol they again moved aside for an enemy cavalry contingent, a few hundred horsemen traveling at a slow trot.

Abruptly their commander, who was obviously of high rank from his flag and standard bearers, reined in his mount. He sat, eyeing the "captors" and their prisoners.

Hanuman had deliberately avoided catching anyone's eye. Now, wondering about the delay, he glanced at the enemy cavalry commander. In the dim light Hanuman recognized the Pariyatra's own flag. The officer wore the cuirass and helmet of a Rajput lord.

The commander smiled thinly at Hanuman.

It was Baldeo.

8

The usurper edged his horse over to Hanuman's. Hanuman readied his sword, though there seemed little point in trying to resist so many men.

"You have a large number of captives," Baldeo said loudly.

Hanuman tried to force his exhausted mind to function. This was the type of threat he had feared most: encountering someone in authority who would recognize him despite the bandaged face. He had been able to devise no good way to manage such a situation. But oddly, Baldeo seemed to be cooperating with the masquerade. Or else the traitor was amusing himself by toying with his deposed brother.

"Emperor's orders," Hanuman replied.

Baldeo raised an eyebrow. He sat gazing at the Pariyatra survivors. At last, Baldeo said, more quietly, "There's a reward for your heads."

"So I understand."

Baldeo grinned broadly. "I was going into the fort to look for you. It was kind of you to deliver yourselves to me."

Hanuman glared at him in disbelief. The slaying of a kinsman a grievous sin for Rajputs. "You'd do *gotra-hatya*?"

"No, no. It's not your heads I want. Although the Emperor might indeed be glad to see you."

"You'd take the reward for your own brother?"

Baldeo laughed harshly. "The reward might be useful, but it's not my main interest. You have something else I need. You know what it is."

Suddenly Hanuman realized what Baldeo was after. His own escape attempt might be finished, but he had no intention of giving Baldeo the final symbol of Pariyatra sovereignty. He shook his head. "I don't carry him any more."

"Then where is he?"

"I unfortunately lost sight of him." Hanuman chose his words carefully, so as not to tell an outright untruth. "There was confusion in the battle. I hope to regain him as soon as possible."

Baldeo eyed Hanuman, obviously trying to decide whether to believe this. "You'd never leave him," Baldeo said at last. "If you give him to me, I'll spare your 'captives.' And I do have a plan for you personally. Otherwise—well, the Emperor's ordered everyone's deaths, you know. He was furious about your marksmen killing so many of our men."

Hanuman said, "If you turn your kinsmen over to the Emperor, it would start a *vair*—a vendetta between your branch of the clan and mine that would destroy us all."

Baldeo said, "There wouldn't be enough of your branch left to be a threat. Anyway, I assume you *already* are angry enough to seek revenge on me if you could."

"You're right on that account," said Hanuman. He sweated as his tired mind tried to function. How could he refuse to turn over the god, if refusing meant the deaths of the people under his protection?

But mightn't Baldeo be bluffing? Though he had seized the *gadi*, he had not shed blood in doing so. "I told you," said Hanuman. "I no longer carry Ekadantji."

Baldeo sat eyeing Hanuman for a time. At last, he said, "Then I want you to show me exactly where you lost him. Or more likely, hid him." He hesitated momentarily, then added, "If we find Ekadantji, I'll let your 'prisoners' go. If not...." He waved toward his men.

"All right," Hanuman said gruffly. "I concede."

"Wait," said Dwarka Das. The bard moved forward, holding a

drawn dagger, its point to his chest. He challenged Baldeo: "If you continue this course, it will be over the blood of a *charan*."

Baldeo's mouth fell open, his eyes wide. A *charan's* life was as sacred as that of a cow or of a Brahmin; if Dwarka Das killed himself, the gods would shower their wrath upon the person responsible. Baldeo said to Dwarka Das, "I offer you the same position you've held with my brother. The main gate at Mangarh is yours again if you wish it."

Dwarka Das said, "You would not like the poems I'd compose for you, Lord Baldeo."

Every Rajput patron dreaded the thought of his bard's tongue turning against him in ridicule. Less certainty in his voice, Baldeo said, "I've already risked the gods' anger. I've gone too far to turn back. Kill yourself if you must. It won't alter my demands. Most of my men aren't Rajputs, so they don't respect *charans*."

Mutters of astonishment came from many within hearing. A Rajput would never dare cross the ban of a *charan's* blood. But the bulk of Baldeo's cavalry was now from Akbar's mixed army, not from the Pariyatra Rajputs.

"No!" said Hanuman. "I value my bard too much." He motioned one of his servant women forward. And he firmly relieved Dwarka Das of the dagger.

He took a large sack from the servant woman. He thought a moment, breathing a prayer to the Ekadantji asking for understanding and forgiveness. Then he reluctantly handed the bag to Baldeo.

His brother opened it, and Hanuman saw the flash of silver. Baldeo inspected the image to ensure he had the genuine god. Then he smiled. "I thought you said you no longer carried him."

"Yes. But I never said he wasn't with my party."

Baldeo grinned. "With your cleverness, Ekadantji must have been on *my* side for me to have succeeded so well. And of course, the priest must come with me, too."

Ekadantji

Hanuman considered. At last he said. "If he consents." He turned and motioned the bound Hara forward.

"You and the others may go now," Baldeo said to Hanuman. "On one condition."

Hanuman wondered if he'd heard correctly. "You're letting me go, too?"

Baldeo laughed. "Unless you'd rather I take you to the Emperor." He glared at Hanuman and said roughly, "First, give me your oath you'll never again enter Pariyatra territories."

Hanuman stared at him. "Never again see our *bapota*? Exiled like Lord Rama?"

"How could I dare let you go otherwise?"

"But to never again enter our forefathers' lands!" Hanuman shook his head. "Kill me now. What you ask would be the same as death."

Baldeo scowled and appeared to think. "Then swear you'll not, so long as you live, approach to artillery distance of Mangarh fortress—nor of Baldeogarh. Nor anyone leading an army on your behalf."

Hanuman tried to focus his exhausted mind. How could he retake his capital if he couldn't even get close to it? How could he stand to never so much as visit his beloved town of Mangarh or the fort in which he'd been raised? How could he build his eagerly anticipated wing to the fortress palace? He would even be barred from the adjacent valley where he planned to create the artificial lake and the summer palace.

This exile could be even worse than Lord Rama's. Rama, at least, had a time limitation of fourteen years. Hanuman's oath could very well last the remainder of his life.

He saw a small group of Mughal officers approaching, apparently curious about what was occurring. No more time to think. Hanuman said bitterly, "I swear. On Ekadantji."

Baldeo nodded, seemingly satisfied. He said loudly, for the benefit of his men, "The Emperor should be pleased with so many heads!" He kicked his horse forward. His troops followed.

Hanuman could not quite believe he was free to go, even given the horrible precondition for the release.

So blood counted with Baldeo after all.

Hanuman doubted he himself even wanted to leave under such a sentence of exile. If it weren't for all the people who were depending on him to lead them in the escape, he would prefer to participate in the *jouhar*. He wearily beckoned his people on, away from the fortress.

9

Hanuman worried that even with the facial bandage he might be recognized by someone who had seen him when he had led the negotiating delegation to Akbar. But the fact that the Mughal encampment was so chaotic at this time, with most of the inhabitants hurrying toward the fortress in hope of gaining loot, aided him in leading his procession slowly through the area without challenge.

Hanuman did not dare to pause for more than a few hours' rest for fear of pursuit by Akbar's army if the escape should be discovered, or even by Baldeo if he should change his mind. The devastated plains of Mewar made it seem as if the fleeing Pariyatras were still on a vast battlefield. At Rana Udai Singh's command, the fields had been burned to deny food and fodder to Akbar's troops, and the farmers had left their villages to take refuge in forts in the hills. For many *kos* around Chittorgarh the huge invading army had cut all the trees for firewood and for timber for the *sabats* and other needs of the siege.

For two days of exhausting, dusty, hungry travel Hanuman's party crossed the Mewar plains. First one of the wounded men died, then another. And another. At last the escaping army forded the tributary of the Banas River marking the border of the Pariyatras' own territories. Abruptly green groves of trees appeared, and golden fields richly carpeted with winter wheat ripening for harvest.

The party halted to bathe themselves and the elephants in the river, and to drink. Hanuman's attendants brought forth the green Pariyatra flag and standards, the red royal umbrella, the flywhisks, the kettledrums.

When they once again resumed their march, the fleeing refugees had become a royal procession, albeit an exhausted and defeated one. At the sound of the drums and the sight of the long line of elephants and horses and marchers, women paused from drawing water at the wells to come look and give their *mudras*. Farmers, unsure of who was now in power in their lands, paused from their chores in their plots of land to give obeisance to the passing lord. Always before, Hanuman had felt a deep peace, a great satisfaction, upon returning to his own homeland. He would have taken pleasure at the sight of the peasants' activities on the plains, or at the

view of the jungle covered, game-rich hills not yet singed dry by the upcoming hot season. But this time Hanuman was returning in defeat, and he had been ousted from his own throne.

At least Mangarh had been saved from Akbar; perhaps he should be grateful to Baldeo for that. Judging from the experience of the Kachhwaha Rajputs of Amber, Akbar was as good for his friends as he was bad for his enemies. In hindsight, perhaps Hanuman himself should have made an effort to forge an alliance with the Emperor, long before getting entangled at Chittorgarh. But it was too late for that now.

Or was it? He had the nagging feeling he had overlooked something important. About Baldeo. About Akbar.

Akbar was clever, reputed to be an excellent judge of men. The Emperor highly valued loyalty. And he wanted to pacify the Rajput states. Why would he place a man of proven disloyalty on a *gadi*, especially knowing it would create conflict and unrest in the very region he wanted to have quiet?

Suddenly Hanuman saw hope. It was a slim possibility, but nevertheless real.

He was abruptly less weary as he led his convoy up the winding, narrow rock-strewn road into the hills to Amargarh village, dominated from high above by the castle of his uncle Mahendra. The fortress was a severe rectangle of heavy stone walls, with rounded bastions at each corner. It dominated a sheer cliff on two sides, with a tiny stream curving around the bottom, and steep, jungle-clad hillsides in the other directions.

In the late afternoon heat Mahendra and his men descended the switchback trail on horseback to welcome their returning clansmen. Hanuman saw with concern that one of Mahendra's sons had to assist the white-mustached old man in dismounting. Mahendra had previously been vigorous despite his age; now, as he came forward to welcome Hanuman with his greeting of "Rama, Rama," his movements were slow and his eyes held a vacant look. When they embraced, Hanuman noticed a trembling in his uncle's hands. Mahendra's body felt thin under the short coat. Hanuman felt certain the change was due to Mahendra's humiliation at so easily losing the fortress of Mangarh and the post of chief minister.

In the atmosphere of dejection the men said little. Mahendra remounted with a boost from his eldest son, and the group slowly clattered up the rocky path to the fort of Amargarh. Hanuman dismounted to enter the gate on the traditional red carpet which had been laid in honor of the ruler's visit.

Not all could squeeze into the small courtyard, so Ajit's men and the Bhils camped in a tree shaded ravine opposite the western wall. Mahendra silently led Hanuman to the guest apartments, while the servants took charge of the remainder of the refugees and installed Hanuman's wive's in the women's quarters.

After Hanuman had bathed and rested, he had a short but serious discussion with Dwarka Das. He then went out to the courtyard, where his own chiefs and those of his uncle had gathered. The customary red *shamiana* had been raised to shelter the *gadi*, and Hanuman seated himself there. Mahendra offered the traditional gift of an elephant to Hanuman, who graciously returned the animal. Mahendra's vassals then offered their own gifts to Hanuman. He returned these offerings also; normally he would have kept them but bestowed his own items to honor the men. His situation had now changed drastically.

The ceremonies concluded, Mahendra dismissed his own men, and Hanuman convened his council of chiefs before the red awning. As Mahendra offered the cup, Hanuman examined the men and saw faces that were exhausted.

Only the conviction that he must act quickly enabled Hanuman to summon the strength he needed. His words shattered the silence that had hung heavy in the gathering: "Brothers, we must retake Mangarh as soon as possible. Before the usurper's hold gets too firm."

His chiefs were slow to respond; as yet only Dwarka Das knew of his scheme. Dewa the Bhil sat hunched over, apparently asleep. Elderly Mahendra said, seemingly with great effort, "You know, Maharaja, that Lord Baldeo left a garrison of Akbar's troops at Mangarh town. Not more than two or three hundred. But our clan lost half its men at Chittorgarh."

Again there was silence. The only movements were of men tipping their wine cups. Eventually, Ajit turned his smallpox ravaged face downward to look at Dewa, and asked in his deep voice, "Would the Bhils help?"

The chieftain straightened and opened his eyes, showing he had merely been resting, not sleeping. He nodded and said to Hanuman, "I pressed the *tika* upon *your* forehead, *Annadata*, not your brother's."

Ajit now said, seemingly more in an effort to show support for Hanuman than out of any real conviction the fort could be retaken, "Baldeo himself may still be with some of his men with Akbar, rather than returning to Mangarh. That could weaken the defenses."

More silence. Then Ajit said, "You've sworn not to get close to the fortress, *Annadata*. Who'll lead us now?"

Before Hanuman could reply, Mahendra absently toyed with his white mustache and said dully, "Another problem, Maharaja. Even if we retake the town, what stops Akbar from besieging us and taking it back again whenever he wishes? He can send enough troops for that and never miss them."

After waiting to be certain no one else wished to speak, Hanuman said quietly, "Uncle, I agree with you. It would be hard to retake the fortress even if Baldeo is gone at the moment. And we could hold it only so long as the Emperor let us."

He saw flickers of interest as the men wondered what he was leading up to. "So I intend to try a different approach." He fell quiet and watched the interest grow. Then he said firmly, "I'll visit Akbar himself, and petition him to return Mangarh. Naturally, I'll have to swear allegiance to him on behalf of our clan."

The men gaped at him, clearly wondering if they had heard correctly. One by one they turned so their eyes met each other's. Finally, they sat in stillness, their faces registering dismay.

Ajit said hesitantly, "Highness, it's been a difficult time for you. Perhaps we should reconsider the matter after you've had more rest."

Hanuman smiled thinly as he said, "I haven't lost my mind, brother. We all agree that even if we retake the fortress, the success will be temporary. In a sense, Lord Baldeo's approach was correct—if our clan is to thrive, we must ally ourselves with the strongest power. There's no doubt that's Akbar. We must accept the fact and try to use it to our advantage."

Ajit said, his agitation overcoming his weariness, "But *Annadata*, the Emperor wants our heads. We were lucky to escape with our lives. How could we possibly ally with him?"

"Akbar will act in his own interest. Hopefully, he'll now see that we can be useful to him."

Ajit said, slowly shaking his head, "We've been allied with Rana Udai Singh. Our honor is probably stained already by our avoiding the *jouhar*. How can we now switch our alliance to Akbar?"

Hanuman replied, "We've done our duty to Udai Singh. Half our men died for him. Now we must consider our own clan's interests."

Mahendra said, as if trying to reason with a stubborn child, "Baldeo's one of the Emperor's own commanders. You can't expect Akbar to take Mangarh from him and hand it to you instead."

Hanuman pressed his lips together tightly. Then he said, "Uncle, I know I'm taking a risk. But I've learned a lot about Akbar in recent months. I question whether Baldeo's position is as strong as we've assumed. The only way to be certain is to ask the Emperor to choose between us."

When Hanuman returned to Chittorgarh, he led a small retinue of only two dozen men. His party might be taken as prisoners, even killed if Akbar's orders still stood. Dwarka Das, too, came. Hanuman had tried to discourage him, but the bard insisted he wanted to witness such an important event, which had the potential to be a key portion of his epic.

On the way, they occasionally met refugees from Chittorgarh. When questioned, each told of how the massacre at the fortress had continued until midday. Akbar's men had searched the city and slaughtered thousands, everyone they could find, soldiers and nonsoldiers alike.

Hanuman was less confident of his reception at Akbar's camp than he had pretended to his chiefs. His apprehension grew as he heard the stories told by the refugees. Still he continued toward Chittorgarh. If the Emperor intended to prevent him from ruling Mangarh, it was best to find out now.

He took care to hide his fear when he boldly identified himself to the imperial guard outpost as the Raja of Mangarh and requested an audience with the Emperor. The officers treated him as a respected high ranking visitor and escorted him to the red tents of the royal encampment. There, Man Singh of Amber, the son of Raja Bhagwant Das, met him.

Hanuman had earlier been favorably impressed by the seventeen year old Man Singh, who no doubt would one day succeed to the *gadi* of Amber. "My father sends his apologies," the sturdily built Man Singh said with poise and calm, showing no surprise at seeing Hanuman. "He's on a special assignment from the Emperor. But he asked that I assist you however I can. You arrived just in time. The Emperor leaves soon on foot for a pilgrimage to Ajmer, to give thanks at the tomb of his saint."

"Then I can see His Majesty today?" asked Hanuman.

"I see no reason why the Emperor should not grant an audience, Highness." Man Singh shook his head and smiled as he added with clear admiration, "His Majesty was furious when he learned of your escape. But I think he now regrets his own men killing so many defenders after taking the fort. Hopefully, he no longer wants revenge."

Hanuman allowed himself to relax just slightly. If true, that was one obstacle removed. But there were others.

Baldeo stood with a crowd of nobles at the audience pavilion. The brothers avoided each other's eyes. Hanuman was glad there was only a short wait before the drums sounded, signaling the Emperor's approach.

Like everyone else in the area, Baldeo made his three *taslims* when Akbar entered. This time, so did Hanuman.

When Akbar had seated himself, he looked down at Hanuman with an unreadable expression. Man Singh whispered to Hanuman, "You may present any gifts."

One of the Pariyatra men held forth a buckler, on which rested Hanuman's finest sword, in the family five generations. Hanuman took the sheathed weapon and extended it toward Akbar.

The Emperor took the sword himself rather than having his official receive it, thereby honoring Hanuman, to his relief. Akbar pulled it from the scabbard, examined it with interest, nodded, and set it aside. The symbolism was obvious—no elephants this time; only a single sword.

Man Singh acted as translator when Akbar said, "I'm pleased you survived my siege. Your escape plan was clever. I admire such daring." He smiled tightly at Hanuman.

Hanuman replied, "Your Majesty, I'm honored at such kind words, especially from one so renowned at strategy as yourself."

Akbar said, "However, I will confess—I was angry at the deaths dealt to my laborers by your Pariyatra marksmen. I wanted to capture them so I could repay them in kind."

Hanuman said, with only a hint of apology, "They merely did their duty, Your Majesty."

"Of course. As did all the defenders. I'm grieved now that I permitted my men to kill so many after the fort fell. But what do you wish of me?"

"Your Majesty, I understand your troops now hold my capital. I wish them removed."

Akbar smiled; amusement shone in his eyes. But he said levelly, "In other words, you want me to restore you to your throne."

Hanuman now risked the argument that would make him or ruin him, depending on whether or not his hunch about Baldeo's relationship with Akbar was correct. "May it please Your Majesty, in fact I have never been deprived of my *gadi*. It was awarded to me by my father, and ratified by our clan's council of *sardars*. The council has never rescinded its decision. In accordance with Mangarh tradition, the chief of the Bhils placed his thumb mark upon my forehead with his own blood. He will never do so for my brother."

Hanuman paused for emphasis and took a deep breath. He said boldly, "Therefore, I am still Raja of Mangarh. As such, I now wish to offer my allegiance to you, in exchange for your ordering your troops withdrawn from my capital."

Akbar's eyes gleamed with delight at being presented with this fascinating dispute between two brothers. He looked at Baldeo. "I assume you have something to say in this matter, commander?"

"I certainly do, Your Majesty!" Baldeo's voice boomed even louder than usual as he told the Emperor, "I took Mangarh while my brother and his troops fought against you at Chittorgarh. Now, he has the effrontery to come to you to ask for it back, after I captured it as one of the spoils of war."

With no hesitation, Akbar said, "Since Mangarh is one of my spoils of war, commander, I can award it to whomever I wish."

Abruptly Baldeo looked worried, rather than merely angered. "I suppose that's true, Your Majesty. But I can't imagine you taking it away from the very officer who seized it for you."

Akbar said evenly, "I never ordered that Mangarh be taken. That was your own initiative. I merely gave my consent when you requested to use the troops under your command. And I haven't yet issued a *farman* naming you as Raja."

Hanuman let out the breath he had been holding. He had guessed correctly.

A sheen of sweat appeared on Baldeo's forehead. He said quickly, and too loudly for someone addressing his Emperor, "May I respectfully point out, Your Majesty, that my brother has taken an oath never to enter the capital in his lifetime. So it would be of little use to him even if it were his."

Akbar smiled broadly. He looked at Hanuman. "Is this true? How could you use a city you can't even enter?"

Hanuman said forcefully, "I would hope my brother will release me from my oath. But if not, Your Majesty, then I will rule from outside the walls."

Akbar examined Hanuman closely. "Fascinating. You Rajputs are so true to your word, to your duty, to your loyalty. That's one reason I value you so much. However, it would seem that not *all* Rajputs esteem loyalty." He turned to Baldeo. "Commander, I appreciate your gift of a kingdom to me as 'war spoils.' As your rewards, I hereby double your income. I give you an additional robe of honor and a new mount. I increase your command to seven hundred fifty horse."

Baldeo's eyes grew wide as the Emperor continued, "However, you may know I make a practice of not deposing a ruler unless I feel he'll cause me difficulties later. Your brother is clearly a man of his word. If he swears loyalty to me, I'm confident I'll never regret having granted him that opportunity." By implication, Akbar was apparently conveying that he did not trust Baldeo to keep his word. Baldeo's treachery against his brother had come back to defeat him. There were rustlings as the onlooking nobles glanced at each other in surprise, although etiquette required they not speak to each other while the Emperor was conducting an audience.

Akbar directed his gaze at Hanuman. "You now have your kingdom back, Raja Hanuman Pariyatra. I order the withdrawal of such of my troops as are in Mangarh." He looked back at Baldeo. "Commander, are you willing to release Raja Hanuman from his oath, so he no longer feels compelled to remain away from his fortress?"

Baldeo's face had turned purple with fury. He stood stiffly, his fists clenched. Eyes blazing, he replied, "Absolutely not, Your Majesty! He gave his oath and he must live with it. Unless he decides to break it."

Akbar looked thoughtful. "I doubt he'll break it, commander. You're sure you won't relent?"

"*I—will—not—relent.*"

Akbar turned back to Hanuman and again smiled. Hanuman thought there was sympathy, as well as amusement, in the Emperor's expression. Akbar said, "Raja Hanuman, since you have sworn allegiance to me, and you can no longer use your own capital, I shall find duties for you elsewhere. I can always use experienced commanders. However, under the circumstances, I think it best to assign you and your brother to separate campaigns."

Akbar turned to a nearby official. "I award the Raja of Mangarh a *mansab*: commander of two thousand horses. Present him with his robe of honor and kettledrums. His horse and elephant. The other gifts." He looked back at Hanuman. "We'll hold a formal investiture within the week. However, you now have full ruling powers within your domains."

Baldeo said nothing, and when they had done their three *taslims* and left the Emperor's sight, he turned his back on Hanuman and stalked quickly away.

Man Singh led Hanuman out to receive Akbar's gifts. Among them was a magnificent elephant. Hanuman's eyes lit with pleasure and he exclaimed, "Chanchal!" He strode over and affectionately rubbed his old friend's trunk. Akbar was devilishly clever, thought Hanuman. The Emperor certainly knew how to inspire loyalty, at least among the vassals he wanted to have serve him in the long term.

Hanuman turned to Man Singh. "Can you show me to my brother's camp?"

"Of course, sir."

When they arrived, several hundred armed horsemen waited in the compound surrounding Baldeo's large tent. Baldeo emerged from the doorway and eyed Hanuman, Man Singh, and the few men of Hanuman's escort.

Hanuman remained astride his horse. "I want Ekadantji," he called to Baldeo. "And our priest."

Baldeo stood glaring. He said, "That wasn't part of the Emperor's command. And you don't have enough men to take them from me."

Hanuman said calmly, "I can make the request to the Emperor. You know he'll grant it."

"That won't be necessary," said Man Singh boldly. "As one of the Emperor's aides, he's delegated certain authorities to me implementing this decision. I interpret His Majesty's award as including your clan's deity and attendants."

Face contorted in fury, Baldeo stared at Man Singh. At last, he motioned to one of his men. "Bring Ekadantji. The priest, too."

After some moments, Hara emerged, his face tense as he blinked his eyes in the bright light. The young Brahmin held the silver statue in his arms. Hanuman beckoned him forward. "The god and you are both all right?" he asked when the priest stood near.

"We've been treated well, Your Highness," Hara replied quietly.

When they left, Baldeo stood glowering, his knuckles white as his hand gripped his sword.

10

Satehpur Sikri, near Agra, eight years later. February 1576.

On an afternoon almost eight years to the day after the fall of Chittorgarh, Hanuman and Bhagwant Das and Man Singh sat playing *chaupar* with the Emperor in a room adjacent to Akbar's private audience chamber.

On the stone floor lay the cloth playing board in the shape of a cross, each of its arms composed of three rows of eight squares. Each player, paired with a partner, moved his four pieces around the board in accordance with tosses of the three dice. The participants had placed small wagers on the outcome.

Akbar was fond of games of all kinds. Any high nobles in attendance at the court eventually found themselves playing *chaupar* or chess or *chandal mandal* with the Emperor. Hanuman, paired with Man Singh, now threw the combination needed to move one of his pieces into the large square at the center of the cross.

Much had happened in the years since the battle at Chittorgarh. The furious Baldeo resigned from the Emperor's service and entered the employment of other rulers outside Akbar's territories. Hanuman himself, now forty-five years in age, had become one of the Emperor's most trusted confidants, with the high rank of four thousand horse.

As the Emperor's vassal, Hanuman spent much of each year in attendance upon Akbar, and like the other nobles attached to the court, accompanied the Emperor wherever he traveled. Akbar frequently was away from his capital of Agra; every year, he made a pilgrimage to Ajmer to the tomb of the Sufi saint, Khwajah Muin-up-din Chisti. Both the Sisodia and the Bundi Ranis accompanied Hanuman on the journeys, and life in the big tents in the encampments was usually quite comfortable.

The Emperor had called upon Hanuman and the Pariyatra army to fight for him on a campaign in the southwest to subdue Gujarat, and also far to the east in Bengal. Each time other Rajput commanders, including Raja Bhagwant Das of Amber and his son Man Singh, also participated, and they became good friends with Hanuman.

Four years after the events at Chittorgarh, Akbar completed rebuilding the massive Red Fort on the Jumna river at Agra. The Emperor then moved his stonemasons and his court to a ridge at Sikri, seven miles west of Agra, where he began to construct a new capital called Fatehpur, "the City of Victory." The buildings in the royal compound were of red sandstone quarried from the ridge itself. Akbar had provided funds for the nobles of his court to build their own mansions nearby, and Hanuman constructed a small palace, designed by his architect Kishen Lal, on the northern slope of the ridge with a view of the artificial lake.

This particular day Hanuman was the first player to reach the center of the *chaupar* board. Akbar smiled mischievously and said, "Still the Rajputs are challenging me."

"Are you referring to *chaupar*, or to Mewar, Your Majesty?" Man Singh asked.

"Which do you suppose?" Akbar replied, still smiling.

Hanuman, now fluent in Persian, interposed, "Knowing how seriously you take your games, Your Majesty, I would assume you're referring to *chaupar*."

Akbar slowly nodded as he shook the dice and threw. "While I'm playing *chaupar*, my attention is solely on it." He moved his pieces, then looked directly at Hanuman. "And on the other players. I learn a lot about my commanders from how they play their games. Are they patient? Impulsive? Can they shift strategies quickly? Are they trustworthy? Do they get so obsessed with winning that they make unnecessary mistakes? They reveal much about themselves in the way they play their games. Especially if the game is long and drawn out, so the players are tired and less on guard."

Hanuman replied with a strained smile, "I suspected as much, Your Majesty."

"I'm sure you did."

Hanuman strove to keep his face calm. Everyone knew the story of how Akbar had actually dismissed and exiled a favored *wazir*, Muzaffar Khan, because the minister had lost his temper after losing heavily at a lengthy game of *chaupar*.

Akbar said, his face now serious, "As you know, I do think a lot also about the problems of the remaining Rajputs."

"Rana Pratap in particular, Your Majesty," Man Singh said casually. It was his turn to throw. He did so and moved his pieces.

Akbar said, "Yes. Rana Pratap. How can I bring him to submit to me?"

In allying his own clan with the Mughal Emperor, Hanuman was one of several Rajput rulers to follow the lead of the Kachhwaha Rajputs of Amber. Jodhpur, Bikaner, and Jaisalmer also saw the wisdom of acknowledging Akbar as their supreme sovereign and gave him daughters in marriage.

However, Mewar, under Rana Udai Singh, continued to hold out against the imperial might. Although the Rana had never regained his capital of Chittorgarh, he established a new one—named Udaipur—on the shore of the Udai Sagar, an artificial lake.

When Udai Singh died four years after the fall of Chittorgarh, his son and successor, Rana Pratap, took a solemn oath to always resist the Mughals. He and his men vowed to eat only leaves, to sleep on straw, and never to shave their beards until the land of Mewar had been freed. Pratap ordered that the kettledrums which normally preceded him should instead follow in the rear, to symbolize his determination to turn previous defeats into victory. With his firm resistance no matter how overwhelming the odds, he and his horse Chetak became heroes to all who resented the Mughal domination of their lands.

Man Singh, as he threw the dice, now replied to the Emperor, "I've thought about that considerably, Your Majesty. I think it would be best to lure Rana Pratap out of the hills, so he fights on our own terms."

"And if he won't come out?"

"We have to go after him. I don't say it will be easy, Your Majesty. But only decisive action has any chance at all."

"You've given up on negotiations?" Akbar was smiling broadly in enjoyment of Man Singh's discomfiture. For Man Singh had visited Pratap as Akbar's informal envoy and was humiliatingly snubbed. Among other tasks, Man Singh had been given the job of obtaining for Akbar a prized elephant which Pratap owned, the great "Ram Prasad," but Man Singh failed to convince Pratap to part with the animal.

"He's taken an oath, Your Majesty. He won't break it. Ever."

Akbar shook his head, sadly. "He'd be so much better off under my protection than fighting me." He turned to Hanuman. "Isn't that true of the Pariyatras?"

"Quite true, Your Majesty," Hanuman replied, seizing the dice for his own throw. "Now that no one dares to attack us, our lands have prospered as never before." Indeed, Mangarh state itself had been peaceful and the harvest plentiful. Hanuman himself and his chiefs had greatly increased their wealth from booty taken during the Emperor's campaigns. For Hanuman, the only major source of discontent—aside from the important one of being barred from his own capital—had been the fact that his wives had still not yet given him an heir, despite regular prayers at the tomb of *pir* Mahmud.

"You can even indulge your passion for building," said Akbar.

The Emperor shared Hanuman's interest in architecture, as did young Man Singh. "Again true, Your Majesty," said Hanuman. "Although it's hard to find builders who'll come to Mangarh, when there's so much work here in Fatehpur Sikri. You've monopolized all the best architects."

Akbar laughed at Hanuman's good natured barb. He then looked intently at Hanuman. "What do you really think of my buildings here?"

Were they finished discussing Pratap, then? Hanuman wondered. He replied, "I approve completely, Your Majesty. Although your palace here is much grander and more spread out, the style is reminiscent of the Gwalior palace, which I've always admired."

And, he added silently to himself, similar to the wing I'd build at Mangarh if it weren't for that damned oath Baldeo forced on me. Only weeks ago, Hanuman had learned Baldeo was now fighting with Rana Pratap. What if Hanuman himself should find himself fighting Pratap, and therefore Baldeo? At times, he felt he could gladly kill the brother who had brought him so much trouble. Other times, he still resisted the thought of spilling the blood of his own kin.

Suddenly he realized he'd better pay more attention to the game and to the conversation. It would be embarrassing if Akbar noticed; the Emperor took delight in imposing nominal fines on nobles who were inattentive.

Akbar was musing aloud, "I sometimes think my own buildings aren't as successful as those at Gwalior. Perhaps it's the color of the stone. At Gwalior, that pale gold color, like ripening wheat, shows off the contrasts between light and shadow more than the dark stone here."

The honey colored stone at Mangarh was quite similar to that of Gwalior, and Hanuman again felt the extreme frustration of not being able to undertake the projects at his home city. "The Gwalior stone is attractive, Your Majesty, no doubt of that," Hanuman replied. "But the red stone here has its own appeal. It has more weight. More dignity."

Akbar slowly nodded. "I agree." He was silent for a time, while the moves continued on the game board. Then, he said, "It's fascinating the way Indian architects have chosen for centuries to use stone almost as if it were wood. They carve the rock into posts, into beams, into lintels, even floorboards. The pieces are then put together much like a wooden structure. And the sculptors carve each part as if it were wood. Not like the Persians at all."

Man Singh said, "I hadn't thought about it that way, Your Majesty. Maybe because I grew up with the method. It seems so natural I never questioned it. But I see your point. Maybe stone should be used as its own nature dictates, like the blocks in the wall of your Red Fort. Not trying to imitate wood or any other material."

Akbar took the dice. Hanuman had assumed the Emperor exchanged the topic of Rana Pratap for the topic of architecture. But the

Emperor clearly was thinking about Pratap still. In a sudden conversational twist he said with a tone of finality, "Pratap needs no buildings. All he needs are hills to hide in. But I think soon I'll have to put an end to his resistance." He turned his head to face Hanuman. "What does your great *Ramayana* have to say that might help me?"

The Emperor knew of Hanuman's admiration for the Hindu epic. Hanuman thought a moment and replied tactfully, "As you know, Your Majesty, Lord Rama was a ruler who always did his duty, always put the interests of his people first, just as you do. But still Fate imposed many obstacles, many problems for Rama. His exile, the abduction of his wife, the war to get her back, the test of her virtue at the end. Always Lord Rama faced his difficulties with forthrightness, acted in accordance with his *dharma*. The solutions to a problem may vary, but one simply does one's best to meet the challenges."

"Your advice is admirable, but it is quite general in nature," replied Akbar. "Not very helpful with a particular dilemma. Our *Qur'an* and other Muslim writings are more specific."

"The *Ramayana* is not principally a book of rules, Your Majesty, so maybe it's not valid to make a comparison." He smiled at the Emperor. "If I may make a suggestion, Majesty, you may wish to consider having your Translations Department make a rendering of the *Ramayana* in Persian. It might be more meaningful if you could listen to it verse by verse."

Akbar gave a slight nod of acknowledgment, and he appeared to be thinking. "Maybe I will, Raja Hanuman." He smiled at Man Singh. "Pratap requires more thought. But I'll add Ram Prasad to my elephant stables yet."

In spite of his own alliance with the Emperor, Hanuman realized he hoped Rana Pratap would somehow continue to resist Akbar's almost overwhelming strength. There was much to admire in the Rana's struggle to remain free no matter the obstacles and hardships. However much Hanuman might question the practical wisdom of Pratap's choice, the Rana embodied Rajput valor at its highest ideal.

11

In April, when Hanuman and Man Singh were attending Akbar at Ajmer, the Emperor ordered that a campaign be undertaken to subdue Rana Pratap. Akbar appointed Man Singh, who had shown brilliance as a commander, to lead the operation. But perhaps because of Man Singh's relative youth, or maybe because Man Singh was a Rajput challenging another Rajput, Akbar assigned a number of other generals to aid him, including Hanuman. Ironically, Rana Pratap's own estranged brother Sukta was among the imperial officers.

That it was the height of the hot season seemed to matter little to Akbar. For two months the Mughal troops gathered at Mandalgarh, a fortress to the east of the Pariyatra domains. Hanuman's wives accompanied him, although staying comfortable in the tents was difficult in the heat. By remaining there for a time, Man Singh hoped to lure Pratap into the open plains to fight. But Pratap wisely stayed within the protection of the hills.

At last, Man Singh led the Mughal army of five thousand men southerly to the village of Molera, near Pratap's current capital of Gogunda. Early on a morning in late June, Man Singh marched his army southward across the Banas River, the water level low after so many months of rainless heat. Hanuman, with Ajit and the contingent of Pariyatra cavalry, rode horseback in the center formation near Man Singh himself, who commanded from an elephant's howdah. Many of the Rajputs had imbibed opium to enhance their fearlessness in battle. Hanuman and Ajit and Man Singh, however, had refrained.

"What are the bards saying about Rana Pratap?" Hanuman asked Dwarka Das, who rode by his side.

Dwarka Das gave an appraising look. "Are you certain this is a good time, Highness? You may not appreciate hearing, just when you are about to fight him."

"I can guess that they praise him highly."

"They also criticize those who have allied themselves with Akbar."

Hanuman's lips tightened. Then he said, "That's to be expected."

Dwarka Das gave a slight shrug. "I will recite a few couplets, Highness:

> *For the sake of comfort all the Hindus have surrendered*
> *to Akbar like jackals.*
> *But the angry lion, Rana Pratap does not budge at all.*
>
> *Akbar is an unfathomable ocean in which all the Hindus*
> *and Muslims have drowned.*
> *It is only Rana Pratap of Mewar who is floating like a*
> *lotus flower.*

"And another:

> *Rana Pratap retrieves the lost honor of the Hindus, as*
> *the sun restores light out of night."*

Hanuman did not respond to the recitation. It merely reinforced his feelings of ambivalence. But he would be true to his salt, do his duty.

They slowly crossed a desolate area of sand and rock, where the soil crunched underfoot and powdery dust rose into the air. Then the army reached a flat area, dotted here and there with *babul* and mango trees, and closely surrounded by rocky hills.

Hanuman saw two horseback scouts ride up to Man Singh and report. The commander nodded, then signaled for Hanuman and the other generals to approach. Man Singh looked down from his elephant and told them loudly, "The Rana is in the hills up ahead, through that small pass of Haldighati. The scouts estimate he has around three thousand men. Arrange your troops as we discussed earlier. If he doesn't come after us by midmorning, we'll need to go find him. I'd like to finish the fighting before noon if we can. The sun's already getting too hot."

The generals dispersed to their units, and the army spread across the little plain, which was actually too small for an ideal arrangement of troops. While they waited, Hanuman talked with Ajit and Dwarka Das, also on horseback. Once again the bard had chosen to wear arms, rather than to rely on his status to protect himself. Hanuman knew that Dwarka Das wanted to be able to come to his aid if needed in battle, and he was both pleased and bemused that the bard would have feelings toward him which exceeded the normal duties of loyalty.

Ajit said, "*Haldighati.* Do you know why the pass is called that, *Annadata?*"

Hanuman shook his head, and looked to Dwarka Das.

"Because of the yellow color in the soil, Highness," said the bard. "The dust from the rocks looks like *haldi,* turmeric spice."

They turned to watch the dromedary corps, with swivel guns mounted on the camels' backs, lope toward the pass.

The men were already perspiring in the blazing sun. The heat was hard on the horses and elephants, too, with the only significant water source, the Banas River, well behind now. Ajit removed his steel helmet, wiped his brow, and said, "Do you ever wish for the old days, when we fought only in winter?"

"Sometimes."

"It seemed more of a sport then, with its own season. Less of a burdensome duty."

"I always viewed it as a duty myself."

Ajit did not reply. Eventually he said in a tone that was undecipherable, "I wonder if we'll see Lord Baldeo."

It seemed likely Rana Pratap would be accompanied by most of his army, so there was a good chance Baldeo would be here, too. Hanuman had worried about the possibility of encountering his brother. What would he do if he met Baldeo in battle? What would Baldeo do? Hanuman intensely disliked the thought of one brother spilling another's blood.

He had tried to find inspiration in the *Ramayana.* That epic, of course, emphasized the loyalties between brothers. When Prince Rama had been exiled, his brother Lakshmana had accompanied him, enduring the same hardships. And Rama's other brother Bharata had refused to accept the throne which he considered to be rightly Rama's. When Rama had insisted, Bharata had agreed only to rule on Rama's behalf. Why couldn't such loyalty exist in Hanuman's own family? How could Hanuman and Baldeo have come into such extreme conflict?

The sounds of shouting and clashing of weapons came from far ahead. Suddenly Hanuman saw riders emerge swiftly from the narrow mouth of the pass. Thundering down the slight incline, they appeared to be fleeing. Other riders pursued them, the sun glinting off swords and spear points. Ajit said, "The Rana's men must have overwhelmed our vanguard!"

Even now, more of Rana Pratap's cavalry were charging into the Mughals' left wing. The air was filling with yellow tinged dust as imperial troops fled from the impact of the ferocious onslaught. Man Singh quickly ordered the main body of his army to move forward toward the enemy.

So far the Pariyatras were too far back to participate in the fighting. But now came what must be the main body of Pratap's forces, for through the dust Hanuman saw the Sisodia standard with the golden sun emblem and the red royal umbrella in the midst of the riders who were charging directly at the Mughal center, where Man Singh and Hanuman rode.

The weight of Pratap's charge carried the Rana's men far into the imperial formation. Suddenly the Pariyatras were engaged in fierce fighting. The uneven, rocky, ground with thorny bushes hindered movement. In the confusion of charging horses, swinging swords, flying arrows, Hanuman saw with amazement that some of the Muslim troops were actually shooting at their own Pariyatra allies!

He shouted at them in outrage, but then he became too busy defending himself to see if they had realized their error. He measured swords with a Rajput warrior. The man was much younger, but he relied on strength more than skill. Hanuman feinted a blow to the man's left, then quickly switched and slashed deeply into the quilted coat on his opponent's right side. The man's eyes bulged. He slumped and pitched from his horse.

Breathing hard from the brief but ferocious encounter, Hanuman wiped the dusty sweat from his right palm so he could get a firmer grip on his sword. God, it was hot! To his right, Dwarka Das was being hard pressed by an opposing horseman. The bard was parrying the blade well with his shield, but he was obviously tiring fast. Hanuman started to move to aid him, but Bhupendra, eldest of the retainers, saw the trouble and dispatched the enemy with his lance.

Hanuman looked about, trying to make sense of the battle. Off to the left, Ajit was regrouping his men. Many of the Mughal troops were retreating before the vigorous assault by Pratap's Rajputs. Man Singh was shouting for his own men to regroup and stand firm, but still they gave way. Hanuman realized Rana Pratap had cleverly outmaneuvered the much larger imperial army by using the narrow pass to maximum advantage.

Several elephants accompanied Pratap's charge, and the imperial elephants had moved forward in challenge. Hanuman heard men shouting, "Ram Prasad! Ram Prasad!" He saw a true giant of an animal flying the Gwalior colors in the center of Rana Pratap's other elephants. This must be the great elephant the Emperor had coveted, ridden now by one of the exiled Gwalior princes who had allied themselves with Pratap. Two imperial elephants faced Ram Prasad, who charged furiously at one.

Suddenly a heavyset enemy cavalryman attacked Hanuman, forcing him to vigorously defend himself.

Deafening blows smashed onto Hanuman's shield and glanced off his helmet. He swung his own sword again and again, parrying thrusts, striving to strike the enemy at a vulnerable spot. In the intense heat, he was tiring quickly. He hoped the wet stickiness that soaked his clothing was sweat, not blood.

At last, with great relief, he struck the man down with a blow at the neck, just as Kesari moved near to help. The retainer raised his blood-tinged sword in a brief salute, which Hanuman acknowledged with a nod.

He heavily gulped gritty air scented with blood and horse sweat, while he looked quickly about to see if anyone else posed an immediate threat. He became aware of the loud beating of drums. It must be Mehtar Khan leading the reserves in the rear, coming at last to assist the main body. Hanuman heard men shout, "The Emperor! The Emperor's coming!"

Impossible, he thought. Akbar was too far away. It had to be Mehtar Khan with reinforcements.

Most of the fighters appeared to believe the Emperor himself had arrived. Hanuman could sense the invigorating effect of the new occurrence sweeping through the dusty air as the imperial troops took heart and renewed their efforts.

At the same time Pratap's Rajputs appeared to lose hope. With unbelievable swiftness, Hanuman saw the tide of the battle turn. He and his men drove off their own attackers, who headed toward the pass to retreat.

The pursuers were smashing into each other as they tried to follow in too great numbers for the narrow valley to accommodate. No enemy were near now, so Hanuman paused, calming his breathing. He examined himself and decided he'd been fortunate so far; his only wound seemed to be a gash in his leg that bled slightly and was not deep.

He looked toward where the great elephants still battled. Chanchal and two other beasts faced Ram Prasad, whose howdah was now empty of fighters. Ram Prasad's mahout, astride the animal's neck, suddenly toppled to the ground with an arrow in his chest. An imperial elephant Hanuman recognized as Gajmukta moved near, and Hussain

Khan, Akbar's Superintendent of Elephants, leaped onto Ram Prasad to take control of the prize.

Man Singh would be pleased. So would Akbar.

Hanuman looked at Man Singh, a short distance away. He was amazed to see Rana Pratap's umbrella and gold sun standard immediately in front of Man Singh's elephant. A blue horse that must have been the Rana's famous charger Chetak reared up with a bulky warrior, who could only be Pratap himself, astride him. The horse's forelegs struck at the elephant's head.

Hanuman spurred his own mount toward the Rana. Pratap thrust a spear at Man Singh, but Man Singh ducked into the howdah. The blow glanced off the steel frame and struck the mahout. Then one of the small swords attached to the elephant's tusks sliced Chetak's foreleg, and blood appeared.

Hanuman and his men crowded toward Pratap. But several of the Rana's own fighters had formed a protective barrier, and on the other side of them Hanuman saw Pratap's banners and umbrella move swiftly away. Many of Man Singh's men gave chase.

Hanuman wove his way through the nearest fighters in time to see the Rana's standards fall, as the small party was overwhelmed in the midst of the melee of attacking Mughal cavalry.

It appeared certain that Rana Pratap was captured, possibly wounded or killed. Hanuman could not help but feel regret at such a valiant opponent's defeat. Pratap had fought so long, so tenaciously, facing adverse conditions and heavy odds. The bards would long tell of his heroism.

Hanuman saw Dwarka Das sheath a bloody sword as he moved closer. Hanuman said to him, "You shouldn't have given up your immunity again."

Dwarka Das smiled. "For my own protection. In the thick of fighting, it's difficult to see if I'm *charan* or Rajput. And some of the Muslims on our own side were shooting at us as if we were the enemy."

Hanuman frowned and gave an abrupt nod. There now seemed little for him to do. He looked about to see if he could spot Ajit. Instead, off to the edge of the battlefield, he spied a bulky figure riding swiftly off on a blue horse that appeared to be limping.

Hanuman instantly recognized the warrior. Pratap! How could the Rana have escaped such a mass of opponents? He realized one of the Rana's men must have taken over the standard and umbrella and pretended to be Pratap, giving the ruler a chance to flee. None of the Rana's enemies had yet realized the King was still free and was slipping away.

Hanuman nudged Bajraj into a gallop. His duty was to try to prevent Pratap's escape, but he briefly wondered what he would do if he actually caught the Rana. Time to think of that later. He sped over the rough, stony ground, intent on his prey, not looking backward to see if Dwarka Das or any of the retainers followed.

A small defile lay ahead, with a tiny stream. Near it, Pratap's wounded horse stumbled and fell.

Hanuman felt sudden anguish: he himself might be the one to take Pratap's surrender. Or, he might have to duel with the Rana, who was undoubtedly a better swordsman.

A horseman appeared ahead on the left and rode swiftly to block Hanuman's way. Hanuman raised his sword and spurred his own mount to greater speed, trying to reach Pratap first.

Something about the newcomer seemed familiar.

Baldeo! In the intensity of the battle, Hanuman had temporarily forgotten about his brother fighting on Pratap's side.

The two riders converged, momentarily riding side by side. Baldeo did not attack, and Hanuman slowed, his sword ready.

Baldeo, too, slackened his speed, looking with an odd expression at Hanuman.

Half forgetting Rana Pratap, Hanuman reined to a stop.

Baldeo halted, and sat staring at him. His face wet with sweat, he appeared much older, thinner than when Hanuman had last seen him several years before. Strangely, Baldeo's sword hung limply from his hand. It was then Hanuman saw that blood flowed heavily from a wound in Baldeo's side.

"Saw you leave," Baldeo rasped. His breath came in gasps. "Need to talk."

Hanuman could not think of a response. At last he said, "You need help. Your wounds are bad." He was vaguely aware that a few of his Rajputs and Dwarka Das had ridden near and sat watching.

Baldeo forced a grim, wincing smile. "Too late for me."

"Maybe not."

Baldeo have a quick shake of his head. He seemed to struggle for words, as he said, "Exile from my clan—too high a price. My sons must pay now." His eyes met Hanuman's. "Release you—from vow." He toppled from his horse.

Hanuman hurriedly slid from his own mount and knelt to examine Baldeo. It was as his brother had said. Too late.

Hanuman raised his head. In the distance, another horseman, leading a riderless steed, had joined Rana Pratap. The man had dismounted, and the Rana was embracing him. Chetak, the Rana's beloved horse, still lay on the ground. Rana Pratap climbed on the new mount and sat, looking down at Chetak for a time. A small group of other riders, no doubt the Rana's Rajput retinue, arrived.

Rana Pratap slowly turned his new horse and, accompanied by

his escort, galloped off through the hot, stony hills.

Oddly, the man who had first aided Pratap did not remain with the Rana; rather he rode swiftly back toward the fighting. Suddenly Hanuman recognized the man: Pratap's estranged brother, Sukta, who had been fighting for the imperials. An odd coincidence, this reconciliation of *two* sets of brothers after fighting on opposite sides.

"Highness, shall we chase them?" asked Bhupendra, the senior of Hanuman's Rajputs who were present.

Hanuman knew his own duty required him to pursue Rana Pratap. He fleetingly wondered what Lord Rama would have done, had he knelt at the side of his own brother who had just died.

Realistically, he knew he could do little against Pratap now that the Rana had again acquired an escort to protect him. For once, Hanuman decided, he would ignore his duty, just for a short while. "No, let them go," he replied. He removed his steamy helmet and lowered his aching body to sit on the ground by Baldeo.

He wondered how many more battles the Rana would fight against Akbar. He glanced at Dwarka Das. The bard should have interesting material for his epic.

Ajit rode up, looking hot and exhausted, but apparently not wounded. Several Pariyatra Rajputs, some bleeding, all disheveled, accompanied him. They silently gazed down at their Raja, and at Baldeo's body.

12

Hanuman looked out from the palace balcony, down over the walled town of Mangarh. His own exile had been less than the fourteen years of Lord Rama, but it had been long enough. At last, after eight years, Hanuman could gaze at his beloved capital. For the celebrations honoring his return the inhabitants had freshly whitewashed every house. The city wall had not been enlarged, but within its confines, the prosperous times had resulted in a number of fine, tall mansions built by nobles and merchants, and in several small but new temples whose spires enhanced the view.

Upon their arrival, Dwarka Das had said with his impish smile, "Highness, if you'll recall, I've often advised you to be patient."

"Yes," said Hanuman, grinning back, "as you said, problems are often outlived."

"With your permission, Highness, I'll take up my post at the main gate."

"You've earned it, *charanji*."

Both the Bundi Rani and Sisodia Rani were relieved to resume permanent residence in their former apartments after the eight years of absence.

Aside from the new construction, little had changed at Mangarh. The sounds of children crying, vendors selling their wares, dogs barking, swordsmiths beating metal, still drifted up from the town. It was almost as if those eight years had never happened. Although he would soon be required to leave Mangarh again to fight yet another battle for Akbar, he now felt at peace.

One problem, however, still nagged at his mind. He returned to the room where his architect had left the drawings for the new wing of the palace. He gathered them up and went to his senior wife's apartments.

At last, though almost forty years of age, the senior Rani was swelling with a child. The fact gave Hanuman great relief and satisfaction. She smiled more frequently now. But he was puzzled that she was not continually aglow with happiness after becoming pregnant.

She stood watching, obviously curious, while he spread the plans on the carpet. "The drawings for the new wing," he said.

She came over with a jingling of anklets, stood by them with her bejeweled and red-soled feet, and gazed down over the bulge of her belly.

He said, "You know I'll have to leave again soon. It won't be practical to take you along, since we'll be traveling quickly through rugged country."

She nodded, then continued looking at the plans. "An elaborate building," she said, apparently intrigued. "Those four towers along the facade...."

"I need someone to oversee the construction when I'm gone."

She looked up at him. "You have a master builder for that. Didn't Kishen Lal draw the plans?"

"Yes. But someone has to watch the finances, make certain the funds aren't squandered."

"Your Treasurer, of course."

"Yes. However, he has other concerns. I trust him, but he has no interest in construction. I'm not convinced he'll watch the outlays as closely as I'd like." He let this sink in. Then he said, "Also, Kishen Lal is competent at building strong, well balanced structures. But I've found him weak on ornamentation."

She stood in silence. At last: "Then who?"

"I was thinking of you."

She stared at him.

He said, "You keep tight control on the palace finances. I think you could do the same on the construction. You have good artistic sense. You're interested in building decoration. I trust you to ensure the stone carvers do a masterful job."

More silence. Then she asked, "How could I supervise the work, when I'm not supposed to walk around openly among men?"

"Kishen Lal can report to you every day, bring the accounts to you, show you the plans. And I see no reason why you can't visit the site briefly every day, since it's for an important purpose, so long as you don't linger among the workmen."

He saw the realization grow in her eyes that he was quite serious. A smile spread across her lips. "You'd actually entrust me with this."

"You're by far the best choice."

The excitement in her face appeared even greater than when she had told him she was expecting a child. He was puzzled, but also pleased, to know that this type of responsibility was apparently what she had needed all along.

Hanuman thought again of how he hoped to please her one day with a major gift—the lovely little summer palace on the shore of the lake he planned to create in the valley to the west. She should definitely be involved with him in the design of both the building and the lake. As if embarrassed at being caught with such a look of joy, she quickly returned her gaze to the drawings.

And out in his post above the main gate, near the timekeeper's balcony, Dwarka Das was composing the final lines of his epic.

***

Future generations of Rajputs, when taking an oath, would often swear by "the sin of the slaughter of Chittor." Allegedly 74 ½ maunds of sacred cords were taken by Akbar from the necks of the dead Rajput defenders of Chittorgarh (likely a bard's exaggeration, as a maund varied from 40 to 75 pounds, depending on the locality). The numbers "74 ½" became considered accursed, and it was the practice to write them as a seal on banker's letters to invoke calamity on anyone who would violate the terms of the letter.

Rana Pratap would continue his resistance against Akbar for twenty more years, until the Rana's death in 1597. The recapture of Chittor became a goal of future rulers of Mewar.

Centuries later Rana Pratap would remain popularly known as a great fighter for the right of Indians to rule themselves, and among many Hindus, as a champion of the Hindu faith against those Muslims perceived as oppressors. Pilgrims would travel to Haldighati to see the battlefield and the monument to Pratap's horse Chetak, and they would smear the yellow dust of the pass on their foreheads. In Mewar, Rana Pratap and Chetak are still often depicted in murals painted on houses, and a bronze statue of them overlooks Udaipur from a hilltop park.

Historians generally view Akbar as the greatest of the Mughal emperors of India, due largely to his political astuteness in consolidating and administering a vast empire, his intelligence, and his tolerance for differing religions. In common with most of the other Mughal monarchs, he was also an enthusiastic patron of scholarship and the arts. Like other autocratic rulers, he did have flaws in his character, some of which were depicted in the preceding story.

The
Mangarh Treasure
Eight

20

Vijay had known of Raja Hanuman and his brother Baldeo, from growing up in the state and from comments by Kaushalya Kumari. But he merely nodded, to encourage Rajendra Singh to continue.

The Thakur of Baldeogarh asked, "You know of the god, Ekadantji, whose temple is in the palace in Mangarh?"

"I do, sir."

"Then you might know that Ekadantji was involved in the dispute." Rajendra Singh gave a wry smile. "I think that to this day, the Maharaja's branch of the Pariyatra clan may fear that we will try to steal back Ekadantji from them."

"Can you tell me," asked Vijay, "if His Highness' branch was indeed so wealthy as the rumors say? At least some time in the past?"

"How could they not have been wealthy? They had the revenues from vast landholdings. Far more than my own lands, and my family did quite well. Even more importantly, His Highness' ancestors fought as allies of the Mughal Emperors for many years. They brought back great wealth from their military campaigns. The treasure of Maharaja Madho Singh, in Emperor Aurangzeb's time, is legendary. But that was centuries ago."

Rajendra Singh paused a few moments, looking out over the village. He turned back to Vijay. "Obviously, His Highness' family has been hurt by the land reforms and loss of political power after Independence. So has my own branch of the clan. But do they have a great deal of concealed, undeclared wealth? I'm afraid they don't let me in on their secrets."

Vijay took another sip of *lassi*. He could not tell if the Thakur was being evasive. What Rajendra Singh said sounded perfectly reasonable. How, indeed, could the man be expected to know inside financial information concerning the ex-Maharaja's family? "You must have at least heard rumors, sir, about the hidden wealth. The so called 'Mangarh Treasure.'"

Rajendra Singh shrugged. "I've heard rumors, of course. There are rumors about a fabulous treasure at Jaipur, also. Neither one has been found yet. Until someone does, it's just speculation."

"Many of the well-known jewels formerly held by the ruler seem to be no longer around."

The Thakur again shrugged. "Maybe they were sold. Maybe they were sent abroad. Who knows?"

Vijay made a last attempt. "Sir, if you were in their place, and you did have something to hide, do you have any ideas as to where you might conceal it?"

Rajendra Singh looked amused. He chuckled. "I know where I would put it. But I don't care to speculate with you. If Lakshman Singh ever found out that I told you, even as a guess that turned out to be correct, he'd never forgive me. Then we really would have a rift between our houses again!"

Vijay hesitated. He had a hunch. No. More than a hunch—a definite intuitive feeling—that Rajendra Singh knew more than he was letting on.

What to do? The search could successfully end in only a few hours if Rajendra Singh gave him the necessary leads. He said, "No one need know the source of our information, sir."

The Thakur shook his head. "Word would leak, or someone would guess." His eyes shifted away. "Anyway, I don't think I really know anything useful to you."

Vijay sensed, strongly, that he was close to the information he needed. He said, hating himself as he did so, "I feel I owe it to you to make sure you realize, sir, that we can subpoena you as a witness. If you don't fully cooperate, it could mean that my superiors in New Delhi might wonder if you, yourself, have something to hide. Your own records might be subpoenaed, and your home could be searched."

Rajendra Singh stared at him. Eventually, he said evenly, "You people don't have much subtlety, do you? I expected better of you, Mr. Singh."

Vijay felt his face growing warm. He, too, had expected better of himself. He drained the last of the *lassi*, and said, "I was just being realistic, sir, and making sure you were aware of the possibility. I don't make those decisions myself."

"I wasn't born yesterday, Mr. Singh. I know how things work in this new Raj of ours, and I don't like the methods. You can send your raiders here if you want, but I won't betray my friends just to make it easier on myself."

Vijay sat a moment longer but could think of nothing more to say.

Rajendra Singh smiled. "More *lassi*, Mr. Singh?"

Vijay mumbled, "Thank you, sir, but no." He awkwardly took his leave from the Thakur.

From the castle's balcony, Rajendra Singh watched Vijay Singh drive away in the jeep. The Thakur was certain he knew where at least one part of the wealth was concealed, and he hoped nothing he'd said to the tax officer was a clue that would reveal the hiding place.

As for the rest of the rumored hoard: he'd had his sources of information in the palace in the days before Independence. He hoped, for Lakshman Singh's sake, that the ex-Maharaja had gotten rid of the potentially embarrassing contents of at least one hidden storage vault.

21

Mangarh, 8 July 1975

Vijay had begun to imagine himself as being in a sort of duel across the centuries, with Maharaja Madho Singh, who had likely hidden the bulk of the treasure, as his antagonist.

But he also had at least one present day adversary, who was sitting across from him at the table in the *dak* bungalow. Ghosali fingered his pipe and said, "Our second week is almost up. The pressure must be quite intense upon you to find something."

"Upon all of us," said Vijay. "We're all part of the team, you know." He had noticed that Ghosali was carefully rationing his bottled water, with the search continuing so long.

"Ah, yes, of course. But it must be especially hard on the man in charge, so to speak."

Vijay shrugged. "It goes with the job." What was Ghosali up to? Not showing sympathy, that was for certain. Maybe needling Vijay was Ghosali's way of expressing annoyance over not being in charge himself.

"You are from Mangarh," stated Ghosali, peering at Vijay through the large-lensed eyeglasses.

"Yes, from a village. Not from the city."

"Why have you not yet visited your family? Surely your duties would have allowed a few hours some evening."

Vijay fought the urge to tell him it was none of his business. Instead, he said calmly, "As you know, I've been rather preoccupied. It's somewhat inconvenient to get to the village. Be assured I'll visit there before returning to Delhi."

Ghosali studied his pipe. "I see." Then: "You are Rajput. Did your family rule the village?"

Vijay shook his head no. "It's a small village of little importance. We weren't major lords." He hated being forced into specifics in his deception. What if Ghosali asked the name of the village? Any hesitation on Vijay's part might cause suspicion. Yet, identifying a particular village provided a fact which could be checked on, whether the name was real or fictitious.

Ghosali was staring at him. "I see." The Brahmin rose from the table, picked up his water bottle. Vijay relaxed a little; apparently the questioning had ended for now. Ghosali said in parting, "One's background is of prime importance in determining his character, so to speak. Do you not agree?" He walked toward his room, not giving Vijay a chance to respond.

Vijay struggled to maintain his composure. What did Ghosali mean by that? Did he suspect the lies about being Rajput? Or was it mere intellectualizing?

Vijay indeed felt the pressure of time. Almost two weeks, and nothing had been found. Where could the treasure be? Did it even exist? He once again tried to put himself in the place of Madho Singh, three hundred years ago, with a huge quantity of captured treasure. Where would he have put it?

Certainly not far away. Some, maybe most, of the loot would have been stored in the state treasury. But Madho Singh had a reputation for both greed and cleverness. He would have been unlikely to put his entire wealth in such an obvious spot, however well guarded, where it could have been an invitation to invaders or corrupt officials.

Madho Singh must have expended some of the treasure on the addition he had built to the palace, the Madho Mahal. And he used much of the money on his workshop of artists. But he would not have spent all of it.

Madho must have kept some of the wealth readily accessible to enjoy by looking at and handling. And to take with him if it should ever become necessary to flee due to an invasion or a coup. The Madho Mahal seemed the most likely location. Madho Singh had built the structure for his own living quarters, and incorporating a hidden treasure vault at that time would have been relatively simple.

Vijay sought out Ranjit and found him carefully examining the pool area of the garden terrace atop the Madho Mahal. The Bhil guard captain, Surmal, stood nearby, obviously keeping an eye on him. One of the striped squirrels sat beneath the *pipal* tree, watching them all. "We're putting everyone into the Madho Mahal," Vijay told Ranjit. "I want the entire building measured, inside and out."

Ranjit smiled. "So it's here, is it, *yaar*?"

"Damned if I know. But that's my best hunch at the moment."

"The building's so complicated, not to mention the size. Measuring will be difficult."

"But not impossible. There are distinctive areas, you know—sleeping apartments, rooms for leisure, courtyards....I think we can divide the building up into the major sections, measure each one as a whole, then add them together and see how they match up with the outside walls. Then start subdividing each area with internal measurements."

Ranjit nodded. "It will take a good while, but it should be feasible." Ranjit turned sober. He glanced around, and said in a lowered voice, "It's probably none of my business, but I thought maybe I should tell you: I overheard Ghosali on the telephone last night. He was talking to someone in Delhi he called 'Batraji.' It almost sounded like he was giving a report on our progress."

Vijay tensed. Could Ghosali actually be spying for Batra?

"Maybe," Ranjit was saying, "Ghosali was only talking to an old friend."

"I suspect there's more to it than that."

Ranjit narrowed his eyes, nodded, and went to get the others.

Vijay stood thinking for a time. Dev Batra could mean a great deal of trouble.

The team began with the tape measures. Despite the country's recent change to the metric system, the Income Tax Department hadn't yet gotten the funds for new equipment, so the tapes were still marked in inches and feet.

Vijay periodically checked on their work, occasionally helping hold one end of a tape or writing down measurements. He helped Ghosali and Krishnaswamy for a time on the inside of the building. Ghosali was doing the drawings, somewhat cruder than Vijay would have preferred, but acceptable. Ghosali's handwriting when he recorded the measurements was sloppy though readable.

Ranjit and Mrs. Desai and Shanta Das worked on the outside of the building, although occasionally the monsoon showers forced them to take cover. Vijay found Ranjit bending over a balcony rail and lowering a string with a weight on the end. The Sikh looked at Vijay, grinned, and said, "This seemed the best way to measure these tall vertical distances."

Vijay nodded. "Good idea." Ranjit always did well on these practical, mechanical jobs.

Mrs. Desai was measuring the length of the terrace. Shanta Das was drawing the plan and writing down the measurements. Vijay glanced at her sketch. The rendering of the building plan was in clear, crisp lines, the labeling neatly done. "Nice work," he said.

She smiled at him, said simply, "Thank you," and continued her recording. Vijay couldn't help but compare her work with Ghosali's sloppiness. For all the Brahmin's airs of superiority, Vijay thought, Shanta was worth at least two of him.

The other groups seemed to be making slow but satisfactory progress. Even with all of them working, it took over a day to chart the huge structure.

The rains had stopped for most of the next morning, so when the job was done they spread the diagrams out in the courtyard, where the sun had dried the paving stones. The two striped squirrels kept cautiously distant, occasionally watching from partway up the trunk of the *pipal* tree.

"I hope someone can make sense out of this mess," said Ranjit. "I know I can't."

Vijay felt under too much tension to feel any humor, but Shanta laughed. The dozens of sheets of rough sketches, splattered throughout with the penciled numbers from the measurements, looked like some beginning architectural student's nightmares. Shanta's stood out as by far the most readable.

It was the first time the drawings had been put together in one spot. The team members all examined them for a time. The timekeeper's gong sounded by the gate, but they had grown accustomed to it and paid no attention.

Vijay pondered the drawings with a growing frustration. Short of building a model in three dimensions, which they had neither the skills nor the time for, it seemed almost impossible to make meaningful comparisons of the inner and outer measurements. He glanced around at the other team members. Shanta was wearing a perplexed frown. She whispered to Mrs. Desai, who shrugged and shook her head.

Ranjit said, "I've been looking at the measurements of the basement levels. That seems the most likely place for a hidden vault. It might even be underground in the hill. See how thick these walls are? Easily enough to hide something in them."

Ghosali drew deeply on his pipe and said, "I disagree. Whoever had something to hide would also expect that area to be searched. Consequently I would like to concentrate on the upper levels. A hidden strong room would be more likely in the living quarters, where the Maharaja could have kept a closer watch on his gold and jewels."

"Do you see any discrepancies in that area of the building?" asked Vijay.

Ghosali appeared annoyed. "Perhaps. Some of the measurements do not seem to add up. Particularly near the outer walls. But with so many corners and irregularities, to be certain we would need to make better diagrams, exactly to scale, so to speak. That would take time."

Shanta Das said, "Sir, I've added the inner and outer measurements along the front facade. It doesn't make sense. The inside is bigger than the outside."

Everyone stared at her. She had used no paper or pencil to calculate. Vijay asked, "You're sure?"

Mrs. Desai said, "Shanta is quite fast at doing figures in her head."

Ghosali said, "I measured that part of the inside myself. With Krishnaswamy's help, of course. I assure you we made no mistakes."

Ranjit raised an eyebrow. "I measured the outside of that part with Mrs. Desai and Miss Das. I don't see how we could have gone wrong, either."

Ghosali said, "Obviously you did do something wrong. I suggest you do it over."

Ranjit glared at him. "We will—if you will, too."

Ghosali snorted. "Of course not."

Vijay was examining Ghosali. Could the Bengali have deliberately sabotaged the effort to make Vijay look bad? It seemed unlikely. But there was that call to Delhi. He sighed mentally; there was probably no way to know. It seemed more likely that Ghosali's crude drawings would be more in error than Shanta's well-done ones. He said in frustration, "We don't have time to do it all over again. Can't anyone figure out where a mistake might have occurred?"

"We were so careful," said Mrs. Desai, looking distraught. "We checked each other's work to be sure."

Ranjit walked over to the measuring tapes, examined them. "I haven't seen this tape before," he said. "Where did it come from?"

"That's the one Krishnaswamy and I used," said Ghosali, in an irritated tone. "It was lying with our other ones when I selected it."

Ranjit had Krishnaswamy take one end, and they stretched the tape straight. Then they laid another one out beside it. "They don't match!" Ranjit said. "At the ten foot mark, they're a good four inches off!"

"That could add up to a big error on a building this large," said Vijay. "How could they be so different?"

Ranjit was examining a tape. He said, "They all have government inventory numbers on them. Except for this one that reads four inches longer at the same distance." He looked around the courtyard, and his gaze settled on one of the Bhil guards. Light dawned in his eyes. "I have a feeling—" he stopped.

"What?" prompted Vijay.

"You know maharajas used to take important guests on tiger hunts. Sometimes they used a special tape or chain to measure the kills. It made the guest think he'd shot a bigger one than he really had. I think the guards played a trick on us."

Ghosali looked like a volcano ready to erupt. "You mean I used a tape that they planted!" He held his pipe rigid at chest height and stared at the Bhil guard, who appeared to be paying no attention to the group of raiders.

"Maybe the question we should ask is, 'Why?'" said Vijay. "Was it only a joke to harass us, or do they want to confuse us because they're hiding something here?"

He was angrier over the deception than he let on. If the guards were trying to divert them from the Madho Mahal, their trick had exactly the opposite effect. He squatted in front of a couple of the drawings and pointed. "See here. Below the ruler's apartments, there are all these storage rooms on the ground levels. The inner walls are cut into the hillside, but the outer walls overlook the view. Even though those walls are vaulted, they still have to be thick to support all the stories towering above. But if I were the Maharaja, I'd have a secret staircase from my apartments, going down inside one of these walls. Down into the walls between the storerooms, and right down into the rock below." He paused to glance at his people.

"Those lower walls are incredibly thick," agreed Ranjit.

"So let's concentrate there, for now," said Vijay. "Take the diagrams of that part with you. Miss Das, I'd like you and Mrs. Desai to remain a moment."

The team members moved off, except for Vijay and the two women. He had come to have considerable respect for Shanta's judgment, in particular. To think, she had done all those computations in her head! "I'm glad you found those discrepancies," he told her. "Have you seen anything else you'd like to mention?"

Shanta gave her attractive smile. "Nothing else at the moment, sir. If you'd like, it won't take me long to revise Mr. Ghosali's measurements on the diagram. I'll just subtract four inches for every ten feet."

Vijay nodded. "Good." He asked both women, "Do you agree with my assessment of where to search?"

Mrs. Desai replied simply, "It's a difficult question. I naturally support your decision. Especially if the guards might have been trying to hide something there."

Vijay looked to Shanta. She said, "I think it's a good analysis, sir. We need to narrow the focus to one place. I agree with your selection."

Vijay nodded. He had needed the reassurance, he realized. It was hell to have everything riding on his own shoulders.

Mrs. Desai excused herself to make a phone call from the office before going to help continue the search. Shanta knelt with a pencil before Ghosali's diagram.

"I wonder," Vijay mused aloud. "Did the princess or her brother put the guards up to trying to confuse us? Or did the Bhils do it on their own initiative?"

Shanta replied with a sober look, "I can't be sure, sir. But I get the feeling the princess is playing straight with us for the most part. Maybe she really doesn't know about the treasure."

Vijay stared at her. He nodded. "It's possible, I suppose." They heard a car noisily ascending the bumpy hill of the approach road, and they both turned to face the fort's main gate. The timekeeper's gong again rang, as if to announce the arrival of the shiny new white Mercedes Benz which sped through the archway and braked to a quick stop in the courtyard. The car's front fenders each held an Indian flag on a short metal staff. The black license plate bore no numbers; instead it sported a large gleaming chrome replica of the famous sculpture from the top of one of the pillars raised by Emperor Ashoka, the image of the lions' heads and the Wheel of Dharma, the official seal of the Indian government.

A tall, bushy haired, glum-faced man slid from the front seat and opened a rear door. An overweight man dressed in white *khadi* and wearing aviator-style sunglasses slowly stepped out. Vijay walked toward him.

"Income Tax Officer Singh?" the man asked.

Vijay joined his palms in *namaste.*

The man returned the greeting perfunctorily. "Dev Batra."

23

Vijay froze for a moment. Recovering, he tried not to show his unease as he said, "Welcome to Mangarh, Mr. Batra."

Batra stared at him from behind the sunglasses. "I had hoped it would not be necessary for me to come. But here I am. You know I hold a number of positions in Delhi. Today, let us say I am representing the Finance Minister, among other persons." Batra smiled. "Including Mataji." He seemed to take great pleasure in alluding to the Prime Minister. "I have come to see why you have not yet found anything."

Vijay had feared as much. Batra pulled a packet of Marlboros from a pocket, shook one out and placed it between his lips. His assistant quickly stepped forward and held a lighter to the end. "As you know," Batra said, his voice muffled by the cigarette, "I gave you an additional week after we arrested the Maharaja. The time is up."

"I realize that sir. We've been trying our level best."

Batra had been eyeing Shanta while he took the initial puffs on his cigarette. Vijay had heard the man was a notorious womanizer. "Miss Das," Vijay said, "why don't you join the other searchers now. You can finish redoing the measurements later."

"But I shall be needing a guide," Batra said, the cigarette still between his lips so his words were slightly slurred. "Perhaps the lady—Miss Das is her name?—could be assigned to assist me." As if to see her better, he slowly raised his sunglasses and perched them so the lenses were above his forehead.

Vijay swore to himself, but said aloud, "Miss Das is needed inside, I think, but I'll be glad to help you all I can myself, sir."

Batra removed the cigarette from his mouth. "No, no, I insist. No offense, Mr. Singh, but Miss Das is much prettier than you."

Vijay grimaced inwardly as he thought. "Maybe we both can guide you around."

Batra laughed. "Excellent. The best of both worlds. Now, then, Mr. Singh, what exactly are you doing here?"

Vijay summarized the search to date. He was almost done, when Batra interrupted, casting the partly smoked cigarette to the paving stones with no effort to extinguish it. "But Mr. Singh! Why are you not tearing the buildings apart if you haven't found anything yet? You had only to ask, and we would have sent hundreds of workmen to help you."

"But sir—these buildings are of great architectural and historical value. We felt we had to proceed carefully."

Batra shrugged. "What for, Singhji? Start tearing hell out of the place. I'd guess that will make the owners much more eager to cooperate. They'll be only too glad to show you where they are hiding their gold when they see their buildings come tumbling down."

"Undoubtedly," said Vijay without humor, "that would be effective. However, it would be costly to hire so many workmen. I was trying to save the government money. And I think we're taking an approach now that will give results without being quite so destructive." He explained how the team was concentrating on a more thorough search of a carefully selected portion of one structure.

"I see," said Batra, sounding unimpressed. "By the way, Mr. Singh, is the princess, Kaushalya Kumari, away in Delhi still?"

Something in the way he asked the question sounded strange to Vijay, but he had little choice but to reply, "Yes, she's been gone a few days now."

After a time, Batra said, "I'm acquainted with her, you know. We have been seeing each other. I believe she is becoming rather fond of me. Quite a beautiful girl, as well as rich. And of course, there is nothing quite like bedding royalty."

Vijay gaped at him. That such a slimy thug could hold any appeal for someone as refined, as perceptive, as Kaushalya Kumari was beyond belief. And what was Batra doing meeting with her anyway, with the government searching for her family's hidden assets, and her father arrested?

As if reading his thoughts, Batra said, "I'm giving her the impression I'd like to help her get her father freed, if only she'll cooperate in telling us where her family's treasure is. So far I've not been successful. But you see, I'm working on the problem in Delhi, at the same time you're working on it here."

"I see."

Batra waved his cigarette toward Surmal, who was standing at a distance watching. "These guards. Have you questioned them about the treasure?"

"Yes, sir. They say they can't tell us anything."

"Ridiculous! They have to know, or they couldn't do their job."

"It would seem so."

"Then why have you let them get away without telling you?"

"We don't have much choice, sir. Being realistic, we have no way to force them to talk. They're just being true to their salt, as they see it."

"Hmm. We'll see. Give my own men a half hour alone with one of them, I'll bet he'd be begging to tell us everything he knows."

Vijay stared at Dev Batra, wondering how to respond. Batra was obviously talking of using physical threats—maybe even torture—

to intimidate the guards. Aside from the morality, it would be totally illegal, but he doubted that would stop Batra. Quickly, he tried to divert the man. "Would you care to look over the fortress, sir?"

"I'd rather see the new palace. Old buildings are so unpleasant. Always full of trash and bats and they smell like piss and shit. Only good for salvaging carved windows and doors. I can see why His Highness lives in the new palace. Let us go look at that one now."

"As you wish," said Vijay, silently damning him and the interference. "Miss Das, would you go inform officer Ranjit Singh that we're leaving for the Bhim Bhawan Palace?"

Batra's eyes followed her until she was out of sight, his sunglasses remaining high above his forehead.

Anil Ghosali appeared from a doorway and walked slowly over. He pressed his palms together in greeting.

"Ah, Ghosaliji," Batra said casually. "So good to see you again. How are your wife and all your daughters? And your parents in Calcutta?"

"They are all quite well," said Ghosali. "I'll be sure to tell them you asked."

"Please do. I understand things are not going so well here in Mangarh, however. Perhaps if an energetic Bengali were placed in charge they might go better."

Vijay tried to hide his anger. Could Batra really put Ghosali in charge of the search? Maybe he could, if he truly represented the Finance Minister.

"We're doing our best," replied Ghosali, taking his pipe from a vest pocket. "It's a difficult job."

"So Singhji here tells me. But I do not want your best only, you realize. It is results I want."

"Of course. Of course," said Ghosali. He began lighting his pipe.

"Good. I am glad we are understanding each other," said Batra. He turned to Vijay. "Ghosaliji and I are both disciples of Swami Surya, you know. It is a bond between us."

Vijay glanced at Ghosali, uncertain how to reply. Swami Surya was both famous and controversial. His lifestyle might be labeled "jet-set," and he attracted a wide range of followers, from cinema stars to rich businessman to government ministers. For every person who considered him a saint, someone else thought him a con artist. In any event, the fact that both Ghosali and Batra were disciples seemed to have formed some sort of connection between the two.

Batra turned to watch Shanta Das approach across the courtyard. "She is lovely," he murmured.

Ghosali turned and saw to whom Batra referred. His eyebrows rose in shock. He whispered to Batra, "But she's Harijan! See how dark she is?"

"Who cares?" said Batra. "They all feel the same in bed." He gave a short laugh.

Bloody hell! thought Vijay. He had enough worries without having to keep Batra's sweaty hands off Shanta. There seemed nothing he could do if Batra were indeed seeing Kaushalya Kumari. But if the man harassed Shanta Das, probably the most valuable member of the search team along with Ranjit....

Batra started to walk over to the Mercedes, with the others following. He stopped abruptly, staring at Airavata. "What's an elephant doing here?"

Vijay said, "He's sort of a member of the royal family."

Batra said, "Maybe we can get him to help tear down the buildings. He should be plenty strong."

Again Vijay tried not to show his annoyance.

Batra walked over to the elephant. "Bring me some candy, Sen. Let's have a little fun."

His tall, wild-haired assistant strode to the car, came back with a small cardboard box. Batra opened it and took out a greenish, ball-shaped sweetmeat. Holding it concealed in his palm, Batra extended his hand toward the elephant. Airavata reached with his trunk and touched its tip to Batra's hand. Batra stepped backward until the elephant, chained as he was, could not quite reach the treat.

Then Batra opened his hand, holding the candy in view. Airavata tried again to reach it but was unable to. Batra began to laugh.

The elephant stopped trying. He stood there, his eye on Batra. Dev Batra took a step closer, again extended his hand with the candy. The elephant's trunk darted out, but Batra moved backward just fast enough that Airavata again missed. The elephant let out a low rumble.

"I think I am making him mad," said Batra unconcernedly. He took a few steps away. Then, casually, he cast the candy to the ground, just out of Airavata's reach. Batra stood and watched, smiling.

The elephant eyed the sweetmeat a few moments. Then Airavata quickly lowered the tip of his trunk to the ground and squirted a blast of air. The candy shot to the nearby wall, rebounded and rolled back across the paving stones to within reach. Airavata extended his trunk, seized the candy, and thrust it into his mouth.

Batra stood with his own mouth hanging open. "I'll be damned. I'd never have believed it."

He grinned, reached out a hand toward his assistant Sen, who held the opened box to him. Batra looked into it, grabbed another sweetmeat. A rectangular one, this time. Batra tossed it toward the elephant— out of reach again, this time much farther away from the wall.

Airavata stared at him. Then the elephant raised his trunk and trumpeted what was clearly a blast of annoyance. Batra jumped at the shrill sound. Then he grinned as if embarrassed at being startled, turned and walked toward the car. The elephant stood frozen, the sweetmeat untouched, tauntingly unreachable.

Shanta Das went over, picked it up, held it toward Airavata.

The elephant slowly extended his trunk, took the sweetmeat from her. He clutched it a moment, as if trying to decide what to do with it. Vijay could hear Shanta talking in a low voice to the elephant. At last Airavata thrust the candy into his mouth.

By now Batra was at the car. Sen held open one of the rear doors for him. Shanta came over, and Dev Batra gestured for her to climb in first, clearly intending to sit by her. Either she did not see him or pretended not to, as she instead quickly opened the front door and slid into that seat.

Batra scowled, and he climbed into the rear. Vijay went around to the other side. He said to Ghosali, "Keep searching." Ghosali opened his mouth as if to protest being left behind. Then he closed it and stepped backward, away from the car.

Vijay got in next to Batra. He was momentarily startled at how far he sank into the pillowy softness of the new-smelling leather upholstery. It was such a contrast to the hardness of the jeep's seats.

"That poor man," Batra said.

Vijay gave him a questioning look.

"Ghosaliji. He has five daughters, five dowries to worry about. Can you imagine the expense? No wonder he looks for every opportunity to advance himself."

Vijay tried to think of an appropriate response, but gave up. As the vehicle reached the bottom of the hill, he was briefly puzzled at how cool it was becoming inside. Then he suddenly realized: *air conditioning*. It was the first time he had ever been in an air conditioned car.

Clouds were moving in, and a heavy rain had begun to fall by the time the Mercedes arrived at the Bhim Bhawan Palace. When the car had halted, Batra's driver hurried to open the door. But Batra continued to sit. He looked at Vijay. "You like this motorcar?"

Puzzled, Vijay said, "It's very fine." That seemed inadequate, so he added, "Quite luxurious."

"It could be yours," said Batra in a quiet voice.

Vijay sat frozen.

"Just find something I can use against this Maharaja," Batra said. "Anything. I don't care how you do it. I will see you are rewarded. If you help me long enough, you will be promoted until you get to use one like this. Or one day you will be rich enough to buy it yourself."

Without waiting for a response, Batra stepped out. Wondering if Shanta had heard, Vijay glanced toward her. She was already away from the car and may have paid no attention.

Vijay slowly followed. Could Batra be serious? A Mercedes cost an absolute fortune. Vijay could save all his life and never begin to earn enough to buy one. He hesitated at the top of the stairs, turned and glanced down at the long, gleaming motor car. The idea of owning one was absurd, of course. Some day, after he'd paid for the school in his village and it was operating successfully, he might be able to afford an

Indian-made Ambassador. But what would he do with an imported Mercedes? Air conditioned, no less! He probably couldn't even afford the taxes and operating costs on it. Only if he became a top government official—unlikely, given his lack of interest in politics—would he ever have the use of such a car.

He continued into the palace, his stomach in a knot at being told it didn't matter how he went about getting the incriminating evidence. Did Batra really think that if a real basis for a case couldn't be found, Vijay might manufacture and plant something false?

Apparently, yes. And there was the threat of removing him as team leader and replacing him with Ghosali, who had clearly been reporting to Batra, possibly right from the start of the search.

How did he deal with someone like this?

The gloomy weather made the interior of the palace feel even more like an old Mughal tomb. Batra showed little interest in the public rooms, insisting on going directly to the Maharaja's private apartments, where he tried out the furniture, sitting in the most elaborate chairs. He opened the jewelry boxes and examined the pieces. Vijay watched him closely, but Batra didn't try to take anything. He opened closets, examined the clothes. He opened the dresser, and fumbled through the underwear. He glanced at Vijay. "I suppose everything here has been inventoried?"

"Yes, sir."

Batra shook his head. "Ah, well. He has so much, he would never miss some of it. Assuming he gets out, of course." Abruptly, he gazed at Vijay. His voice changed to a higher pitch. "The, uh, princess. Her apartments are here, too, I assume?"

Vijay nodded. "In the next wing over."

"I will see them now."

Vijay took a deep breath. "Of course." Batra was headed out the door. Vijay's eyes met Shanta Das.' She raised an eyebrow, and shrugged almost imperceptibly. Vijay smiled stiffly, and shrugged also.

Kaushalya Kumari's suite was decorated with well coordinated, brightly colored Rajasthani block print fabrics, many of them with a typical pattern of tiny round inlaid mirrors. The cushioned platform swing and the canopied bed dominated their respective areas. The many books and paintings lining the walls somehow went well with the other furnishings.

Batra stood near the doorway, his eyes taking in every detail. Then he walked to the center of the bedroom and slowly turned around, as if soaking in the atmosphere. He went to the mirrored vanity table and picked up a photo of a young man in a military uniform. Vijay knew it was Kaushalya's older brother who was now dead, but he did not tell Batra. Batra replaced the photo. He picked up another one of Mahendra Singh, then put it back. He glanced at one of the Maharaja, then he looked for a time at a photo of an attractive woman. Kaushalya's deceased mother.

Batra stared for a moment at a photo of a robe-clad, partly bald, middle aged man. A garland of dried flowers draped the photograph, and a small incense burner stood before it. Obviously, the man was a swami or guru whom the princess followed.

Batra picked up a perfume bottle and sniffed at it, but did not remove the stopper. He examined a hair brush, sniffed at it also, and pulled at a dark hair on it. He replaced the brush on the desk.

He opened a jewelry box and removed a pearl necklace. He ran his fingers along part of its length, then replaced it in the box. He walked over to a dresser, opened the top drawer.

Increasingly anxious to stop the unnecessary intrusion on Kaushalya Kumari's privacy, Vijay asked Shanta for Batra's benefit, "This room was searched thoroughly, wasn't it?"

Shanta nodded. "Yes, sir. Quite thoroughly by Mrs. Desai and myself. We found nothing whatsoever that raised any questions."

While she was replying, her gaze turned away from Batra, Vijay saw the man snatch a pair of pale pink panties from the dresser and quickly thrust them deep into a pocket. When Shanta turned back to him, Batra was closing the drawer. He opened another, glanced in, then closed it again.

Batra stood eyeing Shanta Das for a moment. "Mr. Singh," he said, "you undoubtedly have other work to attend to. Miss Das can stay here to show me in detail where she has searched, and what she has found." He turned to smile at Vijay. "I'm sure she'll be a most useful guide."

Vijay clenched his teeth. How could he keep Shanta away from this lecher? "I'm quite happy to stay with you also," he said, while he tried to think of a better approach.

The Maharaja's ADC appeared at the door. Again Vijay felt the familiar panic at the possibility of being recognized by Naresh Singh. But the ADC merely announced, "Mr. Singh, there's a call for you from the fortress. I've transferred it to this extension." He turned and left.

Vijay thankfully picked up the phone by the bed and said, "Singh here."

"Vijay," came Ranjit's voice, "why are you never around when anything happens? Your hunch was a good one. Only it's not the type of hoard we expected."

"You found something?"

"Did we ever. A whole arsenal, in an underground vault. Enough weapons to fight Pakistan and China combined."

Weapons? What in the world was going on?

Vijay looked over at Dev Batra, who was smiling as he eyed Shanta Das. Vijay would very much have preferred to keep the matter quiet until he had analyzed its implications. But he couldn't leave Batra alone with Shanta. He took a deep breath and said, "Good work, Ranjit. We'll be there straightaway."

24

A narrow stone stairway descended steeply from a concealed floor hatch in an anteroom of the old royal bedchambers. The steps were squeezed inside the walls of the basement and subbasement. Surmal, the Bhil guard captain, stood near the opening, clearly unhappy at his powerlessness to interfere with the searchers.

"We shouldn't have overlooked that trap door before," Ranjit said. "But it looks just like any other paving stone when its closed. I only discovered it when I poured water over the floor."

At least, thought Vijay, it was Ranjit rather than Ghosali who made the find. The Brahmin would have been insufferable if it had been his doing.

At the bottom of the stairway stood a heavy steel door opening into a large underground chamber chiseled from the solid rock of the hillside. Stack after stack of wooden cases filled the room from floor to ceiling, except for some narrow aisles. The faint scent of gun oil mingled with the musty, somewhat foul odor of a seldom visited basement room.

"There's another chamber about the same size opening off from this one," said Ranjit, "but it's empty. We checked all the walls, even the ceiling; no more doorways."

The searchers had already pried open a random selection of cases. Vijay, Shanta, and Dev Batra examined them by the light of the lanterns. "Most of these boxes hold rifles," said Ranjit. "But there are cases of grenades and machine guns, too. And bazookas."

"Pakistan!" exclaimed Batra. "He is in league with our enemy! I heard the Maharaja wanted to join them, rather than India in the first place." He beamed at Vijay, his face glowing in the lantern light. "We have got our man now! He will never get out of prison."

Vijay was reluctantly coming to that conclusion himself. But he examined the black stenciled lettering on the boxes. "These seem to be British manufacture," he said. "And judging from the dust on all the boxes, they've been here a long time."

"Vijay," said Ranjit, "I know a little about weapons, from hunting with my uncles and being around the army and police. These must be thirty years old or so. There's a lot of firepower here, but none of them are the latest stuff. Not even close. See, these Mark I carbines were standard issue in World War II. And those Sten submachine guns are the same vintage. So are the Bren automatic rifles."

"Interesting," mused Vijay. He abruptly turned to Batra and said, "Whoever stored these here has probably half-forgotten about them by now. If he intended any use for them, it would have been years ago."

"So what?" said Batra jubilantly. "Nobody has to know that. Hell, nobody would even believe it. You do not keep enough weapons to equip an army unless you plan to use them. Anyway, it is illegal to be keeping unregistered weapons, regardless of what you are intending with them."

Vijay felt numb; he was forced to agree with the latter statement, but he said nothing.

Dev Batra started up the stairway, one of the Brens in hand. "I am telephoning Delhi."

Vijay took a last look around the cavern. Seeing nothing to investigate further, he reluctantly turned and followed Batra up the stairs. One-by-one, the other members of the team left also.

Shanta Das was the last to depart. Electric torch in hand, she was examining the walls of the other chamber minutely. She saw only rough-hewn rock. She turned her attention to the floor. Like the walls, it was roughly carved stone. Dust had gathered in the depressions.

With the toe of her sandal, she stirred some of the dirt in the corner of the vault most distant from the doorway. Small fragments or chips of stone were mixed in with the dust. One of them, near the surface, had a thin, rounded edge. She bent and pulled it loose.

It was a disk, heavy for its weight. She rubbed off the dust, and found gleaming, embossed metal beneath.

A gold coin.

She stood, thinking, when Ranjit Singh's voice drifted down the stairway, "Shanta! Are you coming? We need to put our seal on the door."

She hid the coin in her hand as she hurried out. She waited until Dev Batra was on the telephone to Delhi, and then she called Vijay aside.

From inventorying many strong rooms, Vijay had at least a general acquaintance with the forms in which wealth was kept. "It's a gold *mohur*, from the time of the Mughal Emperor Aurangzeb," he said as he examined the find. He looked at Shanta. "Great work! I'm glad someone kept enough wits about them to think beyond the fact we discovered an arsenal."

"A gold coin would have been a small fortune for anyone but the rich," said Shanta. "Either someone was in the vault with it and lost it from a purse, or it must have spilled out of a cache so large that no one missed it."

Vijay thought a few moments. "Those chambers were treasure vaults at one time," he said at last. "I'm sure of it, with that iron door, and the only access from the Maharaja's apartments. But when was the treasure removed? At the time the weapons were stored there? Or earlier?"

"Or later?" asked Shanta. "That coin was barely beneath the surface. Someone might have dropped it accidentally, and unknowingly buried it by stepping on it. Even that smaller room alone could have held a huge fortune, after the other room was filled with weapons."

The thought that the wealth could have been removed relatively recently had not occurred to Vijay. After a time, he nodded. "An intriguing idea. But why would it have been removed? And where would it have been taken? It's hard to imagine a place more secure than that underground vault."

Shanta had no answer.

New Delhi, 9 July 1975

When the news came of the discovery of the arms cache, Mahendra and Kaushalya fell into despair. "How could he have been so foolish?" Mahendra muttered, "He should have gotten rid of them long ago. This is just what Madam and her son need to help justify the Emergency. More proof of a 'conspiracy' against them!"

"Father couldn't have expected that."

"Of course he didn't. But you know who controls the press now. And the courts, it seems."

Kaushalya said, "I think we should see Ashok Chand again."

"What good would that do?"

"Maybe none. But he knows Father. And he took a risk when he helped us get the audience with Madam. We probably owe it to him to tell him about the development before he hears it from someone else. It will be in the press and radio soon, if it hasn't been already."

Ashok Chand answered the door. To Kaushalya, his face appeared tense and strained. "Please come in," he said. "You know my wife, of course."

Kaushalya gave a nod as Jaya Chand, an attractive, charming woman in her mid-fifties, entered the room. She was possibly the most highly regarded lady lawyer in Delhi.

After the exchange of greetings as they removed their shoes, they seated themselves in the living room. Mahendra told them about the discovery of the arms cache.

Ashok Chand scratched his head. "I was once quite familiar with the documents involved in Mangarh's accession to India, you know. It seems to me there was something in it about weapons."

"That's right," said Jaya Chand. "I remember it because I wondered at the time if there was any purpose to it. The Maharaja reserved the right to freely import arms."

Kaushalya was ecstatic. "Then they're perfectly legal!"

"Probably," said Jaya. "It depends on when they were acquired. But I wouldn't be very optimistic. The government will try to find some loophole, like saying the weapons should have been declared later, even if they were legal at the time."

"What will we do?" asked Kaushalya.

"Put your lawyers on it right away," said Jaya Chand. "But don't expect too much."

Mahendra sat in thought for a time. Then he asked Jaya Chand, "Is there a possibility of your taking on this aspect of my father's case yourself? Your prior knowledge may be useful. Of course—" he glanced at Ashok Chand "—I realize it could be awkward, with your connections to Congress."

"I'm flattered you asked," said Jaya Chand. "And I'd normally be most happy to help, Congress or no. But," she glanced quickly at her husband, "I think we may have other obligations that could interfere. Not exactly conflicts of interest, but certain other activities. However, I'd be most glad to advise your other lawyers if they think it useful."

"I understand, certainly," said Mahendra. "I'll pass your offer on to them."

Mangarh, 9 July 1975

After the excitement of discovering the armaments, continuing the search seemed anticlimactic. Vijay could see that the other team members were reluctant to resume what might well be a fruitless effort, even when he and Shanta displayed the gold coin. But Vijay firmly insisted the job wasn't done, and by midmorning the next day, the officers were again systematically searching the Madho Mahal. Nothing was found in the half hearted attempt.

That evening, as they sat around the dining tables in the *dak* bungalow, Ranjit asked Ghosali, "Just how did Dev Batra come to have so much power?"

Ghosali removed his pipe from his mouth. He was looking at Vijay as he said, "If you know a man's origins, you know what he is."

Vijay tried to appear unperturbed at yet another statement about "origins." Did Ghosali in fact suspect the deception?

Ghosali resumed, in his lecturing tone, "Dev Batra's background is not without interest. He is self-made. His family was from the Punjab. They lost their lands there at Partition, when the area became part of Pakistan. At the same time, his father was killed and his sister violated, so to speak, by Muslims. Dev saw it all happen. He was perhaps four or five years old at the time. The survivors fled to Delhi, taking little Dev with them. They had lost all their wealth." Ghosali paused and looked about, obviously for dramatic effect.

The others waited expectantly. Even Shanta and Mrs. Desai were listening from their table.

Ghosali continued, "When I met him many years later, he and I had both became followers of Swami Surya. Swamiji uses his powers to ensure the success of his disciples. Devji became involved with the Congress Party and a friend of Sanjay Gandhi. His rise was then extremely rapid." Ghosali smiled dryly. "The lesson is there, for those who wish to get ahead."

For quite some time no one looked at anyone else.

"I won't ask how Sanjay got his own power, when he's never even held political office," muttered Ranjit at last, eyes on his mixture of rum and Campa Cola.

"By having the right mother. And grandfather," said Krishnaswamy, swirling the liquid in his Limca bottle.

There was an awkward silence. Ghosali rose, emptied his pipe by tapping it on an ashtray. "I must attend to some matters," he said, and left.

"Maybe we should all become followers of Swami Surya," said Ranjit, with a grin. "No doubt he can use his powers to find the treasure for us."

Most of the others, Vijay included, smiled, but it would have been inappropriate to joke too much about such a prominent religious figure, and the conversation soon turned to a comparison of the dust and heat of Mangarh with that of Delhi.

The following morning, just after Vijay arrived at the old fort, he received a telephone call from Deputy Director Prasad. Through the noisy trunk line connection, Vijay heard, "News for you, Vijay. You're all being recalled to Delhi. The raid's over."

"The raid's off?" Vijay asked loudly, wondering if he'd heard correctly, with all the interference on the line.

"That's affirmative. It's from the Finance Minister himself. Confidentially, I understand he wasn't been too pleased with the raid from the start. But he went along with it because of pressure from the PM's office. Now that the weapons have been found, he feels enough is enough."

"But what about the treasure?"

"What treasure? You aren't onto something now, are you?"

Vijay hesitated, thinking about the gold *mohur*.

"Hello? Hello?" shouted Prasad through the noise.

"I'm still here!" Vijay said loudly.

"I repeat, have you found anything more?"

Vijay hesitated another moment, before responding, "Not really. Nothing conclusive."

"Then I'll see you in the office when you get back. As soon as you brief me, you can take a few days off. I'm sure you can use them."

"I'll look forward to them," Vijay replied, still trying to comprehend that the search was truly finished.

When Prasad had broken off, Vijay still stood for a time with the receiver in his hand. Then he absently replaced it in the cradle. He was relieved to be leaving Mangarh, to be greatly lessening the risk of having his past exposed.

But he thought about all those jewels in the portrait of Maharaja Bhim Singh. Where had they gone? And had the gold coin Shanta found been only one of a vast number?

He'd had a strong hunch that there was, in fact, considerable wealth somewhere near. He'd felt almost certain that, given time, he would find it. Now he would never know. He wondered briefly what it all meant for his chances for promotion. As an income tax raid, the whole thing had been a fiasco. As an instrument of political revenge, well, apparently it had been a success.

He thought about Kaushalya Kumari. Almost certainly he would never see her again, and he regretted that.

Ranjit, when told about the raid ending, said, "I can't say I'm sorry. I don't think His Highness and the Princess deserve all this trouble."

"Nor do I. I confess I feel a bit dirtied by my own role in the whole matter. I find myself wishing I could somehow tell them I'm sorry."

"I know what you mean. Still, I'd love to have found that treasure! Will you visit your family now that you don't have the pressure on you to perform?"

"Yes, I'm overdue for it." He looked away. "Of course, I'd like to have you to come with me, but I'm, uh, afraid it's a rather bad time. Normally my family would be delighted to welcome you, but some problems have come up that I need to attend to, and it could be awkward." He added lamely, "I hope you understand."

Ranjit was clearly surprised, but he said, "I hope it's nothing terribly serious."

"No, just awkward. I'll tell you about it some day, but right now I need to find out more myself. I'm sorry I can't take you with me, when you're so close at hand."

Ranjit shrugged. "Well, I understand. I hope it all works out all right."

"I'm sure it will."

26

Gamri Village, near Mangarh, 10 July 1975

"Stop here," Vijay told Akbar Khan when the jeep reached the mango grove half a kilometer from Gamri. "Park in the shade and wait for me."

"Yes, sir."

"I may be a few hours. Do you have something to drink while you're waiting?"

Akbar Khan wagged his head "yes."

"You'll no doubt be questioned by children or farmers wondering why you're here. Just tell them it's government business."

"Yes, sir. No problem." Khan grinned. "I'll put them to work helping me clean the dust off the jeep."

Vijay smiled. "That job is never done."

"I don't mind, sir. It's my duty."

Vijay nodded, then stepped to the ground and strode away without looking back. He wore a pale blue sport shirt and brown slacks, and *chappals* on his otherwise bare feet, which quickly acquired a coating of dust from the rutted lane. He wanted to look well-off, but hopefully not so prosperous as to attract undue attention from the higher castes of the village, who could ask embarrassing questions—and investigate further if they weren't satisfied with his answers. This was also his reason for not driving up to the village in the jeep.

His own people, on the other hand, would be enough in awe of him and his obvious success in the big city that they would accept whatever he chose to tell them.

Vijay's people, the five families of Bhangis, the scavenger-sweepers, lived segregated at the very edge of the village, next to the Chamars, the leather workers. Though the latter were also classed as ex-Untouchables, they considered themselves superior to the Bhangis. Working with leather was not so polluting as carrying nightsoil from chamber pots and disposing of animal carcasses.

It had been half a year since he'd visited his own home. The village reminded him too much of past humiliations. There was also the possibility, although its likelihood had grown less, that he might even have to suffer some new humiliation by a member of a higher caste.

He'd known he must visit his mother and other family before returning to Delhi. But this time there was the increased risk of exposure—not only by inquisitive villagers who might be envious enough to want to find out more about him, but also by Ghosali or other tax team members who might see him going there and wonder the reason for his visit.

He felt great anxiety at not visiting his mother or uncle or cousins more often. He sent a letter and a generous sum of money to his mother every month, but he knew that wasn't all she needed from her only son. He had purposely never given anyone in his village his Delhi address, preferring to pick up any mail from them through general delivery. The writers who would transcribe and address the letters for his illiterate relatives also did work for the upper castes and might spread gossip about him.

Although he felt a frequent nagging guilt, he had never aided any of the persons here who asked for help in seeking more lucrative employment in the big city. A visit to him in New Delhi by someone from the village would carry far too great a risk of embarrassment and exposure.

Hopefully, he was making up for it at least somewhat with the well. And with the school, and possibly even a small medical dispensary, he would build here when he'd accumulated enough savings.

The outskirts of the village looked much the same as before:

mud-walled huts with thatched or crudely tiled roofs, the buildings almost the same dun color as the sandy soil from which they appeared to grow. Except for a couple of clusters, barely a tree in sight to break the monotony of the flat landscape.

But by the fields he noted a new tube-well, with an electric line running to a pumphouse. In one of her letters his mother had excitedly told of electricity coming to Gamri. His own people were too poor to acquire much other than a single light bulb per house, but to them even that was great progress.

He walked past the well his own funds had built, the traditional kind, with a bucket hanging from a rope strung over a wheel between two stone uprights, and a masonry basin area for animals to drink from. He had tried to keep his role in paying for the project secret, but word had gotten out, and he was embarrassed that those who benefitted from the well looked up to him as such a major philanthropist. He stopped a moment and eyed the bucket and pulley. Should he try to come up with the money for a diesel or electric pump? There seemed no need, really, unless one were going to sink another deep tube-well to use the water for major irrigation of the fields. That could come eventually, but not yet.

He stopped and stood a moment, eyeing the piece of ground that he hoped to buy for the school site. Although it was owned by a Rajput, the area was not considered part of any particular caste's territory. It was slightly elevated, which meant it wasn't ideal for farming since no water would collect on it, but for that same reason it was a good site for building. It lacked trees, but those could be planted, and if well tended, they could be large enough to provide some shade in several years.

He should begin negotiating for the land soon, he decided. He had enough money saved to buy it, and enough for a basic one room building that could be added onto later. The main problem was the teacher's salary. Recently he'd been toying with the idea of trying to recruit young college graduates as volunteers to come to the village to teach for a month or two at a time. That would mean a series of teachers throughout the year; not an ideal arrangement, but certainly better than no teachers at all.

He continued on. Two naked children, a boy and a girl of perhaps three or four years old, were playing in a rubbish heap at the side of one hut. They looked up at him with curious eyes. The girl stuck her thumb in her mouth and sucked on it as she examined the newcomer. Vijay recognized them as being from a family of Chamars, leather worker caste children.

He walked swiftly down the narrow, dusty lane toward the house where he had grown up. Several older children came running to greet him: "Vijay *sahib*! Vijay *sahib*!"

"Have you come from Delhi?" asked Hanwant, the eldest.

"Did you come by the jeep up by the grove?" asked Bhanwar, probably the brightest of the group.

Vijay ignored the questions. "You should all be in school," he said. "If you had a school here in the village, so you didn't have to go so far, would you attend it?"

"If it doesn't cost very much," said Hanwant, indifferently.

"Of course!" said Bhanwar. "But we might as well wish for motor cars—neither's likely to happen." Then he saw Vijay's seriousness. "Is it?"

Vijay said, "Motor cars, no. School, well, maybe." He continued on, refusing to say more.

His family home was a small rectangular hut with a roof that sagged in the middle, and an equally small attached walled courtyard. Despite the money he sent regularly, not much had been used to improve the house itself. It had only one glassless window and one door. He stood, looking over the low wall. His mother, her skin leathery from over fifty years of work in the harsh sun, sat bent over the flat cylindrical grinding stone which she was turning with one hand while she fed grain (*bajra*, he assumed) into the hole in the center. A young woman, his cousin's wife Roop, sat nearby, sorting through a shallow pan of the grain, looking for rocks or other contaminants.

Roop saw Vijay, and spoke to the older woman. His mother looked up. Vijay smiled and stepped through the gateway.

"Son! It's really you!" said his mother in wonder. She stood up with a vigor that surprised Vijay, and ran to embrace him.

"Tell me about the city," said his mother, watching him as he tore off pieces of the thin, round, flat bread made of *bajra* grain and stuffed them into his mouth. "No, wait—wait until your uncle and his boys come. Then you can tell us all at once." Vijay's cousin's wife had gone to summon the menfolk to come and greet the returning hero.

Vijay stopped eating. Not meeting his mother's eyes, he said,

"I can't stay long, Ma. My boss expects me back at work tomorrow morning."

"You can't stay? You came so far just for a few hours?"

Vijay flushed. He couldn't very well tell her that he'd been in Mangarh two weeks, that he'd even passed near the village twice. He had to be careful not to hurt her feelings further. And his mother, though illiterate, was no fool. "I had some urgent business here for my work," he said. "I had to come in haste. And unfortunately, I have to get back quickly, too."

"To Delhi?" asked his mother.

Vijay hesitated. He didn't want them to know he lived in Delhi almost all of the time; one of them might go there, and with a little effort might be able to locate him. "You know I travel much of the time," he said. "I have some work in Mangarh tomorrow. Then I have to leave right away. I'll soon be in Bombay for a few weeks, I think."

His uncle Surja appeared, a short, stringy man, his back bent and his skin dark and wrinkled from a lifetime of hard outdoor labor, his face marked from a contest with smallpox long ago. With him were Vijay's two cousins Yogesh and Govinda. All wore *dhotis* and turbans grimy from work. Yogesh, in his early twenties, had little interest in schooling, but Vijay had paid the education costs for the younger Govinda through secondary school.

"Nephew!" said Surja. "Welcome home. It's been so long!" Vijay rose and they embraced vigorously. Surja smelled of sweat from working in the sun.

After cousins Yogesh and Govinda likewise hugged him, the men squatted on their haunches. "I still can't get used to seeing him without a turban," Uncle Surja said to Vijay's mother.

"Nobody wears turbans in the city," said Vijay. "Except Sikhs, of course."

"My son was telling me about his work," said his mother.

"Your job must be very big, very important in the government," said his uncle.

Vijay shrugged. "Not so big. Not so important." What would they think, he wondered, if they knew he'd been harassing the Maharaja himself? That he'd even spent considerable time in the company of the beautiful *rajkumari*? He'd love to be able to see the look on their faces. But it would be too risky to say anything about it.

"Tell me more about your work," said Uncle. "You write? You work with papers?" Uncle was illiterate, and his son Yogesh had learned to read only minimally. It was Govinda who was the student in that family.

"Yes, of course I do, uncle. It's office work."

"And you also travel?"

"Some. When I have to." He looked at his mother, who was listening eagerly. "But it's very demanding. It keeps me much busier than I'd like—too busy to get away for visits, unfortunately. Much as I want to."

He doubted they fully believed him. But maybe the explanation would lessen the hurt at least a little, give his mother something to grab onto, since she would want to believe it hadn't been his own choice.

Govinda said, "We heard the police arrested the Maharaja! Have you heard about it?"

Naturally word of the arrest would get around, so Vijay was prepared. "Yes. I heard about it."

"What is the world coming to these days?" asked Uncle Surja. "That never would have happened when I was young. And some tax collectors from Delhi are searching the palaces, too!"

Govinda said, "My mother's nephew Arvind is a gardener at the new palace. He said he was sure one of the tax men was you. But I told him it couldn't be, since none of us had seen you here. Was it you he saw then, after all?"

Vijay had hoped the question wouldn't come up, but he again was prepared if it did. "It might have been me. I had to do some urgent work with the tax men before I could get leave to come visit here. I wanted to come here sooner, but my boss wouldn't let me go until my work was done."

His mother asked, "So you helped the government look for the treasure in the palace?"

"That was part of my work for a short time. But nothing was found."

"So you do work for the tax collectors?" asked Uncle Surja.

"In a way. That's one thing I do."

"Are you a tax collector yourself, then?"

Although Vijay was reluctant to tell too much about his job, he was also averse to direct lying. "I don't collect taxes, exactly. I try to find men who have cheated and not paid the taxes they owe. Then someone else tries to collect the money."

"Then you have lots of work to do! *Everyone* tries to keep from paying taxes." His uncle laughed, and the cousins joined in.

Vijay smiled along with them. "It's true, I'll never run out of work."

"A tax collector!" His mother, smiling, shook her head. "My son is a tax collector!"

"Who would ever have believed it?" asked Uncle Surja.

"Did you get my letters?" asked Govinda, as Vijay had known he would. "I wrote twice to you. I sent them to Delhi."

Vijay tried hard to meet the eyes of his handsome cousin. "The Delhi post offices are terrible about losing mail. And I'm only there sometimes. I got one of your letters and intended to reply, but then I got too busy. I'm sorry."

"Can you help me get a job with the government?" asked Govinda. "That was what I was writing you about."

"Of course, I'll be glad to try. But it may take a long while.

Jobs are hard to find there, too."

"How about in your office? You know I can read and write well."

"Yes," put in Vijay's uncle. "At night he reads to us from the *Ramayan* and the *Mahabharat*, just as you used to."

"I remember those days so well," said Vijay's mother. "Sometimes when we couldn't afford oil for the lamp, the neighbors would bring their paraffin lantern, so you could keep up the reading. They all liked it just as much as we did."

Vijay saw her eyes glisten with moisture at the recollection. He looked quickly away. Much as he resented his difficult childhood, he, too, had fond memories of the nightly readings. The sessions had often interfered with his studies, but he had enjoyed being the focus of attention by villagers of all ages and bringing so much pleasure to the others. He looked at Govinda, the inheritor of that particular tradition. "I'll put in a good word for you," Vijay told him. "But it's up to my boss. I don't have any say in the hiring."

"Maybe I can come stay with you while we look. After the crops are in, of course."

Vijay took a deep breath. "Certainly. I'll be glad to have you." The situation was getting increasingly awkward with Govinda; Vijay realized that maybe he should let Govinda in on his secret of passing as higher caste. Govinda was the one relation who, if he were cleaned up and dressed appropriately, might well be able to pass as Rajput himself.

"What is it like where you live?" asked Yogesh. "Do you have your own house? I understand many people in Delhi live in rooms in big buildings."

Vijay glanced at his cousin. The homely man was the father of two children. "I live in a small flat," Vijay said. "A couple of rooms in a large building." At least that was the truth.

"With an indoor latrine?" his mother asked. "One that you don't have to empty?"

He tried not to show his annoyance. In her earlier years, his mother had carried out the nightsoil from the chamber pots of high caste ladies who lived in *purdah* in some of the Mangarh mansions. The job was the lowest possible one any outcaste could have taken on, and the fact embarrassed Vijay. He also felt considerable humiliation on his mother's behalf. "Yes, Ma. I have a flush toilet."

"One with a high seat? Like those I've heard about in Maharajaji's palaces?"

"No, Ma. It's the hole-in-the-floor kind. Like most people have in the city."

His mother was quiet for a time. Then she said, "Those toilets put many of us out of work. But maybe that's not such a bad thing now. Maybe it's better that we have to find different kinds of work. Your father would have wanted that."

"Yes. I know he would."

"He was a brave man," said his mother. "Maybe foolhardy, but brave." She was silent a moment, her eyes growing vacant. "I wish you could have known him," she murmured.

"My elder brother was a very brave man," agreed Uncle. "He fought hard for the rights of us all."

Vijay remained silent. This was more of his past he preferred to avoid. In fact, his father's fate had convinced Vijay his own best course was to escape from his past, to create a new history for himself.

His father, influenced by the teachings of Mahatma Gandhi, had worked with Ashok Chand and other reformers to fight for the advancement of the Untouchables. But Chand, a member of one of the higher castes, was now a very important man, a former minister in the central government.

Vijay's father, on the other hand, had been killed for his efforts. The lesson had not been lost on the son. The way to succeed wasn't to fight as an Untouchable for your rights. The way to succeed was to work like hell. And to pretend you were higher caste.

Only—why did he have to live in constant fear of exposure? And why did he have to feel so guilty about his deception?

His mother at last asked the one question that was inevitable, unavoidable: "When are you going to let us find you a wife? You should have been married years ago!"

"Yes," said his uncle. "Everyone asks us why you haven't gotten married yet. It's very embarrassing."

Vijay gave the same answer he'd given before every time he'd been asked. "I'll consider it when I get enough money saved and stop traveling so much in my work. And I must have a wife who's been to university, so we can talk about things together."

"That may not be possible," his mother said. "I keep my ears open, but I never hear about any suitable girls with an education from university."

"Nor I," said Uncle Surja.

Vijay's mother said, "Ram Das' brother's wife is looking for a husband for her younger sister. The girl is said to have all the homely skills. Can I tell her you'll at least think about it?"

Vijay shook his head no. "That wouldn't be fair, Ma. I can't think about it yet. Anyway, if she hasn't had the proper education, I couldn't consider her."

"You make it very difficult for us," his mother said.

"Impossible, is more like it," said his uncle.

Everyone was silent for a time.

"Tonight," his uncle asked at last, "can you read to us from the *Ramayan* like you always did before?"

Vijay thought about the waiting jeep. "I can't," he said, surprised at the reluctance he felt at refusing. He, too, had liked those readings. But as team leader, he needed to return to the *dak* bungalow.

Even if the search was officially suspended, he should be available to the tax officers in case any difficulties arose while they were still in the field. "I need to get back." He pretended not to see the disappointment in their faces.

27

New Delhi, 28 July 1975

When Lakshman Singh had been confined in Tihar for a month, the family's attorney called Mahendra to say that a visit would now be allowed. Mahendra and Kaushalya immediately left for Delhi, where they applied for, and received, the necessary permission to go to the jail.

The Tihar complex lay along a main highway at the western edge of New Delhi. Kaushalya had an odd feeling as she and Mahendra approached. Never before in her life had she entered a prison. Rows of living quarters, perhaps unrelated to the jail, lined the busy road, screening the high fence from casual view. But over the roofs of the housing units she could see glassed-in guard towers, and beyond them on tall pylons were large arrays of lights.

The only building actually fronting upon the highway straddled the entrance gate, and with its squat central tower it resembled, she thought, the main terminal buildings at some of the smaller Indian airports. Two or three floors high, rather stark and utilitarian in design, but better maintained than she had expected. The national flag flew above it, a fact which Kaushalya found annoying, a desecration of what should be a symbol of all that was best in the nation.

The guards at the steel gate made a slow check of Mahendra's identification, then Kaushalya's. At last a guard beckoned them through a smaller door. It was narrow, and so low that Kaushalya and Mahendra had to stoop to keep from hitting their heads.

At an office inside, they tried to be patient as they answered questions posed by an official who slowly filled out several sets of forms. Next they were taken down a hallway crowded with other visitors to the office of the jail superintendent. The superintendent himself sat behind a table that served as his desk. A slim man of medium height with a neatly trimmed mustache, he stood to greet them. "Please be seated, Highnesses. Please be seated." He waved at two chairs. After so many brush-offs by other officials, Kaushalya was surprised at how accommodating the man seemed.

"I want you to know," the superintendent said, "I'm doing all I can to see that your father is comfortable." He smiled as if in self-deprecation as he continued, "Unfortunately, my hands are tied by regulations. That is the reason for only one half-hour visit per month, by no more than two persons who must be close relatives. And why the inmates are allowed to send out only two postcards per week, censored by the deputy commissioner's office."

"My father can receive all the letters we send?" asked Mahendra.

"Oh, of course. Of course. We distribute letters twice a week. But you should know that the incoming mail goes first to the deputy commissioner for censoring. Sometimes it's delayed in his office." The superintendent smiled ingratiatingly. "Again, I have no control over that aspect." He looked out the door. "I see your father is here. Regulations also require that your visit be in the presence of someone in authority. In this case, I will serve as that person. You may hold your visit here in my office."

"Thank you, sir," said Mahendra, glancing at Kaushalya. Apparently, she thought, he, too, had his doubts about whether or not the superintendent was really doing them a favor.

Now they waited on the bench for their father to be brought in. A guard approached escorting a tall, bent elderly man.

"Daddyji!" gasped Kaushalya as she ran to touch his feet. An strange odor hung about him, like disinfectant. He smiled his old smile at her, but it had a hollow, forced feeling about it. Then Mahendra, too, was bending to touch his father's feet.

"How are they treating you, Daddyji?" asked Kaushalya, filled with anxiety at his appearance.

He lowered himself to the bench. "Not so bad, Kaushi. It could be worse."

"Do you get enough to eat, Father?" asked Mahendra.

"Oh, yes. It's not exactly up to our own cook's standards. A little heavy on *rotis* and watered-down *dal*." He forced a grin. "And on flies. But I can get it down."

"Flies?" asked Kaushalya.

"Yes, we eat on the ground in the courtyard."

"You don't have a table?"

"Regrettably, no."

"But its rained several days—what do you do then, Daddyji?"

Lakshman Singh glanced at the superintendent, then shrugged. "The ground gets soggy—there don't seem to be any drains. So we bring our *durries* to sit on." Suddenly he coughed several times.

She couldn't imagine her father under those conditions, especially in ill health. She turned to the superintendent. "Can't you do something about the dining conditions?"

The man frowned. "My funds for such things are very limited. But certainly I'll look into the matter, Princess."

She turned back to her father and said, trying to sound cheerful, "I brought some of your favorite sweets, Daddyji." She withdrew the white cardboard box from a shopping bag and started to hand it to him.

"I beg your pardon, Princess," interrupted the superintendent.

"I'm afraid I can't allow any gifts of sweets unless a magistrate has given permission."

"What?"

"Regulations, Princess. The permission must specify exactly what kinds of sweets, and how many of each kind. We check those things carefully."

I don't believe it, Kaushalya thought. How petty! But she struggled to keep her face calm. This man could make it difficult for her father if he became offended.

Lakshman Singh, seemed unconcerned by the matter. He managed to chuckle. "Those inmates with sufficient funds seem to be able to get all kinds of things from the outside, vast quantities of sweets included."

The superintendent was looking down at papers on his desk, pretending not to hear this unsubtle allusion to bribery among his staff.

Kaushalya quickly asked her father, "Do you have your own room?"

He smiled at this. "I'm afraid I have to share my quarters. But my roommates are good companions. Most are in jail only for their politics, like me."

"Is your room comfortable, Daddyji?"

"Like most of the barracks, it's pretty basic. I have a string cot to put my *durries* on when I sleep."

"It must get hot," said Mahendra. "I'm sure there's no air conditioning!"

"There's a fan," said Lakshman Singh. "But only one. It doesn't do much to keep away either the heat or the mosquitoes."

"Daddyji! It sounds terrible!" said Kaushalya. The superintendent was again watching and listening, and she turned to him. "Can't anything be done about these things?"

He straightened and said in a tone of apparent concern, "This is the first I've heard of these problems. But I'll look into them right away. We'll spray for the mosquitoes at once."

Lakshman Singh said to him, "We've complained before that there are also not enough latrines. The odor gets quite fearful by the end of the day. Could something be done about this, too?"

The superintendent looked annoyed at such an embarrassing request by a prisoner, but he replied, "Of course. I'll inquire about the matter."

Kaushalya felt furious. It was the superintendent's job to know what was going on in his facility! Why did he have to wait until someone brought it to his attention? But she realized it could be counterproductive to antagonize him, so she kept her anger in check. As if sensing her thoughts the superintendent said defensively, "I personally tour the entire jail every Monday, you realize, so I can know what is going on. But conditions can arise quickly."

"Father," Mahendra said, "we're trying to get you out as fast as possible. Our lawyers have filed a *habeas corpus* petition in the Delhi High Court. But it's not easy. Many of the judges seem afraid to act. Things have changed." He lowered his voice, glancing at the superintendent, who seemed to be absorbed now in the papers on his desk. "Father, that weapons cache didn't make things any easier. Whatever did you keep it all for?"

Lakshman Singh looked worried for the first time. In a quiet voice he said, "I stored those at the time of Independence. I was sure it was only a matter of a few years at most before the Indian union would fall apart, before the people would demand their old rulers back. I thought some arms might be useful then, in case there were troubles and I needed an army again to restore the throne."

Mahendra sighed. "You must have changed your mind by now."

Lakshman Singh shrugged. "As time went on my doubts grew. But what could I do? How do you dispose of that many weapons without revealing you've had them? It was easier just to hope they'd never be found." He looked at Kaushalya and smiled weakly. "I hoped Kaushi would divert the tax people enough so they wouldn't look there."

Frustrated, Kaushalya said resignedly, "Maybe if I'd known about the weapons, I could have done just that, Father."

"They were legal, you know," said Lakshman Singh. "They were permitted under the Instrument of Accession when I aligned Mangarh with India."

"Yes, Ashok Chand and his wife told us that," said Kaushalya.

Lakshman Singh gave a shrug. "If those charges are dropped, I have a feeling they'll find something else. There's still the so-called foreign currency violation. Even though I haven't been abroad in twenty years."

They sat in silence.

After a time, Kaushalya asked, "Do you need anything, Father? More bedding?"

"They gave me some *durries* when I came. They're adequate, at least until the weather turns cold."

"You'll be long gone from here by then, Daddyji," said Kaushalya.

Lakshman Singh sat motionless. "Maybe. Maybe so."

Mahendra said, "Father, I brought some bank drafts for you to sign. To help us carry on with the household expenses."

"Excuse me, sir, and madam," said the superintendent. "I'm extremely sorry, but that's not permitted unless you have a magistrate's authorization."

"What?" asked Mahendra.

The superintendent spread his hands in a gesture of helplessness. "The Government has frozen many accounts. I have no way of knowing if yours are included. I'm sorry, sir."

Lakshman Singh again coughed several times, but acted as if it were of no consequence.

"I regret to say," said the superintendent with a glance at his watch, "your time is up."

Kaushalya opened her mouth to say that they'd barely had any time at all. But she realized there was no point in objecting. "Daddyji, we'll keep trying everything we can to get you out of here."

"I know," said Lakshman Singh with a fond look.

Tears came to her eyes, and she and her brother embraced him until the superintendent insisted they really must leave.

28

New Delhi, 12 December 1975

The Emergency continued, month after month.

Vijay was stunned when the Prime Minister removed the Income Tax Department from the Finance Ministry, and put it under a new Ministry of Revenue and Banking. A new Chairman loyal to the Prime Minister was appointed for the Central Board of Direct Taxes, the agency charged with overall supervision of the Income Tax Department. The number of tax raids that appeared to be politically motivated soon increased.

On a sunny day in mid-December, Deputy Director Prasad called Vijay to his office and waved him to a chair. Sober-faced, he said, "I wanted to let you know you're returning to Mangarh, Vijay."

Vijay tensed. "Mangarh again? What for, sir?"

"To resume looking for concealed assets. For the 'treasure.' Apparently our new Board Chairman wants to pursue it further. Finding the hoard of weapons wasn't quite the same as finding concealed wealth."

Vijay struggled to conceal his anxiety. Mangarh again.

Prasad said, "We're sending a much larger team now." He looked out the window, and Vijay had the impression the DD was uncomfortable as he continued, "I thought you did a fine job last time, Vijay. I wanted you to be team leader again. But before you find out from anyone else, I want you to know that you won't be in complete charge this time. Batra's overseeing the operation himself, representing Kishore Lodha, the new Revenue Minister. But he won't be there all the time, and he wanted Ghosali to be in command in his absence."

Damn! thought Vijay.

Prasad went on, "Batra said he doubted you had your heart in the search because you're a Rajput from Mangarh yourself. He thought you might not be enthused about working against your clan's former ruler. Confidentially, I did my level best to get you put in command again, but I got overruled. After I kept pointing out that, after all, the team was under your charge when the weapons were discovered, Batra finally did agree to give you equal authority with Ghosali."

Vijay couldn't recall a similar situation before in the department. He wet his lips. "A bit awkward, I think, sir."

"I agree completely. I don't like shared authority. It muddies up the chain of command. Who does an officer go to if he needs a decision? How does anyone know who gets the commendation when things go right? And the blame when things go wrong? Anyway, we seem to be stuck with it this time. Batra says any disagreements between you and Ghosali are to be referred to him immediately. Or to me if he's not available."

Tight lipped, Vijay reluctantly gave a nod.

Prasad continued, "It was Batra and the Revenue Minister who are insisting on resuming the search. Your discovery of the arms cache whetted their appetites. They're determined to tear the fort apart. The government's claiming the entire fortress area under the Ancient Monuments and Archaeological Sites Act."

"What? Wasn't it listed as the Maharaja's own property under the agreement merging Mangarh state with Rajasthan?"

"It was. But somehow the government's ignoring that. I've heard Kishore Lodha has some sort of grudge against Lakshman Singh." He paused, and added significantly, "And I'm sure Batra will have his own ideas of how to speed up the search."

Vijay swore to himself. "I'm sure he will."

He would be glad to see Kaushalya Kumari again. But the visit would not be pleasant for her.

Mangarh, 15 December 1975

On the first day of the new search, more than a hundred laborers swarmed about the fortress, while over twenty tax officers supervised them. The two newly recruited *panch* witnesses appeared fascinated by the operation. A half dozen Bhil guards were scattered about, watching with stern expressions, but not interfering.

As in Delhi, the weather was much better in Mangarh in December than it had been in July. The day was pleasantly warm, but not overly hot even in the open sun. Vijay wore his new sunglasses; he felt slightly more at ease hiding behind them, though far from completely secure.

Dev Batra stepped from his Mercedes onto the stones of the courtyard. He looked about with a satisfied air. Then he said to Vijay and Ranjit Singh, "This is more like it! I think we'll finally see some results."

Kaushalya Kumari appeared, accompanied by Captain Surmal. She stormed over to Batra. "What is going on here?"

Batra replied, turning sober, "Unfortunately, Kaushalyaji, the PM's office has grown impatient. I regret that I'm unable to convince them to back off on the search. Since neither you nor your father have told us the location of your treasure, the government had no choice but a higher level of effort. However, should you become more helpful, all this work will become unnecessary, and I have the authority to send these men home."

"Why so many men? They may damage the buildings!"

"I would regret that, Kaushalyaji. No one would be happier than I if we could stop work. But after all, it *is* the government's property now."

Kaushalya stared at him. "Whatever do you mean?"

Batra took on a look of surprise. "Then you've not heard? Your family no longer owns the fortress. It belongs to the government now."

Her mouth dropped open. "That's not funny."

"I'm quite serious. The government is claiming ownership of the fortress as of three days ago."

"What utter nonsense! You know it's been my family's for centuries!"

"That's no longer relevant, I'm told. Everything is changed now, Kaushalyaji."

"That's ridiculous! You have no right!"

Batra looked sad. "I do understand how you must feel. You may remember that I lost all my own ancestral property at Partition."

"This is totally different! The government's acting illegally and it can stop at any time!"

"Possibly."

"This is absurd! You've really gone too far now. I must insist you stop your men until you've gotten good legal advice!"

"I understand your being upset, Kaushalya. But let's talk it over in a more friendly way. Where is the famous Rajput hospitality? You might offer me some refreshment. It has been a long drive from Delhi."

"You have no right to claim the fort! None whatsoever!"

"Really, Kaushalyaji, please calm down. We'll talk it over. If we can come to terms, I may very well be able to get the men to stop."

"Stop them now, or I'll have the guards throw them all out!"

For the first time, Batra appeared taken aback. He glanced at Captain Surmal, who wore a tense expression, then over to where a couple of other Bhils stood with their rifles. He quickly recovered his composure. "That would not be advisable, Kaushalya. You must calm down. You're doing no good for your cause."

She lowered her voice, but her tone was steel. "Get your men out of here."

"Kaushalya, I can't just order them out. How could I explain sending all these men away with no results? Let's talk matters over. I'm sure we can come to agreement. You could tell me where you think the treasure might be, to narrow the search. Or—you could decide to be much more friendly with me. Maybe visit me tonight?"

She glared at him. "You stop the search right now, or I'll tell Captain Surmal to have the guards escort your people out of the fort."

Batra stared at her. "I almost think you're serious. But you must know it would be foolish for you to start a little war. People could get hurt. I do not think your guards with their antique rifles will be much of a match for the police or the army."

Kaushalya's face was flushed, her eyes blasting. Then, her shoulders sagged a bit, and she quickly looked away.

"Anyway," said Batra, "you might treat me more kindly for your father's sake. I'm still well positioned to help him. All I need is to show the PM's office that you're cooperating. Fully, of course." After some moments of silence, during which Vijay felt embarrassed and awkward, Batra said in a tone obviously meant to be soothing, "Let's talk about this later, Kaushalyaji. At the moment I need to discuss a few details with Mr. Vijay Singh."

Kaushalya abruptly turned and stalked off a few steps, where she conferred with Surmal.

Batra looked over at the elephant Airavata. "There is my old friend." He laughed, apparently trying to lighten the atmosphere. "I wonder if he remembers me and my little joke?"

"The phone call you wanted to make, sir?" reminded Sen.

"Oh, yes," said Batra. "I'll use the one in the guard house." He strode toward the small office.

Abruptly a powerful stream of water blasted him in the back.

Batra shrieked, and screamed, "WHAT THE HELL?!" He whirled about, just as the torrent moved up to drench him square in the face, the excess cascading onto his shoulders and chest. "GodDAMMIT!" he spluttered. "GodDAMMIT!!"

The stream of water continued a moment, then stopped. Airavata lowered his dripping trunk and eyed Batra with a smug air.

"Well," said Ranjit to Vijay, "I guess that answered his question about whether the elephant remembered him."

For the first time that day, Kaushalya laughed. Then she turned her back on the furious Batra and walked away.

A couple of hours later, a white Ambassador delivered Guru Dharmananda to the fortress courtyard. He stood a moment, taking in the scene. Then, white robes flowing, he strode toward Kaushalya, with his assistant Peter Willis and his driver hurrying to keep up.

"Kaushalyaji!" said her guru. "I heard the tax men were here again and I came to see if I can help."

Kaushalya bent and touched his feet, straightened. "It's good of you to come, Guruji. I could use a miracle if you have one to spare."

He smiled warmly at her. "I left my bag of miracles behind at the ashram. But maybe I can help at least a little anyway. Isn't that Dev Batra over there?"

Kaushalya glanced at Batra's small group, the members of

whom were eyeing the guru, as if uncertain what to do about his arrival. "Yes. He's talking to Mr. Ghosali. The other man is Vijay Singh. Both are tax officers. Can you believe it—they say the fort belongs to the government now!"

"How absurd." Guru Dharmananda stared at her a moment, then at Batra's group.

"Batra's also threatened to make things worse for Daddyji if I don't tell him where we've hidden our treasure. And," she looked meaningfully at the guru, "uh, spend time with him."

The guru frowned. "Does that mean what I think it does?"

"Unfortunately, yes."

He shook his head. "All this will pass, Kaushalya. Don't do anything you'll regret."

She looked away, nodded.

He abruptly strode toward Batra and the others. Kaushalya slowly followed.

"Mr. Batra!" said the guru as he arrived within hearing range. "How good to see you!" He glanced at the other two. "And Mr. Ghosali and Mr. Singh, I believe."

Batra, whatever reservations he might have, hurried to bow and touch the guru's feet. Vijay and Ghosali did likewise. The guru calmly accepted the gestures of respect and said, "A tax man's work is never done, I see. You have enlarged your operation considerably, I think."

Batra looked past the guru, an odd smile on his face, as if uncertain how to answer at first. Then he replied, "Very true, Guruji. The government is persistent when it feels success is just around the corner."

"You are close to finding what you seek, then?"

"Quite close, I believe," said Batra. "It can be only a matter of a very short time, with such a concerted effort."

"But are you sure there is something here to find? Even with such a massive effort, you can not find something if it isn't here."

Batra cleared his throat, his eyes shifting uneasily. "We are operating under the assumption that there is indeed hidden treasure here, Guruji. So if our assumption is correct, we will find it."

"Undoubtedly. If your assumption is correct. If not, though— aren't you expending a great deal of money, time, and manpower? Plus causing a great deal of distress for Kaushalya Kumari and her family?"

Batra looked away. "Maybe so, Guruji. But we have to act on our information and hunches." His face lit as he looked back to Dharmananda. "Speaking of which, Guruji—you are famous for your own intuition. Maybe you could help us."

"Help you find the treasure?"

"Exactly!" Batra made a broad gesture intended to include the fortress as a whole. "We have a large area to cover. It could save us considerable time if you would use your powers to tell us where best to look."

"I see. Unfortunately, I fear my powers are greatly overrated. Still..." The guru narrowed his eyes slightly, and he slowly turned in a half circle. Then he fully opened his eyes and faced Batra. "As you know, in my own small way I like to help people with their difficulties. I have no intuition as to the location of any treasure in the fort. I do feel, though, that even if you succeed in your search here, it will not be so great a success as you expect."

"How do you mean?"

The guru gestured at the now deserted buildings. "At one time this place was full of people, full of horses and elephants, full of activity. Look at it now. Virtually empty. Likewise, at one time there was immense treasure here. But surely you, yourself, must sense that most of the wealth, too, has fled from this place?"

Batra's eyes darted about the fortress, with its peeling paint, its air of abandonment.

The guru resumed, "You now have the difficulty of finding the treasure. And the princess and her family have the difficulty of your searching their property."

"This fort belongs to the government now," Ghosali put in.

"Indeed! After so many centuries. How interesting. I assume that the government has adequately compensated the former owners?"

Batra was silent.

"Well, even so," said the guru, "I'm sure you can understand that your presence here is causing Kaushalyaji and her family considerable distress." There was more silence. The guru asked, "Do you have a time limit on your operation?"

"Not as such, Guruji," replied Batra. "We will continue until we either succeed or feel there is nowhere left to search."

"Mmmm. I would think prudence would dictate that after a point you cut your losses and give up if you haven't found anything."

Batra did not reply.

"Can we agree on a reasonable time limit, for the sake of both parties?"

Batra glanced about, clearly uneasy. Yet, the proposal seemed harmless, maybe even prudent. "I suppose, Guruji, but—"

"Good! What is a reasonable time limit? Another day or two?"

Batra gaped at him. Ghosali appeared shocked. Batra said, "That is not realistic, Guruji. It is a very big fortress. A month or two would be more reasonable."

Kaushalya scowled at him.

"A month or two!" exclaimed the guru. "You'd keep all these people here that long, in this abandoned place? Is it truly worth so much risk? All the expense?"

Batra frowned. "Possibly we could agree to something less."

"Much better!" The guru turned to Kaushalya. "Can you stand a week, as opposed to one or two months?"

"Even an hour is too much! A minute is too much!"

The guru turned to Batra. "One week?"

"No." Batra shook his head. "That's obviously unreasonable."

The guru glanced at Kaushalya, then back to Batra. "Ten days, then. Surely with so many men you can search all the most likely places in ten days."

Batra hesitated, clearly unhappy. But respect for a great holy man outweighed his reservations. "The search is tying up considerable resources that could be used elsewhere. I think perhaps I can agree to ten days."

The guru looked at Kaushalya. "It seems maybe a ten day limit is better than no limit at all."

Kaushalya pressed her lips tightly together. At last she said quietly, "I suppose."

"Good! No one is completely happy, but everyone benefits at least a little."

His gaze lingered briefly on the faces of each of those present. "So much unhappiness," he said. "And all so unnecessary. It's a pity."

He abruptly turned and swept toward the car. Kaushalya eyed Batra uneasily, then turned her back and followed. "I'm sorry, Kaushalya," the guru said over his shoulder. "I think I did the best I could."

"I'm grateful," said Kaushalya. "I suppose I can stand even this for ten more days."

The guru looked compassionately at her before getting into the car. He said, "Unfortunately it may get worse. I understand how Dev Batra thinks. He is a follower of Swami Surya, you know?"

"Yes."

"I think you're aware of my opinion of the Swami. Not the most spiritually enlightened of our holy men. Anyway, I wish you well. Be sure to call on me if you think I might be able to help in any way."

Kaushalya gave a nod.

"I'll pray for you and your father, as always."

She stood for a time, then gave another quick nod. The guru entered the car. She watched as it slowly left.

Mangarh, 17 December, 1975

As Vijay was about to climb into the jeep after visiting the Bhim Bhawan Palace, Naresh Singh came down the steps. "May I have a word with you, Mr. Singh?"

Vijay tensed, still fearful of recognition. Then he tried to compose himself. "Of course." He moved away from the jeep, out of hearing of Akbar Khan.

Naresh Singh glanced about, saw that no one was near; the

princess had disappeared back inside the palace. The Rajput Thakur's son grinned, gazing at Vijay. "I remembered where I've seen you before. A number of times, years ago. You're from Gamri village."

29

Vijay stopped breathing, and his head felt light.

Found out. After all this time, all the energy put into his deception. His worst fear realized.

Should he deny ever being in Gamri? Naresh Singh seemed so certain.

Vijay wiped his sweaty palms on the sides of his slacks. He desperately searched for a way out. He could think of none.

Naresh Singh was standing near, waiting.

Vijay's voice was weak, and it sounded as if it belonged to someone else. "Yes." He swallowed. "I was in Gamri a long time ago."

"I thought so," Naresh Singh said, peering at him. "Why did you say you didn't remember me?"

Vijay strained to pull his thoughts, and his voice, under control. "I, I was afraid you'd tell everyone."

Naresh raised his eyebrows. "Tell them what?"

He again swallowed. "That—I'm a Bhangi."

Naresh shrugged. "So what? You've obviously done well for yourself. It's quite impressive how far you've come in your career." He waved at the palace. "No doubt you earn a higher salary than I do here."

Vijay's throat muscles were tight as he managed to say in a quiet voice, "No one else knows my background."

Naresh Singh stared at him. "No one knows?"

Vijay replied hoarsely, "They know I'm from near Mangarh. They don't know what village. Or that I'm Bhangi."

Naresh smiled, appearing embarrassed. "Well, no problem. I won't tell."

Vijay could hardly believe his secret was still safe. He examined Naresh Singh, wondering if the man was sincere.

Naresh sobered. "I thought I overheard the princess say something about you being Rajput, though?"

Vijay tensed again. Did he dare admit masquerading as high-caste? As a Rajput himself, the ADC might take offense, with some justification.

"It's all right," Naresh said with a shrug. "Don't tell me more if you don't want to. I promise you I really won't say anything. Why should I? No point in making things difficult for you personally, even if you are here raiding my employer."

Vijay worried for a moment about the possibility of blackmail. Could Naresh, for example, threaten to expose Vijay if the search were not prosecuted with less vigor? But Vijay could do little to change the course of the tax raid anyway. He decided there was probably nothing more to lose. He took a breath. "I've pretended to be Rajput," he confessed. "I thought it was the best way to get away from my background. I didn't want everyone to continue looking down on me for being Untouchable."

Naresh Singh, one of the particular Rajputs whom Vijay had modeled himself after, gazed at him wide eyed, mouth open. His expression changed to gleeful admiration. "No! You mean you carried that off all this time, with no one suspecting?"

Vijay nodded. "No one until now." Unless, of course, Ghosali was truly suspicious.

Naresh laughed heartily. "That's bloody marvelous! I'd never have believed it could be done. Not for such a long time! Congratulations!"

Vijay grinned tightly. "It hasn't always been easy."

"I'm sure it hasn't!" Naresh shook his head, as if still disbelieving. Then, "I say, you aren't the one who paid for that well for the Bhangis and others, are you?"

Vijay thought briefly of denying it. There seemed little point in doing so now, not to Naresh Singh, anyway. "Yes, I sent the funds for the well. I'd like it not to become general knowledge, though, so I'd appreciate your not telling anyone about that, either."

Naresh was watching him, an incredulous expression on his face. "If you don't want me to, I won't. I suppose if everyone knew, someone might start wondering about you, and it might come out that you're not Rajput. Still, that well was a generous gift, and I hope someday you get the recognition you deserve."

Embarrassed, Vijay said, "I'd rather my involvement were never known. There's no point in people knowing."

Naresh shook his head. "As you wish. Well, good luck. I assure you, I won't tell anyone."

Vijay was still trembling as he climbed into the jeep.

He was reasonably sure Naresh Singh would keep the secret. The ADC gave every impression of being innately trustworthy. It was a fortunate escape.

He returned to his room for a few hours to give himself a chance to recover from the trauma. Then, when he felt back in control, he thought again about the old fortress.

He pictured in his mind the huge bulk of the Madho Mahal, which had yielded a secret vault full of weapons. They'd stopped searching there soon after the weapons were found. But Vijay had concentrated the search there in the first place because that portion of the old palace had been built by Maharaja Madho Singh, and Madho Singh had also been reputed to have accumulated great wealth.

And Shanta had found the gold *mohur*. Had they given up too soon on the Madho Mahal? He couldn't help but wonder if the spirit of Madho Singh was watching them from somewhere, laughing at them, as they followed one false trail after another.

There was one possible source of information he'd been thinking about, though, that hadn't yet been tried.

Vijay stepped from the jeep into the narrow, shop-lined street and glanced quickly about, fearful that someone who had previously known him might recognize him in spite of the dark glasses.

He thought again about how lucky he'd been with Naresh Singh. The sinking feeling in his gut was still a vivid memory.

But there were plenty of other chances to be identified by someone from the past. The streets in the city were especially risky. Vijay saw no familiar faces at the moment, so with relief he turned his attention to the shop. He had never before been to this particular spot in Mangarh. He had envisioned the store of one of the leading gem dealers in Rajasthan to be larger, like some of the shops in New Delhi that catered to the wealthy and the foreign diplomats and tourists. But there was little to differentiate B. Mahajan and Sons from the other small jewelry shops on the narrow lane.

A voice at his ear startled him: "Are you here on personal business, Singhji, or is it connected with the search?"

He whirled his head and saw Anil Ghosali calmly drawing on his pipe.

He took a deep breath, straining to calm his nerves. "Connected with the search, of course, Ghosaliji."

Ghosali eyed the jewelry store. "You would of course inform myself and Batraji if you found any gems?"

Vijay made no effort to hide his indignation. "Naturally. How could you think otherwise?"

"May I ask what brings you to a gem dealer?"

Vijay toyed with telling Ghosali it was none of his business. But it wasn't a completely unreasonable question; after all, Ghosali was co-leader, with a stake in the outcome of the search. "I thought a gem dealer might possibly know what happened to some major items of jewelry that no longer seem to be in the palace."

Ghosali puffed on his pipe. "I see. Do you mind if I go in with you?"

Vijay did indeed mind, but there was nothing to be gained by saying so. "Not at all, Ghosaliji. I welcome your company." He wondered if Ghosali had followed him here. Otherwise, it seemed an unlikely coincidence for Ghosali to appear at this particular spot in town, at this very moment.

They removed their shoes at the threshold and stepped onto the white cloth covering the floor. Realizing that wearing his sunglasses indoors might arouse curiosity and hence closer scrutiny—precisely what he didn't want—Vijay took them off and held them in his hand.

On the right, three clerks sat behind glass-topped counters. Ceiling fans churned the air but seemed to make little effect in dispelling the oven-like atmosphere. "Is Sri Mahajan available?" Vijay asked. Never, when he had been living in a village outside of Mangarh, had he dreamed he would come into this shop and ask to speak to perhaps the richest merchant in the city.

"I am empowered to deal on his behalf, sir," said a clerk, after a brief appraisal of Vijay. "How may I help you? You wish to look at some gemstones?"

It was Arjun Oswal, the face from the past whom Vijay had seen before on the street. His tormentor at school.

Vijay's throat tightened as he fought to suppress utter panic. How could such a meeting have happened *here*, especially with Ghosali present? And so soon after the shock of the incident with Naresh Singh!

Rather than try to say anything more when his voice might betray his panic, with a trembling hand he quickly held up his identification for Oswal to see.

Ghosali pulled out his own ID and thrust it at the clerk.

"Oh, yes, sirs," said Oswal, squinting to read the print. "Income Tax Department."

The identification folder now held Oswal's attention, and Vijay abruptly realized another danger. The first name "Vijay" was clearly typed on the card, almost an invitation to connect the face with the boy from the past. He jerked the folder away and closed it, half expecting the clerk either to protest not having enough time to read it, or to recognize him.

However, Oswal swiftly rose to his feet, barely glancing at Vijay and Ghosali. "A moment please!" said Oswal as he hurried through a door.

Vijay glanced about the shop, torn between fighting the urge to flee and trying to think of a way to prevent Oswal from again seeing his face. Did he dare to put on the dark glasses? It might appear ridiculous in the dimly lit indoors, especially to Ghosali. But if Oswal should wonder why Vijay now had the Singh surname, and if he should start asking questions, with Ghosali right here....

The other two clerks were staring at them; naturally they didn't have income tax officers visit every day. Vijay forced himself to breathe deeply, to try to stay calm.

A rotund man dressed in a white *dhoti* and white shirt and black vest appeared, follow by Oswal. The heavy man pressed his palms together. "I am Bharat Mahajan. Please come this way, sirs."

Pretending to have forgotten Oswal, Vijay followed Mahajan into an office almost as large as the shop. A huge strongroom door hung half open. Along one wall stood a row of three big safes. Mahajan said, "Please be seated, sirs." He ordered tea from a peon who had appeared instantly. "How may I help you?"

Oswal remained in the outer shop. Vijay and Ghosali showed Mahajan their identifications. Vijay struggled to thrust aside his worries over whether he'd been recognized yet. His voice seemed calm, but it sounded somewhat distant to himself, as he said, "Sir, you may be aware that the Income Tax Department is investigating the ex-ruling family of Mangarh. As a routine part of that investigation, we are talking to everyone who may have any familiarity whatsoever with the family's finances."

He suddenly realized he wasn't sure he remembered what he'd just said. He fervently hoped he wasn't repeating himself as he went on, "It was suggested to me that perhaps you, as the principal gem dealer of Mangarh, might have had some transactions with Lakshman Singh—either selling items to him, or even purchasing from him." He realized he was still holding his sunglasses; he set them on a corner of the desk.

Mahajan sat for some moments staring at Vijay. Then, he said, "Mr. Singh, in the absence of a subpoena, I'm not sure how appropriate it is to discuss these matters with you. However, I will say it's true that our firm has had occasional dealings with the rulers over the years—both with the current Maharaja and his father, and with other members of the family. Any dealings in recent years have been quite minor however—repairing settings, that type of thing. There have been no large transactions in many years."

Vijay had concentrated hard to remain focused on what the man was saying. He asked, "Approximately how long, sir, since you had the last dealing?"

Mahajan shifted in his chair. "I seem to remember His Highness purchasing a diamond ring from me, oh, maybe ten years ago. It was not of extremely unusual value as diamond rings go—perhaps five carats or so. I think it was a gift for his daughter. Before that, well, I'd have to check my records. However, the family has not been what I'd call a 'major' customer of our firm since prior to Independence."

Ghosali asked, "Are you aware of them dealing with any other companies?"

Mahajan appeared pained. "They would deal with us if they dealt with anyone. And I'd hear of it if they did go to someone else. Unless, *perhaps*, it was in Bombay or Calcutta. But my impression is that they don't have any more dealings in gems or jewelry than other families of substantial means. Maybe less so."

Vijay said, "But sir—the family must have considerable gem holdings of their own. The state jewelry, as well as their own personal items. Most ruling families had huge amounts."

Mahajan straightened himself in the chair and ran his fingers through his hair. He said, "Mr. Singh, it's no secret that a lot of rulers sent much of their wealth out of India around the time of Independence. Maybe that's what Lakshman Singh did. If it's any help to you, I did approach His Highness on a couple of occasions in the 1950s, offering to buy any items he wanted to dispose of. He assured me he had nothing he wished to sell, but that I'd be the one he'd contact if he ever did wish to dispose of anything."

Vijay mulled this over, managing with effort to keep his mind on the topic and not on the potential danger in the next room. He said, "But in the old days. Before Independence. The ruling family must have had considerable dealings in jewelry."

Mahajan shrugged. "So I was told by my father. Not in my own time, however."

Ghosali said, "Could you kindly tell us what your father told you about these dealings."

Mahajan again sat silent for a time. At last, he said, "I'm not sure I recall all the details, Mr. Ghosali. Or that it would be appropriate in the absence of a court order to relate them if I did remember."

Vijay sat staring at him. Eventually, he said, "Such an order could be obtained, Sri Mahajan. Also subpoenas of your records. It would be quite inconvenient for us, however. And inconvenient for you and your firm."

Mahajan digested this. Vijay knew it would be a rare gem dealer who would not mind scrutiny of his books by the Income Tax Department. There was too much danger of the tax officers finding discrepancies, whether intentional or accidental on the part of the person audited. "Mr. Singh," he said at last, "I'll try to answer your questions, at least up to a point. But can you be more specific?"

Vijay said, "Sir, at least four items of jewelry I know of seem to be missing: a large emerald turban decoration, a necklace of five-strands of large pearls, and a large ruby ring. These items were in a portrait of His Highness' father. And in a miniature painting, I saw one of His Highness' ancestors examining what appeared to be a huge diamond."

"Ah," said Mahajan, smiling for the first time, apparently in amusement. "The 'Star of Mangarh.'"

"Whatever is that?" asked Ghosali.

"The Star of Mangarh," Mahajan repeated. "One of the largest diamonds ever discovered." Mahajan's eyes brightened in excitement. "It was like the Great Mughal diamond that later disappeared, or the Koh-i-noor that's now in the crown jewels in London. It was legendary. One of the Mangarh rulers—Maharaja Madho Singh—captured it as loot on an expedition in the Deccan. But he almost never displayed it to outsiders. People in the business such as my own family would talk about it. But none of us has ever actually seen it." He said more calmly, again with the amused smile, "Assuming it existed, it's probably lost now, or stolen in the 1800s in some Maratha raid, or smuggled abroad, or cut up into smaller gems. If it had resurfaced, I'd have heard about it."

Ghosali said, "You're certain no dealer's seen it since Mughal times?"

Mahajan shook his head. "Not to my knowledge. And it's my business to know those things." Again excitement came to his voice. "If I could obtain custody of a stone such as that—even only as an agent for the seller! It would be the culmination of a lifetime in the field. But," he smiled in dismissal of the idea, "whatever happened to that diamond, no one in Mangarh's likely to see it again."

Vijay asked, "What about the other jewelry I mentioned?

Mahajan again shifted in his seat. "The necklace was quite well known," he said after a time. "It was generally referred to as the 'Mangarh Pearls.' Everyone knew which pearls were referred to. Matched pearls of that size are extremely valuable. The ruby was called 'the Blood of Shivaji.' Supposedly Madho Singh captured it from Shivaji in the famous raid at Surat. And the emerald was merely known as the 'Mangarh Emerald.' Everyone knew which emerald was meant. There aren't many others of comparable size in the world."

I knew it! Vijay thought. Stones like that couldn't go unnoticed. What had Lakshman Singh been trying to prove by pretending he knew nothing of their whereabouts?

"As to where they are now," Mahajan was saying, "I regret I can't say. Maybe they're still in His Highness' vaults. Or maybe they were sold abroad. They've never been part of any sales transaction in India, that I can assure you!"

On the way out Vijay pretended not to notice Arjun Oswal, who was eyeing him, as were the other two clerks. He half expected Oswal to call, "Excuse me—aren't you my old schoolmate Vijay, from Gamri village?"

But Oswal said nothing, even during the several seconds while Vijay and Ghosali were fumbling to put their shoes back on. Outside the shop, Vijay breathed deeply in relief at the apparent escape.

He groped in his sportcoat pocket for his sunglasses. They weren't there. But he did not want to linger so close to Oswal, especially with Ghosali present. He strode toward the jeep. Ghosali followed. "Would you care to ride back to the fort with me?" asked Vijay, knowing Ghosali would do so anyway.

"Of course."

Then Vijay remembered exactly where his sunglasses were: he'd left them on Mahajan's desk. He shot a quick look toward the shop. Did he dare go back for them? He still did not know if he had been recognized. His appearance had changed some; he was almost twenty years older and several pounds heavier. He wore a Western style sportcoat and tie, rather than *dhoti* and shirt. And he was an income tax official, rather than an Untouchable school boy.

There was no way to know if Oswal had realized his identity. Vijay doubted it, but he dreaded giving him another chance. Particularly with Ghosali nearby.

He looked into the jeep, where Akbar Khan waited patiently. Trying to be casual, he climbed into his seat. "Oh!" he said. "My sunglasses." To Khan he requested, "Would you go to the shop and ask if I left them there?"

Akbar Khan glanced at Vijay. His bosses frequently asked him to do personal errands, so he didn't find the request unusual. "Of course, sir." He got out of the jeep and hurried toward the shop.

Vijay waited, anxiety eating at his gut.

"Ah, yes," said Ghosali. "Your sunglasses. I don't recall your ever wearing them before."

"I didn't. My eyes seem to have recently become more sensitive to light."

Ghosali said, sounding reluctant, "A clever idea to question the gem dealer. Unfortunate it did not pay off."

"Yes."

Akbar Khan returned with the sunglasses, handed them to Vijay. Vijay put them on.

He felt taut as a sitar string. The sooner the search was completed so he could leave Mangarh again, the better.

30

Vijay forced himself to return to the new palace to see how Krishnaswamy was coming in examining the account books. Naresh Singh had left for the day, so Vijay did not have to face the embarrassment of seeing the man who had so recently learned his secret.

Krishnaswamy was going back as far as the late 1950s in the hope of stumbling upon something useful. He felt somewhat hindered by the clerk still being on extended leave of absence, but he was able to get a general picture anyway.

"Anything interesting?" asked Vijay.

"I was surprised," said Krishnaswamy. "If I read these books right, this family must be near to a cash crisis."

"How so?"

"As you know, most of their wealth is non-liquid assets. Their income is from rents of farm lands, and from selling crops on the part of the land they farm themselves. The family expenses are high compared to the income, though. All those employees, plus pensioners. And the continual upkeep on the palaces. Those buildings are like gigantic holes that swallow all the money poured into them."

"Then how has the family been managing?"

"By using up their bank deposits and selling off paper-type investments. But the bank deposits are almost gone, and according to the books, there are virtually no stocks or bonds left to sell."

"Hmm. I suppose that really doesn't tell us anything about *hidden* assets, though, does it?"

Krishnaswamy frowned. "I suppose not, sir."

Vijay rubbed his jaw as he thought. "They could be relying on hidden wealth to carry them through in the future. Or, they could just be hoping for a miracle."

Krishnaswamy shrugged. "I don't see any way to know."

"Nor do I. Anything else of interest?"

"Not much. I've been reviewing charitable gifts. The overall trend is downward, which makes sense, given the income crunch. Of course, some of the donations are through the family's trusts. But I've been concentrating on gifts from the personal funds at the moment." He shoved one of the books over. "Maybe you'd be interested in seeing for yourself, sir. This one lists charitable donations for 1956 through 1960."

Vijay sat down, indifferently opened the book and flipped through several pages. The donations were as expected: substantial amounts to schools, temples, hospitals, an orphanage. Most of them in Mangarh.

Then his eye fell on a donation to an individual. He stifled a gasp of dismay:

Vijay, son of Ram, Gamri Village. Rs 25. Tuition as per H.H.'s authorization of 28/8/55.

"See something interesting, sir?" asked Krishnaswamy.

Vijay shot him a quick look. "Uh, no. Just surprised at an amount."

"Yes, sir, some are quite generous. I wish *I* had this much to give away."

Vijay was not listening. He at last knew the identity of the anonymous donor who had paid the costs of his schooling. The "H.H." in the ledger referred to His Highness, Maharaja Lakshman Singh.

Vijay had been working to incriminate the very man who had made his education feasible, the man whose grants had made it possible for Vijay to conceal his caste origins.

Why would Lakshman Singh have done it? The most likely explanation was that the Maharaja had felt some guilt, or at least some responsibility, for his police killing Vijay's father.

Did Lakshman Singh know, now, who Vijay really was? His voice hoarse, he asked Krishnaswamy, "Do you have the more recent lists of donations?"

"Yes, sir." Krishnaswamy selected more ledger books and handed them to Vijay.

Vijay leafed through them. He caught his breath. A 1961 entry said, next to one of the payment amounts, "Recipient enrolled Delhi University under name Vijay Singh."

Vijay wiped the perspiration from his forehead. He continued turning pages: 1962, 1963, 1964...

The final entry concerning himself was dated 1966. The ledger was accurate when it stated that the grants to him had stopped then, the year Vijay finished his university training and took his exams for government service. The final notation read:

> *"Authorization terminated at direction of H.H.—*
> *Recipient obtained position with central*
> *Income Tax Department, New Delhi."*

Vijay sat in a daze.

Lakshman Singh knew.

He slammed the ledger book closed. "I—" his voice was hoarse, so he tried again: "I'm not feeling so well. I think I'll head back to my room and go to bed early."

31

In the morning, Kaushalya drove up to the fort to check on what new mischief the tax raiders might be involved with.

The workmen were filing into buses, and the two *panch* witnesses were climbing into a taxi. She approached Vijay, who was just sending a couple of his tax officers off. "What's going on?"

He looked at her with an odd expression. "I'm sure you'll be pleased to know the search is over. Again."

"It's over?"

"Yes. The Deputy Director called from Delhi. Even though we've found nothing further, the Revenue Minister has ordered the search ended." His eyes searched hers. "I wish there was some way I could adequately apologize for the trouble we've caused you."

After a time, Kaushalya asked caustically, "So why did you stop searching this time? The deadline Guruji got Batra to agree to?"

"Probably. I don't know for sure, so I'd better not speculate."

She hesitated, and asked, in not quite so hostile a tone, "Then you'll be leaving for New Delhi?"

Vijay nodded. "As soon as I've wrapped up the loose ends here. Probably tomorrow morning." His eyes gazed into hers. He said carefully, "You've been very cooperative, under difficult circumstances. I'd like you to know I've appreciated it. And for what it's worth, would you please convey my sincere apologies to your father?"

She stood, looking at him, then lowered her eyes. There was an awkward moment, and she nodded. She turned and left.

Early in the morning Vijay directed Akbar Khan to stop the jeep some distance from Gamri village. "I'll walk from here," he said.

"Is this your home, sir?" asked Akbar Khan. "Where your family lives?"

Vijay glanced sharply at the driver. It was a natural assumption for Akbar Khan to make. Vijay had assumed that if anyone from the tax team asked questions about the visit, he would brush them off by saying he was going to the village as a favor to a friend. But Akbar Khan was not a talkative man; he would likely say little even if anyone should ask him. And somehow, Vijay felt more comfortable sharing the information with a servant than with a fellow tax officer who might become too inquisitive. "Yes," he said. "I have relatives here."

Akbar Khan smiled as if pleased. "I thought so, sir, since you visited here before."

"I'd appreciate it if you didn't say anything to the others."

"I'll say nothing, sir." He cast a hesitant look at Vijay, and added, "Ghosali *sahib* asked me a couple of times where I've driven you."

Vijay went numb. He struggled to act casual as he asked, "What have you told him?"

Akbar Khan grinned. "I told him everywhere I drove was on official business, but I couldn't tell him the places without authorization from you. I asked him if he wanted me to ask you for authority. He told me to forget he'd said anything."

Vijay gave a fleeting smile. "Good." Then, "I may be a couple of hours."

Akbar Khan nodded; the largest part of his job was waiting, not driving. And the waiting gave him ample time to polish the jeep.

Vijay turned and slowly walked toward the village. How much did Ghosali know? Was he merely fishing for information that he might use to discredit Vijay? Or did he truly suspect Vijay of being something other than he claimed? There seemed no way to be sure.

Once again, Vijay had awkwardly made excuses to Ranjit for not inviting him to come along. Ranjit was obviously puzzled, maybe even a little hurt, but he had said he understood.

As Vijay approached the village, the usual group of children ran out and began to follow him. They should be in school, he thought. He really needed to get busy on building it. For certain, without education, the lower caste children of Gamri could never follow his own path.

Dammit! Did he even want anyone else to follow his path? Where had it gotten him? He'd succeeded—and yet he hadn't. He had a good position, earned it on his own merits, not on any reservation or quota system. But he was still living a lie, and he was still terrified he'd be exposed and humiliated.

He could never pursue a possibility of marriage to a woman of one of the higher castes. Her family would follow the usual procedure and investigate his background. And he would quickly be found out.

Almost as difficult would be arranging a marriage to a lower caste woman. His co-workers would all wonder why a Rajput with a good government job would marry so far beneath himself. And wedding festivities themselves under those circumstances would be unthinkably awkward, with all his rural Untouchable relatives clearly revealing his own background to any higher caste guests from the city.

He glanced around at the mud houses. Bathed in the warmth of the early morning's winter sun, the village appeared so peaceful. Crows were cawing as they fluttered from tree to ground after scraps of refuse. Cows were being led out to pasture, their bells tinkling. At the tank, the women were bathing and doing laundry. The *whack whack* sounds of the wet clothes being beat against the rocks carried through the stillness. The air smelled clean and fresh, so unlike the rank odor of diesel exhaust that polluted New Delhi.

But to him, the peacefulness of the setting concealed the underlying reality of oppression and degradation. At any moment he might encounter a Rajput—a *true* Rajput—or a Brahmin who would take offense if he did not show the proper deference. The village's only shopkeeper would not allow him to enter the shop. There were wells where he did not dare drink if he valued his life. And there were shrines where he did not dare pause for worship.

Those were the real reasons he could no longer live here.

After sharing a meal with his mother and uncle and cousins, he made the excuse that it was a long way to Delhi, and he needed to get started.

As he left the village, he again passed the well he had built. The wooden pulley wheel squeaked as a Bhangi girl pulled on the rope stretched over it, hoisting a bucket from the depths. An older woman was talking with the girl while waiting her own turn. Vijay was reminded of one of his tax officer's arguments that treasure was so often hidden in a well or near water. He smiled lightly at the thought of anything truly valuable being hidden in the well at his own village, so far away from the palaces.

Of course, the search was over, so there was little point in speculating. He wasn't even sure he wanted to find anything, now that he knew Lakshman Singh had funded his education. But the habit of thinking about the treasure and its hiding place died hard.

Vijay stopped, looked about at the mud houses. Was it possible? Could the treasure have been hidden in a village? Maybe not this one, but another? Maybe in a well, or maybe not.

There were problems with the idea. Certainly no treasure would still be in a village if Madho Singh had been the one to hide it. Too many centuries had passed to keep such a secret. And over the years, whole villages sometimes even changed location for one reason or another.

So if the treasure was still hidden in a village, it would likely have been put there in more modern times, and as a relatively temporary measure. Maybe hidden at the direction of Lakshman Singh.

But how to get the treasure hidden without everyone in the village knowing about it? True, the villagers often held their ruler in awe and might be fiercely loyal to him. Still, if it involved so many people, how could it be kept secret? By hauling it at night?

A stash so far from the palaces would be inconvenient. How to get access to the treasure when needed, without a lot of eyes watching?

Vijay absently eyed the squeaking pulley at the well. The stone supports on each side of it were reminiscent of the ones on the walls of the old fortress, similar in design. But in the palace area of the fort, there were no wells at the bottom of the wall; the water had to be piped in from the reservoirs.

No wells near the wall there. Why did that fact nag at him?

He remembered looking at that very wall through the Maharaja's telescope.

Suddenly, he knew why someone had been watching that particular wall so carefully. He knew where the treasure lay.

He might be wrong, but he'd bet almost anything he wasn't. He turned and hurried toward the jeep.

"Vijay, the raid's over!" said Ranjit in a half whisper so the other tax officers wouldn't overhear. "You can't just keep looking."

"It was over because we hadn't found anything. But now I know where it is! I'm sure of it!"

Ranjit stared at him. In a low voice he said, "Do you have some sort of personal vendetta against the Maharaja now? Or against the princess? You always seemed almost sympathetic to them, or to the princess at least."

Vijay looked away. "I don't like the idea of hurting them further at all. But we have a job to do. You know we can't let personal feelings interfere."

"Even when we're ordered to stop?"

Vijay took a deep breath, beginning to have more serious doubts. "Keep on and you'll probably talk me out of it." He met Ranjit's gaze. "Don't you want to find the treasure? It's the chance of a lifetime."

Ranjit examined him. At last, he sighed. "All right. Where?"

Vijay did not feel like wasting time to explain, and then maybe to argue the matter. "Come, I'll show you. Bring the others, and our usual tools for prying things open. I'll meet you out at the jeep. We'll grab a couple of new witnesses on the way."

Ghosali had approached and overheard part of the exchange. "What's the meaning of this? Why did you not get agreement from me first?"

"Sorry, Ghosaliji. I'm afraid my excitement got the better of me. But I'm sure you don't object?"

"Of course I object! The raid is over. Batraji and the others are even now getting ready to leave for Delhi."

Vijay smiled. "Feel free to go. I'll let you know if we find anything."

"This is nonsense. If we haven't found the treasure in all this time, we're hardly likely to now."

"Maybe so. I'm willing to take a chance on one last look."

"Batraji should know about this," Ghosali muttered. He hastened off.

"We'd better hurry, I think," said Ranjit quietly. "Just in case Batra decides to interfere."

"Right."

Shanta and Krishnaswamy were clearly puzzled as the party sped toward the old fortress, stopping only long enough to recruit two surprised old men as *panch* witnesses. At the fort the crowded jeep roared through the gates, past Airavata the elephant, and braked to a stop in the courtyard.

What if we find it? Vijay wondered. Was this the way to repay the man who had financed his education? And Kaushalya Kumari would never understand; not after he'd told her the raid was over.

But he had his duty, he told himself. It was his obligation, even his *dharma*, to prosecute the search with all the possible zeal he could command. If a promotion resulted, that was incidental. Surely Lakshman Singh would understand, even if his daughter didn't. The former ruler might not be happy about the matter, but surely he would understand the importance of doing one's duty, being true to one's salt. He wasn't even supposed to know Lakshman Singh had financed his education, he reminded himself with some relief. So Lakshman Singh need never know that Vijay had found out. And with some luck the Maharaja and the princess might never even know he had been the one to get the idea about the treasure's location and pursue it.

That line of thinking wasn't entirely satisfying, but there was no time to dwell on it now.

On foot, Vijay quickly led his team and the witnesses up through the Madho Mahal to the lovely courtyard plaza overlooking the city, then into the adjacent doorway and down the steps to the storerooms. He shoved open one of the ancient wooden doors. "Here!" He announced. "Did you ever wonder what these baskets were for? And these old pulley wheels? And the ropes?" He didn't wait for a reply. "Help me carry them all up."

A pair of Bhil guards had been watching them; now one hurriedly left. A little annoyed at having to handle the dusty items, but intrigued at the same time, the others helped Vijay cart the objects up the stairs. It took some time to haul everything to terrace.

"Over here, by the wall," said Vijay.

"Oho!" exclaimed Ranjit. "I think I begin to see!"

"Help me with this rod," said Vijay.

He and Ranjit wrestled one end of the thick, round iron rod out of its bed in the stone upright. The other end then easily pulled free. Vijay slid the pulley wheel onto the rod, and with the help of Krishnaswamy and Ranjit, he replaced the rod in its masonry housings. Ranjit shook it. "Seems sturdy enough."

Next, they carefully examined the rope throughout its length, tugging hard on it, and inspecting it minutely. Using a triple knot, Vijay tied it to the handle of the largest basket, a massive, sturdy one.

Caught up in the excitement, the team carried the basket to the pulley and threaded the rope onto the channel in the outer rim of the wooden wheel. They suspended the basket so its upper edge was at the height of the wall parapet. "How about a few tools?" asked Ranjit.

"Right," said Vijay. Ranjit dropped in a pry bar, hammer, cold chisel, an electric torch.

"With someone in it, it might be too heavy for us to hold as it is," said Ranjit. "But the rope's plenty long enough to wrap it around a couple of times around one of those marble pillars in the pavilion. Then there'll be enough friction we can easily manage it."

"*Accha.*" Vijay helped Ranjit and Krishnaswamy rig up the arrangement. Then he turned. And stopped.

Kaushalya Kumari stood at the edge of the terrace, a look of disbelief on her face. She had apparently been called by the guard who had left. She hurried to stand before him. She was breathing heavily, her face flushed. "What's the meaning of this? Your raid is supposed to be over!"

Vijay felt the color rise in his own face. "The warrant is still in effect, Princess."

"Did Batra or someone in Delhi tell you to start again?"

"Not exactly. But they would approve, I'm sure—"

"Did you deliberately try to put me off guard?"

"I assure you, Princess, that's not the case. I was in fact told the raid was over. But things have changed now."

Her eyes flashed fire. "How have they changed?"

Vijay's eyes shifted away as he tried to come up with an explanation that might mollify her. He truly didn't want either to hurt her or to damage her opinion of him.

Ranjit and Shanta and Krishnaswamy and the witnesses were waiting, watching him. He gave up and told Kaushalya Kumari, "I now have an idea as to where the treasure might be."

"So you'd look for it even after you're told not to? What are you trying to do to me and my family?"

Vijay said quickly, "I don't want to do anything to injure you, Princess. You must surely know that by now. But we have our job to do. I'm sure the only reason the raid was called off was because we weren't getting results. I could telephone Delhi and get authorization again, but that seemed unnecessary."

A familiar voice came from off to the side: "Indeed it is unnecessary while I'm here. I'm glad to authorize another search."

They both whirled around. Dev Batra and his two men and Anil Ghosali approached. Batra grinned.

"Just—tying up some loose ends," said Vijay.

"Literally," said Ranjit, gesturing toward the rope.

Kaushalya demanded, more shrilly than Vijay had ever heard from her, "What is he doing here again?" She was looking at Batra.

Batra smiled at her. "Maybe I came just to see you, Kaushalyaji. What do you have against me? I'm only doing my duty."

Kaushalya snorted and turned away.

Abruptly, Batra strode over to look at the heavy line, then at the pulley. He slowly nodded, a smile on his face. "I begin to see." He turned to Vijay. "You've found another vault?"

Vijay hesitated, trying to think of a way to steer Batra away. It seemed impossible at this point. "Not for sure," he said. "Just an idea I wanted to try before we leave."

Batra was peering at him. "I think that's bullshit, Singh. I think you've know where it is. And I'm going to have a look myself."

"Devji!" said Ghosali. "This is absurd. It's ridiculous to think anyone would want to use a—a *basket* to get to their treasure!"

Batra grinned at him. "Is it? We'll soon know, won't we?"

Vijay thought furiously. If the treasure were indeed in a hidden vault accessible only from a basket hanging over the wall, he didn't want Batra, of all people, to take the credit for finding it. Especially when he himself had already paid the price of ruining Kaushalya Kumari's opinion of him. He glanced toward the princess. The Bhil guard captain, Surmal, was whispering to her. She looked worried. That fact reinforced Vijay's hunch that he was correct about the treasure's location.

"It may be dangerous," Vijay said to Batra. "We haven't tested the basket yet. Better let one of us go first."

Batra frowned. He slowly stepped to the basket, grabbed the rim, and gave it a hard shake. Then he turned, took hold of the rope, and examined a couple meters of its length. "Looks plenty strong to me," he muttered. More loudly he said to Vijay, "My own men will hold the rope along with yours. Just to make sure."

Vijay felt desperate. Dammit, it wasn't just having his idea stolen so brazenly that infuriated him. But by Batra!

"Everyone take hold of the ropes," Batra ordered. He looked at Shanta, who had been quietly waiting on one side. "Except the princess and Miss Das, of course. Want to come in the basket with me, Princess?"

Kaushalya folded her arms and turned her back on him.

Batra raised his eyebrows and shrugged dramatically. "Oh, well. I'll pursue you later, Princess." He turned to Shanta. "How about you, Miss Das?"

Shanta said grimly, "No, thanks."

Batra grinned. "I'll go first. But when I'm in the vault, Miss Das can be the next to come down and explore it with me. No one will able to see what we're up to. I've never made love in the middle of a pile of gold before." He laughed at Shanta's shocked expression.

Vijay tightened his fists and moved forward. "Don't speak that way to her!"

Ghosali said loudly to Vijay, "You're out of line, Singh! Apologize to Batraji."

Dev Batra stared at Vijay. "You realize who you're talking to?"

"You—just leave her alone!" Vijay was surprised at himself. But it felt good. Whatever the outcome, he was glad he'd spoken up. Batra had no right to treat Shanta so disrespectfully, whatever powerful position he held.

Batra looked to Shanta and back to Vijay. "Well! I think you must fancy her yourself. Can't say I blame you."

Taken aback, Vijay glanced at Shanta, who was clearly dismayed. Her eyes briefly met his, and her expression turned calm. "Please, never mind," she said quietly to Vijay. "It's not worth making a fuss over."

Batra shrugged, seeming unperturbed. He said, "We do have more important matters." He turned and climbed onto the wall.

Vijay relaxed slightly, but he felt strange. He had actually dared to challenge Dev Batra to his face! Batra seemed to be letting it pass, but he might well remember and take his revenge later.

And Vijay had done it because of Shanta. He looked at her, and he saw that her eyes were on him, and there was a slight, bemused smile on her face. He smiled back, but it was strained. He turned to watch Batra.

The basket hung next to the railing, and it was easy even for the overweight Batra to step in as he grasped the stone uprights for safety.

Once in the basket, he moved from side to side slightly, testing the balance, the sturdiness. "All right. Lower away. But slow!"

They inched the basket downward. Batra disappeared from view. Kaushalya stood back with Surmal. Shanta leaned slightly over the rail to watch the descent. Ghosali and Vijay took hold of the rope to help, Ghosali looking annoyed that Batra was continuing with the idea.

Abruptly, Batra shouted, "Bloody hell!"

"What is it?" called Shanta.

"Bees! Millions of 'em!"

Vijay now remembered the huge, black hives clinging to the outer side of the wall, under the parapet. "Better come up," he shouted. No reply came from Batra for a time. Then, "There's a door here, painted the same color as the wall. Right by the hives. It's got a lock on it. A big one!" After a pause: "The wood looks old. I'll try to pry the lock off."

Vijay said to the others, "There are plenty of us to hold him. I'm going closer so I can see." He released his grip on the rope and hurried to the wall by Shanta. He bent over the thigh-high edge, and below he could see Batra's back and part of the basket. The door itself, and the bee hives, were concealed from his sight by the overhang of the parapet.

He saw Batra straining, working with one end of the long bar to pry on the lock. "Shit!" yelled Batra. "It's harder than it looks." Then, "Bloody hell! I hit one of hives! Get me up! Get me up!"

"Pull!" shouted Vijay. He started to move back to give a hand on the rope. Then he heard the buzzing, saw the horde of bees swarming out, a big dark cloud of them. He froze. Batra was now in full view, and as the basket rose, he flailed with both hands to keep the ferocious mass of insects from his face.

Suddenly, the basket bumped the lower lip of the parapet. Batra lost his balance. A thick black halo of bees engulfed him as he began falling over the side, the basket still rising, scraping against the stones of the railing. He screamed, waving his arms in an effort to recapture his balance.

Vijay had moved slightly from the rail to avoid the bees. He jumped back to the railing and seized Batra's wrist with one hand. His other hand grabbed the stone upright support, and he braced his foot against the base of the rail and pulled backwards with all his strength. Bees now swarmed around him, too, and he felt a sharp burn on his forehead, another on his cheek, another on the back of his hand.

Still screaming, Batra fell toward him over the rail, almost knocking him down. Batra landed sprawling on the paving stones. Vijay let go of Dev Batra's arm, and instantly Batra was up on his knees, frantically waving away the bees. Vijay moved off, brushing wildly at the insects himself.

Batra leaped to his feet, and ran toward the entrance, the bees still attacking.

Only a few of them remained around Vijay, and by moving away, he seemed to be able to keep them off.

He was breathing hard from the unexpected exertion. He shouted to Batra's men, who were looking at each other uncertainly. "Better go after him—he may need to go to the hospital!" Both rushed after their boss. Ghosali hesitated a moment, then followed them.

Shanta Das hurried to Vijay. "Are you all right?"

His face and hands burned fiercely. He glanced at his hands, saw only a few red welts. "I think so. I got off easy."

Shanta examined her own arm, where she, too, had been stung.

Kaushalya Kumari was standing nearby. Vijay looked at her, unable to read her face. Surprise and concern, mixed with at least some little satisfaction?

32

Mangarh, the next day, 20 December 1975

Batra, in shock and a serious reaction from the hundreds of stings, had been treated in the Mangarh hospital before being taken to New Delhi.

Ghosali stridently protested resuming the search, insisting it was foolish to risk more people. Only a series of phone calls to Delhi had resolved the matter. Now Ghosali stood back, glumly watching, making it clear that Vijay bore the blame for any further fiascos.

Smoke rose from a fire some Bhil tribals—not related to the guards—had built at the base of the wall. With a rope, another pair of Bhils held a smoldering bunch of leaves suspended below the top of the parapet. They and their ancestors had taken honey from hives on the rock cliffs in the hills for centuries, and this was a time-tested way of inducing the bees to temporarily abandon their homes.

"I'm sorry," Vijay said to Kaushalya. "It's something I have to do."

Kaushalya nodded silently. Her face was expressionless. She was elegantly dressed in a traditional Rajput long skirt outfit of orange silk, and she wore a diamond nose stud and diamond earrings, a gold bracelet, and gold sandals. If her family's ancient treasure were discovered, she wanted to appear as a worthy representative of the lineage.

"You're sure you don't know where the key is?" asked Vijay.

Kaushalya said, "I'm sure. My father would be the only one who could help."

One of the Bhils said, "The bees are mostly gone now, *sahib*. You should hurry before they come back."

Vijay nodded.

"Let me be the one to go down, Vijay," said Ranjit.

Vijay hesitated. The Sikh was definitely stronger, better able to deal with the lock. But as Batra had shown, there were risks involved. "Thanks, Ranjit, but no," he said firmly.

Krishnaswamy stood by to help. An annoyed-looking Ghosali watched from several steps away, puffing on his pipe.

Vijay cautiously climbed into the basket, holding on tight first to the stone uprights, then to the handle of the basket. He deliberately avoided looking at the pavement far below. He signaled, and the men began lowering him—cautiously. The thick smoke was an annoyance, but not nearly so annoying as the bees would have been. The hives were huge, and so close he could touch them.

He shouted when the basket was even with the bottom of the doorway, and the motion stopped.

The padlock, he saw, was in good condition. The wood the bolt was attached to was weathered, but quite solid, with scratches and indentations where Batra had tried to pry the lock off.

Working slowly and carefully under the awkward conditions, it took him a good ten minutes to chisel away enough wood to pry the lock loose. By then, bees were beginning to reappear. He had his crew raise him, and he rested his strained muscles while the Bhils again applied the smoke. Kaushalya Kumari silently watched him, her lips tightly set in a straight line.

Then the men lowered him again, and once more he pried at the door. It gave. It swung inward, so there was no need to maneuver the basket out of the way. In the dimness through the doorway he saw a largish room containing stacks of small metal bound wooden chests and big round metal pots. Vijay instantly recognized the pots as the traditional containers for holding coins.

Carefully gripping the door frame for security, he stepped from the basket to the stone floor. Relieved to be on a solid surface, he quickly examined the boxes and the coin containers. All bore wax seals with the imprint of the Mangarh royal family's coat of arms.

Vijay moved to the door and, trying to keep the excitement from his voice, called, "It's here. Send Ranjit down—and a witness."

"I'll go down," said Kaushalya immediately. She adjusted her *odhni* so it was more secure on her shoulders. With the heels so high on her sandals, she felt awkward stepping into the basket, so she slipped them off.

The wicker floor of the basket felt oddly irregular on her bare soles. She held tightly to the side as the basket was lowered; she did not like the sensation of being suspended by a single rope, in the same basket from which Dev Batra had nearly fallen to his death.

Vijay Singh seemed to understand; he extended a hand for her to steady herself as she extended her foot and stepped to the stone threshold. Relieved to be back on a solid floor, she was only vaguely aware that she was standing in dust and gritty fragments of stone, or that the air in the concealed room was musty and stale. She looked about at the items illuminated by a lantern and by the light from the open door.

So this was her family's legendary Treasure at last.

These chests and coin jars had survived centuries, protecting their contents while strife swirled about them. Invading neighboring princes. Maratha armies. Power struggles among the Mangarh nobles. Weak rulers and strong rulers. Treaties with the British. Corrupt and thieving officials. The accession of Mangarh to the Indian union.

Now, after all that, the treasure would be revealed to the world by government bureaucrats and politicians.

She watched as Vijay Singh broke the seal on a coin container and Ranjit Singh helped him pry out the lid. They looked in, then moved aside so she could see. It was full of gold *mohurs*.

Rather than opening the other containers in the room, Vijay decided to lift them by means of the pulley and set them out on the lawn of the garden terrace.

Back up on the terrace, Kaushalya wiped her gritty feet on the grass, stepped back into her sandals, and watched numbly as one-by-one the chests and coin pots were hoisted and placed in neat rows on the grass. It was hard work, for all the containers were heavy. She had feared that a hoard such as this would be discovered, and she had hoped that it would not. She wondered how much the government would take. Would they argue it all belonged to the old Mangarh state and should therefore have been turned over to the new government of Rajasthan?

For certain, at the very least, there would be a substantial penalty. And it might delay her father's release from jail.

Vijay Singh approached her. He seemed almost embarrassed, she thought, as he asked quietly, "Princess, do you think you could find the keys to the chests?"

She straightened herself, trying to look royally composed, rather than deflated and depressed. "I've already asked my father's staff. None of them know anything about this. I'm not even certain my father was aware of it. It could have been put there by one of our ancestors."

"You're sure the Bhil guards don't have keys?"

She started to say no, but then said, "I'll ask again." She abruptly turned and went to where the guard captain stood watching at the door, his expression one of resigned unhappiness. He instantly came to attention and saluted her sharply, aware of all the eyes upon him and obviously intending to perform his role to the utmost perfection.

"Captain Surmal," she asked, "do you know of any keys for these chests?"

"No, *Rajkumari*. Only Maharaja *sahib* would know of this."

She returned to Vijay Singh and shook her head. "If you could get my father out of jail, I'd wager he could help."

Vijay smiled grimly. "I'd like nothing better. But I don't think we can wait. I must apologize, Princess—we have little choice but to break them open. My warrant authorizes that, of course."

She did not reply.

Ranjit Singh was expert at breaking locks off chests. One by one the contents were revealed:

Cloth-wrapped bundles of swords and daggers with exquisitely inlaid handles.

Silken robes embroidered with pearls and gold threads.

Jewel-encrusted children's rattles and toy carts and horses.

Trays containing pearl necklaces.

Diamond necklaces.

Diamond and emerald necklaces.

Diamond and ruby necklaces.

Turban ornaments, bracelets, rings, with all combinations of precious gemstones.

Silver walking sticks.

Pots of silver coins. Smaller quantities of gold ones.

A chest full of gold ingots.

On and on it went, the longest inventory in Vijay's career.

Ghosali watched, looking as if he had swallowed something distasteful. He refused to help in the recording, apparently unable to face Vijay's success after arguing so insistently against resuming the search of the wall chamber.

Kaushalya Kumari also watched silently, her face expressionless, as she saw all these treasures for the first time: the legacy of her ancestors, revealed to the world by outsiders.

At least she had no doubt about Vijay Singh keeping an accurate inventory, or properly safeguarding the items. When the last gold bar had been recorded and replaced in its container, she turned and walked away. She beckoned for Gopi to join her.

It was time to go to visit Guruji at the ashram.

33

New Delhi, 26 December 1975

Vijay's superiors gladly ignored the fact that he had exceeded his instructions by continuing the search; after all, the warrants themselves had never been withdrawn.

He was relieved, of course, to return to New Delhi. And as word of the find spread, he became somewhat of a hero to his fellow income tax officers—with the natural exception of Ghosali, who avoided him.

The press interviewed both Vijay and his superiors, including Dev Batra, about the fantastic haul worth *crores* of rupees. The headlines called it "The Find of the Century," and "The Fabulous Golden Treasure of Mangarh," and "The Last Great Royal Hoard."

Prasad invited Vijay into his office to congratulate him. They chatted a bit about how Vijay had come to think of the location. "It was an ingenious hiding place," Prasad said, shaking his head. "The treasure would still be there if it hadn't been for your inspiration."

Vijay smiled tightly and did not reply.

"I heard," Prasad continued, "that you stood up to Batra at the last. To protect Miss Das."

Vijay's face grew warm. He shrugged. "It was nothing. He might have been able to give us orders, but I felt he didn't have the right to insult our people."

Prasad nodded judiciously. "Good. Good. It's ironic that you saved his life, but fortunate. I doubt he'll try to punish you now."

Word had spread to the rest of the officers, too, about how Vijay had stood up for Shanta. To his embarrassment, a number of his fellows, after congratulating him for discovering the treasure, mentioned the matter.

All the recognition given Vijay for locating the Mangarh Treasure was gratifying. But something nagged at him, bothered him about the discovered wealth. Late that same night, as he lay awake thinking it all over, he realized what was disturbing him.

The next morning at the office, he sat thinking at his desk, ignoring the many stacks of files bound in red tape. He decided he needed to discuss the Mangarh matter with someone. Shanta had been the one who had worked most closely with him on the historical detective work. He asked her to come in. She accepted with a nod and her usual broad smile.

He shoved back the drape covering the doorway opening and stood aside as she entered. "Like some *chai?*" he asked when she was seated.

"Yes, tea would be good." The low winter sun shone through the window, and she turned slightly to avoid looking directly at it. She wore the same green sari as when they had gone to look at the Harappan village near Mangarh. It went well with her coloring, he thought, as he summoned the peon and ordered the tea.

"I wanted to know what you think of something," he told Shanta. "About the Mangarh Treasure." He spoke in a low enough voice that no one out of sight in the hallway would be likely to hear.

She gave him a puzzled look. "Of course." He was pleased to realize that she never called him "sir" any more, and he vaguely wondered when she had stopped.

"Did you ever wonder," he asked, "that despite all the jewelry we found, we never located any of those pieces shown in the portraits of the Mangarh rulers?"

She frowned. "Yes, I did notice. But I hesitated to mention it. It seemed so minor, compared to the actual discovery. Anyway, I don't have a clue to where the jewelry might be, so the matter seemed academic."

Vijay ticked off the missing items on his fingers: "No five-strand pearl necklace. No giant emerald. No big diamond and ruby turban ornament. And definitely no 'Star of Mangarh' diamond."

Shanta smiled, this time in irony. "When you put it that way, it seems we only accomplished part of the job."

The tea came, and Vijay shoved aside a few of the files to make room for the glasses. "If the rest of the jewelry is still in Mangarh," Shanta asked, "Do you have any ideas where it might be?"

Vijay shook his head. "None. I wonder if Lakshman Singh's having the last laugh on us. Even in jail." He took a sip of tea.

"I doubt he's laughing in jail, poor man." Shanta looked toward the window. "Well, maybe we found enough anyway. I'm sure the princess would think so."

Vijay glanced at her, then stared at his tea glass.

Shanta said quietly, "I think you were quite impressed by her. She's very beautiful, as well as talented."

Vijay sat for a moment. Then he looked at Shanta and smiled. "Yes, she's a remarkable young woman. But she's not the only outstanding one around."

Shanta stared at him, a half smile on her lips. "Do I take that as a personal compliment, or were you making a general statement?"

Vijay grinned. "I meant it as a compliment."

Shanta looked down at her glass. "Well, thank you. Mentioning me and Kaushalya Kumari in the same breath is praise indeed." She sipped at her tea.

Vijay was puzzled to see that her hand was trembling.

But so was his own.

Shanta rose, smiled at him with warmth in her eyes, hesitated momentarily as if she were waiting for him to say something more.

He almost did, but he suddenly realized he didn't know just what it was he wanted to say.

She left, and he thought for some time about what was going on.

He shook his head, trying to clear it. Maybe it was time to get back to the stacks of files on his desk. They might be dull, but at least he didn't feel he was getting out of his depth with them. He'd think again about Shanta later.

In the sequel, India Fortunes:

Indira Gandhi's State of Emergency remains in effect, and the saga of the Mangarh Treasure continues, with Vijay Singh and the other tax officers returning to Mangarh to search for the remainder of the wealth. At Dev Batra' orders, workmen begin demolishing the fort.

Kaushalya Kumari is still desperate to free her father—and she and her friends the Chands are themselves arrested.

Vijay's life is at risk when he is trapped in riots in Delhi. And he is at last exposed as an Untouchable, in the presence of the income tax office staff. But he moves farther toward a romantic interest and a wife.

Desperate to finance a temporary exile from India, Dev Batra and his men abduct Kaushalya. In a long chase through the old fortress of Mangarh, she attempts to flee from her captors to save her own and Gopi's lives—as well as the life of Airavata the elephant, whom the vengeful Batra intends to kill.

In the Mangarh-related stories from earlier eras, in the same volume:

A master builder in the 1600s, forced to work for a Mughal Emperor he despises, designs and constructs the masterpiece that will be known as the Taj Mahal.

Maharaja Madho Singh leads a raid against the legendary King Shivaji in 1663 and seizes the loot that will comprise much of the Mangarh Treasure.

A farm boy from a village near Mangarh is involved in the founding of the Sikh religion.

A Brahmin priest, allied with the Rani of Jhansi in the Revolt of 1857 against the British Raj, struggles for his life against a murderous English officer.

Vijay Singh's father, working for the rights of the Untouchables in the 1930s, confronts Maharaja Lakshman Singh's brutal police.

Ashok Chand, a follower of Mahatma Gandhi and protege of Jawaharlal Nehru, agitates for reforms in Mangarh and is imprisoned by Lakshman Singh.

In 1947, the Maharaja fights the currents of history to preserve Mangarh's place in the new, independent, democratic India.

Ashok Chand leads his family, Hindus trapped in the newly created Muslim nation of Pakistan, in an escape to save their lives in a perilous train ride.

General Notes

Cartographers have not placed the Mangarh of this novel on maps other than those in this book. For travelers who wish to search for the town in Rajasthan, it might be wiser to be satisfied with experiencing other Rajasthani cities and villages similar in spirit to Mangarh. Likewise, historians and other chroniclers have not written of the Pariyatra Rajput clan or the other inhabitants of the former princely state of Mangarh. However, many other residents of the Rajasthan region and their ancestors have lived much as described in this book.

When portraying characters and incidents based on recorded history, I tried to be as accurate as possible. I often created fictional events to illustrate a historical occurrence or time period, and in those cases I went to considerable effort to be true to the spirit of the actual times and places involved. When portraying actual historical personages taking part in incidents created by my own imagination, I tried to be true to their personalities to the extent those can be revealed by research. In the following notes, I specify for each story which were actual historical characters and events, and to what degree I used my imagination.

My interviews with actual persons for background information are covered in my Acknowledgments. I personally visited almost all the sites I have written about in India, some more than once.

I consulted literally thousands of references over roughly fifteen years. To minimize the length of this book, a bibliography listing the major sources I used, and the ones I found most helpful, will be posted on my web site, www.garyworthington.com. As an alternative, I'll mail a printed copy of the bibliography to anyone who sends me a self-addressed envelope with sufficient postage for around three ounces of materials.

Notes on the Particular Stories

THE MANGARH TREASURE: The Time of the Emergency

A number of people named in my separate Acknowledgments section contributed significantly to my ability to write this story. I am deeply grateful to each of them.

The events taking place during the Emergency are fictionalized in this book, but most are based on similar actual occurrences. Of course, Indira Gandhi and Sanjay Gandhi actually lived, and they reportedly acted on occasion in that time period similarly to how I depict them. All other characters are fictional except the briefly mentioned imprisoned national leaders, Jayaprakash Narayan and Morarji Desai. No other characters are based on any real persons, living or dead, although the creation of some characters was inspired by a combination of two or more actual persons. For those who may wonder, I don't follow sports and had never heard of the golfer Vijay Singh until long after the story was completed.

With regard to written sources, I'm especially indebted to the following four books for inspiration regarding royal treasures during the Emergency, and regarding the Indian Income Tax Department:

1. Crewe, Quentin, *The Last Maharaja: A Biography of Sawai Man Singh II, Maharaja of Jaipur*. London: Michael Joseph, 1985. Part of the book describes income tax raids on the Jaipur royal family, including the lengthy, and unsuccessful, search at the Jaigarh Fort for the legendary Jaipur treasure protected by guards of the Mina tribe. Both the current Maharaja and the previous Maharaja's wife, the well-known Gayatri Devi, were jailed at Tihar for a long period during the Emergency.

2. Kasbekar, Sushama, and Palekar, Balachandra, *The Tax Dodgers*. Bombay: Popular Prakashan, 1985. A novel about the Income Tax Department and its raids. As mentioned in my Acknowledgments, coauthor B.B. Palekar, a former Deputy Director of the Directorate of Inspection (Investigation), was extremely generous with his time in writing detailed answers to my many questions.

3. Malgonkar, Manohar, *The Princes*. New York: Viking, 1963. An outstanding novel about the last days of a royal family before Indian Independence, partly involving the family's legendary hidden treasure protected by a tribe of Bhils.

4. Scindia, Vijaya Raje, with Malgonkar, Manohar, *The Last Maharani of Gwalior: An Autobiography*. Albany: State University of New York, 1987. Extensive details about the Maharani's tribulations during the Emergency when she and her family endured a lengthy raid by tax officers searching for hidden wealth. The incident in my story involving waste-removal tunnels beneath the palace, as well as some other details, were inspired by actual occurrences involving the Maharani's family. Like the previously mentioned Jaipur royal family members, the Maharani was jailed during the Emergency, part of the time at Tihar.

THREE PEOPLES: The Vedic Age

General Notes
I first wrote this story almost two decades ago, and much of the knowledge about the time period was, and still is, conjecture. The work of some recent scholars, although controversial, claims to have changed what is known of the identity of the inhabitants of the Indus Valley civilization (also called the Harappan or Mohenjo-Daro civilizations, after those major excavated cities) and why those peoples disappeared. Some periodical articles related to these revisionist views are cited in the bibliography available elsewhere, as mentioned above.

The prior, conventional explanation for the fall of the Indus Valley civilization, blaming it in large part on Aryan invasions, has been challenged by these recent scholars who cite the archaeological and geological evidence of: the destruction of the cities and their irrigation works by floods and earthquakes; significant climatic change; a decline in trade due to major shifts in the courses of rivers; and no on-site indications of violent attacks or warfare.

Some scholars have also relatively recently made cases that an early form of Sanskrit was spoken by the inhabitants of these civilizations and that their script, hitherto undeciphered, can now be translated. And, although natural disasters and climatic changes may have influenced the native peoples to move to more hospitable areas, the peoples may never have migrated so far as the southern part of the subcontinent and therefore may not, as was commonly thought, be ancestors of the Dravidian civilizations of the south.

But there is still considerable evidence that something similar to the invasion and migrations described in my tale may have happened, although perhaps spread out over a number of centuries, and maybe less far-reaching geographically, and possibly less violent. I suspect there will always remain a high degree of uncertainty about major aspects of the civilization and its fate. So I decided to let my story remain as previously written, with only minor modifications.

Kanur is a fictional village, and no such towns have yet been discovered so far to the southeast. All characters in my story are fictional, as is any connection between Bhira and worship of the god Bhairava or Bheru. The Bhils may or may not have inhabited the Aravalli range at such an early date; I extrapolated backwards from current information. It does seem certain that the area was much more heavily forested in those days, and the climate was more moderate. Wildlife was much more abundant and widespread. Lions, which are now extinct except for a small preserve in Gujarat, were common.

Acknowledgments
The excerpt from the *Rig Veda* quoted on the first page of the story is from: Griffith, R.T.H., *The Hymns of the Rig Veda,* I, pages

645-47, Benares: E.J. Lazarus, 1920, as reprinted in: Embree, Ainslee T., *The Hindu Tradition: Readings in Oriental Thought*. New York: Vintage Books, 1972.

The excerpt from the *Rig Veda* quoted at the beginning of the third section of the story is from a translation by Roth, Geldner Kaegi, apparently from *The Rigveda* by Adolph Kaegi, Boston, Ginn & Co., as excerpted in: Gopalacharya, Mahuli R., *The Heart of the Rigveda*. Bombay, Somaiya Publications Pvt. Ltd, 1971.

I misplaced the sources of the other three excerpts quoted in the story. I sincerely apologize to any translators and authors affected. If I find the identity of the sources, I will try to include that information in future editions.

A MERCHANT OF KASHI: The Time of the Buddha

The statements the Buddha makes in his teachings in the story are a composite of statements he allegedly made at various times. For the most part they are taken, with some modifications, from: Marshall, George N., *Buddha, The Quest for Serenity*. Boston: Beacon Press, 1978. All other characters in the story are fictional.

MAHOUT: Ashoka and the Mauryan Empire

Emperor Ashoka Maurya, a major and influential figure in Indian imagination and in world history, is perhaps the person most responsible (other than the Buddha himself) for Buddhism becoming a world religion. He quite possibly lived much as depicted, although many details of his time period are sketchy and conjectural. Many of his fascinating inscriptions survive on rock faces and stone pillars throughout South Asia. The other characters are fictional. The Kalinga war indeed occurred, although its true details aren't known.

This story is written to complement my historical novel, *Ashoka: A Novel of Ancient India*, presently still in manuscript form.

THE ART OF LOVE: The Gupta Age

The actual artist who painted The Dying Princess at the Ajanta Caves is unknown, and the characters in my story are fictional.

BRIDE'S CHOICE: Prithviraja Chauhan

Prithviraja III is an important figure in Indian, especially Rajput, history and imagination. Some historians have questioned whether his abduction of Samyogita actually occurred, and she is called by other names in some sources. Various sources give contradictory details of Prithviraja's later capture and his death after his second battle against Muhammad of Ghur.

THE PRICE OF NOBILITY: The Sultanate of Delhi

Ali Aruzi and Mahmud Aruzi and their family and servants are fictional. All other major characters actually existed. The major historical events depicted in the story actually occurred. Sultan Muhammad bin Tughluq submitted himself for judgment and punishment much as described.

SAFFRON ROBES: The Mughal Empire: Akbar and the Rajputs; Rana Pratap

General Notes

According to the chroniclers and historians, most of the major incidents at Chittorgarh and Haldighati apparently occurred mostly as I have described, but with participants other than my Raja Hanuman and his associates from Mangarh. The excerpts from Dwarka Das' epic about Raja Hanuman are from my own imagination.

The actual historical incidents include: the attacks on Chittorgarh by means of the mining and the *sabat* at the Lakhota Gate; the emissaries who tried to negotiate with Akbar; the death by a musket ball of Jaimal Rathor and the resulting demoralization of the defenders; the *jouhar* involving the deaths of all the Rajput women; and the escape after the battle of Chittorgarh by a party of defenders (apparently from Kalpi in actuality) pretending to be captives.

Rana Pratap in fact carried on his long struggle to retain the independence of his state just as depicted.

Acknowledgments

I greatly appreciate the following of those sources listed farther below for quotations used in my story:

Muni Lal's biography *Akbar*, for the folk song about Akbar on page 479 (Lal's version, which does not cite an original source, was a continuous paragraph; I realigned the phrases to more resemble verses).

Dr. P. Lal's translation of *The Ramayana of Valmiki* for the excerpt on page 490.

Manohar Prabhakar's *A Critical Study of Rajasthani Literature* for the translation of the first two couplets about Rana Pratap on page 523.

Dr. Hiralal Maheshwari's *History of Rajasthani Literature* for the subsequent two lines quoted about Pratap on that same page.

Character Lists

*The names of the characters of most importance to the stories are in **bold** type. Pronunciations are very approximate; many sounds in Indian languages do not have a corresponding sound in English.*

The Mangarh Treasure

The Mangarh (MAHN gar) royal family:

Lakshman Singh (LUX mun Singh), ex-Maharaja of Mangarh, Rajput caste.
Kaushalya Kumari (Koh SHAL ya Ku MA ree), the Maharaja's daughter, Rajput.
Mahendra Singh (Mah HEN dra Singh), the Maharaja's son, Rajput.

The income tax raiders:

Vijay Singh (VEE jay Singh), male senior income tax officer, Untouchable claiming to be Rajput, from village near Mangarh.
Anil Ghosali (Un NEEL Go SA lee), male income tax officer, Brahmin caste from Calcutta area of West Bengal, Vijay's rival.
Ranjit Singh (Ran JEET Singh), income tax officer, Sikh religion, Vijay's friend, from Delhi. Ranjit's wife: Vimala Kaur.
Shanta Das (SHAHN tuh Dahs), young woman income tax officer, Buddhist, from Untouchable background in Agra.
Dilip Prasad (De LEEP Pra SAHD), Deputy Director of Inspection.
Krishnaswamy (KRISH nah SWA mee), young income tax officer, Tamil from South India.
Mrs. Janaki Desai (JAHN uh kee De SAI), woman income tax officer from Delhi.
Akbar Khan (UK bar KHAN), male jeep driver, Muslim from old area of Delhi.

Other characters associated with the royal family in Mangarh:

Gopi (GO pee), Kaushalya's maid/companion.

Shiv (Sheev), Maharaja's elderly retainer.

Naresh Singh (NAHR esh Singh), Maharaja's aide de camp
(ADC)/personal secretary, a Rajput; his father ruled Vijay's
village.

Bhajan Lal (BHA jun LAHL), driver for royal family.

Surmal (Sur MAHL), Captain of Maharaja's Bhil (tribal) guards at
old fortress.

Airavata (Air ah VAT a), the elephant.

Characters in Gamri village:

Manju (MAN ju), Vijay's mother, a Bhangi (Untouchable sweeper
outcaste).

Surja (SURJ), Vijay's uncle, a Bhangi.

Govinda (Go VIND a), Vijay's cousin, a Bhangi.

Yogesh (Yo GESH), Vijay's cousin, a Bhangi.

Roop, Yogesh's wife, a Bhangi.

Hanwant (HAN want), Bhanwar (BHAN war), young village boys,
Bhangis.

Other Mangarh area characters:

Guru Dharmananda (GOO roo Dhar ma NAND a), guru of
Kaushalya and her father; a Brahmin from Himalayan
foothills, former medical doctor.

Peter Willis, Guru's American assistant.

Dr. Savitri Chand (SAH vi tree Chand), lady medical doctor,
Kaushalya's confidante and aunt of Kaushalya's best friend
Usha Chand, Arora caste from the Punjab.

Arjun Oswal (AR jun OS wal) , former schoolmate of Vijay's, clerk
in gem showroom.

Bharat Mahajan (Bhar AT Ma HA jan), gem dealer, Jain religion.

Rajendra Singh (Ra jen dra Singh), Thakur (TAH ker) (ex-ruler) of
Baldeogarh village area, a Rajput.

Delhi area characters:

Dev Batra (Dev BAHT ra), unscrupulous high level political
worker, crony of Sanjay Gandhi, originally from Punjab
area.

Gulab (Gu LAHB), one of Dev Batra's assistants/henchmen.

Sen, one of Dev Batra's assistants/henchmen.

Usha Chand (OO shuh Chand) , Kaushalya's best girlfriend, university student, Arora caste.

Ashok Chand (Uh SHOK Chand), former cabinet member and Congress Party politician, famous worker for India's freedom from British rule, originally from village in Punjab, Usha's father; Arora caste.

Jaya Chand (JAY a Chand), prominent lady lawyer, Ashok's wife/ Usha's mother, Arora caste.

Pratap Singh (Pra TAHP Singh), graduate student, son of ex-Maharaja of Shantipur, a Rajput, friend of Chand family and of Kaushalya Kumari.

Amar (AH mar), *chowkidar* (watchman/gate-keeper) of Mangarh royal family's Delhi house.

Indira Gandhi (In DEER a GAHN dhee), Prime Minister of India; daughter of Jawaharlal Nehru, India's first Prime Minister; no relation to Mahatma Gandhi.

Sanjay Gandhi (SAHN jay GAHN dhee), Indira Gandhi's son.

Three Peoples

Characters from the Indus Valley civilization town of Kanur:

Sumbari (Sum BUH ree), eleven year old girl.
Pippru (Pipp ru), Sumbari's five year old brother.
Varchin (Var CHIN), Sumbari's father, a carver of stone seals.
Namuci (NAH mu chee), a potter.
Balbutha, wife of the potter Namuci.
Chumuri (CHU mu ree), a wealthy merchant.

Characters with the Aryan invaders:

Bhira (BHEE ra), an Aryan warrior.
Visala (Vee SAL a), Bhira's wife.
Trita, Aryan warrior, a rival of Bhira.
Santanu (SHAN ta noo), a wealthy cattle herder.
Kasu (KAH soo), an elderly Aryan warrior.

Characters of the Bhil (Bheel) tribe:

Gajlyo, the Bhil chieftain.
Surio, a Bhil man.

A Merchant of Kashi

Samudradatta (Suh moo dra DUHT ta), a wealthy merchant of the Vaishya class.
Arthadatta (Ar ta DUHT ta), Samudradatta's elder son.
Durvasas (Dur VA sas), Samudradatta's younger son.
Ambalika (Am BAL eek a), Samudradatta's wife.
Chamikara (Cha mee KA ra), a wealthy merchant friend of Samudratta's.
Jajali (Ja JA lee), Samudradatta's manservant.
Sudeva (Su DEV a), Samudradatta's priest, of the Brahmin caste.
Siddartha Gauthama (Sid DAR ta GOW ta ma), **the Buddha.**
Mahavira (Ma ha VEE ra), founder of the Jain religion.
Vairochaka (Vair OHCH uh kuh), the land pilot, a guide for desert caravans.
Paravata (Pa ra VAT a), a merchant who disappeared when his caravan was lost in the desert.

Elephant Driver

Characters from Mangarh:

Jimuta (JIM uh ta), boy, age 15 at beginning of the story.
Jimuta's Uncle, a farmer; and Jimuta's Aunt.
Suchaka (Su CHAK a), Jimuta's boy cousin, age 17.
Chekitana (Che ki TAN a), Jimuta's boy cousin, age 16.
Kuvera (Ku VER a), a village boy.
Pushan (Pu SHAN), a village council member.
Ambika (AM bee ka), a village girl molested by The Crocodile and his men.
Rudra (RU dra), male elephant, age 45 at beginning of the story.
Kumbha (KUM bha), Rudra's former driver, accidentally killed by Rudra in a battle.
Raja Balarama (RA ja Ba la RAHM a), ruler of Mangarh, Kshatriya (warrior) class.
Vasu (VA su), Raja Balarama's Chief Minister, Brahmin class.
"The Mugger" (MUG ger), "The Crocodile," a Kshatriya warrior serving Prince Aja.
Darsaka (Dar SHUK a), The Crocodile's manservant.
Kumara (Prince) Aja (Ku MAR a AH ja), Kshatriya warrior prince, brother of Raja Balarama, ruler of several villages including Jimuta's family's village.

Uttara (OOT a ra), elderly elephant driver.
Nakula (NAH ku la), boy elephant driver.
Kunala (Ku NAHL a), elephant driver.

Characters on the Journey:

Shantanu (SHAN ta nu), merchant, age 48.
Agastya (Ah GUST ya), Shantanu's manservant.

Characters at Pataliputra:

Ashoka Maurya (Uh SHOK a MOWR ee a), the King, a Kshatriya,
    ruler of the Mauryan Empire.
Siddharthaka (Sid DHAR ta ka), a Kshatriya warrior, King
    Ashoka's confidant.
Vidura (VI du ra), an elephant driver.
Gajendra (Guh JEN druh), a male elephant, Rudra's friend; driven
    by Vidura.
Rajasena (Ra ja SEN a), commander of ten elephants.
Devrata (Dev RA ta), older boy, assistant in caring for Rudra.
Mangala (MAN ga la), Devrata's younger brother, assistant in
    caring for Rudra.
Satyavati (Suh TYUH vuh tee), a courtesan.
Renuka (RAY noo ka), girl, age 16 when Jimuta meets her;
    Satyavati's protege.
Bhasuraka, a guard, protecting Satyavati's house and Renuka.
Also: Vadhukha (Va DHU kuh), King of Kalinga, Ashoka's enemy.

The Art of Love

Guhasena (GOO huh say nuh), an artist, age 21, Vaishya class, son
    of a wealthy trader of the city of Ujjain.
Dhavala (DHA va la), Guhasena's valet, age 41.
Shashiprabha (Sha shee PRAH bha), Guhasena's beloved, age 17,
    daughter of a wealthy trader.
Menaka (MEN a ka), Shashiprabha's favorite maidservant.
Vasudatta (Va soo DUT ta), Guhasena's father, a wealthy trader of
    the Vaishya class.
Buddhila (Boo DHEE luh), a young man, Guhasena's friend.
Dharmagupta (DHAR ma GOOP ta), Shashiprabha's father, a
    wealthy trader.
Jeta (JEE tuh), a young Buddhist monk.
Devasharman (DEV shar man), a senior Buddhist monk.

Bride's Choice

Samyogita (Sum YO gee tuh), a princess, daughter of King
  Jayachandra of Kanauj.
Lakshmi (LAHKSH mee), Princess Samyogita's younger sister.
Chitralekha (Chit truh LAY kha), Princess Samyogita's elderly
  maidservant and confidante.
Sita (SEE tuh), Samyogita's younger maidservant.
Jayachandra (Jay uh CHAN druh), Samyogita's father, the King of
  Kanauj, a Rajput.
Raja Man Singh (RAH juh MAHN Singh), ruler of the Pariyatra
  Rajputs of Mangarh.
Prithviraja Chauhan (PRIT vee RAH juh Chow HAHN), Rajput
  King of Ajmer and Delhi.

The Price of Nobility

Amir Ali Sarajuddin Aruzi ("Ali") (Uh MEER AH LEE Sar aj
  ood DEEN A ROO zee), a nobleman and magistrate, age 28
  at the story's beginning; a disciple of the Sufi saint Shaikh
  Nizamuddin Auliya.
Malik Mahmud Aruzi (Ma lik MAH mood A ROO zee), Ali's
  father, age 75, wealthy nobleman and chief *sadr* (minister of
  religious affairs) for the Sultanate of Delhi.
Ishaq (Ish AQ), Ali's servant, a eunuch.
Ayesha (EYE shuh), one of Ali's two wives.
Halima (Hah LEE muh), the other of Ali's two wives.
Ziauddin Barani (ZIA ood DEEN Ba RAHN ee), a young noble-
  man, a friend of Ali's and another disciple of the Sufi saint
  Shaikh Nizamuddin Auliya.
Shaikh Nizamuddin Auliya (Shakh Ni ZAHM ood DEEN AWL
  lee uh), the famous and highly respected Sufi saint, in his
  90's.
Amir Khusrau (Uh MEER KHOOS row), the famous poet, a
  disciple of Shaikh Nizamuddin Auliya.
Amir Hasan (Uh MEER Ha SAN), a poet, somewhat less famous
  than Amir Khusrau, also a disciple of Shaikh Nizamuddin
  Auliya.
Ghiasuddin Tughluq (GHEE us ood DEEN TOO guh LOOK),
  Sultan (ruler) of Delhi.

Muhammad bin Tughluq (Muh HAH muhd bin Too guh LOOK), a Sultan of Delhi, son of Ghiasuddin Tughluq. He was earlier known as **Malik Jauna** (JAU na); then he was known as **Ulugh Khan** (OO lug Khan) after his father's accession as Sultan, until he himself succeeded his father as Sultan.

Shaikh Burhanuddin Gharib (Shakh Bur HAN ood DEEN Gha REEB), a Sufi saint.

Nasiruddin bin Malik Mall (Nas IR ood DEEN bin MA lik Mall), a young nobleman at Daulatabad who brought a lawsuit against the Sultan.

Saffron Robes

Characters from Mangarh:

Raja Hanuman Pariyatra (HAH new mun Pah YAH truh), Rajput ruler of Mangarh, allied with Rana Udai Singh of Chittorgarh against the Mughal Emperor Akbar.

Dwarka Das (DWAR kuh DAHS), Raja Hanuman's *charan* (bard) and advisor.

Dewa (DAY wuh), chief of the Bhil tribals allied with Raja Hanuman.

Hara (HA ruh), Raja Hanuman's Brahmin priest.

Kishen Lal (KISH en Lal), Raja Hanuman's architect and master builder

Rajput chiefs under Raja Hanuman:

Ajit (ah JEET), Raja Hanuman's senior military commander, a Rajput Thakur (local ruler), member of Mangarh council of chiefs.

Baldeo (Bal DE oh), Raja Hanuman's younger brother and rival, Rajput Thakur of Baldeogarh.

Govinda (Go VIN da), a young Rajput Thakur, member of Mangarh council of chiefs.

Karan (KAR an), a senior Rajput Thakur, member of Mangarh council of chiefs.

Mahendra (Muh HEN druh), Raja Hanuman's elderly uncle, Rajput Thakur of Amargarh, governor of Mangarh in Hanuman's absence.

Rajput warriors serving Raja Hanuman:

Bhupendra (Bhu PEN druh), eldest of Hanunan's Rajput retainers.

Kesari (KAY suh ree), youngest of Hanuman's Rajput retainers.
Shyam (Shyam), one of Hanuman's Rajput retainers.
Bheron (BHER ohn), one of Hanuman's Rajput retainers.

Raja Hanuman's wives:

Sisodia Rani (Si SHO dia RAH nee), **Sarasvati**, Raja Hanuman's
     senior queen, Rajput.
Bundi Rani, Bundiji (BOON dee RAH nee), **Champa**, Raja
     Hanuman's junior queen, Rajput.

Non-human characters:

Chanchal (CHAN chal), Raja Hanuman's favorite elephant.
Fateh (FAH teh), an elephant.
Bajraj (BAJ raj), Raja Hanuman's favorite stallion, a Kathiawari
     bay.
Ram Prasad, a war elephant coveted by Akbar.
Chetak (CHAY tuk), Rana Pratap's horse.

Other characters:

Akbar (AHK bar), the Mughal Emperor.
Jaimal Rathor (JAI mal Rah TOR), Rajput, the senior commander
     of Chittorgarh.
Rana Udai Singh (OOH day Singh), Rajput ruler of Mewar state
     and its capital of Chittorgarh, enemy of Mughal Emperor
     Akbar.
Kumar Bhagwant Das (Ku MAHR BHAG want DAHS), Rajput,
     son of the Raja of Amber, ally of Mughal Emperor Akbar.
Man Singh (MAHN Sing), Rajput, son of Bhagwant Das of Amber,
     ally of Mughal Emperor Akbar.
Rana Pratap (RAH nuh Pruh TAHP), Rajput, ruler of Udaipur and
     Mewar state, enemy of Mughal Emperor Akbar.

Glossary

A note on spellings:
For place names, I generally used the modern form, although sometimes I used an earlier name when it seemed appropriate in a particular story, such as Kashi for the city that later became Benares and Varanasi. Since even the latest events in the book take place before the adoption of "Mumbai" for Bombay, I've used "Bombay" throughout.

Many Sanskrit words, as well as names from earlier historical times, end in a short "a" sound. This final "a" has been dropped in modern Hindi and its dialects. Thus, for example, Rama becomes Ram, and Ashoka becomes Ashok. In each story I have usually tried to adopt the form in use during that particular historical period, although occasionally I departed from the practice for consistency and simplicity.

Also, transliteration from the Indian languages into English is only very approximate, so the same word often has two or more commonly used spellings in English. For example: *sati* and *suttee*; Shiva and Siva; Ashoka and Asoka; and Mughal, Moghul, and Mogul. In writing this book I have usually adopted the form I felt to be most common in recent writings for general audiences.

Pronunciations (when shown) are very approximate; many sounds in Indian languages do not have a corresponding sound in English. Since the book is intended mainly for a general public readership, I haven't attempted to use any of the diacritical marks that are standard in scholarly works.

accha: All right, okay.
ADC: Aide-de-camp, a military officer (usually relatively young) acting as an assistant to a ruler.
Agni: The Vedic god of fire; the sacred witness of Hindu rituals such as marriage.
Akbar: Probably the greatest of the Mughal Emperors; ruled from 1556 to 1605 C.E.
Amber: Fortress and city, the capital of the Kachhwaha Rajput clan before the capital shifted to Jaipur.
ankus (an kush): Elephant goad, usually a stick with a curved metal point on one end.
Annadata: "Giver of grain"; honorific form of address for certain rulers.
amir (uh MEER): A Muslim chief or nobleman ranking below a *malik* during the Sultanate. Later used for nobles in general.

Apehi! Apehi!: In the Mauryan age, "Get out! Get out!" shouted by an elephant driver or charioteer to warn other persons to move out of the way.

apsara (AHP suh rah): A nymph of Indra's heaven.

Aravallis: Range of low mountains stretching diagonally across Rajasthan.

arti (AR tee): Worship of a god, especially by waving lights in front of the image.

Aryan: Literally "noble." Relatively light-skinned nomads—horsemen and cattle herders—who have been believed by most scholars to have invaded and conquered the Indian subcontinent c.1500-1000 B.C.E. (the theory has been increasingly questioned in recent years).

ascetic: A holy man who practices self-denial as a spiritual discipline.

Ashoka (Uh SHOH kuh): Famous Emperor of the Mauryan dynasty; ruled almost all of the Indian subcontinent from 269 to 232 B.C.E.; credited with making Buddhism a world religion.

ashram (AHSH rahm): A guru's place of retreat for meditation and instructing disciples; an abode of ascetics and *sadhus*.

assalaam aleicum (uh suh LAHM oh uh LEH koom): Muslim greeting.

Auliya (AH lee ah): A title for a revered Muslim saint.

babul: A hardwood tree, often scrubby in nature.

bagh: A garden. Used as a suffix, as in Golbagh, or "Rose Garden."

Bai: Lady; title added to women's names.

baksheesh: Largesse, a tip or bribe.

bajra: Cereal grain, a type of millet.

Bania: A small merchant, shopkeeper, or moneylender.

banyan tree: A type of fig tree; it can grow quite large, with numerous air roots and multiple trunks, which often cover a wide area.

Bapu (BAH poo): Father.

Bapji (BAHP jee): Respected Father.

bazaar: A shopping area.

B.C.E.: Before Common Era; an increasingly preferred alternative abbreviation to "B.C." (which has obvious Christianity-related connotations), even though the years are counted exactly the same way. Also see the entry for "C.E."

Benares: Banaras (Kashi in ancient times), city on the Ganges River.

betel (BEET uhl): The leaf used in *paan* for chewing.

Bhagavad Gita (BUH guh vud GEE tah): "Song of God," a section of the great epic *Mahabharata*, containing a long dialogue between Krishna and Arjuna, the "Bible" of Hindus.

Bhai: Brother.

Bhangi (BHAN ghee): Member of the sweeper caste; traditionally "Untouchable" scavengers and disposers of human body wastes.

bhawan: Building or house.

bhikkhu (bhik KHU): A Buddhist or Hindu monk, a mendicant.
Bhils, Bheels (Beels): Race inhabiting the hills and forests of much of western India; the aboriginal tribal people of Rajasthan.
bhisti: A water carrier.
bidi (BEE dee): Handrolled cigarette.
big man: A man with considerable influence or prestige or wealth.
bindi: A dot or other mark worn on the forehead by many Hindu women; it has no particular religious significance; often a matter of fashion. Sometimes erroneously called a "caste mark."
Brahma: Great god of creation; a member of the Hindu trinity.
Brahmin: Member of the highest caste, traditionally priests and scholars.
budmash (BUD mash): A criminal or bad person.
burkha (BUR kha): Head-to-toe robe worn by orthodox Muslim women; because it covers the face, it has a mesh area or eye holes to see through. Also called a chadr or chador.

Campa Cola: A popular cola soft drink.
caravanserai: An inn for caravans or travelers.
caste: A hereditary group in Hindu society, ranked in status in comparison to other castes. Traditionally, members of a caste usually marry only within the same caste, and members follow the same or similar occupations (this is increasingly changing in modern times).
C.E.: Common Era (Christian Era according to some); an increasingly preferred alternative abbreviation to A.D., which is from the Latin *anno Domini* ("in the year of our Lord") and hence connotes a reference to Jesus Christ. However, the years are counted in exactly the same way.
chai: Tea.
chaitya: A Buddhist place of worship.
Chamar (cha MAR): An Untouchable caste whose duties traditionally include working with leather.
chandalas: Untouchables who cremated dead bodies.
chappals: Heavy leather sandals.
chappati (chuh PAH tee): Round, flat, thin, unleavened bread.
charan (CHAH run): Member of a particular caste of bards or poets.
charpoy (CHAR poy): A simple cot or bedstead, usually with stringed webbing on a wood frame.
Chauhan (CHOW han): A major Rajput clan.
chhatri: A dome supported on columns (literally umbrella); often used for memorials to rulers or chiefs.
chital: A deer.
chitra shali: A picture gallery in a palace.
chowkidar (CHOWK ee dahr): A watchman.
Congress: A national political party.
crore (krohr): Ten million; 100 *lakhs*.

dacoit (da COIT): Bandit, robber.

dak **bungalow**: Resthouse maintained by the government for traveling officials. "*Dak*" means "mail."

dal: Lentils.

Dalit (DAL it): Literally "Broken People," a relatively recent term for Harijans, Untouchables, or Scheduled Castes.

darshan (DAR shan): The sight of a saint, deity, ruler, or holy place.

dasas, dasi (DA see): A slave or black person.

Deccan: Hilly plateau region of south-central India.

devanagari (de va NAH ga ree): The script used to write Sanskrit and Hindi.

dewan (DE wan): Chief minister.

dharma: Hindu duty or divine law; a person's *dharma* is determined by his caste, sex, position in the family, etc. Also refers to the teachings of the Buddha.

dhobi (DHOH bee): Washerman.

dhoti (DHOH tee): A wide length of cloth, usually white, wrapped around the lower body of Hindu men; commonly worn in rural areas of northern India, and traditionally worn at home and for worship.

Divali (dih VAH lee): Hindu festival of lights in October/November.

Diwan-i-Am: Public Audience Hall in a ruler's palace.

Diwan-i-Khas: Private Audience Hall in a ruler's palace.

doab (do AB): An alluvial plain, often between two rivers.

dupatta (duh PAH tuh): A head scarf, often long and diaphanous.

durbar (DUR bar): A royal audience, court, or assembly.

durry: A small cotton rug.

Dussehra (Duh SAY reh): Hindu festival in October/November when the battle between Rama and Ravana from the *Ramayana* is acted out (the *Ram-lila*).

farman: An official written proclamation by a ruler.

feringhi (fer IN ghee): Former term for outsiders, including Europeans or foreigners.

gadi (GAH dee): Cushion or bolster used as a ruler's throne.

Ganesha: Elephant-headed Hindu god of wisdom and good fortune. As the Remover of Obstacles, he is prayed to before major undertakings.

Ganga (GAHN gheh): The Ganges River as a goddess.

garh: Fort, as in Mangarh.

gecko: A small, harmless lizard; commonly found indoors on walls in the tropics.

ghagra (GHAH grah): Full skirt commonly worn by village women of various castes in Rajasthan.

ghat (ghaht): Wide steps leading down to water for bathing; also the slopes of a range of hills.

ghee (ghee): Clarified butter, often used in a liquid form in cooking, also used in rituals.

gur: Raw brown sugar.

gurdwara: Sikh temple.

guru: Spiritual teacher or master; also a founder of the Sikh religion.

halva (HAL va): Sweet dish made from flour, sugar, and *ghee*.

Hanuman (HAH nuh mun): The monkey who helped Rama in the great epic *Ramayana*; later considered a god.

Hara, Hada: Rajput clan of Bundi and Kota in Rajasthan, a branch of the Chauhan clan.

harem: Women's quarters in a house or palace.

Harijan: Literally "child of god," Mahatma Gandhi's term for an Untouchable.

Hathi Pol (HAH tee pole): Elephant Gate.

haveli (huh VEH lee): Large urban house or mansion.

Hawa Mahal (ha WAH ma HALL): Hall or palace of "winds," with latticed windows to catch the breeze.

Hindi: The general language of much of northern and central India.

Holi (HO lee): Major Hindu festival marking the coming of spring; people throw colored powders and water on each other.

hookah (HOOHK uh): Type of pipe with a large bowl and hose, in which the tobacco or marijuana smoke is drawn through water. Also called a hubble-bubble.

howdah (HOW dah): Seat or cabin carried on the back of an elephant.

huzoor: Literally "the Presence;" "sir;" an honorific form of address.

imam (ih MAHM): Leader of prayers in a Muslim mosque.

Indra: Vedic god of the sky or heaven, and of lightning, thunder, and rain.

inshallah (in sh ahl LUH): "God willing."

jai: "Victory."

Jains: Religious sect founded in the 6th century B.C.E. by Mahavira. One of its emphases is on *ahimsa* or noninjury to living beings. Because this is interpreted to prevent Jains from engaging in agriculture and many other occupations, traditionally numerous Jains have been traders and (later) industrialists. Consequently, Jains as a whole are wealthy and influential out of proportion to their actual percentage of the population.

jelabi (juh LEH bee): Syrup-filled sweetmeat.

jati (JAH tee): Indigenous term for a caste.

jagir: A hereditary assignment of land granted by a ruler.

jagirdir: The holder of a *jagir*.

ji (jee): Suffix added to a name to show respect; also used separately as "yes."

jouhar (jou HAR): Mass suicide by women to avoid capture in war.

jowar (jo WAR): A millet grain.

kanchli kurti (KANCH lee KUR tee): Traditional outfit worn by Rajput women in Rajasthan; *kanchli* refers to a bra-like piece, and *kurti* to a blouse; worn with an ankle length skirt and a long head scarf.

Kachhwaha: A Rajput clan, it ruled the former Jaipur state and Sikar. Amber was the capital before Jaipur.

Kailasa (kai LASH a): Himalayan mountain, home of Lord Shiva.

kamdar: Manager or revenue agent of an estate.

kameez (kuh MEEZ): A fitted tunic worn over baggy trousers by both men and women (also see *shalwar-kameez).*

karma (KAR ma): In Hinduism, Buddhism, and Jainism, the law of cause and effect in which every act results in consequences in this life or in future lives.

Kashi: Ancient name for the city of Benares or Varanasi.

khadi (KHA dee): Rough textured, hand woven cloth. Wearing it became a symbol first of opposition to British rule, and then of adherence to the Congress Party.

khanqah: The monastery or religious center of a Muslim mystic teacher, with a hospice for meals and lodging for the poor.

khan: During the Sultanate, a nobleman of the highest rank. During the Mughal Empire, a title of distinction awarded by the Emperor. Later, many nobles began using the title as a hereditary privilege.

kharif (kha REEF): Crop of the monsoon or rainy season.

kite: Hawk-like bird of prey.

kohl (kohl): Eye make-up made from charcoal.

Koran, Qur'an (Kuh RAHN): The Muslim holy book, written in Arabic.

kos: A variable unit of measure for long distances, assumed to equal approximately two miles for the purposes of this book.

Krishna: Popular Hindu god, an incarnation of Vishnu.

Kshatriya (kuh SHUH tree yuh): Member of the warrior and princely caste, ranking just below the Brahmin caste.

Kumar, Kunwar, Kumara (koo MAR): Heir of a *raja*; term used for a son during a father's lifetime.

kurta (KUR ta): Long, loose, collarless sleeved tunic or shirt.

lac: A red dye made from insect shells.

lakh (lahkh): One hundred thousand.

Lakshmana: Rama's loyal half brother in the great epic the *Ramayana*. The fictional Pariyatra Rajput clan of Mangarh consider themselves descendents of Lakshmana.

lassi (LAH see): A cool drink made from yogurt, sweetened or salted.

lathi (LAH tee): Long bamboo staff with iron on the tips, used as a weapon by police.

Limca: A popular soft drink.

lingam, linga: An image of the erect male reproductive organ, often simplified and stylized, the symbol of the god Shiva.

lota: A small, round metal pot for carrying water.

Maa-Baap: "Mother and Father;" honorific term of address for certain rulers.

maha (MA ha): Prefix meaning "great."

Mahabharata (ma ha BAH rah ta): One of the two great Hindu epics (the other is the *Ramayana).*

Mahadeva (ma ha DAYV a): "Great God," another name for Lord Shiva.

mahal (ma HAL): A palace, or an apartment within a palace.

Maharaja (ma ha RAH ja): "Great King," highest ranking of a hereditary ruler of a Hindu princely state.

Maharajkumar: Son of a Maharaja.

Maharana (ma ha RAH na): Ruler of the princely state of Mewar or Udaipur.

Mahavira: Founder of the Jain religion, a contemporary of the Buddha.

mahout (muh HOOT): An elephant driver.

maidan (my darn): An open park, field, or plain.

mali (MAH lee): A gardener.

malik (MAH lik): During the Sultanate of Delhi, a nobleman ranking above an *amir* and below a *khan.* During Mughal times, it often meant a *zemindar* or large landlord. Later broadened to mean a "master" or landowner-employer.

mandapa (MAN da pa): Hall of a Hindu temple, usually pillared.

mandir (MAN deer): Temple or palace.

Mangarh (MAHN gar): In this book, a city and state in the Rajasthan region. "Man" means "respect" or "prestige;" "garh" means "fort."

mantra (MAHN tra): A repetitious prayer or incantation or a verse. The words have mystical or magical powers.

Maratha (ma RAH tah: Native of the Deccan.

Marwar: "Land of the Dead," desert region that was the kingdom of the Rathore Rajput clan of Jodhpur.

Mauryan: The dynasty and empire founded c. 323 B.C.E. by Chandragupta Maurya, at its height in his grandson Ashoka Maurya's rule, 269 to 232 B.C.E.

mekhala (mek HA la): A girdle worn around the waist in earlier eras.

mela (ME la): A festival or fair.

Mewar: Formerly the kingdom of the Sisodia Rajput clan of Udaipur.

minaret: Tower in a mosque from with the Muslim faithful are called to prayer.

mleccha (mlech a): Foreigner, impure or unclean. Sometimes formerly used by Hindus referring a foreigner such as a Muslim invader.

mohur (MO hur): Obsolete gold coin.

moti (MO tee): Pearl.

mudra (MOO dra): A hand gesture with meaning or symbolism, as in worship or dancing or drama.

muezzin (moo EZ in): Person who calls Muslims to prayer five times a day from a mosque.

mugger (MUG ger): A crocodile.

Mughal (MOH guhl): Also Moghul, Mogul. Term for the Muslim dynasty which ruled most of India from the 1500s to the 1700s.

mullah (MOO luh): Muslim priest.

mujra (MOOJ ra): A formal salutation.

munshi (MOON shee): A clerk.

nagar (NA gar): Town.

nalika: In the Mauryan age, a time period equal to 24 minutes.

namaste, namaskar: The traditional Hindu greeting, meaning "I bow to you in respect." The palms of the hands are pressed together and the head bowed as if in prayer.

Nandi: The bull on which Lord Shiva rides. A statue of Nandi is common in Shiva temples.

nazar (NA zar): Gifts or coins offered to a ruler on ceremonial occasions as tribute or tokens of respect or allegiance.

neem: An aromatic tree with a fine, comb-like foliage. Its leaves are a natural insecticide; twigs are used for brushing teeth.

Nirvana: Buddhist term for Enlightenment.

niwas (NEE was): An abode, small palace, or apartment in a palace.

odhni (ODH nee): Also *orhni;* the shawl or long veil worn by Rajasthani women over the head.

paan (pahn): Also *pan*; a chew of betel leaf wrapped around slaked lime, areca nut, and spices.

padika: In the Mauryan age, a military commander of ten elephants, ten chariots, fifty horsemen, and 200 foot soldiers.

Padshah (PAD shah): Emperor.

pallav (PAL lav): The portion of a sari that is left over after wrapping the body. Usually draped over the shoulder, sometimes it is first pleated and then pinned into position.

palanquin: A covered litter for conveying wealthy or prestigious persons, usually carried by four or more men.

panch: Five.

panchayat (PAN cha yat): A committee which decides or governs village or caste affairs, traditionally with five members.

panch **witnesses**: Citizens recruited to act as impartial observers of a government raid.

pandit (PUN dit): A Hindu scholar, wise man, teacher. The term is often used before a name as an honorary title, as in Pandit Nehru.

Panditji (Pun dit jee): Honorific form of *pandit*.

pani (PAH nee): Water.

Pariyatra (pa ree YAH tra): Early name for the Aravalli mountains; in this book, the Rajput clan, with its home territory of Mangarh state.

peon: An office boy or messenger.

pi (pee) dog: Abbreviation of *pariah* for common mongrel dogs.

pipal (PEE pal): A sacred fig tree; the Bo tree of the Buddhists.

pir: Muslim saint or religious teacher.

pol: A gate.

prasad: Food blessed by a priest in a temple.

puja (POO jah): Hindu worship or ritual to a deity.

pukka PUK kuh): Proper or strong, so a *pukka* road is a paved one, and a *pukka* house is one of brick rather than mud.

pundit: See *pandit*.

punkah PUN kah): A ceiling fan, in earlier times, it was often a large, hanging flap of cloth operated by hand by pulling a rope.

pur (pour): A city, as in Jaipur, Udaipur, Jodhpur.

Puranas: Ancient Hindu sacred texts of historical myths and legends, dealing with the lives and exploits of gods and goddesses.

purdah: The veiling of women and/or their seclusion in homes.

qazi (KA zee): A judge.

Qur'an, Quran, Qu'ran (Kuh RAHN): Alternate, more currently preferred, transliteration for Koran.

rabi: Crop of the winter or dry season.

raga (RAH guh): An instrumental music piece.

Raj (RAHJ): Reign; British rule in India.

Raja (RAH ja): A king or ruler inferior in rank to a Maharaja, which means lit. "great king."

Rajasthan (RAJ as tahn): "The land of kings," the name for the modern state which encompasses the former princely states of the Rajputana region of northwestern India.

Rajasthani: Language spoken in the Rajputana or Rajasthan region; its many local dialects are considered to be variations of Hindi.

rajkumari (raj ku MA ree): A daughter of a Raja.

Rajput (RAHJ puht): Literally the son of a king; a Hindu of certain clans of the Kshatriya or warrior caste in northern, western, and central India.

Rajputana: Name given by the British to a region ruled mostly by Rajputs in northwestern India, west of Delhi. Most of it later became the state of Rajasthan.

rakshinah: In the Mauryan age, a municipal police officer.

Rama (RAH ma): Hero of the *Ramayana*, a prince who is an incarnation of the god Vishnu, idealized by Hindus as the embodiment of a dutiful, selfless, dedicated ruler.

Ramayana (Rah MAH ya na): Great epic poem; its hero is Rama and its heroine is his wife Sita. In the epic, the demon Ravana kidnaps Sita, and Rama must recover her from Ravana's palace on the island of Lanka.

Ram Rajya: The reign of Rama as King, a legendary ancient golden age. Often said to be the ideal toward which a ruler should aim.

ram, ram (rahm rahm): A form of Hindu greeting, saying the name of Lord Rama.

rani: A queen, wife of a raja. Maharani is the wife of a Maharaja.

Rana (RA na): Title of the ruler of Rajput state of Mewar or Udaipur.

rasa (RA sa): Flavor or sentiment, a particular emotion that a piece of art arouses in the viewer.

Rathor: Rajput clan ruling Jodhpur and Bikaner.

Rig-Veda: See Vedas.

roti (ROH tee): Round, flat, thin, unleavened bread; commonly made from *bajra* grain in the Mangarh region.

RSS or **RSSS**: The Rashtriya Swayam Sevak Sangh, or National Service Society, a militant Hindu revival organization.

rupee (ROO pee): Abbreviated Rs.; the standard unit of Indian currency. In the mid-1970s, worth roughly fourteen U.S. cents (seven rupees to one U.S. dollar).

sabat (SAH bat): A tunnel, as used in tunneling into a besieged fort.

sabha (SAH bha): An assembly.

sacred thread: The cord worn over the shoulder and across the chest by males of the three upper Hindu classes, awarded to them as boys in initiation ceremonies.

sadhu (SAH dhu): A Hindu ascetic, often a wandering holy man.

sagar (SAH gar): A lake.

sahib: Also *saheb* (Approximately pronounced suh HIHB or SA'ab). A term of respectful address to a superior, similar to the English "sir." Applied to European men in India, but also to natives of higher status, in which case when used in Hindi after a person's name it roughly means "Mister."

salaam (suh LAHM): A respectful greeting.

sama: Music and dancing of the *sufis*.

samand: A reservoir.

sambhar (SAM bhar): A large deer.

samosa (sah MO sa): A pastry filled with vegetables or meat.

sannyasin (sann YA sin): An ascetic who has renounced worldly life to follow a spiritual discipline.

Sanskrit: The classical ancient language of India (except for the south); studied in schools and used in rituals; otherwise no longer spoken.

Sarasvati: The Hindu goddess of the arts and learning.

sardar: Rajput chief, nobleman or lord; honorific for a Sikh man.

sari (SAH ree): Also *saree*; draped traditional women's garment, it consists of six or more yards of a single length of fabric. The style of wrapping varies from region to region.

sarpanch: Elected head of a village.

sati (SA tee): Also *suttee*; the self-sacrifice of a woman on her husband's funeral pyre. Also refers to a woman who has done so.

Sat Sri Akal: Sikh greeting and rallying cry: "God is Truth!"

senapati: In the Mauryan age, a military commander-in-chief, or a commander of a hundred elephants with their associated horsemen and infantry.

serai (se RAI): An inn for travelers.

shaikh (sheek): A Muslim mystic spiritual teacher.

shalwar (shahl WAHR): Baggy trousers.

shalwar kameez (shahl WAHR kuh MEEZ): Also *kamiz-salvar*; women's outfit of baggy trousers and long shirt or tunic; originally from the Punjab, it has spread to much of India; commonly worn by Muslim village women in Rajasthan.

shamiana: An open-sided tent pavilion.

sharia (shuh ree YAH): Muslim religious law.

shastra: A sacred text or treatise on a subject.

sheesh mahal: Lit. "hall of mirrors," a hall with its walls and ceiling covered with thousands of tiny mirror pieces.

shikar: Hunting.

shikhara (shi KHAR ra): The tower of a Hindu temple in northern India.

shilpa shastra: Sacred text on architecture.

Shiva (SHEE va): Great god of destruction and re-creation, a member of the Hindu trinity. He is usually symbolized in temples by a stone *lingam*. He is also often represented as Nataraja, the Lord of the Dance, with the dance representing creative energy. He rides on the bull Nandi. His wife is called by various names in her different aspects, including Parvati, Kali, and Durga. Shiva is often called by other names, such as Mahadeva, "Great God."

Shivaji: Deccan ruler who unified the Marathas and resisted conquest by Mughal Emperor Aurangzeb; lived 1627 to 1680 C.E.

shraddha (shraad): Ceremonies in honor of the dead.

Shudra: The lowest of the four Hindu broad classes, traditionally servants and manual laborers.

Sikh religion, Sikhism: The faith established in the 15th century by Guru Nanak and continued by his nine successor Gurus, ending with Guru Gobind Singh. Sikhs believe in one God, and a sacred text, the *Granth Sahib*. Their temples are called *gurdwaras*. Most men wear beards and turbans and use the surname "Singh" ("Lion"); women use the surname "Kaur" ("Princess"). Sikhs are concentrated in their homeland of the Punjab region of northwest India, but many have migrated elsewhere.

Singh, Sinha, Simha: "Lion," a last name adopted by Rajputs and by male Sikhs, as well as by others.

Sisodia (shi sho dee a): The Rajput clan ruling the former state of Mewar, including its capitals of Udaipur and Chittor.

Sita (SEE ta): Hindu goddess; Rama's wife and the heroine of the *Ramayana*. Considered as an example of the ideal wife because of her selflessness and loyal devotion to her husband.

sitar (SIH tahr): Stringed musical instrument.

soma: An intoxicating plant juice in Vedic times, used as an offering to the gods and a drink of immortality by worshippers; its precise identity is now uncertain.

stambha: A pillar or tower.

stupa: A masonry-covered hemispherical mound of earth, tumulus-like, containing Buddhist relics.

sufi: Muslim mystic and ascetic.

Sultan: Originally the equivalent of a Muslim king or emperor. The title later degenerated until rulers of even very small territories called themselves sultans.

sura (SU ra): An alcoholic drink in Vedic times.

svayamvara (svay YAM va ra): "Self-choosing," in which a princess would choose a husband from a gathering of suitors after a contest.

swami: A holy man or spiritual teacher, an advanced member of a religious order.

tabla (TAH bluh): A small drum.

tank: An artificially constructed pond or lake.

tanka: A unit of currency during the Sultanate.

tapas (TA pas): Literally, "heat." Ascetic practices, hardships and austerities designed to conserve one's energies to be focused in desired channels.

taslim (tas LEEM): A form of obeisance to a ruler in which one touches the ground and then places the palm of the hand on one's head.

thali (TA lee): A circular metal plate used to serve food.

Thakur (TAHK er): Local ruler or village lord.

thikana (ti KAN a): A hereditary estate, sometimes quite large, headed by a Thakur.

tilaka (TIL ak): Mark of blessing or caste made on the forehead with a colored paste. Applied to the forehead of a ruler at the time of coronation, sometimes with blood.

tonga (TAHN guh): A horse-drawn, two-wheeled carriage.

torana (tor RAN a): A gate or archway.

tulsi (TUL see): A basil plant, sacred to the god Vishnu.

turban: Traditional men's headwear; a long length of cloth wrapped many times around the head. Worn now mainly in villages, and by Sikhs. The styles of wrapping traditionally varied from area to area and with the wearer's status.

Untouchables: Persons so low in social ranking as to be traditionally considered outside the caste system. Close contact with them is said to "pollute" persons of many higher castes. Although the practice is now illegal, it continues in many rural areas.

ulema: The experts in Muslim religious law.

Upanishads (oo pa NISH shads): Books of Hindu philosophy and metaphysical speculation, probably composed c. 800 to 300 B.C.E.

urs: Festival at the anniversary of the death of a Muslim saint.

Usas (USH a): The Vedic goddess of the dawn.

ustad (us TAD): The master of a craft.

vaidya: Physician.

Vaishya: The third in status of the four broad Hindu classes, below the Brahmins and Kshatriyas, but above the Shudras; traditionally traders, businessmen, and artisans.

Varanasi (va ra NA see): Alternate name for the city of Kashi, the great Hindu pilgrimage center, Anglicized as "Benares."

varna: One of the four traditional major class divisions; the four *varnas*—Brahmins, Kshatriyas, Vaishyas, and Shudras—were each subdivided into many castes (*jatis*) and subcastes.

Vedas: Lit. "revealed wisdom." The earliest and most sacred scriptures of the Hindus, probably composed c. 1500-900 B.C. The *Rig Veda* consist of religous poetry; the *Sama Veda* of hymns; the *Yajur Veda* is a priests' manual of ceremonies; and the *Atharva Veda* consists of magical spells.

vihara (vi HA ra): A Buddhist monastery, with living quarters.

vina (VEE na): A popular stringed instrument.

Vishnu: A great god, the preserver of the universe, member of the Hindu trinity. To set things right on earth, he is said to have incarnated as an avatar in a material body nine times—including as the Buddha, Krishna, Rama, and Jesus Christ. He rides on Garuda, a huge bird.

yaar: "Friend."

yogi: A Hindu ascetic; practitioner of yoga.

yoga: A system of exercises or meditation with the goal of gaining control of the mind and body. There are many different variations.

yuvraja (YUV ra ja): An heir apparent, crown prince (of a Hindu state).

zenana (zuh NAH nuh): Women's living quarters or harem, usually forbidden to males except children and close relatives.

Acknowledgments

In a book this long and which was written with the help of so many individuals and libraries, the acknowledgments must also be lengthy.

In America

My wife Sandra has been incredibly supportive, patient, accepting, and tolerant of me and my work over the years as this book grew into a much longer, more demanding, and sometimes more frustrating project than either of us anticipated. At the beginning of the writing of this novel, I closed a law practice in order to concentrate more fully on the book. Sandra has never complained about becoming our main financial support through her teaching job and other means. I am truly fortunate.

I hope our son Shaun will enjoy the book enough to compensate for having lived with an often-preoccupied father.

I am indebted to the late James A. Michener's historical novels, especially *The Source*, for the concept of writing a book using the format of a series of stories in chronological order and tied together by a story set in modern times.

My family and friends have shown me encouragement and interest throughout. I am deeply grateful to all of them. My sister Gale, in particular, has frequently sent me useful clippings related to India.

Gayatri Devi generously read the entire manuscript, part by part, and gave me numerous and detailed insights. Sushma Goyal and Surya Vir Singh, both of whom grew up in Jodhpur, gave me much helpful feedback on "The Mangarh Treasure" portions of the book.

I doubt I would have had the tenacity to complete such a project if it had not been for the encouragement and editorial help of a number of local writer friends. The book is far better because of them. Throughout the years, from the earliest stages, Melinda Howard, Janet Fisk, and Rudy Martin generously gave regular, insightful advice as well as much needed moral support. The justifiably now celebrated author Thom Jones commented on many parts and provided welcomed encouragement. Published book authors Judy Olmstead and Tom Maddox, as well as Gene Barker, Ruth Ann Lonardelli, Beth Fern, Claire Davis, Dennis Held, Keith Eisner, and Tom Grissom gave me valuable suggestions regarding portions of the book. Ernie Bunnell gave detailed and valuable feedback on "Elephant Driver."

Our long time friend Yagya Sharma has given me the benefit of his Hindi and Sanskrit knowledge, especially helpful in the Character List and Glossary, as well as useful background information about his life in a Brahmin family, and being trapped in Lahore at the time of Partition (especially relevant to my sequel novel, *India Fortunes*). Friends Umesh and Veena Vasisth have shared with me their experiences growing up in India, and their own troubles in Lahore at Partition. Our good friend Zahid Sharif helped with the Muslim perspective, including at Partition. Our wonderful Sikh friend Charanjit Singh Sodhi has long been helpful. Har K. "Kris" and Suman Gupta have helped throughout the years in many ways, including contacts both in India and locally. Jagdish and Shanti Rohila greatly helped with contacts in India. Raj Laksmi Phoha gave me useful background information about her life in India. Purshotham Singh Mokha provided useful information about the Sikhs. Many other persons originally from India, including Pran Wahi, Niranjan Benegal, and other friends involved with People for Progress in India of Seattle, have also helped.

Dr. Richard Salomon and the late Dr. Alan Entwistle, both at the University of Washington, Seattle, have been generous to me in sharing their expertise related to Indian languages, and Alan in particular with regard to information about Rajasthani *charans* (bards).

I could not have written nearly as detailed a book without convenient access to the extensive collection of books related to India in the Suzzallo Library at the University of Washington in Seattle. Many of those books were provided by the Library of Congress Special Foreign Currency Program. Irene Joshi, formerly the long time South Asian Librarian at the University of Washington, was helpful on a number of occasions.

Locally, I have made extensive use of the Olympia Timberland Library's interlibrary loan services; the Washington State Library; and The Evergreen State College Library.

Dr. Paul Tate of Idaho State University read the "Three Peoples" portion of the book and gave me the benefit of his knowledge of the period and of Sanskrit. Poorvi Vora also read the same tale and gave useful comments.

Dr. Lloyd I. Rudolph of the University of Chicago provided valuable email advice related to names of Rajput royalty. He and Dr. Susanne Hoeber Rudolph coauthored a book I found highly useful for background, *Essays on Rajputana*. Dr. Lindsey B. Harlan of Connecticut College, author of another book I found helpful, *Religion and Rajput Women*, gave me advice on clothing of young Rajput noble women.

Bruce Upchurch and Ken Morgan at the elephant exhibit, Woodland Park Zoological Gardens, Seattle, were very helpful in sharing their expertise on elephants. Roger Henneous, Phil Prewett, and Jay Haight at the Washington Park Zoo, Portland, Oregon, also provided useful information from their experience with elephants.

Several persons have generously given me technical and practical advice regarding printing and publishing. In particular, Ewald Wuschke Jr. has spent considerable extra time giving me detailed explanations in reply to my email questions about graphics work and printing.

At Central Plains Book Manufacturing, account representative Steve Pate, and Kevin Clark and Valerie Littou in the digital prepress department, have cheerfully answered my many questions regarding preparing the book for printing.

In India

Many, many people have helped me in India during several lengthy travels there. Below are listed most of those who contributed substantially in some way to the writing of this particular book. My wife Sandra has been included in the hospitality extended during many of the visits and meetings; at other times our son Shaun or my sister Gale Schwarb and her husband Marcel were also included. We've been glad for the opportunities to host some of these Indian friends in our own home on their visits to the United States.

Col. K. Fateh Singh and his wonderful wife Indu have both been incredibly helpful hosts during a number of stays at their Megh Niwas Hotel in Jaipur. Colonel Singh has been responsible for many of my best contacts in Rajasthan and much of my knowledge about Rajput life. He has been an excellent guide on excursions to villages and other sites in the Jaipur region. Indu Singh provided useful information from her own childhood as the daughter of a major Rajput thakur. Their sons Udai and Ajay have also been helpful.

Kr. Jaivir Singh and his delightful wife Ila have hosted me in their impressive family fortress at Palaitha in the Kota area. Jaivir's father, Lt. Gen. K. Bahadur Singh, and mother, and many other family members welcomed us in Kota. Jaivir is a concerned citizen, knowledgeable about wildlife, and he has been a good friend, a valuable source of contacts and of information about Rajput life and farming, and an excellent guide during excursions around Kota and Bundi and at Ranthambhor Wildlife Refuge.

Darshan Singh Bhinder has been a helpful source of information about Sikhs, as well as a good friend, guide, and host. He and his family have entertained us on many visits in Delhi and Agra.

Jagdish Parikh, a good friend and a philospher with a social conscience, has been the source of many stimulating conversations. He and his family have been excellent and helpful hosts in Mumbai (then Bombay). Our good friends Kamal and Mita Parekh and family, including daughter Radhi Parekh, were also extremely generous and helpful hosts in Bombay.

Our good friend Arya Bhushan ("A.B.") Bhardwaj, founder of Gandhi-in-Action, has been helpful and inspiring in talking of Gandhian work and modern politics, including background information about the period of Emergency when he was jailed for his own activities. He and his wife Rani and their children were most hospitable during our stay with them in New Delhi.

In the Jodhpur area, the inspiring L.C. Tyagi, founder of the Gramin Vikas Vigyan Samiti (Village Development Rural Sciences) or Gravis, took me on an long jeep tour of his organization's impressive projects to help the rural poor in the deserts. He and his wife Sashi were also quite helpful to us in making various arrangements during a Jodhpur stay. Dr. Manorama Patwardhan, a Gravis volunteer, went far out of her way to help when my wife had a medical problem. Dharamveer Parihar and family have been extremely hospitable; Dharamveer and his friend Heeralal Singhal have shown me many of the sights of the Jodhpur area. Maharaj Swaroop Singh, proprietor of the Ajit Bhawan Hotel in Jodhpur, was an interesting guide on a rural jeep tour and provided useful insights into Rajput royal life.

Balwant Singh Mehta of Udaipur, an energetic worker in the freedom and reform movements from the 1920s onward, and later a draftsman of the Indian Constitution and holder of high government posts, gave me both useful background information and inspiration. His son Bhagwant Singh Mehta assisted us in many ways, including escorting us on a visit to a Bhil village and arranging for Surmal, a Bhil student, as a helpful guide.

In Udaipur, the late R.S. Ashia, Curator of the Bhartiya Lok Kala Mandal (Folk Museum) in Udaipur, was a helpful and generous friend, and he and his wife and family were very hospitable to us in their home. I'll personally miss him greatly. Dr. R.K. Garg was an excellent host and guide to the environmental community and projects in Udaipur. Through him I met Dr. Vyas and other persons affiliated with both the Vidya Bhawan Rural Institute and the Environment Community Centre. Dr. Garg also arranged an excursion with Dr. Bhandari to view reclamation and reforestation work at the Hindustan Zinc smelter.

Thakur Sajjan Singh of Ghanerao, another charming host, provided much useful information about life in the headquarters of an important *thikana* while we stayed with him in his Ghanerao Royal Castle hotel.

Mr. B.B. Palekar of Mumbai, who became a friend through correspondence, was extremely generous and helpful in providing me with details of the organization and operation of the Income Tax Department. Any errors in interpreting those details are of course my own, and he bears no responsibility whatsoever for the subject matter or the plot of the story or the characters depicted. Mr. Palekar also introduced me by mail to Mr. Ramdas Bhatkal, Managing Director of the Mumbai publishing house Popular Prakashan Pvt. Ltd., who was helpful with information about the Emergency period when visiting Seattle.

An Income Tax Department official in a Rajasthan city was extremely generous in providing background information about the workings of the department and about the organization of tax raids. He preferred to remain anonymous, but I nevertheless greatly appreciated his detailed and valuable assistance.

Long before I thought of depicting income tax officials in my novel, we visited both the office and the home of Ballwant Singh, an Income Tax Commissioner (now retired) in New Delhi, and his wife and family. Although he has not been one of my direct sources for income tax information, the background details from visits with him has been most helpful, as were other useful contacts through him at that time.

Bhagwan Singh Sodha was a very helpful and genial guide in Jaisalmer. His brother Tane Singh Sodha, their mother, and other residents were most hospitable in their desert village of Khuri.

Kr. Teej Singh spent considerable time showing me around his family's manor house and the village of Mundota near Jaipur.

Amrendra Singh, proprietor of the excellent and efficiently run Chandralok Hotel near Saheli Bagh in Udaipur, was a helpful host during our stays at the hotel.

The following people have been hosts in whose homes we stayed. Most of them went far above the call of duty in treating both myself and members of my family royally, and I learned much from them which I have used as background in the book: Gyan and Madhu Narula and their children Manju, Alok, and Vivek in Navin Shahdara, Delhi; and their neighbor Gopal Krishna Arora, his daughter Deepti, and family; Dr. Shakuntala Deshpande and her husband and family, and Dr. Subi Chitale and Ashok Chitale and family, all in Indore; Dr. S.N. Mehrotra and wife and family in Gwalior; Mrs. Shankarkumar Sanyal and family at the headquarters of the Harijan Sevak Sangh in Calcutta; Y.D. Sharma and family in Ajmer, his son Desh Bandhu Sharma in particular, and their tenant, P.R. Chaturvedi.

Yaduendra Sahai, Director of the Maharaja Sawai Man Singh II Museum in Jaipur, was quite helpful, especially in teaching me some characteristics of old manuscripts.

Mr. Verma, Chief Instructor of the Western Railway Training School in Udaipur, gave a helpful demonstration of the railway switching systems, which I make use of in the sequel book, *India Fortunes*.

A large number of people have kindly hosted us in their homes for meals and/or significantly helped us in other ways; I have learned something from each of them. In New Delhi these include S.P. Syal and wife Lalita; T.R. "Raj" Kathuria; and Dr. Desh Bandhu, President of the Indian Environmental Society.

Jag Mohan Bhatia was a most helpful friend in Jaisalmer. In Bedla, near Udaipur, Ravi Kant Sanadya and his family were very hospitable. Other kind hosts were Dr. G.S. Deodhar, daughter Savita, and family, in Puna; K.A. Khan and family in Agra; and S.K. Mohanty and wife in Bhubhaneshwar. Keshav and Shobha Jadhav, son Sangram, and daughter Shefali, were very hospitable in Bombay.

A Note on the Type

The body of the text of this book is in 11 point Times New Roman. This font might considered overused in general, since it has become so common on personal computers. However, it was adopted for this book partly because of the easy readability, and also because the narrowness of the letters allows more words per line than most fonts—a major consideration in a book that is so much longer than average. Paragraphs are indented more spaces than usual, in order to give a feeling that the text is less dense.

The ReMinder 106, Rebound ttnorm, and Clark ttstd fonts used for titles, headings, subtitles, running heads, and captions are copyright 1994 by ImageLine Incorporated. After considerable effort, the publisher has been unable to contact the copyright holder to see if any permissions are desired. No infringements whatsoever are intended, and the use of these fonts is gratefully acknowledged.

Reading Group Discussion Guide

The first page of questions should help start and maintain a discussion. The remaining questions offer additional options.

1. How many meanings can you find for the word *Treasures* in the book's title, keeping in mind the novel's topics and themes?

2. In the "Mangarh Treasure" story, what do the attitudes and actions of these characters illustrate about an individual's duties to the family:
       (a) Kaushalya Kumari; (b) Vijay Singh.
The actions of Samudradatta and of his sons in "A Merchant of Kashi"?

3. Vijay Singh feels forced to hide much of his true self in order to pretend to be something different. Do all persons wear a facade that conceals certain aspects of themselves? If so, how is what Vijay does any different?

4.   (a) What importance does Vijay Singh place upon money?
     (b) What importance do you think Maharaja Lakshman Singh places upon wealth?
     (c) How do you think a poor Indian villager would feel about the importance of money?

5. In "The Mangarh Treasure" story, what do you think are the symbolic or metaphorical meanings of:
     (a) The old fortress of Mangarh. E.g., could it be symbolic of a way of life that is no more? Of a flamboyant, highly decorative style of architecture that might not be considered "cost effective" to build now? Of the larger mysteries of the universe?
     (b) Elephants.
     (c) The timekeeper and his gong.
     (d) Ruins, such as the Indus Valley era town and the Buddhist *stupa*.

6. Is there a parallel in Western cultures to the concept of karma (a person's deeds in one life resulting in rewards or punishment in a future life)? E.g., do we "reap what we sow"?

Themes

1. Do you think the search for the Mangarh treasure could parallel any quests in the lives of people in general? Can the treasure itself be a metaphor or symbol?

2. In "Three Peoples," Sumbari finds her way home by means of a constellation, and in "A Merchant of Kashi," the caravan nearly perishes after the guide fails to be properly attentive to the stars. Do you think humanity in Westernized and urbanized cultures has lost anything by generally ignoring the night sky?

Cultural differences

1. What are the relative merits of arranged marriages compared to marrying only for love? E.g., consider Kaushalya's situation, and Vijay's, in "The Mangarh Treasure."

2. Some individuals show considerable initiative toward achieving their desires, e.g., Vijay Singh and Dev Batra in "The Mangarh Treasure," and Jimuta in "Elephant Driver." Do you think those characters' opportunities to advance are typical in Indian society? (For some help, see page 187 in "Elephant Driver.")

3. What do the following illustrate about the importance of religious teachers in Indian society?
    (a) The role of the Buddha in "A Merchant of Kashi."
    (b) The roles of Guru Dharmananda (whom Kaushalya follows), and Swami Surya (whom Dev Batra and Ghosali follow), in "The Mangarh Treasure."

4.   (a) Discuss whether there any parallels in Western cultures to the Kshatriyas, the caste of warriors and princes (e.g., as depicted in "Elephant Driver" and "Saffron Robes"), for whom warfare was a *dharma* (or duty) and a way of life throughout Indian history.
    (b) Does the *jouhar* (mass suicide by fire of Rajput women on the losing side of a siege, as in "Saffron Robes") have any parallels in Western culture?

Indian Society

1. How is the importance of caste in Indian society illustrated in "The Mangarh Treasure?" In "A Merchant of Kashi"?

2. The *Ramayana*, a great Hindu epic, has had a significant impact upon the psyche of many individuals in India, as illustrated by Raja Hanuman in "Saffron Robes," and by Vijay Singh's earlier readings to fellow villagers. Can you think of parallels in Western societies? In your own family's traditions?

3. "Three Peoples" illustrates the great economic importance of cows in Vedic times. How do you think this may have evolved later into a religious reverence for cows in Hinduism?

4. How does the nature of the Indian government in modern times differ from these governments of earlier eras:

(a) Ashoka Maurya's empire as depicted in "Elephant Driver."
(b) The Sultanate of Delhi in "The Price of Nobility."
(c) The rule of Rajput chiefs and rajas in "Saffron Robes."

5. In "The Mangarh Treasure," Anil Ghosali's desire for a job promotion is due in part to a perceived need for a higher salary to pay for the dowries for his five daughters. Although dowries are illegal in modern India, in actuality their use is still pervasive among many castes.

What do you think of the practice?

Many persons do refuse to go along with the expectation of a dowry. Why do you think more families and individuals don't refuse to participate?

Characters

1. In "The Mangarh Treasure:"

(a) Does Vijay Singh's search for the treasure have any parallels in the quests of mythical heroes?

Do you agree with Vijay's choice to adopt a new identity as a member of a higher caste? What are your reasons?

(b) The approach by Shanta Das to dealing with being a member of a "Scheduled Caste" is quite different from Vijay's. Is her way preferable?

(c) Kaushalya Kumari lives in at least two worlds: in Mangarh where her family and the traditional society have strict expectations for an unmarried Rajput princess, and in the more modernized world of attending university in New Delhi and in America. How well do you think she adapts to these quite different situations?

Many immigrants to the West from India and elsewhere have to bridge two quite different sets of societal expectations. Do you have any parallels in your own life, or in that of your ancestors or friends?

To what extent might Kaushalya be an archetype of the "Beautiful Princess"?

(d) Dev Batra might be considered representative of many persons in the official bureaucracies of many societies in which personal influence and bribes are an integral part how the system operates.

How typical do you think he is?

How do you think such a system develops? Are there any benefits to the society at large?

2. From earlier time periods:

(a) Is Emperor Ashoka in "Elephant Driver" an archetype of the "Wise King" whose reign is "The Golden Age"?

(b) Is Raja Hanuman in "Saffron Robes" another "Wise King"?

Why do you think so many rulers or politicians through the ages have failed to place paramount importance on the good of their people as a whole?

The Arts

1. What types of buildings from humanity's architectural heritage do you think are important to preserve? Although many old mansions and palaces in India have been converted into tourist hotels, often older buildings are considered impractical to use and uneconomical to maintain. As Dev Batra illustrates, many of the historic structures are being stripped of items such as carved doors and windows, which are shipped abroad and sold. What do you think of this practice?

2. In Western cultures, is there anything comparable to *rasas*, as depicted in the scene of a classical Indian drama in "The Art of Love"?

3. Are there any parallels between the traditional subject matters of paintings in India and the subjects of Western artists? (Consider the subjects of paintings as depicted in "The Art of Love," "Saffron Robes," and "The Mangarh Treasure.")

About the Author

Gary Worthington has been an attorney in private practice, for the Washington State House of Representatives, as an officer in the U.S. Navy, and more recently helping develop the unique new Cama Beach State Park on a historic waterfront resort site formerly operated by his wife Sandra's family on Camano Island, Washington.

He and his wife have traveled extensively in India and elsewhere, often gaining insights into cultures through staying with families in the Servas volunteer host network. He is involved with People for Progress in India, a Seattle-based organization funding projects in India that help people become economically self-reliant.

His wide range of interests include personal spiritual growth, graphic arts, the night sky, and reading; and issues such as international peace and economic justice, population stablization, environmental preservation, and vegetarianism. He designed the home he and his wife live in, on a forested site near Olympia, Washington. An adult son, Shaun, lives elsewhere.

India Fortunes, the author's sequel to *India Treasures,* is scheduled for publication in 2002.

He strongly encourages your comments regarding this book. Please write to him in care of the publisher, or by e-mail through his Web site at GaryWorthington.com.

The sequel to this book, *India Fortunes*, will be available in 2002.

Prints of the *India Treasures* cover art and of many of the drawings in both books will also be available for purchase at reasonable cost, as well as a color print of a painting based on the Mangarh aerial view map near the front of each book.

If you would like to be notified when *India Fortunes* can be ordered, or if you are interested in information about purchasing the art prints, please furnish the publisher the following:

> Your name
> Your address
> Your email address, if available
> Whether you want information on *India Fortunes*, the
> art prints, or both.

There is no obligation to buy, and all information will be kept confidential.

You can easily send the information on-line:

> Email: info@TimeBridgesPublishers.com
> Web site: www.TimeBridgesPublishers.com

Or:

TimeBridges Publishers LLC
1001 Cooper Pt. Rd. SW, Ste. 140-#176
Olympia, WA 98502
Phone: 360-867-1883
Fax: 206-965-2758

Quick Order Form

Orders are shipped within 24 hours from New Hampshire. For expedited shipping or international orders, request additional information.

Order toll free: 800-345-6665. Have your Visa or MasterCard ready.
Secure online orders: www.TimeBridgesPublishers.com
Mail orders: Pathway Book Service, 4 White Brook Road, Gilsum NH 03448
Fax orders: 603-357-2073. Fax this filled-out form if you wish.
International phone orders: 603-357-0236

Ordered by:
Name _____
Address _____
_____ Zip _____

Phone number: _____-_____-_____
Email address: _____ (in case of questions)

Ship to: (Only if different from above)
Name _____
Address _____
_____ Zip _____

Please send _____ copies of India Treasures
                              $15.95 each $_____
      Add shipping: $3.95 for first book
                    ($1.50 each additional book)   _____
WA State residents: 8% sales tax ($1.28 per book)   _____

Payment: **TOTAL** $ _____
___Cheque enclosed
Credit Card: ____Visa ____MasterCard

Card number: _____ Expir. date _____

Name on card: _____

Your signature _____

To contact **TimeBridges Publishers** direct, for information only:
1001 Cooper Pt. Rd. SW, Ste. 140-#176, Olympia, WA 98502
Phone: 360-867-1883; Fax: 206-965-2758
www.TimeBridgesPublishers.com

The sequel to this book, *India Fortunes,* will be available in 2002.

Prints of the *India Treasures* cover art and of many of the drawings in both books will also be available for purchase at reasonable cost, as well as a color print of a painting based on the Mangarh aerial view map near the front of each book.

If you would like to be notified when *India Fortunes* can be ordered, or if you are interested in information about purchasing the art prints, please furnish the publisher the following:

> Your name
> Your address
> Your email address, if available
> Whether you want information on *India Fortunes*, the
> art prints, or both.

There is no obligation to buy, and all information will be kept confidential.

You can easily send the information on-line:

> Email: info@TimeBridgesPublishers.com
> Web site: www.TimeBridgesPublishers.com

Or:

TimeBridges Publishers LLC
1001 Cooper Pt. Rd. SW, Ste. 140-#176
Olympia, WA 98502
Phone: 360-867-1883
Fax: 206-965-2758

Quick Order Form

Orders are shipped within 24 hours from New Hampshire. For expedited shipping or international orders, request additional information.

Order toll free: 800-345-6665. Have your Visa or MasterCard ready.
Secure online orders: www.TimeBridgesPublishers.com
Mail orders: Pathway Book Service, 4 White Brook Road, Gilsum NH 03448
Fax orders: 603-357-2073. Fax this filled-out form if you wish.
International phone orders: 603-357-0236

Ordered by:
Name _____
Address _____
_____ Zip _____

Phone number: _____-_____-_____
Email address: _____ (in case of questions)

Ship to: (Only if different from above)
Name _____
Address _____
_____ Zip _____

Please send _____ **copies of India Treasures**
                                          $15.95 each $_____
  Add shipping: $3.95 for first book
     ($1.50 each additional book)   _____
WA State residents: 8% sales tax ($1.28 per book)   _____

Payment: **TOTAL** $_____
___Cheque enclosed
Credit Card: ____Visa ____MasterCard

Card number: _____ Expir. date _____

Name on card: _____

Your signature _____

To contact **TimeBridges Publishers** direct, for information only:
  1001 Cooper Pt. Rd. SW, Ste. 140-#176, Olympia, WA 98502
  Phone: 360-867-1883;   Fax: 206-965-2758
  www.TimeBridgesPublishers.com